QUITS!

JEMIMA MONTGOMERY
BARONESS TAUTPHOEUS

Traviata Books

QUITS!

by

JEMIMA MONTGOMERY
BARONESS TAUTPHOEUS

TRAVIATA BOOKS
2005

First published 1857
This edition 2005

Published by Traviata Books Ltd

Introduction and editorial matter
copyright © Traviata Books Ltd 2005

ISBN 1-905335-00-8

Produced by Studio 401 Limited 01935 813176
Printed and bound by Biddles Limited

Cover illustration: Caspar David Friedrich (1774-1840):
Landscape in the Riesengebirge: Pushkin Museum, Moscow

www.traviatabooks.co.uk

Contents

Introduction

JEMIMA MONTGOMERY was born on 23 October 1805[*] in
Donegal, Ireland. Her family were related to the Anglo-
Irish writer Maria Edgeworth (1767-1849), author of
novels on Irish life such as *Castle Rackrent* (1800) and *The
Absentee* (1812); and Jemima was sufficiently proud of the
connection to give the name Edgeworth to her son.[†] The
prospect of a predictable life—if a little less philistine than
most—among the hard-riding, hard-drinking Anglo-Irish
gentry was overturned however when on 29 January 1838,
in her early 30s, she married Cajetan Freiherr (Baron) von
Tautphoeus, Chamberlain and Ministerial Counsellor to the
King of Bavaria. From then on her life was divided between Munich and the mediaeval fortress of Marquartstein,
overlooking the village of the same name[‡] in the Bavarian

---

[*] According to the inscription on her grave and to her husband's entry
in *Genealogisches Handbuch des in Bayern immatrikulierten Adels*, Neustadt an
der Aisch 1967, Vol IX p. 293. *The Dictionary of National Biography*, however, prefers 23 October 1807.

[†] Rudiger Edgeworth von Tautphoeus (1838-1885) who became Bavarian Minister to Rome.

[‡] It may be of interest that some years after the Baroness's death the
village became the home of Richard Strauss, who composed many of
his early works in a house below the Castle and married his wife, the
singer Pauline de Ahna, in the Castle's tiny chapel.

Alps, just a few kilometres north of the frontier with Austrian Tyrol, which she and her husband repaired and turned into their country residence. She died in Munich in her late 80s,[*] and was buried with her husband and son, both of whom predeceased her, in the graveyard of St Martin's Church in Unterwössen, the next village south after Marquartstein along the valley of the Tiroler Ache. Recent modernisation of the churchyard has obliterated the vault and its elaborate wrought-iron entrance; but the plaque has survived and is now fixed to the outer wall of the church.

Baroness Tautphoeus, to use the name with which she signed her work, published four novels: *The Initials* (1850), *Cyrilla* (1853), *Quits!* (1857) and *At Odds* (1863). In their day they were admired by Thackeray, and Henry James wrote nostalgically and admiringly of *The Initials*.[†] There is also evidence that her work was known to another Anglo-Irish writer of more lasting fame. In *The Initials*, when Crescenz Rosenberg is about to become formally engaged to Major Stultz, her "certificates of birth, baptism, vaccination, and confirmation" are laid out for his inspection. Similarly, in Act III of Oscar Wilde's *The Importance of Being Earnest* (1895) Jack Worthing assures Lady Bracknell that he possesses his ward Cecily Cardew's certificates of "birth, baptism, whooping cough, registration, vaccination, confirmation and the measles—both the German and the English variety". The identical wording, even if extended for comic effect, and the sly hint at an Anglo-German origin, seem too much for coincidence.

---

[*] The *Genealogisches Handbuch* and the *Dictionary of National Biography* agree on 12 November 1893 while the grave states 12 November 1895.
[†] The "art-things" of Munich "exhale, ever so kindly, one scarce knows what faint fragrance as of our early perusals of 'The Initials' of the Baroness Tautphoeus, so adored and so forgotten." Henry James, *William Wetmore Story and his Friends* (1903), Vol I p 187.

Like many English novelists of her day, Baroness Taut-phoeus wrote in the format of the "three-volume novel"* meeting the demands of the great lending libraries, which provided family evening entertainment rather as video rental shops do today. Mudie's and other libraries displayed their stock in London and in centres such as Bath, and des-patched parcels to subscribers around the country.† Novel-ists at the top of the profession were able to avoid this strait-jacket: Dickens and Thackeray issued their novels in monthly or even weekly parts, and once established Trol-lope was usually able to negotiate first publication of his as magazine serials. But many authors had to produce up-wards of 1,000 pages—of admittedly quite large type—keeping the story going until it was ready for the great cli-maxes at the one-third and two-thirds points which the li-braries hoped would have the customers coming in eagerly for the next volume. In the work of such novelists the reader can sometimes detect padding and a tendency for the story to sag a little. But the libraries were important cus-tomers, and the standard price of one-and-a-half guineas for a three-volume novel prevented large sales to the gen-eral public. George Meredith, even when he had attained the status of Britain's leading novelist, suffered significant financial penalties when his novels were rejected by the cir-culating libraries for excessive frankness on sexual matters.

Meredith's experience shows that, as well as dictating to novelists how they should structure their works, the librar-

---

* *At Odds* was in fact first published in two volumes.
† Including, before we leave the subject of *The Importance of Being Earnest*, to the Manor House, Woolton, Hertfordshire where Cecily Cardew and her governess exchange views on novels sent them by Mudie's circulat-ing library. "Never speak disrespectfully of the three-volume novel, Cecily," says Miss Prism, "I wrote one myself in younger and happier days."

ies are open to the accusation of encouraging self-censorship; but given the shocked claims during their heyday that much of what they circulated was "sensational" it is doubtful that they added much to the discretion within which 19th-century novelists already operated. Meredith's notoriously difficult style may have disadvantaged him with the libraries as much as his fearless defence of women exploited sexually and financially by their husbands. Certainly in the Baroness's case the physical repugnance Cyrilla comes to feel for Edouard von Zorndorff is clear enough —even if the author leaves the door open for less experienced readers to attribute her disgust only to his attempts to intimidate her. In a practical German way which leaves little to the imagination of any but the most innocent, she describes too the temptations (and not only the threats) to which attractive middle-class girls like Hildegarde and Crescenz Rosenberg are exposed.

While her novels are not didactic, the Baroness is frank whenever she decides the country of her birth has something to learn from her adopted homeland. Women are indeed exposed to male threats and intimidation—more seriously in *Cyrilla* than in *The Initials*—but the relationship between the sexes is shown as freer and more natural in Germany. She implies that this is in part due to greater mutual respect. There is an incident in *Quits!* where Leonora Nixon, temporarily left unescorted in the National Gallery in London, is molested by men who presumably think she is one of the high-class prostitutes who paraded in such public places. The passage is not developed, but clearly hints at the author's distaste for the constraints forced on the independence of respectable women by the blatancy of the contemporary sex industry. She also portrays class distinctions as less rigid and extreme. Both in *The Initials* and in *Quits!* the Bavarian aristocracy are shown as less haughty, and less separated from the peasants by dress and language, than their British equivalents—especially as represented by "Mr Torp". While the under-employed young students and officers who cluster around the Rosenbergs in *The Initials* are hardly heroic, at least there is no suggestion that one could not risk introducing them to one's sister—unlike the raffish young English aristocrats cultivated by Arthur Nixon in *Quits!*.

All of the Baroness's novels did well enough in their multi-volume first editions to justify republication. In the book-trade of the time this normally meant one-volume reprints at 6 shillings or so directed at general book-buyers like Stephen Nixon in *Quits!*, with some scope for rewriting if the author had really chafed at the restrictions of the libraries. There was also the possibility of overseas publication. This did not often lead to payment: in the absence of international copyright agreements American publishers pirated British authors ruthlessly. Inclusion in the Tauchnitz paperback series, which voluntarily paid fees to its authors, was more welcome: these volumes were published in Leipzig ostensibly for the convenience of English-speaking travellers and residents on the European continent; but were often sold, rules or no rules, also in England. Leonora Nixon has been reading a Tauchnitz novel when we first meet her on the Rhine steamer—an early example of what is now called "product placement". All four of the Baroness's novels were republished in one-volume British editions, in pirated American editions, and by Tauchnitz.

In *Quits!*, the Baroness's third novel, she returns to the Bavarian setting of her first. But the book opens with a long prologue in which the suddenly orphaned Leonora Nixon returns to London at the age of sixteen from the life she has been leading on the European continent. She is re-

lated through her mother's first marriage to the aristocratic
Medway family, and is at first accepted by them; but the
sickly Lord Medway's infatuation with the beautiful Leonora is seen as dangerous by his brother, the Hon. Charles
Thorpe, and she is packed off to her Nixon relations. Her
life thereafter as a virtual prisoner in the Russell Square
house of her widowed uncle Stephen, a wealthy business-
man, gives her the opportunity to strengthen further the
self-reliance and resilience which will be so evident in her
character as the novel progresses. The prologue, therefore,
far from being irrelevant to the Bavarian scenes which follow, shows the creation of a mature and strong-minded
character which, if presented to the reader fully formed
without explanation in Chapter XV, might seem implausi-
ble.

Having inherited Stephen Nixon's fortune Leonora is at
last able to return to her beloved Bavaria, travelling with
another uncle, Gilbert Nixon, and her two cousins.
Whereas in *The Initials* the Baroness was concerned to present her adopted homeland to the English reader, with the
local people largely shown as part of the exotic mountain
scenery, in *Quits!* her heroine becomes deeply involved in
their affairs—perhaps reflecting the author's real-life activi-
ties as the great lady of Marquartstein Castle. Nonetheless
she continues to describe Bavaria with much observant detail, the account of the 1850 Oberammergau Passion Play
being of particular interest—even if the argument over the
propriety of presenting Biblical characters on stage will
hardly absorb the modern reader.

The main plot however turns on Leonora's resentment
at the high-handed behaviour of Charles Thorpe—now
Lord Medway—in ejecting her from his family, and
whether having won her revenge she will indeed call it
quits. In gradually bringing the two characters together the

author is plausible and skilful, not relying on the dramatic scene in Chapter XXVIII when Thorpe rescues Leonora from an attack of vertigo. In fact her momentary weakness makes her all the more determined to keep him at arm's length. As for Thorpe, it is not the physical contact with Leonora which brings him to the realisation that he loves her, but her charming appearance in local costume; and her elegance when he sees her formally dressed at the Benndorffs' ball (subtly described only by implication through contrast with the obviously overdressed Irene Schaumberg) convinces him that she would furthermore do him credit as Countess of Medway. It remains marginally uncertain at the end whether Leonora will in fact exchange her beloved Bavarian mountains, her plan to buy and renovate Waltenburg Castle, and the company of the amusing and artistic Count Waldemar Benndorff, for life among the mid-Victorian aristocracy whose arrogance and shallow hedonism her creator found so unsatisfactory.

Baroness Tautphoeus's occasionally unconventional spelling and individual punctuation have generally been retained except where they might cause confusion. Her own footnotes have been given the signature "JvT".

—Adrian Thorpe

CHAPTER I

In the Midst of Life we are in Death

THE bell of the steamer tolled. A hissing sound of escaping vapour, and the gradual cessation of even the slight motion of a Rhine boat, informed the passengers that they had reached their destination for the night, and induced those who had taken refuge in the cabins from the heat of a July afternoon to commence a tumultuous rush on deck. Stretched on one of the sofas in what is called the pavilion, and perfectly unmoved by the bustle around him, lay a young Englishman, apparently in a precarious state of health, and in such very deep mourning that some inquisitive tourists took the trouble to make inquiries about him, and, without much difficulty, discovered that he was a nobleman returning home to take possession of his estates on the death of his father. Yet great as had been the attention lavished on him during the day by most of the English travellers who had become acquainted with his name and rank, they now all hurried past him without word or look, so wholly intent were they on securing their luggage, and obtaining apartments at the usually crowded hotels. Two persons who had entered the steam-boat but a couple of hours previously, stopped, however, at the door, looked back and spoke to each other, but in tones so low, that no sound reached the invalid's ear, though, from the direction of their eyes, he had little doubt that he was him-

self the subject of discussion. Father and daughter they
seemed to be, and had attracted his attention directly on
their entrance, from the evident desire of both to remain
unobserved. The gentleman had the remains of considerable beauty of face and person, disfigured by an unusual
degree of corpulence, which, however, he seemed in no
way disposed to lessen, for during his short sojourn in the
steam-boat he had left the pavilion no less than three times
to strengthen and refresh himself with soup, beefsteak, and
coffee, each time inviting his daughter to join him, and receiving for answer a quick shake of the head, followed, after he had left her, by a still closer drawing into the corner
of the sofa, from which she never moved, and a pressing
nearer to the adjacent window, while she raised towards it,
to catch the waning light, a volume of Tauchnitz's edition
of British Authors.[*] Perhaps this last circumstance, as much
as the mysterious whispering of the travellers, had excited
his lordship's curiosity, for he concluded that if she were
not English, she at least understood the language, and perfectly too, as her quick reading and expressive changes of
countenance proved beyond a doubt. Certain it is that his
eyes had seldom wandered from the face of the young girl
from the moment of her entrance; and a charming youthful
face it was, with its small undefined nose, lustrous black
eyes, well-formed mouth, and high intellectual forehead
partially covered by braids of raven hair. But it was the
smile that had most of all attracted, for it was the brightest
he had ever seen, and the more remarkable as the general

[*] Bernhard von Tauchnitz (1816-1895) founded in Leipzig in 1841 a
publishing house which produced an English-language paperback series
for the convenience of foreign travellers in Germany and elsewhere in
continental Europe. The series continued well into the 1930s. Baroness
Tautphoeus's four novels were all included.

expression of the countenance was pensive. She stood now leaning against the cabin door, while her father satisfactorily proclaimed his country, by offering, in very good English, to secure rooms for the invalid, in case he should reach the hotel before him.

"Thank you—you are very kind," he replied, slowly rising, "but as I have discovered that this boat goes on with us to-morrow, I have made arrangements for remaining in it. Landing, or rather getting myself under way so early in the morning, fatigues me too much."

He advanced towards them while speaking, and then followed them up the stairs to the deck, where their perfect composure during the scene of confusion that ensued proved them to be experienced travellers. They exhibited none of the anxiety about their luggage, that put the whole ship's company into commotion when the tarpaulin was removed, which had during the day-time covered the innumerable trunks, boxes, bags, and portmanteaux that had lain heaped together, not a few, as is usual on such occasions, without an address, or even the name of the proprietor. It seemed as if each individual expected at once to have his property, and the murmuring, growling voices of the men mixed strangely with the sharp, impatient tones of the women. Many, though surrounded by packages of all kinds and dimensions, neither trusting their eyes nor memories, imagined that something must still be failing, and eagerly watched each piece of luggage as it was drawn forward, while the different emissaries from the hotels thrust cards into their hands, and vociferated recommendations into their bewildered ears. Some oddly-shaped cases, that seemed to have once belonged to a carriage, were pointed out with a silent gesture by the Englishman, and then instantly seized by the nearest porters, while he turned to the invalid, and, taking off his hat, politely hoped to have the

pleasure of seeing him the next day. A few minutes afterwards, he and his daughter disappeared in the long procession of travellers, emissaries, porters, and truck-drivers,
who hurried towards the different hotels.

An unusually brilliant sunset had left a bright orange-
coloured sky, that served to render the chief buildings of
the town still conspicuous, and which, reflected in the
broad tranquil river, gave the warmth of colouring and distinctness of outline to the numerous boats and their picturesque rigging that are supposed to be peculiar to warmer
climes. That recollections of similar places crowded on the
memory of the traveller, as he stood alone near the rudder
of the steam-boat, is possible, but not very probable, for
Englishmen are not prone to meditations on past scenes or
scenery; it is more likely that he was thinking of home, and
what awaited him there, while his eyes followed slowly the
golden ripple on the water, or rested in reverie on the
lounging figures of the surrounding boatmen. The colours
of evening changed imperceptibly from violet to blue, from
blue to grey; but it was not until the landscape had faded in
the twilight, and lights from the suburbs of the town began
to glimmer redly through the intervening mist, that he
turned away and descended to the pavilion.

It is unnecessary to follow him. We have but to record
that he was reminded of his dark-eyed countrywoman by
finding the book she had been reading where she had
probably placed it when putting on her bonnet. The name
written on the yellow cover was "Nixon," and, though neither euphonious nor remarkable, it seemed to attract his
attention in no common degree, for he repeated it several
times, and then murmured, "Surely a relation of ours married a man of the name of Nixon—yes—certainly, that was
the name—and it was Harry Darwin's mother—the man a
merchant, or something of that sort, who became a bank-

rupt, or—no—squandered his fortune and was obliged to
live abroad—that was it. Harry never liked speaking of his
mother's second marriage or his stepfather: however, I am
rather surprised he did not mention this half-sister of his,
whom he must have seen repeatedly, for before he began to
live in his yacht, he was continually making excursions
abroad, and especially to Germany. I wonder is this the
man I mean! My mother said he was a vulgar parvenu—
parvenu he may be—vulgar he is not—and as to his daughter—one of whose grandmothers I strongly suspect to have
been the black-eyed Susan* of nautical celebrity—she is the
nicest creature I have seen for an age, and may turn out to
be a relation of ours. Let me see; her maternal and my paternal grandfather having been brothers, we should be second cousins—or first cousins once removed—or third
cousins—or—At all events the name is a sufficient pretext
for commencing an acquaintance with both of them to-
morrow, and that I shall certainly do."

At a very early hour the next morning most of the passengers of the preceding day, reinforced by many others,
began to crowd noisily into the steam-boat; not one however, descended to the cabin until long after the boat had
left her moorings, and our traveller was given more than
time to finish his breakfast in undisturbed solitude. Tapping
rather impatiently on Mr or Miss Nixon's book, which he
had placed beside him on the table, he awaited the entrance
of a group of English who seemed to have chosen the stairs
as the place for discussing the events of the previous night;
and the words that he overheard proved them to have been
of no common-place description:—"Dreadful—awfully

---

* *Sweet William's Farewell to Black-eyed Susan*, ballad by John Gay (1685-
1732).

sudden—enormously stout man—looked apoplectic—must have taken place just after he went to bed—the body was quite cold when they broke open the door this morning—the poor girl fainted—I saw her being carried across the passage to her room." With a degree of anxiety and interest that surprised himself, he approached the speakers, and learned from them that Mr Nixon, their fellow-passenger of the previous day, had been found dead in his bed about half an hour before they had left the hotel.

"And is his poor daughter quite alone?" he asked, compassionately.

"It seems so, but really I had no time to make inquiries," answered a gentleman, endeavouring to pass into the cabin.

"Oh, I dare say the people at the hotel will do everything that is necessary," observed a lady, apparently of a more inquisitive and communicative disposition; "and, at all events, the young lady seemed to me extremely well able to take care of herself under all circumstances. We joined the table d'hôte yesterday, when we found that we could not procure a sitting-room, for you know it is only Germans or French who can drink tea in a bed-room! She and her father were not far distant from us, and my attention was attracted towards them by the variety and quantity of meat and sauces devoured by him in the course of half an hour. Poor man! I did not know it would be his last dinner or supper, whichever he called it—nor he either, of course. But I must say, at a public table I should be sorry to see *my* daughters so perfectly at their ease as she seemed to be. The manner in which her father made acquaintance with all the people about him was quite extraordinary, and the young lady joined in the conversation with a fluency scarcely becoming her years, and not at all English!"

"I wish," said the invalid traveller, languidly, "I wish I had gone on shore yesterday evening. I might, perhaps, have been of use. Going back to the aw—aw—town, what's its name? is aw—out of the question now, as my return home has already been provokingly protracted one way or another."

"Very kind of your lordship to feel so much interest about a stranger," rejoined the lady, "but you may be assured the people at the hotel will pay the greatest attention to this Miss Nixon: my daughters were actually refused a room they particularly wished to have, in order to let her be near her papa, and the whole household was so occupied with her this morning that we came away without breakfast."

This seemed to have been the case with many other passengers also, and a clattering of cups and saucers, and a hurrying to and fro of waiters ensued, which apparently disturbed his lordship's meditations, for he went on deck and watched this swift motion of the steamer, as, aided alike by art and nature, it hurried forward with the stream, the water widening, the banks sinking, and windmills serving as landmarks from the time they entered the territories of Holland.

Flow on, river, as you have done for ages! press forward, steam-boat, to complete your daily task—forward as quickly as your impatient passengers can desire—there is but one among them who in the course of the day bestows a passing thought on the orphan girl whose sudden bereavement had that morning so unpleasantly reminded them that "In the midst of life we are in death."

CHAPTER II

A Short Pedigree

THOUGH few people could be induced by the sudden death of a stranger at an hotel to protract their journey in order to be of service to the survivor—even supposing that person a young and helpless girl—a return to the town on the Rhine, and a short delay there with the daughter of Mr Nixon, will scarcely be objected to by any humane novel reader. After the body of the deceased had been examined, and the cause of death ascertained, the civil authorities requested an interview with Miss Nixon, and questioned her respecting her parents, her age, her past life, and future prospects, exhibiting very evident satisfaction on learning that she had two uncles in London, was related to the Earl of Medway, and had a step-brother whom she described as being of no profession, but a gentleman and a baronet. On being advised to write to this brother without delay, she was obliged to confess that she did not know his address—her mother had always sent her letters to him under cover to Lord Medway, who had been his guardian, and who had also managed all their English affairs for them. She had never corresponded with her uncles, but had written to inform Lord Medway of her mother's death, which had taken place some months previously, and she had received a very kind answer; her brother also had written, but had not come to see them—he and her father had never been on good terms.

These few particulars had been in a manner extorted from the poor girl, as, scarcely recovered from this shock she had so recently received, she leaned her head weeping on the table beside her; but when, on being asked if she had money to defray her expenses to London, she silently produced a purse full of English sovereigns, they recommended her, without further hesitation, to the care of the landlady of the hotel, who was present; and after a whispered proposal to the latter to give her, in some more convenient place, the necessary directions about the interment of the Englishman, they all withdrew, and Leonora Nixon found herself, for the first time since she had known her bereavement, alone.

She instantly sat upright, pushed her dark hair from her pale face, seemed to listen intently to the sound of the retreating footsteps; and, when silence was restored to the corridor, she rose, and murmuring the words, "Once more —I must see him once more," left the room, and ran quickly towards a door at the opposite side of the passage, which she opened with a precipitancy that proved the violence of feelings she had thought it necessary to control in the presence of strangers during the preceding hour. In the doorway, however, she stood amazed, at first incapable of uttering an articulate sound. No trace of her father was there; the bed in which he had died was deprived of all its furniture, and a woman with water and a brush stood scouring the interior, as if death had infected the very boards. Strips of carpet hung pendent at the wide-open windows, from which the curtains had been removed, and a housemaid was deluging the painted floor with fresh water, after having placed the chairs and tables in an adjoining room. Somewhat startled by Leonora's sudden appearance, the girl stopped her work, and leaned on her long-handled brush, while Leonora advanced, stammering, "Where is—is —my—father?"

"The room must be got ready for the steam-boat passengers this evening, Miss," answered the girl, evasively.

"Where have they laid him?" she asked, with assumed calmness.

"Surely, miss, you don't want to see the corpse again after being so frightened this morning?"

"I do wish to see it," said Leonora, "and you must take me to the room directly."

"But I have got orders not to let anyone into it until the coffin comes."

"Such orders cannot concern me. Give me the key, and I promise to give it back to you in half an hour."

"I must first ask the landlady," said the girl, evidently impressed with involuntary respect by Leonora's decided manner; and passing her quickly, she was soon after heard speaking to her mistress at the other end of the passage. They then both advanced towards Leonora; and after a few words of remonstrance on the part of the landlady, which of course made no sort of impression, the latter proposed herself accompanying the orphan to take leave of the remains of her parent.

They descended the stairs, traversed a broad corridor, and, to Leonora's infinite surprise, entered the ball-room. She looked round her with a bewildered air, while her companion slowly and reluctantly unlocked the door of an adjoining refreshment-room, and then silently pointed to a long table, where, stretched on a mattress, and covered with a linen cloth, the outline of a human figure could be distinguished.

The windows were open, but the green jalousies so arranged that little light fell on the features, uncovered with eager haste by Leonora's trembling hand. If the landlady had dreaded being witness to a violent ebullition of grief, she was soon convinced that her apprehensions had been unnecessary. Large tears gathered slowly in the eyes of the youthful mourner, and fell heavily on the face of the dead: —alas! that we should have to record they were the only tears likely to be shed for Frederick Nixon! No bad criterion of our worth and usefulness in this world would be these tears, could they but be collected; and not without deep meaning were the Roman lachrymatory and many funeral customs of other nations of antiquity. In the present civilised states of the world it has become a sort of maxim that of the dead we should only speak advantageously. The Egyptians thought otherwise; and their *post-mortem* trials, where every one was at liberty to accuse the deceased, and the defence alone depended on the good will and affection of surviving friends and relations, may often have found a place in the thoughts of the living, and prevented many a sin of omission as well as commission.

Not few would, in such a case, have been Frederick Nixon's accusers, his sole defender the orphan girl, who, with the prospect of dependence on unknown relations before her, and uncertainty as to her reception among them, nevertheless sincerely mourned the parent who had squandered her inheritance and left her homeless. We regret the necessity of recording the story of his life, which, in its dismal details, is too common either to create interest or serve as warning.

His paternal pedigree had been of a more respectable than brilliant description, until his father became a man of importance in the commercial world. This father had commenced his career in the manner hereditary in the family, that is, as shop-boy in *his* father's old-established house in the city, and had wisely preserved through life a vivid recollection of having carried parcels to their destination, and considered it an honour when permitted, in his turn, to stand behind the counter and weigh sugar and spice for the numerous customers; or, on receiving an "order," to make up with dexterous hand the various packages, and consign them to the care of his successor in office, the attendant boy, who had been especially commanded to say "Sir" to him. Being without brothers or sisters, he found himself, on the death of his parents, in possession, not only of an extensive business, but also a considerable sum of money: the latter he increased by a judicious marriage, and, being of an enterprising disposition, engaged in successful speculations during the war, which raised him to a state of opulence quite beyond his powers of enjoyment; so that the accumulated money amounted, by means of interest and compound interest, to sums of such magnitude that the shop was at length closed, and an emigration commenced beyond the precincts of the city. He had now an office and warehouses, and when death deprived him of his wife, he found no difficulty in obtaining the hand of one of the very handsome daughters of an Irish gentleman of wonderfully ancient family and distinguished poverty, whose name, preceded by the euphonious particle O, satisfactorily proved that he belonged to one of the illustrious races said to be of royal lineage.

In the course of time, Mr Nixon was made fully to comprehend that a name is by no means so insignificant a thing as Juliet Capulet supposed it to be; for his wife, ardently desiring to regain what she considered her proper position in the world, made many and desperate efforts to rise in the social scale, and, as a first step thereto, increasingly endeavoured to induce her husband to remove to the "West End." From the house in Russell-square, purchased and furnished at the time of their marriage, he could never be induced to move; neither would he give up old friends or habits, and to the last day of his life continued proud of having been Lord Mayor, and gloried *bonâ fide* in the title of alderman.

The two sons of his first wife, born and educated while he was still a hard-working man, acquired his tastes and habits, and in process of time became his partners; but the only son of his second wife, when rendered unmanageable at home by indulgence, had been consigned to the care of,—

"A clergyman, married, of much experience, with extensive premises at the WEST END," who would "receive into his family EIGHT YOUNG GENTLEMEN. The course of Instruction securing a solid preparation for the universities, &c, &c, &c. The treatment of the pupils truly parental."

Parental it was in one sense certainly, for parents are almost always careless instructors; but while lazily construing Virgil and Homer, Master Frederick grew healthy and handsome, and acquired tastes, habits, and manners that his mother pronounced exquisite, and which raised expectations of future triumphs in life, the disappointment of which was spared her by an early death.

With half a dozen of the "*eight young gentlemen*" Frederick Nixon afterwards went to Oxford, where he proved notoriously idle and indolent. Good-humoured and lavishly profuse in his expenditure, he was, however, universally called and considered a "capital fellow," and in this opinion his father probably concurred, for he paid his debts without expressing much astonishment at their amount, was easily convinced that his son's talents were more of a military than civil description, got a commission for him in the Guards, and dying soon afterwards, used his plebeian privilege of dividing his fortune with perfect equality among his sons, thereby leaving them all well provided with what is but too generally considered the greatest blessing in life.

The step-brothers, unlike in disposition, temper, education, and habits, dissolved partnership, and in the world of London seldom met again. Frederick, freed from all restraint, possessed of a large fortune and handsome person, fell at once into the disorderly, if not actually profligate, mode of life of his companions and nominal friends, and, without being worse than others, contrived to give himself an unpleasant kind of notoriety by the numerous foolish things he said and did to obtain tolerance, if not a position, in society where a total want of connection nevertheless ever caused him to feel himself isolated. His efforts to remedy this latter evil were unremitting, and at length partially successful, when he persuaded Lady Darwin, the widow of a baronet of good family, and daughter of an Honourable Augustus Thorpe, to become his wife. It is true, her cousin, the Earl of Medway, did not receive his new relative with any demonstration of satisfaction; it was even said that he had openly pronounced him to be a weak-headed spendthrift, and given Lady Darwin to understand that, in consequence of her marriage, he should consider it necessary to send her only son (his ward) to school without further delay. She resigned the youthful Harry to the care of his guardian, and perceived not at all the boy's gradual but total estrangement, as year after year he spent less of his holidays with her, and began completely to identify himself with the Medway family.

Lady Darwin was still young and handsome, and for some years her career was as brilliant as apparently inexhaustible wealth could make it; but Frederick Nixon had, even before his marriage, considerably encroached upon his capital, which, placed in the Funds, was completely at his disposal; and, totally averse to business of any kind, he continued to supply all deficiencies of income in the same manner. His wife, purposely kept in ignorance of the state of his affairs, thought not of making retrenchments; and, in the course of time, was eager to plunge deeper into the dissipations of the world to escape from the society of her husband, who, after having frittered away a noble fortune in the vain pursuit of selfish pleasure and ostentation, began altogether to lose the good temper for which he had once been so remarkable. He became irritable and restless, continually changing his place of residence, and relieving immediate want of money by the sale of one house, while incurring debt, at the same time, by the purchase of another: and thus he struggled on until the crash, long foreseen by every one, took place; when the sale of his effects, and his wife's resignation of thirty thousand pounds, his wedding gift to her, having satisfied his creditors, he was at liberty to retire to the continent, there to live on her jointure from her first marriage.

They had lost many children while in England, but Leonora, born at a quiet town in Germany during the time of their first fresh grief, lived; and the change produced in their small household, and cares imposed on them by her birth, turned their thoughts into a new channel, and greatly alleviated their useless regrets. While, however, Lady Darwin quickly resigned herself to her loss of fortune, and continued to devote herself exclusively to her child, her husband, suffering intolerably from ennui, began, by degrees, to indulge in the roving propensities common to his countrymen when they have left England in search of a foreign home. As far as was possible, too, he fell into his former habits, and squandered, and wandered when and where he could during his wife's lifetime. Her death, just as his daughter had attained her fifteenth year, left him and his child in a state of painful destitution, and to the two brothers he had so openly despised in the days of his prosperity, Frederick Nixon was at length obliged to apply for assistance. It was not refused; each brother consented to give an annual sum of money for his support; and in order to be near England in case of pecuniary difficulties, he had commenced a Rhine pilgrimage, uncertain where he should finally establish himself with his daughter, and contrive to live on an income, of the smallness of which he complained as only those do who have spent but never earned.

His faults and follies were alike forgotten by his mourning daughter, as she bent over the well-known face, and drew towards her the cold stiff hand that, but a few hours before, had, warm with life, pressed hers. The landlady's various movements of impatience—jingling of keys, opening of windows, and displacing of furniture in the adjacent room—were unheeded by Leonora until she became conscious of the approach of two men, who, talking loudly, and walking heavily, carried between them a coffin of large dimensions. As they deposited it on the end of the table, they took off their caps and looked towards the landlady for orders. Leonora shuddered, and allowed herself to be led from the room without remonstrance, receiving a chilling sort of consolation from the assurance given her that her father should be interred with all the consideration due to his rank.

That this promise had been fulfilled she had no doubt, when, a few days afterwards, the bills were laid before her by the hostess. In fact, the purse of sovereigns which had afforded such general satisfaction a few days previously, became so greatly reduced in its contents, that she felt it was time to decide on her future plans, and, having bolted her door, she drew towards her, and unlocked, her father's writing-desk. It contained even less money than she expected, and some letters which shocked and grieved her beyond measure, for, from their perusal, she ascertained that her father had already considerably overdrawn the allowance made him by his brothers. His bills had been honoured, but the letter informing him of the fact contained, from his eldest brother, not only a reprimand of extreme severity, but a threat of retaining payment by instalments on any future similar occasion. An angry correspondence had ensued, followed by a quarrel, and Leonora at length discovered that she had been during the last two days unconsciously on her way to England, where her father had hoped, by his presence, to appease the ire of his justly-incensed step-brothers.

Leonora perceived clearly, and at once, that her father had been in the wrong; nevertheless her dislike to her City uncles (for so her mother had invariably denominated them) increased tenfold. She remembered all she had ever heard of their purse-proud vulgarity; called to mind the various anecdotes of ludicrous economy and ignorance of fashionable life on their parts, so often related, most probably with exaggeration, by her father; saw all, and more than all, she had ever heard, confirmed by the packet of well-written, business-like letters before her, and resolved never to apply to such men for assistance. Her thoughts naturally turned next to her step-brother, Sir Harry Darwin, although her acquaintance with him was but slight, and her father had done everything in his power to prejudice her against him, never naming him, when her mother was absent, otherwise than "that self-sufficient egotist," or "that good-for-nothing puppy Darwin." She had seen him but twice during her life. Once, when she was a mere child, at Heidelberg he had joined them, intending to enter the university there, and remain for a couple of years: he had, however, for reasons at that time unknown to her, resided with them but as many months. The second time was several years later, at Vienna, but he had then come to their house as a stranger might have done, and never without having received a note from his mother to let him know at what hour her husband would be absent from home. He had associated with people unknown to them, and lived altogether with Lord Medway's second son, the Honourable Charles Thorpe, who had just then commenced his diplomatic career as *attaché*.

This last meeting had occurred so recently that Leonora had been old enough to perceive the mutual antipathy of her father and step-brother. She had been disposed to like the latter, though he had taken but little notice of her, and had one day, when she was present, observed to his mother, in a slighting manner, that "her daughter was a thoroughbred Nixon, without apparently a drop of Thorpe blood in her veins: he feared he never should be able to consider her as in any way belonging to *their* family." When taking leave of them he had given his mother a considerable sum of money, telling her, without an attempt at reserve, that on his becoming of age, his guardian, Lord Medway, had pointed out to him the folly of increasing her jointure, as it would only benefit her husband, or rather encourage him in his extravagance; that he had therefore resolved to assist her privately, and trusted she would wisely keep secret his having done and intending to do so. With a deep sigh Lady Darwin had acknowledged the justness of Lord Medway's remark, and fully determined to follow her son's advice; but a few days after his departure, when goaded by her husband's ironical observations about the "extraordinary generosity of her son, Sir Harry," while he pointed to and pretended to admire some trifling gold trinkets that had been his ostensible present, she had confessed all, and produced, with short-lived exultation, the money, which was incontinently taken possession of by Frederick Nixon. He, however, in the excess of his surprise and satisfaction, had overseen a purse of sovereigns, and she had not thought it necessary to point it out to his notice, but dropping it into her pocket with much of the trepidation of a criminal dreading detection, it had been from that time forward carefully concealed, not again seeing the light of day, until, on her death-bed, she had privately consigned it to the care of her daughter, with the injunction to reserve it for some occasion of imminent distress, and when all other resources should fail. Often, when her father was subsequently in embarrassments, had Leonora considered if the designated time were not come for her to produce her treasure, as often had the last clause of her mother's speech deterred her. Other resources had been found, silver, furniture, books, had been sold, until, as her thoughtless parent observed with a light laugh, "They were at last travelling in the pleasantest manner possible, with nothing but their respective wardrobes to care for."

The time had suddenly arrived when Leonora had no doubt as to the necessity of using the contents of this purse. She held it now, much diminished in worth, in her hand, and having counted the remaining sovereigns and some Prussian dollars, perceived that she should just be able to await the answer to the letter which she prepared to write to Lord Medway to tell him of her desolate position, and request him to forward an inclosed letter to her stepbrother, of whose address she was in utter ignorance.

From Sir Harry she expected but little sympathy or brotherly love, and her whole trust was in Lord Medway, of whose kindness and excellence she had heard so much from her mother, that she scarcely knew whether she most loved or revered him. She carried the letter herself to the post-office, and before parting with it breathed a short prayer that God would raise up friends to her in her time of need, and not long leave her homeless.

CHAPTER III

Down the Rhine and Up the Thames

THE return of the post brought Leonora the anxiously-expected answer to her letter. Her eagerness at first impeded her powers of comprehension, and she was obliged to read it twice over before she understood that she was without delay to repair to Lord Medway's house in London, where her affairs would be considered and discussed with the necessary attention, and her plans for the future arranged as advantageously as possible. Energetic on all occasions, she sprang from her seat, tied on her bonnet while rapidly descending the stairs of the hotel, and went, without a moment's delay, to the office where places were to be procured in the steam-boat that was to leave the next morning for Rotterdam.

It was not until after her return to the hotel, and the first excitement of acting for herself had partially subsided, that she again carefully and calmly perused the letter. She had previously not observed that it was written on paper with the very broadest of black edges, a mourning which it now occurred to her was deeper than that likely to have been considered necessary by Lord Medway for her mother, and for her father she never expected him or any of his family to mourn outwardly or inwardly. Again she examined the letter, imagined the handwriting changed—firmer, and at the same time more careless; but as she knew he had been ill, she supposed it not unlikely that he had employed an amanuensis. The signature appeared quite the same as usual, and she put it aside, packed up her clothes, and went to bed, resolved to sleep off the cares and anxieties which crowded on her mind at the near prospect of undertaking, for the first time in her life, a journey alone. Such, however, was the buoyancy of her mind, that all her perplexities were chased by vivid surmises as to the personal appearance of Lord and Lady Medway, their sons and daughters; and her last thought, in falling asleep, was of the Charles Thorpe of whom her step-brother had spoken incessantly, and who seemed from his account to be idolised, not only by his own family, but by all the world besides.

The next morning Leonora and her antiquated carriage cases were carefully committed to the charge of the captain of the steam-boat by the hotel-keeper and his wife, who had shown her much kindness and attention during her ten days' sojourn with them. They remained as long as they could with her, and when parting put into her hands a basket full of grapes and cakes, hurrying away afterwards without listening to her thanks, and from the shore bowing and waving their hands and handkerchiefs as long as she remained in sight.

"These strangers have been kind to me," thought Leonora; "why should I fear that those on whom I have some natural claims will prove otherwise?"

Of the kindness of strangers she had no further proofs worthy of notice for a couple of days. The route by Rotterdam is that of home-returning families burdened with luggage, or commercial travellers: the latter scarcely observed her presence, the former did not approve of the appearance of a girl so young being quite alone; and prudent parents frowned down the incipient attempts of sons willing to offer civilities to eyes so dark and face so fair.

It was well for Leonora that she was in mind less youthful than in appearance, and that her knowledge of various
languages helped her through the little difficulties which
invariably fall to the lot of a solitary female traveller at the
much-dreaded foreign *douane*, and the infinitely more disagreeable English Custom-house.

Her ideas of the vastness and commercial importance of
London were certainly not decreased by her passage up the
Thames. All foreigners should choose that approach to the
metropolis if they wish to receive new impressions; even
those from maritime countries cannot fail to be struck with
the endless rows of ships that form a floating world around
them. The word foreigner, as applied to herself, would have
been most offensive to Leonora, whose pride in being an
Englishwoman, and admiration and reverence for everything English, were as unbounded as her ignorance of the
manners and customs of the country which she pertinaciously called her "native land." Unwilling that even her
fellow-passengers should suspect this to be her first passage
up the Thames, she sat on the still damp, green benches in
the stern of the Dutch steam-boat, a perfectly silent observer of all that was new to her. Through a rather dense
yellow fog she first saw the great ships of war; then more
clearly the merchantmen in apparently interminable lines;
large steamers rushing past, containing perchance persons
and papers of incalculable importance; smaller ones darting
in all directions, filled with people and things of less note;
and many crowded with gaily-dressed pleasure-seeking parties. Innumerable boats of various dimensions and forms
plied across the river from ship to ship, or supplied the latter with fresh provisions; each and all afforded her endless
interest, while from the colliers alone she turned away as
children are wont to do from chimney-sweepers. It was
Sunday, and she saw both ships and crew in their best at-

tire. There was none of the usual hurry and bustle, and as
the sailors leaned lazily over the gunwale of their ships, or
descended smartly dressed into attendant boats in order to
go ashore, she found more resemblance to other places and
people than she perhaps desired; while the dark-looking
wharfs, stores, and warehouses not a little disappointed expectations of the banks of the Thames, that partiality had
unconsciously raised to a par with the beautiful quays of
southern cities of less note.

All comparisons with other lands were soon, however,
lost in wonder at the apparently endless number of ships,
which, as they proceeded, seemed to increase, and at last
close around them; so that when the noisy escape of steam
convinced her that they had reached their mooring-place,
she still saw beyond her an interminable extent of masts
and rigging, with a dark background of massive buildings
becoming gradually clearer in the rays of red sunshine that
struggled through the slowly-dispersing fog.

In the year 1840 there was no St Katharine's Wharf to
facilitate the landing of travellers, and Leonora's contempla-
tions were interrupted by the arrival of the Custom-house
officers. Her luggage was detained, her carpet bag, after a
severe examination, returned to her, and having dragged it
to the side of the ship, she waited patiently for an opportunity of descending into one of the numerous boats surrounding them. There was a great deal of shouting, and
swearing, and pushing, and pulling, and loud dialogues carried on in a language unintelligible to her, though an occasional word made her aware that it was intended for English. An elderly French gentleman, who had been invisible
during the voyage, having been drawn forward by the
crowd, began slowly and carefully to descend the side of
the ship, and when about half way attempted, in very broken English, to make a bargain for the transporting of him-

self and *sac de nuit* to the hospitable shores of old England. He was, however, immediately somewhat rudely pushed forward by two sailors who stood at either side of the ladder, and who then looked up with grinning faces to see who would come next. There was a pause, no one seemed disposed to follow, and Leonora, taking advantage of the open space, directly advanced. She was politely requested "not to be afeard," then fairly lifted into the boat very much in the manner of a package marked "Glass—keep this side up"— deposited beside the Frenchman, and though the boatmen evidently expected and wished for more passengers, they were, in spite of their vociferations, pushed aside and forced to pull towards the landing-place. It was at a short distance further up the river, and they reached it in about ten minutes; but as the French gentleman prepared to step ashore he was desired first to pay his fare, and the evidently much-valued *sac de nuit* drawn from his reluctant hands as a pledge for the same. He gave two shillings—four shillings—six shillings—and then looked with an expression of astonishment at the impudent laughing faces of the boatmen. When, however, he closed his purse, and endeavoured to gain possession of his property, they waved him off, and explained by words and the extension of so many fingers, that for less than eight shillings he should not enjoy the privilege of landing on British ground.

"Dat is four *pour* mademoiselle and four *pour moi?*"

They explained, with imperturbable insolence, that *poor* or rich ma'mselle must pay eight shillings as well as mounshier, and they seized her property also, to explain alike their determination to persist in their claims, and fully to explain their meaning, which they doubted her understanding, as they had only heard her speak French to her fellow-traveller. Leonora instantly paid the eight shillings, without an attempt at remonstrance; and then, in better

English than was perhaps quite agreeable to them, hoped at least that one of them would carry her bag and place it in a carriage for her. After a few words of advice to her travelling companion to follow her example, she ran up the landing-place, and was soon after rolling rapidly towards B—— Square.

CHAPTER IV

Leonora Nixon Lands—and Forthwith Finds a Guardian

ONLY those who have travelled, and not unfrequently themselves remained stationary for some time at various places on the continent of Europe, can form an idea of the numbers of British subjects who, from necessity or for economy, or pleasure, reside there. The wanderers, scarcely deserving the name of residents, are perhaps still more numerous, and to both classes children are born, who, educated and not unfrequently married without having ever been in England, nevertheless persist in calling it their *native* land, denominate themselves English, and think it incumbent on them to be peculiarly and even sometimes ostentatiously patriotic.

One of these pseudo-English was Leonora Nixon. England was to her the land of promise, the home of her imagination. Her father had ever taken a sort of pride and pleasure in abusing foreign habits and manners, even while himself unconsciously acquiring them. He had impressed on her mind so exalted an idea of England, both as country and nation, that she supposed ignorance alone enabled her still to value what she saw elsewhere; and his brilliant and somewhat boasting reminiscences of his life in London received too much confirmation from her mother's fond recollections of the same scenes, not to be listened to with profound and eager credulity. During the long private con-

versations between the mother and daughter, it was especially the glory and excellence of the Medway family that
had formed the topic of discussion—the worth and dignity
of Lord Medway, the beauty and grace of Lady Medway,
her enviable position in the world of fashion, her charming
children, the magnificence of Thorpe Manor, and even the
humbler beauties of a villa on the Thames called The Willows. Of her paternal relations, the Nixons, Leonora had, as
has been observed, heard nothing that had tended to raise
them in her estimation—vulgar, purse-proud, city people.
She wished to forget their very existence, and pretty nearly
contrived to do so as she drove along the silent, empty
streets of London, internally applauding the evident keeping holy of the Sabbath day, and doing no manner of work,
which the still unopened shutters of the windows so satisfactorily demonstrated.

Her predetermination to admire everything English was,
during this early Sunday morning drive, put hardly to the
proof: there were no open warehouses, with their marvellous display of costly goods to attract her attention; no bustling crowd to amaze her with its endless swarms; no pal-
ace-like buildings, such as had been familiar to her eyes
from childhood; and as she glanced curiously up at the interminable rows of dingy brick houses, with their unorna-
mented façades of three and four windows, she was obliged
to recall to her mind all her mother had told her of the luxury and domestic comfort which could only be obtained
when each family, as in England, possessed a house alone.

The prospect brightened as she advanced westward. The
squares were succeeded by long, wide streets; buildings of
some extent became visible in the distance; there were occasional glimpses of the parks; more rows of shopless
houses, trees, grass, iron railings, and at length the cab
stopped. A knock, and instantaneous opening of a large

handsome door followed; but although two servants became visible, neither moved beyond the threshold, and the
cabman returned to Leonora for orders.

"Ask if I can see Lady Medway."

The man came back directly with the answer, "Her l'ship
has left town for The Willys."

"Perhaps Lord Medway is still here," suggested Leonora,
getting rather nervous.

She saw the servants look at each other, and then at her,
and half smile as one of them answered, "His lordship is in
town, but not up; he always breakfasts late, and it would be
better if the young lady were to call again."

"Oh! if he be but at home, that is all I want," cried
Leonora, joyously springing up the steps to the door; "I can
wait until his usual breakfast hour, and do not wish him to
be disturbed on my account."

One of the footmen now whispered a few words to a
servant out of livery, just then about to ascend the stairs: he
turned round, looked deliberately, almost inquisitively, at
Leonora, and then asked her name.

Not apparently much enlightened by hearing it, he nevertheless opened the door of the breakfast-room, and requested her to wait while he informed Lord Medway of her
wish to see him.

Leonora was too anxious to take much notice of the
room or its furniture; she stood with her eyes fixed on the
closed door, listening for the sound of returning footsteps,
which the well-carpeted stairs rendered inaudible; but so
intense was her attention that she soon after heard a low
voice say distinctly, "All right, Williams, take in the travel-
ling-bag and dismiss the cabman." A moment afterwards
the door was opened, and she was respectfully informed,
"That his lordship was up, and would come down as soon
as possible; he hoped Miss Nixon had had a good passage

from Rotterdam: had he known when she was likely to arrive he would have sent a carriage:—begged she would breakfast without waiting for him."

All this was very satisfactory; and with a sigh of relief Leonora took off her bonnet, and for some time calmly watched the quick yet noiseless preparations for breakfast. They were, however, no sooner completed, and she was once more alone, than her uneasiness and anxiety returned, and after walking for some time up and down the room, she threw herself into a chair, and awaited the coming interview with a sort of desperate resolution that enabled her effectually to overcome the faintness that befell her as the door at last opened; and advancing towards her she saw— not the benevolent-looking, venerable friend she had expected, but the invalid traveller of the Rhine steamer!

"Miss Nixon," he said, in a low and rather weak voice, "I know you did not expect to find in me your late correspondent. Let me assure you that nothing but the fear of filling your mind with doubts, and creating useless difficulties, prevented me from informing you of my father's death when I answered your letter."

Leonora, who had risen for a moment, again sat down, struggled with her feelings of regret, disappointed hopes, and personal annoyance for a few seconds, and then burst into tears.

"I—I did not know that you had been personally acquainted with my father," said Lord Medway: "from some letters found among his papers I was led to suppose that he had corresponded with your mother, and chiefly as guardian to her son. In fact, I imagined you in want of an adviser and friend, both of which my father would have been to you most undoubtedly had he lived. I hope I have not erred in proposing to take his place, or supposing that my services would be as acceptable to you as his."

"He was my only friend," said Leonora, in a voice nearly choked by emotion, "the only one of our family who ever remembered my name, or seemed conscious of my existence."

"And when did you last see him?" asked Lord Medway, leaning his elbow on the chimney-piece, and watching with an air of mixed surprise and commiseration, the uncontrolled expression of her almost passionate grief. "When did you last see him?"

"I never saw him," she answered, looking up, and at the moment the utter selfishness of her sorrow struck her so forcibly that she compelled herself to overcome it; and removing the traces of tears from her face, she stood up, and in a tolerably composed voice informed him of his father's kind letter to her after the death of her mother, and offers of friendly services should she ever be in want of them. "I mention this," she added, "that you may not think I applied to him without a right to do so: his loss to me is just now irreparable, as it obliges me to apply to my step-brother, who, I fear, will have little inclination to assist a person he could scarcely learn to tolerate even for his mother's sake."

"You don't mean that Harry does not like you?" said Lord Medway.

"I once heard him say," answered Leonora, "that the name of Nixon would stifle any feelings of regard he might ever be disposed to feel for me. You have, I hope, had the kindness to forward my letter to him, and if you will now only let me know where he is to be found—"

"You could scarcely ask me a more puzzling question," answered Lord Medway, smiling. "I forwarded your letter to my brother Charles, who is at Vienna: he keeps up a desultory correspondence with Harry, and generally knows something of his whereabouts—he believes him to be now at some place on the coast of Syria, in his yacht; but when your letter will reach him is very uncertain."

"What is to become of me?" cried Leonora, covering her face with her hands, while visions of her city uncles and their plebeian families floated distractingly before her haughty imagination.

"You will of course remain with us—with my mother, until you hear from Harry," suggested Lord Medway.

Leonora instantly caught at this idea. "Can I go to Lady Medway to-day?" she asked, quickly.

"My mother is at present from home on a visit to some relations," he answered, "and only my youngest sister is at The Willows. I shall, however, have great pleasure in taking you there to-morrow."

"And why not to-day?" she asked, a little anxiously.

"I'm sure I don't know. I aw—suppose—there is nothing to prevent us from driving there after we have breakfasted, and aw—been to church."

He rang the bell, and afterwards, during a *tête-à-tête* of more than an hour, they strode towards intimacy with seven-leagued boots, Leonora being perfectly communicative on every subject excepting her uncles; and Lord Medway informing her that he had been a sad, idle, worthless fellow; but now intended to reform, and, if his health allowed him to winter in England, proposed becoming a pattern country gentleman. He evidently considered a regular attendance at church as a first and very important step towards the meditated change, and nothing could equal the gravity and decorum of his manner, as he accompanied Leonora to church, and his attention to the service when there. She did not at all believe that he had ever been idle or worthless, and when he rose from his knees at the end of the Litany, apparently exhausted, tears of genuine compassion dimmed her eyes to think that so excellent a young man seemed doomed to an early grave. This feeling must have been in some degree participated by a large proportion of the congregation, if one might judge by the looks of interest which reached them from the remotest corners. The carpeted and well-cushioned pews of the Chapel of Ease, as it was called, were occupied by a congregation who were all either sufficiently acquainted to speak, or who at least knew each other by sight. Lord Medway's appearance with a young and remarkably pretty stranger, in as deep mourning as his own sister could have worn, created quite a sensation; more eagerly than usual was he surrounded as he left the church, more numerous than ever were the inquiries concerning his health, and plans for the summer; the querists deliberately examining his companion while listening to his languid, negligent answers. To not one did he name her, to not one did he mention his intention of leaving town that afternoon; but drawing her arm within his, increased their curiosity by murmuring a few words of German, and then sauntering slowly homewards.

"I fear," said Leonora, after having seen him throw himself at full length on a *chaise longue*, and resolutely close his eyes, "I fear you will not be able to drive to The Willows to-day."

"Oh, yes; I shall be quite well again after I have slept a little and dined. You won't mind dining with me at two o'clock, will you? I am obliged to keep invalid hours at present."

"I am accustomed to dine early," answered Leonora. "What people call dinner here would be supper to me."

"Ah, true—I had forgotten that you are scarcely an Englishwoman."

With considerable warmth she explained that "she did not think her having by chance been born in a foreign country in any way lessened her right to consider herself one."

"I referred to your habits and education," said Lord Medway, amused at her eagerness.

"Papa's habits were very English, and mamma directed my education herself: I—I only," she added, with some reluctance, "only went occasionally for a few months to a foreign school, when, on removing to a new country, it was necessary to acquire the language quickly."

"What immense advantages you have had!" he observed thoughtfully. "I dare say, now, you speak three or four languages quite as well as English."

Leonora was silent. She could not contradict the assertion; but would have greatly preferred his saying, that she spoke the last-named as if she had never been out of England.

"The only way to learn these languages properly," he continued, "is to live abroad. And with what ease can they be acquired in early youth—with what labour at a later period!"

Leonora just then felt too English to value in the least her linguistic acquirements, and when he again spoke and remarked, that travelling about, as she had done, imperceptibly formed both mind and manners, almost without instruction, and added that she was "charmingly *dégagée*, and not at all prudish, or like an Englishwoman," she rose, and with a formality which seemed to contradict his last words, "feared she was preventing him from sleeping, and would not further intrude upon him."

"Stay, Miss Nixon—stay; I can't go to sleep this half-hour," he cried, starting up; "and as to intruding, I never heard anything so absurd! Why, we are relations, aren't we? Come back, and let us find out in what degree."

These last words were not without effect: Leonora was at the door—she stopped a moment, looked back with a bright smile, and seemed to hesitate; but then saying, "We can talk of that some other time—you must go to sleep now," she resolutely closed the door.

For the first time in her life she had now an opportunity of inspecting a really well-furnished house. She had not unfrequently been the inmate of suites of rooms approached by marble staircases; of airy Italian villas; of apartments with fresco-painted walls, and statue-filled ante-chambers: but cold and comfortless came the recollection of such domiciles, when compared with the perfectly elegant luxury of the furniture of this English home. All that art, and taste, and wealth, could command, or fancy suggest of useful or beautiful was there, and all so judiciously in keeping that the most careless observer must have been charmed. She had not examined half the china, bronze, and ormolu ornaments, the tables, carpets, and book-cases, and was delightedly turning over the leaves of a volume of magnificent prints, when the announcement of dinner obliged her to join Lord Medway.

It was still early when they were seated in the carriage, on their way to The Willows. Once fairly out of the immediate precincts of London, Leonora became eager in her praise of the various crescents, squares, and rows of neat houses which long made the suburb appear a continuation of the metropolis. These houses gradually assuming a country air, diminished in height as their possessors increased their extent of landed property; beginning with the little garden in front, progressing to the small shrubbery, followed by more or less ambitious attempts at avenues; then some trees to shut out the road, and finally the walled domain!

Much as Leonora was bent on finding everything in England supereminently excellent and admirable, she was somewhat puzzled to find any object worthy of condemnation, when their road lay between long walls topped by iron spikes, or hideous fragments of broken glass bottles. The dust seemed forced to hover around them, while the over-hanging trees, giving an idea of green woods beyond, be-came at last so tantalising, that, after a long silence, she could not help drawing a comparison between the road scenery of other countries and England, which was not ex-actly advantageous to the latter.

Lord Medway seemed roused to unusual attention, and replied quickly, "It is quite natural that you should merely glance at things with the eye of a foreigner, and, like them, form hasty conclusions. I can easily understand your disap-proving of these walls; but there are two sides to every question. You have as yet no idea of the extent and popula-tion of London, and were you for some time an inmate of one of these places, you would, for more reasons than I can now explain to you, be very glad to have a barrier between you and a high road such as this!"

Leonora thought this might be true, but was surprised at the warmth of her companion's defence of the ugly broken-bottle topped walls, as he had not only abused everything English during dinner, but had unreservedly laughed at her, perhaps, indiscriminate praises of all she had since seen. She was not yet aware that an Englishman's abuse of his country is about as sincere as his abuse of himself. He may call the laws confused and intricate, the climate atrocious, and so forth; but he does so much as he would call himself a dolt or a donkey, great being alike his surprise and indig-nation at finding any one inclined even for a moment to agree with him.

Leonora begged him playfully not to remind her so very often of her foreign education, and assured him she was quite disposed, in fact, rather expected (with the exception of the walled-in roads), to find everything faultless in Eng-land.

"Then you will be bitterly disappointed," said Lord Medway.

"I do not quite agree with you," she rejoined. "There, for instance, is a village, and here are trees and meadows answering all my expectations."

"That village is not far from The Willows," said Lord Medway, "and at the next turn we shall see the river, and soon after the house."

The Willows was what is called a jointure-house; it was there that all Countesses of Medway took up their abode, inspected schools, were good to the poor, and died respected and lamented by all who had the happiness of knowing them. But it was not there that they were buried—their remains were conveyed to the family vault at Thorpe Manor, there to be solemnly interred in the presence of the surviving family. On former melancholy occasions of this kind, many days had been necessary to convey the coffin and coach full of mourning servants to their destination; on the last as many hours had sufficed for the same purpose per railroad, thereby proving that railroads are curtailers of grief as well as distance.

The Willows had been long uninhabited, excepting occasionally for a few days, when there were races or archery-meetings in the neighbourhood; and the present possessor, having three young and unmarried daughters, was not likely to be as constant a resident as her predecessor. She had already left it, accompanied by her two elder daughters, to spend a few weeks with relations, at whose house a select party of friends had assembled to offer her all the consolation in their power. It had been said The Willows required repair, and some tiles had been put on the roof, the doors and windows painted, and the chintz curtains washed. Further orders had not been given, and perhaps they were not necessary, for the house was comfortably, though not luxuriously furnished. As Leonora drove up the short avenue, so short that it scarcely deserved the name, and gazed up at the long, low, red-brick house, with its ground floor, first story, and high weather-beaten tiled roof, a look of disappointment passed over her expressive face, which was instantly observed by her companion, who seemed to study her countenance as earnestly as Lavater* himself could have done.

"Leonora," he said, smiling, and laying particular emphasis on her name (they had discovered that they were cousins in some way or other, and had become very good friends during the day), "Leonora, this is not one of the disappointments I foretold. Wait until you have seen the other side of the house before you pass judgment on The Willows."

They entered the hall, which was large, and had an old-fashioned fire-place, not far distant from the commencement of a broad oak staircase, rendered almost black by oil and age; they then passed into an ante-room redolent of fresh flowers in vases and pots, concealed by green wicker-work stands, and thence into a long drawing-room, with windowed recesses, that seemed to belong to octagonal turrets, each forming a sort of separate apartment, while between them glass doors led into a garden terminating in shrubberies with groups of forest trees.

The undoubtedly antiquated furniture of the room was covered with a gay-coloured chintz: its want of elegance of form being, however, amply compensated by its variety and

---

* Johann Kaspar Lavater (1741-1801), Swiss poet and Protestant clergyman; author of *Physiognomische Fragmente zur Beförderung der Menschenkenntnis und Menschenliebe (Physiognomic Fragments on the Encouragement of Human Understanding and Philanthropy)* (1775-78), promoting the theory that facial characteristics were clues to personality.

comfort. This chintz, perhaps, concealed more costly material, for each succeeding dowager had added some favourite
pieces of furniture, so that the covers now served but to
give them all the necessary uniformity. The setting sun
shone brightly into the room, and lighted the figure of a
fair-haired girl of about fifteen, who, after uttering a slight
exclamation of surprise, sprang forward and embraced
Lord Medway with an emotion that wavered strangely between joy and sorrow.

"My dear Severton—a—a—I mean Med—"

"Never mind that, Jane. Let me introduce our cousin,
Leonora Nixon, to you."

Lady Jane looked round hastily, gazed half inquiringly,
half amazedly at Leonora, saw nothing repelling, perhaps
something the contrary, in her appearance, and held out her
hand, murmuring something about having so many cousins
that she scarcely knew all their names.

It was hardly to be expected that she should know Leonora's, never in all her life having heard it; but, without waiting for an answer, she turned to her brother, and said—

"How kind of you to come and see me; I gave up all
hopes from the time mamma went to you!"

"If you promise to be very attentive to me, perhaps I
may stay here for a few days," he answered, smiling.

"Oh, so attentive!" she exclaimed, pushing a large chair
towards him, and seating herself on a footstool beside him,
while Leonora walked to one of the glass doors, "so attentive and obedient! You may send me twenty messages in an
hour, and I shall not grumble or pout my lips, as you used
to say I did."

"Twenty messages in an hour! Surely I never was so un-
conscionable!"

"Indeed, you were; but I was often disobliging enough
too—however, that was all a hundred years ago. Tell me

something about yourself now. Mamma and Grace wrote to me after they had seen you, and said you had grown rather thinner, but that you were getting much better, and they hoped you would be induced to remain in England this winter."

"If not," answered Lord Medway, "I intend to propose your all spending the winter with me at Nice."

"Oh, how delightful! nothing I should like so much as going abroad. I really at times feel quite ashamed of never having left England."

"And there is your cousin Leonora, who is quite ashamed of never having been here."

"Never been in England?"

"No. She was born and has spent all her life, hitherto, on the continent."

"Do tell me how she is our cousin," whispered Lady Jane.

"She is step-sister to Harry Darwin—her mother and our father were cousins, you know."

"Oh!"

"So you see—she is second cousin or a—aw—first cousin once removed, or a—something of that sort—a cousin at all events."

When Leonora perceived the gradual lowering of the voices to a confidential whisper, she stepped into the garden, and having walked a short distance, turned round to take a view of the house. It might have been originally at this side also a long, low, red-brick building, but changes had been effected, and additions made, until it had assumed the appearance styled Elizabethan; and as Leonora's wondering eyes wandered along the puzzlingly irregular façade, seeking symmetry and finding none, she was fully impressed with the idea intended to be given to all beholders unlearned in such matters, that the mansion was of great antiquity.

She was soon after joined by Lord Medway and his sister, and commenced a walk through gardens and shrubberies kept with a neatness perfectly new to her. The grounds, running along the banks of the Thames, were tastefully and advantageously laid out, and contained fine specimens of forest and other trees, single and in groups, and among them sufficiently conspicuous, and near the house, some splendid weeping willows—which had probably given the place its name. Under these trees were seats, and there they sat down to watch the approach of night.

It was a calm, warm evening, and a pleasing glow spread over the whole scene as the sun disappeared, and left the sky covered with fantastic-looking bright red and yellow clouds, that were distinctly reflected on the clear surface of the river. Occasionally a heavily-laden barge glided slowly past, or a light wherry darted across to the landing-place of some other villa, but it was not until a succession of boats filled with a gay party returning from a pic-nic came close beneath the willows that they moved. Lord Medway had accosted some friends, and great was their surprise, as they said, to see him there, looking so well, and able to sit out so late on the damp banks of the river. On this hint a hasty retreat was made to the house, Lady Jane openly expressing her anxiety, and hoping and trusting he had not caught cold, to prevent which she ordered a fire in an odd-shaped little room, where they drank tea and spent the evening together very gaily.

CHAPTER V

The Willows

ONE week, and then a second, and then a third passed over calmly and pleasantly at The Willows. For some undoubtedly good reason, which Lord Medway did not think it necessary to communicate to his companions, he had from day to day deferred writing to his mother, and Leonora, after being desired somewhat authoritatively to "leave everything to him," concerned herself no further about the matter. Lady Jane was too young, and had much too exalted an idea of her brother's wisdom to offer either advice or remonstrance, and having yielded at once to the boundless admiration for Leonora with which she had suddenly been inspired, informed every one who chose to hear it, that she liked her better than all her other cousins—that she was the most dear, darling, clever creature she had ever seen, the only one who suited her exactly for a companion, and could make her quite contented to stay at home until Grace or Louisa was married.

To all this Lord Medway listened approvingly, agreed with his sister in thinking it would never answer to let Harry Darwin take charge of Leonora, even if he proposed doing so on his return to England, and when they were alone together, "hoped" his mother would allow her to remain with them until—until—

"Until Harry is married," suggested Lady Jane. "Oh, I

am sure mamma will have no objection when I promise to speak French constantly, and to learn German from her; do you know, I think German does not sound at all disagreeably when she speaks it; and then she sings such lots of pretty little songs—but she says they sound better to a guitar—I wish you would send to town for one."

"Of course I shall," he answered, "and in the mean time she must sing to me with a pianoforte accompaniment. I dare say she plays famously!"

"Not exactly—it is rather in an odd sort of way, for her father did not like to hear her practise, so she learned altogether differently from other people."

"How so? I heard her playing some sacred music very nicely."

"That's it!" cried Lady Jane, "she has learned theoretically, and can go on playing chords and composing for herself whole hours together."

"A much pleasanter kind of accomplishment for a private performer than rattling eternally at those dreadful fantasies and variations like Grace and Louisa," observed Lord Medway. "Tell her to come here, Jane; say I want her to write letters for me, as I am too much fatigued to sit up any longer."

He stretched himself on a sofa as he spoke, and when Leonora appeared, pointed to a table beside him on which were writing materials. He dictated, and she wrote, sealed, and addressed, as he directed her; the last letter was an order for a guitar with case, strings, &c, and then she looked up inquiringly.

"For you—to serenade me with," he said, nodding his head, and Leonora smiled and folded the letter, with a slight increase of colour, that he thought became her exceedingly.

The guitar arrived the next evening, and was carried into

the garden, where, to Lady Jane's infinite delight, Leonora hid herself behind a clump of trees, and by a few chords or a verse of a song, attracted the attention of all the passers-by on the river. At a later hour she played at serenading, too, sitting outside the drawing-room window, and recalling distant scenes and persons to Lord Medway's mind by a succession of light French, sweet Italian, and melodious German airs. When she re-entered the room he seemed to be indulging in a deep reverie, while Leonora, drawing a chair close to Lady Jane's, and unconscious of being watched or listened to, yielded without reserve to the gaiety inspired by her own music, and sang, laughed, talked, and related some travelling adventures with such humour, that Lord Medway, irresistibly attracted by her amusing gaiety, moved unperceived his chair behind hers, and she was first made aware of his vicinity by a hearty fit of laughter on his part that startled himself by its mirthful boyish sound.

This had taken place very shortly after her arrival, and a slight sketch which she afterwards gave of her short but not unadventurous life, seemed at once to remove all barriers to intimacy, and their intercourse thenceforward lost every trace of new acquaintanceship.

Lady Medway's letter announcing her intended return home, gave pleasure to Lady Jane alone—"She so much wished Leonora to know dear mamma, and darling Grace and Louisa, and then they could have some nice little pic-nics in the neighbourhood, and—" but here she was stopped by Leonora asking anxiously if there were no mention made of her in the letter.

Lady Jane had not observed the omission; she glanced once more at it, and then her look of inquiry, though less intense than Leonora's, was turned towards her brother.

His pale face became unusually flushed, and there was a good deal of nervous irritation in the manner in which he suddenly rose from the breakfast-table and said, "I have not yet written about you, Leonora, but I suppose I must do so to-day; there is, however, time enough—and I feel better now than for some time past—more equal to the exertion."

He had ever found his health so impenetrable a shield against reproaches implied or expressed, that he never failed to use it; and Leonora was not only silenced, but even felt great compassion a couple of hours afterwards, when she saw that he had written an unusually long letter, and appeared extremely fatigued.

Lady Medway arrived the ensuing week. She was what is generally termed "a fine woman"—that is, she was tall, handsome, and distinguished-looking, and inclined just so much to *embonpoint* that, with the partial loss of symmetry of figure, she had preserved a good portion of the freshness and beauty for which she had long been remarkable. Lady Grace and Lady Louisa resembled their mother a good deal in appearance; they were lady-like, and had already enjoyed several seasons in London, which had given them considerable knowledge of the world, and what is called *à plomb*.

They all received Leonora kindly, putting her at once at her ease by seeming to consider her being at The Willows the most natural thing possible. She was very much pleased, and very grateful, and thought Lady Medway the most charming person she had ever seen, the most amusing person she had ever heard talk—especially when seated beside her son's sofa, her feet stretched out before her on a footstool, she related all that had occurred in their family during his absence abroad. She touched but once, and then lightly, on his not having been able to return home for some time after his father's death, ending by assuring him with a warmth that made no small impression on Leonora, that dearest Charley had supplied his place to them all, and that nothing could equal his attention to her, or energy in business of every description.

"Charley was always a capital fellow," murmured Lord Medway, in reply.

"We thought him greatly improved in appearance, too," she continued.

"I think him much the same as ever," he rejoined; "very like you in face, very like my father in figure, and his manners all his own."

Lady Grace and Lady Louisa joined their mother in pronouncing Charley's manners perfect.

"Well, I believe he is pretty generally considered a gentlemanlike sort of fellow," he observed, indolently; "people even admire and applaud his eccentricities, perhaps because they are essentially English. For my part I sincerely rejoice in all his faults and foibles, as I should consider a paragon younger brother a decided bore."

"Has he done or said anything to offend you?" asked Lady Medway, quickly.

"Quite the contrary; he has saved me such an infinity of trouble that I have forgiven him for having called me a lazy hypochondriac, and recommending a course of his own rough exercise to a man in my state of health!"

"Perhaps," began Lady Medway, hesitatingly, "perhaps my dear love—a little exertion on your part occasionally might be beneficial to your—"

"Do you, too, begin to consider me a *malade imaginaire?*" he asked, peevishly. "Do you think the life I lead at present is agreeable? I tell you it is not; and if," he added, rising and walking towards the door leading into the garden, "if I could with half my fortune purchase health and a constitution such as Charley's, I would do it to-day, without waiting for to-morrow."

As he stepped out of the room his mother sighed, and turning to her eldest daughters, observed, "Is it not melancholy to see such terrible want of energy? His desire to be considered an invalid has become a positive mania."

Leonora did not hear the answer, she followed Lord Medway and Lady Jane into the garden, and began to collect flowers to make a bouquet for the former, such as she knew he liked. His mother had since his arrival so completely monopolized him, that for several days she had scarcely had an opportunity of speaking to him. When he now sat down under one of the willow trees, she placed herself beside him, and while arranging her bright-coloured verbenas and pelargoniums, hoped he could bestow a few minutes of his precious time upon her—just enough to tell her if his mother would permit her to remain at The Willows until she received an answer from her brother Harry —she had not courage to ask Lady Medway herself.

"It will be long before Harry gets your letter," he replied, evasively, "still longer before you can have an answer to it. Suppose you should be obliged to pass the winter here?"

"I should be but too happy," said Leonora, looking up with a smile.

"And do you not find it dull in this place, after the gay, wandering life you have hitherto led?"

"Dull in such society? Oh, no—I wish I could spend the rest of my life here."

"Indeed! and how much of that wish may I place to my own account?"

"A large fifth portion," she answered, twisting some bast round her bouquet,—"a large fifth portion. I like Jane best—you next—then Grace—then Louisa—and then Lady Medway—I am a little, a very little, afraid of her still, because—because I don't think she quite likes me."

"You are mistaken, Leonora; she likes you very much, but—"

Leonora looked up anxiously.

"She thinks you ought to have been more candid with me in the first instance, and not concealed the fact of your having two uncles living in London, able, and probably willing, to be of use to you, but who may now reasonably be displeased at your avoidance of them. She even fears they are in ignorance of your present place of abode. Is this the case?"

"It is," answered Leonora, her eyes filling with tears; "but, oh! if you knew how I fear and dislike these uncles—"

"Are you personally acquainted with them?" he asked, surprised.

"No; but I have heard of them all my life from mamma and papa: they are purse-proud, vulgar men; and in papa's writing-desk I found such severe letters from my uncle Stephen to him that I quite dread a meeting. It is true papa had over-drawn his allowance, and was rather in the wrong; but under the circumstances the threats were so ungenerous, so ungentlemanlike, that—"

"Let me see these letters," he said, interrupting her, and Leonora, throwing her half-finished bouquet and remaining flowers over his crossed arms, ran into the house.

She soon returned, and then with heads bent together they pored over uncle Stephen's epistle; Leonora reluctantly admitting her father's error, but eloquently commenting on the harshness of the manner in which he had been reproved.

"It is the letter of an angry man of business," said Lord Medway, folding it up and returning it to her. "I believe, Leonora, the less we say about this matter the better. What sort of a man," he added, after a pause, "what sort of a man is your other uncle? Gilbert I believe is the name."

"Rather less disagreeable, but infinitely more vulgar, according to papa's account," she answered; "but you see the letter is a joint concern—he says, 'my brother Gilbert and I,' throughout."

"True," said Lord Medway, musingly, "I must explain all this to my mother—it would never do—careless as Harry is, he would scarcely approve of his sister's being sent to people among whom we should completely lose sight of her."

"My uncle Stephen's house is in Russell-square," began Leonora, despondingly, "so except when you happen to be in town I should be very far away from you and Jane."

"And even then you would be very far away from us," he observed, smiling, "so far, that I refuse my consent to any arrangement beyond letting your uncles know where you are now living. Perhaps, however, in the excess of your patriotism you would prefer any residence in England to one on the continent just at present?"

"You think," said Leonora, "I shall have no answer from Harry before you go abroad?"

"I am sure you will have none," he replied, with emphasis. "Now listen to me, Leonora. You have very exalted ideas of England and the English, and I have no desire to lower either in your estimation; for this reason, and perhaps some others also, I do not wish you to go to Russell-square. On the contrary, I hope to be able to induce you, for my sake, to leave England again for some time. My mother and sisters spend the winter with me at Nice—promise me to go there with us."

"If Lady Medway have no objection—" began Leonora.

"She will be *my* guest," he interposed quickly, "and you, Leonora, will be the same—for—some—time." While speaking he took her hand, and drawing her towards him looked earnestly into her face while he added, "But you must tell me that you will leave England without regret, that you can do so willingly, because you know that you will add to my happiness—"

"And Jane's," said Leonora, smiling.

"No Janes," cried Lord Medway, impatiently, "you must think of me and me alone!"

At this moment a low soft voice immediately behind them said gently, "Is it prudent your remaining out here when it is so late and so very damp?"

He turned round, evidently not pleased at the interruption. It was his mother, who stood close to them. She might have heard the latter part of their conversation, but there was nothing in her manner to lead any one to suppose so. Her eyes were fixed on the dusky fog that now seemed to be slowly drifting along the river towards them, while she added, "One feels that it is September, and that winter is approaching. Let us go in and sit round the fire, the pleasantest place by far on such an evening as this!"

"It is damp, but not cold," said Lord Medway, rising. "Come, Leonora, you shall read the papers to me. I want you to acquire a taste for politics."

"Let me or Grace read to you," said his mother, "we shall ourselves be interested while so employed, while to Leonora it will be an unnecessary trial of patience. She and Jane can take a walk in the shrubbery—the evening fog will do them no harm."

Leonora had no particular fancy for reading newspapers, nor did she fear the fog, so she turned back to Lady Jane, who was springing along a gravel walk with a small spaniel barking at her heels, and followed her slowly with thoughts full of having to leave England before she had seen almost anything of it—of returning to Nice, where she had already spent two winters with her dying mother—of Lord Medway's unusually earnest manner, until her companion suddenly ceased playing, and, snatching up her dog in her arms, breathlessly exclaimed, "Oh, Leonora, only think! After all you may see Charley before we leave England!"

"How so?" asked Leonora, with an eagerness and interest only to be accounted for by the fact, that, added to what she had already heard of him from her step-brother, he had been latterly the subject of constant conversation between her and her friend Jane.

"Because, you see, mamma wrote to Charley the day after she came here, and an answer arrived this morning."

"Well?" said Leonora.

"Well, I heard mamma say to Grace and Louisa, that she would write again and request him to come to England, if only for a fortnight, as she required not only advice but assistance."

"About what?" asked Leonora.

"I'm sure I don't know—something concerning Medway, I should think, as they talked of the necessity of getting him off to Italy* without delay."

"He has asked me to go with you," said Leonora.

"And you will go—oh, say yes!"

"Of course I shall, if Lady Medway have no objection."

"What objection can she have?"

"I don't know."

"Nor I either. Do you, Azor?" she cried, appealing to the struggling little animal in her arms, bending down her face and speaking with closed teeth. "Can you think of any possible reason why Leonora should not go with us to Italy? No! you see he is quite delighted at the idea," she added, when, having let him spring to the ground, he began to caper round them, barking with all his might, as if inviting them to join in his gambols. Repeated gestures of pre-

---

* Nice (Nizza) was at that time part of the territory of the Counts of Savoy; it was ceded to France under the Treaty of Turin in 1860.

tended anger, various grimaces and shakings of the head having failed to silence him, a chase began, and soon after the sound of youthful laughter, intermixed with Azor's sharp barks, reached the drawing-room through the still unclosed windows. Lord Medway became singularly inattentive to his mother's reading—begged she would not give herself so much trouble—the papers were really not worth reading just now—scarcely anything going on at home, and nothing at all elsewhere—he believed he wished for tea—and—would it not be better to send to Jane and Leonora, and desire them to come in?

CHAPTER VI

An "Enemy" Procures Leonora an English Home

L ADY MEDWAY'S attention to her son became from
day to day more assiduous: she was ably assisted by
her two elder daughters, and Lord Medway, consti-
tutionally indolent, and sincerely attached to his mother and
sisters, was exceedingly gratified, and only occasionally a
very little bored. Some weeks elapsed without his having
found a convenient opportunity for renewing his interrupted conversation with Leonora, though he had not unfrequently, in an impatient, pettish manner, said, that "He
chose to have Leonora to sit beside him," or "He wanted to
speak to Leonora." On such occasions, a place in his immediate vicinity was instantly ceded to her; but the attention then bestowed on the youthful guest completely overpowered her. Even Medway himself felt a sort of reserve
creep over him, in the presence of so many apparently eager listeners. Lady Medway invariably laid down book or
work, and whether near or distant, turned her face towards
them with a benignant smile. Lady Grace pushed forward
her embroidery frame, and Lady Louisa, with a playfulness
for which she was remarkable, never failed to seat herself
on a favourite footstool at her brother's feet, and kindly
request Leonora to relate her life and adventures—

> Whereof by parcels she had something heard,
> But not intentively.[*]

Leonora would *not* consent, however, and the conversation was in the end carried on between Louisa and her brother, or Lady Medway advanced to the rescue, and allowed Leonora to slip away to her friend Jane or the garden, the first convenient opportunity.

Letters of importance began to arrive from London for Lord Medway, and it became evident that he would be obliged to spend some days in town. He prepared to do so most unwillingly, tried to persuade his mother that it was necessary they should all accompany him, and received for answer, that she must remain at The Willows until various unavoidable arrangements, before leaving England for so long a time, were completed; if the arrangements could be made in the course of the ensuing week, she would follow him to town without delay, or to Paris, should he think it advisable to precede them. For her part, she thought it very desirable that he should reach a warmer climate before the weather became wintry.

Lord Medway said, he would "think about it," and did so, perhaps, occasionally, for some days; at the end of which time a messenger was sent late one evening from London, to inform him that his brother Charles had just arrived from Vienna, had but one week to spend in England, and hoped that he would leave The Willows and join him in B—— Square without delay.

Lady Medway expressed more surprise at her son Charles's arrival than Leonora expected, after having heard from Jane that her brother would probably come to Eng-

* *Othello* Act I scene iii lines 154-155.

land, in consequence of a pressing request from his mother. Her look of inquiry was answered by Jane in a whisper: "I suppose Charley first said he could not come, and after all has managed it; some way or other he always contrives to do whatever he likes."

"I suppose I *must* go to town to-morrow," said Lord Medway; "but, with Charley's energetic assistance, we may manage to start for the Continent in a week or ten days! I dare say," he continued, glancing towards Leonora, "he can tell us something about brother Harry; but at all events," he added, turning to his mother, "nothing shall now interfere with the arrangement for Leonora, about which I spoke to you yesterday."

"Of course not," she replied, dryly; and rising abruptly, she walked towards a writing-table at the other end of the room, and there found occupation until it was time to separate for the night.

When leaving the next morning, Lord Medway begged his mother to follow him as soon as possible, told Jane she might take Azor to Italy with her, and then, turning to Leonora, hoped she had not forgotten her promise about going to Nice, and assured her that being at some place on the coast of the Mediterranean was her best, if not only, chance of seeing her brother for years.

When she looked towards Lady Medway, hoping for a word or look of at least acquiescence, her ladyship seemed altogether engrossed by some directions which she was giving to a servant about a letter that he was to deliver without delay to her son, Mr Thorpe.

Some few words Lord Medway then added in a whisper to Leonora—"He feared he should find the time pass very dismally without her, even for one solitary week, he was convinced he should be bored to death; most probably he would return in a few days, and bring Charley with him—

entreated her not to forget him—and made her promise to try and like him better even than she liked Jane!"

Leonora promised, and hoped he would bring Charley to The Willows. And she did hope this with all her heart, for if the truth must be told, she had taken a singular fancy to the boy portrait of him that hung beside that of her brother Harry, in the breakfast-room. Often, when she was supposed to be looking at the latter, had her eyes been fixed on the miniature of the proud, manly-looking boy with his whip, and his dog, and his great grey eyes; and then, when Jane told her of his wild pranks, and his courage, and extraordinary strength, Leonora feared—yes, feared—she should prove ungrateful, and like him better, far better, than her kind and gentle friend, Medway!

Lady Medway's silence respecting the projected journey during the ensuing week surprised Leonora much, as the intercourse of letters was apparently incessant. Lady Jane told her, in confidence, they were almost all from Charley, adding mysteriously, that he did not appear quite to approve of their plan of their going to Nice for the winter. Leonora attached infinitely less importance to this remark than it deserved, and forgot it completely a few evenings afterwards, when at tea-time, a packet of notes arrived, with one for herself from Lord Medway. He informed her very briefly, that all his arrangements were completed, and that, urged by his brother, he had consented to leave England in the course of a few days—that he should not, however, go further than Paris without them all, and, therefore, hoped she would forthwith have her "coffers," as she called them, packed up, as he found it impossible any longer to exist without the society and services of his charming little secretary.

Lady Medway's eyes were fixed on Leonora's smiling face, as she stood by the fire-place and read these hurried lines. Explanation of some kind respecting the journey to Nice was now inevitable, and to promote it Leonora silently handed the note to her ladyship, who was sitting unusually upright on an adjacent sofa.

"It is a fortunate circumstance, my dear girl," began Lady Medway, after a pause, "a most fortunate circumstance, that you so greatly prefer England to the Continent; were it otherwise I really should be extremely embarrassed at this moment."

Leonora's face said more plainly than her words, "I do not understand—"

"It is a curious coincidence," her ladyship continued, in her softest voice, "that I, this very morning, received a letter written by your uncle Stephen, to say that he would send a—a person here to-morrow, to take charge of you, and convey you safely to his house in Russell-square."

"My uncle! but I—I did not ask him to send for me—I have not written to him since I have been in England!"

"So I perceive from his letter, and I must say, Leonora, it was very injudicious your so openly neglecting such a rich relation."

"But his riches can in no way concern me," suggested Leonora hurriedly.

"It seems, however, he offers you a highly respectable, and a—a—comfortable home—one which may lead, in all probability, to the possession of future affluence," observed Lady Medway.

Leonora felt greatly inclined to say that she would not go to her uncle, that she should greatly prefer spending the winter at Nice—when it suddenly occurred to her that the announcement had been made without a word of regret, and that perhaps Lady Medway was unwilling to add another member to her family. Bending forward, she therefore said in a low voice—

"*You* do not wish to take me to Nice?"

"Most willingly, my dear Leonora, would I take you with me, if I should not, by doing so, deprive you not only of the protection of your nearest relations, but also of the chance of hereafter inheriting from them."

Leonora made an impatient gesture.

"Why not?" continued her ladyship. "This uncle of yours is, by all accounts, so rich, that he could provide for you without injuring his own family in any perceptible manner; and let me tell you, dear Leonora, that I cannot do so. We all like you, for Jane you are a charming companion, but after having made you sacrifice your relations, and probably considerable pecuniary advantages, what have I to offer you? Literally nothing. With two already grown-up daughters, and a third, who, in a couple of years will also expect to be introduced to the world, myself a widow, and consequently reduced in circumstances, what could I do with a young person such as you are?"

She paused, but Leonora made no attempt to answer her question, and after a moment's hesitation, her ladyship, gently compelling her to sit down beside her, enlarged with eloquence on the same theme, ending by an appeal to her good sense, and an assurance of unalterable regard on her part.

A good deal softened by this speech, Leonora sat for some moments silent and motionless, her eyes fixed intently on the floor. The necessity of resignation to her fate, and the certainty that Lady Medway would not take her to Nice, had become so evident to her, that Lord Medway now reigned paramount in her thoughts. She feared he might suppose that she had joined in deceiving him in order to remain in England, and she continued this train of ideas when, taking his note from Lady Medway's hand, she murmured, "What will *he* think of me? What will *he* say?"

"Very little, Leonora," answered her ladyship, quietly; "I am sorry to be obliged to undeceive you respecting Medway, but a—his wish to have you with him is a most reprehensible instance of selfishness—he merely wants something to interest him—some one to amuse him—and thinks you may answer both purposes for the next six months. I regret to say, this is not the first time he has acted in a similar manner!"

Leonora did not quite comprehend what the "similar manner" meant. She believed Lord Medway to be her only sincere friend, and was not disposed to resign him without a struggle. She could not understand why he should not be made acquainted with her removal to her uncle's, if the plan were so very desirable for all parties. A wish for further information made her ask to see her uncle's letter, and Lady Medway evidently prepared for the request, drew it from her pocket, placed it in Leonora's hands, and walked towards the tea-table where her daughters were seated, the two eldest speaking to each other in a low, indistinct manner, the youngest listening anxiously and following with her eyes all her mother's movements.

"There is some mistake," said Leonora, hastily, advancing a few steps, "this letter begins 'Sir'."

"It is addressed to Charles," answered her ladyship, without turning round, "it was he who undertook and carried on the correspondence."

"So," thought Leonora, "there has been a correspondence, and my uncle was perhaps unwilling to receive me."

Yet there was nothing in the letter to confirm this idea. It informed Mr Thorpe, in the very fewest words possible, that a trustworthy person would be sent to The Willows for Miss Nixon, who would not so long have been left there to cause embarrassment, had either of her uncles been earlier made acquainted with her address.

"I think," said Leonora, after a long and painful pause, "I think as this 'trustworthy person' will be here so early to-morrow, I had better go to my room now and commence packing my clothes."

"Oh, no—dear Leonora, no—wait until after tea," exclaimed the Ladies Thorpe together. "Jennings will pack everything for you in an hour or two to-morrow morning."

"No thank you," said Leonora, in a scarcely audible voice, but walking with an appearance of unusual calmness to the door. A strong effort of the mind will enable most people to control the outward signs of emotion as far as they are expressed by the movements of the body; to retain the colour of the cheek—to restrain the flashing of the eye and quivering lip—is however not so easy, and Leonora's deadly paleness greatly alarmed Lady Medway. She first advanced a few steps with outstretched hand as if to detain her, and then, as the door closed between them, hastily motioned to Jane to follow.

Breathless the two young girls stood together at the top of the staircase.

"Jane—I—wish to be alone—I cannot—speak—even to you—just now," gasped Leonora.

Jane's answer was a tearful embrace, from which Leonora released herself somewhat impetuously, and then ran into her room. Her thoughts, as she afterwards impatiently paced up and down the apartment, were for some time quite chaotic: anger, mortification, and disappointment predominated by turns. One moment she resolved to write to Lord Medway, the next blushed at the mere idea—wished she had expostulated with Lady Medway, then rejoiced she had not done so. Suddenly an undefined terror of the meeting with her uncle took possession of her mind. Had he sent to inquire about her? or had her place of residence been notified to him with the request that he would relieve the Medway family of an—incumbrance? She feared the latter; and what a reception was likely to be given to her under such circumstances! The thought was dreadful. Overwhelmed by the consideration of her perfect helplessness, she yielded for a few minutes to a violent burst of grief, from which she had not quite recovered when Jane stood at her door praying for admittance. Leonora for a minute or two appeared inclined to be inexorable; she employed the time, however, in opening her wardrobe, drawing forth various articles of apparel, and throwing them on the sofa and chairs in a manner to give the room all the uncomfortable appearance that generally accompanies the preparations for packing. Even after the entrance of her friend she continued her occupation with averted head and an expenditure of energy that someway began to impress her companion with a feeling of awe and dismay.

Lady Jane's voice was very tremulous as she observed, "I hope I shall see Charles, and have an opportunity of telling him how very unkindly he has acted."

"I rather think he has only done what Lady Medway desired him," answered Leonora, continuing her occupation without intermission, "and I do not blame her, on reflection, for wishing to get rid of me; but she ought to have consulted me and let me make the application to my uncle myself."

"That is exactly what Grace said just now; but Charley, it seems, disapproved from the beginning of your being spoken to. He said nothing but your extreme youth could excuse your having come here with Medway, and that nothing but the strongest and most energetic measures would now insure your going to your uncle; and if given time even to write to Medway, the consequences would inevitably be most disagreeable to us all."

"I do not see how," said Leonora, turning round with a

look of astonishment, and standing upright before her companion; "for if Lady Medway declined to take me with her, there must have been an end of the matter. I could not," she added, petulantly, "I could not have gone alone to Italy with your brother, could I?"

"I suppose not," said Lady Jane.

"Well, then, had I been able to consult him, there is no manner of doubt that he would have mediated between me and my uncle more kindly than Charles seems to have done."

"That is true," said Lady Jane; "but Charles does not choose Medway to mediate, or to know anything about the matter, for he has written to say that he hopes to get him off to Paris to-morrow, and then mamma must write to him and pacify him with promises and plans for next summer."

"What promises and plans?" asked Leonora.

"They said something about proposing to ask you to return to The Willows when we come back to England, but—" here she hesitated.

"But what?"

"Charley says that Medway's fancy for you will be long over by that time."

Leonora could not or would not believe this. She clung to the idea of Lord Medway's regard as the drowning mariner to the floating wreck, thoughtless of the force of the surrounding waves, and hoping against reason.

Lady Jane continued sorrowfully—

"From the day that I heard of Charles's disapproval of our winter plans I was sure that another arrangement would be made. In his letter to mamma this evening he says that from some conversations he has had with Medway, he expects to find him troublesome at Paris, but by dint of ridicule and judicious procrastination, he has no doubt all will be right in a few weeks."

"I cannot understand what all this means," said Leonora,
with a puzzled air; "Lady Medway's reasons for not wishing
me to reside with her are quite within my comprehension:
but why Charles, who has not yet seen me, should so dislike
me, is what I shall never be able to make out."

"Or I either," said Jane; "but he says expressly in his last
letter that mamma must be firm, and rather spend the winter in England than consent to take you with her to Nice."

At that moment a feeling of strong resentment sprang
up in Leonora's mind against Charles Thorpe: a positive
personal dislike to him for what she considered his
officious and unkind interference in her affairs. She pictured him to herself as a stern arbiter of her fate, an intrigu-
ing, calculating man of the world; in short, her secret, powerful, and implacable enemy; and, though she wished him
no actual evil, the wild desire presented itself that she might
in the course of her life have an opportunity of making him
feel, if only for a short time, as acute mortification as she
had suffered that evening. It was a vague wish, prompted
by anger, and without a thought of intervening obstacles;
yet she remembered it years afterwards, when experience
had taught her to understand the motives of his conduct,
and knowledge of the world and its ways, made her judge
him rather more leniently.

"Jane," she said slowly, "all this manoeuvring and writing was most unnecessary. A few rational words from Lady
Medway, such as she spoke this evening, would at any time
have been sufficient to have induced me to apply to my uncle, and leave The Willows voluntarily."

"Charles did not choose to have it so," murmured Jane.

Leonora shrugged her shoulders, and began in an absent
manner, to collect her books.

"I believe, Jane," she said at length, looking round her

with some dismay at the disorder she had created in the room, "I believe, after all, it will be better to let Jennings pack up all these things for me to-morrow morning."

"Oh, much better! and now, dear, you will come down to tea, won't you? Mamma is so sorry, you can't think!"

"I must hope, and not think, for the next twenty-four hours," said Leonora, making an effort to appear cheerful. "As to going downstairs, and talking on indifferent subjects, after all that has occurred this evening—that is beyond my power; so you may say good night for me: I wish you could say good-bye, also, and that I were now far, far away from The Willows!"

"Oh! Leonora," cried Jane, vainly endeavouring to restrain her tears, "I cannot bear to think of your leaving us! but we shall continue friends for ever, promise me that at least."

Leonora warmly gave the assurance required.

"And when we go to town," continued Jane, " I shall be sure to see you and spend hours with you—and I shall write to you—oh, that puts me in mind—mamma desired me to find out if you intended to write to Medway."

"No," said Leonora, "I leave it to you to explain this affair to him, and then—perhaps—he may write to me. I wish, with all my heart, I had never come here—but there is no use in thinking of that now. Good night."

The door closed, and Leonora was once more alone, and how confused and unhappy only those can know who have been in their youth homeless, and unceremoniously forwarded from one house to another. For some time a feeling of utter desolation, a sensation of even more complete loneliness befell her than when first, an orphan and among strangers, she had written the short formal letters to her uncles, and the long explanatory one to Lord Medway, on whom all her hopes then centred. What would he have

been to her had he lived? Would Charles have dared to—
but why complain—his successor had proved as willing to
befriend her as she could have desired; it was the unexpected opposition on the part of his brother and mother
that now made him unable to do so. And then hope began
to whisper that he would not desert her completely, that he
would write to her; perhaps even return to England, if only
for the purpose of securing her a pleasanter position in her
uncle's house. Had he not said repeatedly that he liked her
better than any of his sisters?—told her never to doubt his
interest in all that concerned her? and assured her that his
father's offer of protection should be carried into action by
him in the most surprising and satisfactory manner? Some
doubts of his power to do this just now were reluctantly
admitted; but with all the careless confidence of youth and
inexperience, she dwelt long on the chance of being invited,
kindly and willingly invited, to spend the ensuing summer at
The Willows. That Lord Medway would still desire it she
felt sure, and she took it for granted that by that time she
should have sufficiently conciliated both her uncles to satisfy even Lady Medway's scruples. In short, were the
dreaded interviews with her relations once over, she believed she should, after all, have no very great objection to
spend, on any terms, the winter in London—it would be
something so novel, so interesting to her! Opening a guide-
book that lay on the table, she spread out the map of London before her and studied it attentively, until she had her
finger on Russell-square. It seemed to her just the central
sort of place for seeing and hearing everything. Yes; she
should see Westminster Abbey and St Paul's, the Docks,
the Tunnel,* the Zoological Gardens, the Tower, and the

* The railway tunnel between Rotherhithe and Wapping constructed by

Museum! It was so odd that her mother had lived so long in London and had never been to see the Museum! She could not expect her uncle to go everywhere with her—he was too old, past sixty she believed—but his son Arthur—here Leonora sighed, and wished she were going to her uncle Gilbert, who had a daughter or daughters about her own age—vulgar most probably—but she believed she could like any one now who would receive and treat her kindly. Yet even while this humble thought passed through her mind, appalling visions of corpulent, red-faced, loud-voiced uncles, with shopmen-looking sons, rose vividly before her imagination, which, it has been already observed, was of the most fertile description; and the forms, when they had acquired gigantic proportions, were in their turn chased, phantasmagoria-like, by painfully contrasting groups of tall, graceful, gentle-mannered Thorpes. Among these, however, Charles at length stood so prominent, that anger effectually put to flight all the intruding phantoms; her pride was roused, and, starting from her chair, she resolved whatever her fears for the future might be, to conceal them; not even to Jane would she breathe a word of complaint, or show a particle of the deep regret with which she left a family, whose habits and manners were so congenial to her own; and her thoughts centred, during the greater part of a sleepless night, in the consideration of how she could now leave The Willows with at least a semblance of dignity.

Sir Marc Isambard Brunel (1769-1849) between 1825 and 1843.

CHAPTER VII

A City Uncle

LEONORA'S composure the next morning surprised Lady Medway not a little. The arrangement of her clothes, and the hasty finishing of some trifling fancy-work which she had undertaken for Jane and her sisters, seemed to occupy her so completely, that she appeared quite unconscious of the grave faces around her, or even Jane's tearful eyes, as she followed her from place to place with Azor in her arms; bestowing on the dog the caresses she no longer ventured to offer Leonora, who seemed to have changed in some strange manner during the night. Yet once more their eyes met with the wonted look of intelligence, and a mutual sympathetic paleness overspread their features as the carriage was announced which was to separate them for a time—nominally indefinite, but which both, with anxious forebodings, feared for that reason might prove long.

Lady Medway desired to see the "person" who was to take charge of Miss Nixon: and as Leonora left the room to prepare for her journey, she stopped for a few minutes in the hall to look at the monstrous yellow carriage sent by her uncle, and the strange figure that descended from it. She had been closely followed by Jane; and, under almost any other circumstances, laughter would have been irrepressible on their parts; but all inclination to gaiety was subdued by grief, and merely an expression of wonder pervaded the countenances of the young girls, as their eyes followed the thin form of the elderly woman, who tripped rather than walked across the hall. A glimpse of her face had shown them a pair of prominent, restless, dark eyes, a nose of large yet sharp proportions, slightly inclining to the left, and partaking amply of the dappled colours that flushed her cheeks, and all surrounded by a cap of innumerable lace frills, pressed down upon her forehead by a bonnet of amazing proportions, and in form resembling a coal-scuttle—the date of fabrication was beyond the recollection of either Leonora or Jane; and the extreme freshness of the materials for a moment staggered their judgment, and made them fear it was some terrible importation from beyond the Channel, which they and every one must, in the course of time, copy and adopt. It was a relief to their mind when the removal of a muffling cloak disclosed a black silk dress, fresh as the bonnet, but which, even to their youthful eyes, betrayed its age in those unmistakable ciphers—the sleeves. Old as was that gown, the folds from the shop might still be distinctly traced in its thick rustling plaits: it was a curious fact, the cause of which was made but too evident to Leonora at a later period.

While her bags and boxes were being placed in and outside the carriage, she put on her bonnet; and on returning to the hall was met by Lady Medway, who, with a slightly flushed face, turned to her and said, "I hoped you would have been able to remain until after luncheon, but this—a—person—says that she has received directions to avoid all delay here, and is to stop at the Toy in Hampton Court to rest the horses. I suppose your uncle's orders must be obeyed, dear girl."

"Oh, of course!" answered Leonora, breathing quickly, as they all advanced to take leave of her.

Jane, in an agony of grief, laid Azor in her arms, and with difficulty articulated, "Keep him for my sake."

The gift was already accepted with eager gratitude, when the "person" interfered, observing that "Mr Nixon could not abide dogs, which certainly were 'orrid hanimals in a town 'ouse."

Leonora reluctantly resigned the proffered treasure, and Azor displayed considerable enjoyment at recovering the liberty of which he had been deprived for so long a time in order to be ready when required for the meditated sacrifice to friendship.

Turning hastily away, Leonora entered the carriage; and then, leaning back in a corner, remained silent and motionless, until, on arriving at Hampton Court, her companion proposed having luncheon and walking in the palace garden. Leonora declined both, and was left unceremoniously enough to sit alone with her luggage, her feet on the opposite seat, her head bent on her clasped hands.

How long she thus remained she had not the least idea; for, in complete oblivion of all around her, she had lived over again in thought the last two months of her life, recalling, with an accuracy sharpened by regret, all she had seen, and heard, and felt during that time. Pleasant were the recollections of the various afternoon tea-parties beneath the willows with Jane and her brother; interesting the drives with Lady Medway in the neighbourhood, where people and scenery were equally strange and new to her. A certain small dog cemetery at one place they had visited rose distinctly before her; for among the graves of pet pugs and poodles she and Lord Medway had spoken of the contrast between German and English churchyards—the pious remembrance of lost friends displayed in the carefully-cultivated graves of one country, the apparent forgetfulness, in the neglect of them, so common in the other. Her description of a foreign village churchyard he had called poetical prose, while she had obstinately refused to believe his perhaps exaggerated account of some London burial-places. Then there had been quiet boating-parties to neighbouring villas, whence friends of the Medways came for them in their own wherries: expert and handsome boatmen, who had all been, as Leonora ingeniously expressed it, "extremely kind to her." She was in the midst of an excursion to Claremont,* then untenanted by royalty, was in imagination standing before the picture of the Princess Charlotte† in the dining-room, the white satin, well-fitting shoes again provokingly attracting her attention, when—the horses were led out to be put to, the carriage door was opened, and her travelling companion entered, apparently greatly refreshed by her luncheon. She carried in her hand a paper bag, filled with tempting-looking biscuits, which Leonora, who had breakfasted very slightly, found it impossible to refuse, and they formed the commencement of a conversation, that gradually, from a description of the excellent mutton-chops to be had at Hampton Court, led to an enumeration of the things most suitable for luncheons; dinners followed, and market prices, until Leonora had no longer a shadow of doubt that she was enjoying the society of her uncle's housekeeper, or cook, or both united in the person of Mrs Ducker, which she now learned was the

---

* House and garden near Esher, Surrey, built and laid out by Sir John Vanburgh (1664-1726) and Charles Bridgeman (?-1738) from 1715 but both extensively redesigned by Lancelot "Capability" Brown (1716-1783) from 1768. Crown property from 1816, the house was briefly occupied by Louis-Philippe, King of the French, following his exile from France in the 1848 revolution.
† Princess Charlotte (1796-1817), only child of King George IV and Queen Caroline.

name of her companion.

Indeed, Mrs Ducker, who probably saw no reason for either concealment or silence on the present occasion, informed her soon afterwards, at some length, that she had risen to her present high position in Mr Nixon's family from having been nurse to his only son, Arthur (so named after the Duke of Wellington, who, however, she believed, was not his real godfather). Arthur she loved as if he were her own child; she might say, indeed, that she had been a mother to him since Mrs Nixon's death; and he never forgot her—never came home from foreign parts without bringing her a handsome silk dress. The bonnet she then wore was from Paris, given to her by him, and was so well made that it was quite as good as new after years' and years' wearing: but then, to be sure, she took remarkably great care of her clothes. Here an admonitory glance was darted at the unconscious Leonora, who while crunching her biscuits, was carelessly lounging in the corner, and allowing her crape bonnet and its light decorations to rub against the side of the carriage.

"I wonder my uncle did not marry again," observed Leonora, on whom the history of the bonnet had made but little impression.

"Why should he?" asked Mrs Ducker, rather tartly. "I was there to take charge of the 'ousekeeping. Our Arthur had gone to school, the little girl died of the measles, and Missus was after all but a poor thing, always unealthy, and the doctor never out of the 'ouse as long as she lived. Master had no fancy to take another wife—never thought of such a thing, *I'm* sure!"

"He is very old now, is he not?" asked Leonora.

"Between sixty and seventy," answered her companion, thoughtfully; "they said he was past thirty when Arthur was born."

"So Arthur is also quite old!" exclaimed Leonora with a look of disappointment.

"A man is young at thirty, Miss Leonora, and your cousin is young and 'andsome too, though he 'as red 'air like his mother."

"Red hair! oh, now I am sure I shall never be able even to tolerate him," cried Leonora, with a light laugh.

"You're not likely to see much of him, I suspect," rejoined Mrs Ducker, with flashing eyes: "he can have his choice of company, I can tell you, and will not be in any hurry to leave Rome, or his friends, Viscount Torpid and the Marquis of Witherington!"

This was said almost triumphantly, and in the manner of a person who plays down a well-reserved trump at cards. Leonora, however, had known too many viscounts and marquises, and was still too little English in her ideas to attach the expected importance to such titles. Indeed, the chances and changes of foreign life enabled her to number some dukes and princes among her acquaintance; she was, therefore, neither astonished as her companion intended, nor at all interested in the given information—it merely sent her thoughts, with the swiftness of lightning, to Italy; and, as answer to the pompous announcement, she observed with a smile, "I liked everything at Rome excepting —the fleas."

"So! you have been there, too!" cried Mrs Ducker, with a look of surprise; and then piqued, and, provoked perhaps, by Leonora's silent nod and mouth full of biscuit, she added, "It *will* be a change for you, going to school this Michaelmas Term!"

"To school!" repeated Leonora, amazed, and instantly sitting up as erect as her companion could have desired.

"Yes; to the same where Miss Georgina 'as been so well heducated. Oh, you may think yourself very well hoff, for there's a carriage for the young ladies to go a hairing in and to the riding-school, and a French *fem de sham*, and they learn to make curtseys, and receive visitors, and are only a limited number, and the daughters of people of fortune and family!"

"Georgina is my uncle Gilbert's daughter?" said Leonora, half interrogatively.

"Who else could I mean?" asked Mrs Ducker; "but she's Miss Nixon, by right, since our little girl died; and most uncommon haccomplished she is they say—plays long variations on the pianer, and sings hopera songs, and draws 'eads in chalk; but of course you can do all this too!"

"No," answered Leonora, "I am not at all accomplished;" and, to say the truth, she had no particular wish to become so at that moment, if, for the purpose, she must again go to school. Had Mrs Ducker expressed herself properly, and said that "A lady would receive her into her circle," or that, "A vacancy having occurred in a select ladies' establishment, &c," the plan might have appeared less revolting; but to be sent to school when she considered her education finished, was a stroke of fate for which she was not prepared; and though her companion began, in consequence of her confession, loudly to applaud Mr Nixon's intention, she paid no sort of attention, merely ejaculating during the first pause, as if in continuation of her thoughts, "Why could he not let me live with him?"

"And what," demanded Mrs Ducker, "what could a gentleman, at his advanced time of life, do with a young person such as you are?"

"Do with a young person such as I am?—" repeated Leonora, thoughtfully, "just what Lady Medway said—no one knows what to do with me."

"Of course not," said Mrs Ducker, her face flushing vividly. "Why you couldn't make yourself useful—and fill my place, and undertake the 'ousekeeping, could you?"

Leonora's natural powers of observation had been strengthened by practice. She instantly perceived that Mrs Ducker dreaded finding in her a rival, and was ill-disposed towards her in consequence. She hastened, therefore, to remove all such suspicions from her mind, by some very truthful confessions of both uselessness and inexperience on her part, which were received with amusing satisfaction; a very perceptible softening of manner taking place after she had murmured, "Oh, I thought, perhaps, as you wasn't accomplished—"

"I ought to be useful—" interposed Leonora, with a smile. "I have led too wandering a life, and my acquirements are merely in foreign languages and literature, not, I much fear, in any way likely to recommend me to my uncle."

"Well, I don't think he has any partikler hobjections to forring heducation; but Mr Gilbert 'as, and couldn't at all be persuaded to let you be sent to him, which master would of course have preferred."

"So," said Leonora, "my uncle Gilbert refused to have me; every one rejects or tries to get rid of me."

"Perhaps, however," said Mrs Ducker, softening as Leonora's insignificance became more and more apparent to her, "perhaps, after all, you may not be sent to school. Master didn't seem quite decided, and only desired me to send to Mr Gilbert for the Prospects of Mrs Howard St Vincent's establishment. If he doesn't find you troublesome, he'll not mind you at all after the first week or two."

This was poor consolation, and Leonora thought long before she again spoke; when she did so, it was with the wish to conciliate her companion, who, she began to suspect, was a person of importance in her uncle's house. "I dare say," she began, with some hesitation, "or rather I am sure, that having lived so many years with my uncle, you have great influence with him—"

"No one has the least, excepting Arthur," interposed Mrs Ducker. "I couldn't venture to offer an opinion even about a salad, or lobster sauce! He orders everything from market himself, and excepting at the greengrocer's, and the fruit shop, I never buy anything for the 'ouse."

This, and some other remarks about her uncle's habits, gave Leonora so much subject for thought, that they were driving through the streets of London long before she again began to look around her. The endless rows of shops, the crowds of busy pedestrians, the carriages, carts, and omnibuses, seemed to multiply as they advanced, and became at last so confusing, that she felt a sort of relief as they turned at length into a succession of quieter streets, and she was informed that they were drawing near home. She looked out eagerly, and saw soon afterwards a space of ground neatly inclosed by iron railings; within which were a few dark-looking trees and shrubs, some dried-up dusty grass, and a weedless gravel walk, whereon several nurses and children were sauntering sorrowfully, like prisoners taking exercise. The high surrounding houses appeared to Leonora perfectly alike; and so they were, in fact, the only difference being in the number of windows in front. They stopped, and while a loud knock announced their arrival, Leonora looked upwards, perfectly unconscious what sort of rooms were lighted by the rows of bright-paned carefully-blinded windows above her. Not so the English reader, for so great is the uniformity of British town architecture, that it will suffice to say, the house of Mr Nixon was one of the largest sized, three-windowed, long-balconied, description; and immediately the edifice stands erected with its discoloured bricks, and plate-glass windows outside—its dining-room, drawing-rooms, bed-rooms, and attics, within.

Mrs Ducker commenced gathering together the stray parcels, and then said—

"Miss Nixon—please—will you step out?"

Leonora did as she was desired—ascended the stone steps to the door, and entered the hall. It was large and lofty, and at the end of the first flight of stairs she perceived a stained glass window of a brilliant kaleidoscope pattern, calculated effectually to shut out the view of stables and the backs of other houses, and perfectly harmonising with the yellow and red striped stair-carpet. A remarkably portly butler, with a white waistcoat and red face, was at first so occupied with Mrs Ducker, and giving directions to a youthful footman about the proper places for Leonora's luggage, that she herself appeared to be completely forgotten after having received from him a stiff obeisance on entering; but when she opened a door near the foot of the staircase, and looked into a perfectly dark room, he advanced, saying—

"That is the dining-room, Miss Nixon—will you not walk into Mr Nixon's study, where there is a fire?"

He preceded her, while speaking, into the large, handsomely furnished front parlour, drew up the window-blinds, moved a chair towards the fire-place, and informing her that Mr Nixon would be home in about an hour, left her to examine at her leisure the furniture of a room which was so different from what she had expected, that she found it necessary to call upon her imagination for a new portrait of her uncle. Handsomely bound books in glass cases completely covered the walls, a round table was heaped with new works, pamphlets, magazines, reviews, and newspapers. There was a writing table of large dimensions, and near one of the windows, globes, and a telescope on pedestals. About a dozen luxuriously comfortable arm-chairs and a *chaise longue* were covered with green morocco leather to match the colour of the curtains and carpet; the chimney-piece was loaded with handsome ornaments, and in the midst of them, a clock of singularly beautiful workmanship. Leonora had ample time for observation, and used it while there was light sufficient to discern the objects around her. As the evening drew to a close, she walked towards one of the windows and looked at the square and the surrounding houses, and watched the various groups of people, who resided in the neighbourhood, returning to their homes. Candles glimmered red and rayless in the opposite houses, lamp-lighters began to hurry to and fro, and when, at length, a broad gleam of light fell on the window where she stood, and the stone steps immediately before her, she saw a man slowly ascend the latter, while deliberately drawing from his pocket a key, which he applied to the hall door. A moment after she knew that only a few steps separated her from her much-dreaded uncle.

During the hour she had just spent alone, the silence in the house had been unbroken, but now the opening and shutting of doors not far distant from her became audible, and soon afterwards the study door was opened, and she turned round, with a beating heart, to meet—Mrs Ducker, who came to inform her that Mr Nixon having gone to dress for dinner, she supposed it was time for Miss Nixon to do the same, and she had come to show her to her room. Leonora followed her into the gas-lit hall, and up four long flights of stairs, in silence; then Mrs Ducker pointed to the door of the back bed-room, and whispered "Master's room," whereupon Leonora turned to the other doors, but finding them locked, perceived that she was to follow her guide up a narrow, uncarpeted continuation of the staircase, which led to the attics, where she was put in possession of a large, wild-looking room, called the nursery.

Her toilet was quickly made, and without giving herself time to become frightened again, she rapidly descended the stairs, fervently hoping to reach the study before her uncle. She was disappointed, he was already there, his elbow leaning on the chimney-piece, and his tall, stiff figure turned towards the door, on which his eyes were fixed with piercing keenness.

Leonora's previous life had been of a description that was calculated to early form her manners and give her unusual self-possession for her age; but the gentlemanly appearance of the erect old man before her, with his well-formed, expressive features, full lips, high forehead, prolonged by baldness, and snow-white, curling hair, was so unlike the "City" uncle of her dread and dreams, that she stopped blushing, and uncertain how to approach him. After a long and painfully scrutinising glance, he slowly extended his hand towards her, and, as she had expected, his first words were a reproach.

"It would have been better," he began, coldly and severely, "it would have been better, and infinitely more decorous, had you applied to me or your uncle Gilbert for advice and assistance after your father's death, instead of forcing yourself upon the notice, and seeking the protection of a young and unmarried man like Lord Medway."

Leonora was so shocked at this view of her conduct, that it was with great difficulty she explained the true state of the case, and assured him, she had supposed Lord Medway's father still alive when she came to England, and that he having been in constant correspondence with her mother, had, by letter, offered to protect and assist her should she ever be in want of a friend.

"When you found out the mistake," said her uncle, calmly, "there was still time to remedy it; but I have reason to know that you purposely kept Lord Medway in ignorance of our being in existence."

"So," thought Leonora, "Charles Thorpe's correspondence has been of a nature to create a strong prejudice against me—that was unnecessary cruelty on his part." Mr Nixon pausing, with provoking patience, for an answer, she stammered a few words about the letters in her father's writing-desk having made her unwilling to apply to either of her uncles.

"A plausible defence," said Mr Nixon, his features relaxing a little; "but," he added slowly, "the letters in question related altogether to pecuniary affairs, and in no way concerned you."

"I could not be sure that you would not visit the failings of the father on the child," answered Leonora, beginning to recover from her embarrassment, "and besides, after all, the Thorpes are also relations of mine, and—"

"They are very distant ones," interposed Mr Nixon, "but you would, no doubt, have preferred a residence with them had they been disposed to keep you."

"They told me I was a second cousin," began Leonora, her eyes filling with tears, "and I was very happy at The Willows, for they were very kind to me, and I found a companion of my own age."

"You would have found the same in your uncle Gilbert's family," rejoined her uncle, dryly; "however," he added, while ringing the bell twice in an expressive sort of way, that probably conveyed some order to the regions below stairs, "however, on this disagreeable subject I shall, in consideration of your youth, now only observe that you have acted foolishly, perhaps I should say childishly, did not the Thorpes view the matter in another and more serious light: of that, and of them, we need speak no more, for you will scarcely seek or desire further intercourse with a family who, in order to get rid of you, have shown so little consideration for either your feelings or wishes."

Leonora blushed deeply, and he continued—

"I have been considering how best to dispose of you; my first idea was to send you to a Mrs Howard St Vincent, with whom your cousin Georgina will probably remain another year for the completion of her education; it has since occurred to me, that the advantages you have probably had abroad will make this unnecessary. You are old enough to judge for yourself; the establishment, as they call it, is very expensive, so if you prefer remaining here with me—"

"Oh, I should greatly prefer it!" cried Leonora, hastily.

"Then you may do so. I require and expect nothing from you, excepting that you will be punctual in your hours, and not interfere with habits of regularity which have become necessary to my health and comfort."

Leonora was about to answer, when dinner was announced, and her uncle, with polite formality, offered his arm, and conducted her into the adjoining room. It was an enormously large apartment, containing massively carved mahogany sideboards, tables that might be drawn out to an astonishing length, carpet and curtains of a rich crimson colour, chairs to match, and even the walls were covered with paper of the same warm tint, on which the gorgeously gilt frames of some family pictures shone resplendent. Over the fire-place hung the portrait of Mr Nixon's father, a handsome, healthy-looking man, in a buff waistcoat, with a bunch of ponderous seals pending over his portly paunch. On the long wall opposite were hung Mr Nixon's own portrait, taken some thirty or forty years previously, when he had, evidently, dressed very carefully for the occasion; that of his wife, a sickly-looking woman, with short frizzled curls of red hair; and also that of his son, likewise red-haired and not handsome—yet so full of life, and so eminently well painted, was his picture, that Leonora was instantly attracted by it, and her uncle, with a wave of his hand, and the words, "Your cousin Arthur," introduced her to it, much as if it had been a living person.

"Painted at Rome, by a very eminent German artist," he added, seating himself at the dinner-table; after which words the most profound silence reigned, rendering audible the eager snorting sound that accompanied Mr Nixon's hasty devouring of the viands before him, and which proved to Leonora that her uncle's gastronomic propensities greatly resembled those of her late father. Either the previous conversation, or the bag of biscuits, had so effectually deprived her of all appetite, that she had time to examine and study the appearance of her now perfectly unobservant relation. She saw with more dissatisfaction than surprise the pale face flush with avidity, the veins near the temples swell, and at length, as he bent over a plate full of curry, large drops of perspiration trickling down his white intellectual forehead! While seeking his handkerchief to remove them, he perceived Leonora's eyes fixed gravely on him, with an expression that he mistook for astonishment, and probably intended to reply to her thoughts, when he said, "If you had worked hard as I have done since ten o'clock this morning, and had had no luncheon, you would perhaps be quite as hungry as I am."

Leonora turned away, and pretended to eat.

"You don't like curry," said her uncle, after having, in his turn, observed her for a short time.

"It burns my mouth," she answered, "worse, even, than English mustard."

"You will soon learn to like it," said Mr Nixon, amused at her wry faces and glistening eyes, "very soon—it is a taste that must be acquired, but like all such, when acquired, is frequently stronger than what we feel for simple natural food."

Leonora shook her head incredulously.

"You do not understand me," he continued, helping

himself again copiously, and eating quickly while speaking slowly. "What I mean is, one never hears—of habitual excess—in the gratification, of—of the inclinations towards—bread, milk, water—or even wholesomely-cooked meat, but often, very often, in the acquired taste for brandy, tobacco, wine, opium, and so forth—"

"But I should think all these tastes better avoided than acquired," observed Leonora.

"That I shall not attempt to deny," he answered, glancing quickly from his plate towards her, with a look of keen intelligence; "but my pleasures in this world are very limited, and their variety consists almost exclusively in a change of dishes on this table, and of books on the one in the next room. Both acquired tastes, for which my relish is, I confess, at times more intense than it ought to be."

Leonora attempted no answer, but watched with some interest the, to her, novel operation of removing the table-cloth, admired the highly polished wood beneath; and when the dessert was arranged, following a sign from her uncle, she rose and took the chair placed for her at the side of the fire-place, opposite him.

When they were alone, he asked her a few questions about her former mode of life and places of residence; told her, in a parenthesis, not to put more powdered sugar on her plate than she could eat with her orange; sipped unremittingly glass after glass of the wine placed close beside him by his attentive butler; and when the contents of the crystal jug began to wax low, he stretched out his feet to the adjacent fender, sought and found a comfortable resting-place for his head on the well-stuffed back of his large arm-chair, and from a doze imperceptibly fell into a profound sleep.

Leonora's position was so new to her, that she did not know whether to leave the room or remain in it; but having at length decided on the latter, she leaned her head on her hand, gazed pensively at the glowing coal-fire, and recalled the events of the previous evening at The Willows with painful minuteness. Stealthily she drew from her pocket the letter she had then received from Lord Medway, and having read it carefully over, tried to convince herself that she should hear from him again and soon. Yet, while she mused, it seemed as if all around began to assume an appearance of home: already she felt that she was not, as at The Willows, a mere passing visitor in her uncle's house; he had offered, and she had tacitly accepted his protection. She looked along the walls of the room, and the portraits, warmed by the light of lamp and fire, appeared to return her glance with the freedom of long acquaintance, her cousin Arthur's fiery brown eyes seeming to ask her opinion of the vase on which his hand rested, the form of which was far more familiar than that of any of the fruit-dishes on the table beside her.

At the end of about an hour, her uncle awoke, expressed some surprise at finding her still in the room, rang the bell, and opened the folding-door into the study. There they found the preparations for tea, which Mr Nixon made and poured out himself, retiring with his cup to a seat near the fire-place, and taking up a book, in which he read without intermission until bed-time. Leonora had silently followed his example, which seemed to please him, for as they separated for the night, he observed, that he was glad to perceive she liked reading, and, after a pause, added, "You will find the key of the bookcases on my writing-table, and near the window there is a collection of foreign works, which belong to my son. Though *I* cannot read them, you of course can. They are well chosen, I am sure—in fact, the names of all the authors are familiar to me, and I have read translations of most of them. We breakfast at nine o'clock, *pre–cisely*. Good night."

"Good night," said Leonora, turning into the hall while he remained to extinguish the lamp and rake up the embers still glowing in the grate.

CHAPTER VIII

How Leonora's Name Came to be Shortened

ACCUSTOMED to early rising, Leonora was dressed the next morning before seven o'clock, and was considerably puzzled how to employ her time for the ensuing two hours before breakfast. Half that time sufficed for the unpacking and arrangement of her wardrobe, and then, having placed her little writing-desk on a table ready for use should she hear from the Medway family during the day, she went to the window, counted the houses of the square and their windows, speculated dreamily on the families in the neighbourhood with whom she was likely to become acquainted, and at length sauntered towards the staircase, intending to inspect the drawing-rooms, which, from the appearance of the lobby, and the lofty doors, she concluded, must be unusually splendid. She found the doors locked, and while deliberating about the propriety or necessity of returning to her own room, she continued to descend the stairs, her lingering irresolute steps bringing her at last to the door of the study. She entered and advanced to the glass cases, to examine the books that had so strongly attracted her attention the day before. The door into the dining-room was ajar, and she started slightly on perceiving her uncle already seated at the breakfast-table reading a newspaper, his spectacles poised on the end of his nose, and his chin slightly raised as if to keep them there: glancing over them he made some guttural sound as answer to Leonora's morning greeting, and then continued his occupation until the clock struck nine. As he deposited *The Times* on the table the door opened, and every requisite for a substantial breakfast was noiselessly placed within his reach—a large tea caddy, as on the previous evening, being rolled towards him, out of which he not only took the necessary quantity of tea, but also a massive silver sugar basin. He did not himself invite Leonora to join him, but made some sign to the servant to do so; and when she seated herself at the table, after having pushed towards her a cup of tea, he helped himself to each thing before forwarding it to her, as if at once and for all to show that he had no intention of playing politeness with so young a person and so near a relation. Leonora made a few attempts at conversation, which seemed to surprise him amazingly, but they proved completely abortive, his answers—with a mouth full of egg and buttered toast, or voice half smothered in a teacup of immense proportions—being perfectly unintelligible.

At length he rose, received from the servant, who was waiting in the hall, his paletot, gloves, hat, and walking-stick, while looming in the distance stood Mrs Ducker to receive his orders for dinner. His conference with her lasted some time, and seemed to interest him deeply; the moment it was ended he left the house, and Leonora did not see him again until he was dressed for dinner.

These particulars are not interesting, and would not have been forced upon the notice of the reader, had it not been necessary to give an idea of the tenor of Leonora's life for a longer—much longer—period than she had expected. So completely did one day resemble the other in Mr Nixon's house, that it merely remains to name Sunday as an exception, scarcely however worth mentioning. On that day Mr

Nixon did *not* go to his office, and *did* go to church accompanied by Leonora, having procured for her a place next his own in a part of the building where the light was not too strong for his eyes, or, as Leonora soon shrewdly suspected, where he could occasionally close them unremarked by other members of the congregation. When the service was over, she was consigned to the care of Mrs Ducker, while he went to take a walk at the "West End," from which, however, he returned home at precisely the usual hour—dining, sleeping, reading, and going to bed without the slightest further deviation from his wonted habits.

Leonora did not willingly or even patiently resign herself to this unsociable life,—the change was too great from the freedom and incessant variety to which she had been accustomed. That she had been perfectly happy for a couple of months in the dignified seclusion of The Willows, with a companion of her own age and a young man such as Lord Medway, was quite natural, the more so as, to add a charm to her intercourse with the latter, there had been a sort of consciousness that his friendship had been mixed with a large proportion of personal admiration. Her hopes of hearing from him or his family sustained her for some time, but when weeks passed over without a line even from Jane, an uncontrollable impatience began to prey upon her mind. Like a newly-caged bird, she moved about restlessly in her prison, wandered from one window to the other, rushed up and down the stairs, wondered if ever her uncle would have time to take her out to walk, or if she should ever have courage to ask him to show her something of London. So great was at length her want of a companion, that she even made desperate efforts to obtain the friendship of Anne Ducker, descending to the housekeeper's room, and offering, nay entreating to be allowed to hem rubbers or mend stockings as an excuse for remaining there. Mrs Ducker's jealous fears, however, had returned directly she found that the school plan had been set aside, and she repulsed Leonora's offers of usefulness so ungraciously that the poor girl retreated, mortified and offended, to the lonely study, and after yielding for some time to a despondency that deprived her cheek of every trace of colour, and caused an unconquerable lassitude to pervade every movement of her drooping form, she at last sought and found in the library, placed by her uncle at her disposal, occupation for her time, and solace for her solitude.

At first she read slowly, almost listlessly, but the works were all of the best kind, and there were critical journals of every description to guide her choice. She began to discover that she was extremely ignorant, to rejoice in having so much leisure for reading, to like the quiet room with its comfortable ponderous furniture, to be surprised at the quick flight of time, and even wonder if her uncle had not come home too soon when the turning of his now well-known Chubb key in the hall door interrupted her studies. It is astonishing what a variety of literary inclinations the careful perusal of reviews and magazines gave her, and what knowledge of the world—that is the English world— she acquired by reading not only the works of fiction already in her uncle's possession, but each new novel as it appeared. As regularly as the newspapers these works were laid on Mr Nixon's table, for, like thousands of men in his position in England, he felt the necessity of relaxation for his mind, and perhaps also a natural longing for some intercourse (though but in fiction) with a world from which, either from choice or necessity, he lived so wholly apart. Leonora was needlessly surprised at the interest which he took in the fate of the various heroes and heroines of these works, for it is not unfrequently those who concern themselves the least about the life struggles of the persons immediately around them, who sympathize most unreservedly in the joys and sorrows of fictitious personages. At all events, novel reading was the usual evening occupation of both uncle and niece, and served effectually to banish the sleepiness which the nocturnal silence in the room and house might have produced.

Leonora at last succeeded in completely gaining Mrs Ducker's heart by submitting to a regimen of slops to cure a cold caught during the winter on one of the very few occasions that presented themselves for going out: she also discovered why that worthy woman's bonnets and silk dresses retained the lustre of newness, while their forms denoted an unusual age for such articles—they were used but once a week, and then only when the weather was propitious. A walk for pleasure or health was a thing scarcely understood by the members of Mr Nixon's family, but, indeed, had it been otherwise, Mrs Ducker would not easily have found leisure for what she unhesitatingly pronounced waste of time. Her activity at home was unceasing, amounting almost to restlessness; she was domineering, addicted to scolding, yet a kind and even warm-hearted woman, perfectly illiterate, yet possessed of both good sense and intelligence. Her jealousy of Leonora once overcome, she scolded and petted her alternately—her ire being generally provoked by Leonora's carelessness about the rents in her clothes, her affection continually increased by the gentleness, growing cheerfulness, and, it must he added, beauty of the young girl, whom she began to consider in some degree dependent on her for bodily comforts. Her visits to Leonora in the study, at first "short and far between," were in the course of time frequently prolonged by a forcible retention in a chair while the whole story of a new play or poem was retold. It is even on record that a strong piece of cord was once used for that purpose, the knots laughingly tied

being afterwards found of a Gordian description, and the
operation of cutting them still uncompleted when Mr
Nixon's step was heard in the hall: Mrs Ducker, or, as she
was then called "Duckey," was obliged to make her escape
into the dining-room with the chair still fastened to her person.

Leonora's efforts to understand her uncle's character
were at first not quite successful. The unbroken regularity
and seclusion of his life astonished her, and his want of all
inclination for society, or anything approaching to amusement, was incomprehensible to one accustomed to the sociability and gaiety of foreign life. Winter, spring, and summer passed over without his ever even mentioning to her
the familiar words concert or theatre, and from the papers
alone she knew that such entertainments were not uncommon in London. His taciturnity yielded, however, by degrees to her winning ways; she had a good deal of feminine
tact, and never put herself in competition with *The Times*
during breakfast, or the *entremets* at dinner; but after having
breakfasted he sometimes voluntarily entered into a short
political discussion, or he delayed his slumber after dinner
to criticise a new book; occasionally, too, he lingered over
his tea in the evening for the same purpose, and as time
wore on, and intimacy increased, he spoke of foreign countries and manners; and though in both giving the preference
to England, his opinions were those of a man who had read
and thought, his prejudices the natural consequences of
want of personal experience. His ruling passion was ambition—he himself would have said love for his only son, of
whose long and frequent absences he nevertheless evidently
approved. He told Leonora that Arthur was a man of unusual artistical and aesthetical tastes, which were more easily
satisfied on the continent than at home; but he refrained
from adding that he could there also make acquaintances,

English and foreign, quite out of his domestic sphere, and
that they both concurred in an ardent desire to rise in the
social scale, and hoped to secure this desirable end through
the wealth perseveringly increased by the one, and the judicious marriage of the other.

The first interruption to the quiet monotony of Leonora's life, was a grand dinner given on Christmas-day by Mr
Nixon to his brother Gilbert and his family on their return
from the country. He invited to meet them his commercial
partner, William Plumpton, his wife, sons, and daughters;
and again to meet them, and render the party complete,
several young men in their mutual employment. The preparations for this dinner were of the most extensive description; the furniture of the drawing-rooms was uncovered,
and Leonora examined and admired the carefully preserved
chairs, sofas, and tables, carpets, lustres, and alabaster vases,
as much as she perceived Mrs Ducker expected. The glasses
over the chimney-pieces were of enormous dimensions,
fixtures, as Leonora was informed, and bought with the
house, some earl or marquis having had them built into the
wall when Russell-square had been one of the most fashionable parts of London.

Leonora felt a good deal of curiosity to see her uncle
Gilbert and his family, about whom she had, by degrees,
obtained some information from Mrs Ducker—her utter
ignorance of the names and ages of her cousins appearing
to the latter perfectly incomprehensible. Not without surprise had she learned that there were Gilbert Nixons in
both the East and West Indies and Australia, all well-to-do
in the world, and likely to be as rich as their grandfather in
the course of time. Of the fourth son, Mr Sam, who had
received the "heducation of a lord, had been to Hoxford,
and was a barrister with chambers," Mrs Ducker spoke with
respect and reserve, but she dwelt long and feelingly on the

restlessness and ill-conduct of Master John when "at 'ome for the 'olidays." Miss Georgina was considered very helligunt; but by far the best of the family, in her opinion, had been Miss Leonora, who had died of a heart complaint a few months previously.

Leonora, ashamed to confess that she had never heard either of the existence or death of this cousin, considered it a sort of expiation to make the most minute inquiries respecting her namesake, and learned that she had been about her own age, but from childhood so delicate that she had constantly resided at her father's country house, Beechfield, which was at a convenient railroad distance from London; that even in winter she had been seldom long separated from her family, her father especially regularly passing part of each Saturday and all Sunday with her. Though greatly inferior to her sister Georgina in talents and acquirements, she had avowedly been his favourite child, and he had by no means recovered from the grief occasioned by her death when he first saw his niece on Christmas-day. Similarity of name and age, perhaps also some personal resemblance between the two Leonoras, seemed to strike him forcibly and painfully; tears started to his eyes, and, unable to control his emotion, of which, like a true Englishman, he was heartily ashamed, he abruptly left the room, and did not return until just before dinner was announced.

"Papa cannot yet bear to hear the name Leonora," observed Georgina, who had swept into the room and seated herself on one of the sofas with astounding gracefulness, "but I dare say in time he will learn not to mind it."

"It may require longer than you suppose," said Stephen Nixon, gravely. "I have not yet been able to pronounce my niece's name without an effort."

"Ah! true—my aunt's name was Leonora," said Georgina, "I had forgotten that she was godmother to our poor dear Leonora."

"I had also a daughter of that name," observed Mr Nixon.

"But," rejoined Georgina, "she was such a mere child when you lost her!"

"She lived long enough," he answered, slowly, "to make the name doubly dear and familiar to me."

Leonora now recollected that during the three months she had resided with her uncle he had scarcely ever addressed her by her name, that he had even used some ingenuity to avoid doing so, and had peremptorily desired the servants to call her "Miss Nixon," when, with the nice perception of rank peculiar to the English, they had shown their knowledge, that the daughter of the youngest son of Samuel Nixon was in fact only Miss Leonora, until after the marriage or death of her cousin Georgina.

"Why do you not call me Nora?" she now said, turning suddenly to her uncle; "I never was called otherwise until I came to England."

"And you never shall be called by any other name in future," he answered; "we shall drink your health after dinner to-day, and give you again the name I have no doubt you like better than any other."

Nora, as she was henceforward called, had not time to become much acquainted with her relatives during the evening. Her uncle Gilbert appeared to her more good-natured, but less gentlemanlike, than her uncle Stephen. In fact, good living had made him stout, and prosperity cheerful—at times almost jovial—though ever with a certain pomposity of demeanour, which he imagined equally English and dignified. He had suited himself with a wife early in life, and had often facetiously declared that she had been one of his best speculations. They had lived very happily together, and, after having attained an immense size, she had died from the effects of good living and want of exercise. Time had enabled Gilbert Nixon to get reconciled to this loss, but there was another which he never ceased to regret, and unceasingly and loudly to deplore—the want of a classical education. While his brother, however, had endeavoured to supply this loss by an extensive study of every branch of English literature, Gilbert had never attempted to read anything but a newspaper, in which, strange to say, the fashionable intelligence was apparently of nearly as much importance to him as the state of the funds. Fortunately this intelligence was not scanty in detail, so that he had frequent opportunities of rejoicing in balls and dinners, given by and for the entertainment of people, with whose *names* at least he was familiar. The queen and princes seldom rode or walked out without his being in the same way made acquainted with the minutest particulars; and, feeling deeply interested in such communications, he invariably spoke of them with a mixture of pride and exultation, the cause of which might perhaps by a circuitous route be traced to the fact that the balls and dinners were given and frequented by *his* countrymen, the queen was *his* queen, the princes were *his* princes!

Gilbert Nixon was, according to the English fashion, essentially patriotic, being not only deeply impressed with the invincible power and boundless wealth of England, but perfectly convinced that there never had been, and never would be, a nation in any respect capable of bearing a comparison with her. Personally he was strongly prejudiced against all foreigners, calling the French dirty and the Germans dull, without ever in the course of his life having become acquainted with an individual of either nation. Nora's continental education he considered a great disadvantage, but was more then half reconciled when a nearer acquaintance made him aware of her still unbounded admiration for everything English.

Nora found the Christmas dinner tedious and tiresome, and the plum pudding by no means so excellent as she had expected. She was somewhat perplexed, too, how to find amusement for her guests in the drawing-room, and much regretted her cousin Arthur's having removed the piano-forte to the attics, and let it fall to pieces there, merely because the form was old-fashioned, and the more so as Mrs Plumpton informed her more than once, that both her daughters "played with extraordinary execution," and that the Plumpton family were all remarkably musical! Nora's efforts to please were, however, too sincere to be unsuccessful, and before her uncle came upstairs she and Mrs Plumpton had made great strides towards a better acquaintance, the latter having already hoped to see her soon at *her* house, and promised to give her an excellent receipt for mock-turtle soup.

The Misses Plumpton were slim, quiet girls, no longer very young, and Nora had thought them sensible unaffected women until she observed their efforts to attract the attention and flirt with the half-dozen young men who, flushed with wine, hovered round the tea-table at a late hour. Not so Georgina; *she* seemed to consider Nora alone worthy of notice, disdained the female Plumptons altogether, and leaning back in an arm-chair, repulsed even the advances of that very fine gentleman Mr Percival Plumpton, so that he withdrew in disgust from the contemplation of her little saucy turned-up nose, and bestowed his condescending attention on Nora for the remainder of the evening.

In due time an invitation to dine with the Plumptons reached Mr Nixon, in which Nora was included. The party was of a gayer description than that given by her uncle, for, as Mrs Plumpton observed, "Where there are young girls in a house, music and dancing are a matter of course." Many people came to tea, and the Misses Plumpton commenced an impromptu concert with what they called "pieces" of Thalberg and Herz.[*] They were succeeded by some timid young ladies, who trembled forth the newest and most popular ballads, and then a stout gentleman shouted out the bass of a duet from a well-known opera, but with such utter contempt of all the rules of music, that when people whispered, "Lablache[†] to the life," Nora innocently supposed his performance a parody, and laughed and nodded her head with the others. During the waltz on the carpet that followed, she came to the hasty conclusion that Englishmen considered it beneath their dignity to learn to dance, and then unwillingly admitted to herself, that as specimens of the first nation in the world, they were wonderfully awkward in their manners.

Yet this evening often recurred to Nora's memory, as week after week, and month after month, passed over without another invitation. Her uncle Gilbert spent all his spare time at Beechfield; Georgina had returned to Mrs Howard St Vincent's Establishment; Mr Sam Nixon lived at his chambers; and John had gone back to school. The Plumptons called one day, and said they were going to Margate, which was a delightful place, and from that time forward, excepting to church on Sunday, or to take a solitary saunter in the square, Nora never left the house.

[*] Sigismond Thalberg (1812-1871) and Henri Herz (1803-1888), both virtuoso pianists and composers of popular salon pieces.
[†] Luigi Lablache (1794-1858), celebrated bass singer who performed frequently at the King's (later Her Majesty's) Theatre, London, between 1830 and 1852.

CHAPTER IX

A Practical Lesson on the Force of Habit

SOON after the commencement of the second year of Nora's residence with her uncle, a transaction took place that seemed likely to change her prospects in a very unexpected manner. Stephen and Gilbert Nixon had joined in some railway speculation that had proved fortunate beyond their most sanguine expectations. Gilbert, who had been manager on the occasion, called by appointment late one afternoon, and brought with him his daughter Georgina, now returned home "for good," as he expressed it.

The two girls retired to one of the windows, where Georgina, putting her hand on Nora's shoulder, hoped they were soon likely to be much together, and become very good friends.

"If you can manage to come here occasionally," began Nora.

"No, dear, you must come to us," said Georgina, interrupting her hastily. "Russell-square is quite out of the question—Ultima Thule, as one of my friends called it the other day!"

"But my uncle has strictly forbidden my going out, excepting to walk in the square," said Nora, "or with Anne Ducker, who has so seldom time—scarcely ever, in fact!"

"Oh, we don't want old Ducker at all," rejoined Georgina, laughing, "we only want you—that is, *I* want you, and hope to be of use to you. Papa has been so lucky with his railway shares, that he has at length yielded to my entreaties, and bought a house in Eaton-place, and given me *carte blanche* for the furniture! I have chosen amber-coloured silk for the drawing-rooms, green and gold for the dining-room, and Mrs Savage Wayward says, if papa will only give dinners, she can introduce us to all the first people in town, and that her friend, Lady Robert Botherton will present us—that is, you and me—at the next Drawing Room; but you, I suppose, will prefer Lady Medway, as she is a relation."

"Who? I? Lady Medway!" repeated Nora. "I—I do not even know where she is at present!"

"Surely," cried Georgina, much astonished, "surely, you must be aware that they are all returned from Italy."

"How should I know?" asked Nora, with a faint smile.

"Because it was in the papers a week ago," answered Georgina. "Do you never read the fashionable intelligence?"

"Very seldom."

"What an odd girl you are! But you will soon think and feel differently about all those things. Wait only until our establishment in Eaton-place is in order. I intend to begin very quietly, to prevent people from talking too much about us, or forming a league to laugh at us, also to give papa time to get rid of all his tiresome, old-fashioned habits. My brother Sam is a provoking plodder, and John is still a mere child—both of no sort of use to me, and I have not courage to brave the difficulties of working my way in the world of fashion quite alone. With you, however, for a companion, and plenty of money, it will be very odd if I cannot contrive, not only to brave, but even to overcome them. You see I am candid, and tell you that I want you. It

would undoubtedly have been more worldly-wise, had I
pretended perfectly disinterested motives for this offer of a
home—such as a wish to save you from a continuance of
your present dull life, and a desire to promote your marrying advantageously; but I take it for granted that though a
couple of years younger than I am, you have seen enough
of the world to understand me, and like me all the better
for being plain-spoken."

Nora smiled with a look of such perfect intelligence that
Georgina continued—

"There is but one thing likely to interfere with our plans;
I fear—I greatly fear—that my uncle Stephen may take it
into his head to object to your leaving him."

Nora almost laughed at the idea, and assured her cousin
that her uncle Stephen would scarcely observe her absence.

"I am glad to hear it," said Georgina; "papa will speak to
him directly about you. I suppose," she added abruptly, "I
suppose you will be glad to see the Medways again, and can
introduce us to them? You must know them well after having resided in their house so long."

"I *knew* them tolerably well," said Nora with a slight
blush, "but they have never come to see me—never even
written to me since I have been here."

"Of course not," said Georgina, lightly, "how could you
expect such a thing?"

"I thought Jane at least too young to have any absurd
prejudices."

"She must do as her mother desires," rejoined Georgina;
"but you will soon see her, as she is to be presented this
year, when Lady Grace marries Mr Cardwell."

"Why, you know all about them!" said Nora, surprised.

"I saw them yesterday evening at the Opera, where I
went with the Savage Waywards. Lord Medway was there
too, looking so indolent and ill; people say it is quite unpar-

donable his requiring such a length of time to die!"

"Oh, Georgina, how can you speak with such levity!"

"Mr Wayward's words, not mine," she answered; "but hush," she added, turning towards her father and uncle, "they are talking about us now, and I suppose we may listen."

A look of intelligence passed between her and Gilbert Nixon as in an off-hand kind of manner, and without any circumlocution, he proposed to relieve his brother of the charge of their niece, Nora, assuring him with evident sincerity, "that he and Georgina had taken a fancy to her; that she should never want for anything, and that without offence he might say they had a gayer and more eligible residence to offer her than the old house in Russell-square!"

Mr Nixon did not listen to this speech unmoved; the colour forsook his lips, and, perhaps to conceal some feeling so unexpected on his part that he hardly understood it himself, he turned towards the fire-place, bent his head on his hand, and seemed to consider long before he answered slowly, "With you Nora will undoubtedly be happier than here, and I have no right to retain her if she choose to leave me."

This answer was pretty much what Nora had expected, but Georgina seemed equally surprised and pleased at an acquiescence so unconditional, when she had prepared herself for downright steady opposition. She thanked him warmly, and asked when Nora might remove to Eaton-place.

"When she pleases," answered Mr Nixon, stiffly.

"Let us take her with us at once," suggested Georgina, eagerly.

To this, however, he objected with strangely flashing eyes, and Gilbert interfering, proposed the following day, to which no objection being made, he added, while shaking his

brother's hand, "To-morrow then let it be. I'm glad to find
you so ready to part with the girl, Stephen; Georgy was
afraid you might wish to keep her, and," he added, turning
round at the door, "and I myself enjoy so much having
young people about me, that I thought it very likely you
might some way or other have got fond of her, and used to
her company and all that sort of thing. Of course, I should
not have pressed the matter had this been the case, but
Georgy would have been terribly disappointed, I can tell
you. Good-bye, Stephen; God bless you. So you won't join
me in the shares I intend to purchase to-morrow?"

Mr Nixon shook his head, the door closed, and Nora
stood in the middle of the room, stupefied at the sudden
and perfectly unexpected change in her prospects. "Youthful companions—a gay house—balls—operas—concerts—
a presentation at Court—perhaps she should meet the
Medways, and Lady Medway might *now* be kind to her, as
she no longer wanted to live with her! She believed she
could pardon Lord Medway's having forgotten her—but
Charles Thorpe, if in England, should be made to feel the
whole weight of her displeasure. She would not dance with
him, or look at him; and if he asked her to forgive him, she
would say *'Never!'* or—no; she would laugh, and refuse to
listen to his excuses; or, still better, she would—but there
was time enough to think of all that. How different her life
would be in Eaton-place to what it had been in Russell-
square; and yet the quiet study and the well-known books
had to a certain degree become dear to her, and even her
uncle—" Here she raised her eyes, and found his fixed on
her with an inquiring, penetrating glance. He was standing
precisely on the same spot where she had first seen him,
somewhat more then a year before: again he stretched out
his hand towards her; but this time no words of reproach
followed.

"Nora," he said, calmly, "my brother was right when he supposed I should 'get fond of you and used to your company:' you do not know with what reluctance I resign you."

"You are very kind to say so," answered Nora, with a slight flush of pleasure; "but I cannot flatter myself that you will miss me in the least."

"You are mistaken," said Mr Nixon: "I shall miss you greatly, and wish I had a right to insist on your remaining with me."

"That right you have," rejoined Nora. "When I was homeless you received me into your house, and I feel bound in gratitude—"

"I received you into my family as a duty," said Mr Nixon, interrupting her; "and I resign you now for the same reason."

He rang the bell in the deliberate manner that Nora now knew denoted an order for dinner, and she was but too glad to consider his doing so a sign on his part that he wished to end a conversation that was likely to embarrass her extremely.

Of the charms of change Nora had perhaps an exaggerated idea—of the force of habit a very faint notion. With the docility that generally accompanies a fair proportion of intellect, she had accommodated herself to the customs of her uncle's house; but as she stood occasionally at one of the study windows, or sat alone there after dinner by firelight, her thoughts had wandered far and wide, and not once had it occurred to her that happiness, or even contentment, could be felt by any one who was immured within the walls of one house. From the day of her arrival in Russell-square, she had never for one moment lost the feeling of imprisonment that had thus taken possession of her; but it was ever so mixed with a hope of release at some time indefinite, that she had seldom, even to herself, mourned over a captivity of such uncertain length, and, taken all in all, so endurable in its details. The eve of this long-expected time of freedom had arrived; and, to continue the contrast with the day of her arrival, she and her uncle seemed to have, in a manner, changed places. While she dined, he watched her intently; so much so, that he scarcely ate anything himself, causing thereby some consternation on the part of Biggs, the butler, who lingered unusually long in the room, to satisfy himself that the claret would not be disdained, as the various viands had been.

That evening, too, Nora waited in vain for her uncle's accustomed sleep, during which she was in the habit of retiring to the study: though he stretched out his feet, and leaned back his head in the usual manner, his eyes askance were still fixed on her, until, at length, murmuring something about not disturbing him, she thought it better to leave the room. He followed her almost immediately, sat down to read near the fire; but a few minutes afterwards, starting up, he dashed the book on the table, and returned to the dining-room. A good deal surprised at conduct so unusual, Nora sat musing on the probable cause, until she heard the bell ring for tea, when he again entered the room, and, without speaking, commenced walking up and down in an uneasy, impatient manner.

"Nora," he said, at length, abruptly stopping before her, "the nomaden-like life that you have led, until very lately, will, I fear, prevent you from understanding me if I speak of the—force of habit."

"Perhaps so," she answered; "my life has been as you say, nomaden-like. I do believe I have never yet been long enough stationary in any place to know the true meaning of either the word home or habit."

"Pre—cisely," said Mr Nixon; "I thought so. It would be absurd," he added, with ill-concealed embarrassment, "absurd my expecting you to have found anything congenial to your disposition in my house: you naturally rejoice in the prospect of leaving it—and me."

"Not you," answered Nora, quickly; "for though our daily intercourse has been very limited, and you have seldom found me worthy of any kind of rational companionship, I have by no means remained so indifferent towards you."

"Indeed!" said Mr Nixon, with a look of extreme satisfaction, as he seated himself at the table beside her. "Now see, Nora, my taciturn habits alone have prevented me from enjoying your society as I ought to have done; but I have been by no means insensible to the pleasure of having a young and cheerful girl to greet me in the morning, and to meet me on my return home in the evening. Surely you must have observed that I come home from my office a whole hour earlier than formerly."

"Certainly, I remarked it," answered Nora, smiling; "your return has been the only daily event of importance to me—my life has been positively regulated by it!"

"Can you not imagine," said Mr Nixon, gravely, "that coming home to silence and loneliness will now be very disagreeable, if not painful to me?"

"I think," she answered, beginning with some anxiety to suspect the drift of his discourse, "I think that your old habits will soon resume their preponderance, and that you will forget an interruption which certainly, at first, was anything but pleasing to you."

"Very well reasoned, indeed," said Mr Nixon; "it seems you know more of the force of habit than I supposed. Let me, however, tell you that your presence has been no interruption to my habits, and a very great embellishment to my home—that, in short, you have become necessary to my comfort and happiness, and—and—I wish you would consent to remain with me."

Nora's countenance fell so instantaneously and perceptibly that her uncle hastened to add, "I shall, of course, undertake to provide for you respectably, and promise to make a codicil to my will for that purpose to-morrow."

What did Nora know about codicils? What did she, with youth, health, and beauty, care for a respectable provision? She sat beside her uncle in a painful state of embarrassment, a vague feeling of gratitude alone preventing her from refusing at once a proposition so unwelcome and perplexing. All things considered, her gratitude was without much foundation; Mr Nixon had but tolerated her presence in the first instance, as the least expensive mode of disposing of her; and if he had felt otherwise, at a later period, she had in no way been made aware of the change. This he knew and understood better then Nora, who only remembered that she had been received without demur, and permitted to live without molestation. He made a very slight impression when he assured her that the happiness she expected to enjoy in his brother's house might prove of a very mixed, if not uncertain description; that Gilbert and his family were about to labour up the hill of fashion, and would, undoubtedly, meet with stumbling-blocks in the form of rebuffs and annoyances, the mere description of which in books alone had effectually deterred him from ever even attempting to increase or *improve* his small circle of acquaintances! It was the concluding sentence of his tolerably long oration that at length had the effect he desired; it was when he earnestly, yet gently, entreated her to stay with him, and not force an old man back into a loneliness that had become distasteful to him, that she consented to remain in Russell-square, and of her own accord, before she went to bed, wrote an explanatory note to her cousin Georgina, which he took particularly good care should reach its destination at a very early hour the next morning.

CHAPTER X

Arrival of, an Addition? Or, an Acquisition?

MR NIXON in no way concealed the satisfaction he felt at having secured Nora's society "for the remainder of his life," as he unhesitatingly said to his brother a few days afterwards; adding confidentially, "The fact is, Gilbert, I am growing old, and were I to became infirm, Anne Ducker is not the person I should like to have about me. The wife likely to be chosen by my son Arthur will never consent to live in Russell-square; and, in fact, I make no pretension to acquiring a daughter when he marries—on the contrary, rather expect to lose him altogether."

"You have very nearly done that already," observed Gilbert, bluntly.

"By no means," said Mr Nixon, quickly; "I expect him home very soon to spend some time with me."

"Perhaps he will condescend to visit us now that we have moved westwards," observed Gilbert, with some pique. "He was formerly much too fine a gentleman to notice or know me in the Park or at Kensington when he happened to be surrounded by his grand acquaintances."

"I have passed him in the same places without a nod of recognition," said Mr Nixon, smiling: "one look of intelligence is all I expect on such occasions."

"Oh, if he cuts his own father, I have no right to be offended," rejoined Gilbert, laughing; "only one of *my* sons had better not attempt anything of the kind with me."

"Arthur and I have come to the most perfect understanding on these subjects," observed Mr Nixon, calmly; "he must endeavour to rise in the world, and he can do so much more easily when not hampered by an old father, whose very existence is unknown to many of his acquaintances."

"I have no notion of being put aside in any such way," said Gilbert, flushing a good deal. "I should think there was nothing to prevent him from rising in the world as well as my son. Money's the main point, and that I have, and intend to keep too as long as I live."

"It won't do what you want," said his brother, in the same calm, thoughtful manner: "the rise in the social scale is only perfected in the third generation. We are a decided improvement on our father in manners and appearance, and in both, as well as in education, our sons are an improvement on us."

"Ah, I knew you would say something about our want of a classical education! *That* indeed is a loss never to be repaired; but do you know, Stephen, Georgy tells me that people of rank do not quote Greek or Latin excepting in parliament, and she thinks even if they did, I might pull out my handkerchief, like the people on the stage, and pretend to understand, and—"

"And look like a fool!" said his brother, interrupting him.

"That's it," said Gilbert, laughing good-humouredly; "after all, it's better to 'tell the truth and shame the devil,' eh?"

"It is better to keep quiet and make no pretension of any kind," answered Stephen. "Let your sons and daughters work their way in the world; your wealth will help them on, but you yourself will be a dead-weight on their hands, and with all their affection for you, they will find your presence in society a nuisance."

"No, I cannot believe that," exclaimed Gilbert, walking up and down the room a good deal chafed; "though not as good looking as you, I may at least say that I have the manners and appearance of a—gentleman."

Stephen Nixon neither assented nor dissented to this observation; he seemed relieved by the entrance of Nora, to whom his brother instantly turned, exclaiming, "So, Miss Nora, you prefer Russell-square to Eaton-place after all, it seems!"

"My uncle Stephen prefers my society to being alone," she answered, with a smile.

"Now, I wonder," he continued, with some asperity—"I wonder if you would give the same answer to Lady Medway, supposing her ladyship took it in her head to wish for your company!"

The possibility of an invitation to spend the summer at The Willows had again partially taken possession of Nora's mind, from the time her cousin Georgina had informed her of the return of the Medways to England. She looked eagerly and inquiringly towards her uncle Stephen, who apparently understood her thoughts, when he answered, "Gilbert is jesting, Nora; no letter or message has been sent by the Medways, nor is there the slightest chance of your hearing anything of them until your brother returns from the Mediterranean; *he*, I suppose, will take some notice of you, but I have no fears of his ever proposing to take you from me altogether as your uncle Gilbert would have done."

"For which I shall ever feel grateful," said Nora, extending both her hands to the latter.

"Well, well," cried Gilbert, looking exceedingly pleased, "it's a good thing to have 'two strings to one's bow,' Nora;

so when you are tired of Russell-square you can come to Eaton-place, and *vicy vercy*. In an establishment such as mine, one more or less is of no importance, as Georgy said, when she engaged the fellow who is to wear powder, and indeed everything would be right if I could only get used to the new fashions and the late dinner-hour. Georgy chooses to keep the cloth on the table, too, and won't let us after-wards sit round the fire to crack our nuts comfortably, as I have been used to do ever since I have had a house of my own—but I suppose it's all right, for Mrs Howard St Vincent told her that such customs were now considered quite antidelerium."

Mr Nixon rubbed his upper lip to conceal a smile, and said, "You are a younger man than I am, Gilbert, and can perhaps change all your habits to please your children. Nora has fortunately been able to accommodate herself to the old-fashioned usages of my house, though I have no doubt, many of them are diametrically opposed to what she has been accustomed to. Take care that Georgina does not learn to dictate more than you may find agreeable hereafter."

"Oh, she's so clever," responded Gilbert, with evident pride, "such a manager, that she would turn even you round her finger in no time if she were here. It was her plan our inviting Nora as we did last week; she said, if we took you by surprise, and spoke in Nora's presence, you would be ashamed to refuse your consent, it would appear so egotistical on your part; and, egad, she was right, but she did not reckon on your flinching when our backs were turned."

A flush passed over Mr Nixon's face while his brother continued—"she was exceedingly provoked at Nora's note of refusal, and would not come here with me to-day, as she said, she could not possibly refrain from telling you that it was uncommon selfish your burying poor Nora during the best years of her life in your front parlour here, and depriving her of any chance of settling advantageously in the world."

Gilbert, in his eagerness to prove the cleverness of his daughter, evidently forgot the presence of his niece; not so, Stephen, who, with difficulty, repressed his anger, as he answered, "Georgina seems a person of extraordinary penetration, and I am happy to be able to relieve her anxiety by giving her the information that she need give herself no further concern respecting her cousin's settlement in the world. I shall so provide for Nora, that aw—in short, Georgina may bestow all her thoughts and care upon herself and her own affairs in future."

"That I shall certainly tell her, Stephen, you may depend upon it; for she desired me to sound you on that very subject, and point out to you the necessity of doing something handsome for Nora, after her having consented to remain with you in this dismal old house!"

"Have the goodness also to tell Georgina from me," said Mr Nixon, his face flushing and eyes flashing, "that I consider her advice on this occasion extremely impertinent, that I forbid all future interference on her part between Nora and me, and to prevent the possibility of anything of the kind, that I shall feel greatly obliged by her absenting herself altogether from my dismal old house."

"Now don't be offended," said Gilbert, half apologetically; "that the idea was not bad is proved by your having already done of your own accord what she desired me to suggest. You don't yet know what a clever girl Georgy is; if you only heard her talk you would be astonished!"

"At her flippancy? I dare say I should."

"Come, come, Stephen, you must not be angry with my girl for knowing a little of the world and its ways. Mrs St Vincent assured me, when I left Georgy with her the additional year, that she would make her capable of presiding over any establishment in England, and I must say she has kept her word. Georgy might be a duchess!"

"I hope she may be," said Stephen, with a grim smile.

"It won't be her fault if she's not," said Gilbert, "she has ambition enough for us all. But now I must go—won't you take a look at my new carriage? It's a very nice turn-out, I can assure you; Georgy says, quite complete and in very good style."

"Chosen by her, of course?" half asked Mr Nixon.

"Certainly. Nothing would have induced her to enter our old coach since her return from Mrs St Vincent."

"Oh—indeed!"

"I can afford it, Stephen, afford it well," cried Gilbert, provoked at last by his brother's manner; "and I don't see why my daughter should not have her own carriage as well as your son his cab and riding-horses, to say nothing of all the expensive fooleries on which he spends so many thousands every year!"

"Your ignorance, alone, excuses the word fooleries," said Mr Nixon, with a smile of contempt.

"I know I am ignorant, Stephen," cried Gilbert, too angry to understand the less offensive meaning of his brother's word, "but there is no necessity for your telling me so continually. All the Greek and Latin ever learned at Oxford or Cambridge would not have taught us to make money like the writing and arithmetic that you pretend to despise."

"You misunderstand me—" began Stephen.

"No I don't. You sneer at me and my family because we are about to make at home the same efforts that your son has been for years making abroad."

"By no means," said Mr Nixon. "Don't suppose I blame the young people for endeavouring to rise, or even for making desperate efforts to push themselves forward in the world; they may succeed, but you will only be ridiculed for your pains."

"And why so?" asked Gilbert. "Did not Nora's father—"

"You have chosen a bad example," said Stephen, interrupting him; "Nora's father sacrificed his fortune to fashion, and died—a pauper."

"Take care that Arthur does not do the same," said Gilbert.

"I have no anxiety on that subject," answered Stephen, nodding his head. "Few fathers are on more confidential terms with their sons than I am with mine. Arthur has seldom exceeded his allowance, and when he does so, it is only for objects of *vertu*."

"Virtue, indeed!" exclaimed Gilbert, laughing ironically. "You know very little about him or his virtue, during the last twelve years, I suspect! My sons Sam and Jack shall remain at home, and never wear a moustache on pain of being disinherited!"

"Oh, it's the moustache that has given offence!" said Stephen, smiling.

"No offence at all," rejoined Gilbert; "but I have heard enough of your son's doings to make me resolve to keep my sons at home as long as I can; and if going abroad be so necessary as people seem to think now-a-days, why I shall go with them, and follow them about too, wherever they go."

"I advise you to set about learning French, with all convenient expedition," said Stephen, with a sneer.

"I shall have a *coureer*," retorted his brother.

"And a tea-kettle—" suggested Stephen.

Gilbert took up his hat, with evident signs of extreme irritation.

Stephen rose and laid his hand on his brother's arm.

"Come, Gilbert," he said, "let us understand each other, and not part in anger. You are a clever, clear-headed man, as I have reason to know, having often enough profited by your advice."

The other, with a look of returning satisfaction, attempted to disclaim.

"I say, you are an unusually clever man of business," persisted Stephen; "but you are no man of the world, and never will be—or I either, though I know more of it from books than you do. Try it for a few years, and painful experience will convince you that I am right. As to our children—it is evident you feel no great regard for my son, and to tell you the truth, I do not desire the society of your daughter, either for myself or Nora. Let us, therefore, as heretofore, meet daily in the City, and but rarely at our respective houses. Our roads are no longer parallel, and Georgina will explain to you before long that your servants need not be made acquainted with the fact, of your having a brother who lives so much nearer the City than the West End."

Gilbert looked conscious, as if he had already heard something to that purport, and endeavoured to conceal his embarrassment by asking when Arthur was expected home.

"In a week or two," answered Stephen. "He and Lord Torpid are travelling together, and have reached Paris by this time."

"Ah—indeed! I read this morning in the paper, that it was generally supposed his lordship would shortly lead the beautiful and accomplished Lady Louisa Thorpe, to the—the—hymn—hym—him-alay-an altar!"

Nora thought her uncle meant to be facetious, and laughed. Such was not his intention; he had some slight misgiving that he had blundered a little in the pronunciation of a hard word; but, otherwise, considered his speech as very correct, and probably classical.

"That may be true," observed Stephen, suppressing a smile. "Lord Torpid was at Nice, for some weeks, when the Medways were there. Arthur can tell you all about the Thorpes, Nora, if they still continue to interest you."

"I believe I had better try to forget them, as they seem to have forgotten me," answered Nora, blushing.

"The Medways are a very distinguished family," said Gilbert, as he walked towards the door, "very distinguished, indeed! Yesterday evening, her ladyship entertained a select party, at her house in Grosvenor-place, at which were present the Earl and Countess of Witherington, the Ladies Martingale, Lord Augustus Jockey, and other members of the aristocracy. It is not improbable that I may become acquainted with the Medways during the season, Nora; and you may depend upon my speaking of you the first opportunity that occurs."

He left the room with a pompous wave of the hand, and an oddly contrasting good-humoured smile.

This conversation made a deep impression on Nora, from having given her more insight into the characters of her two uncles than all the previous months of careful observation. Mr Nixon never referred to it; but the knowledge that Nora was not altogether in his power, that others were as desirous as he was of having her to reside with them, unconsciously raised her in his estimation, and made him anxious to relieve the tedium of his house. That same evening, he requested her to preside in future at the tea-table, proposed her writing once a week a list of the books she wished to read, promising to procure them for her with his own, and, in a fit of kind thoughtfulness, actually surprised her with a present of a pianoforte, which with difficulty found a place in the study. She saw his efforts to make her feel herself at home, and unostentatiously met them half way; so that by the time her cousin Arthur arrived, she had pretty nearly obtained the position of a daughter in his father's house. It was his arrival that first made her painfully conscious of the very reduced state of her wardrobe: her mourning was completely worn out; she had outgrown all her other clothes, had no money to replace them, and could not overcome the repugnance she felt to an explanation with her uncle on this subject. From week to week she had hoped he would observe her wants, and say something when on the way to church, during the cold, damp, autumn Sundays; but he had no idea that her crape bonnet that had borne the dust of two summers, could not also sustain the sleet and rain of the succeeding winters.

Nora's embarrassment was greatly increased by the unusual preparations made for the reception of her cousin. The drawing-room windows were opened, the furniture uncovered, and fires lighted; Anne Ducker informing her that their dear Arthur could not endure a house looking only half inhabited. The treasures of the front bed-room, and adjoining dressing-room, which were his, were then too, for the first time, completely disclosed to her admiring eyes, and she was permitted, at her leisure, to examine the choice pictures that covered the walls, the inlaid cabinets and tables, bronze statuettes, vases, and other objects of art with which they were crowded. The day of his arrival, light once more fell on the splendid service of plate, and the silver vessels of various forms, that had decorated the sideboard on the occasion of the Christmas party; but when Nora at last perceived that new and handsome carpets were being laid on the stairs, she thought it time to inspect her wardrobe, and endeavour to discover some dress appropriate for the reception of a person of such evident importance. She possessed a black velvet gown that had belonged to her mother, and though a foreign prejudice had hitherto

made her unwilling to wear what she had learned to consider a matron's dress, she was now glad to have it, with its
valuable old lace appendages, unconscious, when her toilet
was completed, and she reluctantly left her room, that she
had never in her life looked so picturesque and pretty, so
graceful and dignified, as while leaning for a moment over
the banisters of the staircase, to ascertain whether or not
her cousin had arrived.

He had arrived. Ostentatious as had been the preparations for his reception, nothing could be more simple and
quiet than his entrance. Having joined his father at his office in the City, they had returned home together, and he
had then expressed so much more desire to see Mrs Ducker
than his cousin Nora, that he had retired first to the apartment of that much-flattered woman, and then to his own,
making hastily the slight alterations to his dress which he
considered sufficient for his father and the young relation
whose acquaintance he was about to make. He seemed,
however, rather to waver in the latter opinion, as, immediately after leaving his room, his eyes rested on the charming
figure in black velvet, that he saw preceding him downstairs, and he would, perhaps, have retreated to effect some
advantageous change, had not Nora looked up and—
smiled, smiled as if she already knew him.

In a moment he was beside her, and they entered the
drawing-room together, where they found Mr Nixon enact-
ing *grand seigneur* with all his might for the laudable purpose
of gratifying his only son.

The dinner, as far as conversation was concerned,
proved almost a *tête-à-tête* between Nora and her cousin; but
she left the father and son together directly afterwards, and
sitting down beside the fire in the drawing-room (where she
felt rather as if in a strange house) she came very quickly to
the conclusion that Arthur was very decidedly gentle-

manlike. She thought his hair, too, rather auburn than red; and if the colour of his beard admitted of no doubt whatever, it did not prevent him from being good-looking: he was agreeable, too, and would be a pleasant addition to their small party, an acquisition to her as well as to her uncle.

A very short time elapsed before he joined her, and, drawing a chair close to hers, said—

"My father is sleeping, and, I suppose, will continue to do so for half an hour longer. Let us have coffee, and tell me all you know about Lady Louisa Thorpe: she is going to be married to a friend of mine—one of the quietest, best-natured fellows in the world, and I hope you can tell me that he has not drawn a blank in Hymen's lottery."

"I know very little of Louisa," answered Nora; "but I should think Lord Torpid had not made a bad choice."

"So you know all about it!" said Arthur; "very natural—to be sure—of course."

"Do not misunderstand me," rejoined Nora, quickly. "A paragraph in one of the papers, repeated by my uncle Gilbert, gave me all the information I possess. That Lord Torpid and the Marquis of Witherington are *your* intimate friends, Anne Ducker has impressed upon my mind by dint of eternal repetition of the words."

Arthur half laughed as he exclaimed—

"Dear old Ducker! I hope you like her, Nora. In fact, you must, for she loves you beyond measure, and has already assured me that you are a 'hangel;' I, too, feel rather inclined to think this must be the case now that my father has told me you refused to go to Mr Gilbert Nixon's, in order to vegetate here with him. It was an immense sacrifice on your part; and what this house must have appeared to you, coming from the Medways, I can well imagine!"

Nora played with her fire-screen, and made no attempt to disclaim.

"You expected," he added, with some hesitation, "to return to—them?"

"I confess I had some foolish hopes of the kind for a month or so," answered Nora, with a freedom from embarrassment that encouraged her companion to go on; yet he looked at the fire and not at her, as he observed—

"You did not know Lord Medway's wavering character, and expected him to carry through his plans concerning you with firmness."

"I hardly knew what I expected," she answered, leaning back in her chair, and gazing thoughtfully at the ceiling; "I did not expect to be so completely forgotten, certainly; but, after all, the plan was impracticable, you know, without his mother's consent."

"I know no such thing," said Arthur. "Her ladyship's consent was, undoubtedly, desirable, but by no means necessary to a man in his position. Our cousin Georgina would, in your place, have played her cards differently, and gone to Nice as—head nurse—hired by his lordship himself—as Lady Medway, in short!"

"I do not understand—" began Nora.

"Is it possible you did not know that he intended to marry you? that his brother had the greatest difficulty in keeping him in Paris? that he refused for a long time to see his mother, who was obliged to propitiate him by making all sorts of promises about you for the ensuing summer, the fulfilment of which her son Charles assisted her in evading?"

"Are you quite sure of all this?" asked Nora, earnestly.

"Perfectly certain."

"And," continued Nora, "and they returned to England last year?"

"Oh, no! I don't think anything but the marriage of her two eldest daughters would even now have induced Lady Medway to return. In her present position as a widow she finds Paris, Naples, or Rome, pleasanter places of residence than London; besides which, she wished to have the Channel for some time longer between you and Medway, being much more afraid of the effects of your *beaux yeux* than even her son Charles, who told a friend of mine, in confidence, that a very short separation would be sufficient for their purpose, as you were merely a—a—"

"What?" asked Nora, smiling.

"Something so very different from what you are, that for his sake I am glad he gave the name of his informant."

"And who may that have been?" asked Nora.

"Your step-brother, Harry Darwin, who most probably has not seen you since you were a child."

"Harry never liked me," said Nora, with some emotion; "but that is of little importance to me *now*. As to Charles Thorpe, I dislike him intensely."

"You would not if you knew him," said Arthur; "he is a fine, resolute fellow, and knows perfectly what he is about. As to his not particularly wishing his brother to marry, why—aw—a—hum—"

"Oh! as to that," said Nora, "my studies in English novels and tales of fashionable life since I have been here have given me such an insight into the present state of society that I can perfectly understand his motives."

"And partly excuse them, perhaps," said Arthur, "when you consider his brother's state of health, and that he did not know you personally."

The entrance of a servant with coffee prevented her from answering, and Mr Nixon joining them almost immediately afterwards, the Thorpes were not again mentioned.

CHAPTER XI

Battledore and Shuttlecock

I T was not long before Nora began to discover that her internal rejoicings at the agreeable addition to their family had been somewhat premature. Arthur Nixon left home every morning directly after breakfast with his father, sometimes accompanying him to the City, more frequently directing his steps westward to the Club, where he not only received his notes and letters, but also his friends; and in the course of time the numerous invitations he expected for dinners, *soirées*, and balls. The evening after his arrival he went to the Opera; and from that time forward, for several weeks, seldom dined at home, excepting on Sundays. He informed his father daily at breakfast of his evening engagements, spoke of every person and every thing he saw without the slightest reserve; and on such occasions exhibited a degree of satire eminently calculated to lead the uninitiated to suppose that in his heart he had learned to despise the rank and fashion, in the pursuit of which he was squandering the best years of his life.

Nora and her uncle returned to their old habits, and the study, and Arthur became to them merely an occasional but always an acceptable and agreeable guest. As the spring advanced his engagements multiplied; and though he complained frequently of being bored and fatigued, he seldom made arrangements for a day of rest; gravely assuring Nora, when she jested on the subject, that if he remained at home for even one week, he should run a great chance of being "clean forgotten, like a dead man, out of mind."

One rainy afternoon, towards the end of May, he returned home at an unusually early hour, and instead of going directly to his room, as was his custom, turned into the study. That he expected to find Nora there is certain, but so little did her absence concern him, that he took up a book, without even inquiring whether or not she were in the house; and, throwing himself into a chair, rather rejoiced in the feeling of being alone. Scarcely, however, had the slight noise produced by his movement of books and chairs ceased, than he heard the sound of irregular, eager, almost breathless counting in the adjoining dining-room—98—99—300!—301—302—-3—4—5 and so on.

Cautiously opening the door of communication between the rooms, he perceived that Nora, adroitly avoiding the tables and chairs, was amusing herself with a solitary game of battledore and shuttlecock, her anxiety lest the latter should fall to the ground being so great that his intruding head remained long unperceived. It happened that one of her greatest personal advantages was a perfectly-formed figure, and nothing could be more graceful or fascinating than the unstudied and various positions into which her game compelled her to place it, while her upturned face, with sparkling eyes, lips slightly parted, and cheeks into which exercise had forced the clearest and brightest colour, made her, for the time being, the most beautiful creature he had ever beheld. He watched with intense interest every movement, followed with a sort of nervous anxiety the wavering flight of the shuttlecock as it sometimes approached, sometimes receded from his vicinity, and started when at length it alighted on his head, and Nora stood before him.

"Oh, why did you open the door?" she exclaimed, in a

tone of jesting reproach; "if your tiresome head had not been there, I could have completed my fourth or even fifth hundred without interruption. Surely you must have returned home a full hour too soon to-day!"

"An hour earlier—but I hope not too soon," he answered, with heightened colour.

"Oh, I have said something you don't like to hear, or you would not correct my English," observed Nora, smiling archly as she continued to play with her shuttlecock. But it now began to fall continually, and after Arthur had raised it from the floor at least a dozen times, he said he supposed she must be tired.

"Not at all," she answered, quickly; "it is dividing my attention between you and the shuttlecock that makes me so *maladroite:* I am never tired until after my fifth hundred."

"What on earth do you mean by your fourth and fifth hundred?" asked Arthur.

"Why, you see," said Nora, tossing the shuttlecock towards the ceiling and pursuing it afterwards with a look of sportive eagerness—"you see I am not accustomed to be so completely confined to the house (bump, bump), as if I had been born and bred in London (bump).—So when I first came here I used to run up and down the stairs a good deal (bump, bump, bump); but without any object in view, it was all too tiresome (bump). Then I made a ball for myself (bump)—broke the windows (bump, bump)—and had no money to pay the glazier!" Here the shuttlecock fell to the ground, and she raised it herself, as Arthur repeated—

"Pay the glazier?"

"Yes, for I did not wish my uncle to know that I was so childish as to play at ball, so Duckey paid for me (bump, bump), and did not write it in the account book. She also (bump) gave me this battledore and shuttlecock last Christmas (bump, bump, bump)."

"Ducker!" exclaimed Arthur.

"Yes, Ducker," said Nora, coming towards him, and with light touches of her hands keeping the shuttlecock constantly in the air just before her face, after the manner of the most expert juggler. "You have no idea how kind she has been to me."

"Or how generous you have been to her," said Arthur; "yet she has shown me a brooch and earrings given her by you, which were certainly intended to deck a fairer person than good old Ducker's."

"Earrings are a barbarous ornament," replied Nora, smiling, "and I never wear them. Other trinkets I value in exact proportion to my affection for the donors. The brooch that so delighted Ducker was worthless to me, given carelessly and accepted unwillingly. I can only rejoice in its having at last found a possessor who will value it, both intrinsically and fictitiously."

"You have raised my curiosity concerning this brooch," said Arthur. "Have you any objection to tell me the name of the donor?"

"None whatever—it was my step-brother, Harry Darwin."

"Do you feel so very indifferent towards him?" asked Arthur.

"I have reason to do so," answered Nora. "He never cared for me, and the letter I wrote to inform him of my father's death and my unpleasant position was not answered for six months!"

"It may not have reached him so soon as you supposed," suggested Arthur.

"It was forwarded to him immediately by Charles Thorpe, who must have given him some information concerning me at a later period, as in his answer, though he passed over my father's death as an event of no importance, he expressed very great satisfaction at my being so well provided for; and recommended me to conciliate my uncle Stephen in every possible way, and to make myself generally useful in his house."

"When you again write," said Arthur, "you can tell him that you have made yourself indispensable to my father."

"Our correspondence is at an end," said Nora, as she entered the study. "I could read between the lines of his letter his anxiety to avoid all further communication with me, his fear that I might become a burden to him."

"For a young unmarried man, like Darwin," began Arthur, "an orphan sister is rather a—a—"

"An incumbrance?" suggested Nora. "Harry shall never find me one."

"I should not exactly have used that word," said Arthur, laughing, "and only wished to point out to you, that Darwin only acted as a—most other young men in his place would have done. He disliked your father, I believe—knew very little of you, and therefore—"

"You need not go on," cried Nora, interrupting him, indignantly. "After having attempted a justification of Charles Thorpe's conduct the very first evening of our acquaintance, I can hardly be surprised at your now excusing Harry's neglect of me! In a worldly point of view they are both patterns of prudence, no doubt, but I can never like them—or you either," she added petulantly, "if you can speak and think in this manner."

"Forgive me, Nora," said Arthur, gravely, " for not being able to find fault with men whose conduct, whether reprehensible or not, has been the means of bringing you under our roof." He sat down at the writing-table, and hastily wrote a few lines, while Nora, half vexed, half flattered, retired to her room to dress for dinner.

Great was Mr Nixon's surprise, and (must it be confessed?) not inconsiderable his annoyance, when his son entered the study a few minutes before dinner-time, and carelessly saying that he had written an excuse to the Savage Waywards, and intended to dine at home, sat down beside Nora, and peered over her shoulder, while she examined a book of engravings containing views of various mountainous parts of Germany, but chiefly the Tyrol.

"If you had mentioned your intention of remaining with us a little earlier," said Mr Nixon, "we could have had a fire in the drawing-room; in fact," he added, hastily turning round, "it is not too late, and the—"

"Let me entreat that no change may be made for me," cried Arthur, springing towards him. "I am really not such a bulky fellow that you cannot find room for me in your snuggery here."

"But," said his father, "I know you dislike this room, and when we have drawing-rooms, why not use them?"

"Why not, indeed?" exclaimed Arthur, laughing, "but, on the present occasion, I do not choose in any way to interfere with your or Nora's habits, nor do I choose to be treated as a visitor any longer."

"I assure you, however," said Mr Nixon, "that when the weather begins to get warm I have no sort of objection to going up stairs in the evening. I only turned in here when I was quite alone, you know."

"Yes, but you have continued here with Nora, and she likes this room better than the others, I am quite sure;" he turned to Nora while speaking, but without waiting to hear her answer, Mr Nixon left the room to give some orders about Rhine wine and ice, while Arthur, resuming his place beside his cousin, bent over the engravings and murmured, "I wish I were at any of these places."

"So do I," said Nora, vainly endeavouring to suppress a sigh.

"You are, probably, well acquainted with them all?" he asked.

"I have spent several summers among these mountains," she answered, "and know the banks of the Inn, and Innsbruck, far, far better than the Thames and London!"

"I suspect you have as yet seen scarcely anything of London," he observed.

"Rather say nothing at all," she replied; "I have not even had a glimpse of St Paul's and Westminster Abbey."

"You shall see both to-morrow," he said, smiling.

"Oh, thank you—I should like so much to see the Tower, also, if—if—" here she stopped, for it suddenly flashed across her mind that she had no dress in which she could appear in public with her cousin. To hide her embarrassment she turned over a leaf and forgot it altogether as her eyes rested on a view of Meran, with its beautiful suburb of Obermais. "There, there we lived," she said, her colour rising as she extended her hand to the print, "just beside that church—I do believe these are the windows of our little drawing-room—we could see the Zenoburg and the road to the Castle of Tyrol from them. You have been to see the ruins of the old castle?"

"Yes," said Arthur, "the view from that long room, which, by-the-by, is not at all ancient looking, is the most beautiful imaginable—without water."

"But there is the Adige," cried Nora, eagerly; "one can follow the course of the river for miles."

"True, but it looks like a silver thread; and to satisfy me, half the valley ought to have been under water in the form of a lake—I dare say it was, once upon a time."

"If you were not enchanted with that view, just as you found it," said Nora, "we must never travel, nor even look at prints together," and she prepared to close the book.

"Surely you will allow me to differ from you in opinion

occasionally," he said, preventing her from doing so; "if we always thought alike there would be an end to all conversation."

"But," said Nora, "I am afraid you are like most travelled Englishmen, and will contrive to find something to criticise everywhere."

"Try me," said Arthur.

"This is Rametz," she said, pointing to a castellated building. "You know Rametz?"

Arthur nodded.

"And the very fat Italian doctor to whom it belongs?"

"No."

"The son of a peasant of Meran, who studied in Italy, became a celebrated physician, saved money, returned home to purchase the ruins among which he had played as a boy, and restored, and rebuilt, and added—"

Arthur laughed. Nora stopped, and looked at him inquiringly.

"I had not time to find out all this," he said; "but it accounts most satisfactorily for the confusion of architecture, which you must allow to be rather evident in the edifice."

"What do I care for the architecture?" said Nora. "I did not go to Rametz to see a Gothic church or Grecian temple; I went with gay friends to sup under the vines, and to stand on the balcony after sunset, and watch the shadows of evening spreading over the valley—I have stood there until the mountain tops were lighted by the moon, and—" here she stopped again.

"Go on," said Arthur.

"No," answered Nora, "you are laughing at me. You do not understand me, and cannot comprehend the distinctness with which I can recall these scenes, and remember every word I there heard spoken."

"I can, I do," cried Arthur, eagerly; "the terrible monotony of your present existence makes you return to and live in the past. Nora," he added, lowering his voice, though they were alone in the room, "are you very unhappy here?"

"No—oh no—by no means—only a little lonely sometimes; but that is the fault of my education, I suppose. Had I been born and brought up in London, I dare say I should have quite enjoyed being shut up—that is a—rather confined to the house as I now am."

"Do you go out so very seldom?" asked Arthur.

"Not at all, excepting to church, and occasionally to walk in the square," she answered, and then fearing a renewal of his proposal to take her out the ensuing day, she again bent over the prints, and pointing to Schoena, asked if he had been there too.

"No, I had not time; in two days one cannot go to all these places."

"I am sorry you did not go to Schoena, for the architecture is quite correct there, I believe. A stronghold of the middle ages, with massive walls, small windows, vaulted corridors, armoury hall, and so forth. I don't understand much about these things, and confess that the history of one of its last possessors, before it was purchased by the Archduke John, interested me more than the place itself."

"And what was his story?" asked Arthur.

"*Her* story, you must say," answered Nora. "She married a peasant, and retired with him to a small house, which she built lower down on the hill."

"Some handsome fellow, no doubt," observed Arthur.

"I did not ask," said Nora, thoughtfully; "they said she was not happy—"

"I dare say not," interposed Arthur. "A descent, or rather a fall in rank, is always a dangerous experiment for a woman, and a *dame châtelaine*, who becomes a peasant's wife, has a very difficult lesson to learn; the sort of love, too, which induces her to take such a step is not of a description to last long, or enable her to bear her unavoidable trials with patience."

"The peasant, who spoke to us about her, seemed to be of your opinion also, and evidently disapproved of the match; he would have told us more, perhaps, had papa been disposed to listen. Almost all the old castles about Meran have not only ancient but also modern histories, some of them quite romantic; at Fragsburg, for instance, one of the most isolated of them all, where we went in the hope of seeing a curious collection of family portraits described in Seawald's *Tyrol*, we found a widow with a son and daughter, obliged by circumstances to reside there constantly, hardly able to keep the great pile of building in repair, yet clinging with affection to the very stones. The ancestors' pictures had been disposed of in the Charles Surface* manner, and no rich uncle having made his appearance as purchaser, they—"

Here dinner was announced; but Arthur only waited until his father slept afterwards to return to Nora, professedly to hear the remainder of the story, but, in fact, to talk of other things, and find out as much as he could of the mind and attainments of a relative, who, in the very heart of London, was nearly as much alone as the young shy girl she so graphically described standing beneath the old fig-tree in the dilapidated court at Fragsburg.

Arthur had an evening engagement, but seemed in no hurry to leave home; the announcement of his cab was received with an impatient wave of his hand, nor did he again

---

* Character in the comedy *The School for Scandal* (first performed Drury Lane 1777) by Richard Brinsley Sheridan (1751-1816), who is willing to sell off the portraits of his ancestors until rescued from poverty by his rich uncle.

think of it, or the Countess of Allcourt's ball, until his father had gone to bed, and Nora parted from him in the hall. Even afterwards he stood watching her ascent of the stairs, compelling her frequently to look over the bannisters, and answer his reiterated "good-night."

It was remarked that Arthur paid very little attention to the countess's daughter, Lady Emmeline, that evening; the young lady herself seemed to consider an officer in the Blues a very good substitute; but her mother thought otherwise, as she was by no means unwilling to bestow one of her numerous progeny on Nixon the millionaire, a man of such undoubted talent that it was generally supposed he could become anything he pleased. Arthur was not ignorant of the favourable opinion entertained of his fortune and intellect, and in no way endeavoured to lower it; he called himself a "marrying man," spoke of purchasing landed property, and hinted an intention of entering Parliament the first convenient opportunity. Once only that night did he address Lady Emmeline, and when she was afterwards questioned by her mother on the subject of his apparently interesting though short conversation, she assured her he had spoken of nothing but the charms of—battledore and shuttlecock, which he pronounced to be the most perfectly graceful game ever invented, and one that rendered a handsome woman, when playing, irresistibly captivating.

The fact was, Nora's face and figure had that day taken Arthur's heart by storm, and he could only wonder at his previous insensibility; while thenceforward, without the slightest consideration of the consequences, or the faintest attempt to overcome the headstrong passion that he felt taking possession of him, he yielded to every impulse, and before many days had elapsed, made Nora perfectly aware that his heart was hers, and that he wished her to know it.

There are few things that ought to be less gratifying to a

woman than becoming the object of a sudden and violent
passion of this kind, yet there are not many who remember
that the feeling has its source in an exaggerated estimation
of mere personal beauty, and remain unflattered by it. Nora
attempted no analysis; she received Arthur's homage as
willingly as it was offered; and found that his earnest devotion contrasted pleasantly with her recollection of Lord
Medway's languid regard. He soon began to remain much
at home, at first ostensibly to direct her studies in English
literature, of which she fancied herself unusually ignorant,
afterwards to improve himself in German, which she undoubtedly understood better than English, though nothing
annoyed her more than being told so. Both occupations
were dangerous, for they led to mutual discoveries of talent,
that, in the common intercourse of life, might long have
remained concealed; and when Arthur in time learned to
appreciate her mind even more than her person, and began
to meditate a sacrifice in her favour of his long-cherished
matrimonial plans, the very idea of which would have appeared incipient madness to him a few months previously,
Nora, not for a moment doubting his intentions, gave herself an infinity of trouble to return his affection, as she
thought it deserved, and laboured not unsuccessfully to become reconciled to what her foreign education made her
contemplate without much aversion, a *mariage de convenance et
raison*.

The weather had become sultry, windows and doors
were opened, the large drawing-rooms in use by common
consent, and either Nora remained longer in the dining-
room, or her uncle's drowsiness was increased by heat, for
she was seldom more than a few minutes alone after dinner
before Arthur was again at her side. She had learned to expect this, and many other little attentions of so unobtrusive
a nature, that though perfectly understood by her, they

were completely unobserved by her uncle.

One day, before and during dinner, Arthur had used all his eloquence to induce his father to go abroad, if only for a few weeks, during the summer, promising to show him scenery, of which he had not yet even an idea; pictures and statues of which he had but read descriptions; and ending with the assurance that none of his habits should be interfered with, none of his usual comforts forgotten; he and Nora would undertake to make him enjoy himself perfectly, and travelling was now so easy!

"Rather too easy, Arthur," replied Mr Nixon, dryly. "As to my ever leaving home, that is out of the question; but that you want to take flight again is evident enough. Now, without intending to dictate, let me tell you that I should be glad to hear you had at last begun to think seriously of establishing yourself in your own country; half my fortune is yours whenever you choose to do so."

"I cannot—say—that I feel—any great inclination just now to—accept your—really very—liberal offer," said Arthur, with some hesitation and evident embarrassment.

Mr Nixon, who had already begun to stretch and compose himself for a doze, suddenly raised himself upright in his chair, and, fixing his eyes on his son, observed, "You have remained at home a good deal lately, Arthur; I hope that no quarrel with Lady Emmeline has been the cause, or that any difficulty on the part of her family is likely to interfere with our plans. You did not seem to apprehend anything of that kind when we last spoke on this subject."

"Nor do I now," answered Arthur, with all the confidence usually manifested by his sex on such occasions; and he glanced towards Nora, as he added, "Any delays or difficulties that may henceforward occur are likely to be on my side."

Now this was the first time that Lady Emmeline had

been so mentioned in Nora's presence; and though not by any means as yet deeply attached to her cousin, she had so completely made up her mind to become his wife, that she could not hear unmoved so plain an intimation that he was engaged, or nearly so, to another woman. She looked alternately at her companions in a bewildered, inquiring manner, felt herself blush intensely, and then rising, with as much calmness as she could command, murmured something about leaving them alone to discuss affairs of such importance, and walked towards the door, to which her cousin sprang before her, and where he bent forward as she passed him, in the vain hope that she would look at or speak to him.

Before Nora had reached the drawing-room, her consternation at what she had just heard began to abate. No one but herself knew what she had expected and intended, and no one ever should know the efforts she had made to return the affection of a man, who, it was now evident, had only been amusing himself with her. Was it right or honourable that he had done so? It is true he had never uttered the *word* love, or spoken of marriage, but—but—no matter —men were undoubtedly at liberty to act in this manner if women allowed them. With her, at least, no one should ever trifle again; she had received a painful and mortifying lesson, but had reason to be thankful that she had not been wounded in a manner to destroy her happiness irretrievably. It was, after all, a disappointment in marriage, and not in love—a disappointment unknown to all the world, easily concealed, not *very* hard to bear, and she believed she should in future distrust all mankind, and despise and dislike that portion of it to which Arthur Nixon belonged.

Having come to this conclusion, she walled into the back drawing-room, opened wide one of the windows, and gasped for breath in a manner that strongly resembled a succession of deep sighs. The evening was oppressively warm; and being dressed, for a reason already mentioned, in the indestructible black velvet, she naturally concluded that the sensation of suffocation proceeded altogether from her unseasonable attire. This led her to long reflections on poverty and dependance, that were by no means exhilarating; so that as she stood half on the balcony, half in the room, now growing dusky in the twilight, her anger subsided slowly into a despondency, that better suited the scene around her. A strong current of air made her aware of the opening of the door of the front room: it ceased immediately, and she was provoked to find her heart beating violently, her hands cold and trembling, as she pressed them together in the agitation and dread of a meeting, and, perhaps, explanation, with Arthur. She wished to get out of the room, but could not do so without passing the open folding-door and being seen. Suddenly she remembered having heard her mother say, that to prevent an untimely exhibition of agitation, there was no better remedy than a severe pinch administered to the back of the neck, which pinch was to be repeated until it took effect. She raised her hand, and—was it the pain, or hearing her uncle's voice, that so effectually tranquillised her? She knew not, nor had she time to consider, for, unfortunately perceiving the room unoccupied, the first words that Mr Nixon uttered were of a nature to compel her to remain where she was, in order not to embarrass him, and place herself in an intolerably mortifying position. She therefore endeavoured to put herself out of sight and hearing by standing on the balcony, while her uncle continued—"No one can be more sincerely attached to Nora than I now am: she is a good and a clever girl—yes, a very clever girl, and pretty, and interesting, and all that you have said, but such a connection for you would destroy all our plans and hopes of rising in the world. I am sorry to perceive that your opinions on this subject have begun to waver: be yourself again, Arthur, and follow the course that will enable you to found a family, and *obtain* a name! This first step is of the greatest importance, and any attempt to evade it will place you in my position, and force you to realise your ambition in the person of your son. Want of fortune may easily be overlooked on our side, but want of rank—never!"

"I thought," began Arthur, hesitatingly, "that perhaps my own numerous personal friends, and her relationship with the Medways—"

"They all but deny the relationship," said his father, interrupting him: "Lord Medway, indeed, attracted probably by her youth and good looks, wished his mother to retain her in the family, but her ladyship was, in consequence, rendered even more anxious to get rid of her on any terms. She even sent for her son Charles, who was at Vienna, to manage the affair. You shall see his letters to me; they will show you in what light the Thorpe family view the relationship! Nothing could be more downright than his statement of facts; and it was not flattering to Nora, I can tell you: but I neither blamed him nor his mother for acting precisely as I should do myself in a similar case."

"Were I to be the object acted upon," said Arthur, "such plans would most certainly fail; but Nora was young and inexperienced, and Lord Medway an indolent, wavering fellow, who always has been, and always will be, completely governed by those about him. I have yet to discover the man who can rule me openly or covertly."

"You prefer being ruled by women," observed his father, sarcastically. "But come: the most perfect confidence has hitherto existed between us, and will, I trust, continue as long as we live; believe me, this foolish fancy for your black-eyed cousin will pass over, as others have done. I know that your ambition fully equals mine: marry this Lady Emmeline, get into Parliament, and let me see you a man of consequence, if not of rank, before I die."

"Had you so spoken a few weeks ago," said Arthur, gloomily, "your words would have found an echo, if not in my heart, certainly in my head; but now——"

"You surely do not mean to say that you have deliberately been making a fool of yourself for that length of time, Arthur?"

"I mean to say that I then admired, but now love Nora—sincerely, deeply, passionately—as I have never loved before, and never shall again. I fear—I—cannot forget her."

"Time will enable you to do so," said Mr Nixon, quietly. "Time must do you this good service, Arthur, for I will never give my consent to your marriage with her. To all your other follies I have been more than indulgent, and am now prepared to make any sacrifice to give you a position in the world; it seems to me, also, that you have already paid this Lady Emmeline too much attention to be able to draw back with honour——"

"Oh, no!" cried Arthur with a slight sneer: "in this world of fashion that we value so highly, one is not so easily caught and bound as elsewhere. I consider myself still quite at liberty."

"Oh, indeed!" said his father. "Then, perhaps, you prefer one of the daughters of Lord Witherington? Having never seen any of these young ladies, I do not venture to give an opinion; in the latter case, you will, of course, go abroad again, and—Nora can then remain with me."

"That she can do at all events," said Arthur. "After what you have just said, I cannot speak to her, and everything remains as it was, before this foolish confession of mine."

"Not quite," said Mr Nixon, "for if you do not decide

on either marrying Lady Emmeline, or joining the Witheringtons at Baden, where you told me they now are, I shall
consider it necessary to send Nora, for some time at least,
to your uncle Gilbert's. He and Georgina will I know be
quite pleased to have her."

"I dare say they will," replied Arthur; "but I am much
mistaken if they ever let her return to you."

"Gilbert will scarcely interfere with me, after my having
told him of my intention to give her two thousand
pounds," said Mr Nixon.

"Have you done so?" asked Arthur, quickly.

"Certainly. The very day after she consented to remain
with me, I placed the sum in the Bank for her."

"Then," rejoined Arthur, "I think you had better henceforward allow her to receive the interest of this splendid
fortune, for this morning, when I was angry with her for
persisting in her refusal to go out with me, Ducker told me
in confidence, that the poor dear girl had outgrown all her
clothes and had no money to replace them."

"Why did she not tell me?" said Mr Nixon; "the slightest
hint would have been sufficient."

"I do not think Nora likely ever to hint a wish of the
kind," said Arthur; "but you are bound to supply her wants,
and make her existence as endurable as possible, after having refused to resign her to your brother, or give her to me;
—after having, in short, deliberately resolved to bury her
alive in this house."

"I really do not understand what you, and Gilbert, and
Georgina, mean by eternally harping on the horrors of this
house," said Mr Nixon, testily. "Nora's life is not more solitary than that of thousands of others in London. I cannot
perceive why she is such an object of pity—her time is at
her own disposal, I give her a home, and—"

"And," said Arthur, sarcastically, "and food, and even

raiment, perhaps; but you seem altogether to forget that her previous life has been spent in the enjoyment of bright skies and magnificent scenery, gay society, and all that art can offer to improve and refine the taste. As to comparing her to those who have been born and bred in London, it is absurd. Canaries reared in a cage are happy there, knowing no gayer kind of life; but other and rarer birds mourn their captivity, and find the shelter and food given them a poor exchange for liberty."

"In order to answer you in the same strain, Arthur, let me tell you, that you will compel me to set my rare bird at liberty, if you do not soon begin to think and speak more rationally than you have done for the last hour. I cannot, however, say," added Mr Nixon, walking towards the fire-place, and from habit leaning on the chimney-piece, and gazing into the grate, "I cannot, however, say that I feel in the least uneasy as to your ultimate decision; the question is rather, now, whether you go abroad or remain at home."

"I shall remain here," answered Arthur, sullenly.

"And," said Mr Nixon, in the same calm voice, "and propose for Lady Emmeline without further delay?"

"To-night, or—never," he replied vehemently, and then strode across the room and stepped out on the balcony.

His father followed him, and Nora seized the opportunity to glide unseen past the open door, and escape up stairs to her own room.

CHAPTER XII

To Marry,—or Not to Marry,—That is the Question

I T was with some slight trepidation that Nora descended to breakfast the next morning. Before her return to the drawing-room the previous evening, Arthur had left it, and probably the house also, and while afterwards awaiting the striking of ten o'clock, with an open book in her hand, her thoughts had been completely occupied by surmises as to how he and his father had parted. All her doubts on the subject were at once removed when she saw them standing together at one of the windows of the dining-room amicably engaged in the discussion of money matters. The words "purchase" and "settlement" were frequently repeated as she employed herself making tea at the breakfast-table, and while she was still considering whether or not Arthur's manner was that of a man who had taken the important step that had been so peremptorily enjoined him, her uncle advanced towards and informed her, that having, according to promise, placed two thousand pounds in her name in the Bank, she could draw the interest of that sum as she pleased, and when she pleased in future.

Prepared for this announcement, Nora thanked him warmly and appropriately; but when, sitting down beside her, he thrust a bank note of large amount into her hand, saying that was for immediate use, she felt distressed, and stammered and coloured as a feeling that he was paying her for her disappointment flashed across her mind. Her uneasiness was, however, almost immediately relieved, when he turned towards Arthur, who stood with his back to them looking into the little garden, and observed, with a jocularity of manner very unusual to him, but denoting a satisfaction too great for concealment, "Who would think now, Nora, that that man there was a bridegroom elect, the accepted lover of one of the prettiest girls in London?"

Nora perceived that her uncle had not thought at all of her on this occasion, so she looked up and observed quietly, "Lady Emmeline, I suppose?"

Now this was said with a composure that gave infinite satisfaction to herself, but struck Arthur as something so unexpected that he turned his flushed face round, and stared at her in astonishment.

"I don't know what is the custom in England, Arthur," she continued, bending slightly over the table as she poured out the tea, "but abroad you know people expect to be congratulated by all their friends, and therefore—"

"For heaven's sake, spare me all such heartless formalities!" he cried, interrupting her vehemently, while he seated himself further from her than had of late been his custom, and snatched up the nearest newspaper.

There are few women, even at the age of seventeen or eighteen, who have not the power of concealing annoyance, disappointment, and mortification, if a strong motive make them desirous to do so: some hours' reflection had enabled Nora so effectually to overcome the portions of all these feelings that had fallen to her lot, that she not only looked but felt calm, and she experienced a strange sort of satisfaction in showing her cousin that the commiseration he had perhaps intended to bestow on her would be quite thrown away.

Now Arthur really loved Nora; but such is the

selfishness of man's heart, that he was disagreeably surprised and beyond measure indignant to find that he had
not made her as unhappy as himself.

"Let me show you the advertisement of the sale of the
house I spoke of just now," said Mr Nixon, supposing his
son to be in search of it, when he saw his eyes wandering
up and down the columns of the paper with impatient uncertainty. "It is there, just at the end of the page before
you."

"I know the house well," said Arthur, after a pause; "it
belongs to Lord Trebleton's young widow. I suppose her
jointure is not sufficiently splendid to enable her to keep it,
and that she intends to return to her family."

"Do you know her?" asked Mr Nixon.

"Of course I do—she is a daughter of Lord Witherington, and by many degrees the handsomest of the family.
She is somewhat extravagant in her tastes, fond to excess of
all kinds of gaiety, but altogether one of the most charming
women of my acquaintance. We very nearly fell in love with
each other, just before she was engaged to Lord Trebleton."

"Would the house suit you?" asked Mr Nixon, but little
interested in the history of its possessor.

"I should think so," answered Arthur, "for undoubtedly
no expense has been spared to make it perfect."

"Then let us see about it this very day, before I go to the
City," said Mr Nixon, beginning his breakfast without further delay.

Nora attended little to the conversation that followed.
She was considering if the very great change in Arthur's
manner were necessary—if, instead of the murmured good
morning, and scarce perceptible bow when she had entered
the room, he might not have given her his hand as usual,
and looked at her and spoken to her. Perhaps he had some

idea that he had not acted honourably—but no—he had observed the evening before, that in the world in which he lived, men were not bound as elsewhere, and he had certainly not in any way committed himself—had said, in fact, even less than Lord Medway: there was some similarity in the two cases, and Arthur, she now remembered, had not blamed him in the least, had rather approved of the interference of Charles Thorpe, and had undertaken his defence the very first time he had ever spoken to her alone. Perhaps he was glad that his father now compelled him to be prudent! One thing was certain and evident to her, that however much she might be admired or even loved, there was that in her position in the world which precluded all chance of marriage; this fact she resolved should not again escape her memory.

A few days afterwards Arthur received as a gift from his father the spacious and completely furnished mansion of Lady Trebleton: all the treasures of his rooms in Russell-square were conveyed to it, and various new and costly purchases added, so that between his house and visits to Lady Emmeline, he had little time to spare for home. When there, he was rather low-spirited, and failed not whenever an opportunity offered, and he chanced to be alone with Nora, to assure her that he was the most wretched of human beings, a martyr to the prejudices of the world and parental authority.

Yet he hurried forward the preparations for his marriage with an energy that gave great satisfaction to the heads of both families, his father merely smiling ironically when he persisted in assuring him, he only wanted to have it over. Nora, in the mean while, apparently forgotten, had full leisure to renovate and improve her wardrobe. This she accomplished with judgment and taste; her decision when purchasing and giving orders astonishing Mrs Ducker, who conducted her to some of the large warehouses in the City, and to the Soho Bazaar, at her leisure hours, viz., between seven and nine o'clock in the morning.

It is not alone simple Bob Acres[*] who has discovered that "dress does make a difference." The first day that Nora laid aside her mourning, and when dressing for dinner put on white muslin and rose-coloured ribbons, her glass told her something to the same effect, and it must be confessed she herself was more than satisfied with her appearance, as she looked at the reflection of her fair young face and graceful figure. She thought it probable her uncle would say something on the occasion, and prepared a little speech of thanks, but on entering the drawing-room all thoughts of herself or her dress were lost in surprise and anxiety, when she saw Mr Nixon walking up and down the room, with pallid face and purple lips, and Arthur astride upon a chair, his head bent down on his hands, which seemed to clutch the back of it as if cramped, while he muttered, "Infernal affair altogether!"

As Nora closed the door, he looked up, started from his seat, and added, "Hang me if I care much after all, were it not for my legion of friends and acquaintances!"

"Cross the Channel until the affair has blown over," suggested his father, following towards the door.

"No!" he answered fiercely, "I will face and brave them all; not one shall dare to pity me!"

The door closed, and Nora was left alone until dinner was announced. At table her uncle and cousin talked of politics and public affairs; but she suspected they did so on account of the servants, and was confirmed in this idea

[*] Character in the comedy *The Rivals* (first performed 1775), by Richard Brinsley Sheridan (1751-1816).

when profound silence followed their absence. For her own part she was so convinced that something very unpleasant had occurred, and so perfectly at a loss as to its nature, that she scarcely uttered a word, and left the dining-room almost immediately after dinner. Arthur and his father joined her at tea-time; the former went out as usual, the latter read, or seemed to read, until ten o'clock, when Nora went to bed, feeling herself forcibly reminded that she was still a stranger in her uncle's family.

Too proud to show a particle of curiosity, she scarcely observed the next morning that both father and son were poring over a paragraph in one of the papers as they stood together at the window; but she could not help remarking afterwards that they were endeavouring to outstay each other, and that a serious kind of manoeuvring was going on, which ended by Mr Nixon asking his son abruptly if "he intended to tell Nora."

"Certainly," he replied; "it is no secret, and I am very anxious to know what she will say."

Mr Nixon fixed his eyes on her, while Arthur, folding the morning paper into a small form, placed it so before her that her eyes instantly fell on a paragraph headed "Marriage in High Life," in which the engagement of Lady Emmeline Wary to her cousin the Marquis of Torrisford was announced in the usual manner.

It was some moments before Nora could stammer, "How is this? was she not betrothed to you?"

"We have no betrothals in England," replied Arthur. "She was engaged to me publicly enough, and I thought willingly too; but yesterday morning she informed me that she had long been attached to her cousin Torrisford, and entreated me to release her from a promise that had been in a manner extorted from her by her mother. Could I refuse? I felt myself atrociously and notoriously jilted, but any attempt to seek redress after such a confession on her part would only have served to render my position still more ridiculous; so having told her I was sorry her cousin had not known his own mind, and rewarded her constancy a few weeks earlier, I resigned my claims, and prepared myself to face the world's dread laugh as well as I could on such short notice."

Nora's colour mounted to her temples, and she paused for a moment before she observed, "This is a most unexpected—a most undeserved indignity, Arthur. I am sincerely sorry for your disappointment."

"I shall get over that easily enough," he answered with a slight sneer; "my heart was wonderfully little engaged in this affair."

Mr Nixon walked across the room, and placed himself behind Nora's chair, directly facing his son.

"But the vexatious mortification—the—the publicity"— continued Nora, indignantly.

"Well," he said, with a forced smile, "I suppose I shall get over that too. Emmeline's avowal of an attachment to her cousin is infinitely less distressing to me now than it would have been after our marriage: she assured me he was in ignorance of her engagement to me when he wrote the letter from Naples, which she offered to show me, but which I declined reading. I suppose, however, that I must believe her; and I have serious thoughts of giving a proof of my good faith and exemplary patience by requesting an invitation to the wedding, which will be celebrated a few weeks hence."

So Arthur spoke to Nora, so also to all his friends and acquaintances, by no means avoiding them or the subject that formed the chief topic of discussion for nearly nine days, after which it was forgotten by all but those personally interested in the affair. But though Arthur jested lightly and laughed good-humouredly at his "disappointment in marriage," as he pointedly called it, he was greatly irritated and deeply mortified, proving it to all thoughtful observers by his continuing to parade his indifference long after the effort had ceased to be necessary. His father wished him—urged him—to go abroad for a few months, in vain; he was determined to stay out the season, and employed himself chiefly in the purchase of pictures and furniture for his house, no wish of his being left ungratified by his father, who secretly blamed himself for having precipitated his son's choice of a wife, and thereby drawing him into his present painful position.

One day when Arthur at dinner was expatiating on the excellence of a picture that was for sale at an artist's in Piccadilly, his father, who had, at his request, been to see it, at first hesitatingly "supposed his son might be right, as he had experience in such things," and then commenced a criticism that was as distinguished for sound sense as want of technical language. Arthur laughed, while Nora, with a smile, assisted her uncle to express his opinion in proper words, and then playfully sided with him as much as her want of knowledge of the object of discussion would permit.

"Two against one is not quite fair," said Arthur at last, turning to his father; "but as Nora has seen most of the best pictures in Europe, and I really believe knows something about the matter in question, I am ready to make her umpire between us. Shall I drive her down to Piccadilly tomorrow, and will you abide by her decision?"

Mr Nixon instantly agreed, and Nora had no reason and no wish to excuse herself. Arthur was in waiting exactly at the appointed hour the next day—he examined her dress with a critical eye, bestowed on it some words of approval, on herself a glance of undisguised admiration, and then devoted his attention for some time to the rash movements of his high-stepping horse.

Nora's opinion of the picture was quickly given; she agreed with Arthur in considering it worthy of much commendation as a work of art, but scarcely adapted for a private collection intended to decorate the walls of a dwelling-house. The subject was hackneyed (nymphs bathing); and the very excellence of the flesh-tints would make it, to her at least, an unpleasant picture to have constantly before her.

"You are a genuine Englishwoman after all, Nora," said Arthur, smiling, "and somewhat prudish too, for the painter, by means of water, rocks, and trunks of trees, has managed to make this picture the least exceptionable of its kind that I have ever seen."

"Perhaps so," she answered, turning away, while he, half-petulantly remonstrating against her "absurd objection," followed her to an unfinished portrait at a little distance. There she stopped, and said in a low voice, "Those other people, and the presence of the artist, prevented me from saying all I thought of the picture. The richness of colour is an exaggeration of nature; did you not observe how very freely he has used vermilion?"

"N—o—I don't know much about the mixture of oil colours. You do, I suppose?"

"A little—that is, I studied it for some time, until either the smell of the materials or the sedentary occupation disagreed with me. I was a mere copyist, but learned enough to have some idea of the browns of Rembrandt and the flesh-tints of Rubens."

"That's it," cried Arthur; "the colouring in that picture strongly resembles Rubens."

"And are you aware that, to copy a head of his, the colours on your palette must be different from those required for any other master? that the flesh-tints are all mixed with vermilion, which gives a wonderful and almost unnatural freshness?"

"But I like this wonderful freshness," said Arthur.

"Unfortunately, however," observed Nora, "time fades, or perhaps changes, some colours and darkens others, while the vermilion remains bright and glaring."

"You—you don't mean to say that you have the audacity to depreciate Rubens!" cried Arthur, laughing.

She nodded her head, and then said, "The colossal proportions of his women I cannot admire, and the too great use of vermilion I cannot approve; but remember, I don't want to force this opinion on you; it is altogether the result of my own experience and observation, and I may be altogether in error."

"My nymphs have lost the power to charm me at all events," rejoined Arthur, taking advantage of some new arrivals to pass out of the room; and when they reached the street, he said gaily, "Come, Nora, let us take a drive in the Park, and you shall also have a short walk in Kensington Gardens."

Nora made no objection. She was amused and pleased, and giving words to every idea that presented itself to her mind, so delighted her companion that he resolved to enjoy again and frequently the same pleasure. That day at dinner he proposed taking her on the following one to see Westminster Abbey; and though Mr Nixon was too much pleased with her opinion of the picture to make any objection, Arthur prudently waited afterwards for some days before he observed, with well-assumed indifference, "that he had an hour to spare on Wednesday, if she still wished to see St Paul's." Unobserved by Nora, the invitations were subsequently given when his father was not present; there was something new to be seen continually, and three or four times every week Arthur's cabriolet whirled her from

Russell-square to Hyde-park, Kensington, the Zoological Gardens, or wherever the crowd was greatest and gayest.

Arthur asked her one morning if she had any inclination to go to the Royal Academy, in Trafalgar-square[*], and receiving a joyous assent, as she sprang lightly into his cab, they drove there. He had been a good deal gratified at the sort of sensation which her appearance with him so frequently in the Park had created among his acquaintances, but he had taken care never to allow any of them an opportunity of speaking to him when she was present, and to the questions afterwards asked him, he gave such short unwilling answers that a very considerable degree of curiosity had been excited. It was so late in the season, that he had not expected to meet any of these inquisitive persons, and his annoyance was therefore great, when, after an hour of pleasant loitering and discussion with Nora, he perceived a group of well-known inveterate loungers enter. Scarcely bestowing a glance on the well-furnished walls, they scanned with astonishing rapidity the appearance of every person within sight, occasionally uttering a few indistinct, but as it seemed significant monosyllables to each other, as they strutted along, feeling or fancying themselves the "observed of all observers." Arthur's first inclination was to seize Nora's arm, and attempt an escape, but there were two among them of rather enterprising dispositions, who had already threatened to force an introduction to his fair incognita the first convenient opportunity, and he therefore whispered to her hurriedly, "I see a lot of men of my acquaintance, to whom I must speak—it wouldn't do to in-

---

[*] The Royal Academy of Arts, founded by George III in 1768, was at that time housed in the National Gallery in Trafalgar Square. In 1869 it moved to its present home in Burlington House, Piccadilly.

troduce them to you, so go on quietly looking at the pictures, without turning round, and when you have reached
the door, stand still, and I shall join you instantly."

Nora did as she was desired, undisturbed by the English
cause of uneasiness, the "being without a gentleman," for
her recollection of foreign galleries, where the appearance
of a woman alone merely leads to the supposition that she
has come to study, prevented her from feeling either annoyance or embarrassment. But her quiet self-possession,
joined to such evident youth, the graceful, fashionably-
dressed figure, without the appendage of a protector, so
necessary in London, soon made her as much an object of
impertinent curiosity as admiration, and before long she
found herself, to her infinite surprise, surrounded by a
number of men, some of whom continued to follow her
from place to place, with an assiduity that astonished without in the least alarming her. Those nearest her were well
dressed and elderly, and the one who had secured a place at
her left elbow was a particularly stout, fatherly-looking sort
of personage, with a grave face, and very grey hair. Nora
felt quite comfortable in the vicinity of so much respect-
ability, until a low voice, which seemed to come from the
grey head, slowly pronounced the words, "Are you Maria?"

She did not answer—he had mistaken her for some one
else, would perceive his error, and go away.

But he did not go away: on the contrary, he came still
nearer, and again, in a mysterious whisper, repeated the
words, "Are—you—Maria?"

"No!" she answered, turning to the querist a face in
which amazement was so legible that the bystanders with
difficulty suppressed their laughter, and Nora, blushing at
the unexpected rudeness of her much-respected countrymen, sought refuge at the place near the door assigned her
by Arthur. He joined her immediately, and they were soon

on their way to his new house, which he had promised to show her. She related what had just occurred, but Arthur was apparently so occupied with his house that he answered not a word, and wondering at his taciturnity, she added, "Had the old gentleman asked me if my name were Brown or Smith, I should not have thought it so odd, but inquiries about one's Christian name are certainly rather uncommon!"

"Very," said Arthur.

"Perhaps the man was mad," suggested Nora.

"By no means impossible," he responded.

"I am beginning to think," she continued, "that some things abroad are better than in England."

"Picture galleries, for instance," observed Arthur.

"Yes," she answered thoughtfully, "and the manners and habits of those who frequent them. People there look less at each other, and longer at the pictures; and works of art have a sort of current value which makes them universally respected even by the ignorant—much as jewels of high price and ingots of gold would be here."

"Far be it from me to attempt a defence of either our galleries or their visitors," said Arthur, laughing; "rather let me point out to you the delightful comforts of the interior of our houses—see this is mine, and," he added, drawing up his horse, "and strange to say, Nora, the only property I possess in the world; this my father gave me as a reward for implicit obedience a few weeks ago, but for the means of living in it I am still altogether dependent on him."

"The dependence of a son upon a very indulgent father is easily borne, I should think," answered Nora, with a smile, as she walked up the steps to the hall door.

On the staircase she would have stopped to admire a conservatory, but he hurried her forward to one of the drawing-rooms, not giving her time to look round her until she had reached a window there.

"Oh, how light, how airy, how cheerful!" she exclaimed, eagerly. "London at the West End—is not that what you call it?—and London—at—at—in the middle, are as different as—day and night."

"Almost," said Arthur, thoughtfully. "I wish I were less conscious of the difference."

"Wish no such thing," said Nora; "you possess this house, and should rather desire to be able to enjoy it to the fullest extent."

"But I must do so alone, or with a companion chosen by my father."

"Not exactly," said Nora, quietly, "for I believe he requires nothing but rank, and you are free to choose among the nobility of England. Not a very hard fate, I should think."

"And yet, Nora," he answered, gloomily, "I have lately begun bitterly to regret not having a profession, or rather not having joined my father in business. I should have been, by this time, in all probability, either quite independent, or a partner in his house, and, in either case, able to marry the only woman I can ever really love."

He paused; but Nora made no attempt to answer, and he continued—"Obtaining my father's consent to *this* marriage is out of the question—to await his death would be odious."

"Very," said Nora, perceiving that he paused more determinately then before.

"Oh, if ever I have a son!"—he began, passionately.

"If you have," said Nora, interrupting him, "you will act precisely as your father is now doing. Your son and son's son must seek connection, until the name of Nixon has made itself of note, or become but the family name of a noble house; such is the open or covert ambition of all rich rising men like you in this free country of ours. Your father is already in treaty for the purchase of landed property; you acquiesce in his well-devised plans, and are not one bit in earnest when you speak as you have just now done."

"You wrong me, Nora; I am in earnest—*now*—understand me—to-day—*this* day—to-morrow, perhaps—that is, after having given my father a solemn promise never to marry without his consent, I shall be put in actual possession of a noble fortune, but bound in a manner that may—that will blast my future happiness. I have planned this opportunity to speak to you alone, without the chance of interruption, in order to ask your advice, while I am still at liberty to mar or make my own fate."

"And why ask the advice of so inexperienced a person as I am?" asked Nora, almost coldly, for the eager, inquiring expression of Arthur's face made her suspect he was putting her feelings towards him to the test.

"Because I place the most implicit reliance on your intellect and good sense."

"And," said Nora, gravely, "supposing me to possess these estimable qualities, do you think it possible that I would venture to give you advice? Should I not prove myself wanting in both by the mere attempt?"

"No—for I see that you perfectly understand my position in the world, my habits, and disposition. From you, educated abroad, I have no fear of hearing English twaddle about a home, and cheerful firesides, contentment, domestic bliss, and so forth."

"Yet I have dreamed of all this," said Nora, "as much, perhaps more, than many an Englishwoman who has never left her home."

"You have!" cried Arthur, eagerly. "Then you think that you—that I—that we—I mean that a man brought up as I have been, and with my expectations, could be happy in poverty with the companion of his choice? You think that luxurious habits can be overcome, visions of ambitions pushed aside, the longing to be of importance in the world of fashion altogether subdued? for oh, Nora, I am ashamed to confess, that this last would be to me the hardest task of all!"

"Is then the love of fashion so inveterate?" she asked.

"Almost inextinguishable among the upper classes of the inhabitants of cities," answered Arthur. "No weakness, no folly, is so prevalent as this, which, like a moral pest, infects the soundest understandings, and not unfrequently prostates even genius itself! But why," he added impatiently, "why talk to you of what you cannot possibly comprehend? Why force on your notice my own weaknesses or the absurdities of a world still unknown to you?"

"Not so unknown as you suppose," said Nora; "young as I was, the struggles of my father and mother to get into, what is called, the best society abroad, were perfectly evident to me—were made so by the presentations at Court, the introductory letters to the different ministers, residents, or ambassadors, some of whom were civil to us, some not; in the one case we were induced to live beyond our means, in the other, we shortened our stay, exceedingly disgusted at the inhospitality and unkindness of people who were given their places, as my father continually affirmed, for no other purpose than to assert the rights of British subjects, and be polite to travelling English people! At the best, however, it was a miserably unsatisfactory sort of life. Mamma often complained, that she had not a friend in the world, that she spent her life getting introduced to people who invited her to their balls and routs, but never spoke a word beyond the mere civilities of society, showering visiting cards upon her without asking if she were at home, and sliding past her with a '*Bon soir, madame*,' when they met her elsewhere."

"I suppose she talked over all these things in your presence," observed Arthur.

"Of course," said Nora, "and without the slightest reserve. I remember quite adoring the people whom she rather liked, and intensely hating those who had been rude to her: for my own part, I was, as a child, singularly fortunate, being not unfrequently the playmate of various little royal and serene highnesses, and feeling, I assure you, immensely flattered at the distinction. From all, however, that I have heard from mamma and her visitors, I believe there must be a great deal of envy, hatred, malice, and all uncharitableness, in this world of fashion that you prize so highly."

"No doubt of it, Nora—no doubt of it. *Mais, que voulez-vous?* I have laboured for years, and not unsuccessfully, to obtain some rank in it; to support rank of any kind and anywhere, money is necessary; married, I require more than single—so you see, dear girl—"

"I see," she observed, with a smile, "that you want no advice from me, or any one else, having already made up your mind on the subject."

"Don't speak so lightly and look so cheerful, Nora," cried Arthur, greatly displeased; "that is, if you would not have me think you totally heartless!"

Nora's short upper lip became still shorter as she shrugged her shoulders and turned away, with a slightly contemptuous smile.

"Nora, what do you mean?" he cried, catching her hand.

But she had so completely understood him from the beginning, and so well managed to avoid betraying consciousness, that she now greatly desired to end the conference.

"Nothing, nothing," she answered hastily. "It is late, Arthur. Let us go home."

As she leaned back silently in the corner of the cab, she thought to herself, "The fear of paining his father, or the thought of having acted dishonourably towards me, has had no weight with him. Is he thoroughly selfish, or—or—is this the way of the world?"

CHAPTER XIII

All Serene

THIS explanation (for such he chose to consider it) afforded Arthur great relief of mind; he was quite unconscious of the insufficiency and selfishness of his excuses; and on his way home planned a continuation of his former pleasant intercourse with his cousin, under the name of friendship.

Nora, however, began quietly, and at first imperceptibly, to avoid him. When he returned home before his father, she retired to the long, low building that extended nearly the length of the garden wall towards the stables, the greater portion of which was in possession of Mrs Ducker, under the name of store and housekeeper rooms. The apartment which she occupied was rather gloomy, and not rendered more cheerful by its green paper, representing luxuriant vine-leaves, or its wide, iron-barred windows. Here, however, Nora contrived to amuse herself very satisfactorily with a canary bird, that had been born and bred in the large green cage that rested on the rickety work-table. A cheerful little animal it was, this canary bird; and Nora having assisted in rearing it, not a particle of fear, or even timidity, was perceptible in its play with her: it hopped on her arm and shoulder, picked grain from her lips, was desperately jealous when she took notice of the other birds, stretching out impatiently its quivering wings, and twittering

in a melancholy, reproachful manner, being afterwards pro-
portionately happy and flattered when she showered kisses
and caresses on it, and seizing the first opportunity to perch
on the top of the looking-glass, or the handle of a work-
basket, there to stretch its little throat almost to bursting
while warbling a song of ecstasy.

To Anne Ducker's room, however, Arthur began not
unfrequently to follow Nora, feeling himself peculiarly at
home and unrestrained there, surrounded by the well-
known, old-fashioned furniture of his nursery, a choice collection of his former playthings serving for chimneypiece
ornaments, and the high wirework fender, though freshly
painted, still bearing evident marks of the violent kicks bestowed on it by him in various fits of juvenile rage. The
book-shelves, too, brought crowds of old remembrances to
his mind: beside the large-print Bible and Prayer-book,
there were still the well-known copies of *The Mysteries of
Udolpho*,* *The Children of the Abbey*,† and the awful and never-
to-be-forgotten *Tales of Wonder*.‡ Some of these last had
made a terrible impression on his youthful mind, and
caused him many sleepless nights; his recollection of them,
as read aloud by Anne Ducker in a nasal, melancholy tone,
while he sat perched beside her on his high chair, was so
vivid that they had become fixtures in his memory for life.
He could repeat, with provoking accuracy, "Alonzo the
Brave and the Fair Imogene," remembered the ever-
renewed horror with which he had awaited the words, "Be-
hold me, thou false one!" addressed by the dead Alonzo to

* Novel (1794) by Ann Radcliffe (1764-1823).

† Novel (1798) by Regina Maria Roche (1764-1845).

‡ Verse anthology (1801) written and collected by Matthew Gregory
Lewis (1775-1818), better known from his most famous work as
"Monk" Lewis.

the faithless Imogene, as she sat at her marriage-feast, the bride of another. The story of Rudiger had had something more personally interesting for the anxious-eyed, open-mouthed boy, who breathlessly listened to the recital of the cruel father proposing to give his only son, instead of himself, to Beelzebub. But Anne Ducker's favourite tale was "The Maid of the Inn," beginning—

Who is she, the poor maniac, whose wildly-fixed eye, &c &c

and relating how the said maid went out by moonlight, and beheld a corpse carried by murderers, one of whom drops his hat, which she picks up, and

—the 'at of her Richard she knew!

All this, and much more, had Arthur related to Nora, ending with a dissertation on the cruelty of reading or relating such tales to children, who, almost always endowed with vivid imaginations, recalled them when left alone at night, suffering, in consequence, frightful paroxysms of shivering fear and glowing terror. For his part, if ever he had a child likely to visit Mrs Anne, he should consider it both a duty and a pleasure to consign to the flames volumes so destructive of sleep, and suggestive of painful dreams.

In the vicinity of Anne Ducker, Arthur seemed to return to his boyhood; he sat on the table at the window, swinging his legs, and gazing complacently into the dismal, high-walled, little garden, while making jesting remarks on the rank grass, stunted gooseberry-bushes, and smutty London-pride and pensées, that contended for the honour of forming a border to *the* flower-bed; or he peeped into cupboards, and stole guava jelly, tamarinds, and preserved ginger; or, opportunity and an open drawer favouring him, he dressed himself in the antiquated, carefully-hoarded silk garments and pyramidal-crowned bonnets, mounting afterwards, with Nora's assistance, to the top of some high press, and awaiting, with a look of intense glee, the return of Anne, who invariably threatened vengeance, and scolded loudly, while it was easy to perceive that she was not a little flattered at the liberties taken with her, and was more than willing to have these troublesome children, as she called them, in her room on any terms.

It must be confessed that Nora was sorry, when it occurred to her, that spending an hour with her cousin quietly in the study was far less objectionable, in their relative positions, than the same time passed in the very free-and-easy intercourse of Anne Ducker's room—a freedom which seemed to increase from day to day, for Arthur could be amusing when he chose: he sang scraps of songs, imitated actors, actresses, popular orators, and all his friends and acquaintances—men, women, and children—sparing, as Nora laughingly observed, neither age nor sex, but making himself so entertaining, that one day, after having carried on for some time a suppositious conversation between his uncle Gilbert and cousin Georgina, Nora asked him if *he* had been able to steer clear of all the absurdities he ridiculed so unmercifully; and desired to know what sort of person he was himself in society.

"Nothing very brilliant," he replied, with perfect sincerity.

"But you are feared, most probably," suggested Nora, "on account of this extraordinary power of imitation that you possess."

"Why—no, for I reserve the talent, if such it may be called, for the amusement of my most intimate friends, being well aware that it is no sign of genius, quite opposed to originality, and usually the resource of mediocre intellects. In society, I believe, I generally affect a mixture of the *blasé* and cynical, having found it the easiest mode of procuring a sort of respect from fops and fools."

"But you are not really either the one or the other?" she asked.

"No—if I had not become a votary of the phantom, Fashion, and had not been encouraged in my worship by my father, I believe I should have been a respectable hard-working man, with some qualities of head and heart that might have won me what are called 'golden opinions,' and perhaps, also, a larger portion of your esteem than I have now the faintest hope of ever obtaining."

Nora did not choose to continue the conversation. She placed her bird in its cage, again played with it for a few minutes, and then left the room.

That day, at dessert, Mr Nixon informed his son that he had completed the arrangements for the purchase of the estate in Suffolk, and that it should be his on the day of his marriage.

"And not before?" asked Arthur, pretending to jest, but evidently surprised and offended. "I understand that a promise on my part—"

"I have been advised," said Mr Nixon, interrupting him,—"advised by your uncle Gilbert to trust no man, not even my own son. He said he considered it a foolish thing, under any circumstances, my resigning so much property to you, and making you so completely independent during my lifetime; but with my views it is unavoidable; and, indeed, until very lately, I never doubted that our wishes and intentions on all subjects were perfectly similar."

Arthur's face became crimson: he pushed away his plate, threw himself back in his chair, crossed his legs, and while impatiently moving backwards and forwards the upper one, observed, "Oh, then, in fact I am precisely in my old position—that is, if my uncle Gilbert permit you to continue the liberal allowance which I have hitherto enjoyed. I had no idea that his advice had such weight with you, or I should have cultivated his acquaintance more assiduously of late, though he *is* such an ignorant, pompous noodle!"

"He is a very shrewd man of business," said Mr Nixon, frowning, "and this very day realised no less than twenty thousand pounds in railway shares. I greatly regret not having joined him in the speculation, and intend to take his advice without hesitation on such occasions in future."

"Do so by all means," said Arthur; "but I request he may never again interfere between us."

"I am afraid he knows you better than I do, Arthur; he has seen you more frequently than you suppose."

"And," observed Arthur, sneeringly, "and is offended at my not stopping to speak to him, most probably!"

"Ah," said Nora, "then it *was* my uncle we saw in the Park—that day—you know, Arthur—"

She stopped, instinctively feeling that something was wrong; her uncle looked at her sharply, and said, stiffly, "Young Plumpton, too, saw you every day."

"It seems you have been making inquiries," said Arthur, flushing with anger.

"I heard more than I wished without asking a question," answered his father.

"I don't think I can stand being watched and schooled in this manner," continued Arthur, with increasing irritation; "so, if you have no objection, sir, I shall leave England to-morrow."

"Do so, Arthur," cried his father, quickly—"do so. The very proposal on your part is reassuring, and dispels at once my doubts and fears. I now feel convinced that you have not deceived me, or—or—betrayed yourself—in short, that you have acted honourably and kept your promise."

Arthur shrugged his shoulders, drew his plate towards him, and as he bent over it, observed bitterly, "I am still for sale if that be what you mean. Next time we must manage matters in a more business-like manner, as, were I thrown on your hands again, I should fall immensely in value. As it is, I think we might now be satisfied with an Honourable Blanche or Beatrix."

"Arthur!" said his father, reproachfully.

And a silence ensued, during which, uneasy and feeling uncomfortably conscious, Nora left the room.

Four-and-twenty hours afterwards, Arthur was on his way to Baden-Baden, his rooms were closed up, and Nora and her uncle sat in the study, sipping their tea and reading alternately, to all appearance as if nothing had ever occurred to interrupt the even tenor of their lives. Mr Nixon felt perfectly contented; his son was out of the reach of the dark eyes and bright smile that, even he, as he glanced occasionally over his teacup, began to suspect might reasonably put a man's prudence to the test: he and Arthur, too, had parted in perfect amity, and he had little doubt that the wish for independence would induce him, before long, to think again of marriage. Nora's feelings were of a less satisfactory description, when the door had closed that morning on her cousin; her uncle's home had once more assumed, in her eyes, the aspect of a prison, the little liberty she had enjoyed having served but to make her more impatient of her thraldom. She had become perfectly aware of the insurmountable obstacles that separated her from a world of luxurious enjoyment and brilliant gaiety, and if her intellect prevented her from exaggerating the pleasures of which she was deprived, her education had at least taught her to appreciate some of them more highly than they deserved. She made one desperate, energetic effort to induce her uncle to move closer to his brother, but failing completely, she once more resigned herself to solitude and study, sincerely hoping that nothing would again occur to disturb either.

A few months later, Mr Nixon informed her that Arthur was engaged to be married to Lady Trebleton, the widowed daughter of the Marquis of Witherington.

"Was it not from her that you bought his house?" she asked, perceiving he expected her to say something.

"Yes. He writes that he supposes she had accepted him in order to get possession of it again: but he informs me also, towards the end of his latter, that she has confessed she would have married him seven years ago had he asked her before Lord Trebleton."

Nora remembered having heard Arthur make some remark to this effect, and also his having said that she was young and handsome.

"Very handsome," said Mr Nixon, "and as they are to be married immediately, and do not return to England until spring, Arthur has sent me her picture in miniature."

With undisguised interest Nora examined the portrait placed before her by her uncle: it was that of an extremely pretty woman of about five or six and twenty, magnificently dressed, and all her personal advantages so judiciously displayed that it was impossible not to suspect her possessed of more than a common portion of coquetry. Yet it was a pleasing, insinuating countenance, and Mr Nixon was supremely satisfied with it; he talked of his son's choice doing him credit, of the double connection acquired among the Witheringtons and Trebletons, doubted not that Arthur's house would become one of the most fashionable in London—Lord Trebleton's had been so, whose fortune had not been so large as Arthur's would be—rank was a good thing, riches better, both together ruled the world—he wondered what Gilbert would say?

Gilbert, who had not unsuccessfully studied the peerage for some years, and knew the family name and arms of every nobleman in the United Kingdom, was a good deal amazed, and expressed infinite satisfaction at the prospect of a marriage which, as he expressed it, would give them all a "lift" in the quarter where they most wanted it. A fortnight afterwards, however, he drew his brother aside, and whispered that he had better limit Arthur's power over the estate in Suffolk, for that he had heard that Lady Trebleton could spend money faster than most men could make it, and Arthur had never been in the habit of denying himself any gratification that wealth could procure.

CHAPTER XIV

Seven Years Later

FEW things are more difficult than in the space of six
or eight lines to give the idea of the lapse of as many
years. Were we to follow the career of Arthur Nixon,
some events, though of no particular interest, might be
found to mark the passage of time; but his fate, it is to be
hoped, can only interest the reader inasmuch as it affected
that of Nora, and this was at first very little—apparently.
He returned to England with his wife, who immediately
repaired to Russell-square, and effectually gained her father-
in-law's heart by a freedom from affectation and an ease of
manner that delighted him beyond measure. She dined with
him on all the great church festivals, and also on his birth-
day; invited him to her house with persevering assiduity;
and though he almost invariably, and with polite formality,
refused the invitations, he liked to receive them, and to be
able to think and say, that the first society in England was
accessible to him whenever he chose. Unable to conceal his
satisfaction, he pointed out to Nora with triumphant mien
the paragraphs in the papers describing the dinners, balls,
and soirées given during each succeeding season by his son
and daughter-in-law; but that was all she ever knew about
them, for Lady Trebleton's first invitation to her had been
refused by her uncle in a manner to prevent a repetition.

Arthur, in the course of time, entered Parliament, but

proved a less brilliant member than had been expected; he
was useful and hard-working; and as such men, though
necessary, are seldom valued as they deserve, after having
been passed over on various occasions when he hoped for
and expected place and power, he became disgusted with,
and retired altogether from, public life, seeking, unfortunately, occupation in the indulgence of one of the most expensive fancies of the present day—building. Not satisfied
with the handsome old house on his recently-purchased
estate, he commenced erecting an edifice which was to
make Morris Court one of the handsomest places in England. Magnificent it was when completed, but—Arthur had
become an embarrassed man: he furnished it splendidly,
and found himself deeply in debt. Lady Trebleton, who had
never for a moment thought of making the slightest re-
trenchment in her town establishment, and whose inclinations and habits were of the most expensive description,
continued, with a levity incomprehensible to prudent
minds, to give dinners and balls as long as she could find
tradesmen willing to supply her various wants. Many were
the plans resorted to by both to procure money; but their
efforts ware abruptly terminated by the arrest of Arthur one
afternoon for a few hundred pounds, which serving as a
signal to his other creditors, so many detainers were lodged
against him, and for such large sums of money, that his father, on hearing it the next day, was struck with palsy, and
taken home more dead then alive. On regaining consciousness and the partial use of his arms, Mr Nixon sent for his
partner, Plumpton, and made the necessary arrangements
for paying his son's debts, and restoring him to freedom. In
the immediately subsequent meeting, Arthur was received
without a word of reproach, but the sight of his father's
shaking head and paralysed limbs so overcame him, that he
burst into an uncontrollable passion of tears, and was long

quite inconsolable. Nora, whose presence had been desired by both, at length found means to tranquillise her cousin's grief and uncle's agitation, and induce them to discuss calmly the state of their affairs. Arthur insisted on selling the house in town as well as Morris Court; and Mr Nixon heard with surprise and satisfaction his son's declaration that he intended to reside in Russell-square, and supply his father's place at the office as long as might be necessary.

"But your wife, Arthur—your wife—what will Lady Trebleton say?"

"Very little," he answered; "she proposes remaining in Paris until I join her."

"Do you not think she would like to come here if my uncle wrote to her?" asked Nora.

"No," sighed Arthur; "Alice could not live here—nothing would induce me to make such a request to her; but if she remain in Paris, I can cross the Channel occasionally, and, in point of fact, see her quite as often as during these last three years, which you know I have spent almost entirely at Morris Court."

"I supposed her very much attached to you—" began Mr Nixon, gravely.

"Oh, well, so she is," said Arthur, "and I like her too—amazingly. All things considered, we got on very well together; but aw—she likes living in the world, and being admired, and all that sort of thing—and even if she did consent to come here for a while, she would disturb you and put the house in confusion with her eternal visitors, and, in all probability, go out every night, and return home late—and, in short, it would never answer."

Mr Nixon was silent, and seldom spoke of her afterwards. He soon recovered sufficiently to be able to get up and be moved downstairs, where the dining-room was converted into a sleeping-apartment, and he could he rolled into the study in a chair; but months passed over without the slightest further change in his state becoming apparent, and he grew captious at last, and impatient, and greatly worried poor Nora, now his constant companion. Eagerly she daily watched the return of Arthur from the City, his presence alone having the power of restoring his uncle's equanimity, and gladly she left them after dinner to discuss their complicated affairs, Mr Nixon requiring the most accurate information on every subject. Arthur, wholly bent on satisfying his father, devoted himself completely to business, and so successfully, that he already began to rival his uncle Gilbert in fortunate speculations. The exultation of Mr Nixon on these occasions was unbounded: he shook his son's hand every ten minutes, drank his health in champagne, and encouraged him to go on while fortune favoured him. And he did go on; but while doing so, undermined his health completely. The sedentary work at his office, the constant mental excitement, and the climate of London, proved in the end too much for one who had hitherto led a life so different. He caught cold, neglected it, became hectic, and after having refused to consult the family physician or use any of Anne Ducker's remedies, quietly told Nora one evening as they sat alone together, that he believed he was—dying.

At first she thought him jesting, but when he told her that his mother and all his maternal uncles and aunts had been the victims of consumption before the age of thirty, and that he had already in early youth been threatened with the treacherous disease, she entreated of him to see some eminent physician, and not treat so serious a matter lightly.

"I have already been to Dr X—, who gives me just one winter if I remain here; but promises me a tolerable lease of life in a warmer climate."

"Then, Arthur, you must leave England this year—at once."

"Impossible, Nora; my presence just now is of the greatest importance."

"I have no doubt of that; but if my uncle for a moment suspected that it was attended with danger to your life, he would urge—insist on your leaving him."

"He would be incredulous, Nora—would doubt the danger, and think I was merely tired of work. My proposal that we should close accounts with Plumpton, and retire altogether, was evidently most offensive to him, and I shall never renew it."

"And for what purpose is he accumulating all this money?" asked Nora, impatiently.

"He says it is for me," answered Arthur; "and had I a family I could, perhaps, understand him. For my own part, my only wish is to replace what I squandered on Morris Court, and that once accomplished, I am ready to—die; for in good truth, Nora, I have little left to make life desirable."

"Arthur, how can you say so?"

"It is a melancholy fact," he continued, drawing his chair close to hers; "and now for once in my life I wish to speak to you without reserve. My life, Nora, has been a failure—a complete failure. I will not blame my father—he meant well; but my education was a mistake from beginning to end; yet, when it was supposed to be completed, I had still time to redeem the past had I been so inclined, instead of which I plunged into a life of folly, idleness, and dissipation, and so frittered away my best years in the pursuit of pleasure and novelty—making acquaintances, valued solely by me for their names, and by whom I was merely tolerated for my wealth."

"Arthur, I cannot believe this either of you or your acquaintances."

"You may," he said dejectedly, "for the exceptions were few, though I gloried at one time in knowing 'every one' in London! Yet I was not without intellect, Nora; you may remember how I scorned and condemned the life I was leading, when we first met."

Nora remembered that he had done so in words, but not in acts, and could not give the ready assent he perhaps expected: he observed her silence and answered it.

"Yes, Nora, I saw and understood my position perfectly, and think—in fact I am sure—that a marriage with you then might have saved me from myself."

"Arthur!"

"We are talking of what happened or might have happened ages ago," he continued, quietly. "I don't say that you were in love with me, Nora; but you liked me, and would have married me."

"Not without your father's consent, Arthur; and having confessed so much, let us end this useless retrospection."

"It is not useless," he rejoined, gazing gloomily into the fire. "I loved you as I believe a man seldom loves more than once in his life, and had my father consented to our marriage—"

"Arthur," said Nora, rising, "I cannot listen to you, if you talk in this way."

"I have done," he answered: "my father refused his consent: without it we should have been poor; and I was an egotist—unworthy of you—incapable of making a sacrifice even for—well—well—I know—you would not have accepted me. Be it so, and let me tell you, that was my last chance of becoming a useful member of society—my life since then has been a troubled dream."

"Not so," said Nora, compassionately; "you were of use to your country when in Parliament, and—"

"Merely served to fill the house," he said, interrupting

her. "I did the work that any paid official could have done as well; gave my vote to those whose political opinions co-incided with mine, and from whom I hoped, in time, to ob-tain place or power; and when I was disappointed, I retired to Morris Court, to lead a still more worthless and selfish life."

"You judge yourself too severely," interposed Nora.

"Scarcely," said Arthur, without looking up. "Of the thousands lavished on the house and furniture intended for my own enjoyment, not one guinea was spent on the im-provement of my tenantry. I knew nothing about them or their wants or wishes, understood nothing of agriculture—what business had I with landed property? Could I but spend my life over again—or—part of it; could I, with my present experience, but return to the time when we first met, what a different life I should lead!" He paused, and then added, "I believe it is now seven years, Nora—seven years and some months since we first sat together, as we are doing now?"

"Seven years," she repeated, thoughtfully; "how long they *were*—how short they now appear!"

"I remember our meeting on the stairs," he continued, and that first evening, as if it were but yesterday. You were dressed in black velvet and point lace—an odd dress for a girl of sixteen; but it made you look like one of those charming pictures by the old masters on which one can gaze for ever."

"The dear old dress!" said Nora, pensively; "it would certainly appear less unsuitable to me now!"

"Yet you are wonderfully little changed," said Arthur; "and every perceptible alteration is for the better."

Nora smiled. "A great internal change has, I hope, taken place," she said, quietly; "I should be sorry to think that seven or eight years' uninterrupted reading and meditation have been quite lost upon me."

"That they have not been lost, I am sure," observed Arthur. "With such a foundation as you had to build upon, I have no doubt that by this time your information and learning far exceed those of most women."

"I make no pretension whatever to learning," answered Nora; "and have, I assure you, only arrived at a consciousness of my profound ignorance on the subjects I understand best, and at not at all doubting it on all others."

"And this is the result of eight years' steady reading in the three most literary modern languages!" said Arthur.

"Not quite: I have learned the meaning of the words, 'Vanity of vanities, all is vanity'."

"So have I," said Arthur, with a sigh; "but *my* knowledge has been obtained by painful personal experience."

"Some experience I have had, too," observed Nora; "without it, the words of the preacher would have made less impression on me: he says, 'Of making many books there is no end; and much study is a weariness of the flesh'."

"Go on," said Arthur.

She continued: "Let us hear the conclusion of the whole matter—'Fear God, and keep his commandments: for this is the whole duty of man'."

At this moment the door opened, and Mr Nixon, in his chair, was slowly rolled towards the tea-table.

When Nora, the next day, was alone with her uncle, she spoke to him very seriously of Arthur's state of health; but found it extremely difficult to make him believe that anything could be the matter with a man so full of energy and activity as his son. "His cough? that was constitutional. No one was exempt from colds and coughs during a London winter; and she might remember what he had himself suffered from the influenza the preceding year, though he had never allowed it to detain him one day from his office."

Mr Nixon was most unwilling to lose either his son's services or society; in the end, however, Nora's influence prevailed, and Arthur left them to meet his wife at Strasburg, and spend the winter and spring at Meran.

When taking leave, he spoke so long and so warmly in praise of Nora to his father, that Mr Nixon at length said, "I understand you, Arthur; you think I ought to make some small addition to her fortune?"

"Some great addition," replied Arthur, earnestly; "she has devoted the best years of her life to you—has been to you a daughter; never think of her hereafter in any other light."

From Nora he parted early in the morning, before his father was up. She had made breakfast for him in the study, and prepared to follow him into the hall, when he stopped suddenly, turned round, and said, "You told me you had a commission for me, Nora, in case I should go up the Rhine, and, I think, even said I could confer a great favour on you by undertaking it; that your saying this has been an inducement to me to choose that route I need scarcely assure you; yet in the pain of parting I had nearly forgotten all about it."

"I—have changed my mind," said Nora, with evident embarrassment, "and prefer asking you to undertake this commission for me when you are on your way home."

"Nora, I may never return home, and that you know as well as I do. You spoke of Dusseldorf, where, I believe, your father lies buried; speak out, like the pious German girl that you are, and tell me to visit his grave, and let you know in what state it is. The commission will not make me die one day sooner; and I see by your face that I have guessed it rightly."

"Dear Arthur," said Nora, with tears in her eyes, "I shall

be so much obliged to you if you will perform this act of friendship. I have long been in correspondence with the landlady of the hotel where he died; and as soon as I had saved sufficient money to enable me to erect a monument, I sent her a drawing of my mother's tombstone, requesting her to have a similar one made for my father. It is this," she added, taking a paper from her work-table; "I should have preferred leaving the space at the base altogether for flowers; but when no friends or relations are near to see that the grave is properly cared for, and supplied with fresh plants—"

"I know—I know," said Arthur. "The neglected graves of the English in foreign churchyards have always grieved me by their contrast to the others; but one has, at least, the certainty of being left undisturbed to turn to dust there. For this reason," he added, mournfully, "wherever my life ends I shall be interred; and you, Nora, must now promise me, before we part, to visit my grave, to have a tombstone such as this erected for *me*, to plant flowers at its base, and with your own hands to place a wreath of evergreens on this ornament so evidently made for the purpose. Will you promise?"

"Life is uncertain, Arthur," said Nora, making a great effort to speak calmly; "but should I outlive you—" She placed her hand in his and turned away.

"Don't waste a tear on me now, dear girl," he continued, "but bestow a few on the earth that will cover me some—years hence, let us say; for, after all, if Alice take good care of me, who knows but I may hold out as long as Lord Medway, who, to my certain knowledge, has been dying these eight or nine years?"

Most unwillingly Nora wrote to recall Arthur the following spring, when her uncle's declining strength made his return home, for some time at least, desirable. But they never met again; for, after a somewhat hurried journey through Tyrol, he was obliged to stop at a village in the Bavarian highlands, and there, after a few days' illness, ended his life, and was buried, as he had desired, in the tranquil churchyard of the place. His wife returned to England, and related circumstantially to the broken-hearted father every incident of his last moments; she was also the bearer of letters from him to Nora, to remind her of her promise to visit his grave—to his father, requesting him to increase Lady Trebleton's jointure, and hoping he would henceforward consider Nora his adopted daughter, and provide for her as his now only child.

When Nora showed the letter *she* had received to her uncle, and spoke of her intention, at some future time, to make a pilgrimage to the church at Almenau, he took both her hands, and answered, with a solemnity that often afterwards recurred to her memory, "I shall take care to supply you with money for the journey, Nora."

Not long after she found herself, on his demise, one of the richest heiresses in England, for, with the exception of some legacies to the servants, her uncle had left her everything he possessed. The care of erecting a monument to the memory of his son was intrusted to her; and this, added to her own strong feeling of having a sacred promise to fulfil, made her long for the expiration of the time that must intervene before she could set out on a journey abroad, which she secretly resolved should end in a residence of some duration in the land, which (ever prone to extremes) she now began to call hers, and to prefer to England!

CHAPTER XV

Return to Germany after Ten Years' Absence

NORA did not at first comprehend either her complete independence or immense increase of importance. She felt deeply having lost the only two relations to whom she had had an opportunity of becoming attached during the nine years she had spent in Russell-square, for of the Gilbert Nixons she, as yet, scarcely knew anything. Her uncle Stephen had taken a dislike to Georgina, and, in a manner, forbidden her his house; Mr Sam Nixon, as contrast to his son Arthur, he could scarcely learn to tolerate; and it was more to please Nora than himself that he endured, occasionally during the holidays, the visits of his brother's youngest son John.

John had been, during the first years of Nora's acquaintance with him, as restless, noisy, and rude a schoolboy as could well be imagined, then he had changed into a bashful, awkward hobbledehoy, had afterwards become a wild and idle collegian, and had, latterly, begun to talk incessantly about a commission in the Guards, which was to make a man of him. Through all these periods of his life, a steady and undisguised affection for Nora had induced him to visit at his uncle's house, and, in return, she had crammed the schoolboy with fruit and sweetmeats, supplied the collegian with small sums of money, and had, for some time, listened patiently to the ravings of the future hero, without in the least participating in his longings for "a good smart war likely to give a fellow something to do."

It had never occurred to Gilbert Nixon that Arthur might chance to die before his father, and when the event took place, he greatly regretted that Sam and Georgina had never been on good terms with their uncle, and that even John had by no means succeeded in making himself agreeable to him. The evil could not, however, be remedied; therefore, though not pleased, he was scarcely surprised to find that Nora alone was his brother's heiress. The fortune was certainly too large for a woman; but he thought it not improbable if she came to live with them, that she might eventually become attached to, and marry one of his sons. Sam was a steady, sensible fellow, likely enough to please such a quiet girl, and for Jack she had for years avowed her affection: it was a pity the latter was so much younger then she was, but if she had any fancy for him, she might have him; the boy required someone to keep him in order in a rational way! So, after the funeral, Jack was sent to condole with her, Sam to assist her in looking over her uncle's papers, and Georgina to invite her to remove to Eaton-place.

With John she went to visit her uncle's grave, and was shown the large damp flag, beneath which the remains of the Nixon family had been laid for two generations. It was in a dismal, high-walled churchyard, with undertakers' establishments in the neighbourhood, and John, who stood at the gate, soon grew tired of the gloomy objects around him, and called out, "Come away, Nora, there's no use in your making yourself unhappy about the place; he chose to be buried here, and one churchyard is just as good as another in my opinion."

"But not in mine," said Nora.

"Too soon for you to be thinking of such things; and, for my part, I hope to die in a field of battle, but not until I

have become a colonel—or, no—a general—I might be a
general at fifty, Nora, and after that, a man has not much to
live for, eh?"

"I—don't—know," said Nora, who had not heard a
word that he said. "Have they no flowers in the churchyards here, Jack?"

"Not that I know of," he answered. "Now do let's go
on, Nora—Sam is waiting to help you to look over the papers, you know; and the sooner you come to live with us,
and give up thinking in this uncomfortable way about
churchyards, the better."

Among Mr Nixon's papers, Nora found a small packet,
on which were the words, "Correspondence with the Hon.
Charles Thorpe concerning my niece Leonora." It was immediately transferred to her pocket, and kept for perusal
when alone in the evening; the ink was pale, and the paper
yellow with age, but the unkind construction put on her
actions by Charles Thorpe, and the cold worldly tone of his
letter, had still the power to produce a deep blush, and renew the strong feeling of resentment against him, that had
now for some years lain dormant.

"I wish him no evil," she murmured, as if in reply to the
reproaches of her conscience; "I believe I have learned to
forgive him too—but he need not have blamed *me* for his
brother's infatuation, as he calls it, and the remark about
my foreign education, making me by no means a desirable
companion for his sister Jane, was altogether unnecessary.
This letter closed my uncle Gilbert's door against me at
first, and accounts completely for the coldness and suspicion with which, for such a length of time, all my efforts to
please were here received. I know we should 'love our
enemies, and do good to those that hate us'—and I think I
could do good to Charles Thorpe if an opportunity offered,
but like him I never can. Never!"

At the end of a few weeks Nora was glad to remove to her uncle Gilbert's more cheerful house. It did not occur to her to make any extraordinary additions to her wardrobe, or to expect the undivided services of a maid; she thankfully received the little assistance she required from Mrs Nisbett, her cousin's *femme de chambre*, was surprised at her obliging manners, and never for a moment suspected that the worldly little woman was already speculating on entering the service of the heiress. It was only by degrees that Nora learned her new position in the world and in her uncle's family, and discovered that she had become an object of speculation to all around her. Georgina merely hoped and expected that she would make a brilliant match, which would secure them a new connection; but her uncle observed more frequently than was agreeable, "that it would be a pity to let such a fortune as hers go out of the family, and he hoped she would take a fancy to one of his sons some day or other; that, for his part, he had always liked her, and, as she must remember, would have taken her 'for good,' and made her his daughter eight years ago, if his brother Stephen had given his consent." The conclusion of the speech always made Nora forgive the want of delicacy of the commencement, and she thanked him, over and over again, for his former generous intentions towards her, ending with the assurance, that she never should forget his kindness on that occasion. With regard to herself, or rather, as she suspected, her fortune, she gladly seized an opportunity of being explicit, when, one morning, John, in his boyish way, sounded her on the subject in his sister's presence.

"I say, Nora," he began, whipping his polished boots very diligently with a small cane, "I say—it must be pretty evident to you, that our governor expects you and Sam to make a match of it some of these days!"

"I cannot believe that he seriously thinks of anything so

absurd," she answered, quietly.

"Just what Sam himself said," observed John, laughing. "Why, you'd as soon, perhaps sooner, think of marrying me!"

"I have just as much idea of one as the other, my dear Jack."

"But you like me, Nora? I know you do."

"Be assured of it, Jack," she answered, extending her hand to him; "I like you better than any one else in the world just at present. We have liked each other for ten years, and I have no doubt shall continue to do so as long as we live."

"I suppose, Nora, you agree with Georgina here, in thinking that Nixon marrying Nixon would never answer."

"I think," said Georgina, looking up from her embroidery, "that Nora may now aspire higher, and you and Sam had better try to improve our connection."

"I suppose that will be easy enough, now that our family has turned out to be so ancient. You know, of course, Nora, that we are of Saxon origin?"

"No," she answered, with some surprise. "I really was not aware of the circumstance."

"Why, our very name is German, our crest but a play upon the word."

"I don't quite understand—"

"Because your father, I suppose, took the arms of the other numerous Nixon families with whom we have, in fact, no sort of relationship; but my father and Georgy never rested until we had arms found, sketched, and painted at the 'West End Practical Heraldic Office,' parchment a yard long and everything complete. It was easily made out, for you know *Nixe* is the German for water-sprite, water-fairy, nymph."

"You don't mean to insinuate that we are the descendants of a naiad?" she said, smiling.

"Now, Nora, you must be serious, and listen to what concerns you as much as any of us. Nothing can be plainer than the derivation of our name from Nix—Nixe—Nixy—Nixon! and the name once traced to its Saxon origin, what more natural than to suppose ourselves descendants of one of the ancient possessors of Britain?"

"Our remotest ancestress being the fair Melusine herself," said Nora, laughing. "She who, half woman, half fish, lived in a dark green grotto, waiting for a faithful lover to release her; but, according to the legend, waited in vain, and sank at last all fish beneath the water—or no—I believe we must take the other one of mysterious parentage, who was only occasionally fish or serpent, and who had a lot of ugly sons."

"I see you have learned from our uncle Stephen to laugh at our arms and name," said John, half offended, "but I only wish you would talk a little to Georgy on the subject—she'll soon convince you!"

"I am quite ready to be convinced," observed Nora, smiling. "No one will be likely to dispute our right to the mermaid, or water-nymph, or even Melusine herself as crest. There is also no reason why we should not be descended from the Anglo-Saxons, and if so, we may suppose that an ancestor of ours fell at the battle of Hastings—his body being found near that of Harold, partly covered with a shield bearing the well-known device of a water-nymph!"

Georgina laughed good-humouredly. "Oh, I see you have seized upon our mermaid as eagerly as our father: but you will introduce her to your acquaintance and friends more judiciously than he did, I have no doubt. I assure you I used to feel quite nervous whenever he raised a spoon or fork at dinner, dreading the long explanation that would follow, he understanding about as much of heraldry as—"

"As I do," said Nora. "The naiad is really a very ingenious discovery, Georgy. I should never have found out anything better than a hogshead for our crest."

"A hog's head or boar's head is a very much-esteemed crest, and I am sure I should have had no objection to it," said Georgina: "but I don't quite understand in what way it could be accounted for."

"By the way in which our grandfather made his fortune," answered Nora. "My mother informed me that he dealt largely in hogsheads of Jamaica rum, casks of sugar, raisins, figs, and so forth."

"Hush!" cried Georgina, playfully; "we only speak of the funds and railway shares now: and seriously, Nora," she added, "it is not necessary to tell all the world where we lived, and how we lived in days of yore; my plan has been to keep quiet, and attract as little attention as possible, and I have found it the most efficacious means of securing a position in society in spite of those who so perseveringly laughed at my father, and treated me with insolence. A few years' hard struggling we had, of course, and I often thought the end obtained not worth the trouble bestowed on it."

"I am sure it was not," said Nora.

"If," sighed Georgina—"if one could but practise as well as preach indifference to all these social distinctions! I assure you I feel at this moment as convinced as you or any one can be of the folly of fagging after fashion; but I have only to visit, or be visited by, one of my acquaintances, and I find myself talking, thinking, and feeling as foolishly as ever! The worst of it, I am happy to say, is now over—I have been dragged about and introduced to people who did not want to know me; I have been a beggar for invitations given with ostentatious unwillingness; I have been patronised by Mrs Savage Wayward and her friends, and mortified by their inviting our guests and giving concerts in our house! But from all this I am now emancipated, and you may have observed that our visiting list is quite *comme il faut;* and though you refused to make your appearance at our dinners, you must acknowledge that we have had a very pretty sprinkling of nobility at them!"

"Why, yes," said Nora, smiling a little mischievously, "you have certainly entertained a good many Honourable de Boots and Lady Magnolias, as *Punch* calls them!"

"And do you really and sincerely, Nora, condemn all efforts to make the acquaintance of people of rank?"

"*I* shall never make any effort of the kind," she answered, "and I don't like to see, or let others see *yours.*"

"Nine years ago you thought and spoke differently," observed Georgina. "Had you come to live with us then—"

"I should undoubtedly have struggled with you," interposed Nora, "for it is only lately that I have quite perceived the ruin that this false ambition has brought upon the different members of our family. I shall never sacrifice my happiness to fashion, and never live in what is called the world!"

"My dear Nora, what will your brother say to such resolutions?"

"Everything that is worldly-wise, egotistical, and narrow-minded," she answered.

"Is it possible that you do not like him,—that you are not proud of him?" exclaimed Georgina.

"I know very little about him," said Nora. "He has occasionally paid me a duty visit when in England; but I have ever found him worldly-minded to a degree that was perfectly appalling. The last time I saw him was just after our poor dear Arthur's death, and fancy his saying, 'That it would be a famous good thing if old Nick himself (so he always called my uncle) would drop off quietly, and leave me his fortune, as in that case I should be the very thing for Charley Thorpe!"

"How like him!" said Georgina, laughing; "but you must not be too particular about little speeches of this kind, Nora. Young men have got a habit of talking in this manner, without meaning any harm. Your brother did not exactly want your uncle Stephen to die; he merely thought it probable that he would not live long, and very naturally wished to make you think of Mr Charles Thorpe, to whom by all accounts he is extremely attached."

"He might have spared himself the trouble," said Nora, indignantly. "Charles Thorpe is the very last man in the world I could ever be induced to marry."

"Suppose, however," observed Georgina—"suppose he should in the course of time become Lord Medway; they say his brother cannot survive the winter."

"To me," said Nora, "he will ever remain Charles Thorpe; and as to his brother, he is merely hypochondriacal, complaining alternately of his lungs and liver, and probably encouraged in his fancies by his mother, who wishes to live abroad with him."

"Perhaps you are right," said Georgina; "Lady Medway has been but once in England since we came to live *here*. It was the first year I believe, and I met her frequently, and was introduced to her—you may remember I told you at the time that she inquired about you very kindly, said you were such a nice creature, and was *so* glad to hear that my uncle liked you!"

"Her words," said Nora, thoughtfully, "made more impression than you suppose; they filled my head with thoughts of The Willows, and made me half expect an invitation there."

"I should not be surprised if you received one next year," observed Georgina.

"Nor I either," answered Nora; "but I shall not leave Beechfield until I can go abroad."

And to Beechfield, her uncle Gilbert's villa, Nora went at Christmas, and there remained during the winter and spring. She read in the papers an exaggerated account of the amount of her fortune, and of the perfect seclusion in which the young and beautiful heiress was passing the time of her mourning; but the smile of derision passed from her countenance as her eye glanced to the succeeding paragraph, which announced the death of Lord Medway at Palermo, and the arrival of his brother in England. The same paper informed her, some time afterwards, of the reception of the latter at Thorpe Manor, and at a later period of the return of Lady Medway to The Willows.

It was about this time that Nora informed her uncle of her wish to go abroad, and heard of his intention to accompany her with Georgina and John. He professed himself quite willing to submit to any of the discomforts that might attend a residence of a week or so in the village where the fulfilment of her promise to her cousin Arthur made it necessary for her to go during the summer, and showed actual alacrity in his preparations for the journey. A stupendous travelling-carriage was purchased, with cabriolet before, and cabriolet behind, imperial above imperial, and every contrivance for the disposal of baggage that had been discovered during the previous twenty years. When Nora first saw this vehicle, she shook her head, and said that on the railroads it would be unnecessary, and in the village where they should spend most of their time, such a carriage would be perfectly useless, if not inconvenient to them. But the words of disapprobation were lost in the exultation of her uncle, as, heedless of his rotundity of figure, he sprang in and out, removing cushions, raising boxes, pulling out secret drawers, mounting to the top, and making the car-

riage swing, stooping beneath it, and pointing out the construction of various parts, in language sufficiently unintelligible, to convince Nora that he knew all about elliptic and
cross-springs, and wheels with patent axles, hoops, nuts,
and pins, though she did not.

Gilbert Nixon and his son provided themselves with a
few of those eccentric articles of apparel which serve as
stamps to Britons on the Continent, and Georgina's protes-
tations against them were silenced by Nora's proposal that
every member of the party should be at liberty to dress and
act as he pleased, provided it did not interfere with the personal comforts of any of the others. Half playfully, half
earnestly, she afterwards wrote out an agreement to this
effect, which was unhesitatingly signed by them all, and
four-and-twenty hours later they were in a steamer on their
way to Paris. Mr Nixon and his daughter sat with much
dignity side by side in the spacious carriage: the one declaring he should have crossed the Channel long ago if he had
known it was so easy to do so, and looking alternately at the
waveless sea and the packet of newspapers with which he
had stuffed his numerous pockets before embarking; the
other negligently leaning back, and occasionally turning
over the leaves of a book which she held in her hand, in
order that no one might suspect her of travelling for the
first time in her life, or taking an undue interest in the
things and persons around her. John and Nora, or as they,
to Georgina's infinite disgust, familiarly called each other
Jack and Norry, amused themselves differently: the former
wished to see and hear everything without compromising
his dignity as an embryo Guardsman and an Englishman;
he felt agreeably conscious that he was creating a sort of
sensation, and entertained very little doubt that all the
young and pretty women on board were watching and admiring him. Nora seemed to have become several years

younger; everything she saw was familiar to her eyes, every language she heard familiar to her ear. On landing, the houses, furniture, and people brought thousands of youthful recollections to her mind, and when in Paris, when she had wandered about the well-known places with her uncle and cousins, she felt it impossible, on her return to the hotel in the evening, to join in their querulous complaints of fatigue, or believe in her uncle's assurances that all he had seen had made about as much impression on his wearied eyes and confused mind, as the figures of a magic-lantern on the senses of a drowsy child.

In short, the Nixons "did" Paris in a week, and several other places in still less time, and reached Munich about the month of July. The day after their arrival there, Nora went to the churchyard, and at a stone-mason's in the neighbourhood, ordered a tombstone, such as Arthur had desired to have, but with additional marble ornaments, that she was informed would require at least two months to sculpture. Under these circumstances she ceased to urge her companions to continue their journey southwards, the more so as her brother, on his way to England, joined them and announced his intentions of remaining in Munich as long as they did.

Sir Harry Darwin was a man who had travelled extensively: he had sought notoriety by the ascent of glaciers, had made a faint attempt to discover the sources of the Nile, had ridden on dromedaries, yachted away some years of his life in the Mediterranean, and become a cosmopolite of the purest water. He was a sunburnt, exuberantly-whiskered man, still feeling and looking younger than his actual age, exclusively devoted to the world and its enjoyments, and perfectly satisfied with himself in every respect. His stepsister had risen immensely in his estimation since she had become an heiress; but he was too experienced a man not to take some pains to prevent her from suspecting that she was the magnet that had drawn him to Munich—his first few jesting remarks about her present wealth and importance having been received in a manner that convinced him she began already to doubt the motives, and weigh the words of those who in the most distant manner alluded to her fortune or future plans. His attentions, therefore, were almost exclusively bestowed on Georgina, with whom, in fact, he was far better acquainted than with Nora, having not only frequently met her in society, but being in the habit of dining at her father's house, and flirting with her in a remarkable manner during his occasional visits to England. They had of course many acquaintances in common, much to talk of, and in Munich enough to see that was mutually interesting; and Nora perceived with pleasure his attentions to her cousin, after having heard from her uncle Gilbert that "Sir Harry had long been an adorer of Georgy's, and that she certainly did not hate him, though he had often enough disappointed her when she had expected him to propose." Georgina herself believed he must be in earnest this time, or he would not have gone out of his way to meet them, and devoted himself to her so completely during his stay at Munich; and so Nora thought also: but Sir Harry had no sooner satisfied himself that there was no immediate danger of his sister's bestowing herself and her fortune on John Nixon, than he resolved to announce his intention of returning to England for the grouse-shooting! It was at the Hôtel de Bavière, on a warm summer's evening, about the hour when the party, after drinking tea together, usually separated for the night, that the well-prepared little speech was made, ending with some civilly-expressed regrets that he must at once take leave, as he should be far from Munich before they were up the next morning.

As much surprised as any of the others, Nora watched her brother as he cordially shook hands with Mr Nixon and his son, and then with the most careless friendliness imaginable approached Georgina. She was sitting at one of the windows, and as he drew near she turned towards him, extended her hand, forced a smile, and then looked again into the street. He murmured some unintelligible words about meeting before long in England, and whispering to Nora to follow him, left the room.

Mr Nixon, who had been dozing, or, as he himself would have said, "resting his eyes," was disturbed by this sudden leave-taking, and now sat upright in his chair, looking alternately at his son and daughter, until perceiving that silence was desired and expected by the latter, he again leaned back, and half closed his eyes.

On the countenance of John there was an expression of complete contentment, an air of only half-concealed triumph in his walk, as, perambulating the room with long strides, he passed and repassed the pier-glass, and occasionally stopped to arrange his hair or cravat. On these occasions there was a studied gracefulness and endless variety in his attitudes, denoting a most laudable desire to learn to please on some future occasion, or giving a very amusing exhibition of personal vanity. After a long, last, and, as it appeared, satisfactory inspection of himself, a pulling up of shirt-collar and pulling down of waistcoat, with a slight stamp as he changed the leg on which his body rested, and a curious wriggling of his whole person which showed him his figure alternately in three-quarters and profile, he turned to his sister, and observed in a low voice, "I say, Georgy, it's a devilish good job that Sir Harry is taking himself off in this pleasant, easy sort of way—I don't think I could have stood his quiet impudence much longer! He completely ruled us all lately, and hardly allowed me to speak a word when we dined at the *table d'hôte*. As to our governor, he treated him precisely as if he were a—a—secretary, or something of that sort, good for nothing but to sign his name at the bankers' and supply Adam, the courier, with money."

He paused for an answer, but his sister remained silent, and he continued:—"Of course you cannot dislike him as I do, for he never contradicted or commanded you; but if you think he liked you better for always going against me and approving all his plans, you are mistaken. It's too soon for the grouse-shooting, and all a sham!—he has other game in view, I can assure you; for Tomkins told me this morning, when I was dressing, that be suspected Sir Harry would not remain much longer with us, as he was engaged to be married to Lady Jane Thorpe, and had got a letter to say that the family were now at The Willows."

"Lady Jane Thorpe!" repeated Georgina, turning quickly round.

"Lord Medway's sister, you know. They've been engaged this long time."

Georgina put her hand to her head, and seemed to think intensely for a few seconds, then rising, hastily left the room.

Nora and her brother were still standing in the corridor. "I am glad to find you here," she said to Sir Harry, "for I wish much to tell you that, though I felt rather vexed and surprised at your leaving us so abruptly, when I supposed it was merely for an additional week's grouse-shooting, now that John has told me the real cause of your return to England, I can only applaud your intention, and wonder at your remaining here so long!"

Sir Harry stared at her with a look of amazement.

"Although," she continued, quickly, "although I am personally but slightly acquainted with the Medways, I have

heard them so much praised, and Lady Jane is so universally admired and liked, that I may safely congratulate you
on your choice. Good night. Don't quite forget us while we
are buried in these Bavarian highlands, of which Nora
speaks with such enthusiasm." While saying these last
words, she entered her room, which was close to where
they stood, and as she closed the door with a nod and
smile, Sir Harry exclaimed,

"Well, Nora, I hope you are satisfied now?"

"You are *not*," she replied, with an arch smile. "You
would rather have made Georgina unhappy than have had
the conviction forced upon you, that, while you were
merely amusing yourself, she was similarly employed."

"Not I," said Sir Harry, carelessly; "I have flirted with
Miss Nixon these eight years, more or less, at intervals, and
whatever I may have imagined at the beginning of our acquaintance, I took it for granted that, by this time, her heart
and feelings must be completely worn out from incessant
use and abuse."

"How slightingly you speak of the person to whose
words you listened with such apparent deference this very
morning!" exclaimed Nora, indignantly. "Georgina fortunately understood you better than I did, as I confess I never
doubted your intentions since the day you explained at such
length that a woman necessarily rises or falls to the rank of
her husband."

"That was all intended for you, Nora. I wished to remind you, that if you married either Sam or John Nixon,
you would be neither more nor less than—"

"Than Mrs Sam or Mrs John Nixon," said Nora, composedly.

"Nora—if I could, for one moment, suppose it possible
that you would bestow a thought either on that prig, Sam,
or that donkey, John, I—"

"You would remain here to take care of me—perhaps even accompany us to the mountains? The country would be new even to you!"

"New, inasmuch as I have never seen this village to which you are going," he answered; "but after having been in Switzerland and ascended glaciers, I imagine I should find little to interest me on a Bavarian or Tyrolean alp!"

"I don't know that," rejoined Nora, "for I think a picturesque and well-wooded mountain, with its pasture-grounds, inhabited châlets, herds of cattle, and an extensive view from it, might be nearly as interesting and infinitely more agreeable to most wanderers than a glacier."

"Perhaps so," said Sir Harry. "If the Medways were with us instead of these Nixons, I have no doubt I should find the Bavarian highlands or Tyrol pleasant enough."

"I can scarcely imagine Lady Medway making excursions such as I mean," said Nora, laughing; "and as to Charles Thorpe—I mean Lord Medway—"

"Charley is a keen sportsman, Nora, and nearly as well acquainted with Germany as you are!"

"That is the first good thing I have heard of him for a long time," said Nora.

"And what have you heard to the contrary?" asked her brother, with an appearance of interest that rather surprised her, adding, without waiting for her answer, "Some of his wild doings, years ago, perhaps? but let me tell you, Nora, a man may occasionally put his life in jeopardy for a wager, or undertake daring and eccentric exploits, who can, at other times, be as quiet and gentle as any woman could desire."

Nora smiled, attempted no explanation, and merely said, "I have heard him praised often enough by his own family, but I know him to be an extremely worldly-minded and selfish man."

Sir Harry shrugged his shoulders. "He has lived constantly in the world, and had to work his way in it—that makes the best man worldly in time, and—selfish we all are, more or less. For instance, he would certainly not seek or cultivate the acquaintance of these Nixons, or even tolerate them, as I have done for the last three weeks."

"I am rejoiced to hear it," said Nora, promptly, "as it will prevent me from having the trouble of avoiding him."

"Do not imagine you will have any difficulty in doing so," rejoined her brother, with a malicious smile, glad perhaps to laugh a little at her in his turn, "for I offered you to him after you became an heiress, and he declined the alliance, saying, that your paternal connections would prevent him from thinking of you, even were you twice as rich and twice as good-looking as you were said to be."

Nora felt greatly irritated, but wisely concealing her annoyance, said quietly, "Did it never occur to you that I might also decline the alliance?"

"Why, no—we concluded your foreign education would have taught you to think rationally on such subjects, and I should have trusted the fulfilment of my wishes on this occasion to time and your pretty face. I have lately been inclined to suspect he spoke in that way in order to appear consistent, and that, having prevented his brother from marrying you, he is resolved, notwithstanding your present very different position in the world, to consider the match unsuitable. All this, however, need not prevent you from becoming good friends when you meet."

"Of course not," she answered, ironically; "all you have just said is eminently calculated to remove my prejudices and make me like him! But let us not talk any more on so disagreeable a subject. Jane will, of course, write to me when the arrangements for your marriage are being made, and you can give me hints, at the same time, as to what would be most acceptable in the way of presents. You see I have already learned to play heiress, and know what will be expected from me."

"You are a dear, wilful girl," said her brother, as they parted; "but I still hope you will like Medway as well as I am sure he will like you when he knows you. Good-by."

Nora's room adjoined Georgina's; but though, on entering it, she found the door of communication open, some minutes elapsed before she attended to her cousin's request that she would join her.

"Well, Nora—what do you say to your brother's engagement?" began Georgina, abruptly.

"Had he told us of it immediately after his arrival here," she answered, "we—or, at least I, could not but have approved, for Jane is, by all accounts, what she formerly promised to be, a dear, good creature. His silence was quite unpardonable, and when you joined us in the corridor, I had just been telling him so, and accusing him of duplicity towards you."

"But you did not betray me!" cried Georgina, anxiously; "you did not say that I—"

"Oh, no!" said Nora; "I only spoke of what I had myself observed and expected."

"I hope you think I acted judiciously in following and speaking to him again."

"Quite right," said Nora; "he looked so completely put out that I could not help laughing at him."

"And he never suspected that I was acting?"

"I think not."

"You, of course, understood me directly?"

"Assuredly; and felt for you, and sympathised with you most sincerely. Events of this description, Georgina, are very annoying—very mortifying; and the only means to avoid them is by never bestowing a serious thought on any man who has not, like the lover in old Ducker's song, said, 'Oh, will you marry me, my dear Ally Croker? Oh! will you—'"

"If you can jest—" began Georgina, turning away, offended.

"By no means," said Nora, apologetically; "the words I have just spoken apply, I assure you, as much to myself as you. For my own part, I think it better to reserve every demonstration, and, as much as possible, every feeling of regard, until it becomes time to look over the marriage ceremony, and study properly the meaning of the important words—'I, N, take thee, M'."

"You are quite right to say M, Nora."

"Of course, you know those are the letters used."

"That was not what I meant. I have a strong suspicion that your brother wishes and hopes you may be induced to marry Lord Medway."

"Towards whom," said Nora, a blush adding to the already deepened colour of her unusually flushed face, "towards whom I feel so little elective attraction,[*] as Goethe calls it, that there are few things would give me greater pleasure than having an opportunity of proving how little I desire his acquaintance, or value the rank and station he so greatly overvalues."

"What on earth do you mean?" exclaimed Georgina, surprised at her sudden vehemence; "surely you must know him, whether you like it or not, when you meet, for you are relations."

"The relationship," said Nora, "is not near enough to compel intimacy, and, were it not for this marriage of

---

[*] A reference to *Die Wahlverwandschaften (The Elective Affinities)* (1809), novel by Johann Wolfgang von Goethe (1749-1832).

Harry's, might have been altogether forgotten. As far as I am concerned, it has lain dormant for ten years, and may remain ten more, if any effort on my part be necessary to rouse it. Let us not, however, waste another thought either on my brother or the Medway family, but tell me if you would like to leave Munich to-morrow."

"Very much indeed," said Georgina; "I am quite willing to go to your village whenever you please."

"I fear you will be equally ready to leave it, Georgina; for, as I have told you more than once, there are no grand hotels, or English travellers of distinction to be found in the quiet villages of the Bavarian highlands."

CHAPTER XVI

First Mountain Excursion Attempted by the Nixon Family

NORA'S proposal to leave Munich was received the next morning with evident satisfaction by her uncle; and John's approbation was quickly obtained when she proposed, at the end of the first day's short journey, an ascent of the Peissenberg, to take a panoramic view of the mountains they were about to visit.

"I say, Norry, is this Peissenberg what you call an alp or alm?" he asked, drawing his chair close to hers. "I mean, is it one of those pasture-grounds on the mountains, where you told me the people send their cattle in summer, and pleasant parties are got up, and wild hunters[*] take refuge? I wouldn't give a fig for a mountain, now, that had not alps upon it, with handsome peasant-girls to take care of the cows, and sing the *Ranz des Vaches*,[†] and all that sort of thing."

"The Peissenberg is not an alp," answered Nora; "it is merely a very high hill, rising, promontory-like, into the plain, and consequently commanding an unusually extensive view. There is a church, a priest's house, and a small

[*] An anglicisation of *Wildschütz*, the German word for poacher.
[†] French term (the German equivalent being *Kuhreigen*) for melodies sung or played on the alphorn by Alpine herdsmen to call their cows.

inn on the top; and I think it will in every way suit us as a trial of strength for future excursions."

"What do you say to this plan of Nora's?" asked John, turning to his father.

"Why, aw—if there's a tolerable road, aw—and our carriage—"

"Bless me, sir! you seem to have forgotten all about the Bavarian alps!"

"I never heard of them, that I can remember," said Mr Nixon.

"Don't you remember that Nora talked about them for more than an hour the day we decided on going abroad? and when we were planning excursions to them, you said you thought mountains must appear infinitely grander from their bases than from their summits."

"The remark was good, Jack," said Mr Nixon, "very good. I believe I do recollect saying that; and though of the same opinion still, yet, once in a way, with a donkey or a mule, and a steady guide, I'm sure I've no objection to—"

"You are talking as if we were on a tour in Switzerland, or at one of the much-frequented German springs," cried John, impatiently; "and we have explained a dozen times that we are going to the most out-of-the-way places imaginable. Even this Peissenberg, though so near Munich, is not much known to English travellers, is it, Nora?"

"When I was there," she answered, "there was not one English name in the numerous 'Stranger Books' that had been for years carefully preserved by the priests there."

"I am glad to hear that," cried John; "for a more uncivil set of people than the English I have met since we left home I never saw in all my life—they scarcely answer when one speaks to them."

"Perhaps because you have not been introduced," suggested Mr Nixon.

"Not exactly," observed Nora; "the English avoid each other on the Continent, to the great surprise of all foreigners; but I have no doubt you would, for various reasons, do the same yourself if you had resided a few years abroad."

"For my part," said John, "I don't want to know anything about them. If I could only speak French tolerably I should apply to the Germans; they all understand and speak it well; and when I can't get on in their language, commence talking it as a matter of course: however, it's too late to learn French now, so you must help me on with your 'grunting guttural,' Nora, that I may be able to speak to the people at your village."

Nora laughed, for John wished to be taught German, but would not give himself the trouble of learning it.

"Well, I suppose I may order horses," he continued; "for though this place is not exactly on our way to Nora's churchyard, it is at least in a southerly direction, and there are roads from it to the mountains."

On the evening of the following day they left their heavily-packed carriage to be stared at by the inhabitants of the village at the base of the Peissenberg, and commenced the easy ascent to the church they had long seen in the distance. Their way lay through cornfields and meadows, bounded by woods, and occasionally past an isolated peasant house. Oaks, beech, and on the south side mulberry trees, grew luxuriantly; and this, and the increasing extent of view, Nora pointed out to Mr Nixon, as, with true English determination, he laboured manfully on, heedless of heat and shortened breath, declaring, when he heard that they should soon be at a height of 3,000 feet, that "He rather liked the work, and shouldn't wonder if he became a famous mountain climber."

Nora and John were the first to reach the platform on which the church and adjacent buildings stand. They hur-

ried round them, looked into the former, and then surveyed
the rows of windows belonging to the priest's house, from
the greater number of which groups of inquisitive faces returned their glances. For a few minutes Nora contemplated
the wide expanse of plain that lay beneath them, the forests,
lakes, rivers, towns, villages, and castles that diversified the
level landscape until it reached the distant, thickly-wooded
hills that form a commencement to the chain of mountains
extending along the whole horizon, excepting in the direction towards Munich, where the towers rather than steeples
of the Frauen church were still dimly visible in the grey
cloudy vapour, indicating a long continuation of the plain.

John touched her arm, and with his eyes directed her attention to two figures not far distant from them. One was a
young, middle-sized, well-proportioned man, negligently
dressed in a suit of that light grey summer stuff which de-
fies the power of the thickest clouds of dust to change its
colour. A straw hat shaded his sunburnt face, the features
of which, high and sharply defined, were rather intellectual
than handsome, especially the long, deep-set, dark eyes,
which were of extraordinary brilliancy, and seemed constantly in search of objects to amuse or interest him. His
mouth was scarcely visible, so well cultivated had been the
growth of the black moustache, which covered the upper
lip and joined the *barbe Grecque* that, thick and short, nearly
concealed his well-formed chin. He sat on the low wall
which partly incloses the church and adjoining house, and
on his knee was placed a portfolio, while on a loose sheet
of paper he sketched with extraordinary rapidity and correctness the country around him. At his side stood a handsome, athletic, noble-looking man in the prime of life, who,
with folded arms and head very erect, looked alternately at
his companion's drawing and the distant range of mountains. As John and Nora approached, and the former en-

deavoured to satisfy his curiosity by gliding behind the artist, he bestowed on them a glance of haughty interrogation
that was by no means agreeable, and yet it was on him that
Nora immediately centred her attention: because she
thought he looked like an Englishman. It may be asked,
"What do Englishmen look like?" and I believe it was
Heinrich Heine who said, "Like statues with the ends of the
noses lopped off." Now this man's nose was not deprived
of any of its fair proportions, therefore it could not have
been that feature which had influenced her judgment; nor
on his broad forehead, of which she could just discern the
lower half, was the word Englishman written; nor in the
large eyes and low-marked, meditative eyebrows, though
English enough in their way; nor, nor,—in fact, she could
not tell what it was; but those more experienced in the
study of physiognomy would have at once affirmed that it
was the whiskers that so plainly said *Civis Britannus sum*, and
which, being without that continuation under the chin denominated *barbe Grecque*, were particularly English-looking
in a country where lip and chin beards grow so redundantly
as in Bavaria. In the year 1850 Mr Dickens had not yet
asked the English nation why they shaved; nor had the god
of war procured for the military part of it the permission to
pack up their razors and deposit them in the open temple
of Janus. Most Englishmen's faces were, therefore, still
carefully shaved, and many still remained in ignorance of
the different expressions of countenance that can be produced by a variation in the form of these hairy accessories.
A very short study of this important subject, with the aid of
a few pencil or chalk sketches, will lead to the conclusion
that whiskers *à l'Anglaise*, and ditto with continuations *à la
Grecque*, ought to be abolished, as tending greatly to increase
that most humiliating resemblance between men and apes;
while a moustache may be tolerated from its having the

contrary effect, inasmuch as no ape has yet been found with one; and, indeed, a moustache would be bestowed in vain on animals incapable of discovering the expression of cheerfulness imparted to the face by the turning of it upwards, the serenity by a horizontal position, the gravity by an inclination downwards, the ferocity by a shadowing of the under lip with it! Nora knew nothing of all this, and was so unconsciously an observer of whiskers, that had she discovered herself speculating on the subject she would, undoubtedly, have been very much surprised. Just as she had detected a slightly foreign accent in the few correct German sentences that the stranger addressed to his companion, John exclaimed:—

"Look, Nora, here they come, regularly blown, and Georgy as pale as a ghost."

"Hard work, Nora—hard work," cried Mr Nixon, still panting for breath as he joined her; "but the view is fine—very fine indeed: reminds me of Richmond—greatly. The country not so cultivated or thickly inhabited, eh?"

"Richmond!" exclaimed John, "who could think of Richmond with such mountains staring one in the face? I must say I cannot discover the slightest resemblance."

"Must be, Jack, or I should not have thought of it—green hill—look downwards—beech trees—water—very like Richmond!" Here he walked up to the young man who was drawing, and after having watched him for a short time in silence, he added, pompously, "Hum—aw—draws well —these Munich artists are clever fellows."

The artist continued his occupation, either unconscious or indifferent to the commendation bestowed, until Mr Nixon, unwilling to deprive him of the satisfaction, which he never for one moment doubted the approbation of an Englishman must afford him, touched his shoulder, and first pointing downwards and then to the sketch, signified expressively that he knew perfectly the part of the landscape there represented.

An impatient gesture was all the notice taken of his pantomime; and imagining himself misunderstood, he repeated it, uttering at the same time a succession of those inarticulate, inharmonious sounds or grunts, generally used by dumb persons, while at the same time he nodded his head and smiled good-humouredly.

The young man at last looked up with flashing eyes; but scarcely had they encountered Mr Nixon's bulky person than the expression totally changed, and placing the end of his pencil under one of his front teeth, he deliberately inspected the whole party without an attempt to conceal the amusement they afforded him.

Nora drew back, while John whispered rather loudly, "There's an artist for you, Nora! You say they are better worth knowing than other people; that they are always gentlemanlike in manner and picturesque in appearance! Now how should you like to sit to that chap for your picture?"

"Hush," she replied, turning away from the bright, laughing eyes that seemed to have singled her out from the others. "Don't speak so loud, perhaps he may understand what you say. I am afraid he thinks us very rude."

"Rude to admire his drawing! What can an artist desire more than to have his performances admired? Perhaps, however, you think he is not an artist?"

"He may be," answered Nora, "but he is evidently a gentleman also, and does not like to be the object of idle curiosity."

Georgina took her father's arm and retired into the house, her head even higher than usual.

"I say, Nora," cried John, seating himself astride on the wall, at some distance from the strangers, and beginning to pitch the pebbles, and bits of loose lime upon it, down the hill, "the wonderful sunset you promised us from this place seems rather a failure; those thunder-clouds may be very grand, but they are not pleasant to look at."

"I am beginning rather to fear a change of weather," she answered, "so that we may be disappointed in the sunrise as well as sunset. I am sorry for it, as we are not likely to see so extensive a view again."

"What! not on your famous Alps, which are so much higher?"

"The views from the Alps are generally more confined," she replied, "for the mountains are nearer and more heaped together; and there is seldom such an extent of plain to be seen from them as we have now before us. However, it would never do to keep my uncle up here waiting for a picturesque sunrise, though I should be tempted to remain a day or two myself for the purpose, were I alone. Let us look at your map, and find out the pleasantest road to Almenau."

"I dare say that fellow with the portfolio could tell us all about it," observed John; "but I suspect civil answers are not in his line. He looked furious when the governor touched him, and I cannot say I have any fancy for figuring among his sketches as a caricature; I dare say he had some intention of the kind, or he would not have stared at us so."

"The other," began Nora, "the quiet man, is, I think, an Englishman, and therefore we had better avoid—"

"An Englishman!" he exclaimed. "If that be the case I'll just go at once and—"

"Oh, pray, John," cried Nora, catching his arm to detain him; "I entreat—I—" But he broke from her, and, with feelings of indescribable annoyance, she saw him approach and address their haughty-looking countryman.

What he said she could not hear. That he was allowed to

speak without the slightest interruption, or even a gesture denoting interest, was evident; but the artist, clapping his portfolio together and placing it in one of his capacious pockets, stood up and seemed more disposed to be communicative than his friend. John turned towards him, and a very animated conversation began, which appeared so displeasing to the "quiet man," that he thrust his hands into the pockets of the paletot and walked off.

John's map was then produced, spread out on the wall, and for some time the places and roads on it were evidently the subject of discussion. When, however, Nora perceived the elbows instead of fingers were placed upon it, that the intelligent countenance of the artist assumed an expression of intense curiosity, that he spoke less and listened more than at first, she felt convinced that her friend Jack was becoming more confidential than was necessary, and after a few moments' hesitation she resolved to interrupt the conference.

As she approached she heard the artist say in very correct English, but with a strong foreign accent, "I comprehend perfectly; the old gentleman is to be induced to go to Ammergau—but you suppose he will object to the great mystery. It is a great pity, for it is very interesting."

"What mystery?" asked Nora, her curiosity completely overcoming her reserve.

The artist raised his straw hat, and let the wind blow his hair in all directions, while John answered, "Oh, Nora, I have made out such a delightful plan, if we can only get the governor to consent! This Mr a—a—"

"Waldemar," said the other, with a gay smile, "my name is Waldemar."

"Mr Waldemar says that he and his friend, whom you were quite right in supposing an Englishman, are now on their way to the very place we are going to; and intend to sketch, and fish, and shoot there, until they cross the mountains to the valley of the Inn in Tyrol, where they have friends expecting them some time about the end of the month!"

"But what is the great mystery?" asked Nora.

"Well may you ask what is the mystery," replied John, laughing; "it is a religious play to be performed at a village called Ober-Ammergau, perhaps the only place in the world where such a thing is now to be seen in such perfection. And only think, Nora, it is altogether got up by the inhabitants of the village—the people who carve those famous figures in wood that you and Georgy bought in Munich! and crowds of people are now on their way there, because, you see, these villagers only perform their mystery every ten years, and Mr Waldemar says their stage is quite classical, and all that sort of thing."

"It is certainly well worth your going a little out of your way to see," observed Waldemar.

"In fact," said Nora, "as we have no way to go out of, no settled plan whatever for some weeks, I do not think there is anything to prevent us."

"The governor," said John, shaking his head.

"What objection can he possibly have?"

"Do you really know what this mystery is, Nora?"

"I did not when you first mentioned it; but I understand now that you mean the performance of one of those religious dramas which were as common in the middle ages as they are uncommon now."

"Exactly; but it is the passion of our Saviour—the crucifixion that is to be represented. I am afraid my father will object—will think it improper—profane, perhaps!"

"He can hardly think it profane," observed Waldemar, "when you remind him that the Christian mysteries originated among the ecclesiastics, and were, it is said, first acted by monks in the churches. Bishops, and if I am not mistaken one of the Popes, composed mysteries, and encouraged in every possible way the performances."

"Oh, that would be no sort of recommendation to our governor," cried John, half laughing, while he twisted himself round on his heels. "We'll keep 'dark' about that."

"Then you can tell him," continued Waldemar, "that they were acted in England in the reign of your King James."

"That's a good point at least. Don't forget that when you speak to him, Nora."

"And," added Waldemar, "they were frequently performed at universities and schools."

"Better and better," cried John. "In fact, Nora, you can say that they are most interesting and highly moral performances."

"They may promote morality," said Waldemar, smiling; "but this representation at Ober-Ammergau is not at all what used to be called Moralities."

"I know very little about the matter," said John, "but I confess I should like to see something of the kind."

"Strictly speaking," said Waldemar, "the Mysteries or Miracle plays merely represent stories, according to the letter of Scripture, or the legend to be represented. The Moralities were not altogether destitute of plan and plot, and inculcated a moral by means of allegorical characters."

"Oh, the governor knows nothing about all these distinctions;—we might call it a Morality, Nora, if you think it would sound better."

"No," she answered, gravely; "if I am to speak to him, I must know what I am talking about, and call things by their right names."

"I do not think it is called either Mystery or Morality," said Waldemar, drawing from his pocket a pamphlet. "How would you translate that?" he added, pointing to the title-page.

She bent forward and read aloud—

"The Great Sacrifice at Golgotha; or, The Sufferings and Death of Jesus, according to the Four Evangelists—with Tableaux from the Old Testament for contemplation and edification—"

Either impelled by impatience or curiosity, the Englishman joined them just as Nora thoughtfully observed, "The name appears unimpeachable; whether or not such sacred subjects can be properly used for the stage, without irreverence or—or—profanation—"

"Pshaw, Nora, don't you be squeamish; it was only from my father that I expected opposition—I never thought of your demurring in this way. You look as grave as if we were trying to persuade you to witness a Pagan instead of a Christian mystery."

"Torp," cried Waldemar, turning to his friend, "can you not help us to remove the unnecessary scruples of your countrywoman?"

"No," he answered, gravely, "I can *not*, because I don't think them unnecessary. I feel them myself."

"But you are going to Ammergau all the same!" cried John, with a laugh.

"He is going there to get rid of them," observed Waldemar, with an affectation of gravity; "but Torp is so strictly evangelical in his ideas, that if he see anything to displease him he will be sure to leave the theatre in a manner to mark his disapproval."

"A clergyman, of course?" said John, turning to Torp.

"No."

"Hum—that's a pity—as you could have spoken to our governor, and—"

"Excuse me—" began Torp, loftily.

"Oh, it's of no consequence," cried John, turning away from him; "you can be of no manner of use to us as you are not a clergyman. Now, Nora, just go to my father and tell him exactly what is necessary for him to know, and no more. If *we* don't approve of all we may see at Ammergau, we can walk off you know, as Mr Torp here intends to do."

Still Nora hesitated. "If," she said, musingly, "if it were one of those miracle plays taken from the Old Testament, or a legend, my uncertainty how to act would be at an end; but to see our Saviour represented on a stage—"

"Stay," cried Waldemar, eagerly; "on that subject you have really nothing to fear. You have most probably seen pictures both good and bad representing him in every important event of his life, and especially of his crucifixion. As you have seen him in the best pictures, so you will see him represented by the wood-carver, Pflunger*, in Ammergau, whose appearance and acting, if one can use the word for such dignified tranquillity, are—perfect. But, even if it were not so, the supposition that everything holy must in the representation equal the ideal formed of it, or be profaned, is an error. How impossible would it be to satisfy the expectations of such differently constituted minds as must be found in every mixed crowd of people, or to produce the ideal of such various degrees of cultivation! Fortunately, however, it is not necessary; the imagination, naturally more excited by dramatic representation than by any other means, easily and unconsciously supplies what may be wanting, and satisfaction is the result. I have heard," he added, more quietly, "I have heard a competent judge say, that the performance at Ammergau reminded him strongly

---

* Tobias Flunger, a wood-carver, played the part of Christ in the 24th production of the Oberammergau Passion Play in 1850.

and incessantly of the best paintings of the middle ages."

"Come, Nora, after hearing all this, you can have no more scruples I should think! if you have, I must say it was very improper your spending so many hours looking at those old pictures in the Pinakothek, at Munich."

Nora seemed not to hear, but she followed him slowly into the house.

"So you have advised them to go to Ammergau?" observed Torp, with some displeasure, as soon as he perceived they were out of hearing.

"Of course—I could scarcely do otherwise when my advice was asked."

"Hem! but we shall get rid of them there, it is to be hoped!"

"Hope no such thing, for, by a singular chance, they are going to the same place that we are."

"You are not serious, I hope," said Torp.

"I am," rejoined Waldemar, laughing; "they are going to Almenau, and, in fact, have as good a right to go there as we have."

"Then let me tell you, Waldemar, that you and I must part company."

"Nonsense, Torp! you are not serious."

"Perfectly so, I assure you, for I can scarcely imagine anything more disagreeable than the intrusion of an English family on our privacy. When I accepted your offer of a few weeks' sporting in the mountains, rather enjoying the idea of the deprivations and hardships you told me to expect, I never for a moment doubted that we should be free from every kind of restraint, and now the very first thing you do is to collect an English colony about us! just the sort of people, too, most likely to worry us with attentions directly they find out that you are not a tinker, or I a journeyman tailor!"

"My dear Torp, it is not my fault that these people are going to Almenau. The young fellow told me something about a monument that they were going to erect in the churchyard there."

"Pshaw! you did not understand him rightly. If they have a monument to erect, they must be on their way to Meran, or some such place where our people generally die. Confess you advised them to stop at Almenau on their way, quite forgetting that the inn there is small, and that they will of course require all the best rooms."

"No," said Waldemar, quickly, "and the last annoyance I can spare you by sending an express to the landlady tomorrow, so you may depend upon having the best of everything that is to be had in her house."

"But conceive what a bore it will be having these women meeting us at every turn!" exclaimed Torp, with increasing irritation.

"None whatever," replied Waldemar. "In such places women lay aside some of their formality, and one becomes better acquainted in a week than elsewhere in a year! Their presence makes one overlook a thousand little discomforts, and they give an interest to the most trifling events. You must be greatly changed during the last few years, Torp, if you have any dislike to women's society; and I have a strong idea that if that dark-eyed girl were a German, you would make no sort of objection to her company."

"Perhaps not," said Torp; "but I can tell you I have a very decided objection to becoming acquainted with that intrusive, talkative, vulgar coxcomb, with whom you seemed to be on such astonishingly good terms just now."

"I did not observe any of these qualities," rejoined Waldemar, "and merely supposed him a happy young fellow fresh from one of your Universities. I can make more allowance for high spirits than you, being afflicted with them

myself occasionally, and excuse me for observing, that Englishmen are sometimes much more agreeable companions
before they have put on the pompous dignity of their riper
years. There was a time, Torp, when you would have resigned yourself willingly enough to the society of two such
pretty women, and would have sought rather than avoided
opportunities of meeting them. I have no doubt I shall be
able to persuade that black-eyed houri to meet us occasionally on an alp after a day's hunting, and shall feel trans-
ported into the seventh heaven the first time she prepares
me a *schmarn*,* or a cup of coffee!"

"The English houris are not so useful or complaisant as
the German," observed Torp, half laughing; "you will have
to wait long for your coffee, I suspect, especially if she and
her relations continue to suppose you a poor, wandering
artist, as they evidently do at present."

"Let them think so; I shall get the coffee all the same."

"You may get a cup of tea, per–haps—but—"

"No—coffee—and made by that adorable girl called
Nora—and brought to me by her, and she shall sit by me
while I drink it!"

"Will you bet?" asked Torp, amused.

"Willingly. I shall require a week, perhaps a fortnight, after we have reached Almenau."

"Agreed. A month—two months if you like, and a hundred to one."

"Done."

"Done."

Meantime Mr Nixon's objections to the mystery, as it
was explained to him at some length by Nora, proved, as
she had expected, insurmountable. "He would accompany

---

* A Bavarian or Austrian dish composed of pieces of sweet pancake.

her, of course, to Ammergau, and remain there as long as she pleased—he should not attempt to offer her advice—hoped that Georgina would remain at the inn with him, though John, having had the advantage of a classical education, must be allowed to judge for himself."

The discussion had taken place at one of the windows of the large sitting-room in the priest's house, where they, at first, expected to be alone, but soon found themselves, in consequence of the unusually crowded state of the inn, in the midst of a very mixed company collected in expectation of supper. Nora had much difficulty in consoling Mr Nixon for the want of his tea, which had been forgotten; and even after he had commenced what he called his second dinner, he continued to wonder at the want of civilisation evident on a Bavarian "alp," where tea was an unknown luxury! His son pretended sympathy, all the while bestowing sundry knowing winks and grimaces on Nora and Waldemar, the latter having contrived to procure a place close to them. Mr Torp was at the other end of the long table, and John observed, with some astonishment, that he was engaged in a lively conversation with a German lady and her daughter, and seemed to have altogether laid aside his taciturnity. As they rose from the table, the weather was discussed, and anxious inquiries about it made.

"Is the weather of such very great importance?" asked Nora.

"Undoubtedly," replied Waldemar, "for the theatre in Ammergau is in the open air; if you will go with me to what is called the Belvedere, on the top of the house, we can take a look at the clouds and see what our chances are."

"Georgina, will you go?" asked Nora.

"No, thank you, I am tired, and prefer my bed to any Belvedere on earth."

"Jack," said Nora, looking round; but seeing him engaged in listening and trying to understand what was being read aloud from the "Strangers' Book," she stood with Waldemar watching the group of people who had gathered round the reader as, lazily leaning over the large soiled volume, he sometimes read, sometimes made remarks, which were not unfrequently received with peals of laughter.

"Is that 'Strangers' Book' so very amusing?" asked Nora.

"It depends upon the reader," answered Waldemar. "A dull person would, perhaps, discover but little subject for laughter, but a lively mind finds amusement in the characteristic remarks and odd effusions with which it abounds, as the bee finds honey in the flower over which the stupid fly hovers in vain."

"He has looked towards us two or three times," she observed; "perhaps you know him?"

"By name and reputation, very well," he answered. "He is a Dr X——, very clever, very witty, and one of the most popular men of his profession in Vienna."

"A doctor! he does not look at all like one."

"Indeed! Have doctors in England any particular appearance?"

"Oh, no, of course not, but—a—one could not—at least I could not imagine that man soberly feeling pulses and writing prescriptions."

"I dare say not," rejoined Waldemar, amused, "nor has he, during his life, done either the one or the other. He is *Doctor Juris*, not *Doctor Medicinæ;* and has studied law, not medicine."

At this moment someone touched Nora's arm, and, on looking round, she perceived Georgina, who, drawing her aside, whispered,—

"Nora, dear, forgive me, but as I am older than you, and have been so much more *out*, you must allow me to tell you that you are acting against all *usage du monde*, talking in this way to a stranger, a person who has not been introduced to you—of whose name you are ignorant—"

"Who could introduce him here?" asked Nora, laughing. "He told Jack that his name was Waldemar, gave us very good advice about our journey, and—"

"I knew," cried Georgina, interrupting her, "I felt quite sure, that as soon as your brother Harry left us, John would bring you into all sorts of embarrassments. It is quite provoking to see him talking to all these people as if they were his best friends! What must they think of us?"

"They are not thinking of us at all," answered Nora. "It is quite a common thing in these sort of out-of-the-way places for people to speak to each other without waiting for introductions; for instance, one of those priests inquired, without the slightest hesitation, if we were going to Ammergau, and if we had rooms there."

"And you, of course, told him all our plans?"

"Of course; and he and his companions informed me that they had bespoken their rooms three months ago, and that we had but little chance of finding a place to lay our heads."

"If that be the case, would it not be better to change our route? I assure you, Nora, nothing is so destructive to the health and appearance as want of rest."

Nora laughed. "I only mentioned this to you," she said, "in order to prove the advantage of speaking occasionally to strangers when one is travelling as we are now. These most polite priests have advised us to apply to a M. Zwink, a wood-carver, and the person who is manager and director of the theatre at Ammergau, and should *he* not be able to arrange everything to our satisfaction, I am to inquire of him for Pater Ignaz. Now you see this Pater Ignaz is one of those who spoke to me without an introduction, and who, having received a civil answer from me, may perhaps be

very useful to us in the sort of place to which we are going."

"And in what way do you intend to make use of the
young artist with the fiery eyes?" demanded Georgina,
ironically.

"As ambulating guide-book," replied Nora, demurely. "I
find him even more amusing than Murray!*"

"I suspect he will not be satisfied with that arrangement," said Georgina. "He seems to me to expect to be
considered as a—gentleman."

"Well," said Nora, "and that he undoubtedly is."

"But," persisted Georgina, "it is even more than that—
in fact, he appears to imagine himself quite equal, if not su-
perior to us; his manner to John just now was more that of
a person conferring a favour than one on whom a favour
was being conferred."

"But I don't exactly see in what way we *are* conferring a
favour."

"You don't choose to understand me, Nora, and are annoyed at what I said just now about introductions."

"Not in the least, I assure you," she answered, moving
aside to allow some people to pass her. A young and pretty
girl looked back and smiled, while her mother, politely ad-
dressing Georgina in French, asked her if she would accompany them to the Belvedere, to see what chance there
was of fine weather for the next day.

With a look of affected astonishment at being addressed
by a stranger, Georgina drew herself up, and coldly declined
the proffered civility.

"I should like to go very much," said Nora, perceiving

---

* Series of guide-books produced, from 1820, by the publisher John
Murray.

that her cousin John was just then too much engaged to be at her service.

"Oh, pray come," cried the younger stranger, eagerly. "I know you are a foreigner, but my governess was an Englishwoman, and I can explain everything to you in your own language."

Nora moved on while Waldemar looked away, and seemed to have no inclination to accompany them, although she had observed that, on entering the room, he had appeared well acquainted with both her companions, and had introduced his friend Torp to them.

Mr Nixon was sitting near the door in a lamentable state of bewilderment. "Oh, Nora," he cried, despondingly, "these doings don't answer for a man at my time of life! Whether it's the second dinner, or the jabbering about me which I don't understand, I can't exactly say, but I never felt so oddish in all my life. My tea, if I had it, would have set me all to rights, I am sure. What that cooreer, that French fellow, Adong, was thinking about when he forgot it, I'm sure I can't tell, for I don't understand a word the moustached rascal says to me! If Jack had got an English cooreer, as I asked him, this would never have happened, and I don't and won't believe a word about his not being able to find an Englishman! I only wish we had given the tea in charge to Tomkins, or even Mrs Nesbitt—I'll answer for it—it would not have been forgotten! Why, they will be just as much inconvenienced as I am, and what we are to have for breakfast to-morrow, *I* don't know!"

"Coffee," answered Nora, consolingly; "and pray don't make yourself unhappy about Tomkins, who can take care of himself, or Nesbitt, who will be taken care of by Adam;" then bending down, she whispered, "Don't you think it would be a good plan if you went to bed now?"

"Perhaps it would; but as there is a doctor in the room, I

think I'll just ask if I ought not to take something."

Nora did not wait to hear his answer; and no sooner was he joined by his daughter than he approached Dr X—, and having bowed in a pleasant, condescending manner, drew a chair to the table, and sat down beside him. Imagining he wished to see the "Strangers' Book," the doctor politely moved it towards him. Mr Nixon shook his head mournfully.

"Can I in any way be of use to you?" asked the doctor, in French, vainly endeavouring to suppress a smile.

Again Mr Nixon shook his head, sighing out the words—"English, English."

"My father can only speak English," explained Georgina.

"Ah!" said the doctor, leaning on his elbow, and pausing for a moment, before he added, "Well, I can speak English. Do you wish me to interpret for you?"

"Sir!" cried Mr Nixon, with that feeling of relief which only those who have heard unknown tongues spoken around them for some weeks *can* experience on again unexpectedly hearing their own—"sir, I am delighted to make your acquaintance!" and with a good-humoured laugh he continued, "When I saw you reading these books full of names to the company, I desired my son to find out who you were; and he has just now informed me that you are the celebrated Dr X—! I know, sir, that men of your profession do not like to be asked for advice when they are travelling for their amusement: but, as they say, 'Necessity has no laws,' and 'Needs must when the devil drives'."

The doctor turned to an acquaintance at the other side of him, and muttered between his teeth, "Mad, or not mad?—that is the question."

"Now the fact is, doctor," continued Mr Nixon, "I have always been a remarkably healthy man, and though, when our travelling-carriage was being built, I consented to the portable medicine chest, it was with the firm belief that none of the patent medicines would ever find their way down my throat. Now, my daughter, Miss Nixon, is quite different—she likes medicine, and takes her pill every night regular."

"Is it possible?" asked the doctor, slowly, and looking with unfeigned astonishment at Georgina, whose face became crimson: "is it possible you like eating pills?"

"Papa is only jesting," she answered, in a voice tremulous from vexation.

"Not a bit of it, Georgy. I assure you, doctor, no apothecary could manage the little scales, or weigh and measure with greater nicety than my daughter; she can make up pills, and—"

"Good night, papa," said Georgina, in that distinct, quick manner, which is so very demonstrative of female displeasure.

"Stay, Georgy, stay; I have only a few words to say to the doctor, and then we can go together."

She sat down at a little distance, slightly contracting her brows, and biting her under lip, while her father continued, in a low, confidential tone—"you must know, doctor, that late hours never did, and never will, agree with me. I like living at the West End, and being in good society, amazingly; but only those who have been brought up to it, like my son and daughter, can find riding in the Park, and dining at eight o'clock, and going to evening swarries, quite easy and natural. I moved too late in life, and can't get used to it, especially the late hours; so that I often wish myself back again in—in—the street we used to live in, as my daughter says. We knew many pleasant, sociable people there, who dined at rational hours, and better and more plentifully than at more fashionable places. *My* father used

to dine at five o'clock; by degrees, to please Mrs Nixon, *we*
got on to six o'clock; my daughter has brought us on to
seven or eight; and I suppose my grandchildren will dine at
nine or ten, as I have done to-day! But it has disagreed with
me, doctor—disagreed in the most uncomfortable manner.
Perhaps the walk up the alp may have increased my appetite—I *may* have eaten more than usual: the fish and the
omelettes were good, the beer excellent, but the wine was
sourish; all Rhine wine *is* sourish. Give me the curious old
sherry, ever so many years in bottle, or even Cape, good
and clever, such as we used to drink when alone in—in the
street we used to live in. Now, doctor, you see, the late—
the second dinner and the wine having disagreed with me, I
should be very much obliged to you if you would tell me
what I ought to take before I go to bed."

"Punch," said the doctor, who had listened to him with
undeviating attention.

"What?" cried Mr Nixon, opening his eyes as wide as
the lids would permit.

"Punch," repeated the doctor, nodding his head.

"Hush!" cried Mr Nixon, with a wink and a gesture of
his thumb towards his daughter, to whom he then turned,
and affectionately observed, "I say, Georgy, dear, I'm keeping you up a great deal too long; you had better not wait for
me any longer;" adding, in a whisper, "Uncommon clever
man, this doctor; he thinks I ought to take something before I go to bed, and is just going to prescribe for me."

Glad to be released, Georgina immediately left the
room; and Mr Nixon, drawing still closer to the table and
the doctor, observed, "My daughter does not like punch."

To this observation no answer was made. The doctor
did not seem to think it of any importance whether or not
Miss Nixon liked punch; and Mr Nixon continued, as it
were in explanation, "She may, for all I know, in point of

fact, like the taste of punch, and it may be only the vulgarity of the thing that she so specially abhors—"

"Vulgarity!" repeated the doctor; " I never heard that punch was vulgar."

"Why, sir," cried Mr Nixon, "my daughter says it is so shocking vulgar, that since we left the—street we used to live in, and came to Eaton-place, I have never been allowed to see anything of the kind at my table. I can conscientiously say that I have not tasted punch for nine, or perhaps ten, years; but if you recommend it, I shall have no sort of objection to try a tumbler—medicinally, you know, medicinally. I say, just order the materials, will you?"

"I know nothing about the materials," said the doctor; "but I can order the punch if you wish it." He made a sign, while speaking, to a girl who was in waiting; and before Mr Nixon could express half the satisfaction he felt on hearing that punch was not considered vulgar in Germany, the waitress returned, carrying a covered glass in one hand, and a plate, on which was a large slice of cake, in the other.

"Hey? ha! what's that? Must I eat that with it?" asked Mr Nixon, hastily.

"Not if you do not choose," answered the doctor, with a smile, quite unconscious that he was being consulted as a physician, and thinking his companion singularly simple for a person who looked so intelligent.

Mr Nixon accordingly made a negative motion with his hand towards the cake, uttering some of the "grunting gutturals," which he seemed to consider so like German that they might pass for the language, and then took the glass, remarking that "It was very small, and did not deserve the name of tumbler."

Just as he had pronounced the punch excellent, and deposited his glass on the table, he caught his son's eye fixed on him from the other end of the room. He pushed the punch towards the doctor, who, however, slightly bowing, refused what he supposed was an English token of conviviality, while he observed, "I prefer beer or wine—it is a matter of taste, you know, or habit."

"Hem!" coughed Mr Nixon, again pushing the glass towards him, "but you see my son is looking this way just now, and—"

"And he thinks punch vulgar, too, perhaps," said the doctor, amused.

"Why, as to that, he must, indeed, we must all, in such things, do as my daughter chooses, for she knows the world and how people live in it, and has for many years had the complete management of my establishment."

"Hallo, governor, what have you got there?" cried John, leaning across the table.

"Why Jack, the doctor here recommended me, after my late dinner, to try a glass of punch."

"Where's Georgy?"

"Gone to bed."

John drew the glass towards him, and seemed to like the contents so well that his father laughed, and desired him to use his German in order to procure a fresh supply. Several of the guests followed his example, and almost all began to smoke. Now tobacco was an abomination to Gilbert Nixon.

In the mean time, Nora and her companions, accompanied by a chamber-maid with a candle, ascended the long steep flight of stairs which led to the roof of the house. There, however, even before they reached the door that opened on the small inclosed space called the Belvedere, the wind, which was blowing strongly, extinguished their light. Yet still they groped on, stepped out on the roof, and even while making some jesting remarks on the inappropriateness of the name, just then their eyes became accustomed to the darkness, and they began to perceive the widely-extending horizon, marked out by vivid flashes of lightning that, playing noiselessly along the dark sky, rendered at intervals the outline of the mountains visible, and showed the distant thunder-storm that was raging among them.

"It looks better than I expected," observed the elder lady. "The thunder-clouds are driving towards Tyrol, and the moon will soon be visible to *us* at least! After all, it may be fine to-morrow."

"It *will* be fine to-morrow and for some weeks afterwards," said Nora, gaily; "I have bespoken fine weather, as we are going to a pretty mountain village where M. Waldemar has promised to show us some beautiful views from the alps in the neighbourhood."

"Oh, Count Waldemar is of your party, then? I understood he was on a hunting-excursion with that Englishman—that friend of his whose acquaintance he made at Vienna so many years ago."

"He is not of our party," said Nora, quickly; "we met him here accidentally to-day; he told us his name was Waldemar, gave us advice about our route, and—"

"And invited you to visit him at his castle in the Valley of the Inn," said the elder lady, laughing; "it would be just like him."

"No," answered Nora; "the fact is, we saw him sketching when we arrived here, and, without further consideration, concluded he must be an artist, and his friend, Mr Torp—"

"Torp," repeated the lady; "that was not the name he said, was it, Sophie?"

"No, mamma, he said Lord Medvey, but he afterwards called him Torp, once or twice; and the name sounded so oddly that I asked him about it, and he told me that the family name of the Medveys was—"

"Thorpe," said Nora.

"Exactly; but as Count Waldemar never could learn to pronounce the 'th'—he called him Torp. He said he had become acquainted with him when his name was Torp, and could not now learn to call him anything else without a great deal of trouble."

The lady and her daughter talked on, and Nora heard the murmuring of voices; but the words conveyed no sense to her mind, so completely had she been surprised by what she had heard. Could it be true that chance had brought her into the immediate neighbourhood of the only person in the world she wished to avoid? Was it indeed certain that he was going to Almenau, where they must necessarily often meet? Would he claim acquaintance when he heard her name? What would be his manner towards her uncle, Georgina, and John? Could she, in fact, receive him with even a semblance of cordiality after her last conversation with her brother? She had not time to answer any of these questions before her companions proposed going down stairs again. At the door of her room she stopped, and, as they wished her good night, hoped she would not be too much fatigued to get up the next morning to see the sun rise.

"Oh, Nesbitt, I am so sorry I forgot to tell you to go to bed," said Nora, when she saw Georgina's maid waiting in her room, and vainly endeavouring to suppress her yawns; "just put my things in order for to-morrow morning, and then you can sleep until Miss Nixon wants you."

"Yes, ma'am, thank you. Miss Nixon does not wish to be wakened for the sunrise, ma'am."

"Nor you either," said Nora, laughing.

"Why, ma'am, Monsieur Adong says that a sunset is

much finer."

"Of course what Adam says must be right."

"Yes, ma'am—only in one thing he is wrong, very wrong—he always calls master, Lord Nixon, ma'am, since Sir 'Arry left us—he says it makes people think more of us."

"But, Nesbitt, you ought to explain to him—"

"So I have, ma'am, but he says he has been so accustomed to travel with noblemen that he cannot do otherwise. It's all very well with the hignorant Germans, who don't know the difference; but when English people hear him, I am so ashamed I don't know where to look."

"There is an Englishman here now—a Mr Torp"—began Nora, quickly.

"Yes, ma'am, and as ill-luck would have it, he and a young gentleman with a face and beard just such as one sees in the pictures of the galleries, ma'am, passed the kitchens when I was getting candles for this room. The young gentleman turned back suddenly, and asked Mr Adong the name of the family he was cooreer to. 'My Lor Nixone,' says he, 'from London,' says he, and immediately the other gentleman, who had walked on very high and mighty, stopped and laughed a little, and said something of the creation, which I did not quite hear, and of a pleasant addition to the peerage, and then he too turned back and said London was a large place, and might contain a great many Nixons; that he knew something about one of that name, and wished to be informed where Mr Adong's present employer lived in London. And no sooner, ma'am, did he hear of Eaton-place than he became more inquisitive a great deal than the other gentleman, and asked if you were all of one fambly, and especially if you and Miss Nixon were *sisters;* and Mr Adong, knowing no better, said, 'yes,' ma'am, that you were 'all one fambly, tray distinguey;' and then they walked away, laughing, and I had the greatest mind to run after them and explain that you, ma'am—"

"I am very glad you did not," said Nora, quickly, "and you will oblige me very much by never entering into any explanation whatever. I am quite satisfied to pass for a daughter of my uncle's; in fact, I prefer it just at present."

Mrs Nesbitt seemed for a moment surprised, remained a short while silent, and then observed, "I suppose, ma'am, you think it better for us while in this wild part of the country to remain incog."

"Exactly," said Nora, laughing; "it is quite unnecessary that these strangers should be informed of my relationship to my uncle; nor can it in any way interest Monsieur Adam either, so for the present let us leave him in ignorance also. In short, Nesbitt," she added, with unusual emphasis and seriousness, "the less you speak of me and my affairs for the next six weeks, the better pleased I shall be."

These words made the impression intended, for Mrs Nesbitt greatly desired to enter Nora's service; and she actually was scrupulously silent during the time required.

The Peissenberg is not a place for tranquil slumbers on a moonlight night, and but a few hours had elapsed before bright moonbeams in her chamber, and on her bed, wakened Nora so completely, that she looked at her watch, rose, slowly dressed herself, and having from her window seen several dark figures already moving about before the house, she descended quietly, and passed through a small gate that opened to the east. The daylight, which began to pervade the horizon, was so faint, and the wind so high, that she returned to the front of the buildings, and had scarcely reached the parapet wall when John sprang towards her.

"Good morning, Nora; I knew you would be one of the first up. Did you hear the row in the house about midnight?"

"No, I slept too soundly."

"The governor was ill—got up a regular scene—thought he was dying!"

"Oh, Jack, if these sort of excursions disagree with him, let us give them up at once."

"Nonsense, dear girl, it wasn't the walk up here, nor the late dinner either, though he still tries to think so—it was—but don't peach—don't tell Georgy—it was the rum-punch he drank; and even that would not have upset him, perhaps, if he had not sat sipping it in a room full of tobacco-smoke. It was too much for me at last; for, though I like my own cigar, I don't choose, as that quiet fellow Torp said, to inhale the—"

"Never mind what he said," cried Nora; "but tell me about my uncle."

"Well, either the punch or the smoke, or perhaps both together, disagreed with him—he really *was* ill for half an hour or so, and then he sent for the doctor."

"How fortunate there happened to be one in the house!" exclaimed Nora.

"So we thought, and sent for him at once; but he refused so obstinately to get up, that I went to him myself and explained, as well as I could do so in German, my father's situation, and the duties of a man of his profession. I did not know, at first, that he understood English, and supposed my German, spoken in a hurry, was not so intelligible as usual; he listened to me, however, civilly enough, said something about being very sorry, drew up the monstrous down bed with which people half smother themselves in this country, and composed himself to sleep in my very presence!"

"How very unfeeling!" cried Nora, indignantly.

"Wait until you hear the end," continued John, laughing. "My father, alarmed as you know he always is when anything is the matter with him, got out of his bed, and in order not to catch cold, took the bright red wadded quilt from his bed and threw it over his dressing-gown. Now don't try to look grave, Nora; his appearance *was* comical, and when, accompanied by Tomkins, we commenced a regular pilgrimage to the doctor, I could not keep my countenance. Some people in our vicinity had been wakened, doors were ajar, and I heard whispering and tittering in all directions. The tassel of my father's monstrous white nightcap—"

"I really could laugh," said Nora, "if it were not for anxiety about my uncle."

"Oh, laugh as much as you like," cried John; "I laughed too, and amused myself making bows to all the half-opened doors as I passed. Now that I know the true state of the case, I cannot conceive why the doctor did not get up and lock his door when I left him. I should have done so in his place; however, it proves satisfactorily that the Germans are a phlegmatic nation. The door was still unlocked, and in the few minutes I had been absent he had actually contrived to fall asleep again!"

"And you were obliged to waken him?" interposed Nora.

"Of course. And after staring at us all for a few seconds, rather savagely, he began to utter the most extraordinary words I ever heard. I did not understand them; but I can imagine their import, and it struck me at the time that the German language was very powerful for the expression of rage. The governor sat down by him, and mildly began a detailed account of his sufferings; but the doctor interrupted him by an impatient and fruitless endeavour to make him understand that, though a doctor, he was no doctor."

"Ah," said Nora, "that was the man who was reading the 'Strangers' Book' this evening; I made the same mistake myself."

"Yes, and if he had only used the word physician, perhaps the governor would have understood him—but I am
not sure—these things are out of his line, you know; so
they kept shouting at each other, doctor or no doctor, until
at length finding English, German, and French insufficient,
he explained, with a couple of Latin words, that he was a
lawyer and not a physician. I understood him, of course,
and with some difficulty made my father comprehend the
state of the case; but no sooner did a light break upon him,
than he thought it necessary, as an apology for having got
up such a row, to commence a history of his neglected education, and how *his* father had considered a classical education unnecessary, and how often he had intended to learn
Greek and Latin, but had never had time for it! The old
story, you know; if Georgy had been there he would not
have been so communicative, I suspect—"

Here they both became conscious that Torp was within
hearing distance of them, and John added quickly, "In
short, all was at last satisfactorily explained, and we left the
doctor in peace—but even then he did not bolt his door—
curious people these Germans!"

At that moment Waldemar advanced towards them, and
while he leaned against the wall, and was still eagerly speaking to Nora, the wind caught his light straw hat, balanced it
a moment high above his head, and then blew it down the
steep green hill. John laughed loudly. Waldemar smiled
good-humouredly, looked after it for a moment, and perceiving that it was already out of sight, continued speaking
as if nothing had occurred to interrupt him. "I scarcely, in
fact, know which I prefer," he said, looking round him, "a
sunrise from a quite dark night, or this protracted struggle
between moonlight and breaking day. But we must go to
the other side of the church, Mees Nixe, if we intend to see
the sun rise in all its glory."

"I wonder," cried John, leaning over the wall—"I wonder how far down the hill your hat is at this moment!"

"If you feel the slightest curiosity on the subject," said Waldemar, "I advise you to gratify it."

John jumped over the wall, and directly he was out of sight, Torp joined Nora and Waldemar. Several groups of people from the neighbouring inn were assembled, all eyes turned to the east. Nora's acquaintances of the previous evening moved towards her, and Waldemar seemed for a moment inclined to retire; but when he perceived that both ladies turned to Torp and began to speak English, he remained standing with his arms folded, his eyes sweeping eagerly over the plain before him, while he began again to speak to Nora, as if in continuation of what he had before said. "Moonlight is more adapted for confined landscapes than for a view like this: there it can produce strong shadow, and make insignificant objects appear grand; here it serves but to create confusion; the eye labours in vain to find a distinct outline or place of repose—just light enough to make us painfully aware of the imperfection of the noblest sense that we possess!—I believe I give the preference to that gradual transition from night to morning which I witnessed the last time I was on this spot at this hour. Impenetrable darkness changed by degrees into grey twilight—the first glimmer of light caught by the mountain tops, and showing their outline in dark masses,—then the boundaries of forest and long dark-coloured lakes became visible—last of all the towns, villages, churches. Do not look again at that pale fading moon," he added, turning once more with Nora towards the east, and fixing his eyes on the spot where, bright and glowing, the sun's disc began to appear above the horizon.

With the others they gazed undazzled on the magnificent fiery orb as long as his rays "shot parallel to the earth," and were tempered by its misty atmosphere. Soon, however, the deep red colour changed to the pale hue of intense heat and light—the admiring eyes were averted, and tongues were loosed and—talked of breakfast.

Nora took advantage of the general movement leisurely to examine Mr Torp. The moment was favourable for him: he was listening to the broken English of her acquaintances of the previous evening; and though none of that suavity of manner which men frequently feel or feign when speaking to women with whom they are but slightly acquainted was perceptible in his person or features, there was an unaffected cordial smile on his lips, and a mirthful glance in his eyes, that made her unwillingly acknowledge to herself that he was handsomer than she had expected to find him. The scrutiny, however, was short, for with that inexplicable feeling of consciousness from which even the most near-sighted are seldom quite free when closely watched, Torp soon became aware that eyes were fixed on him, and turned to meet them. Indifferent and haughty was the glance he bestowed on Nora, but the look that met his, though a mere flashing of the eye, instantly arrested his attention—there was recognition in it, and few are ignorant of the change, which that produces in the human eye. Did it remind him of somebody he had seen before? When? where? Pshaw! Often as he had heard of the Nixon family, he certainly never had seen one of them. The eyes were handsome, very—very handsome, and he rather wished she would look at him again—it would greatly assist his memory. For this purpose he followed her into the house and to the sitting-room; but in vain. Nora would not look at him any more, and seemed altogether occupied with John, who, after a fruitless chase of Waldemar's straw hat, had ordered his breakfast, and now assured her he had had an excellent view of the sunrise from the window opposite him. They then lowered their voices, spoke for a few minutes, and finally left the room together, John to induce his father to get up, Nora to bribe Georgina to exertion, by a proposal to stop at Sultzbad, at the foot of the hill, until they had all had warm baths.

By the time they were ready to commence their descent, not a trace of the numerous travellers of the previous evening was to be seen.

CHAPTER XVII

Peasant Artists

THE road from the Peissenberg to Ober-Ammergau, though not uninteresting, presents little worthy of notice until, after having passed Mornau, the mountains appear gradually to close around it; soon after the summit of the Watterstein rises majestically in the background, and the steep ascent of the Ettal mountain commences. It was here that the carriages, carts, omnibuses, and crowds of pedestrians assumed the appearance of a procession to a pilgrimage, and here that the justness of some of Nora's remarks on her uncle's heavy and unwieldy travelling-carriage first became manifest; for had not the neighbouring peasants been prepared to supply additional horses, they would have been obliged to have either procured a lighter vehicle or have pursued their way on foot. The church and former monastery of Ettal, an immense pile of building, became visible at the top of the mountain, and there they once more found themselves in a valley, above the green hills on each side of which rocky peaks again presented themselves.

A short drive then brought them to the village of Ober-Ammergau, where with much noise and pretension the Nixons' carriage drew up before the door of the inn, and the courier sprang to the ground. Nora, quite prepared for the intelligence that they could not get rooms there, had descended, and was beginning to make inquiries about Herr Zwink and Peter Ignaz, when their acquaintance of the previous evening, Waldemar, advanced towards her, and with the assurance that the inhabitants of the village were quite willing to inconvenience themselves in any way to afford travellers shelter for the night, added that, if they did not mind being separated, he doubted not being able to provide for them some way or other. Nora and John accompanied him in his search, and before long Mr Nixon and his son were put in possession of a small room, Georgina was given one still more diminutive, and immediately under the roof, but in the same house; while Nora, accompanied by the half-wondering, half-discontented Mrs Nesbitt, proceeded to a neighbouring peasant's cottage, where Waldemar observed, carelessly, he and his friend Torp had been so fortunate as to get lodgings for the night.

As is usual in the Bavarian highlands, the houses composing the village were detached, each in its orchard, and generally furnished with a little garden in front. Most picturesque and sanctified they looked, with their low overhanging roofs, ornamented gables, and walls covered with frescos, the subjects of which were all from Holy Writ, while the Ettal Madonna,[*] conspicuously placed, seemed framed as it were in flourishes and ornaments of the most elaborate description.

The interiors of these houses are as similar as their exteriors; there is the long narrow passage leading through the house to the offices, the steep staircase and kitchen in the distance, the doors right and left on entering, one of which

---

[*] A marble statue of the Madonna and Child, brought by Emperor Ludwig IV ("Ludwig the Bavarian") from Rome which he visited in 1328. On his return he founded, in 1330, the Benedictine monastery at Ettal where the statue still is.

invariably conducts into the sitting-room of the family, with its large green stove surrounded by wooden benches that, as fixtures, are continued along the walls of the room, the windows almost covered by luxuriant exotics, and the massive table of well-scoured maple-wood in the corner, where the cross light of a front and side window falls upon it.

The inhabitants of Ammergau are scarcely peasants in the common acceptance of the word; the ground and country about them is not favourable for the growth of corn, they occupy themselves but little with field labour, and neglect the usual resource of other Alpine districts—the breeding of cattle. As manufacturers of toys and carvers of wood they at first appear to have improved their condition, and attained a higher position in the world; but though, in an intellectual point of view, this may be the case, in material well-being they are far behind the other peasants of the mountainous parts of Bavaria. The chief profits fall into the hands of foreign agents and the possessors of warehouses; yet so artistically inclined are these people, and so experienced are they in the carving of wood, that they prefer it to all other occupation. The very children from earliest infancy make rude attempts, and assist in colouring and varnishing the ordinary toys that serve as playthings to little beings of their own age, whose chief pleasure and occupation seem to be the speedy destruction of them.

At the door of one of these houses Waldemar stopped, apparently surprised at finding the benches outside occupied by a row of people who rose as he approached. They proved to be acquaintances, for he extended his hand to an athletic old man in a hunter's dress, made some inquiries about his family, and nodding familiarly to the others before entering the house, he passed Nora in order to open the door of the sitting-room of the proprietor. She heard a hasty discussion about rooms—regret that he had not explained his wishes before the arrival of the Forstward from Almenau, and a proposal to lodge the daughter of the latter elsewhere.

"No, no, no," cried Waldemar, returning to the passage, and requesting Nora to follow him up the stairs.

"Miss Nixe," he said, throwing open the door of a small low room, "this apartment is quite at your service, and I believe I must advise you to take possession of it without delay, as it has already happened more than once this summer that travellers have been obliged to pass the night in their carriages."

"But," said Nora, glancing towards a portmanteau and some already unpacked toilet requisites, "but this is your room, and I cannot think of depriving you of it until you have secured another."

"Torp must share his with me," answered Waldemar, opening the door of the adjoining apartment, and beginning to shove his portmanteau into it with his foot.

Nora motioned to Nesbitt to assist, and perhaps might herself have aided, had not the voice of Torp announced his presence.

"Hollo! what are you at now, Waldemar?" he said good-humouredly. "Have you repented giving me the best room, and come to dislodge me?"

"Not exactly," answered Waldemar. "I only want you to share it with me, as I have resigned mine to"—here he lowered his voice and spoke rapidly in German, "to your fair countrywoman, the naiad, the nymph, the black-eyed Nixie!"

"Better than the old alderman or his son," said Torp, dryly; "but you must refrain from smoking, Waldemar, if you do not mean to cancel the whole obligation, for English nymphs eschew the smell of tobacco, and I am much mistaken if that door will effectually prevent the entrance of the fumes of your cigars, or the most subdued tones of our melodious voices. Singing is out of the question to-night, Waldemar, neither hunting-song nor—"

"Hush, Torp! she's there, and may hear what you say," cried Waldemar.

She had in fact more than heard; she had caught a glimpse of his figure, stretched at full length on a row of chairs, so placed as to represent a sofa, while with arms folded, and head thrown back, his eyes followed his friend's energetic movements with an expression of lazy amusement.

The arrangements were soon completed; and then Waldemar stepped up close to Torp, laid his hand on his shoulder, and whispered, "You're a better fellow than I thought you, Charley. I half expected you to he dissatisfied, as, on our way here to-day, you seemed so strangely averse to any interchange of civilities with your countrymen, or the slightest acquaintance with the family of Nix."

"I shall make no attempt to interfere with your civilities in future," said Torp, quietly; "the more so, as I flatter myself that I can keep these people at a distance, and avoid an acquaintance which I confess *would* be disagreeable, and might be embarrassing to me."

"*Con*-found your arrogance!" exclaimed Waldemar, impatiently turning away.

In the mean time, Nesbitt had been looking round the small apartment rather disconsolately. She could find nothing to interest her in the coloured prints that decorated the whitewashed walls—the painted bedstead, with bright yellow arabesques on the head and foot-board, and the letters IHS above the pillows—or the large wardrobe before which Nora stood, apparently lost in contemplation of the Madonna and Saviour that were painted on the upper panels, and the gaudy flower-vases that decorated the lower.

"I shall send your courier to you for orders," said Waldemar, re-entering the room, "and I hope you may be able to make yourself tolerably comfortable for one night."

"I really do not know how to thank you for resigning your room in this generous manner," began Nora.

"Pray do not attempt it, or even think of it," said Waldemar, smiling, as he took up his hat and the little drawing-book that lay on the window-sill.

"I suppose, ma'am," said Nesbitt, after be had left them, "I suppose he has gone about a room for me now, ma'am?"

"Suppose no such thing," said Nora; "but consider yourself fortunate in getting from me this great feather-bed and a pillow on the floor!"

"Lor, ma'am, you don't mean that you will sleep on the paillasse?"

"Many will have to sleep on straw or hay to-night, Mrs Nesbitt," answered Nora: "do you think the thousands of people now in this village are likely to find beds?"

"P'raps not, ma'am, but peasants—"

"Peasants," said Nora, "are here accustomed to rooms and beds such as we now see. Every one must be satisfied with what he can get to-night, Nesbitt; and you had better now return to Miss Nixon, and make yourself useful, while I find out the people of the house and get acquainted with them."

She found the peasant's wife in the kitchen, preparing supper for her numerous expected and unexpected guests, and was received by her with the warmest expressions of hospitality, and many regrets that her room was not what such a young lady was accustomed to.

Nora assured her she considered herself very fortunate in being so well provided for; she had not expected it when she had seen the crowds on the road.

The peasant laughed, and observed that all the garrets,

lofts, and even barns would be filled with people through-out the whole neighbourhood; and how many would arrive in the morning it would be hard to say! She only hoped there would be places enough in the theatre, for, large as it was, it had already happened that some thousands had to be refused admittance, and the play performed over again for them the day after.

She said all this with such evident pride and satisfaction, that Nora continued the conversation, and soon discovered that there was no inconvenience to which the villagers would not submit cheerfully in order to accommodate strangers who came to see their "play," considering them guests whose presence would serve to increase the brilli-ancy and reputation of the great performance.

Here it may be observed, that no advantage whatever is taken on such occasions by the inhabitants of Ammergau to obtain profit of any kind; they barely allow themselves to be remunerated for actual outlay in the purchase of provi-sions, giving their houses and time willingly to all who re-quire their assistance.

While Nora still lingered in the kitchen, two young girls entered it, followed by the children of the house, joyously shouting, "The miller's Madeleine, and the forester's Rosel, from Almenau!"

This meant that they were the daughters of the miller and forester of that place, and therefore the greeting of the peasant's wife was listened to attentively by Nora.

It was hearty in the extreme—she shook their hands, laughed, patted their shoulders, and then turned the miller's remarkably pretty daughter round and round, declaring she did so to ascertain if she had grown taller since the morning.

The girl blushed and said, if she were not taller, she was certainly happier.

"And when is the wedding?"

"About Michaelmas. I wish Rosel's father would let her marry the Crags peasant's Seppel at the same time."

Rosel did not blush at all as she seconded this wish, adding that "there was little chance, as her father could not forget or forgive Seppel's having joined the other peasant lads in the year forty-eight, and taken advantage of the short time he was at home on leave to shoot the best herd of chamois in the whole district: he said then," she continued, "and says now, that he will never give anyone belonging to him to a—a—wild hunter!"

"Ah, bah!" cried the peasant's wife; "there was scarcely a lad in the village of Almenau, or anywhere else in the Highlands, that did not do the same in forty-eight, and no one thought the worse of them for doing what was allowed by law."

"That's true," said Rosel, "and I have often told him so; for, saving Seppel's brother Anderl, and the miller's man, black Seppel, they were all out more or less."

"No doubt of it, Rosel—and here, too, and everywhere in the land. But now that Crags Seppel has served his six years as cuirassier, and got a discharge that any man might be proud of, your father should overlook his having used his rifle too freely in former times, and let bygones be bygones."

"If it had not been for that unlucky chamois last year, perhaps he might," rejoined Rosel; "I mean the one that came over the mountain from Tyrol, and that father had watched and preserved for Count Waldemar. Game was so scarce just then, and mostly up high among the rocks. As ill-luck would have it, Seppel—"

"No, but he didn't though!" exclaimed the woman, evidently amazed at this instance of temerity.

"I was going to tell you," continued Rosel, "that Seppel just then had to see after the cattle on his father's Alp, and

unluckily took it into his head to go on to the fisherman's at
the Kerbstein lake, passing over the very ground that my
father cannot hear named without avowing vengeance on
all wild hunters. Well, and so he and the count hunted afterwards for two days and a night together without getting a
shot, and went over the mountains into Tyrol, but never
saw or heard more of the chamois."

The peasant's wife seemed to consider this conclusive,
and went on with her cooking.

"It appears to me," said Nora, "that they condemned
this Seppel on very slight evidence. Might not another have
been the offender? Was no one else absent from the village
at the same time?"

"No one but Seppel would have dared to do it," observed the peasant's wife, without looking up.

"Though he may be suspected, he ought not to be condemned without stronger proof," continued Nora.

"So I always say," observed Rosel in reply; "but my father declares that that buck was so old and wary, that no
one in the village but Seppel could have followed and
hunted him down. And you see," she continued—and Nora
fancied she detected a sort of suppressed exultation in the
voice of the bright-eyed girl—"you see Seppel never hunts
anything but chamois, and when he finds them high up on
the rocks, he thinks it no crime to take a shot, and—and—
he never misses, never!"

"That's true," chimed in the miller's daughter. "Every
one says Seppel ought to be made an under-keeper or
wood-ranger, or something of that sort, and then the forester would like him as much as he now dislikes him."

"His being an under-keeper would not be much gain for
Rosel," said the peasant's wife; "he might as well be a cuirassier for all the chance of marriage he would have. I
would rather hear that his old father was going to resign

house and land at the Crags to him, and that—"

Here a loud tapping at the window was heard, which made them all start and look round.

"Bless me!" exclaimed the peasant's wife, "if there isn't Seppel himself, on his way from Munich, and in his handsome uniform, to astonish us all! We greet you a thousand times," she added, springing to the window and throwing it open, while hands were extended, and then eagerly protruded through the iron bars; one of these he retained, giving it an occasional jerk, while he explained that a letter having informed him he should meet friends if he went to Ammergau, he had not required long to make up his mind to see them and the great play at the same time. All he now wanted was to find somebody who would give him shelter for the night.

"Shelter and a bundle of hay you can have, Sepp," laughed the peasant's wife; "I had nothing better to give my own sister's son Florian, when he was here last week."

"I suspect I can sleep better on hay than Florian," said Seppel. "He came to see the great play of course?"

"Yes, and brought his mother with him. It was long since we sisters had been together; but we knew we should see little more of each other when she married into Almenau, and we should hear nothing either if Florian had not taken after our family, and been, as I may say, born an artist. He alone keeps up the relationship now, by coming here so often for one thing or another. Last week he ordered some ornaments to be carved for St Hubert's chapel in the wood. He's been given the renovation of the altars there, and he says it will be a troublesome job, as the new parts must be made exactly to match the rest, which is very curious, and ever so many hundred years old. If you should go to Almenau, miss," she added, turning to Nora, "you ought to make a pilgrimage to St Hubert's."

"I shall certainly do so," answered Nora; "and if you have any message to your nephew Florian, I can be the bearer of it, as I intend to remain some time at Almenau."

"He lives at the end of the village with his mother, who has the shop there," said the peasant's wife, evidently pleased at Nora's willingness to visit her relations. "Any one can show you Meister Florian's studio, for he is quite an artist, and has been at the academy in Munich."

During the last few minutes some hurried whisperings had been going on at the window, which Nora did not consider it necessary to interrupt, or even appear to observe, so she walked out of the kitchen, and turned into the dwelling-room, where she found the peasant himself, finishing a most elaborate piece of carving—a goblet with figures in high relief and Gothic ornaments. He stopped working for a moment, to raise a small Greek cap that covered his bald head, pointed to a seat, and perceiving that she did not intend to interrupt him, continued his occupation, first nodding to a man who was sitting opposite to him, and then murmuring something about wishing to hear the end of the affair.

The person addressed was the elderly man to whom Waldemar had spoken before entering the house. His dress and manner, joined to his bearded sunburnt face, made Nora suppose him a forester or wood-ranger, and she was soon not only confirmed in this idea, but also convinced that he was to be the future father-in-law of the miller's daughter Madeleine.

"The end is soon told," he continued, playing with some carving tools that lay temptingly near his hands. "You may easily suppose that I expected a right good match for my son Franz, after having sent him to the foresters' academy, and secured him a chance of being before long set far above myself, for I have not the learning required for a forst-meister now-a-days. Well, back comes Franz to me as assistant-forester, by way of a beginning, and gets one of our best rooms, and writes, and studies, and is treated with that respect by my old woman, that you would suppose he had taken orders and was priest of the parish at least; all that was wanting was that she should say 'sir' to him. His sister Rosel made much of him too, and it was her friendship with the mountain miller's family, added to the nearness of the houses and long acquaintance, that brought about the match. Now, you see, money there must be on one side or the other. My son has education and good prospects, and the mountain miller's daughter will inherit the mill and a good fortune besides. Franz always had a fancy for Madeleine; but I did not choose to hear of it when he was last at home, for it was well known that the miller's affairs were in a ruinous condition, and so they continued until his mill was burnt down a few years ago. I dare say you heard when it happened, for there was a good deal of talk about it at the time."

"I remember," said the wood-carver, looking up for a moment, "I remember hearing that it was supposed the miller himself—"

"The miller had gone to his brother in Munich when the fire took place," said the forester, interrupting him hastily; "I ought to know all about it, living so near, you know. He came home the day after, and was in a state of distraction, such as I never saw—his brother had promised to help him out of his difficulties, and advance him money for better works, and a new water-course, so that he hoped to have begun a new life, as he said, over and over again. It was an awful sight to see him sitting moaning among the blackened ruins of the old mill, as if quite out of his mind, and indeed he has never been the same man since. We did all we could to console him, took his daughter to live with us until the house was rebuilt, and—"

"People here," observed the wood-carver, once more looking up, "people here said the insurance was high, far beyond the value of the mill."

"Well, it *was* high," replied the forester; "and so much the better for him; he required less assistance from his brother, rebuilt both house and mill, and since that time the world has prospered with him in every respect."

"If," said the wood-carver, putting down his work, "if he were not encumbered with that right-hand man of his— black Seppel, the Tyrolean!"

"I have advised him more than once to get rid of black Seppel," said the forester; "but he says he can't do without him; and the truth is, Seppel certainly does understand not only the management of the mill, but the ground about it, far better than the miller himself."

The peasant artist began to arrange his carving tools in a cupboard; Nora requested him to allow her to examine the goblet on which he had been working, and while she was doing so, he turned to the forester and said, "No doubt Seppel is a clever fellow; but they say he manages the miller as well as the mill, and through him both wife and daughter."

"I suppose Florian has told you all this," said the forester; "perhaps he also mentioned that the miller's brother, the locksmith in Munich, died not long ago, and has left him everything he possessed."

"Of course he told me that, and talked so much of Madeleine, that I suspected he had thoughts of becoming one of her suitors himself."

"Ah, poor Florian! little chance for him when my Franz was in the way. It was all settled between me and the miller this morning, and there is to be a betrothal when we get home."

"And what will black Seppel say?" persisted the wood-carver.

"What business is it of his?" asked the forester.

"Why, many suppose he had an eye on Madeleine himself, and he comes of respectable people, you know—the son of a miller in Tyrol, they say!"

"Yet he must be ill off at home," observed the forester, "or he would not remain so long in service. Men obliged to serve cannot think of marriage."

"Florian says that Seppel remains at the mill on account of Madeleine," rejoined the wood-carver, "and that he watches her better than either her father or mother. Last year at the church festival, when she only danced once round the room with Florian, up he came and reminded her quite sternly that she was not yet eighteen years of age, consequently a Sunday-school scholar, and not allowed to dance in public! and then he walked her off home, threatening a reprimand from the priest."

"I think my Franz will put an end to his interference in future," observed the forester, "and you'll come to the wedding, won't you?"

"I believe," answered the wood-carver, "my wife will be with her sister in Almenau about that time, and we can't well leave home together, not to mention the orders for work that I have lately received."

At this moment John entered the room, and hastily informed Nora that they were waiting dinner for her at the inn. Waldemar was with him, and advanced to look at the goblet still in her hands.

"I should like to purchase this," she said, turning to the wood-carver; "that is," she added, perceiving he hesitated, "that is, provided it be not already bespoken."

"Not just that," he answered "but—we are expected to send these things to the warehouse, where you can have the choice of all the carving in Ammergau."

"Am I to understand that you are not at liberty to sell me this?" said Nora.

"At liberty! O yes, of course; but I don't like to lose, or run the chance of losing, my certain sale at the warehouse for the small advantage of disposing of one or two articles privately."

"Are you well paid for work of this kind?" she asked.

"Well, I suppose so; it is slow gain at best, and I sometimes think that out-door labour, though harder, is healthier, and brings more surely abundance into one's house. Had I turned out a mere toy-maker, I might have given it up perhaps; but, having arrived at carving in this style," he added, looking approvingly at his goblet, "and made a name for myself as an artist, nothing would induce me to turn my hand to any other kind of work now."

"So the hope of fame asserts its rights even in this cottage," observed Nora in English, half to herself, half to John, who stood beside her, a perfect personification of impatience.

"Come, Norry, let's go to dinner," he answered; "I never was so hungry in all my life, and Georgy says she's quite exhausted."

As Nora followed him out of the room, Waldemar joined her, and said, "You smiled at our peasant artist's ambition, Mees Nixe, without knowing the full extent of his aspirations. He dares to hope that his goblet may be deemed worthy of a place at your Great Exhibition in London next year."

"Where it will undoubtedly be much admired," replied Nora; "but I fear the name of the artist is seldom asked, and soon forgotten."

"Perhaps so," rejoined Waldemar; "but it would be cruel to enlighten him on this subject."

"You need not fear my doing so," said Nora; "I shall soon forget his innocent ambition, but not so easily his remark, that out-of-door labour was not alone more healthy, but even more profitable than wood-carving, though of the very finest description."

"And he was right, Mees Nixe: the peasants here and in Grodner Valley in Tyrol are almost altogether manufacturers, and manufacturing districts are never so healthy and seldom so wealthy, in the best sense of the word, as agricultural."

"Many people," said Nora, "suppose that no other peasants but the Swiss and Tyroleans are wood-carvers, and most English travellers have very obscure notions of the boundaries between the Highlands of Bavaria and Tyrol."

"And in fact," said Waldemar, "the scenery is so similar, that if it were not for the Custom-houses, and the black and yellow painted bars and posts, a stranger could scarcely discover that he was in another land. You, however, who have evidently been long in Germany, must be aware of the great difference in the inhabitants."

"Of course I am," answered Nora; "the Tyroleans are a much handsomer, much poorer, and much more melancholy people than the Bavarians."

"Poor and melancholy!" repeated Waldemar. "It is time for me to tell you that I am a Tyrolean from the Valley of the Inn."

"Then you must be aware of the truth of my observation," continued Nora; "for though the inhabitants of your valley, from being on the high road to Innsbruck, may be better off than those of other parts of Tyrol, the contrast on entering Bavaria is too striking to be overseen by any but very unobservant travellers. I do not require to see your Custom-house, or painted boards, to know where I am. The first little inn on the roadside, with its room full of shouting, laughing, and singing peasants, would tell me that I had passed the frontiers, and entered the merry Highlands of Bavaria."

"They do shout and sing a good deal about here," said Waldemar.

"And they do *not* sing much in Tyrol," rejoined Nora, "excepting in the Zillar valley, known to us English people as the birthplace of the Reiner family,* who made themselves rich by singing their Alpine songs all over Europe."

"I am surprised to find that the habits and manners of the peasants can interest you so much," observed Waldemar.

"On the present occasion in an unusual degree," she answered. "I—that is, we—we are about to erect a monument in the churchyard at Almenau to the memory of a near relation who died there, and I have undertaken to find out a family worthy to be intrusted with the care of this grave."

"Ah, I understand. You intend to deposit a sum of money, the interest of which will be paid to the family for that purpose."

"Some such idea has occupied my mind lately," said Nora, as they stopped at the door of the inn; "so you may imagine that the inhabitants of Almenau interest me at present in no common degree."

She did not wait to hear his answer; for perceiving Torp approaching, she entered the inn, and soon afterwards found herself seated at the end of a long table beside her uncle and cousins in a room crowded with the most extraordinary mixture of all ranks of people.

* Singing group best remembered for having popularised the carol *Stille Nacht (Silent Night)*.

CHAPTER XVIII

A Remnant of the Middle Ages

As the evening drew to a close, the melodious bells of the village church pealed long and loudly. The arrivals of strangers became still more frequent, carriage followed carriage, until the street was almost blocked up, and the unwieldy omnibuses scarcely found place to discharge their muffled contents. Mr Nixon and his family had dined, and those around him supped, on precisely the same succession of viands at the crowded table d'hôte of the inn, when the report of cannon and the sound of distant music caused fresh, and, if possible, increased commotion in the room.

Some hurried to the windows, others rushed to the door, among the latter John, followed more leisurely by Nora. They reached the street in time to witness some violent efforts that were made to remove the various vehicles from their places, so as to open a passage for the procession of the Ammergau musicians, who were marching from one end of the long village to the other playing slow and solemn music, intended to remind the assembled multitude that the vigil of the great holiday had commenced. They played well, and created much sensation as they passed by, drawing all the inhabitants of the village to their doors or windows, arid most strangers fairly into the street.

John and Nora were soon separated; and the latter, finding herself in the neighbourhood of the forester's daughter, joined her, and partly to avoid the vicinity of some cattle returning late from pasture, partly to make inquiries about Almenau, she sauntered with her beyond the houses of the village, until she unexpectedly found herself at the one where she was to sleep that night: she might have passed it too without notice, had not the peasant who was seated before the door raised his little cap as she approached, and his wife smiled recognition. Nora's companion pointed to the miller and his wife, who, with the forester, were seated at the other side of the door, the robust frame and face of the latter forming a strong contrast to the emaciated figure and pallid features of the former. The eyes of all were following the steps of the newly-betrothed pair, who, having perhaps left them to join the musicians, now lingered on the road together, unconscious alike of these looks of pride and affection, and the arch smiles and jocose nudges and winks passing among the homeward-bound peasants who hurried along the road.

There was something about the young assistant forester that immediately prepossessed Nora in his favour. The strongly-built muscular figure accorded well with the dark-complexioned and profusely-bearded face, while both contributed to render conspicuous the mild, almost pensive expression of his clear hazel eyes. He was dressed in a loose grey shooting jacket, green waistcoat, and shorts of black chamois leather; his knees were bare, and he wore grey worsted leggings, with fanciful green clocks, that reached but did not cover the ankles, while his feet rested, uncovered by socks, in heavy nailed shoes, seemingly formed to defy all weather and roads: his shirt was scarcely held together by the light black kerchief that served as cravat, and left exposed a large portion of a broad brown chest shining like polished wood. His green felt hat, with its tuft of black-cock feathers, was in the hands of Madeleine, and he smiled while watching her decorating it still more with a gay bouquet of wild flowers. Rosel introduced him to Nora by proudly exclaiming, "This is my brother Franz!" and had his dress led to the expectation of a peasant's greeting, Nora was immediately reminded that education had made him a gentleman. Nothing could be more easy and unembarrassed than his manner, and Rosel's bright intelligent eyes watched eagerly the impression he was making on the English lady, who seemed to speak to him quite as if he were Count Waldemar himself.

Nora had while speaking moved towards the house, and then sat with the peasants and their guests until they retired to the sitting-room, when having been joined by Mrs Nesbitt, and received a tall slim candle, she mounted the steep staircase conducting to her room, and went to bed.

The weather was sultry—Nora's room was over the kitchen, where the peasant's wife, "on hospitable thoughts intent," had cooked the live-long day. The pillows and plumeau, well aired on sunny balcony, rose like mountains on each side of her: they seemed to glow, and though want of rest on the previous night made her painfully sleepy, the heat at length became so intolerable that she sprang from her bed, and threw wide open the little lattice window, actually gasping for breath as she leaned out of it. The sound of voices in the orchard beneath made her shrink back again, but the moon had not yet risen, and the night was still so dark that she need not have bound up so carefully her long hair, dishevelled by the recent tossings on downy pillows, or drawn her dressing-gown so very closely round her, as she once more approached the source of fresh air. A slight odour of tobacco was wafted towards her with the words, "Well, I don't deny that she is pretty and interesting, and that her figure is slight and graceful, but you must allow me to doubt her being so very youthful as you seem to suppose."

"I don't care what her age may be," answered a voice that Nora knew to be Waldemar's; "she's very charming, and I shall take advantage of the first convenient opportunity to tell her that I think so."

"Better not," replied Torp; "for although I have been too seldom in England, during the last ten years, to know much about the pecuniary affairs of these people, I can, at least, tell you that a lot of sons being in the family will prevent this new object of your adoration from having a sufficiently large fortune to induce your father to overlook her want of pedigree. I happened once, by a singular chance, to have an interest in ascertaining that the lineage of these Nixons loses itself mysteriously in the obscurity of that part of the city of London where fogs are thickest and days are shortest."

"What matter?" cried Waldemar, laughing; "that need not prevent me from admiring her to any reasonable extent. I was not so serious as you supposed, notwithstanding my somewhat strong expressions of commendation just now, and merely meditate lending her my heart for a week or two while we are at Almenau, nothing more, I assure you."

"I wish," said Torp, "you would be rational, and do what would be infinitely pleasanter for me than being thrown among these people, and that is, go at once from hence to the Valley of the Inn; your father expects us at Herrenburg, and when these English people have left Almenau there will still be time enough for us to have a few weeks' sport before the end of the season."

"Very likely," answered Waldemar; "but by that time Irene Schaumberg will be with us, and I shall not be able to leave home."

"What! Do you expect the widowed countess with

daughters and dogs from the banks of the Danube?"

"Yes. She comes ostensibly to be present at my brother Carl's marriage, which takes place some time next month; he has been engaged these three years to Lotta Falkner, of St Benedict's."

Nora, who had withdrawn from the window, unwilling to overhear this conversation, found that unless she closed the casement every word distinctly reached her ear in the profound silence of the night. That they had been speaking of her she more than suspected; but she thought not of them or herself either just then, so completely had her interest been absorbed by the name of Irene Schaumberg and the few words following. Back, back, back she went to her earliest recollections, and the ground-floor of a large house in Vienna was her home. In the *bel étage* Count Schaumberg lived, and he had sons—rude boys of whom she was much afraid; they ran after her when she played in the court, chased her up and down the stairs, and one day fairly carried her struggling into their father's apartments, where, pushing her towards a springing laughing little girl of her own age, they exclaimed—"There, Irene, there she is for you; don't let her go, or she'll be off again like an arrow." But when Irene had whispered, "Oh, come and play with me, mamma says we may!" she had gone willingly enough to the drawing-room, and from that time forward they had become constant companions. Irene's parents had probably found the little English girl a desirable playmate for their daughter, and were kind and attentive to her in consequence, while Mr Nixon and his wife had encouraged an intimacy that procured them much pleasant society. Though often, at a later period, separated for long intervals, the regard of the young girls had suffered no diminution; and about a year before Nora had left Germany she had spent some time with the Schaumbergs, and, as a parting service, had officiated as bridesmaid when Irene had married her cousin, the chief of another branch of their family. A correspondence of the most unreserved description had, in the course of time, slowly worn itself out. The brilliant and fashionable inmate of one of the gayest houses in Vienna could have but little in common with the solitary girl whose days were passed in reading, and the contemplation of the dingy vegetation of Russell-square. It gave Nora, however, sincere pleasure to hear that she should soon be so near the person who had supplied the place of sister to her; but her wish to remain unknown to Torp as long as possible made her resolve to defer her inquiries about her friend for some time. While these thoughts passed through her mind, she closed the window in a manner to attract attention, and so effectually that, on opening it again soon afterwards, the speakers had left the orchard, and on the road near the house she thought she perceived two figures sauntering slowly towards the banks of the Ammer.

The drums of the Ammergau musicians proclaimed the break of day. At a very early hour the next morning they beat a reveille through the whole village, which, with the sound of church bells, entering Nora's room through the still open casement, wakened her and her companion most effectually, and about the time she had completed her toilet the band commenced playing in a manner to draw her irresistibly towards the window. As she stretched out her head in eager attention, two other heads from neighbouring windows were protruded also, for the same purpose no doubt, but while one determinately looked away, the other turned towards her to wish a cheerful "good morning," and to hope she had slept well.

"Thank you—quite well. Is the representation about to begin?"

"Not yet. But you ought to see the church and hear high

mass: every one in the village who can sing will assist, and the performers in the drama consider it a duty to begin the day with Divine service."

At this moment the peasant's wife appeared at the door, and told Nora that she would find her breakfast and her brother in the room below.

Waldemar heard, and smilingly observed that brothers were not often so punctual, and he had rather begun to hope she would have required him as cicerone.

Early as it still was when John and Nora had breakfasted, they found the village streets crowded to excess, and hundreds of people already on their way to the theatre to secure places. John persuaded Nora to go there also, assuring her that from day-break the arrival of spectators had been incessant, and that no theatre could possibly contain them all.

Perhaps he was right—at all events figures in Oriental dresses and draperies began to flit about the village; groups of children assembled before the houses to have their costumes inspected; but the report of a cannon from the precincts of the theatre made all turn in that direction; and in the midst of a rather motley multitude, Nora and John found their way to the large inclosure formed by wooden planks, and alone remarkable for its enormous circumference.

A short flight of steps brought them into one of the boxes that were erected behind, and a little above the space that descended amphitheatrically to the orchestra, which contained seats for six thousand persons. The stage was of sufficient extent to suit this theatre, and the great drama about to be performed on it. There was a proscenium of considerable depth, and beyond it a closed theatre of smaller dimensions, for the representation of interior scenes and tableaux from the Old Testament: and this thea-

tre within a theatre had at each side a building, with balconies, joined by arches to the side-scenes of the proscenium.
Through these arches two long streets of Jerusalem were
constantly visible; and when the middle theatre was closed
by its curtain, representing also a street in perspective, the
whole formed a view of the city of Jerusalem.

Crowds of people soon began to pour in at all the en-
trances; and the various costumes of the different parts of
Tyrol and Bavaria found numerous representatives, in the
brightest and freshest colours. John found time to become
an enthusiastic admirer of the black bodices and fantastic
head-dresses of the women; while some vague ideas entered
his mind of procuring for himself one of those loose jackets and picturesque hats, that seemed to make "the commonest fellows," as he expressed it to Nora, "look something like!" She paid little attention to his remarks, being at
first too much occupied with the construction of the stage,
and afterwards with the demeanour of the audience, as they
defiled slowly between the benches, and reverentially took
their places, as if in a church—even their greetings to each
other were subdued; the men exchanged silent nods, the
women whispered gravely, while spreading out their text-
books, and seemed wholly occupied with the great drama
about to be enacted.

It was curious that, on observing all this, Nora's doubts
and scruples about the propriety of witnessing the representation returned in full force, and that she turned towards
Torp, who, with Waldemar, had taken a place in the adjacent box, to see if he shared her uneasiness. Leaning forward, with an elbow placed on his crossed knees, his chin
resting on his hand, he gazed at the landscape beyond the
theatre, with a calm earnestness that might perhaps have
reassured a less careful observer; but Nora would just then
have preferred seeing him watching the progress of Wal-

demar's rapid sketch of the classical stage with its proscenium, or interested in the groups of picturesque peasants
standing immediately below him.

To Waldemar she would not speak: how could a Tyrolean, accustomed from infancy to see his Saviour represented in every possible way, pictorial and sculptural, understand the fear of profanation with which a living representative inspired her? She herself believed she could, ten
years previously, have taken her place among the spectators, with feelings of more curiosity and interest than uneasiness and awe. Familiar then with pictures and images of
the crucified Redeemer, not only in churches and chapels,
on the high-road, and beside the scarcely-trodden wood-
land path, but in every cottage, in every house, almost in
every dwelling-room, while lithographs of the same mild
face might be shaken from among the leaves of most books
of prayer, she would have found far less to shock her in the
representation that now filled her mind with anxiety and
dismay. She recalled to her memory every argument that
could tend to reassure her,—it would be but a succession
of living pictures; she had heard they were eminently well
arranged; the performers were simple religious peasants, full
of enthusiasm, deeply impressed with the necessity of
fulfilling a solemn vow,[*] and with intentions and objects as
pure as could be found on earth.

As the echo of the last cannon was lost in the surrounding hills, the overture commenced. Soon after the chorus

---

[*] In the year 1633, when the village was visited by a devastating and
contagious disorder, the monks of Ettal induced the parish to make a
vow, "That in thankful devotion, and for edifying contemplation, they
would, every ten years, publicly represent the Passion of Jesus, the Saviour of the world." Whereupon the parish that had made the vow was
immediately freed from the pestilence.   —JvT

filled the proscenium, and all Nora's remaining scruples were absorbed in the most intense interest. The stage arrangements possessed all the charm of novelty to her; and, with the assistance of a text-book, she easily followed the leaders of the chorus, as, generally singing, but occasionally reciting, they explained the tableaux represented on the inclosed and smaller stage, or prepared the audience for the next act of the drama, while exhorting them to devotion and repentance.

And this chorus, so fantastically dressed in white tunics, coloured sandals, girdles, and mantles, with crown-like plumed head-dresses, soon became so familiar, as not in the least to detract from the reality given to all else by the bright daylight, the summer sky with its passing clouds, and the pasture-land, hills, and woods, seen beyond the streets and above the houses of Jerusalem.

It would be difficult to describe Nora's feelings as the representative of Jesus appeared on the scene; but so completely did the person and manner of the artist performer satisfy her high-wrought expectations, that dissatisfaction or disappointment was certainly not among them. She perceived instantly that what was then before her would take the place of all the pictures and statues she had ever seen, and remain indelibly impressed on her mind for ever. It was, therefore, this one deeply interesting figure, with the pale face, finely chiselled features, and parted waving hair which has become typical, that she followed with breathless interest and anxiety throughout, and never did the eminence of the character of Christ strike her so forcibly, or the worthlessness of mankind, and the ignoble motives that are the springs of their actions become so glaringly apparent as on this occasion. The monologues of the principal actors, showing the current of their thoughts without reserve, made each as it were a psychological study, yet so simple and forcible, as to be within the comprehension of the most illiterate among the audience. The sending of Jesus from one tribunal to another, the wish of those who knew his innocence to avoid the responsibility of his martyrdom, yet determination that he should suffer, his being forsaken by every friend at the moment of danger; in short, all that habit enables us to read and hear read almost unmoved, and as a matter of history, was brought before Nora with a force so perfectly irresistible, that, various and eloquent as had often been the sermons she had heard, excellent and celebrated as were the pictures she had seen, never had she been moved as on the present occasion. A sceptic might perhaps have followed the representation with criticising curiosity, a less imaginative mind with calm self-possession: Nora forgot herself, time, place, spectators, everything, and saw, heard, and felt, with a vividness that at length completely overwhelmed her. As the crucifixion was completed a shudder of horror passed through her whole frame, a sensation of extreme cold seemed to chill her blood, and after some ineffectual efforts to control, at least outwardly, her emotion, she bent down her head and covered her face with her hands, remaining motionless until roused by a whisper from Waldemar. "Mademoiselle," he said, "allow me to advise you to leave the theatre now; another scene might weaken an impression well worth preserving in all its strength."

Nora rose, looked back for a moment, saw the commencement of the removal from the cross, and soon after found herself outside the wooden building with Waldemar and John, both more tranquil than she had yet seen them, as they walked slowly beside her towards the silent and deserted village.

The pause at the end of the first four hours of the performance had been that day unusually short, in consequence of a threatening thunder-storm, which, however, had greatly heightened the effect of the latter part of the drama, by the gloom cast on the scene from the darkening clouds and the incessant rolling of distant thunder. A favourable wind seemed now about to waft the storm away from Ammergau, and leave the evening sky clear and cloudless.

Followed by Torp at a distance, which his curiosity to hear what they were saying induced him by degrees to lessen, Waldemar and Nora reached the cottage, which they had left much about the same time in the morning. The door was open, and Nora entered, turning into the little sitting-room, while Waldemar, instead of following, remained outside, and leaning on the window-sill looked into the room, apparently continuing their conversation when he observed, "So you have no curiosity—no wish—to see Pflunger? Not even when I can assure you that you will not be at all disappointed by a nearer acquaintance with him? His resemblance to the pictures of our Saviour does not lose in the least by close observation, and there is even something in his manner which accords perfectly with all our preconceived ideas. Let me delay my departure for an hour, and take you to his house."

"No, thank you," said Nora, quickly, "not for any consideration would I see him in another dress. I intend to forget that he exists otherwise than as he appeared to me this day. Not even ten years hence would I desire to witness this great drama again; he will then most probably have lost in appearance some of his present eminent advantages, and I wish to preserve the impression made on me to-day as pure as may be, and as long as possible."

Waldemar seemed to consider this conclusive: he raised his hat without speaking another word, and followed the evidently impatient Torp, who, having caught a glimpse of

John advancing to meet him, had begun to stride towards the village in a more resolute than civil manner.

CHAPTER XIX

Almenau

NORA was perfectly sincere in what she had said to Waldemar; for, much as the artist peasants of Ammergau had interested her, she was so unwilling to weaken the impression of what she had just witnessed by a personal acquaintance with any of the actors of the drama, that she used all her influence to induce her uncle to leave the village without delay. Her account of the classical arrangements of the theatre, its immense dimensions, the hundreds of actors and thousands of spectators, joined to a performance that had lasted eight hours without producing a moment's lassitude, made Georgina half regret her absence; but Mr Nixon continued to condemn, in terms of the strongest censure, what he called "the whole concern;" he would not listen to any explanations, and on reference being made to pictures and statues, declared equally strongly his objections to either in churches, never failing, during their journey of the succeeding days, to express his serious disapprobation of every shrine of the Madonna, or way-side crucifix, that they passed. The wax and wooden images, which abounded in the small inns where they stopped to dine or sleep, he pronounced an abomination, treating with contempt Nora's quotation from Goethe, that they served perhaps occasionally to recall wide-wandering thoughts, and turn them into a higher and better channel.

Travelling for the first time in his life, and strongly imbued with every description of English prejudice, Mr Nixon found much to surprise, still more to condemn, in all he saw; but Nora perceived, with secret satisfaction, that the scenery was beginning to make an impression on him that she had scarcely ventured to expect. He first "allowed" that the country itself was "well enough," then he admitted that the woods were very extensive, and the mountains high and picturesque, and ended by acknowledging that the scenery was grand, very grand. "But he had always known that Tyrol abounded in mountains; on the map it was quite black with them."

"This is not Tyrol!" exclaimed Nora, for the hundredth time; "we are in the Bavarian Highlands."

"Well, well," he answered testily, "it's all the same, you know, to us; but having seen this sort of thing, I'm glad to think that we too have highlands—very. Nora, you're very clever, but you'll not be able to show me anything here that we have not at home—and better."

"Woods and forests, for instance!" said Nora, laughing; "however, as my knowledge of England is chiefly derived from books, and yours of Germany from maps, we had better not attempt a discussion."

What resemblance to England there might be in the beautiful country through which they were travelling, Nora knew not, and could therefore make no mental comparison. She gazed with profound admiration at the vast extent of forest that covered long ranges of mountains; for Almenau was essentially a forest district, and the road as it approached the village, formed in the side of a mountain, presented a wall of blasted stone on one hand, while, on the other, a wooded precipice descended to a foaming torrent that forced its way boisterously through, and over masses of rock. Innumerable alpine plants still flowered luxuriantly wherever the dark heath-mould could find a resting-place, and nothing as yet marked the approach towards autumn.

The windings of the road brought various changes: sometimes an opening showed the rocky-pointed or rugged summits of the mountains, that had appeared far distant but a few hours before, now quite close to them; at others, inclosed in wood, an occasional glade gave an opportunity of admiring the foliage of the beech, birch, and maple, that seemed to have replaced the pine in every sheltered nook. On reaching the top of a long ascent, where on a guidepost the words "Drag-chain, or fine," were printed in large letters, beneath a sketch of something greatly resembling a ploughshare, the postilions having descended and commenced a clattering with chains beneath the carriage, totally indifferent to the courier's entreaties, in broken German, that they would not injure the wheels, Nora learned, between their mutterings about the monstrous weight and proportions of the carriage, that the journey was drawing to a close, and that the next village was Almenau.

Directly before her lay a valley with a river winding through it, and bounded on each side by wooded mountains, beyond which she saw still higher with summits of stone, and still further distant than these last, others partially covered with snow. A tall pointed church steeple formed the middle of the view, denoting the site of the village, and on reaching that part of the road which partially followed the course of the river, some isolated cottages already formed a sort of suburb to it.

"Well now—aw—really—all this—is very pretty," observed Mr Nixon.

"Whose place is that?" asked Georgina, with more than usual animation, as she caught a glimpse of a large building close beside a small but picturesque lake, on the calm waters of which the golden-coloured clouds were distinctly reflected.

"It's the brewery," said the postilion, on being questioned, and Nora, as usual, interpreted.

"But there is a church with Gothic windows and a belfry."

"He says it was a monastery in former times," explained Nora.

"I declare I should not at all dislike living there," continued Georgina. "What beautiful trees! and those little promontories running into the lake make it so pretty! I wonder is there a good neighbourhood here?"

"In that case, perhaps, you would marry the brewer?" suggested John.

Georgina threw back her head, and smiled disdainfully.

"If this place, or anything similar, is to be sold," said Nora, "I shall be tempted to purchase it, and remain here for the rest of my life."

"You are not serious, Nora?" asked Mr Nixon, gravely.

"Perfectly, I assure you," she answered; "but I shall not be in a hurry, for I might perhaps prefer that ruined castle on the hill. You, who understand so perfectly the state of my affairs, will be able to tell me if I can afford to rebuild as well as purchase it."

"I should rather have expected to hear you talk in this way ten years ago," began Mr Nixon, seriously; "but after having resided so long in England—"

"So long in Russell-square, you mean," said Nora, interrupting him, laughingly; "I know nothing of England—but a great deal about such places as this; and even if I return to London with you, I am afraid you will never be able to persuade me to remain long there."

"I perceive that you will marry a foreigner, and desert us altogether, Nora."

"Let me assure you that I have no thought of marriage

at present, though a very strong desire to have a home of my own somewhere or other. By that lake, for instance, or on that hill, in the valley of the Inn, or—or—anywhere, provided I can look at such mountains as these, and feel young again! What wonderful castles in the air I used to build in such places, with my mother, when I was a child! I wish," she added with a sigh, "I wish she were now alive, and able to join me in the more solid kind of architecture in which I may soon be tempted to indulge."

The road had turned from the river, the valley widened perceptibly, the houses, with their long, fancifully painted wooden balconies, and their overhanging shingle-covered roofs, secured from the ravages of storm by large stones placed at irregular distances upon them, seemed to draw closer to each other, until they were at length merely separated by their respective orchards, or a clump of old trees; yet so little appearance of what might be called a street was visible, that they were all a good deal surprised when the carriage drew up before a house perfectly similar to the others in form, though on a much larger scale. It was the inn, and presented a large gable with double balconies to the road; looked very freshly whitewashed, very spacious, and very clean; and a very stout landlady, with a good-humoured face and rosy cheeks, advanced towards them, while the ostler in his linen apron, red waistcoat, black velveteen jacket, and tasselled cap, busied himself about the horses.

The necessary questions about rooms were asked; and Georgina was not a little astonished when informed that she could not have the number she required, and that there was not a single private sitting-room in the whole house. Nora explained in vain that there was a parlour little used by strangers during the day, and that people passed their time chiefly in the open air in summer; and she pointed across the road to a grass garden where, under the shade of luxuriant chestnut and lime trees, tables and benches of every size were arranged, while a long, many-windowed wooden building, equally well furnished, had been erected in continuation of an inclosure for the favourite game of skittles.

Georgina shook her head, and murmured something about the impossibility of existing without a drawing-room; but she descended from the carriage and followed Nora into the house. At one side of the broad passage where they entered there was the parlour mentioned by Nora, containing tables covered with green oil-cloth, glazed cupboards filled with china and silver, a row of pegs for the hanging up of hats on the wall, numerous portraits of the royal family in black frames, and—a guitar. On the other side a wide open door permitted a full view of the capacious peasants' room, where at some of the numerous deal tables about fifteen or twenty men were drinking their evening tankard of beer, and at intervals singing loudly in chorus. Here John remained, while the others ascended the broad staircase, preceded by the landlady jingling a monstrous bunch of keys. She passed by the rooms on the first floor, observing to Nora that they had been engaged some days previously by Count Waldemar Benndorff and his friend Milor Torp.

These last words Georgina understood; and Torp himself had not been more amused when he heard of Milor Nixon than she now was. "I think," she said, laughing, "I think, Nora, we must give him strawberry leaves, and call him the Marquis of Carabbas[*]—he really seems to be everywhere."

---

[*] The Marquis de Carabas, the title invented for his master by the cat in the tale "Puss in Boots" ("Le Maistre Chat, ou le Chat Botté"), published by Charles Perrault (1628-1703) in his collection *Contes de Ma Mère l'Oye* (*Mother Goose Tales*) (1697), in order to impress the king.

The landlady, proud of her house and its capacious corridors, could not resist the temptation to show her ball-room and its adjoining apartments to the strangers, and Georgina would willingly have taken one of the latter for a drawing-room, notwithstanding its bare walls and want of proper furniture, had she not been informed that these rooms were required for weddings and other festivities, and that the church consecration fête was to be celebrated in them before long. Nora, who interpreted, added, "I shall resign whatever room I may get to you to-morrow, Georgina, as I have been offered a lodging at the forester's house, which is close by, and will be a much quieter place than the inn; and now let us lose no more time, for I wish to go to the churchyard before it is dark."

On a well-chosen prominent spot in the midst of the village stood the large massively built church, with its high, pointed, green steeple. An ascent of several stone steps, and a wooden gate, led to it and the churchyard, which was inclosed by a low wall, and appeared tolerably full of monuments both in stone and iron. The wish to be remembered, talked of, and thought of after death, seems much stronger in Germany than in England, and manifests itself in the churchyard of the most insignificant hamlets. Not only the innkeeper, smith, miller, and other leading families of the villages, have their burying-places furnished with handsome monuments, in or near the walls of the church, but every peasant in the neighbourhood who makes any pretension to being well off, possesses likewise his burying-ground, more or less furnished with ornament, and all carefully tended by the survivors. The most common monument is in the form of a cross, frequently of iron, painted, varnished, and gilt; on a plate of copper, in the centre of the cross, one often sees, painted in oil, a miniature full-length portrait of the peasant whose body is mouldering beneath the turf; the

figure generally kneeling with clasped hands, gazing upwards at a Madonna or an ascending figure of the Saviour.
If the village painter be skilful, or chance sends a wandering
artist to the neighbourhood who will undertake such work,
the whole peasant family appear kneeling side by side—no
great demand for striking resemblance in the portraits being
made on such occasions, or any artistical arrangement considered necessary. The dead and living take the places assigned them by custom—father and mother generally
somewhat apart, their offspring before them placed according to size, like organ pipes; and sometimes as background
a rather incongruous pillar and red curtain, which latter,
being draped aside, discloses a view of the village, with its
church and surrounding mountains. English eyes resting on
such a picture would scarcely be able to discover that those
represented with hands clasping a crucifix were deceased,
the other members of the family alive, at least, at the time
the picture in question was painted.

The churchyard at Almenau possessed many such pictures; they were not new to Nora, yet she lingered beside
them—read the long epitaph of the maiden, Marie Maier,
rich in virtue and honour—stooped to decipher the name
of the infant represented being borne in swaddling-clothes
on the arms of a bright-winged angel to heaven—and even
glanced at the unusually numerous triangles in which an eye
of large dimensions was used as an emblem of the Supreme
Being, until the eyes, many of which were newly and well
painted, seemed to turn and watch her as she at length
moved slowly towards the grave she had travelled so far to
visit. It was, as had been described to her, somewhat apart
from the others; and on a black wooden tablet, a couple of
feet above the surface of the ground, and already partially
hid by the long rank grass that grew wildly around it, she
read the name of Arthur Nixon, and the date of his demise.

Having pulled up by the roots some offensively luxuriant weeds, she held them unconsciously in her hand, while
memory brought Arthur before her, with all his worldly
ambition, his self-made cares and sorrows, disappointments
and early death. The end of all a few feet of earth—not
more than was accorded to the poorest peasant in Almenau! Yet he had chosen well when he had desired to rest
in that peaceful churchyard; for a more lovely spot could
scarcely be imagined. Slight as was the elevation, it sufficed
to render visible the course of the river, and to give a view
into an adjacent valley, the mountains of which formed distances that would have delighted a painter, while through
an opening in them the setting sun cast a long bright parting ray of light on the village and its old church, lingering
on Arthur's grave, as Nora observed, with a sort of fanciful
superstitious pleasure, for some time after shade had fallen
on the others.

At length the sun disappeared, but the summits of the
mountains continued to glow in fiery light, changing imperceptibly in colour, and apparently reflecting on their rocky
heights the gorgeous hues of the evening sky, where red
deepened into crimson, with which the darkening blue of
the sky mixed, producing various shades of violet that in
their turn were lost in the neutral tint of night. Before this
last change, Nora had felt the light evening breeze that in
fine weather invariably blows from the mountains to the
plain, heard the rustling of leaves in the not distant wood,
saw groups of labourers returning from their work, and was
slowly roused from the meditations suggested by the place
in which she stood, and the magnificent scenery around it,
by the approach of a noisy party of peasants, who, with
some sunburnt merry girls, passed through the churchyard
on their way home. The laughter ceased, and the loud
voices were hushed, when they entered the hallowed place;

while some walked gravely on, others dispersed to visit the graves that were the object of their constant pious care. One strongly-built healthy-looking girl drew near the place where Nora stood—on her arm a wreath of fresh ivy, and in her hand a bunch of bright blue cornflowers bound together by the stalk of a still green ear of wheat. For a few seconds she stood with downcast eyes and moving lips beside an iron cross, and then prepared to decorate it. The cornflowers had already found a place in the little receptacle for water, and the wreath of ivy was being raised in both hands, when her eyes fell on Nora; and in a moment she guessed that she was the person who was expected to visit the grave of the Englishman. Moved either by Nora's dejected countenance, or a feeling of regret that the stranger's grave should be found in a condition of such obvious neglect, the girl advanced awkwardly, and after a moment's hesitation shyly placed the ivy wreath, so as to form a frame to the space containing Arthur's name and the date of his death.

"Thank you," said Nora, warmly; "I am very much obliged to you; for I have just been regretting that there was no one here to decorate this grave with a few flowers occasionally. It must in future be better cared for than during the year that is past."

"I think it may be something more than a year since he was buried here," said the girl, using her reaping-hook to remove the long grass from the grave. "They say the first thing he did, the evening he came to the village, was to walk to the churchyard here and admire the view from it; and when he was taken ill next day, and there was no hope of his getting better, he said they must bury him at this side near the wall, and that there was *one* who he knew would come to see his grave and have it taken care of, and that's you, of course."

Nora bent her head. Arthur had evidently attached great importance to the performance of her promise—perhaps he had stood where she was then standing, and thought of her. Large tears gathered in her eyes, and, falling on the mound before her, she unconsciously fulfilled his last request as completely as he could have desired.

When she looked up she was alone; but she heard the sound of joyous voices and children's laughter from the nearest houses, mixed with the distant bark of dogs and the tinkling bells of cattle driven out to graze in the woods.

Nora was certainly not a strong-minded woman, for she left the churchyard rejoicing that Arthur's grave was within the reach of all these cheerful sounds.

CHAPTER XX

Saint Benedict's and its Inhabitants

EORGINA was made happy the next day by Nora's resignation of her apartment, which was immediately converted into a sitting-room. Its large dimensions and fine windows made it appear but scantily furnished when divested of everything but its hard sofa, six chairs, round table, and looking-glass between the windows, placed so high that it nearly touched the ceiling, where it slanted forwards in a manner to render it just possible to obtain a glimpse into it from some distant parts of the room. In vain had Nora pleaded the cause of a massive chest of drawers with brass ornaments, and a glass cupboard filled with all that was most precious in the house of gilt china and silver spoons. Georgina wondered how she could think of having such things in a drawing-room.

"But," suggested Nora, "you could put your books on the drawers, and your worsted-work into them."

"I rather expect," said Georgina, "that our landlady will find me some furniture when she sees the room so completely destitute of every comfort."

Nora shook her head. "You had better ask at once for a few tables and benches from the ball-room," she said, smiling; "for if you will not dine in the garden or the parlour, like other people, this one table, though large, will scarcely answer for working and writing, breakfasting, dining, and—"

"I see, I see!" cried Georgina. "Yes, we must have in the deal tables; they will be very ugly, but very convenient; and as we are not likely to have any visitors, it is of little importance of what wood they are made. I hope *you* have got a comfortable room at the forester's. Had you no difficulty in making your arrangements with the family?"

"None whatever. They have a spare room, and even proposed my breakfasting in the garden, where there is an arbour, or on the balcony. The temptation is strong; it would so remind me of old times."

"Oh, Nora, this will never do! If you do not come here every morning, papa will be angry with me, and say it is because I have turned you out of your room."

"I intend to come here every day to luncheon," said Nora; "but in case of rain, it may suit me to remain at the forester's in the morning. Besides, I shall probably sometimes be absent, as I intend to make excursions to all the lakes, waterfalls, and alps in the neighbourhood, and hope to induce you to join me in most of them; though, as you have never lived in a country like this, you can form no idea of the longing that I feel to be again in such places."

No answer was made; for the attention of both, as they leaned together out of the window, was just then attracted by a light carriage, or rather cart, that drove rapidly up to the inn door. There was a sort of cabriolet seat in front, and a peasant driver was perched on its foot-board, his feet hanging in trustful proximity to the hind legs of a horse that seemed to have been taken from the plough or some such agricultural occupation, and forced into the service of a couple of hunters, in whom, notwithstanding their change of costume, it was easy to recognise Torp and Waldemar.

"I wonder who, or rather what, that man is!" exclaimed Georgina, as Torp sprang to the ground, accoutred in English shooting habiliments, of unimpeachable correctness.

"I think his companion infinitely more interesting," said Nora; "he is just now one of the most picturesque-looking men I have seen for a long time."

"You mean the artist? Well, I confess he does look handsome and even gentlemanlike, though he is dressed completely like a peasant."

"Rather like a forester or hunter," said Nora.

"But," continued Georgina, "I have seen several peasants pass the inn this morning with precisely such grey jackets as his, and you see he has a green hat and naked knees, and nailed shoes, and even a leather belt with letters upon it!"

"The baldric or broad belt was formerly worn as a distinguishing badge by persons of high station," observed Nora, smiling. "Suppose, now, he were a prince in disguise—"

"Nonsense, Nora."

"Or a nobleman of high degree," persisted Nora, laughingly; "let me, at all events, advise you not to judge too rashly of the station of men in a dress such as he now wears, while you are in the Bavarian highlands;—it is popular in the mountains here, and I have seen odd mistakes made from too hastily-drawn conclusions."

The innkeeper, his wife, a couple of waitresses with black bodices, into which silver spoons were thrust as badges of office, and some labourers about to return to their work, now gathered round the carriage, and began to peep, one after the other, underneath a cloth of green baize spread over something that was laid in the cart-like back of the vehicle, and which from its uneven surface excited their curiosity in no common degree. Waldemar threw aside the cloth and disclosed a large roebuck and a chamois: the graceful head of the latter he raised, and pointing to a scarcely perceptible wound in it, observed, with a commendatory nod to Torp, "Not a bad shot for an Englishman!"

Now Torp was in all probability exceedingly pleased, but Englishmen generally think it dignified to conceal their feelings, or moderate the expression of them, so, with the imperturbability of a North American Indian, he turned away while Waldemar good-humouredly expatiated on the difficulties they had encountered, and the excellence of the shot, to John Nixon and his father, who had left the garden to join them, dwelling especially on the fact that the chamois had been brought down by a rifle, and at a distance of at least a hundred and fifty paces!

Mr Nixon, to whom this last remark sounded rather ambiguous, inasmuch as he had never in the course of his life had a rifle in his hand, perceived, nevertheless, that surprise and admiration on his part were expected, and therefore murmured some of those ejaculations in which the English language abounds.

"Aw—ah—exactly! Well—really now! Ah—to be sure —aw—capital—hem—famous!"

John wished for further information; but, unwilling to be overheard by Torp, moved quite close to Waldemar, and leaning on the back of the cart, pretended to examine the chamois, while he observed in a low voice, "Well, now, I should have thought it was pretty much the same thing whether rifle or fowling-piece were used."

"By no means," said Waldemar; "there is a great difference between one shot and another. Surely you would rather hit and kill with a bullet, like a good marksman, than perhaps make an ugly wound or mangle with a discharge of shot, and—"

"Oh, I see, I understand," cried John; "I am not a bad shot at a target, or—pigeons, and am sure I should enjoy this deer-stalking amazingly; it must be capital sport in such a country as this, and I wish you would let me go out with you next time!"

Torp's ears were as good as his eyes: before Waldemar could answer, he called out impatiently, "Come, come, Waldemar, let's have something to eat; you seem to forget that you have been complaining of hunger for the last two hours!"

Waldemar turned to the garden, while Torp, stretching himself at full length on one of the wooden benches, added in German, "If you intend to invite that youth to go out with you, let me know in proper time, that I may take my fishing-rod and seek amusement elsewhere, for I strongly suspect he is more likely to shoot one of us than anything else."

These words were spoken so deliberately and distinctly that they were heard by the forester and his son as they approached the inn, and both smiled significantly, while unceremoniously removing the chamois from John Nixon's sight. Nora too had heard, and thought to herself, "Is it worth that man's while being so very ill-natured and rude to us?" and then she called from the window to John, who instantly ran into the house and upstairs to her.

"Did you understand what was said?" she asked, as he took his sister's place beside her at the window.

"Not exactly all the words," he answered; "but it is very evident that this Mr Torp is a disobliging, disagreeable fellow, and won't let the other be civil to us. I must now try to make up to the forester and his son, and if they cannot or will not give me a day's sport, I shall borrow a gun from some one here, and go out deer-stalking by myself."

"No, Jack, you must not do any such thing," cried Nora, quickly; "that would be turning wild hunter, and you might run a chance of being shot yourself!"

"Oh, I don't imagine the danger is so great after all," said John, "and wild hunting sounds uncommonly tempting."

"Call it poaching, then," said Nora.

"No, I won't; because you see there is a fellow here who will help me if I ask him. He was just outside the village breaking a horse this morning, and rode so well that I asked about him, and heard that he had been six years in a cuirassier regiment, and was now a free man as they call it, to the great vexation of the foresters in the neighbourhood, as he is, or was, a notorious *wild-shoots*."

"You mean long Seppel from the Crags," said Nora; "but I can tell you he is not likely to attempt anything of that kind now for many reasons, so you had better leave it to me to speak to the forester for you. I have got a room at his house, and can easily find out what he can do for you, and when this Mr Torp is likely to be out of the way. In the mean time you must take some walks with me, and perhaps my uncle and Georgy may be tempted to join us."

Immediately after their early dinner, or luncheon, as Georgina chose to call it, Adam brought the letters and newspapers that had accumulated for them under the address *"poste restante"* at the neighbouring town: they afforded occupation for a couple of hours, and it was late in the afternoon before Nora could persuade her uncle to walk to St Benedict's, the secularised monastery, with an extensive brewery, the situation of which, beside a small lake, and almost completely surrounded by wooded mountains, had so greatly pleased them the day before.

Their way led them along the banks of a clear stream, in which, from time to time, they could see small trout darting backwards and forwards in all directions, which so interested Mr Nixon and his son that they spent nearly an hour in watching and waiting, and poking long sticks under the banks to dislodge the fish hiding, or supposed to be hiding, there.

They all stopped on a bridge of planks where a boy of

about twelve years old stood fishing, with a rod of such simple structure that John could not repress a loud "Bravo!" as almost immediately after they drew near him he flung a tolerably large trout on the grass.

The young angler was not alone: beside him stood a man in the prime of life, but what his station in the world might be it was at first difficult to guess, as his toilet gave no clue whatever to it. His head was covered by a straw hat of the same materials as those worn by the reapers in the neighbouring fields, nor was it in much better condition than the most of them, being rather dingy and of uncertain form; a black kerchief was very carelessly slung round his throat; he wore one of the loose grey jackets that seemed to be common to all ranks; and his trousers, of the same rather coarse material, were nevertheless carefully turned up above his nailed shoes to prevent them from being injured by the marshy ground or water into which he occasionally splashed with perfect unconcern. The boy called him Ernst, and danced round him while he disengaged the struggling fish and arranged another bait upon the angle, which consisted merely of a piece of twine fastened to the end of a still green branch of hazel-wood.

Mr Nixon's knowledge of fish was confined to a market or a dinner-table; of the art of angling he was utterly ignorant, but it seemed to be such child's play in that clear shallow brook that he was suddenly seized with a desire to become a fisherman, and accordingly advanced with an air of grave interest to look on; while John, in execrable German, wondered that anything could he done with such miserable tackle: he supposed fish must be very plenty thereabouts.

"We are not badly off," replied Ernst, in very good French; "the streams have small fry such as this, the river below the village large trout and greylings, and the lake is well stocked with carp, pike, and so forth."

Nora interpreted to her uncle, but no sooner had the stranger heard her speak English than he turned to Mr Nixon and said, with a smile, "If you are a fisherman you can have much sport here—but Englishman fisherman—fisherman Englishman—is all the same."

"Why—yes—I believe we *are* considered pretty good in that line, but for my own part I have never thought it worth while to fish; the London markets afford such choice and variety that, aw—a man is not likely to think of providing for his table himself, as he might be obliged to do here."

The stranger looked at him with some wonder, and suggested that the sport was generally the strongest inducement.

"Well, perhaps you are right. I can imagine it a pleasant enough sort of pastime in such a place as this, and confess I should like to try my hand at it."

"In that case," said the other, "I may venture to offer you the fishing of this stream and the lake during the time you remain in this neighbourhood."

"You are very kind—very liberal indeed!" said Mr Nixon.

"Not at all," said Ernst, giving his young companion his rod again, and directing him where to throw it, "not at all, for were you what the English call a 'complete angler,' I should probably not have made the offer. One a year is as much as I can permit here, and there is now at Almenau an Englishman—"

"Mr Torp?" said John.

"That was not the name— the note, I think, mentioned a Lord somebody."

"Oh, they call him Lord Torp at the inn—"

"And is he not a Lord?" asked Ernst, turning round.

"Not he!" answered John, laughing ironically, "not more Lord Torp than I am Lord Nixon. Titles are not so plenty in England as in Germany!"

"I suppose you know him well?" said Ernst, half interrogatively.

"No—not at all—and I don't want to," replied John,
with ill-concealed pique.

"Very odd—very odd," murmured the other. "The English, when they meet in a foreign country, always seem to
avoid and dislike each other! Now Monsieur Torp," he
added, laughing, "will perhaps say just the same thing of
you when he comes here to-morrow."

"Very likely," replied John. "I don't myself think there is
much love lost between us."

"It is not improbable," observed Mr Nixon, rather
pompously, "that this Mr Torp is a highly respectable person, but we do not know him; he has not moved in our circle in London, and the name is utterly unknown to us; his
friend, the young German artist, made altogether a pleasanter impression on us!"

"Do you mean Benndorff?"

"They call him Waldemar," said Mr Nixon; "my son says
he is quite a gentleman."

"I should think he was," replied Ernst, almost laughing.

As he spoke they reached the high road from Almenau
to the monastery, and at a short distance perceived, advancing towards them, the two men of whom they had been
speaking.

Nora prepared herself to hear Torp presented to their
new acquaintance by his true name, and to see the change
which she did not for a moment doubt it would produce in
the manner and conduct of all her relations, but John hurried forward, saying, "Let us go on and look at the monastery church that the people in the village talk so much
about."

"Must we not ask permission to see it?" asked Georgina,

speaking for the first time.

"By no means," answered the stranger, stopping to let them pass him; "our churches are always open."

He raised his hat, and then turned to meet Waldemar and Torp.

"Now who may that man be?" soliloquised John, as soon as they were alone.

"The proprietor of the monastery or his son," said Nora.

"That is, you suppose him to be either the brewer himself, or the brewer's son and heir?"

"Yes."

"Might he not be the steward or book-keeper?"

"Certainly not," said Georgina, with more than usual decision.

John laughed. "Well, do you know, I took him, in the first instance, for something of that kind, and as to Georgy, I am sure his hat and hob-nailed shoes disgusted her at once, to say nothing of the way in which he stood in the water and washed his hands. I have known her call a man vulgar for less."

"And yet," said Georgina, "I suspect I discovered that he was a gentleman before you did."

"Because he spoke French, perhaps? but I can tell you that is a common accomplishment here. However, whatever he may be, he seemed very much inclined to be civil, and I dare say would have shown us all over the place if that Torp had not, as usual, come in our way."

They turned from the lake towards the church, the entrance to which was through one of those carved stone Byzantine portals, with mysterious combinations of human figures and animals, that are supposed to represent the triumph of Christianity over paganism; and having found the door wide open, to admit the warm air from without, they

wandered up and down the long aisles, looking at the pictures and monuments, altars and curiously-carved confes-
sionals, until their attention was attracted by a noise in the
gallery, and on looking up towards the organ, they perceived Waldemar, Torp, and their new acquaintance, striding over the musicians' benches until they reached the front
row, where, seating themselves, a whispered conversation
began, which, from the direction of their eyes, Nora
strongly suspected was as much about her relations and
herself, as the church of St Benedict's.

She had been much pleased at the permission to fish
given so unrestrictedly to her uncle; had even begun to indulge a hope that John would, in the course of time, be allowed to shoot on the grounds belonging to the monastery;
and now she beheld her enemy pouring his English prejudices into the ears of the attentively listening Ernst, and, in
all probability, obliterating any agreeable impression that
she and her relatives might perchance have made on him a
quarter of an hour previously.

This time Nora did Torp injustice; he had not spoken
until Ernst had made direct inquiries, giving, as a reason,
that he wished to be civil to the travellers, and show them
the monastery, but considered it necessary to ascertain that
they were people who might be introduced to his mother
and sister, who happened just then to be at home.

Torp's answer seemed to amuse more than enlighten,
when he observed, that he believed them to be highly respectable people, but, as they did not exactly move in the
same circle as his family in England, he had never chanced
to see them until a few days ago.

"The fact is, you know nothing about them," said Ernst,
laughing; "and I had better reserve the acquaintance for
myself, and show them our cells and corridors some other
day. If I had considered a moment, I should not have ques-

tioned you; for how could you give me information concerning a family who, I had already ascertained, knew nothing of you—not even your name?"

"They have not yet heard it properly pronounced," replied Torp; "nor is it necessary that they should. I consider it quite a fortunate circumstance that Waldemar has furnished me with so short and insignificant a *nom de guerre*, and you will oblige me by not entering into any explanations on the subject with any one, especially with any member of this English family. I believe I must add that, though personally unacquainted with these Nixons, they are not altogether unknown to me, and you need have no hesitation in presenting them to either your mother or sister."

"But," said Ernst, hesitatingly, "a day can make no great difference; and my people are going to-morrow to spend a week or two with the Benndorffs, at Herrenburg, in the Valley of the Inn. Waldemar has perhaps told you that his brother Carl has long been engaged to my sister, and their marriage is to take place next month. Carl and I have served many years in the same regiment; we always applied for leave of absence at the same time; he preferred spending his with us, instead of going home, and, as a matter of course, fell in love with my sister. Their engagement has caused great intimacy between our family and the Benndorffs; and if it had not been for Waldemar's arrival, I should have left St Benedict's to-morrow with the others. I mention this to convince you that I really do remain here on his account and yours, and therefore wish you would both take up your quarters with me as I proposed."

"Thank you," said Torp, "I should have accepted your offer, were I not likely to be here for several weeks; and before I leave Almenau your house will be so full of wedding guests that you would scarcely know where to put me."

"We have plenty of cells," answered Ernst, laughing; "and the only person we expect who requires more than a reasonable quantity of room, is the Countess Schaumberg; she generally travels with so many servants, and horses, and dogs, that she overwhelms quiet people such as we are. To do her justice, however, she puts aside some of her grandeur when with us, and can be very charming when she chooses to please, as you know perhaps better than I do, for no friend of Waldemar's could avoid intimacy with the Schaumbergs."

"Yet it was through them that I became acquainted with *him*," said Torp, smiling; "their house was one of the pleasantest in Vienna, and Waldemar almost lived with them!"

"That was natural enough," rejoined Ernst, "as he and Schaumberg had been educated together and were like brothers. Waldemar is now guardian to the Countess's daughter; and I suppose it is in consequence of that, and his intimacy with her, that, directly after she became a widow, people said he was engaged to be married to her. At all events, I know he likes her, and the sooner she comes here the better pleased he will be."

"I don't know that," said Torp, looking towards Waldemar, and smiling, as he observed him leaning eagerly forward, forgetful of their presence, and wholly occupied with the persons moving about in the church beneath. "I rather think that until Waldemar is actually affianced or married, he will always contrive to find some one to interest him, or as he says himself, some one to whom he can lend his heart for a few weeks occasionally."

"One of these, perhaps?" said Ernst, looking significantly downwards.

Torp nodded. "That one standing at the door," he said; "and now, if you feel disposed to show these people your monastery, Herr von Falkner, let me again assure you, that there is nothing whatever to prevent you from introducing them to your mother and sister, should chance bring them together. In the mean time Waldemar must take me to your father."

Ernst called Waldemar, and having shown him a door leading from the gallery into the interior of the building, he himself descended by a narrow staircase to the church, whence he followed and overtook the Nixons, just as they reached the court in which the principal entrance to the monastery was situated.

Unconscious that any one was near them, Nora observed, that this part of the building seemed of much later date than the church, and was neither very ancient nor very modern, as far as she could judge. She believed she was rather disappointed—the monastery certainly looked better when seen from the road, with its dark background and pretty lake.

Mr Nixon said it was a prodigious pile of stone, and would require monastic revenues to keep so many different buildings, and such an extent of roof in order—to say nothing of the innumerable windows!

John thought it must be a confoundedly gloomy sort of barrack inside.

Georgina pronounced it an interesting, fine old place, and declared she should have no objection whatever to live in it.

"Perhaps you would like to see the interior?" said Ernst, who was so close beside her that she started, and left it to the others to accept his offer.

They did so eagerly enough, and followed him as he mounted a handsome stone staircase—their impressions with respect to the immense proportions of the building being confirmed on seeing long, wide, well-lighted corridors branching off in different directions. The one through which they were conducted was decorated with well-painted coats-of-arms, and led to several large, lofty, but simply-furnished apartments; a long row of cells had been converted into bed-rooms, but did not seem to be at present in use; and there were apparently endless suites of apartments quite unoccupied. There was a handsome library, without books; and a music-room, or rather hall, of beautiful proportions, with marble pillars, paintings in fresco, elaborate stucco-work ornaments, and church-like windows, of which the upper parts were of painted glass. The only furniture of this room was a marble fountain, at the end opposite the windows; and Georgina, after expressing unqualified admiration of the apartment, could not help adding, that she wondered it had not become the favourite resort of the whole family.

"My mother thinks it too large for our small household," said Ernst, "and in fact we only occupy ten or twelve rooms at the lake side when we are alone."

"Is it long since you purchased the place?" asked Mr Nixon.

"It has been in our possession as far back as my recollection reaches."

"Then I suppose you cannot tell me what the value of a property of this kind may be?"

"I fear I must refer you to my father," answered Ernst; "the woods and brewery make it rather valuable, but both have long been greatly mismanaged, as until a couple of years ago we never resided here."

"The—vicinity of the brewery—was not agreeable perhaps?" suggested Georgina.

"Oh, not at all!" answered Ernst. "Brewing is a very good business in Bavaria, and my father has quite a predilection for it, but until very lately he was in active service in the Austrian army: I have also been many years a soldier,

and could only get a few weeks' leave of absence occasionally, so there was no one to attend properly to our affairs
here, and the place was going to ruin as fast as possible."

While speaking they had reached the cloisters that were
open towards a small court, in the midst of which a fountain played in the almost eternal shade of the surrounding
buildings, throwing showers of light drops beyond its stone
cistern on the dark grass around.

Here Nora and Georgina stopped, while Ernst, springing lightly up a few stone steps, threw open the nearest
door, saying, "This is my cell: here I do penance for my sins
on rainy days."

Mr Nixon and John followed him, and found so much
to interest and amuse them that a considerable time elapsed
before they again made their appearance; when they did so
they were supplied with fishing-rods, and Nora heard with
infinite satisfaction an appointment made for the next day
at the trout stream near the lake.

They passed soon after through a garden: at one end of
it was an arbour close to the lake, and two ladies were sitting there with Torp, but they did not look round or seem
conscious of the presence of strangers, although Waldemar
and an old man, with snow-white hair, left them, and the
latter, approaching the Nixons, was immediately introduced
to them by Ernst with the words, "My father." Being, however, unable to speak English like his son, he could only
bow to Mr Nixon, and then turn (not as it appeared unwillingly) to Georgina and Nora.

Before they parted he seemed sincerely to regret that
"business and pleasure," as he termed it, obliged him to
leave home the next day; he hoped, however, to find them
at Almenau on his return, and in the mean time offered
them the use of his lake, boat, and garden.

As they slowly walked back towards the village, John observed that it was a great bore not being able to speak either French or German well, adding, "I dare say now the old fellow would have let me shoot on his grounds, as well as fish in his lake, if I could have mustered German enough to have asked him properly."

"Uncommonly civil people indeed," said Mr Nixon; "they evidently wish to become acquainted with us—I suppose because we are English!"

"I rather think that Mr Waldemar has kindly recommended us to them," observed Nora; "but at all events I am glad that you and Jack have found an occupation likely to amuse you for a week or two."

CHAPTER XXI

The Mountain Mill

NORA was put in possession of a cheerful little room at the forester's, and her uncle and John went regularly every day to St Benedict's. Georgina frequently accompanied them, preferring the garden there to that of the inn, which was more the resort of beer-drinking gentlemen and coffee-drinking ladies than she approved.

"It seems," she observed one day to Nora, when preparing to follow her father to the lake,—"it seems to me as if the whole neighbourhood had chosen the place as a rendezvous."

"Not at all improbable," said Nora.

"But surely, Nora, you do not approve of your Germans being so constantly lounging about the inns, as seems the custom here?"

"That entirely depends upon the circumstances in which *my* Germans live."

"I can tell you from personal observation, for I have watched them, that there are some—many, in fact, who come here regularly every day. I begin to know their faces."

"Well?" said Nora.

"The young men amuse themselves rolling those horrid wooden balls that make a noise like distant thunder—quite irritating to one's nerves; the more elderly are occasionally accompanied by wives and shoals of children, but they also frequently come alone, and may be seen day after day, smoking and drinking coffee, while reading a small newspaper that seems to contain nothing but advertisements."

"These people," said Nora, "are probably men who have situations in the offices of the neighbouring town; the distance to this village is about an hour's walk; and as such perhaps they use it daily for exercise and recreation."

"But," continued Georgina, "some who come in the afternoon remain until quite late at night. Even after you have gone to your room at the forester's, and I have dismissed Nesbitt, they may be seen, sitting in the garden, smoking, talking, and singing by candlelight!"

"This," said Nora, "is a southern German custom that I cannot take upon me to defend."

Georgina was silent for a few moments, and then observed hesitatingly, "The custom does not appear to be altogether confined to the *employés* of the neighbouring town. M. Waldemar, and even the Englishman Torp, are sometimes among the company, which is of a very mixed description. I cannot tell you how surprised I was to see that gentlemanlike Austrian officer, Captain Falkner, from St Benedict's, here also."

Nora was not at all surprised, and merely suggested that he might, perhaps, find it dull at home without his family.

"Oh, I perceive you have turned completely German again," said Georgina; "but you manage to keep John very nicely from these beer-drinking parties."

"Who?—I?"

"Yes,—you. I dare say Mr Torp's disagreeable manner to him was at first the cause of his ceasing to frequent the garden, but now we see him regularly every day either go with you, or follow you to the forester's directly after luncheon."

"When he goes with me," said Nora, "it is to take a

walk, but I am much more frequently obliged to engage Rosel as guide and companion, and naturally supposed that when he did not call for me he was fishing at St Benedict's."

"He will never learn to fish," said Georgina, "and does nothing but mutter and grumble, and destroy Captain Falkner's tackle whenever he is with us. Papa, however, is very successful, and yesterday caught quite a large trout at the bridge near the brewery. Captain Falkner was with him, and was so polite and good-natured, that we took quite a fancy to him."

Nora, who had at first turned to Georgina, and listened with marked attention, seemed wonderfully little interested either about the fish or Captain Falkner, so that even when her cousin added, "He remained with us afterwards during the afternoon, and chatted very pleasantly," she scarcely appeared to hear her, and proved her inattention by asking abruptly,

"Has Jack been talking of chamois hunting lately?"

"Not so much as at first," answered Georgina; "it is provoking that the forester takes care of, and rents the game on the lands of St Benedict's, so that Captain Falkner has no longer a right to give permission to shoot on them. He mentioned having used all his influence lately in favour of M. Waldemar's friend, or something to that purport; so you see, dear Nora, this tiresome Torp is again in our way."

"Tiresome!" exclaimed Nora, "he is perfectly detestable —the most complete egotist I ever met. That good-natured M. Waldemar and the forester would, I know, have made no difficulties about allowing Jack to go out with them occasionally, if this odious man had not objected. I heard what he said myself, and as there is no chance of his giving way for some time, there is every probability that Jack will end by making the acquaintance, and hunting with a young man here, who is a noted wildschuetz. Do you not remember his threatening to do so the very day after we came here?"

No. Georgina had no recollection of anything of the kind, nor the remotest idea of the danger to which her brother might be exposed, should he put his threat into execution. Nora did not think it necessary to alarm her, but resolved to endeavour to keep John out of temptation, by communicating her apprehensions to the forester's daughter Rosel, and inducing her to speak to Seppel. She therefore parted from Georgina at the turn to St Benedict's, and, pursuing the course of the stream in a contrary direction, was soon again close to the village, somewhat beyond the last houses of which the forester's was conspicuous, from its dazzling white walls, bright green jalousies, and the gigantic antlers of a stag that decorated the gable beneath which the entrance was placed. It was separated from the road by a trim garden, with a rustic paling, and also by the stream, which here began to give unmistakable tokens of its mountain origin by brawling over large stones, and working its way beneath rocks protruding from the banks, effectually undermining the roots of the few old trees that still remained in its immediate vicinity.

Nora entered the ever-open door, and in order to put her plan at once into execution, requested Rosel to accompany her to the Crags, informing her immediately after they left the house why she wished to go there, and making no attempt to conceal her anxiety about her cousin.

Every trace of colour forsook Rosel's face as she listened. She remembered having seen the young Englishman pass their house frequently; she had observed Seppel standing with him near the inn on Sunday morning; and recollected, with dismay, her lover's unqualified praise of young Herr Nix, whom he had declared to be "a lad of spirit,—up to anything,—afraid of nobody, and the making of a good soldier." Yet a natural inclination to defend Seppel from suspicion, even in the mind of Nora, made her refrain from giving utterance to her misgivings, and when she spoke, it was with a forced smile and in assumed confidence.

"He promised me never to go out wild-hunting again," she said, "and I don't think he will. Not that he wouldn't dare, but his father has been brought round to promise to resign the Crags to him, and with such a prospect in view he will not be easily tempted."

"Don't you think, however, it would be better if you were to speak to him?" said Nora.

"Of course I'll speak to him, but it's hard to know what to say, when he tells me he is no longer a wildschuetz, and that I ought to believe him when he says so."

"At least," said Nora, "you can recommend him not to venture his life, and injure his future prospects, by attempting anything of the kind now, when your father and brother, Count Waldemar, Mr Torp, and Captain Falkner, may meet him any day and at any hour."

"That's not the way to talk to him," answered Rosel; "the danger is just what he likes best. I am more afraid of suspicion falling on him than anything else; there is not much chance of their either seeing or taking him prisoner, for he knows the mountains better than any of them."

"Remember," said Nora, "my cousin will be with him, who, perhaps, cannot so easily make his escape in case of danger, and they may both be fired at as armed poachers, and wounded—"

"Or killed," said Rosel, with a shudder, "killed by my father or brother if they do not instantly stop when called to, and deliver up their rifles on the first summons; and that Seppel will never do, though he knows that when my eldest brother lost his life in an encounter with a wildschuetz, my father swore that in future his second call should be the whistle of a bullet, and he would henceforward hunt a wild-schuetz with as little compunction as if he were a chamois or deer."

"And your father is, probably, a good marksman?" said Nora, half inquiringly.

"Few better," answered Rosel.

"And is it possible that, under such circumstances, there are men in this neighbourhood daring enough to venture out deer-stalking?"

"More than I like to say," replied Rosel, nodding her head; "the danger is the last thing they take into consideration, and many are only prevented from going out by want of time, or the chance that their absence from home might excite suspicion. There is no use in trying to make our young men here look upon this hunting as a crime—only those who have served their two or three years in the army can understand the game laws, and refrain altogether from hunting."

"I thought they were obliged to serve six years," observed Nora.

"So they do, nominally, but when the frequent leave of absence is reckoned, it is in the end not more than half the time. Serving in the army improves and steadies them all, more or less; and even Seppel has become quite another man since he has been in the cuirassiers."

While speaking they had sauntered in slow ascent along the banks of the stream, which began to fall in noisy cascades, and form deep green pools among rocks, that as they advanced imperceptibly assumed larger proportions. The valley narrowed, the high road seemed to dwindle into a pathway far up on the side of the mountain, and a sudden turn brought them so near the mill that they could see the stream splashing over the labouring wheels, which, with all the demoniacal breathless energy of machinery, ground corn in one building, while in another the trunks of trees were sawed into boards with undeviating accuracy.

A little further back, at the base of an abruptly-rising, thickly-wooded mountain, the handsome house of the miller came into view; its balconies, as is usual in the Bavarian highlands in fine weather, draped, as it were, with feather beds and pillows, the size and number of which, with their blue and red striped covers, being considered a sort of criterion among the peasants of the wealth and cleanliness of the inhabitants. Inflated with warm summer air, they presented a so satisfactory appearance to Rosel, that she became loud in their praise and in that of the miller's wife, who was the most active and indefatigable woman in the parish.

"And her daughter?" said Nora, interrogatively.

"Madeleine is young," she answered, evasively; "and, as my father says, has now money enough to make one overlook a little want of steadiness."

"So then," said Nora, "she is not exactly the sort of sister-in-law you desired?"

"My mother and I looked higher for Franz, and my father too, until the miller inherited his brother's fortune. Franz has studied and passed his examinations, and there is nothing to prevent him from becoming a forstmeister and marrying a lady."

"And would that be more agreeable to you than his choosing one of the friends and companions of your youth?"

"A good connection," answered Rosel, "such as the daughter of a counsellor of the forest board, might have helped him on in his profession. My father often said that connection was better than money for a man who wished to rise in the world."

"Must I hear this even *here?*" murmured Nora.

"It is true," continued Rosel, "I have gone to school with Madeleine, and known her all my life. Perhaps I know her too well. In a small village like ours one hears and sees everything that goes on in the houses of one's neighbours."

"And what did you see here to displease you?" asked Nora. "Madeleine seems to be a remarkably quiet and extremely pretty young woman."

"She is not so quiet as you suppose," answered Rosel, "and is always trying to make people love her. I saw myself the trouble she took to please Florian, until he downright asked her in marriage."

"You mean the painter, Florian?"

"Yes; he was as sure of her as my brother himself could have been, but Madeleine laughed, said that nothing was further from her thoughts, and that she had only talked to him because he was less unmannerly than the other men in the village."

"I believe I had better not attempt her defence," said Nora, "though she is pretty enough to be pardoned a little coquetry."

"Florian forgave her, at all events," said Rosel. "He is a kind soul, and bears no malice; but there is another who will not be put off so easily, and that is black Seppel, the Tyrolean."

"Black Seppel!" repeated Nora; "I have heard of him somewhere."

"He is the miller's man, who manages everything, and has lived with him upwards of six years. He is come of as good people as the miller's family, and need not have served if it had not been for an accident that caused a quarrel with his father, and forced him to leave home for a while. I suspect Madeleine is not easy in her mind about him, for she has been lately teasing her father to dismiss him; and it seemed quite a relief to both when he left them to spend a month in the Valley of the Inn. They may expect his return any day now, however, and what he'll say to the betrothal I'm sure I don't know."

"Is your brother aware of all this?" asked Nora.

"I believe," she answered, "Madeleine tells him just what she thinks necessary, and in such a pleasant sort of way, that he only laughs and likes her all the better."

Nora stopped before the house, which looked so clean and cheerful that she was induced to ascend the stone steps to the door. The miller's wife peered out of her kitchen, and then came bustling towards her, leading the way to the dwelling-room with many expressions of pleasure at so unexpected a visit. The room was large; the windows well furnished with geraniums; the clock filled the place made for it in the wall; the great green stove occupied the usual space; the benches round the room, and cross-legged table, were scoured to an unusual degree of whiteness; and in cages at an open casement two canary birds warbled loudly, straining their little throats to drown the voice of the miller's wife, as she repeated her welcome to Nora, and very unnecessarily swept the spotless table with her apron.

"What a very nice house," said Nora, looking round her with unaffected pleasure; "so beautifully situated! so large and airy!"

"Well, the house is one of the best built hereabouts, and ought to be, having cost money enough," answered the miller's wife; "and I don't deny that I could have my pride and pleasure in it if my old man wasn't always wishing for the old house back again, and talking of how happily we lived in it. Rosel knows better, and young as she is, can remember the sorrow and poverty we had to endure there, and the state it was in. I might say the fire that burnt both house and mill was the greatest piece of luck that ever happened to us, if the miller had not quite broken down from fright, and never been the same since. And he grows worse from year to year, Rosel, and takes no interest in anything, so that but for our man, Seppel, the business could not be carried on at all."

"I have heard of this Seppel," said Nora, perceiving that Rosel would not speak, and that an answer of some kind was expected; "he is your head workman, I believe?"

"He's everything," answered the miller's wife; "saved me and my daughter the night of the fire, and when, in the midst of the confusion, I remembered that we had not had money to pay the high insurance, and thought everything we had in the world was lost, never shall I forget his telling me that he had himself gone to the town a month before, and paid it for us out of his own money. From that time he has been like a son to me, and if I had another daughter, Rosel, I'd give her to Seppel."

"People say he would take Madeleine if she would have him," observed Rosel.

"Well, I don't know but he would," she answered, with a smirk indicative of satisfied motherly vanity; "and if she wasn't promised to your brother he'd be worth thinking of, I can tell you. Perhaps," she added, on observing Nora turn from the window and the canary birds towards the door, "perhaps the young lady would like to see the house; strangers often ask to look at it."

Nora smiled a ready acquiescence, and followed her across the passage to the miller's room, when, after admiring some jugs and mugs of china and earthenware in glass cases, the drawers beneath them were pulled out, and she was requested to inspect the Sunday and holiday suits of the old couple. Without explanation much might have escaped Nora's notice, notwithstanding all her quickness of comprehension; but the miller's wife liked talking, and had no desire whatever that the double row of buttons on her husband's coat and waistcoat should pass for ordinary workmanship, when they were good pieces of silver money coined at the mint. This peasant mode of exhibiting wealth was new to Nora, and she showed the necessary portion of respect for the buttons, but was naturally more interested in the wardrobe of the female part of the family. The high heavy fur cap of the miller's wife—a curious grenadier sort of head-dress, worn on state occasions, and too costly to become common—the silk spencers, aprons, black bodices with silver chains and pendent crown-pieces, were all admired in a most satisfactory manner; and then they went up stairs, where, with a look of subdued exultation, the door of one of the front rooms was thrown open by the miller's wife, while she observed with proud humility, "This is our best room, a poor place for a young lady like you to look at, but peasant people such as we are have a pride in it somehow."

"And with reason," said Nora, as she unaffectedly admired the handsome bedsteads and beds, with elaborately flounced pillow-cases and coverlets. As completing furniture to the room, there were tables and chairs, white curtains to the windows, a chest of drawers, and a remarkably large double-doored wardrobe, which last when opened disclosed a sufficient quantity of linen to have furnished a small shop. Carefully bleached and pressed, the pieces were folded and bound round with red tape, as if for sale, and with surprising accuracy the miller's wife could tell the number of ells contained in each, the winter when the flax had been spun, the spring when it had been woven, and the summer during which it had been bleached.

Nora remarked that a great number of wax tapers, gilt and decorated with foil, or brilliantly coloured, were placed in front of the shelves, and soon learned from her loquacious companion that when they disposed of their hives they generally took some wax in part payment. "For it would look poor not to have a store of these," she explained, "and some we want, at all events, for the church. You may be sure, Rosel," she added, turning to the admiring girl, "you may be sure that our Madeleine will not enter your family empty-handed. These silver spoons and my mother's necklace go with her to the Forest-house."

This latter she now held towards Nora. It was composed of twelve rows of heavy silver chains, fastened in front by a rococo clasp of immense dimensions, containing some garnets, topaz, and other gems more remarkable for their colour than intrinsic value.

"Indeed, all that you see will be given to Madeleine when she marries," continued the miller's wife, "for my old man talks of nothing now but selling the mill, and settling in some other part of the country."

"Oh, you must not let him do that," cried Rosel, eagerly; "I could not bear even the thought of having strangers living here, where I have spent the happiest days of my life playing with Madeleine and Seppel from the Crags."

"Rosel," said Nora, looking at her watch, "you have just reminded me that we were on our way to Seppel and the Crags, and I perceive it is much later than I supposed."

Rosel led the way to a steep mountain path, Nora followed, but before they again entered the wood she stopped and looked back.

"What a lovely spot it is!" she said to her companion: "I think I could live here myself with pleasure if—it were a little—less noisy."

"Noisy!" repeated Rosel. "Surely you don't mean the water?"

"Not exactly; I could easily get accustomed to that."

"Or the canary birds?"

"No, I like them; but I think the clatter of the mill, and the grating of the saw, must be intolerable when heard incessantly."

"That is just what makes the mill so pleasant and cheerful," rejoined Rosel. "I love the place and everything in and about it, for it was here I played as a child, climbing over the planks at the saw-mill when they appeared like mountains to me, and running into the mill to be chased out of it by the miller or one of his men, whom we children called the dragons."

"You seem to like the mill better than the Forest house."

"I believe I do. My father was feared by the children of the village, but the miller let us jump about him as much as we pleased, so we got the habit of coming here, and to this day I like to take my knitting and sit on the rocks beside the stream, and think of the years that are past."

"And, perhaps," said Nora, merrily, "perhaps also of those that are to come?"

"I cannot deny it," answered Rosel, moving on, while her cheeks crimsoned with a blush. "It was here that I saw Seppel first and last, as I may say: he used to come down from the Crags when we jodel'd where the echo is."

As Rosel finished speaking, she placed a hand at each side of her mouth, bent her body backwards, and uttered a long, loud, clear musical shout composed of a succession of notes that were repeated, as she had expected, by the echo; but scarcely was the last faint sound lost in the distance, when an equally loud and still more joyous answering shout reached them, and then Rosel, laughing gaily, sprang forward with an ease and elasticity of step that obliged Nora to use some exertion in order not to be left behind.

CHAPTER XXII

The Crags

THE CRAGS was an isolated place, and might, from its elevated situation on the side of a mountain, have been supposed an autumn alp, had not the surrounding cornfields and well-filled orchard proved that the ground was good and the climate temperate. In fact, it was a well-sheltered nook; and, though the upper fields and some extent of pasture land were bounded by the wild, bare, weather-beaten crags, from which it derived its name, a wood of fir and pine trees flourished above them, reaching the summit of the mountain in spite of the frequent interruptions caused by colossal masses of protruding rocks, in the fissures of which not only plants but trees contrived to find sustenance, and grow in the most fantastic and unaccountable manner.

The peasant's house bore evident marks of age, and was picturesque in no common degree; the ground floor alone was built of stone, all else of wood, brown, and weather-stained; the small lattice windows were glazed with round pieces of the most ordinary glass; and so low was the balcony that a tall man standing at the door might easily have touched it with his hand, or even plucked one of the crimson pinks that hung temptingly downwards from the half-decayed boxes on the shelf above the balustrade. There were scarlet geraniums there also, and stiff balsams flowering exuberantly in broken pitchers and cracked earth-enware kitchen utensils, adding more to the picturesque interest of the abode than the inhabitants could easily have imagined.

The barn, an extensive wooden building, forming a continuation of the house, and under the same roof, had an entrance from the fields so constructed that by means of a short and steep ascent the loaded carts could be driven into it. The gate was now wide open, for the corn was being brought home, and seemed to have required the hands of all the household; no one was to be seen, though the sound of cheerful voices and the barking of dogs might be heard at no great distance.

Nora sat down on one of the benches before the house, taking care not to displace any of the bright yellow milk-basins ranged against the wall, and then looking round her, perceived a small house at a little distance, with closed door and window-shutters, evidently uninhabited, though on its diminutive balcony large heaps of peas were drying in their pods for winter use, and some well-grown green and yellow gourds had been placed there for ornament or to ripen their seeds.

"That's the house for the old couple when they resign," said Rosel in a whisper.

"Which for your sake I hope they may do before long," answered Nora; "the place is charming, but the house seems very, very old, and rather neglected too. I dare say it will look quite different when you and Seppel enter into possession."

"A little tidier, perhaps," said Rosel; "but we could not make any great changes as long as the old people live, though a new house would not cost much, as the neighbours would help, of course, and the forest rights are as good here as on the miller's property."

"You must tell me all you know about these forest rights and foresters some other time," said Nora.

"I don't know as much as I ought to do," answered Rosel, "for, after hearing all my life of forest laws, and rights, and revenues, and regulations, I only understand what I have seen with my own eyes."

"Quite enough for me," said Nora, rising; "and now, as these people won't come to us, we must go to them."

"They are taking advantage of the fine weather to bring in their first corn," said Rosel, apologetically. "Seppel will be sure to come to us as soon as the cart is loaded."

"We need not take him from his work," observed Nora, smiling at her eagerness to excuse his absence. "I can ask him a few questions about my cousin, or you can give him a little good advice in the corn-field as well as anywhere else."

They found the whole family working together—father, mother, sons, and servants, all equally busy, Seppel alone perhaps not completely engrossed by his occupation. That his eyes wandered round the field, and that he was the first to perceive Rosel's approach, was remarked by his mother with a laugh as she followed him, when, shouldering his pitchfork, he advanced to meet the visitors. There was much friendliness in the pump-handle hand-shakes that followed; but a good deal less warmth in the manner of the Crags peasant, who continued to give directions to the servants until Nora was close behind him, when, slowly turning round, he formally raised his battered straw hat, and held it pertinaciously in his hand until repeatedly requested by her to replace it. His figure was a good deal bent by age and hard work, his large marked features furrowed with wrinkles; but the red and brown tints of the face denoted health, and contrasted well with the long snow-white hair that hung down to his shoulders: he wore black leather shorts, white stockings, shoes, and a red waistcoat with silver buttons: coat he had none, nor any of the men present, but their shirt sleeves appeared in keeping with every costume, excepting that of Seppel, whose blue cuirassier trousers, forage cap, erect figure, and well-trimmed moustache made the want of coat, waistcoat, and cravat rather remarkable. The peasant's wife was a stout, elderly woman, wearing a black bodice, a red-printed calico petticoat, and a broad-brimmed man's hat of coarse black straw. Her cheerful face was lighted up with smiles, and once in possession of Rosel's hand she kept it fast, swinging her arm backwards and forwards while assuring her that she was delighted to see her, and hoping before long "to be with her old man on a pleasant mission to the forester house."

Nora had walked on with the old peasant, and before long had heard the history of his rheumatic pains during the winter, been made acquainted with his doubts that he would ever again be what he was, and his resolution, in consequence, to resign the Crags to his son Seppel, reserving a reasonable maintenance for himself and his wife, and a sum of money for Anderl, which he expected would be paid out of the dowry that the forester would give his daughter.

The peasant spoke as if he took it for granted that Nora had heard of the projected marriage, and knew the plans of the family; so she nodded approval, and then said, "Shall I tell them you will come down and talk the matter over tomorrow evening?"

"I don't mind if you do," he answered; "they can discourse about it among themselves, and I don't object to your letting them know also that Anderl must have his two thousand florins down before I or my old woman turn into the off house. Anderl has been always a good and steady lad, never caused me a day's trouble since he came into the world, and has as good a right to his share as another, and let that other be who he may!"

This was said in a very determined manner, and was succeeded by a succession of nods of the head, evidently intended to challenge opposition. Now Nora, who knew that the two thousand florins amounted to something less than two hundred pounds English, considered the sum so moderate a provision for a younger son that she remained silent, wondering what he meant, until he continued, "And the money must be raised at once, by hook or by crook— for Anderl, after being, as I may say, master and man here for the last three years, is not likely to turn into a day-labourer on his brother's ground!"

"Of course not," said Nora.

"Yet it's a common thing about here," said the old man, who seemed possessed with a spirit of contradiction. "I've known two or three brothers living on together, so that there wasn't a hired servant in their house."

"Most creditable to the family who so lived," observed Nora.

"Maybe so," he rejoined, peevishly, "but they never came to anything after all. Now my Anderl is ambitious, and intends to make a fortune as ostler in an inn where the custom is good."

"I was not aware that ostlers were so well paid as to enable them to make fortunes," said Nora.

"It's not a bad thing in a house where waggoners stop the night, and there is a regular business on the road in salt, corn, or hides. If you would mention this to the forester it would be doing a service, as he's a sensible man, and will understand why we must have the money paid down, and not put off in any way."

Nora promised, and stopped for a moment to look at the double row of beehives ranged on shelves along the side of the house, while the peasant advanced towards a tall, strongly-built, dark-complexioned man, who with long strides was descending from the Crags directly towards the path leading to the mill.

"Hallo, Sepp," was shouted by the peasant and his sons with stentorian voices, "stop a minute and tell us how you are, and if you have seen our people at the Kerbstein lake."

The man turned back, not very willingly as it appeared, answered the various greetings of the family with ill-concealed impatience, and then informed them that he had been that morning at the Kerbstein lake with their relations, who were all well, and expected a visit from long Seppel the first convenient holiday.

"Which may be next week," observed Seppel, "and perhaps to invite them to my wedding!"

"Oh, ho!" cried the other, glancing quickly towards Rosel, "wish you joy with all my heart—it will be the first wedding in the village this year, and the sooner it takes place the better. A wedding's as good as a church fête any day, and at yours there will be the best music and—"

"Not so fast," cried old Crags, interrupting him, "the betrothal must come before the wedding, and we are not clear about that yet. If the forester does handsomer by his son than his daughter, why, all I have to say is—that the son will be married sooner than the daughter. No offence to you, Rosel; my old woman has of course told you that Anderl must have his portion in hand the day I turn out of this house, and all depends on *your* father now."

"Don't be cast down, Rosel," said the peasant's wife, consolingly, "leave me to manage for you and Seppel. Your brother Franz will be a forester himself in no time, I dare say, and the miller's Madeleine is so rich that a thousand florins more or less just at first will not—"

"Franz and Madeleine?" repeated the Tyrolean, interrupting her, while a dark shade seemed to pass over his features, and his brows contracted into a fearful frown. "What do you mean?"

"That they are to be married at Michaelmas," she answered, "and we fear the forester may do more for his son than his daughter."

"His son will require little from him on this occasion," he rejoined, with flashing eyes.

"Well, that's just what we all said," observed the peasant's wife; "Madeleine is so well off that it cannot be of the least importance when Franz receives what the forester may be able to give him."

"Set your mind at rest," said the Tyrolean, his deep voice trembling perceptibly, while his colourless lips were forced into a smile; "Michaelmas will come and pass over often enough before the miller's Madeleine is the wife of the forester's Franz."

Without waiting to observe the effect produced by his words, he turned to the mill path and was out of sight in a moment.

A few exclamations of astonishment from the peasant and his wife preceded Nora's leave-taking. Rosel and Seppel, who perfectly understood the cause of the Tyrolean's ire, merely exchanged looks of intelligence, and prepared to follow her; they loitered, however, considerably while fastening the rustic gate in the fence towards the wood, in order to give her time to precede them, which little manoeuvre so delighted the peasant's wife, that she showed her appreciation of their tactics by a shout of laughter, and by bawling after them a profusion of those coarse epithets, that the tone of voice in which they are uttered can make alternately terms of intense endearment or virulent abuse.

That Seppel and Rosel had much to talk about, and many hopes and fears to communicate to each other may easily be imagined. Certain it is that the distance between them and Nora lengthened as they proceeded, and that she descended the steep path and reached the mill alone. The saws worked on through the quivering wood with a harsh grating sound, the water splashed over the heavy wheels, and made them labour round, creaking and clattering without intermission, and so great was the din within the corn mill, that as Nora stopped for a moment at the door, the civil requests to enter of the men at work there were perfectly unintelligible, excepting as far as gestures and smiles expressed them.

It was perhaps in consequence of these noises, that she reached the miller's house before she heard the sound of the loud angry voices within, though they were accompanied by a shuffling and tramping of feet, to which was soon added a succession of half-suppressed screams, ending in a loud cry of murder. Then Nora rushed into the house, and the door of the sitting-room being open, she beheld black Seppel, with eyes rolling wildly beneath his frowning eyebrows, and features perfectly livid with rage, holding at a distance the miller's wife with one hand, while with the other he grasped her husband's cravat and shirt-collar, pressing his knuckles on the old man's throat, and shaking him in a manner that threatened strangulation. Breathlessly, and through his fixed teeth, he muttered huskily, "Miserable villain, did you dare to forget that you were in my power? Was it not with your consent that I set fire to your cursed old mill?"

"Ye–ye–yes," gasped the miller, with great difficulty.

"And did you not say I should have your Madeleine as bride the day my father resigned his mill to me?"

The miller made some inarticulate sound, intended perhaps for affirmation.

"Let him go, Seppel, for the love of heaven!" cried his wife, in a voice of agony, while endeavouring in vain to place herself between them.

At that moment Nora rushed forward, and as she vainly tried to remove the rough hand, or even loosen its grasp of the neck-cloth, the miller's wife called out, "Untie it!—untie it, or he will be choked!"

With trembling hand Nora caught the long ends and drew them towards her, but the knot yielded with great difficulty, and only after repeated efforts, leaving both cravat and shirt-collar still in the hands of the enraged Seppel, who, staggering backwards a few steps, dragged the miller after him to the bench beside the table, where with a jerk he released him, and then, as the storm of passion began to subside, gloomily watched the old man's effort to arrange his disordered dress.

To the miller's wife, who had burst into tears the moment her terror had been allayed, and was now sobbing violently, Nora turned and whispered, "Adieu, Frau; I can be of no further use here, and must return to the village."

The woman looked up anxiously, followed her into the passage, and said hurriedly, "You—you have not been here long, I believe?"

"Only a moment before you saw me."

"Did you hear—"

"Not more than a few words," said Nora, anxious to re-assure her.

"It will be better not to mention this quarrel at the forester's," she began, with evident embarrassment.

"Neither there nor elsewhere," answered Nora; "you may depend upon me."

She walked towards the garden, and looked up in the direction of the Crags, but instead of Rosel, perceived Madeleine tripping gaily homewards. She had gone at daybreak to her father's alp, having heard from the forester and his son that they were likely to hunt in that neighbourhood with

Captain Falkner, Count Waldemar, and Mr Torp; and after having done the honours of her hut, by supplying them with cream, butter, and cheese, she had in requital been flattered and cajoled to her heart's content by the mirthful and hungry sportsmen. They had accompanied her down the mountain, parted from her but a few minutes before, and the flush of gratified vanity was still on her dimpled cheek as she approached her home, adroitly carrying on her head a flat basket, in which, covered with a napkin, she had put some fresh butter and a cheese for her parents.

She was still singing a snatch of one of the *Schnaderhüpfeln** with which Captain Falkner and Waldemar had beguiled the time of rest on the alp, and in clear loud tones was offering a bunch of green ribbons to some imaginary deserted lover, when her mother called out, "Hush, Madeleine—hush, or you'll make him as mad as ever!"

"Who?" asked Madeleine, with a careless smile, removing her basket from her head, and then courtesying in her best manner to Nora.

"Seppel. He's within," said her mother.

"Does he know—has he heard—" began Madeleine, and then she paused, raised her apron, and passed it across her face, which became colourless as her mother nodded despondingly, and pointed to the door of the adjacent room.

"I don't see why I should be more afraid of him than any one else," she said, forcing an appearance of courage that her pale lips belied. "I've chosen Franz, and I'm not likely to change my mind for anything Seppel may say."

Impatiently shaking off her mother's detaining hand, she advanced into the room, and, in a half-conciliatory, half-

* Popular Bavarian or Austrian songs in waltz-time.

defiant manner, held out her hand, exclaiming, "Welcome back, Sepp; we almost thought you had forgotten us."

He took her hand, but only to fling it from him with such violence that she reeled to the wall, and with difficulty kept herself from falling.

"Unmannerly boor!" she cried, angrily, "the next time I offer you my hand you'll take it, or I'm much mistaken."

"Madeleine," said her mother, coming forward, "I am afraid he has a right to it and yourself, any day, for the asking."

"I should like to know who gave him such a right?" she asked, saucily.

"Your father," answered the miller's wife, beginning to sob afresh. "I did not know until to-day that he was bound by a promise."

"*I*'ve made no promise," said Madeleine, angrily interrupting her; "and if I had, I wouldn't keep it."

"Have you not?—Would you not?" cried Seppel, fiercely, catching her arm, and drawing her towards him.

"No," she answered, boldly; "and I won't be made answerable for every thoughtless word I may have spoken to you when I was a child."

"Child!" he repeated, in angry derision, "why it is but two years ago, and you were as tall as you are now, and nearly as stout, and quite as handsome, and a deal quieter and humbler; but at that time, Madeleine, you did not know that an uncle would die suddenly and make you rich; you thought that few in the village—and least of all the forester's Franz—would think of you as a wife; and you knew—and right well too—that I was the son of the rich miller at the other side of the mountains. One thing you did *not* know," he added, gloomily, "but your father might have told you any day, that as long as he lives you can never marry any one but me."

"I don't believe you!" cried Madeleine, vehemently; "and if you think I'm afraid of you, you're greatly mistaken."

"You're so completely in my power," continued Seppel, with savage tranquillity, "that I can insist on our bans being published next week, and maybe I'll do it. Your father daren't object; for we've done *that* together which makes us more than friends for life."

"You have no proof," cried the miller, interrupting him, in a harsh, discordant voice; "no proof of any kind."

"Have you forgotten the letter you wrote me from Munich, telling me not to do the deed we had planned together?" asked Seppel, malevolently. "It reached me twelve hours too late, but I have kept it by me carefully, and on my person, ever since. It is here—here!" he said, tapping the breast-pocket of his jacket, "and though, for my own sake, I shall not use it, unless driven by jealousy to revenge myself, you may as well remember that I am not a man to be trifled with. Give me your daughter, as you promised, and—"

"I won't be given to you!" cried Madeleine, passionately; "for I like Franz's little finger better than your whole body. If you had twenty letters from my father I would not marry you."

"Wait till you know what the letter's about," said Seppel, with a bitter smile. "You have worried me enough for more than three years, Madeleine, and I'm tired of this sort of life. As to your fancy for the forester's son, it will pass away, like your love for many another that I could name. I was the first, as you've often told me—I intend to be the last; and the sooner you make up your mind to cross the mountains with me, the better for both perhaps."

He strode across the room, bent his tall figure when passing through the doorway, and as he ascended the stairs to his room, Nora left the garden, to join Rosel and her

companion, too much occupied with all she had heard and
seen, to remember that she had intended to question and
warn the latter about her cousin John. It occurred to her
after he had left them to return to the Crags, and Rosel had
honestly confessed having forgotten to mention the young
Englishman to her lover; but Nora, though greatly provoked at their mutual forgetfulness, had no time to repair it,
as she was obliged to hurry on to the village to dine with
her relations.

Mr Nixon was in high spirits: he had caught a trout of
considerable size, and had invited Captain Falkner to dine
with him and partake of it. Fish and fishing was the chief
topic of conversation, which in no way interested Nora,
excepting inasmuch as she observed John's indifference on
the subject. When questioned by her after dinner, he said
he had no patience for fishing, preferred making excursions
on the mountains, and had been that day at St Hubert's
chapel, and in Tyrol, where, at a shabby little inn on the
frontiers, he had drunk some capital wine, and made the
acquaintance of a miller returning to Almenau.

"Black Seppel?" suggested Nora.

"I don't know his name," answered John; "he is head
man at the new mill outside the village here, and had been
to see his father, who is very old and infirm. He often
crosses the mountains for that purpose, and appeared
known to all the people we met—indeed, he seemed quite
at home at most of the peasants' houses, especially on the
Tyrolean side."

"That was black Seppel, I am sure," said Nora.

"Very likely," replied John; "half the men about here are
called Seppel, or Sepp, which I believe means Joseph. You
have only to call a fellow Sepp on chance, and nine times
out of ten you will be right."

"I saw this man at the Crags to-day," observed Nora,

"and took no fancy to him whatever."

"Nor I either," said John; "so we parted company soon after passing the frontiers, and I returned to the village by St Benedict's. By-the-by, Nora, *that* Torp and the others had famous sport this morning; they were out at daybreak, and, I hear, shot black-cock and a gigantic bird called *Auerhahn*.* Georgy *might* say something for me to Captain Falkner; she sees him every day, and I suspect he fishes with the governor that he may talk to her; but when I asked her to give him another hint about me, she declared she could not possibly do so, it would have such an odd appearance."

Nora smiled. "Have patience, Jack, and you will find that Mr Torp will tire of the village and its inhabitants before long; another week's shooting will probably satisfy him, for the forester told me he had already begun to talk of going to Herrenburg in Tyrol."

"Where the Falkners are?" asked John.

"Yes; and when he is gone the forester and his son will do whatever I ask them. In the mean time you must be satisfied with exploring the mountains about here; and I think you had better not ask long Seppel to go with you as guide, for his father wants him at the Crags, where they have a great deal of field-work to do just now."

"Oh, I know that," he said, impatiently. "I was up there yesterday for two or three hours."

"Jack," said Nora, reproachfully, "you went there to borrow a gun, and ask him to go out with you; I'm sure you did."

John did not attempt denial, and she continued, "If no fears of the consequences, as far as you are yourself concerned, can deter you, have at least some consideration for

* Capercailzie.

this young man, whose prospects would be completely ruined if he engaged in any exploit of the kind just now."

"Do not be uneasy, my dear Norry," said John, evidently wishing to end the conversation. "Your young man has, as you observed just now, no time, and, it appears, but little inclination, to do anything but wield a reaping-hook at present. I never was so disappointed in any fellow as in this long Seppel."

"I am glad to hear it," answered Nora. "It seems that Rosel was right when she supposed a few years' service in the army had quieted him."

CHAPTER XXIII

Ways and Means

NORA returned to the forester's house at an unusually early hour the next evening, having been requested by Rosel to act as mediatrix, if necessary, between her father and the Crags peasant, should any difference arise in their proposed arrangements. She found both families assembled in the little parlour, well supplied with beer, bread, and tobacco, Rosel seated somewhat apart, apparently occupied with her spinning-wheel, but looking very anxious and flushed.

Nora's arrival as inmate of the house caused neither surprise nor embarrassment; they all knew her, some had even learned to pronounce her name from the servants at the inn, and greeted her as "Mees Nora," and Franz and Seppel stumbled against each other in their eagerness to hand her a chair; but after she had drawn from her pocket a piece of crochet-work and bent over it, they immediately resumed their places and the conversation as if no interruption had occurred.

The Crags peasant had a packet of yellow-looking papers in an old leather case before him, and Franz, apparently acting as secretary, sat pen in hand, prepared to draw up any agreement into which they might enter.

"It was in the year twenty," said the peasant, adjusting his spectacles on the end of his nose, "in the year twenty

that I entered into possession of the Crags, and, according
to contract, agreed to give my parents yearly as follows."
He opened one of the papers and read slowly—

"1 bushel of wheat,
2 ditto rye,
1 peck of barley,
18 lbs of butter,
100 eggs,
25 lbs of meat,
6 lbs of linseed oil,
12 lbs of flax,

one quarter of the orchard fruit; cabbage, potatoes, and
turnips as required; a quart of milk daily; wood for fuel, and
the necessary repairs of the off house; a pair of shoes and a
pair of slippers annually and twenty florins a year, paid
quarterly."

"That's all fair," observed the forester, with a nod of approbation. "The ground about the Crags is good, and there
is no mortgage on it, I believe?"

"No mortgage," repeated the peasant, "and therefore I
expect you will make no difficulty about the provision for
Anderl. The young lady there has, perhaps, told you that I
expect two thousand florins for him."

"You must be satisfied with half the sum," said the forester, decidedly, "or—we shall never come to terms. I am
not a rich man, but my daughter will not go ill provided
into your house. Besides her bed and her spinning-wheel,
her clothes and house-linen, she shall have one thousand
florins on the day of her marriage, and perhaps the same
sum after my death; but more than this I cannot give her."

"Then, neighbour," said the peasant, doggedly, "there is
no use in talking longer about this matter, unless you
choose Seppel to raise the money on mortgage, which,
however, *I* cannot take upon me to recommend."

"No," cried the forester, pushing his chair backwards, "no; I know too well that such a beginning would lead to ruin. I cannot allow my daughter, and you cannot advise your son, to commence housekeeping with a debt they may never be able to pay off."

"I don't advise," said the old man, with a peculiarly artful smile; "I said if you chose. It all rests with you. Seppel, in his wish to possess the Crags and marry Rosel, is ready to agree to anything, though I have counted over and over the income and expenditure, and proved to him that a few florins at the end of the year is all he can expect to put aside, and may be thankful, when he has a family, if he can keep clear of debt. Oh no! I don't advise! I leave everything to you."

"Come, come, Crags," said the forester, smiling, "we all know your love of contradiction, but this is going too far. People say you have managed to save money, and I suppose your son can do the same."

"My savings are said to be more considerable than they really are," observed the peasant. "After thirty years' management of the Crags, I have, it is true, contrived to scrape together a few hundred florins, but it is only since my sons could help in the work, and corn and cattle have risen in price. The house is now in want of repair."

"Well," said the forester, "there is no denying you might have kept it in better order."

"What for?" asked the peasant. "Maybe that it might look handsomer when seen from the off house after I had resigned? No, no, forester, you don't know me yet."

"I believe that's true," said Franz, who had latterly been biting the end of his pen, as he sat with his eyes fixed on the peasant. "My father is upright and honest, and speaks his mind, but the devil himself could hardly make out what you're at now. Perhaps you're not willing to resign. If that's it, say so; there's nobody has a right to compel you."

"I'm willing enough to resign," he answered slowly. "After labouring ten years for my father and thirty for myself, I've had enough. And what with the rheumatism and my goitre, and the wish of my old woman to see her Seppel married, I'm at times more than willing; but knowing the income and expenditure, I can't advise the burdening of the land with a debt, and see no way for the young people but your coming forward with the money."

"I can't give what I haven't got," began the forester, angrily; but an appealing look from the two women opposite him, and a glance at Rosel's dismayed face, seemed to appease him. "Let us go a little more into detail," he added, quietly, "and see how matters stand. Perhaps you have got your last year's account, and from it we can make an estimate."

Seppel came forward noiselessly, and added one to the eager faces around the table, as the peasant drew from his pocket a large sheet of paper covered with sprawling writing and figures, and, as if he had been prepared for the request, read without comment an account of his outlay and income during the preceding year, which, being drawn up in a rather confused style, was listened to with but the more intense attention by all his auditors.

When he had ended, no one seemed inclined to speak, and as he laid the paper on the table, and took off his spectacles, he observed composedly, "After deducting the taxes and parish rates from the overplus, the remainder, I take it, will prove somewhat less than was expected."

Old Crags rubbed his chin and mouth very diligently for a few seconds, Nora almost thought to hide a smile of satisfaction at the dismay he had caused, and than began to fold up his papers, and replace them in the leather case.

"The value of your property has been greatly overrated,"

said the forester.

"That's not my fault," answered the peasant; "the truth might have been known any day for the asking. I thought you had lived long enough in the mountains to know that the soil so high up is not always of the best description."

"I know you grow wheat every year," rejoined the forester.

"Well, I don't deny that worse land might be found in the parish than at the Crags," said the peasant; "I don't complain. If I'm not rich, I can at least say that no one ever felt want in my house. There's always enough to eat, and something to spare for a stray guest; my servants are paid regularly, and get their shoes, jackets, linen, and harvest-money at the time appointed. We don't work on holidays at the Crags, and keep our church festival in a becoming manner, and I have always been a contented man, and so was my father before me, and his father before him, and Seppel can live as we have done, and is willing if you'll consent to raise the second thousand on the land. I dare say you'll pay the interest during your lifetime, and in your will make all straight again."

"No," said the forester, rising, "I cannot consent to this arrangement. You seem to forget that I have two children, and whether or not I may live to save another thousand florins, God only knows. My eldest son fell by the hand of a wildschuetz, and such may be my fate any day in the year —there are enough of them in our neighbourhood"—here he glanced for a moment towards Seppel, and amended his speech by adding,—"from Tyrol I mean —and I shall never rest until I have hunted them all down. Now, with regard to this money, you see I can do nothing, and promise nothing. My daughter has not been daintily brought up; she is willing and able to work, and can live at the Crags as others have done. It is hard enough that her fortune is taken from her before she enters into possession, as I may say, and given to Anderl; but as to her commencing with a loan, and having to pay interest for it, perhaps as long as she lives, that is out of the question, and there is nothing more to be said if you will not do something handsome for them."

"I can neither do nor say anything more," observed the peasant, closing his leather case, and dropping it into one of the pockets of a grass-green coat, that seemed to have been inherited from his father or grandfather, the waist being formed by two large buttons placed almost between his shoulders, the remainder of the garment sweeping the floor at each side of his chair, when seated, and hanging down to his heels when he stood up. "I have two children, as well as you, forester," he added, "and I do not see why one should get all, and the other next to nothing."

"But the 'all' is not much," interposed the forester's wife; "Seppel and Rosel will have enough to live upon, and no more. A thousand florins, and what you will give him from your savings, and a home at the Crags, when he chooses to stay there, is surely enough for Anderl."

"Do you suppose," said the peasant, angrily, "that my Anderl is likely to be a day-labourer at the Crags, or to turn wood-cleaver, or charcoal-burner on the mountains here under your husband? We have other plans for him, as the young lady there might have told you, and he shall not come short, let what will happen, for it is only lately that my wife has made me give up my intention of resigning to Anderl instead of Seppel."

"Ah—ah!" cried the forester, with a look of intelligence, "is that your drift?—then indeed there is no chance of our coming to terms. Rosel," he said, turning to his daughter, "you see that no ill-will on my part against Seppel stands between you and your happiness. You know that I cannot do more than I offered just now, and after hearing that the income at the Crags, even in good years, so very little exceeds the expenditure, you must be convinced that I am right in refusing my consent to the proposed mortgage."

"Of course, father—of course you know best," faltered Rosel, "but—but I cannot give up Seppel!" One hand wiped the tears from her eyes, the other she extended frankly to her lover.

Nora, who had followed attentively the calculations of the peasant, and listened to the discussion that had preceded and followed it with the deepest interest, now rose, and laying her hand gently on Rosel's shoulder, said, "I can be of use here, or rather we can be of use to each other, Rosel. You know," she added, turning to the forester, "that I have come to Almenau to erect a tombstone on the grave of a very near relation in the churchyard here. I want some one to take charge of this grave, to plant flowers on it in summer, and decorate it with wreaths during the winter, and consider a thousand florins by no means too much for this purpose. Rosel shall receive the money from me any day you appoint, on condition that Seppel promises for himself, and imposes as a duty on all future possessors of the Crags, to attend to this grave in the manner I have described."

Great was the surprise and delight caused by this speech, the old Crags peasant alone appearing more astonished than pleased. Rosel seized Nora's hand, and stared at her in speechless happiness; the forester bowed repeatedly, and said the proposal was munificent, the engagement should be contracted formally, and an agreement concerning the grave drawn up, signed, sealed, and delivered into her hands; Seppel, standing before her erect, as if about to present arms, first thanked, and then assured her she had not misplaced her generosity, and that no grave in the parish should be better attended to than that of her relation.

The forester's wife and Seppel's mother were loud in their expressions of gratitude, but no entreaties could prevail on the Crags peasant to resume his seat, in order to drink another glass of beer, and wish the young people a speedy and merry wedding.

"Time enough—time enough," he said testily, drawing a black silk night-cap over his head, and taking up his hat, "time enough when the day of betrothal comes."

"But," said the forester, "I hope you'll go to the town, and ask the judge to name a day next week for the drawing up of the surrender and marriage contract; and when all is in order we'll have a little merry-making here, and I dare say Mees Nora won't disdain to join us, or Count Waldemar either."

"I'm not going into the town till Wednesday," said the peasant, peevishly.

"Well, Wednesday is not long off," observed the forester, good-humouredly, "we're not going to be unreasonable; and if Seppel sows the winter corn on his own account this year at the Crags, it's all we want or expect."

Nora had found an opportunity of leaving the room unperceived, and it was evident that the peasant had been put into a more congenial humour afterwards, for as he passed beneath the balcony on which she was standing, when he left the house, she heard him talking and laughing as gaily as the forester and his family, who all accompanied him as he turned into the pathway leading to the Crags.

While Nora looked after the noisy happy party, her mind was so occupied with kind sympathy, and generous plans for future benefits to be conferred on Rosel, that she was unconscious of the approach of Waldemar and Torp, who, having fished with tolerable success in the trout streams near the village, now turned to the forester's house, to inquire about their chance of sport the ensuing day, should they go out deer-stalking.

Waldemar loitered and looked round him, Torp strode quickly forward, for, like most Englishmen, he made a business even of pleasure, and with the most unceasing perseverance fished and hunted alternately, pursuing his sports with an intentness and eagerness that not unfrequently made him overlook the beauties of the country about him, or caused him to consider many of them as mere impediments, which, when overcome, would serve to enhance in his own and others' eyes the triumph of success.

While Waldemar, with head uncovered and upturned smiling face, addressed Nora, and induced her to lean over the balcony to answer him, Torp, scarcely glancing toward her, merely touched his hat, and stalked into the house. He was still employed questioning the stupid old woman, who was rinsing beer-glasses in the kitchen, as to the time when the forester was expected home, when he heard his friend enter the adjacent passage and bound up the stairs three or four steps at a time. It was in vain he cleared his throat, coughed significantly, and finally called to him. Waldemar either did not or would not hear, and Torp, with an impatient shrug of his shoulders, entered the little sitting-room, and naturally turned to the gun-rack, as the object most likely to interest him while awaiting the return of the forester or his son. In order to gain a nearer view of the rifles and fowling-pieces, he pushed aside with his foot a spinning-wheel, and on the floor where it had stood perceived a small patent pocket-book, firmly closed, with patent pencil. He picked it up, examined it for a moment, and though there was no name or initial on the green morocco cover— no engraving on the pale amethyst that decorated the top of the pencil—he knew that it could only belong to Nora Nixon, and therefore pitched it carelessly on the nearest window-stool. This would not be worth recording, had he not afterwards occasionally interrupted his inspection of the fire-arms in order to glance towards the neat little book, and ended by once more taking it up, and then deliberately walking out of the room.

Restoring it to its owner would, he thought, serve to interrupt a *tête-à-tête* that had already lasted long enough; yet he hesitated, and hardly knew how to put his plan in execution, when, on reaching the lobby, he caught a glimpse of Waldemar through the door that opened on the balcony. He was sitting on a wooden bench with Nora, bending forwards, and explaining the last drawings he had made in his sketch-book, which was spread open between them. The noise of the stream before the house prevented Torp from hearing what Waldemar said, when, pointing to some spot on the paper, he observed, "It was somewhere here that Torp shot the black-cock yesterday morning, and with a rifle too! He is a capital shot with a bullet, and hunts with a patience and perseverance that are at times quite incomprehensible to me. I like deer-stalking as well as most sportsmen, and will climb, and creep, and crawl as long as any one; but to stand for hours waiting for a shot, either in the twilight or moonlight, is a thing I can't endure, so I generally leave him with the forester or Franz, and take refuge in the nearest hut. We were last night on this alp, the highest about here: in fact, it can only be used in the heat of summer, and the cattle are to leave it in a day or two; but the view from it is magnificent, and will well repay you for the trouble of mounting."

"Do you think I could undertake such a walk?" asked Nora. "Your drawing gives me the idea of a very wild place."

"It *is* a wild place, and is called the Wild Alp," answered Waldemar; "but I have taken it into my head that you can not only walk, but also climb well, and that difficulties would not easily discourage you."

Nora smiled.

"We have had such remarkably fine weather lately," he continued, "that I may safely recommend you to undertake the excursion; one day's rain, however, would make part of the way impracticable for a lady, on account of the cows' stockings."

"Cows' stockings?" repeated Nora, interrogatively.

"I mean holes in the swampy ground which have been made by the passage of cattle in wet weather, when they follow each other in single file, stepping regularly into these holes, then filled with water, and carefully avoiding the more solid mud around them. After a succession of foot-baths of this description, you may imagine the appearance of the cows."

"I can," said Nora, interrupting him with a laugh, "and understand your hint so well that I shall certainly choose dry weather for an expedition to the Wild Alp."

"Why not make it to-morrow," rejoined Waldemar, eagerly, "and let me accompany you?"

"If I could persuade Jack," began Nora.

"Oh, never mind him!" cried Waldemar. "Take Rosel with you, who can make herself useful, and carry a basket of provisions. You don't mind getting up at daybreak, I hope?"

"Not at all; and you tempt me so strongly that I really must endeavour to make arrangements with both Jack and Rosel to start at four o'clock to-morrow morning. I suppose that is early enough?"

"If Monsieur Jacques go with you," said Waldemar, "you might as well make a two days' tour, and go on to the Kerbstein lake." He placed a sketch before her, in which high mountains inclosed an apparently more deep than extensive sheet of water; towards the foreground some remarkably jagged rock impeded a stream that flowed from it, forming long, low cascades; and in a sheltered nook, the probable opening into a narrow valley, stood a solitary châlet built half of stone and half of wood, fishing nets pending from the balcony, and a couple of roughly-made boats so near that Nora scarcely required the explanation given when he added, "That's the Kerbstein's fisherman's house, where you could remain the night; Torp has already spent a day there, and says the people are uncommonly civil. By-the-by, he might go with us—or meet us at the lake—or something."

"No, thank you," said Torp, who had reached the door to the balcony a couple of minutes previously, and now stood leaning against it. "You seem to have quite forgotten that if we do not hunt to-morrow you proposed going to St Hubert's chapel, and afterwards across the mountains into Tyrol. I know you are expected at Herrenburg."

These last words were uttered with much meaning, and seemed to cause some annoyance to Waldemar.

"I have fixed no time for my return home, Torp," he answered, a little impatiently; "and having been accepted as a guide to the Wild Alp by Mees Nora, you must excuse my leaving you either to hunt with Franz, or inspect the ancient altar at St Hubert's without me."

"I cannot allow you to break an engagement on my account," said Nora, "for if I want a guide, one can easily be found in the village. In fact, the painter Florian has already offered his services through our landlady, and I ought to have gone to see him and his mother long ago, as it was at their relation's house I was so hospitably received at Ammergau." She spoke without looking at Torp; for she was vexed that, having heard her ready acceptance of Waldemar's offer, he had not also been made aware of her intention to decline his being invited to join their party: she felt, too, some natural irritation at his thinking it necessary to defend his friend from the imaginary danger of her society, and not a little increase of indignation at his interference on all occasions.

"Am I to understand that you have changed your mind, and will not accept my escort?" asked Waldemar, rising.

"Precisely," answered Nora. "I shall defer my excursion to the Wild Alp until next week, and spend to-morrow in the village. That old castle on the hill deserves a visit; and when there I can amuse myself rebuilding the edifice in imagination—it will not be difficult, as they say it was inhabited towards the end of the last century."

"So!" cried Waldemar, gaily, "so you build castles in the air occasionally?"

"Rather say continually," replied Nora, laughing; "for since I entered the Bavarian highlands every hill has been supplied with a castle, and every dale with a cottage!"

"And have you peopled your castles and cottages?" asked Waldemar.

"N–o," answered Nora, and a sudden melancholy overspread her features, for the light question had brought strongly to her recollection her depressingly isolated position. Of the few near relations left her, was there one she could ask to live in a German cot or castle with her? Her uncle's treasure was in London, and with it his heart; Georgina would call such a residence being buried alive; Jack was a mere boy, full of youthful frolic, with a decided inclination to enjoy the world and its pleasures to the utmost; his brother Samuel she scarcely knew, and friends she had none! Yes—one—Irene Schaumberg; but what changes might not a ten years' separation have produced in her regard! These thoughts had but flashed through her mind, however, when Waldemar, surprised by her seriousness, said, with a mixture of curiosity and interest,

"Not peopled? not swarming with English friends and relations?"

Nora shook her head.

"So much the better," he said, reseating himself on the wooden bench beside her, and nodding a laughing defiance to Torp,—"so much the better; there will be the more room for Bavarians and Tyroleans! You really must allow me, Mees Nora, to accompany you to this ruin to-morrow: I know something of architecture, and we can build and plan together in the most satisfactory manner imaginable. Now don't refuse, or I shall think it time to be offended."

"I cannot well refuse," answered Nora, smiling, "seeing that the ruins of Waltenburg are quite as much at your service as mine."

"And you will permit me to go there with you, or,"—he added, correcting himself,—"to be there at the same time that you are?"

"Of course," said Nora, as she rose from her lowly seat. "Until the castle is mine, I cannot raise the drawbridge, and refuse you entrance." When passing Torp, who stood in the doorway, she perceived her pocket-book in his hand.

"This is yours," he said, coldly handing it to her; "I found it on the floor in the room below stairs."

"It is mine—thank you," said Nora; and a so unwonted colour spread over her face as she received it, that Waldemar's attention was instantly attracted.

"I wish," he said, "that I had found your book; it evidently contains secrets, and you fear that Torp, in looking for the owner's name inside, may have discovered—"

"I have no fears of the kind," said Nora, interrupting him. "Nothing, I am sure, would have induced Mr Torp to open this book or read a line of its contents. If he had not known it to be mine, he would have left it in the parlour."

Torp seemed to consider even a word of assurance unnecessary.

"You do not deny that there are secrets in it, Mees Nora," persisted Waldemar, "and I would give much to possess it. See, here are my sketches of Ammergau; you have more than once said you wished to possess them. Let us make an exchange—they are yours for the notebook!"

Nora thought over the contents of her little green book, and then dropped it into her pocket. Secrets such as Waldemar perhaps expected to find in it there were none. She had got the habit, during her solitary hours in Russell-square, of taking notes when reading, of writing lists of books, short critiques of those just read, and other matters of an equally unimportant description. A box full of such small volumes had been left in Mrs Ducker's care in England, and any of them, or many of them, she would, without hesitation, have given for the tempting sketches now offered her; but the little green book in question unfortunately contained in its side pocket the letter that Charles Thorpe had written to her uncle ten years previously, and a few memoranda, which, if shown to Torp by Waldemar, would inevitably lead to explanations that she by no means desired.

"I am sorry I cannot make the exchange you propose," she said, turning away; "I wish these sketches had some other price."

"Stay," cried Waldemar, springing after her to the head of the staircase, "listen to me, Mees Nora—the sketches *have* another price; they shall be yours for—for—a cup of coffee made by you yourself for *me*—any day you please on any of the alps about here."

"A cup of coffee!" repeated Nora, incredulously. "You shall have a dozen, if you desire it."

"I shall remind you of this agreement," said Waldemar.

"You need not," she answered, laughing; "I shall take

care not to let you forget it."

Waldemar could scarcely wait until she was out of hearing before he exclaimed, "You see, Torp, I shall win the wager."

"Perhaps you may," he answered, dryly; "that you will make a fool of yourself is, however, even more certain, and I greatly fear that your father will think that I led you into temptation."

"Pshaw!" cried Waldemar, impatiently. "I acknowledge that I am considerably *épris* with this black-eyed nymph of the Thames; but I could go to Herrenburg tomorrow, and in a week—or—let us say a fortnight, I could forget her—yes, I think I could forget her in a fortnight or three weeks."

"Then go," said Torp, earnestly, "go while the effort is easily made, and you will spare yourself and your family a world of annoyance. I have made the inquiries about these Nixons that you desired, and heard to-day, from a friend of mine who knows everybody in London, that this man has undoubtedly a large fortune, but also a large family; there are sons in Australia and elsewhere, one a lawyer in London, and the interesting youth now here, called Jack. The eldest daughter is well known in town from being constantly with the Savage Waywards, the younger my friend cannot well remember—he believes she has resided chiefly in the country; some people supposed her consumptive, others said she was eccentric, and many now assert she is dead. We know that she is neither dead nor consumptive, but I think the word eccentric may be used when describing her. At all events, according to the letter, the young ladies may 'be worth' about twenty thousand pounds a-piece."

"It is the connection and not the fortune I wanted to hear about," said Waldemar, with a look of annoyance.

"My informant," continued Torp, "could not give me

much more information on that subject than I gave you at Ammergau. The founder of the family, according to the legend, was a peasant boy, who wandered to London in the Whittington fashion, and afterwards made a fortune in trade. This is an old story, and a convenient one for finding arms when they become necessary; whether true or not is of little importance, for though love might manage to blind you, your father would certainly put on his spectacles when examining the genealogy of the Nixons, and nothing but the most enormous fortune would induce him to overlook its defects. Perhaps, after saying so much, I ought to add, that one of this family married a relation of ours many years ago."

"Ah!" said Waldemar, "such marriages cause no commotion in an English family!"

"The lady was a widow, and perfectly at liberty," answered Torp, "so though my father greatly disapproved, and indeed opposed the marriage, which turned out even worse than he expected, he could not prevent it. I have spoken to little purpose, Waldemar, if it has not yet become evident to you that one of this family is no match for a Benndorff of Herrenburg, who has every chance of succeeding to a principality and becoming a Serene Highness in the course of time."

"That's it," cried Waldemar, "that chance is what makes my father so hard to please. I hope your succession to an English earldom has served to hamper you in the same way."

"I have not thought much about the matter as far as concerns myself," answered Torp, "but my brother gave me much trouble about ten years ago, when I was obliged strenuously to oppose his making a disagreeable match of this kind. Oddly enough," he added, "it was one of these Nixons, the daughter of that relative of ours of whom I spoke just now, that he took it into his head to marry. The very name of this family is odious to me ever since, for though Medway yielded to my remonstrances in the end, we quarrelled a whole year about the matter. Do not expect me, however, to make the same efforts for you, Waldemar; but I am ready and willing to leave Almenau to-morrow, and share your flight from this nymph of the Thames as you call her."

"No, Torp, I ask no such sacrifice. You are right: I shall order horses for to-morrow morning, and leave without again seeing Mees Nora. In four-and-twenty hours, my friend, I shall be at Herrenburg, admiring the magnificent dress of Irene, Countess Schaumberg, and making grave inquiries about the education of my unruly little ward Adelheid."

"That's right!" said Torp. "I should not have thought a retreat so necessary if I had not seen plainly to-day what has happened to Falkner."

"There is no doubt how that affair will end," said Waldemar, laughing. "Ernst evidently hopes to persuade the other nymph to follow him into Hungary, and if he succeed, she will not be the first Englishwoman who has married into *our* regiment, as we call it, from having so many relations among the officers. My brother tells me that two of his best friends have English wives, patterns of perfection by all accounts, women who stop at home, and all that sort of thing; and I suspect it is the recollection of them that has made Falkner think of Mees Nixie. She is not ill-looking, however, far from it, but not to he compared to Nora—my Nora—our Nora! I wonder he did not choose Nora!"

"I wish he had," said Torp; "or rather, I wish the whole family and their projected tombstone were in some other Bavarian village. After I have hunted on the Wild Alp you may expect me at Herrenburg, as I shall of course miss you greatly, and find it dull here without you. But go you must, Waldemar, and without delay, for I see plainly that this girl is just the sort of person likely to make you more desperately in love than you have ever yet been, and that is saying a good deal."

"Ah—ah! Then you admit that she is charming?"

"She is dangerous," said Torp; "and—a—you will go to the Valley of the Inn to-morrow, old fellow, won't you?"

"I will," answered Waldemar, heroically.

CHAPTER XXIV

A Rustic Studio

NORA was in the village at so early an hour the next morning that most of the inhabitants were at church, for it is there the Highland peasant commences both work and holiday, invoking a blessing alike on toil and pleasure. The sound of the well-played organ induced her to follow some dilatory labourers into the handsome edifice, which, with its showily decorated altar, was the pride of the parish. She saw her companions doff their battered straw hats, stroke down their hair on their forehead, and reverently kneel down, while bright beams of earliest sunshine, finding an entrance through the high narrow windows, passed over their rugged features, and directed her glance to other groups of men and women who, in remote corners or at side altars, forgetful of the presence of those around them, gave an outward expression to their devotions, both in feature and posture, which is said to be a peculiarity of southern nations, but seems common to all votaries of the Roman Catholic religion.

The service was soon over, the congregation, not having time to linger in or about the churchyard as on Sundays, dispersed at once, and Nora turned towards the not far distant house of Florian and his mother. It had rather a smarter air than the dwellings around it, had light green jalousies, and no trees in front, perhaps to prevent the pass-

ers-by from overlooking the shop-window at the left side of
the entrance, which displayed a collection of heterogeneous
articles, such as pipes, coarse cutlery, and writing materials,
thread and tape of the most glaring colours, tobacco, twine,
lidless boxes full of gigantic brass and steel thimbles, harle-
quin leather balls, silk kerchiefs, and samples of sugar, coffee, and liquorice.

The shop itself was a long narrow room, with a very
townlike counter, behind which were shelves reaching to
the ceiling, well stored with printed cottons, woollen stuffs,
and cloths; while on the opposite wall, placed conveniently
within reach of customers, there were various implements
of husbandry, fishing-tackle, wooden toys, and a great variety of straw and felt hats. Madame Cramer, a cheerful-
looking little woman, dressed in a dark cotton gown by no
means unfashionably made, and with partially grey hair
neatly and becomingly braided, bent over the counter, and
asked Nora in what way she could serve her.

Nora requested to see some straw hats, but having,
while looking at them, mentioned that she was the bearer of
messages from Ammergau, Madame Cramer pushed them
aside and began to speak of her relations and of her son, in
amusing forgetfulness of her duties as shopkeeper. Nora
was soon made aware that in Florian all her hopes and affections were centred; on him all the money she and her
husband had saved had been expended; her greatest sorrow
in life had been parting with him, though but for a time.
"For he went to study in Munich," she said proudly, "and is
an artist, and would have remained there until he had made
himself renowned; but the old man died, and the village
wanted a painter, so he came back, though with a heavy
heart; and when we talked over matters together, and he
told me what hundreds and hundreds of painters were in
Munich, and how many more years he must study before

he could hope to be what he intended, I could not help advising him to retain his father's privilege of being village painter, which afforded a good and creditable subsistence, and proposed spending all the ready money I possessed in building an addition to the house. Well, miss, after some hesitation he consented, and for his sake I refused to marry the baker; and what with the building of his own *ately*, as he calls his workshop, and the repairs of altars in the churches, and the gildings, and the carvings, he was wonderfully contented for some time, but," she added, with a sigh, "that did not last long, he could not take kindly to the other work—"

"What other work?" asked Nora.

"The house-painting and varnishing," she answered; "and I cannot blame him, for it is below him, as I may say, now that he is an artist, and paints so beautifully in the style of Michael Angely! You'll step up stairs, I hope, miss, and look at his cartoons?"

"I should like to see them very much," answered Nora; "but it is still so early, that I have time enough to look at your printed calicoes, and choose one of these straw hats for my mountain walks, before we disturb him."

The hat she chose was very coarse, very stiff, and bore a strong resemblance to a flattened extinguisher. She did not, to the great surprise of Madame Cramer, look in the small glass to see whether or not it were becoming; and when some ribbon was afterwards produced for her inspection, she merely said, "Black, if you please," and began an examination of the cottons and stuffs on the shelves behind the counter.

"I shall require some of these things before long," she observed, mounting the little ladder that enabled her to take a view of the contents of the upper shelf, "and then you must tell me the prices."

"If you would like to have the marks explained," said

Madame Cramer, "I'm sure I have no objection. It will not be necessary to have a second price when dealing with you, but the peasants are so accustomed to haggle and bargain, that they would think themselves cheated if I did not reduce my demand; so I always ask a kreutzer or two more than I afterwards take, and then they go away satisfied with themselves and with me."

Nora was amused, and some time elapsed imperceptibly while she learned to keep shop. The mystic numbers and letters were made perfectly intelligible to her, and also, in some degree, the profits and losses of a village trader. She learned that peasants incurred debts quite as readily, and often as thoughtlessly, as people in other ranks of life; some but paid an old account in order to commence a new one; and her proposal to Madame Cramer to insist on ready-money payments in future was answered by a shake of the head, and an assurance that all her customers would desert her, and go to one Hans Maier in the neighbouring town, who had injured her enough already by obliging her to keep many articles in her shop that remained long on hand.

Madame Cramer could not leave her shop, and Nora was conducted up stairs by a remarkably plain, red-haired, and very freckled girl, of the name of Vevey. She was the adopted daughter of Madame Cramer; and Nora, struck by her likeness to some one she had seen occasionally at the inn, asked her if she had any relation there.

"The sennerin on the landlord's alp is my sister," she answered, smiling, "and you have seen her perhaps every Sunday morning. I shall make her guess who spoke of her when I go to the alp to-morrow."

"Rather tell me at what hour you leave the village," said Nora, "for I should greatly like to go with you."

"When you please, miss; it is quite an easy path, and hardly two hours' walk."

"I must choose the latest hour possible," said Nora, "as I hope to induce some others to join us who are not very early risers."

Vevey now led the way along a short passage, tapped rather timidly at a door, and having obtained permission to enter, held it open for Nora to pass her, and then closed it, and withdrew so noiselessly, that Florian continued his occupation, totally unconscious of the presence of a stranger. He was a pale, dark-haired, small man, with a perfectly picturesque beard, open shirt collar, and well-daubed linen blouse, and stood before a cast-iron cross intended for the churchyard. Though only painting it black to defend it from rust, his posture was that of an artist before his easel; and he seemed to encourage the delusion by having hung his pot of black paint on the thumb of his left hand, as if it had been a palette, stopping occasionally to look at the progress of his work, and turning his head from side to side in a manner that greatly amused Nora, until, on a nearer approach, she perceived that there was a small picture in the centre of the cross, which might be supposed to have caused the pantomime.

Nora's visits to artists' studios had been frequent enough in former times to make her acquainted with the almost unavoidable litter and disorder usual in such places, but anything like that around her now she had never beheld. Beside the usual casts of legs and arms in plaster of Paris, half-finished pictures; sketches, palettes, brushes, and colours, there were all the more ordinary requisites for house-painting. Window-frames were placed with portraits against the wall to dry, and near them a couple of small coffins of a bright blue colour, such as were usually placed *over* the graves of children in the churchyard. On shelves round the room there was a large collection of distemper colours in earthenware pots, and numerous filigree arabesque patterns for the decoration of the walls of rooms and ceilings, while angels with broken wings, saints with tarnished draperies, and various pieces of curiously-carved wood, still awaited repairs from the skilful hand of the village artist.

How long Meister Florian might have continued to advance and retire before the black cross, had he not been interrupted by Nora, it is hard to say. He started when she addressed him, made some apology for having supposed her Genoveva, and then, for her use, began to disincumber an old brown leather chair of its accumulated lumber. Nora did not wait for the completion of this operation, but began at once to speak of Ammergau and his relations there, the great drama, and the wood-carvers.

Florian's embarrassment was at an end; he listened attentively, and answered eagerly. She spoke of Munich and his studies there, and asked to see some drawings. Willingly he brought his large portfolio, and exhibited a succession of copies in chalks from well-known busts and statues; but they bore testimony to more assiduity than talent. His attempts in oils were of the same description; and Nora saw that though he might in time, and with perseverance, become perhaps a good copyist, he was no genius struggling with adverse fate, as she had been somewhat romantically inclined to imagine him.

"I wonder you have not tried landscape-painting," she observed, after having patiently listened to his complaints about the difficulty of getting people to sit for their portraits. "In such a country as this you could never be at a loss for studies, and mountains, lakes, and trees must submit to be sketched and painted how and when you please."

"I have not the slightest inclination for landscapes," he answered; "my ambition was to paint altar-pieces for churches, but I have never arrived at composing anything. Perhaps I have not studied enough, for even in portrait-painting I am often at a loss. The miller's Madeleine was the only person who ever sat as often and as long as I wished; but she has since said that I made a scarecrow of her, and that I required a whole morning to paint the mole on her throat; while Count Waldemar, as she expressed it, 'had her down in his pocket-book in a quarter of an hour, as like as two peas, and no mole at all!'"

"It is difficult to paint female portraits satisfactorily," observed Nora. "Women expect to be idealised, and to have their defects either concealed or altogether omitted."

"That mole is no defect," said Florian, "I think it beautiful."

Nora smiled, and observed that he seemed to have employment enough to put portrait-painting out of his head.

"I cannot complain," he answered, looking round his room; "there is employment enough—such as it is!"

"They told me at Ammergau," she added, "that the renovation of the altars at St Hubert's had been confided to you, and that is by all accounts a very flattering distinction."

"True," said Florian, with heightened colour. "I get as much work of that kind as I can manage to do; but you see, mademoiselle, my mother is from Ammergau, and I have a sort of natural talent for wood-carving. These old altars are crowded with figures in alto or basso-relievo, and it is not every one who can supply the lost or broken arms, legs, and even heads, so easily as I can."

"And," asked Nora, "has that never led you to suppose that as wood-carver you might be more successful than as a painter?"

"Yes," he replied, with a sigh; "but wood-carving is a common talent, both here and in Tyrol, and no one ever became rich or renowned by it!"

"Fortunately, thousands of people are very happy without being either," said Nora, turning from him to examine the old altar, with its folding doors and figures about a foot high in alto-relievo, representing the legend of St Hubert being converted to Christianity by seeing a crucifix on the head of the stag of which he had long been in pursuit. The interest she expressed in his careful and judicious reparations seemed greatly to gratify Florian, and he hoped, if she intended to visit the chapel of the sainted huntsman, it would be at the time when he also should be there.

"I may as well confess that I came here intending to propose some such arrangement," she answered; "but, besides St Hubert's, I wish to see the Wild Alp and the Kerbstein lake."

"Seppel will be a better guide to the lake," said Florian, "but to St Hubert's, or any of the alps about here, I can show you the way as well as—as—if I had been out with a rifle, and knew where a wildschuetz was likely to find a welcome and breakfast in case of need."

"And have you never been out in the way you describe?" asked Nora archly, and not much fearing that the suspicion would give offence.

"No," he answered, "though I have little doubt that many would think more of me if I had. A man who cannot handle a rifle has a hard stand here; there is no end to the joking and laughing about him; even the women cannot spare their jibes, and are always making comparisons, and lauding the foresters to the skies! I have heard it said, that in towns the soldiers are made much of by them; but in the villages about here the foresters are better off still—it is forester here, and forester there, and one never hears of anything else!"

Nora pretty well understood the drift of this speech, but she betrayed no consciousness, as she acknowledged having herself rather a predilection for foresters; their dress was so picturesque; their employments so manly; and they had all a certain ease of manner that was irresistibly pleasing.

"Ease of manner!" exclaimed Florian. "I dare say—and no wonder—they keep good company! All the noblemen and bureaucratists of the neighbourhood pay court to them for an occasional day's shooting; and their wives are civil to make sure of getting venison. Old General Falkner, who is as proud a man as can well be, makes no guest so welcome at St Benedict's as the forester; the captain's first visit, when he comes home on leave of absence, is to the Forest-house; and even Count Waldemar himself, who speaks to me whenever and wherever we meet, has not a word if the forester be present, or his assistant only drop a hint about having seen a chamois or roe on the mountains."

"Did you never think of becoming a forester yourself?" asked Nora, wishing to turn his thoughts from his jealous grievances, for such she knew them to be.

"I had not health or strength for it," he answered; "but even had it been otherwise, my whole thoughts were bent on being a painter. As soon as I was free from the day-school, I began to carry my father's paints; when I left off attending the Sunday-school, I learned his trade, thinking, in my ignorance, that it was a good foundation for my future career; and I ended by going to Munich, with ideas so contracted, that I supposed technical skill all that was necessary to make me a celebrated artist!"

"A very natural mistake on your part," observed Nora, "when one takes into consideration the trade you had learned from your father."

"Perhaps so; but coming into a knowledge of one's ignorance is not agreeable, mademoiselle. It seemed as if the more I learned the less I knew."

"That is the case with most people," said Nora, "and is by no means confined to artists and their studies."

"I got into despair at last," continued Florian; "tried portrait-painting, but soon discovered that the photographers were competitors with whom only first-rate artists could contend; so, when my father died, I returned home and established myself as his successor. My mother and Genoveva were made happy, they say, but I'm sure I don't know why, for I give them both a great deal of trouble, and am often ungrateful for their attentions. Vevey especially has had a hard life lately; but my mother is kind to her, and in return she has patience with me."

Nora, who had long been standing beside the half-open door, now took leave. He accompanied her down the stairs, promising, as he opened the door of the shop, to let her know when he had completed the renovation of the altar for St Hubert's.

Great was Nora's surprise to find her cousin John in eager discussion with Madame Cramer about the purchase of some very coarse, dark-green cloth, to make what he called a "rain mantle." "A famous thing," as he immediately explained to her, "worn by all the men employed in felling wood on the mountains." To judge by the pattern, it was a very formless garment, with merely an opening in the centre for the head; nevertheless, some seams it must have had, for it was to be sent to the tailor, and the measure of John's shoulders was carefully taken by Madame Cramer.

"I thought you had all sorts of waterproof jackets and caps?" observed Nora.

"Well, so I have, but I prefer being dressed like other people. There is no use in making one's self remarkable, you know; and I may be in places where being known by my coat might prove troublesome."

"Am I to understand, Jack," said Nora, "that you have found some one to go out deer-stalking with you?"

"Deer-stalking or chamois-hunting, as the case may be," he answered, seating himself on the counter; and in the full security of not being understood by any one but his cousin, continuing, "I have been thinking, Nora, that I must begin to limit my confessions to you; and, indeed, for your own sake, you had better ask me no questions in future about where I am going, or what I intend to do. You see, dear girl, if you know too much, you may in the end be obliged to bear witness against me, and you wouldn't like to do that, I am sure!"

"I thought," said Nora, reproachfully, "I thought you would have waited a week or ten days longer, until Mr Torp had left the village."

"He has no intention of leaving," said John. "I heard him say that the scarcity of game enhanced its value; and that he believed an Englishman liked wandering through a picturesque country just as well as a German, though he might talk less about it. He seems to enjoy himself here, this Mr Torp, and likes wearing his tweed jacket and wide-awake—and hunting and fishing, and playing skittles, and pretending not to see us, and all the rest of it; and I tell you, Nora, he has no more idea of leaving the village than we have. The forester's son is going out to-morrow to look after some chamois that were seen above the Wild Alp; and the day after, Torp and Waldemar are to hunt there. Now they all know I wish to join them, but not one can invite me, because that fellow Torp won't allow them."

"You have not yet tried Captain Falkner."

"Yes, I have," answered John. "He is evidently flirting with Georgy, so I asked him yesterday, point-blank, to let me shoot on his ground—and what do you think he said? His father had given up hunting; he himself was only occasionally at home on leave of absence, and that they had now let their chase to the forester: he had only reserved a right for himself, and was obliged to purchase his own game when his mother wished for it! I saw he was sorry he could not oblige me—more, of course, on Georgy's account than mine; and he even proposed speaking to the forester; but as I did not choose him to know that, at Torp's instigation, I had already been refused in that quarter, I requested him to say nothing about the matter, for that I could amuse myself walking about on the mountains, and making excursions into Tyrol."

"I wish you would, for the present, be satisfied with doing so," said Nora, earnestly.

"I am much more likely to have a shot at the chamois, near the Wild Alp, before any of them," cried John, exultingly.

"Then I may not hope that you will go with me to our landlord's alp to-morrow?"

John shook his head, and turning to Madame Cramer, requested, in broken but very intelligible German, that his woodman's mantle might be made in the course of the next few hours, as he should probably want it that very evening.

Nora left the shop with him, and walked towards the inn without asking another question, or attempting remonstrances that she knew would be useless.

CHAPTER XXV

Treats of Marriage and Other Matters

NORA found her uncle and Georgina still sitting at the breakfast-table, and was at first somewhat provoked at the little inclination shown to join her alp party. Now, though she did not, perhaps, very particularly desire their company, the appearance of separating herself so completely from them as of late was not quite in accordance with her ideas of propriety, so she combated with some pertinacity all Georgina's objections.

"Change of weather to be expected!" she repeated; "not in the least probable for some days. The wind blows out of the mountains in the morning, and into them during the day, in the most satisfactory manner."

"But I have heard," said Georgina, "that the alps about here lie very high, and the excursions to them are, in consequence, exceedingly fatiguing."

"We are not going to a high alp; the cattle have already left most of them. The one I mean is quite easy of ascent."

"I dare say, however," rejoined Georgina, "that there are places without a path, and rocks to be scrambled over, and springs and rivulets in all directions, to wet one's feet."

Nora could not deny the probability of such impediments being in the way, but suggested that strong boots would make the path of little importance, especially after a continuance of fine weather, such as they had lately had.

"They say," persisted Georgina, "that one generally arrives at such places ravenously hungry; and there is nothing to eat but dreadfully greasy messes, such as the peasants here delight in—and they might disagree with papa, you know!"

"I shall take care that no such messes be set before him," said Nora, good-humouredly.

"I'm afraid of nothing but the too warm weather," observed Mr Nixon.

"And I," said Georgina, "am much more afraid of—of—"

"Of what?"

"Of the dirt and smoke," she replied, with a slight grimace.

"But we are not going to sleep there, and I am quite sure that where I propose going everything will be perfectly clean."

"John has had experience, Nora, and he assures me—"

"Most probably," said Nora, interrupting her, "John did not want to have you with him. He does not wish for my company either, but found other means to prevent me from joining him."

"That may be the case," rejoined Georgina, thoughtfully, "for when I first came here I really intended to make some excursions; but he told me at once that they were not the sort of thing I should like, and that a—In short, my feet were better fitted for parquet floors than mountain paths."

"I think," said Mr Nixon, with a smile and a sly wink at Nora, "I think that was said by the captain at St Benedict's, as we were getting out of the boat, Georgy."

"Well, perhaps it was," she answered, her colour a good deal deeper than usual; "he, too, rather dissuaded me from undertaking any expeditions of the kind, and he has a sister—"

"Who," said Nora, "has most probably been on every

mountain in the neighbourhood."

"Yes; but made herself quite ill last year by attempting to follow a Countess Schaumberg from Vienna, who, he tells me, can use a rifle and hunt as well as the keenest sportsman, and from his account must be a specimen of a German masculine woman. In England, when we become manly, we turn completely to the stable, talk of horses, and delight in slang; this countess does not ride, or even drive a pony carriage, but she has a choice collection of fire-arms, and takes her chasseur and dogs wherever she goes."

"When is she expected here?" asked Nora.

"In about a fortnight or three weeks. She comes here for the marriage of Captain Falkner's sister, who has long been engaged to Count Carl Benndorff of Herrenburg Achenanger Drachenthal."

"How well you pronounce these hard words," said Nora, laughing; "one would think you had been taking lessons in German."

"Well, so she has," said her father, with a significant grimace; "she is reading a book of poetry with the captain, and seems to get on famously; but she can't understand other people's German, or talk a word to the little boy who catches minnows for me when I want bait."

"Perhaps," said Nora, demurely, "my proposed alp party might have interfered with the German lessons?"

"Not far wrong, Nora," cried Mr Nixon, with a loud laugh. "Come, Georgy, tell the truth and shame the devil. If Nora had said the day *after* to-morrow you would have made less difficulties—a certain person will be out hunting then, you know."

Georgina's colour again deepened as she said that she had not thought of Captain Falkner when objecting to the alp party.

"Well," said Mr Nixon, nudging Nora as she sat beside

him, "well, *I'm* not ashamed to say that if you will put off your excursion until the day after to-morrow we shall be happy to join you, eh, Georgy? To-morrow, you see, the captain might expect us to—no matter what—we couldn't disappoint him, you know—on no account—he might be unhappy or offended, for the captain is very fond of us, he is! and I, for my part, shouldn't mind confessing to you, if Georgy was out of the way, that I'm uncommon taken with him. He doesn't sit at my end of the boat, and has lately begun to ride on the bench, almost, indeed, turning his back to me; but it's all for the purpose of teaching Georgy German—she has told me so a hundred times, and I must believe her—he has not a thought beyond that book of songs—"

"Sonnets," said Georgina, joining half unwittingly in Nora's merry laugh.

When Mr Nixon left them together a short time afterwards, some minutes elapsed before either of them spoke a word. At length Georgina, while playing diligently with her lace-sleeves and bracelets, observed, "M. Waldemar improves on acquaintance, Nora; we begin to think him very gentlemanlike."

"I never thought him otherwise," said Nora; "he is very unaffected, agreeable, and gay, and forms a most pleasing contrast to our cold proud countryman, Mr Torp."

"Who certainly does give himself wonderful airs for a Mr Torp!" said Georgina, scornfully. "I am rather glad he avoids our acquaintance, though I am inclined to think he is not quite so insignificant a person as I at first supposed; he is not vulgar or pompous, and his insufferable arrogance I now begin to think may proceed from his having a large fortune, and considering himself an object of speculation to designing young ladies. Nesbitt tells me he has a servant who dresses as well or rather better than his master, and walks about all day amusing himself; it seems, too, he imitates Mr Torp in manners as well as dress, declines all the civil advances of Monsieur Adam and Mrs Nesbitt, and was so seldom heard to speak that for a long time people could not find out whether he were German, English, or French!"

"I suppose, however," said Nora, "the interesting discovery has been made at last?"

"Nesbitt says that Adam's abuse of a Russian family with whom he had travelled last year, roused him in so unusual a manner that little doubt now remains of his being a Russian."

"Did you really feel any curiosity on this subject, Georgina?" asked Nora, surprised.

"Only inasmuch as it proves that this Mr Torp has probably travelled about a good deal."

"Oh, if you care to know," said Nora, "M. Waldemar told me that his friend had been for the last ten years almost constantly on the continent."

"I should rather like to know something about him and his family," said Georgina.

"Why?" asked Nora.

"Because one naturally feels curious about a person with whom one has spent some weeks under the same roof in a small village like this. Captain Falkner has seen him very seldom, I believe, and calls him generally 'my friend's friend,' as if to prove that he knows nothing about him."

"I cannot say that I feel the slightest interest or curiosity concerning him," observed Nora, carelessly.

"Perhaps you will not say so when I tell you that M. Waldemar is not, as I supposed, an artist by profession: he is the eldest son of a Count Benndorff, a Tyrolean nobleman of very old family." She paused, as if expecting some demonstration of surprise on the part of Nora.

"Well," said the latter, smiling, "do you not remember

my telling you not to judge of people by their coats or shoes in the mountains here? I said it was even possible he might be a prince in disguise!"

"I do recollect your saying something to that purport," said Georgina; "and it is odd enough that he will probably be a prince in the course of time. Papa says these foreign titles are perfectly worthless; and Mrs Savage Wayward told me, before I left England, that I should find princes, counts, and barons like mushrooms in Germany. They don't seem quite so plenty, after all, which is curious when one considers that all the children inherit the parental title."

"Captain Falkner's instructions," observed Nora, "have apparently not been confined altogether to the song-book, as my uncle calls it."

"No," answered Georgina, "he speaks good English and excellent French, so we have discussed a variety of subjects."

"Such as, for instance—" said Nora, and then she paused, with a look of interrogation.

"Whether I could make up my mind to remain in Germany—'for good,' as papa says when he means for ever."

"And do you feel disposed to resign the pomps and vanities of the London world, and retire to the cloisters of St Benedict's?"

"Unfortunately that is only a happiness in prospective," answered Georgina, "for Captain Falkner cannot or will not give up his profession as long as there is what he calls a chance of war."

"And you like him well enough to follow his regiment, and submit to the discomforts of country quarters in Hungary, Transylvania, or elsewhere?"

"I requested twenty-four hours for consideration," replied Georgina, gravely. "After being so often, and, as you know, so recently deceived in my expectations, I resolved to attach no importance to Captain Falkner's attentions, and was therefore completely taken by surprise yesterday evening. If you had not come here this morning I should have gone to you for advice, knowing no one more competent to give it."

"Had you so spoken ten years ago," said Nora, "I should have discussed this matter in a manner that would have convinced you I was worthy of the confidence placed in my wisdom; for my mother having herself made two love matches, and neither proving particularly happy, educated me in an almost overstrained rational manner, making me not at all disposed to fall in love myself, or fancy others in love with me. At the age of sixteen or seventeen I might have been reasoned or have reasoned myself into almost any proposed *marriage de convenance*, while now, strange to say, at six-and-twenty, I feel myself growing seriously sentimental and romantic, and consider love the chief desideratum."

"I think I may take it for granted that Captain Falkner likes me," said Georgina, smiling, "and I like him, not perhaps quite as well as—one who never really cared for me. But I am tired of struggling in the world of fashion, and am no longer young, have no wish to end my life as the unmarried one of the family; and my chances are few at home, Nora, for the increase of the female population in England is monstrous they say. So all things considered—"

"All things considered," said Nora, laughing, "you have made up your mind to marry, and only ask advice in the hope of being confirmed in your resolution. Now I begin to think that I can scarcely venture to give an opinion on this occasion, having scarcely seen Captain Falkner half a dozen times. In fact, were he to burst upon my dazzled sight in the full glory of his Austrian uniform at this moment, I should positively not know him. Don't you think, instead of the grey jacket and straw hat, you could persuade him to dress himself in all his accoutrements for our gratification, when he comes this evening formally to demand your hand of my uncle? Dress *does* make such a difference, as Bob Acres[*] says."

"Nora, you are laughing at me," cried Georgina, a good deal discomposed.

"I ought rather to envy you," replied Nora, seriously, "for you have evidently gained the affection of an honourable man, who, without knowing anything of your family or fortune, tells you he loves you, and asks you in marriage. I have never had the happiness of being loved in this manner, Georgina; but so highly have I learned to value a perfectly disinterested attachment, that I would willingly give all I possess to be able to inspire any one with such an affection for me. Of this, however, there is now no chance, so I must take the place you decline, and become the 'unmarried one' of our family."

"Then," said Georgina, smiling cheerfully, "then you do not think I am about to do a foolish thing, Nora?"

"Certainly not," answered Nora, moving towards the door, "that is, if you are quite sure that you love him."

On descending to the road before the inn she perceived a number of children just released from school, dispersing homewards; the boys whooped, whistled, shoved and cuffed each other, playing at ball with their caps, hats, and books, as boys will do to the end of time most probably. A madcap girl occasionally attempted to join in the rough sport, but as often retreated, hurt or frightened, to more quiet companions. She was scarcely well received by the groups of little girls, who, with arms entwined, were

---

[*] See note p. 143. Obviously one of the author's favourite quotations.

confidentially whispering to each other their little secrets, or perhaps animadverting severely on her unruly conduct. Two very youthful maidens lingered among the feeding-troughs for horses, ranged along the wall of the inn, and Nora perceived at once that they were imitating their mothers, and enjoying a little gossip.

"It was when I was going to school this very morning that I heard her," said one little chatterbox to the other: "'Adieu, Count Waldemar,' says she, 'and a pleasant journey home,' says she."

"Well, to be sure, the courage that she has!" interposed the other. "As mother says, the boldness of that girl is not to be believed."

"And," continued the first, "'A pleasant journey home,' says she, 'Count Waldemar,' and runs away, and he after her, and laughs and lifts her up ever so high and shakes her."

"I'm glad of it," said number two; "many a shake she gets from her mother, and well she deserves them."

"She didn't mind the shake a bit," said the first speaker, "for the count told the landlady to give her the biggest piece of cake in the house, and she came running after me with a lump of kugelhopf* full of currants and covered with almonds, and she as proud as a peacock."

"Well," said number two, "I couldn't think where she got that cake; it was very good, and she gave me a piece of it, and Catty, and Lina, and—"

"She did not dare to offer me any," said the first speaker, with proud propriety. "I had seen her pertness, and taxed her with it. To speak to the count, and he getting

---

* A kind of cake popular in Germany and also in Alsace, traditionally baked in a tall mould with fluted sides.

into the carriage, and the strange gentleman from England, and all the people of the inn, and the postilion from the town standing by!"

Here Nora, not altogether uninterested in their discourse, moved towards the speakers; but after a hurried frightened courtesy they both scampered off, and she turned to the little romp, who, having been thrown down in a concluding scuffle, was now rubbing the dust and gravel from her pink petticoat and black bodice, while a red-haired boy, riding on one of the feeding-troughs, alone remained to pity or enjoy her discomfiture. She looked up as Nora approached, and showed a pretty, round, sunburnt face, that no doubt had attracted the artist eye of Count Waldemar, and made him acquainted with her. She was not at all shy, and laughed as Nora shook some gravel from her thick curly hair, and asked who had thrown her down.

"Red Hans," said the little girl, pointing to the grinning, freckled-faced boy, who was moving about on the trough in a reckless manner, making movements with his long, dangling, bare legs, as if spurring a horse.

"And who is Red Hans?"

"He belongs to the widow at Waltenburg."

"And you?"

"I'm the hammersmith's Nanerl. Come, Hans, let's go home to dinner."

The boy instantly descended from his imaginary horse and came towards her. "Nanerl won't tell," he said, glancing towards Nora. "She knows I'd get no dinner from the hammersmith if she made a complaint."

"Why don't you go home to dinner?" asked Nora.

"Cause mother's so poor, and the hammersmith said I could have a bit with Nanerl every day."

"I'm afraid you're a very naughty boy," said Nora: "you ought to take care of her instead of throwing her down, as you did just now."

Hans looked embarrassed.

"He's a scamp," said the little girl, promptly. "Father says so, and mother too; but I like him, and we play at wildschuetz together."

"And you are the sennerin on the alp, and take care of the cows?"

"No, I'm a wildschuetz too," she answered. "Come along, Hans, I won't tell; come along."

Glad to escape, he seized her hand and pulled her after him as he rushed down the road into the midst of the village.

Nora looked after them and smiled.

"Now that girl is regularly 'doing the poor'," muttered Torp to himself, as he peered from behind one of the old chestnut trees in the garden, beneath which he had breakfasted. "I suppose," he continued, in soliloquy, "she is waiting for Waldemar, expecting him to go to the ruins with her. 'Mees Nora,' you may wait long; by this time I should think your adorer must be in Tyrol."

Had Waldemar been beside him, Torp would have turned away his head, to prove his total indifference to the presence of so insignificant a personage as a Miss Nora Nixon, whereas he now thought proper to indulge his curiosity without reserve, and for the first time took a long and steady stare at the unconscious Nora, as she stood on the road between the garden and the inn. Dressed, as usual, in a check black and grey silk, he thought her figure as graceful as any he had seen for a long time; and even beneath the hideous coarse straw hat the delicate little face appeared to such advantage that he magnanimously rejoiced in the absence of his friend, and applauded himself for his disinterested conduct.

Just as Nora was about to walk away, she perceived the

forester's son, Franz, coming towards the village; he hastened his steps, and advanced so directly towards her, that she first stopped, and then moved a few steps to meet him.

"Oh, ho! what is the meaning of all this?" thought Torp, as the young man, raising his hat, exhibited a pale, agitated face, and began to speak with an eagerness and vehemence of action very different from his usual tranquil manner.

Nora's cheerful smile faded away, and a look of deep interest spread over her features as she listened, and began to walk slowly along the road with him.

"Madeleine said you were at the mill, mademoiselle," observed Franz, "and that you can bear witness that she told black Sepp she did not care for him, and would not marry him."

"I remember hearing her say so," replied Nora.

"He reminded her," continued Franz, "of some promise that she had made years ago."

Nora nodded assent.

"But," he added, "that is of no importance, for she must have been then almost a child; and she confesses having made promises of the same kind to half-a-dozen others before she was sixteen."

Nora looked grave, but did not speak.

"She would have braved him if she had dared," he continued; "but her father, she says, has entered into solemn engagements with the Tyrolean, who contrived to make himself useful and necessary when the family were poor and in debt. It seems he not only served without receiving wages, but even assisted them in various ways, all, as it now appears, on condition that Madeleine was to be his wife."

"It is incomprehensible to me," observed Nora, "why the miller permitted an engagement with you under such circumstances."

"I cannot say he was exactly willing," said Franz; "it was

my father who urged it at Ammergau, on account of the
fortune perhaps—and other friends helped, and laughed at
the idea of the miller consulting his workman about the
marriage of his daughter! I only thought of Madeleine's
beauty, and the triumph of carrying her off from all the
others, and so it was settled an hour after we came together."

"Has Madeleine broken off her engagement with you altogether?" asked Nora.

"She said she must, for that her father, at black Sepp's
instigation, had withdrawn his consent, and until his death
she would have no fortune; I have none either, and must
wait long to become forstwart."

"You seemed just now," said Nora, after a pause, "to
think I could be of use to you. I cannot, however, imagine
in what way."

"Madeleine thought if you called on the priest, and got
him to speak to her father and black Seppel, it might do
good; they have both a great respect for his reverence."

"Could not her mother explain the state of the case better?" suggested Nora.

"Madeleine tells me her mother takes part with the
miller, and is now more disposed towards the Tyrolean
than me."

"That is not improbable," said Nora, musingly; "and if
you really think that my interference can be of use to you, I
will go at once to the priest."

"Thank you, mademoiselle, you are very kind. His reverence is at home now, I am sure, and either in the garden or
looking after his bees. I should not have given you this
trouble, if Madeleine had not expressly forbidden any interference on my part, which, she said, would do no good, and
only serve to irritate her father. She hoped that you, who
had been so kind to Rosel, would not refuse to help her,

and it seems she was not mistaken."

"Will you wait here to be made acquainted with the result of the conference?" asked Nora.

"I cannot," he answered, "for Count Waldemar sent express for me this morning, to tell me that he was going home, and must trust altogether to me to find sport for his friend from England, as the captain of St Benedict's had said he had no time at present to call on the gentleman, or go out hunting with him; so I must now look after some chamois, said to be in the neighbourhood of the Wild Alp, and I'm glad of the walk, or anything that takes me from the village just now."

He opened the wicket of the priest's garden, bowed low as she passed him, and stood looking after her, when she entered the open door of the house, and commenced a conversation with the old housekeeper, who had advanced to meet her.

Unperceived by both, Torp sauntered along the road, his hands thrust into the pockets of his shooting jacket, his eyes fixed on the sunny summit of the mountain that rose high above the shingled roof of the parsonage.

Light, and airy, and clean, like all the priests' houses Nora had ever seen in Germany, was this one also. It seemed as if everything had been just freshly scoured; and when the door of the reception-room was opened, she found herself in precisely the sort of apartment she had expected. Two side and three front windows were furnished with very white thin muslin curtains carefully draped aside; there were six chairs, a round table, a sofa, and two chests of drawers in the room; on one of the latter, a well-carved crucifix, on the other a pair of silver candlesticks. She had scarcely time to look round her, when the door of an adjoining room was opened, and a middle-aged, intelligent, and rather solemn-looking man advanced towards her; his coat was very long, his cravat very stiff, his high forehead rendered higher by incipient baldness, and his carefully-shaved cheeks and chin remarkably blue-chinned. He approached Nora with a succession of slight, shy bows; and as he stopped before her, and placed his right hand slowly in the bosom of his coat, the peculiar priestly movement betrayed to her at once *his* embarrassment, and removed hers.

Accepting the offered chair, she informed him of as much of the miller's story as she felt herself at liberty to relate, and he listened to her throughout with the most undeviating attention, observing, when she paused for an answer, that "He was not surprised, but sorry for what had occurred, on account of the forester's family; he should scarcely feel justified in speaking to the miller in the manner she desired; and had little hope of influencing the Tyrolean, who was in the habit of avoiding the church in Almenau, by crossing the mountains to visit his family, almost every Sunday and holyday; the man was violent and resolute, and not likely to listen to expostulations from any one."

"I regret to hear this," said Nora, "for he seems to have the miller completely in his power."

A momentary flash of intelligence gleamed in the priest's eyes, but passed as quickly as lightning; and it was with eyes fixed on the ground that he observed, "The miller is a weak —a very weak man, mademoiselle, and has unfortunately left his affairs completely to the superintendence of his chief workman during the last six years, and has become dependent on him: he was very poor when I came to reside here, but has since inherited a good deal of money from a brother, and his daughter as village heiress has been latterly the prize for which all the neighbouring peasants have been contending. She has been the subject of more quarrels, and the cause of more brawls, than she is worth; and knowing her to be an idle, pleasure-loving girl, you must excuse my saying that a separation from her would be the greatest piece of good fortune that could happen to the young assistant forester."

"Unfortunately he does not think so," said Nora, "and he and Madeleine now place their whole reliance on you."

"I shall speak to *him* this evening, and I hope to some purpose," he answered, dryly.

"You will not find him at home, as he is going to the Wild Alp," rejoined Nora; "and if what I have said has led you to form the design of dissuading him from a renewal of his engagement, I have indeed proved but a sorry advocate, and had better cease to plead."

"Mademoiselle," said the priest, politely, "no better advocate could have been chosen on this occasion; I have heard of your generosity to Rosel, and can assure you it is not misplaced; she is, and always has been a good girl; her brother also is worthy of regard, and you cannot be more interested in his welfare than I am. I have hitherto avoided all interference in the marriages of my parishioners; they are generally rational contracts made by the parents, in which the parties most concerned are so little consulted, that the refusal to bestow a cow or calf has not unfrequently broken off a match in every respect desirable. Now I have little doubt that interested motives induced the forester to propose his son to the miller for his daughter."

"I understood," said Nora, "that Franz and Madeleine had long been attached to each other."

"Madeleine's attachments," said the priest, with a contemptuous smile, "have been very numerous. Franz has not lived at home for many years; and though I think it more than probable that he admires Madeleine, who is considered very handsome, I suspect she accepted him for the purpose of becoming, in the course of time, a forester's or perhaps even a forstmeister's wife, and being able to wear a bonnet."

"Wear a bonnet!" repeated Nora, "could she not wear one now if she pleased?"

"No, mademoiselle, a peasant's daughter does not wear a bonnet in this country; but what I meant to express was, that Madeleine's ambition was to become a lady."

"Oh," said Nora, "I understand you now."

"Yet I was not speaking in the least metaphorically," continued the priest; "Franz has been to the forester academy, will receive a place under government, and, as his wife, there is nothing to prevent Madeleine from substituting a bonnet for the peasant hat, or still simpler black kerchief so universally worn here. The sliver-laced bodice, short skirt, and apron will be thrown aside, and replaced by a modish gown, and the ignorant, vain girl will fancy the metamorphosis complete."

"She will look uncommonly pretty in any dress," said Nora. "I have seldom seen more perfect features."

"Mademoiselle," said the priest, almost reproachfully, "you attach too much importance to beauty. I could prove to you that the plainest girl in this village is by many degrees the cleverest and most amiable!"

"Oh, pray tell me all about her," cried Nora, eagerly; "you can in no way oblige me more than by giving me information concerning the people here."

"If that be the case," said the priest, "perhaps you will go to the school-house with me, and look over the judgment-books."

The school-house was not far distant—an unpretending building, in no way differing from the others in the village, excepting that the whole of the ground floor was required for the large school-room, which was amply lighted by side and front windows, and furnished with long rows of benches and desks, suited to the different ages of the pupils, and increasing progressively in height as they receded towards the door. A broad space in the middle of the room served to separate the boys from the girls, and afforded the school-master a place, which he constantly perambulated, to the no small terror of idle or mischievous children.

As Nora and the priest advanced into the school-room, Torp's head might have been seen at one of the open windows, thrust through the clustering leaves of a vine trained against the wall of the house. There was a mixture of curiosity and irony in the expression of his face as he listened to Nora's questions, and saw her poring over the large blue books so willingly presented to her for inspection by the schoolmaster. It is probable she asked questions he had no objection to hear answered, as he remained at the window, and even stretched forward once or twice, as if he also wished to see the contents of the judgment-books.

When Nora took leave, followed to the door by both her companions, she found Rosel waiting for her near the church, and they soon after entered the footpath in the wood that led to the ruins of Waltenburg.

At some distance before her Nora soon perceived Torp. Why he just then chose to go where, from her conversation with Waldemar on the previous evening, he knew he was likely to meet her, she could not well imagine. It never occurred to her that, unconscious of the information she had obtained of Waldemar's departure, both from the school-children and Franz, he felt a mischievous pleasure in the expectation of seeing her sitting on some fragment of the ruin, confidently expecting the arrival of his friend! Yet it must be confessed that this idea had for some minutes served to amuse Torp when he first turned into the wood, and seemed to recur, when, having scrambled to a prominent place on a weather-beaten wall, he looked down with laughing eyes, and watched her progress over the few

mouldering planks that supplied the place of the drawbridge.

Scarcely, however, had she and Rosel entered the precincts of the ruins, and looked over the wall that commanded a view of the high road, than they heard a loud and
joyous jodel, and saw soon afterwards a young man springing up the hill, flourishing his hat in the air, and followed
more leisurely by an old peasant, whose long-tailed, short-
waisted, grass-green coat made Nora instantly recognise the
man now well known to her by the name of "Crags."

Nora's inclination to build castles in the air on the ruins
of Waltenburg instantly vanished, and she turned back to
meet the old man and his son, who were evidently bearers
of good news. With much pleasure she heard that the judge
had appointed the following Tuesday for the signing of the
contract of resignation, and that he would that very afternoon come to Almenau to speak to her.

"About the thousand florins, you know, miss," said the
old man; "for I told him I was sure you were ready to deposit the money in his hands on Thursday, or even sooner,
if it were necessary."

"Quite right," said Nora, smiling at the peasant's cun-
ning way of informing her that she would be required to
keep her promise sooner perhaps than she had expected.

"When I have once made up my mind to do a thing," he
continued, with much self-complaisance, "I do it. And
that's why I did not wait till next week to go into our town,
but says to Seppel this morning, says I—If the young lady is
willing to make that agreement respecting the churchyard,
says I, let's take her at her word, says I, and strike while the
iron is hot."

Again Nora smiled, and he continued: "If it's agreeable
to you, miss, the betrothal can take place at the forester's
on Thursday evening, and before you leave the village I'll

move with my old woman into the off house, and let Seppel bring home Rosel."

"You could not do anything that would give me more pleasure," said Nora.

She had scarcely ceased speaking when, more to her amusement than surprise, Seppel waved his hat in the air, and at the same time raising his right leg, he gave vent to his feelings of exultation in a shout that caused Torp to look in some astonishment at the pantomime being performed on the green hill beneath him.

"This very day," said Seppel, "I'll go to the Kerbstein lake, and invite my mother's brother to come to us on Thursday next."

"The fisherman there is your uncle?" observed Nora.

"And—my godfather too, miss, and has done his duty by me handsome from beginning to end. I would not miss being the first to tell him of my betrothal for any consideration, so I'll just run on, and take leave of my mother, and perhaps I may get to the lake before nightfall; if not, I can turn into one of the huts on the Wild Alp."

"The cattle have been driven down from want of pasture," shouted his father after him, as he bounded down before them. "You will not find a cow or sennerin on the whole mountain now!"

"No matter," he answered, laughing, "the keys of the huts are to be found under the benches before the door, and I can have my choice of the lofts, and the hay in all of them!"

"A spirited and handsome fellow he is, there is no doubt of that," murmured old Crags, as he plodded on beside Nora and her perfectly happy companion. "I sometimes think a little of his life and energy would do Anderl no harm; but one can't have everything one wishes, and in respect of steadiness there's no comparison!"

CHAPTER XXVI

Jack's First Exploit

THE next day was partly spent by Nora in becoming better acquainted with Captain Falkner. She perceived that he knew more of Torp than he was at liberty to divulge even to Georgina, and rejoiced that the incognito was to be continued for some time longer, as she had learned to distrust her uncle's professions of indifference to rank, and feared that Torp's haughty reception of his civilities might put her patience to a severe test.

She accompanied her uncle to the lake at St Benedict's, interpreted for him when he chose to talk to the people about the place, joined Georgina in trying to persuade Captain Falkner to leave the army, and made plans for the future, in which, as possessor of Waltenburg, she was to be their nearest neighbour. She would have spent a pleasant day in the society of companions so evidently happy, had not John's absence caused her much uneasiness. He had left them the day before after a hasty dinner, and laughing congratulations to his sister and Captain Falkner, and not having returned during the night, she feared, and at last firmly believed, that he had gone, as he had said he would, to the Wild Alp. It was there, also, that Seppel had proposed to pass the night, and she knew not whether to suppose a planned meeting on both sides, or an unlucky chance that would inevitably lead to mutual temptation. She remembered, too, with increasing anxiety, that Franz had returned home for Torp during the previous evening, and that Rosel had mentioned having seen them pass the forest-house together just before she went to bed. Their destination was also the Wild Alp, and she dreaded to think what might occur there should a meeting take place.

Long, therefore, appeared the day, still longer the evening, but at last, leaving her uncle, Georgina, and Captain Falkner under one of the trees near the inn, she sauntered through the village, pre-occupied and dejected, responding more laconically than was her wont to the "Good evenings" wished her by the peasants who sat or stood before their doors. Scarcely, however, was she beyond the village, and within sight of the forest-house, when she heard her name pronounced in a low, cautious manner, and on looking towards the place whence the voice came, she saw her cousin John standing far above her, in the deep shade of an old beech-tree. He seemed to have just descended from the summit of the mountain, along the steep side of which the road had been made; but instead of joining her, as she expected, he beckoned impatiently, and then receded still further into the wood, as if unwilling to be seen.

A good deal alarmed at his manner, Nora sprang up the bank, and when beside him looked anxiously into his face. It was still light enough for her to see him distinctly, and, under any other circumstances, she would have indulged in a hearty laugh, so oddly did his disordered hair and smutted face contrast with his smart English walking-dress; but the streaks of soot about the roots of his hair, and the comical prolongation of his eyebrows, produced hardly the shadow of a smile on her countenance, as, reassured of his personal safety by his presence, she said, gravely, "I see, Jack, you have had your face blackened, and been out poaching."

"Call it wild hunting, if you please," he cried, embracing

her somewhat turbulently, "and let me tell you, Nora, that I have no wish to be anything but a hunter of this sort, as long as I may chance to remain in this jolly country, for more exciting sport it is impossible to imagine; I would not have missed last night's hunt, or this morning's fun, for anything that could be offered me. But I have got into a little dilemma, Nora, out of which you must help me, and keep my secret into the bargain."

"A dilemma!" she repeated: "oh, Jack, I hope it does not concern Seppel in any way! You do not know what unhappiness it will cause, if he should be detected, or even suspected just now. I say nothing of the consequences to yourself, but for a mere frolic to destroy irretrievably the prospects of a young man whose father has so lately consented to resign his property to him, that he may be able to marry the person to whom he has been so long—"

"Oh, I know all that!" he cried, interrupting her. "I've promised to dance at his wedding, if he has not to wait another half-dozen years before he celebrates it."

"Should he be brought before the judge as a wild-schuetz," said Nora, "there is an end to all his hopes, for his father will undoubtedly disinherit him!"

"There is much more danger of his being shot by your friend the forester, than brought before the judge," said Jack. "I never saw such a dare-devil of a fellow in my life, to say nothing of his having friends and accomplices at both sides of the mountains."

"And you have induced him to recommence these dangerous and unlawful practices," observed Nora, reproachfully, "after his having refrained from them for upwards of six years!"

"Bosh!" cried Jack. "The people about here may believe that, and think he never touches a rifle now; but he told me —no matter what—a different story, at all events, and I must believe him, for he had his clothes in one house and his gun in another, and knew perfectly well where to find the key to the uninhabited châlet in which we blackened our faces."

"On the Wild Alp, most probably," said Nora, sorrowfully.

"The very place," exclaimed Jack; "but we did not remain long there, for directly after sunset we began our hunt, and were joined by three fellows from Tyrol, who had seen no trace of chamois, although they had been out all the previous night. They proposed, however, giving me a 'stand,' as they called it, near a spot of ground that has been much frequented lately by deer; and, as we had famous moonlight, I had only to keep to leeward of the direction in which they were likely to come. But to get to this place, Nora, Seppel and I had to creep through narrow defiles and over rocks, to clamber uphill on loose sand, through bushes and brambles, and, at last, actually to crawl like worms over stones and trunks of trees, cast about in all directions by one of those mountain-torrents now without a drop of water, though sometimes quite a broad deep stream."

"I can easily imagine such a place," said Nora; "and though I do not exactly understand why you crawled over the stones—"

"To prevent them from rolling, and either alarming the deer or attracting the attention of those foresters, who are perpetually on the look out."

"Well," said Nora, "go on. You shot something, I suppose, or you would not have got into a dilemma? Tell me what happened."

"Oh, that was long after; and I rather expect you will enjoy, or at all events excuse, the scrape I have got into this time, as there is no harm done, and you can easily prevent any unpleasant consequences."

"Tell me how, and let me do it then," said Nora, impatiently.

"I thought you would like to have a full and true account of all that occurred; besides, you cannot be of any use until to-morrow morning."

"In that case," said Nora, "you may be as circumstantial as you please; and while you relate, we can walk towards the inn together."

"By no means," cried Jack, catching her arm to detain her. "I do not wish to enter the village until it is dark, or the inn until I can get to my own room and wash my face without being observed; besides, for reasons which you will afterwards understand, I don't choose any one to know that I have seen or spoken to you."

"This sounds very mysterious, Jack: I wish you would be more explicit."

"Well, don't interrupt me so often," he rejoined; and then having seated himself deliberately on a huge stone, he looked up with an air of extreme satisfaction, and an odd twinkle in his eyes, and asked abruptly, "Do you know what a *schmarn* is, Nora?"

"A sort of omelette, cut up into little pieces," she answered.

"And a woodman's *schmarn?*" he asked.

"Something similar, I believe, excepting that it is made with water instead of milk."

"Right; they call it *holz-muss*; and a better thing for keeping off hunger was never invented. That's what they gave me for supper yesterday evening."

"Where?" asked Nora.

"At one of the houses—I don't know whether it was in Tyrol or Bavaria; very civil people they were—wanted to return me the greater part of the money I gave them."

"Then you were probably in Bavaria," observed Nora;

"but go on."

"It was fortunate I had had so substantial a supper, and carried off a piece of rye-bread in my pocket, for after we came to the 'stand' they had talked so much about, the three Tyroleans left us, and we had to lie ensconced behind some rocks for hours and hours, listening to every sound, distant and near, with fatiguing attention, and peering out continually, to see if we could distinguish anything approaching the green spot at the other side of the nearly dried-up rivulet that ran between the mountains. I think it must have been a couple of hours past midnight, when we heard the sound of rolling stones and gravel, and soon after perceived a stray roebuck descending from the more barren heights to the grass plot nearly opposite us. I could see every movement; and at one time, as he raised his head, and came forward to the very edge of the grazing-place, he was not thirty yards from the muzzle of my rifle. I raised it—my hand was on the trigger—when,—can you believe it, Nora?—I got into such a state of agitation, that I could not attempt to take aim. I don't think I ever in my life had such a palpitation—such a fit of trembling—"

"And this is what you call sport?" said Nora.

"Pshaw!" he cried, starting up impatiently; "there's no use in telling a woman anything of this kind, she can't understand one! In short, he moved about unconscious of his danger; gave me ample time to recover my self-possession;—and—I shot him. The row caused by the report of my rifle is not to be described. Why, just on that spot there should be such an infernal echo, I cannot tell. It may have sounded louder from the long silence that had preceded it—perhaps, also, my wish to do the thing quietly made me more observant of the noise—but it seemed as if a regular discharge of musketry had taken place, followed by a rolling like thunder along the mountain-side, apparently endless; for, even as it gradually died away, a fresh re-port in the distance seemed to rouse the echo afresh, until I was perfectly aghast at the commotion I had caused."

"I suspect," observed Nora, "you are not the first wild-schuetz who would have liked to silence the echoes about him: but stay!" she added, hastily; "you say this happened about two o'clock in the morning. Now, Mr Torp and Franz left Almenau at midnight, and must have been in the direction, and near enough to have heard your shot."

"To be sure they heard it," answered Jack, laughing; "and I dare say did their best to get at us: but, in order to prevent an unnecessary encounter, while I was listening to the echo, Seppel had scrambled across the stream to where the roebuck was lying, nearly motionless, only giving evidence of life by deep breathings and an occasional shiver, while enormous quantities of blood flowed from a wound in his side."

"Poor thing!" said Nora, compassionately; "I hope he did not suffer long."

"Oh, no," said Jack; "his struggles were soon over; for Seppel plunged his dagger into the nape of his neck in a most scientific manner, and he never moved afterwards."

"Well—well—and then?" said Nora.

"And then," continued Jack, "he butchered away for some time in a manner that I need not describe to you, and ended by placing the roebuck partly in his green linen bag, and slinging it, with my assistance, on his back. He after-wards put his fingers between his teeth, and produced a succession of piercing whistling sounds."

"What for?" asked Nora.

"A signal to the other fellows to join us: they had been searching about the rocks above us, as I had promised them something if I got a shot. Seppel said it was better to be satisfied with the roebuck for this time, and proposed going on to the alp, as he believed the forester was out on the mountain, and he was the last person he wished to meet just then."

"What a passion this hunting must be," soliloquised Nora, "not to be able to resist the temptation even now, when so much is at stake!"

"You may well say that," observed John; "for if the old man had seen us, we should have had bullets 'whistling as they went for want of thought.'* They tell me he fires in a very unceremonious manner at every wildschuetz he meets, ever since his eldest son was shot by one somewhere about here."

"The forester was, fortunately, at home last night," began Nora; "but his son and Mr Torp—"

"I know, I know," cried John, interrupting her; "they came upon us at the Wild Alp, just as we had made a fire, and were going to cook our breakfast. One of our Tyroleans was on the watch; and, as we were five to two, we let them come on, and prepared for battle."

Nora looked alarmed, but John's laugh reassured her, and she let him continue without interruption.

"Our sentinel gave the alarm; we seized our rifles, and looked through the window, just in time to see the enemy advancing up the hill, and over the ground tramped into holes by the cattle in wet weather. Torp and his companion sprang behind some rocks, raised their rifles, and shouted to the Tyroleans, who appeared at the door, to deliver up their arms. They were answered by an order to sheer off, if they thought their lives worth preserving. Seppel, in the mean time, kept in the background with me; and I am

* "He trudged along, unknowing what he sought, | And whistled as he went, for want of thought." John Dryden (1631-1700): *Fables Ancient and Modern* (1700): "Cymon and Iphigenia" lines 84-85.

much mistaken if Torp, supposing us to be but three, did not consider himself, with the assistant forester, more than a match for us. At all events he showed more courage than prudence, for no sooner had the Tyroleans retreated into the hut, than he left his place of safety, and rushed after them, notwithstanding the loud remonstrances of his companion, who, nevertheless, seemed to think himself obliged to follow him. You should have seen how Seppel pounced upon the young forester—"

"What!" exclaimed Nora; "surely you must be mistaken!"

"Not a bit," cried Jack: "he knocked his rifle out of his hand, and then they wrestled desperately for a few seconds; but, with the assistance of one of the Tyroleans, he managed to get him down on the ground, and then tied his hands behind his back, and afterwards his feet together."

"And Mr Torp?" asked Nora.

"Torp floored the two fellows who attacked him without any difficulty, and was evidently making for the door, with his eye on his rifle, until I rushed to the rescue; and though I determined not to betray myself by speaking, and didn't say, "Come on," I'm afraid I looked it, for he turned to me at once, and we had a regular set-to, pitching into each other like—"

"Jack, Jack," cried Nora, quickly, "you have betrayed yourself to Mr Torp, and will be completely in his power!"

"You could not expect me to wait until he knocked me down, too!" cried Jack; "I gave him fair play afterwards at all events, for as soon as the others attacked him again, I drew off. I tell you, Nora, you would have died of laughing had you seen him, as I did, struggling on the floor, and giving them all employment before he was pinioned. He's an uncommonly powerful fellow, that Torp!"

"Perhaps," said Nora, "he did not observe any difference in your mode of attack from that of the others, for, after all, his surprise and the confusion must have been too great for him to make nice observations."

"I don't know," replied Jack, carelessly; "I kept out of his way as much as I could from the time he was overpowered by numbers. The young forester kicked, and writhed, and raged, vowing vengeance on us all: Torp never moved from the time that resistance was useless, and actually contrived to look dignified when lying helpless on the ground, fixing his great grey eyes upon us one after another with such scrutinising glances that we thought it expedient to get him out of the way, and had him carried into the little inner room, and laid him on the boards that had served as bedstead to the shepherdess—I mean dairy-maid; that is what they call sennerin."

"And did he not speak a word then?" asked Nora.

"He said that he hoped we would send some one up to release them before they were starved to death; but Seppel answered that he was not such a fool as to run the risk of having his messenger brought before the judge of the district to betray us. Torp then proposed terms, said that he would take no steps to discover us, and if we would release him at once he would even promise to remain three or four hours in the hut in order to give us time to get into Tyrol; but Seppel did not understand such chivalry, laughed in his face, and locked the door of the room."

"Good heavens! what a dreadful situation!" cried Nora; "surely, Jack, you interfered at last?"

"Not I," he said, with a laugh; "they would not hear of the young forester's being set at liberty, and I could not help enjoying Torp's discomfiture, after all his incivility to me. Of course I thought all the while of telling you, and proposing your making an excursion to the alp to-morrow, with one of your numerous peasant friends. You know you can be quite astonished at finding them prisoners, and all that sort of thing. Take plenty of prog with you, for they'll be deucedly hungry, I suspect, by the time you reach them."

"I wish I could go this moment," said Nora, uneasily: "it is horrible to think of their passing the night in such a way!"

"Why didn't Torp let me have my sport by fair means?" said John; "if I can only have it by stealth he shall not interfere with me. You know you have often said he was a selfish, disagreeable man, Nora; and a little punishment of this kind may bring down his pride perhaps. At all events such things are not uncommon hereabouts, and as to their being starved, or anything of that kind, there is no danger whatever, for if the old forester did not go to look for them, he could be sent an anonymous letter, you know. The simplest of all plans, however, will be for you to go to the alp; Torp knows that you are continually making excursions of the kind, and—"

"And," interposed Nora, "and fortunately he has heard me say that I intended to go to this very place."

"Then go," cried John eagerly, "go, and get up a loud scream when you see him—afterwards you can laugh and question him as much as you like."

"I have only to leave Rosel in ignorance of all that has occurred," said Nora, "and she will be astonished and shocked enough for us both. And now, Jack, I must leave you in order to make arrangements with her, and put off my uncle and Georgina, who had at last consented to go to one of the lower alps near the village. The man who was to have been our guide must be told to call for me at three o'clock in the morning instead of eight, and I shall take all the provisions provided for my uncle to your prisoners."

"I say, Nora," cried John, calling after her as she descended to the road, "don't betray me by looking conscious when you see Torp, and avoid answering any questions he may ask you."

Rosel was not much surprised at Nora's change of plan: the excuse was so plausible, that she must take advantage of the fine weather to go to the Wild Alp, as every one said that the path after rain would be impracticable for her, and a continuance of the present warm weather was not to be expected.

And Rosel explained this at some length, not only at the inn, but also when she went afterwards with a pair of Nora's boots to the shoemaker, and requested him, late as it was, to put large nails in the soles, as otherwise her young lady would find it hard to get over the rocks and loose stones on the way down the mountain from the Wild Alp.

CHAPTER XXVII

The Wild Alp

DAY had not dawned, but the moon, though completely screened by the mountains, still afforded a pale grey sort of light as Nora, accompanied by Rosel and an athletic young wood-cleaver named Michael, left the forester's house. Their way was at first through meadows and gently-sloping hills, and woods of beech and maple, past isolated peasants' houses, where, early as it was, the thrashing-flail was already being swung by busy hands. Many were the morning greetings that Nora and her companions received as they passed the open barn doors, and great the surprise expressed when it was known that they were on their way to the Wild Alp, where the huts were uninhabited and the cattle driven home for the winter! Higher up Nora observed fields of corn and wheat scarcely ready for the sickle, and oats still green as grass. By degrees the beech, birch, and maple trees became rarer, and they entered a forest of pine and fir that Nora thought endless, and, in fact, it covered a not inconsiderable mountain, over which they had to pass before they reached the one on which the Wild Alp was situated.

The mountains around Almenau joined those of Tyrol, and not unfrequently the line of boundary between Bavaria and Austria was made evident by a clearance of wood about the width of a road, which might be distinguished for miles through the forest district, seemingly made with as little regard to hill or dale as a line drawn on a map. Nora had been out some hours, and the sun had risen before she arrived at those higher regions whence she could observe this, and look down on the chains of wooded mountains beneath, with their intersecting valleys and winding rivers; then, too, she caught the first glimpse of the long row of glaciers that so deeply interest the Highland tourist, each step rendering visible a greater extent of eternal snow and ice. More and more rugged became her path, while rocks of the most grotesque form seemed to start from the ground in all directions, and as she wound round the mountain on a narrow shelf that had been blasted in the rocks for the convenience of charcoal-burners and cattle, Nora stopped for a few minutes to look down a deep dry water-course, and wonder at the havoc caused by a small waterfall that now, trickling scantily from the heights above, seemed in no way to render necessary the bridge of felled trees over which she stepped; but which in spring or after rain probably swelled to a raging cataract, as it had prostrated trees and carried away everything impeding its course down the mountain. Masses of loose stones, gravel, and sand, forced along by the torrent, had not remained in the bed excavated by the water, but, spreading over a wide space of ground at each side, had created a scene of devastation that widened as it proceeded, until finally lost in the chaos of rocks that vainly opposed the progress of a river far below in the gorge between the mountains.

When Nora turned from this spot and began to pursue her path, she perceived Rosel far above her, kneeling beside a wooden cross that had been placed in a sheltered nook beside a ledge of rock; the sun's first glowing rays fell on it and the bent figure, and as Nora approached she perceived a tablet containing a picture fastened to the cross, and knew

that on the spot where it stood some one had died suddenly, by accident or otherwise. When Rosel stood up,
Nora bent forward and saw a very rough representation of
a man with a blackened face, intended to represent a wildschuetz, but which might also have been the portrait of a
fiend incarnate, as from an ambush he fired at a young man
whose trim uniform showed him to be a hunter and wood-
ranger by profession.

"Your eldest brother, I suppose?" said Nora.

"Yes. My father, who heard the report of the rifle at the
alp, ran on here, and found him shot through the heart."

"And the wildschuetz?" asked Nora.

"He escaped by sliding down the mountain on the sand,
near the waterfall, at the place you were standing just now,
and once in the forest below, there was no chance of finding him. My mother had this picture painted by Florian's
father, and put up here; but I sometimes think it would be
better if she had been satisfied with the churchyard cross,
for every time my father comes on this mountain, he vows
fresh vengeance against every wildschuetz he may hereafter
meet. When he is hunting or inspecting the woods about
here, I can never sleep at night, and was right glad that he
stayed at home, and sent out Franz with the Englishman
yesterday."

"You feared, perhaps, that Seppel, once out on the
mountain, might be tempted to—"

"Oh, no! I did not think of him," said Rosel; "you know
he has gone to invite his people to our betrothal."

"And this is not the way to the Kerbstein lake," said
Nora.

"Not—the—shortest," answered Rosel, with some hesitation; "yet not much out of the way either; but I can trust
Seppel now, and even if he did pass by the alp, it would be
with no unlawful intention."

Nora walked on in silence, so occupied with her thoughts that she took but little notice of the surrounding scenery, until startled by a loud shout from their guide, when she perceived that they had reached the base of the walls of rock that formed the summit of the mountain, while beneath her, with its deserted châlets and rock-bound nameless lake, lay the Wild Alp. There was a gloomy grandeur in the scene that Nora had not expected; no tree or shrub grew on the steep shore of the emerald-green lake, in the wonderfully clear waters of which every cleft in the surrounding rocks was reflected; no rivulet poured itself into the tranquil basin, nor was there any apparent outlet for the water—supplied by hidden springs; equally secret channels conveyed the superfluous water through the adjoining mountains, leaving the lake in unruffled serenity, and rendering distinctly visible the sand, stones, rocks, and plants that afforded refuge to shoals of large and thriving fish.

Nora descended to the lake, clambered along the pathless shore, until she reached the deserted hut of a charcoal-burner, and there remained while her companions went on to the châlets, which were at some distance, on a rising ground. She heard Michael's gay jodel long after he was out of sight, then a pause, followed at intervals by shouts of four or five notes in a descending scale, leaving time between them for an answer, after which all was still.

Had the prisoners called for help, and been able to make themselves heard? Nora thought so, and began slowly to mount the cow path, now dry and hard, but perfectly answering the description given her by Waldemar of the places called cows' stockings; she soon, however, found a way to the short green grass of the alp, and, by a slightly circuitous path, was enabled to ascertain that the door of the nearest châlet was open.

Let not the reader suppose that the word châlet is here

used to designate a building such as is known in England by
this name, or that of Swiss cottage; the common appellation
in Tyrol and Bavaria for these dwellings is *Senner* hut,—
senner (herd and dairy-man) being usual in the former, and
Sennerin—herds and dairy-maid) almost universal in the latter. Perhaps the proper word in English is cowherd's cot;
but these words would scarcely give a correct idea of the
picturesque summer residences of the Bavarian highland
herdswoman. The small gable front, with its door and window at each side, is of stone, and whitewashed; the loft
above is of wood, as also the long adjoining cow-house;
and all are under the same low overhanging roof of shin-
gles, kept steady by stones of dimensions calculated to defy
the storms that rage round the exposed place in winter.
Generally a wide extent of the greenest pasturage surrounds
these senner huts: on the Wild Alp the herbage seemed to
have sprung up among rocks; it was short, thick, and to the
eye of the botanist presented a vegetation quite different
from that of the plains, or even the valleys at the base of
the mountains. No garden or glass-house can furnish more
beautiful plants than are here to be found forcing their way
through moss, or the clefts in the rocks, creeping round the
decayed roots of trees, or luxuriating in the damp atmosphere of some ever-flowing spring. Nora clambered up
among the rocks, and had gathered a handful of these
wonderfully delicate flowers, when Rosel suddenly appeared at the door of the hut with raised arms, called loudly
to her, and then, with both hands pressed to her forehead,
rushed impetuously down the slope, before Nora had time
to descend from her elevated position.

The poor girl's passionate vehemence was so great, that
her relation of what had occurred would have been perfectly unintelligible to Nora had she not previously been so
well informed. She was still standing on a fragment of rock,

as Rosel ended her recital by a burst of tears, and the not unexpected information that her brother Franz had recognised Seppel among the wild hunters, and had vowed he would have him prosecuted, if only to prevent his sister from marrying an incorrigible wildschuetz, who would bring disgrace on them hereafter, and being in league with the Tyroleans, might, for all they could tell, have been the accomplice, if not himself the villain who had shot their brother Philip.

"As if," she sobbed, "as if Seppel would ever have entered our house, or spoken a word to me, after committing such a crime!"

"Don't make yourself unhappy about so preposterous an accusation," said Nora, consolingly; "your brother spoke in anger, and does not, I am sure, entertain the slightest suspicion of the kind. That Seppel was one of the wild hunters is possible—is probable—and we must endeavour to accommodate matters as well as we can, and persuade Franz to forgive—"

"Oh, he won't forgive!" cried Rosel, interrupting her; "I know he won't, for he says that Seppel singled him out, and rushed upon him with a fury that was perfectly incomprehensible."

"But," said Nora thoughtfully, as they walked towards the hut together, "but he cannot prove that it was Seppel, for I suppose he took the usual precaution of disguising himself?"

"His face was blackened," answered Rosel, "but Franz said he could not be mistaken in the tall figure, and thick black hair, and large white teeth, and he is ready to swear that it was Seppel and no other."

"He had better not," rejoined Nora, "for Seppel may be able to prove that he was at the Kerbstein lake with his relations when your brother was taken prisoner. What did Mr

Torp say?"

"The Englishman!" exclaimed Rosel, confused; "I don't know, I did not see him, I never thought of him. Michael helped me to cut the cords that bound Franz, who was so fierce and wild that he quite frightened me, and put everything else out of my head."

She had not quite finished speaking, when her brother suddenly appeared before the hut, and directly afterwards darted past them with a velocity that rendered all attempts to arrest his progress ineffectual. Where the ground had been rendered rough and uneven by the cattle, he stopped, bent down, appeared to rub his ankles in an impatient, hasty manner, and then moved on with a very perceptible limp. Rosel started forward—turned round—spoke a few agitated, scarcely intelligible words to Nora about the necessity of following her brother—rushed after him without waiting for an answer, and a few seconds afterwards they disappeared together behind the rocks.

At the door of the hut stood Torp and Michael, not a trace of displeasure on the face of the stoical Englishman. Nora bowed slightly, sat down on the bench outside the house, and leaned back against the wall, as if determined to rest after her fatiguing walk.

Now though Mr Torp chose to be haughty and repulsive to every member of the Nixon family, he could be very much the contrary with other people, and Nora found him talking in the most unaffectedly familiar manner to her guide.

"I believe, after all," he said, glancing downwards at his feet, "that I was quite as firmly bound as Franz, but my boots saved my ankles, and by remaining quiet I spared my wrists. All things considered, they behaved well enough, brought me my cigars that had dropped out of my pocket during the scuffle, and told me I should find my rifle in the cellar."

"And," said Michael in a confidential tone, "and do you, too, think that long Seppel from the Crags was one of them?"

"If you mean the tall cuirassier, with the black hair," replied Torp, "I think he was."

"No wonder the forester's Rosel took on so," observed Michael.

"She seems a good girl," said Torp, "and did all she could to pacify her brother—at least as well as I could hear what they said from the inner room, for Franz quite forget me in the first burst of his wrath."

"He had cause enough for his anger," observed Michael, "if so be that Seppel did indeed single him out, and fall upon him at once with all the signs of the bitterest enmity."

"I was too busily engaged myself to observe what happened to Franz," answered Torp; "but I dare say his sister will make him pardon this affront, for after all it is little else."

"She may follow him all the way home, and go down on her knees to him, and he will not pardon this insult," said Michael. "I heard him tell her that he could have excused the attack under the circumstances, knowing how much Seppel had at stake; and had he only been overpowered by numbers and made prisoner, why it was not more than might happen to any one; but that as long as he lived he never would forgive or forget Seppel's coming back to the hut after the others were gone, standing grinning at him when he lay helpless on the floor, and then brutally spurning and kicking him, as if he had been a cur or a reptile that he longed to destroy."

"Impossible! he never could have acted so!" cried Nora, starting from her listless posture, and looking up with an expression of so much surprise and concern that Torp opened his eyes wide in wonder at the interest so openly avowed by his countrywoman for a notorious wildschuetz.

"These were the assistant forester's own words to his sister," said Michael, "and grief enough they caused her."

"He must have been out of his senses, unconscious of what he was doing," began Nora.

"Well," said Michael, "it's not unlikely that he did take a glass too much of Tyrolean wine. We are more used to beer than wine in Bavaria, and it may have got into *his* head, though the others did not feel it. The son-in-law of the sexton at St Hubert's, who lives at the other side of the frontiers, has good wine, I am told, for his friends, and the gentleman here says there were four from Tyrol with Seppel."

"*Three*," interposed Torp, with strong emphasis; "the fourth was certainly not a Tyrolean."

"One of the boys from our village?" asked Michael.

"I think it very likely that he came from Almenau," answered Torp, his eye resting on Nora, while he spoke with so much meaning that she perceived he had already begun to suspect that she had been sent to release him.

The interest excited in her mind by the recent occurrence was, however, on Rosel's account, too great to allow her to think of herself, or even John, at that moment; she therefore looked up without embarrassment, and observed, "It is so much more likely that Seppel would endeavour to keep in the background, and avoid being seen on this occasion, that I am inclined to think that Franz, after the first attack, may have mistaken one of the Tyroleans for him. He did not speak, of course?"

"A few words to me," said Torp; "but I do not know his voice."

"Well," said Michael after a pause, "I wonder if they will be able to prove anything against him this time. Often and often has he been brought before the judge, but was always dismissed for want of sufficient evidence against him. If he can contrive to mystify them all this time, why he has the devil's own luck, and they may as well let him alone in future."

"Yet," observed Nora, "the accusation will, I fear, be sufficient to injure his prospects materially. The forester may refuse to give him his daughter, and even Rosel herself—"

"Oh! as to Rosel," said Michael, winking knowingly to Torp, "that will make no difference to her, she likes him all the better for being a scapegrace. It's the way with the girls about here; the wilder a fellow is the more they like him."

Torp looked amused, and Michael continued: "Seppel's what they call here a fresh boy, 'a Frischer,' who never tapped at a window that it was not opened, who never turned into an alp but that the best milk and butter was set before him; and certain it is that no sennerin could ever be made to remember having seen him hunting, or even carrying a rifle."

"You are speaking of many years ago," said Nora, "for since he has been in the army no young man could be steadier."

"He was a cuirassier in the year forty-eight, and took his pleasure on the mountains here as well as any—of us."

"In that year there was no law to prevent the peasants from hunting," observed Nora.

"And a pretty mess they made of it," interposed Torp.

"It was about that time," said Michael, "that I was engaged by the forester as one of the charcoal-burners at the clearance above the Trift Alp, part of which belongs to the miller, whose handsome daughter was there that year as sennerin."

"I was not aware," observed Torp, "that the peasants sent their daughters on the alps as sennerins."

"Often enough about here," answered Michael. "If they go with free will and for pleasure, as many of them do, they call it their 'sommer frisch,' and fresh enough the sennerins were that same year. The Trift Alp is on the frontiers, half Tyrolean, half Bavarian; the miller's Madeleine was there, and Afra, a smith's daughter from Tyrol, that some said was even handsomer. At all events a more frolicsome pair were never seen, and the talk of their beauty was so great that the boys came from far and wide to see them, and none more often than Sepp from the Crags."

"High and low, all—all the same," soliloquised Nora. "He had pledged his troth to Rosel that very year!"

"We found out afterwards," continued Michael, with a laugh, "that he was all the while out after a chamois that was hovering about the frontier."

"Oh, I'm glad to hear that," she said, quickly.

Torp smiled and looked towards her, but she did not observe him.

"And didn't we tease the girls afterwards about him!" continued Michael; "and didn't Madeleine chafe and fume at his hypocrisy, as she called it; and the very next time he tapped at her window only opened it to call him a scamp, and then banged it to with such force that every pane of glass was smashed to atoms!"

Torp and Nora laughed simultaneously. "And what did Seppel do then?" she asked.

"He went on to Afra's, but she neither opened window nor door, and only answered his call by wishing him a pleasant hunt."

"And then?" asked Nora.

"He ate his schmarn at old Nandl's, and shared her coffee, and made light of the girls' anger, and said he'd send a lad to Madeleine to mend the window; and sure enough the next day up came black Seppel from the mill, and was well received, though as dull and dismal a fellow as could be found, even in his country."

"I never heard that the Tyroleans were dull and dismal," observed Torp.

"An earnest people, or at least very little given to cheerfulness, we consider them at this side of the mountains," said Michael; "and the more south you go the less you hear of singing and dancing, until at last both seem forgotten, and a wedding is about as gay as a funeral."

"I believe they avoid all unnecessary revelry from religious motives," began Torp, "and are, perhaps, somewhat fanatical—"

"Eh? what's that?" asked Michael.

"I mean their religion is of rather a gloomy description; but they are an interesting people; the women handsome, the men courageous, and the best marksmen I ever met; not even the Swiss can surpass them in the handling of a rifle."

"Well, I don't think we're behind-hand in that way in Bavaria," said Michael. "I could name a good many in Almenau who have brought home prizes from Tyrol. No one can deny that they are steady marksmen at the other side of the mountains, but they are tardy in taking aim. 'Slow and sure' is their motto, and when a Tyrolean is in the shooting-stand he is in no hurry to leave it. At a target we fire five shots to their three."

"Of course," said Torp, "there is a good deal of rivalry between the two countries on this subject?"

"No doubt of it," answered Michael, laughing, "and about other matters too."

"Which," said Torp, "causes occasional skirmishing at the inns most probably."

"Often enough formerly," answered Michael, "but we can get up a row without the Tyroleans, and require small provocation to take up the cudgels and lay about us. I've got into trouble myself for a trifle."

"And," said Nora, "besides the wounds given and received in these battles, accidents with firearms must be of quite common occurrence here. How can it be otherwise, with guns in every house, and boys longing to use them, after hearing men boasting continually of their prowess out hunting or at target-shooting matches?"

"Yet I don't remember any accident ever happening in our neighbourhood," said Michael, "excepting black Seppel's, and that was in Tyrol."

"What happened to him?" asked Nora.

"One day, about seven years ago, when he was trying a new rifle behind his father's mill, his younger brother came springing towards him unawares, and received a wound in his neck that caused him to bleed to death. Seppel left home, it is supposed, for this reason, and entered into service at our miller's, where he has been ever since, and remains, they say, for love of the miller's daughter. At all events, he has never since touched a rifle, goes out of the way whenever there is a shooting-match, and I shouldn't like to be the man to ask him why he dislikes the smell of powder."

"I wish he would go back to Tyrol," said Nora; "he is exceedingly in the way just now, and Madeleine does not care for him in the least."

"Doesn't she?" cried Michael. "I've heard her say often enough that she liked him, and why she liked him."

"You seem to know her well," observed Nora.

"Are we not from the same village?" asked Michael, "and is not that next to being of the same family? She liked black Seppel just because he was disliked by everybody else, and especially because he was morose to all the world but herself."

"And who is this Madeleine?" asked Torp, with some curiosity.

"The mountain miller's daughter," answered Nora, rising; "and I am afraid I must add, as perfect a coquette as you could find in any London or Paris ball-room."

"Stay, Miss Nixon," cried Torp, perceiving her about to leave them, "or at least before you go have the charity to give me some of the provisions that are so temptingly protruding from your guide's green bag."

"I ought to have thought of that before," said Nora, turning into the hut, "and poor Franz has gone off hungry in all probability!"

"Franz filled his pockets with bread before he left us," said Torp; "and I confess to having stolen a couple of sandwiches, for after having fasted upwards of four-and-twenty hours, the temptation was more than I could resist. I cannot remember ever being so hungry—so ravenously hungry —as at this moment," he added, seating himself on the low hearth, and beginning to eat with so hearty an appetite that Nora continued laughingly for some time to supply him, altogether forgetful of herself or her guide.

"What a profusion of provisions!" he remarked, at last, when she had spread the whole contents of the bag before him. "Quite a banquet for an alp party!" and as his eyes rested on a bottle of wine, and a couple of small tumblers, he added, "One might almost suppose you had had a sort of presentiment, Miss Nixon, that half-famished prisoners would require your good offices!"

Nora saw a provokingly meaning smile playing round his lips, and the eyes that had disconcerted Jack and his companions by their scrutinising glances seemed very much inclined to try their power on her.

"When I desired Rosel to pack up these things," she answered, quietly, "neither you nor your companion were in my thoughts, I can assure you. We intended to have made a family party to one of the lower alps near the village, and the wine especially was intended for—" she stopped, not choosing to betray herself by saying the word "uncle."

"For the old gentleman who fishes at St Benedict's," interposed Michael, as distinctly as his crammed mouth would permit him to articulate.

"Exactly," said Nora.

"And you changed your plan—aw—suddenly—perhaps yesterday evening?" persisted Torp.

"You may remember having heard your friend M. Waldemar recommend me to visit this alp before a change of weather made it inaccessible," she answered, "and fortunately for you I have followed his advice."

"Change of weather," he repeated; "not much chance of that, I should think."

"I would not take upon me to answer for this evening," observed Michael, glancing towards the open door; "those light streaky clouds denote storm."

"Perhaps we had better leave the alp at once," proposed Nora, hastily; "I confess I should not like to be weather-bound here."

"We have had clouds like these continually during the last fortnight," said Torp, "and you will be dreadfully tired, Miss Nixon, if you do not rest after your fatiguing walk before you attempt the not easy descent of this mountain."

Nora said she could rest more pleasantly at the shore of the lake than in the hut, and left them, rather glad on any pretence to escape the further questionings of Torp.

CHAPTER XXVIII

The Forester's Bridge

TORP would have been little flattered had he known with what extreme satisfaction Nora left him to the society of her guide. It had become quite evident to her that he suspected Jack of having assisted in taking him prisoner; and though his wish to obtain some certainty on the subject was natural enough, his quiet attempts to embarrass her had been, to say the least, disagreeable, as she felt very doubtful as to the use he might make of any proof of Jack's guilt, or her connivance, that he might be able to procure. Had Waldemar been in his place, she would without hesitation have told him all she knew of the vexatious affair, and would have requested his good offices for Seppel, and complete forgiveness of Jack's share in the exploit, almost with the certainty that neither would be refused her. Torp's cool self-possession repelled confidence, and her experience led her to consider him a hard, worldly-minded man, who would undoubtedly call a wildschuetz a poacher, and let the law take its course. Her best plan, then, was to avoid him; and as she thought it was probable that the little lake would have more interest for him than any other spot in the neighbourhood of the hut, and might tempt him out even in the noontide heat, she turned her steps in a contrary direction, mounted the rising ground behind the huts, and soon reached the base of the chain of rocks that gave the alp itself the wild appearance whence it derived its name.

Among these rocks Nora climbed with unrelaxing per-severance, until she came to a height from which she could see a great part of the Bavarian Highlands, and far into Ty-rol: then seating herself in a sheltered spot, she overlooked at her leisure a world of hill and dale, forest and rocks,— the last named in such masses, and of such wild and fantas-tic forms, that they must have surprised even those accus-tomed to such scenes. Mountain on mountain rose innu-merable, some rounded, some conical, others long-ridged, but almost all with high rocky summits, occasionally start-ing abruptly out of the pine-forest, but more frequently al-lowing the eye to follow the gradual cessation of vegetation, until the bare stone rose sharply against the blue sky. No stretch of the imagination was required to discover what appeared the ruins of gigantic strongholds or watch-towers; it was rather necessary to call reason to assist the sight, in order to be convinced that the hands of men could never have constructed buildings of such proportions in such places. To an English observer the most striking objects in the view would have been the immense extent of forests, the ultramarine blue of the distant heights, and the long region of eternal snow and ice beyond. For Nora, these ob-jects possessed *not* the charm of novelty, but the far—far more deeply-felt attraction of strong resemblance to similar scenes indelibly impressed on her memory, and treasured in her heart of hearts for ten long years—serving as a solace in hours of London solitude, when the chimneys of the neighbouring houses, and the dusky sky above them, had wearied her eyes and dulled her senses.

That part of Nora's life was now in its turn beginning to appear like a dream—its monotony giving the delusion plausibility, so that the events of a decennium dwindled eas-

ily into the recollections of half an hour, while previous
years expanded, and bright visions of childhood and early
youth flitted before her. Half reclining on the small patch
of moss that she had chosen as a resting place, hours might
have passed, and in fact did pass unobserved by her. The
sun was high in the heavens,—the rocks no longer afforded
any shade, but rather seemed to attract his beams, causing a
feeling of intolerable heat,—the fresh current of air that
scarcely ever fails on the alps was replaced by an oppressive
calm,—when Nora at length started from her recumbent
posture, and sat upright, her hands clasped round her knees
as she gazed intently about her. Had she been sleeping?
dreaming? She could not think so,—for those fields of
snow had not been lost sight of, but had rather given rise to
a long train of recollections ending at the Gross Venediger,
on which she now looked. Years ago, when travelling
through the valley of Pinzgau, she had passed a night at
Mittersill, near that glacier, and had first seen it with the
gorgeous background of a summer evening sky. When they
had arrived at the inn, every one had been occupied with
preparations for the ensuing day, on which the *primitz* of a
young priest was to take place. They call it his *primitz*, that
is, *prima missa*,—first time of reading mass; and as he was
the son of a peasant in the neighbourhood, he had chosen
the inn at Mittersill for the celebration of the fête usual on
such occasions. The guest-chamber and staircase had been
decorated with green wreaths, a room near the kitchen contained a row of tables covered with dishes full of flour,
eggs, sweetmeats, pounded sugar, and other ingredients,
that only awaited the dexterous hand of the cook to change
their nature and their name. As if it were but yesterday,
Nora remembered having entreated her mother to allow
her to be present the next morning at the ceremony in the
church, and the landlady's good-natured offer to take

charge of her. "My little daughter, Marie," she said, "is to be his reverence's bride. He knew what he was about when he chose her, for, of course, I shall do something handsome towards his future housekeeping, to say nothing of my husband, who is his cousin." Nora's father and mother had talked much during the evening of the custom of celebrating the *primitz* of a priest as if it were a marriage, of the useful presents given by the parents of the brides, and much more that she had not understood; but in the morning "his reverence's bride" had come to waken her, and greatly had she admired the demure, rosy-cheeked little girl, scarcely seven years old, and her fresh muslin frock and wreath of white flowers placed like a coronet on her head. The procession to the church had been long and pompous, the crowd there dense, and universal and deep the devotion pictured in the faces upturned, or the heads bowed reverently to receive the blessing of the agitated young man, who with raised arms and flushed cheeks looked down from the pulpit on a congregation above whom his recent vows had placed him so immeasurably high. As the crowd dispersed Nora's attention had been directed towards the glacier by hearing some peasants observe that the "Venediger" was putting on his cap, and they might expect a change of weather before long—and as it had then appeared to her, so it was now. A light mist seemed to hover about the summit, rendering the outline indistinct, and spreading along the snow-fields in a shadowy manner, that made it difficult to decide whether the vapour rose from the snow or was drawn downwards towards it. The more distant glaciers were soon lost to sight, and, as if at a given signal, clouds gathered round most of the adjacent peaks, and higher mountain ridges. All this was at first so distant—so far away in Tyrol—that Nora watched the lights and shadow, and the changes produced in the scenery, with delight and interest, undisturbed by a thought of her own position, until some long light clouds began to rest on the summits in her immediate vicinity, and wreaths of white transparent vapour rose from, and hovered over, the wooded acclivities. Then she commenced a quick descent of the rocks, and met her guide, who said that he and the English gentleman had been looking for her at the lake, and that they had not a moment to lose, if they hoped to get partly down the mountain before the storm commenced.

"Perhaps," said Torp, who was standing with folded arms on a prominent crag, and looking along the horizon with such engrossing attention that he did not even turn round while speaking, "perhaps it would be better to await the storm here, Michael; it seems to me nearer than you supposed; and Miss Nixon will scarcely be able to reach in time the shelter of the first houses on the mountain, though we might manage it by making a violent exertion."

"I am a very good walker," said Nora, rather alarmed at the prospect of spending the night in the hut.

"The alp is greatly exposed," observed Michael, "and in a few hours may be covered with snow. If the sennerins were still here the young lady might stop in the hut for a day or two pleasantly enough; but without provisions we could not attempt it now. The rain that's coming will be no summer shower, I can tell you; and what with the bare rocks on this side, and the waterfall across the way on the other, and the river flooded below, it might be long before any one could reach us, or we make our way down the mountain with the young lady, though she did climb it as well as the queen herself could have done!"

Nora smiled, and observed that climbing a mountain like a queen was very dubious praise.

"Not in Bavaria, Miss Nixon," said Torp, "as Michael would explain to you at some length, if we had time to listen to him."

"Then," said Nora, "having heard that I mounted so
well, you will scarcely doubt my being able to descend also,
and if we hurry forward perhaps we may reach the peasant's house, where the corn was still green."

"Let us try at least to get past the waterfall before the
rain comes down upon us," exclaimed Michael, springing
on to the hut.

He reappeared with Torp's rifle slung over his shoulder,
and busily employed burying in the recesses of his green
pouch the small remains of their recent repast.

A few minutes afterwards they were on their way to the
lake, which Nora scarcely looked at in her eagerness to
leave the valley of the alp and reach a more elevated spot,
where she could better judge of the state of the weather,
and see the approach of the storm.

"This is really a magnificent sight," cried Torp, soon after, warmed into a sort of enthusiasm, as once more the
long range of mountains became visible.

"What a change!" said Nora, contrasting in her mind the
blue sky, cloudless mountains, and sunny valleys, that she
had seen from the same place but a few hours previously;
"what a complete change of scene! One might almost expect to see Woatin himself appear among that chaos of
cloud."

"You mean the wild huntsman, miss," said Michael;
"people say he is out regular in the thunder-storms at the
change of the season, and this may be the last summer
storm. I suppose"—he added, half interrogatively—"I suppose it's the queer-shaped clouds that give rise to the saying
about the wild hunt?"

"Not exactly," answered Nora; "Woatin was, I believe,

supposed to be the god of thunder*, and has in some way been confused with the wild huntsman. I wish whichever brings the last summer storm would at least delay his appearance until we are safely down the mountain."

"And I," said Torp, "wish I could remain here and watch the coming of this storm, which is the very grandest thing I ever saw in my life."

"Are you deterred from remaining on account of the waterfall?" asked Nora. "I am quite sure the danger has been exaggerated, for it would require hours of rain to procure a flood that would fill the space beneath the wooden bridge I passed over on my way here."

"You are not aware," answered Torp, "that the water has been kept back for the woodfall. A few days ago Franz showed me the place that had been dammed up, and the felled wood piled up beneath it. The reservoir was at that time nearly full of water, and he said a few hours' rain, such as might be expected after this sultry weather, would burst the temporary sluice, and save him the trouble of sending up men to hew it down."

"I thought," said Nora, "that most of the timber about here was sledged down the mountain in winter."

"Water carriage is always the cheapest," answered Torp; "enormous quantities can be conveyed, without either expense or trouble, down the mountain with the fall of water; and once in the river below us, it will work its way to the neighbourhood of Almenau, where a grating across the stream stops its further progress, unless it be considered desirable to give it free passage to another place."

* Nora appears to be confusing Odin or Wotan, the highest of the Gods in Germanic mythology, with his son Thor who was, among other things, the God of thunder and lightning.

While they were speaking, a thick white cloud began to wreath itself round the mountain on which they stood, its motion scarcely perceptible as it rolled along, avoiding the bright sunbeams that still lingered on the summit. As the heavens above lowered, valley after valley darkened into deepest shade, a struggling ray of light resting last of all but for a moment on the white steeple of a secluded pilgrimage chapel that had failed to attract the eye in brighter hours. Torp and Nora watched with intense interest the last array of clouds that, rushing across the sky, at length effectually obscured the sun's disc, and caused an indescribable gloom to fall on all around them. Distant lightnings darted through the leaden-hued firmament, and in the direction of the Wild Alp a long stripe of green-coloured sky made itself remarkable.

"That looks like a hail-storm," said Michael, uneasily. "Indeed, Miss Nora, it would be better if you moved on and tried to pass the waterfall before it comes to the worst. In a very short time we shall not be able to see a yard before us, and when you come to the narrow path, with a wall of rock on one side and a steep fall at the other—"

"I had forgotten that place," said Torp, interrupting him, "and wish for your sake, Miss Nixon, that we had taken our chance of starvation in the hut. Franz would have managed, I am sure, to get to us some way or other. Even now," he added, stopping suddenly, "even now we might turn back, and at least secure shelter from a storm that may cause you more discomfort than the wetting for which you are of course prepared."

"Yes—go back,—do," chimed in Michael, eagerly; "and early to-morrow morning, let the weather be what it may, I shall return here with provisions, and Franz and his father; and it will be odd if we can't find some way of bringing you home in safety." He had unslung his green pouch while speaking, and held it towards Torp.

"No, no, no!" cried Nora, "it is not to be thought of: go on. I shall follow you as carefully as I can. If I fall you must help me up again, and for a shower-bath of some hours' duration I am fully prepared."

"On then," said Torp, without the slightest attempt to urge an acceptance of his proposal.

And on Michael went, followed recklessly enough by Nora, who did not choose to be the cause of delay when every moment was of consequence. They had all ceased to look round them, or speak, and were just within sight of the wilderness of rocks around the fall, when a few gusts of wind put the clouds above and below them into commotion, and a few seconds afterwards an impenetrable mist enveloped them. The guide preceding them shouted, Torp answered, and Nora sprang on between them with a fearlessness that was very satisfactory to the latter.

"Keep to the left, Miss Nixon," he said, as the first burst of the tempest swept past them, and the wind seizing her hat, nearly tore it from her head.

"To the left—to the left," he repeated, springing towards her: but the words were unintelligible, and at all events Nora was too much occupied with efforts to retain a covering for her head in such inclement weather to pay much attention to anything else. In vain, however, she raised both hands, and struggled with the wind; the straw yielded in all directions. and even while Torp was speaking, the hat was borne aloft, and she had made an equally fruitless and imprudent attempt to snatch at it.

Another blast of the storm whirled her round until she became perfectly giddy; but she was not immediately aware that, when raised from the ground, the path was no longer beneath her feet, and that she was on her way down the mountain precisely at the spot chosen by the wildschuetz for his desperate slide. The first horrible consciousness of her danger flashed across her mind on finding herself flung on a heap of sand and gravel, that, without affording her a moment's support, began to glide downwards, carrying her amidst a cloud of dust and sand, clumps of loose earth and a shower of gravel, towards the river that she had in the morning seen dashing in cascades among the rocks at the foot of the mountain.

Down, down, down she was carried with a rapidity that increased every moment. Being unhurt, she long retained both consciousness and presence of mind; made no resistance where the fall was hopelessly steep; and endeavoured to grasp whatever seemed likely to arrest her progress, when the decreasing velocity enabled her sufficiently to distinguish surrounding objects. She did not despair even when a deafening hurricane swept through the ravine, carrying with it large branches of trees, and raising the sand about her in palpable masses; but when the forked lightning dazzled, and the instantaneously following thunder pealed above her head—when she once more felt herself raised from the ground, and borne along without the power of resistance, a feeling of utter helplessness took possession of her mind; she expected instantaneous death, or horrible mutilation; and, murmuring a prayer, had scarcely touched the trunk of a fallen tree, before she became completely senseless.

How long she remained in this state she never could ascertain; her return to consciousness was, perhaps, accelerated by the furious raging of the wind, and unceasing rolling of thunder, that was echoed a hundredfold by the surrounding mountains. When she again opened her eyes, Torp was bending over, and watching her, with an expression of such intense anxiety, that a natural impulse made her sit upright and look round her.

"Are you much hurt?" he asked, gravely.

"I—think—not," she answered, putting her hand to her head.

"Thank God!" he exclaimed, fervently; "for never in my life was I so horror-struck as on seeing you lying there, apparently dead."

"I have, indeed, had a most miraculous escape," said Nora, rising slowly, and supporting herself against the stem of a tree.

"If you can walk, let us leave this place," cried Torp, quickly, as he heard the crashing of falling timber behind them, and observed some young fir-trees rolling past, that had evidently just been torn out by the roots. "We are in actual, immediate danger here, and ought to endeavour to cross the fall before the rain cuts off our retreat."

He gave her her mountain-staff, which he had found lying on the ground, seized her hand, and hurried from the unsafe shelter of the wood. But so violent was the tempest, that they had hardly staggered about a hundred yards towards the fall, when Nora was again thrown to the ground. The darkness of night seemed to overspread the sky; a few large, heavy drops of rain preceded a long, whistling gust of icy-cold wind, which was instantly followed by the most violent shower of hail that Nora and Torp had ever in their lives witnessed.

Let not the English reader suppose these hailstones were such as may be occasionally seen pattering against their plate-glass windows. They were compact masses of ice, like stones, and giving a blow that caused actual pain. Torp pulled off his shooting-jacket, and throwing himself on the ground beside Nora, formed with it a partial shelter for her and himself—the more necessary as they were both without covering for their heads—and there they sat together, resigned and silent, during the hail-storm, and immediately succeeding torrents of rain, which poured like a bursting cloud upon and around them. Sheets of water seemed borne along by the wind; and the noise caused by the rushing of the already flooded river below, the still rolling thunder above, and the storm sweeping over the adjacent forests, at first prevented them from hearing the approach of the long-expected, and not a little-dreaded woodfall, which they knew would cut off all communication with Almenau for many hours, and effectually prevent them from returning the way they had come.

When Torp started to his feet, the turbid torrent was thundering down the mountain-side, carrying stones, gravel, and sand, with blocks of wood tossed wildly in all directions; and, while he and Nora were still retreating, the overflowing water spread to the sand on which they were toiling, ankle-deep, half blinded by rain, and blown about by the storm.

"This is hard work, Miss Nixon," said Torp, from whose manner every trace of coldness and indifference had disappeared; "and I am afraid there is still harder in prospect, if you expect to have a roof over your head tonight."

"I suppose," said Nora, as they once more stood in the doubtful shelter afforded by the trees on the skirt of the wood, "I suppose there is no use in trying to climb the mountain, and regain our path?"

"None whatever," he answered; "we cannot ascend on the sand that is now under water; still less here, where the trees grow on terraces, separated by walls of rock. One could not easily have found a more inauspicious place for an accident such as you have met with. Fortunately I know the country about here pretty well, from having fished in the river below us: we must cross it; and once on the woodmen's path, on the other side, a couple of hours will bring us to a few peasants' houses, where we can get a vehicle of some kind or other to take us on to our village before midnight."

"There is a bridge, I suppose—" began Nora.

"One of very primitive construction," answered Torp. "A couple of well-grown trees have been thrown across the stream, for the convenience of the foresters, but it will, I hope, save us from spending the night on the mountain."

While he was speaking, Nora had been employed in pushing back her long braids of plaited hair, now without a comb to keep them in order.

"I am afraid," he added, on observing an expression of pain pass over her features, "I am afraid you have not escaped as unscathed as you at first supposed."

"Only a few bruises," she answered cheerfully; "but we have no time to attend to such trifles now. The storm has abated; it is not to be expected that the rain will cease for some hours; so, if you will lead the way, you may depend on my making every effort to follow you."

He turned at once into the wood, through which they had to toil for some time, over rocks, protruding roots of trees, and an occasional morass of black, slippery earth. Torp at first frequently offered assistance; but it was invariably refused, with a decision that not only effectually silenced him, but in the end induced him to walk on, and only show his consciousness of Nora's presence by stopping at intervals to ascertain that she was keeping up with him.

On reaching a tolerably extensive clearing, Nora perceived that the ravine became narrower as they advanced, and that there was little more than space for the river between the mountains.

It was, however, but at intervals that she could see the foaming stream; for a succession of vapoury clouds rolled through the gorge, giving only occasional glimpses of the opposite mountain, and making it appear of fabulous height and grandeur. At times she scarcely knew whether she were ascending or descending, so rocky and precipitous were the vast masses of mountain-wreck around her—so unceasing her efforts to pass over or among them, without receiving assistance from her companion.

At length they began a descent to the river; but were still about a hundred yards from it, when the forester's bridge came into view, greeted by Torp with an exclamation of pleasure—by Nora, with a start and shudder of apprehension.

The trunks of two tall trees had been thrown across the water, where the stream was narrowed by the rocks; a succession of foaming cascades completely filling the upper part of the gorge, while in the lower the yellow flood spread itself out as far as the ground would permit, successfully undermining many a stately pine: some of these, already uprooted, were being borne off triumphantly by the stream, their green boughs stretching upwards, and waving in the distance, as if in despair; while others seemed to struggle hard for the privilege of death on their native soil, and, with roots entwined in those of the trees around them, resisted the violence of the waves, and were not unfrequently flung by them above the level of the water, where, covered with sand, earth, and weeds, the rain poured in no longer refreshing torrents on their drooping branches.

"Halloo!" cried Torp, "the path is under water! What are we to do now?"

"I'm sure I don't know," answered Nora; "excepting there is some way of ascending the mountain on this side."

"Impossible, without climbing-irons," he said, looking upwards.

"I have pointed nails in the soles of my boots," she observed, stretching out a foot so covered with mud that the material of the said boots might have formed a subject of speculation—"regular hobnails, I assure you," she added, eagerly.

"So I supposed," said Torp, quietly; "otherwise you would not have been able to follow me as you have done this last hour. However, I am happy to say our situation is not so hopeless as you apprehend. I think—I hope—I can take you to the Kerbstein lake on the frontier. In such weather as this, we shall require four—perhaps even five or six hours to get there; but the fisherman and his wife will give us shelter and dry clothes; and you will need both, I greatly fear, before we reach their house."

"Must I cross that—bridge?" asked Nora.

"Yes—but I think I had better first try if it is all safe. In these sort of places it sometimes happens that the trees become decayed, and only the foresters are aware of—"

"Oh, then," cried Nora, interrupting him, "pray don't venture on it!"

But he was already in the middle of the bridge, and putting its stability to the proof by stamping his feet, and kicking away the remnants of mouldering bark and accumulated withered leaves that were likely to make it more perilous than it was already.

"All right, Miss Nixon," he said, returning to her: "you had better follow me as closely as you can, and hold my staff as a sort of rail; for these barkless old trees are confoundedly slippery, I can tell you."

"I know it," replied Nora; "yet were they anywhere but over that foaming water, I could walk upon them without the assistance of either your staff or mine."

"Of that," said Torp, "I have no doubt, after having seen you spring along the rocks on the shore of the lake to-day."

"A fall into such shallow water would have been of little

importance," she answered; "but here—" she stopped, embarrassed.

"You think one might easily find a pleasanter place for a plunge than this just now," said Torp, smiling as he placed one of his feet on the bridge and held his staff towards her.

"Here it would be death," said Nora, "and a horrible death too; the very thought of it makes me giddy!" and she leaned over a rock and looked down into the river, that immediately under the bridge flowed in an unbroken sweeping current.

"You must not look at the water if you are subject to vertigo," said Torp; "but I can scarcely think you are, after having seen you walk so fearlessly on the brink of a precipice not two hours ago."

"You forget," answered Nora, "that I had then a wall of rocks on one side to give me at least a feeling of security, while here—" she paused, and then asked abruptly, "Is there no way of overcoming this sensation of giddiness? Surely when it is not caused by weakness or actual illness, a strong resolution must conquer it! I must not give way to such folly—go on, and I will follow you."

"Take my staff to steady you," said Torp, not quite liking the manner in which she changed colour, "and don't look at the water."

Nora took the staff, but before they had advanced half-a-dozen steps on the bridge, Torp felt it tremble so violently that he stopped.

"Go on," said Nora, faintly.

"Rather let us go back while we can," he rejoined, turning round and catching her arm.

Nora sprang from the bridge, covered her eyes with her hands, and exclaimed in a tone of the deepest chagrin, "I cannot—cannot cross the river on those trees: they seemed to glide from beneath my feet, and the water to rise until I felt choking. Mr Torp, you must go on to the lake without me, and send the fisherman and any peasants you can procure to take me out of this place."

"I shall require at least four hours to reach the lake," answered Torp; "the fisherman and his son four more to return here; and in the mean time you propose to sit alone and wait for them in this deluge of rain?"

"I dare say it will clear up presently," said Nora, looking round her rather disconsolately.

"It will not," replied Torp. "There is a fresh storm coming from the south-west, and even supposing you had a constitution to bear eight hours' exposure in such weather, without the necessary movement to save you from cold, it would be evening—night, in fact—before assistance could reach you. Few, excepting the foresters about here, could find their way to the lake after nightfall, and of what more use the fisherman and his son could be to you than I can, I am at a loss to discover."

"True, most true," said Nora, despondingly; "I only thought that with one at each side of me I should feel more secure perhaps—"

"I doubt it," said Torp; "and as to our remaining here all night, or my leaving you in such a place, it is not to be thought of. The case is urgent, Miss Nixon, and something must be done. Give me your handkerchief," he added after a pause; "I believe I must blindfold you."

Nora drew her handkerchief from her pocket, and bound it herself over her eyes.

"Are you quite sure that you cannot see?" asked Torp.

"Quite," she answered, holding out her hands towards him in a groping manner, evidently expecting to be led forward.

A moment afterwards she felt an arm thrown round her, and found herself raised from the ground before she had time to utter a single word of expostulation. In another moment she knew they were on the bridge, knew that her feet were suspended over the water she had so much dreaded; but so strong was the arm, so steady the stride of her bearer, that not a particle of fear mixed itself with or ameliorated the acute sense of mortification she felt at having yielded to a weakness that had made such a step on his part a matter of necessity.

"I beg your pardon, Miss Nixon," said Torp, as he deposited her safely on the opposite side of the river; "I shall never take such a liberty again without permission, but it could not be helped this time."

"I am sure," answered Nora, greatly disconcerted, and blushing deeply, "I am sure I ought to be very much obliged to you."

"But you are *not*," said Torp, smiling, for he had been perfectly aware of her previous unwillingness to be assisted by him, "and," he added good-humouredly, "there is no reason why you should be. The rest of the way, Miss Nixon, though long, would be pleasant and interesting enough in fine weather for so good a walker as you are, but in storm and rain like this a march across the mountains to the lake will probably prove an excursion that neither you nor I shall forget for some time."

Nora was already convinced of this as far as she was concerned, but she answered cheerfully that she was prepared for anything excepting passing over rivers on foresters' bridges; and though the storm Torp had foreseen just then burst over their heads, she declined his proposal of seeking temporary shelter, and followed him up the steep rugged side of the mountain that rose abruptly before them. Not one word of complaint did she utter while scrambling through the pathless forest, heedless alike of the showers that the wind shook from the dripping trees upon her bare head and saturated clothes, or the slimy mud and treacherous moss that caused her to slide and slip, stumble and even fall, repeatedly. They reached the ridge of the mountain; but, unable to see more than a few yards before her, Nora could only follow her companion as he wound round or climbed over the rocks there, without having the slightest idea of the appearance of the country beyond or beneath the spot on which she stood. Their descent was rapid, and Torp showed considerable knowledge of human nature in general, and Nora's in particular, when a shallow, turbulent stream was to be crossed, by splashing into it at once, and taking it as a matter of course that she could and would follow him, though the water reached to her knees, and was of a rather repelling dirt colour.

A succession of marshy meadows succeeded, where the ground seemed of sponge, scarcely offering resistance enough to the foot or staff to afford a resting-place for one moment, the water springing up on all sides, and forming a little pool in each footstep. The ascent of a number of hills was a relief, and a narrow pass beyond them, with a stony path through it, made Nora hope they were approaching some dwelling, until Torp informed her it was the cattle road to an alp already deserted: they should reach it in about an hour, he said, but in case she did not wish to rest there, they could pass by without going to the huts. If not too much for her, he should recommend going on, as the lake was on the other side of the mountain on which the alp was situated, and it would be evening before they could reach it, at all events.

Nora made no objection. Wet through as they were, an uninhabited alp offered no advantage, and as yet the weather showed not the least likelihood of clearing up. Thunder-storms and showers succeeded each other unceasingly, the latter filling to overflowing the dried-up rivulets, and causing innumerable nameless waterfalls to foam down the mountainsides, or, blown into spray by the tempest, to mix once more with the rain from which they had derived their origin. The clouds hung so low on the mountains that Torp could with difficulty find the way. Once they were obliged to turn back, and on another occasion to wait until a storm had passed over, in order to look for the alp and mountain that lay between them and the lake.

These delays, the various impediments to be overcome, and the labour of walking on wet and slippery ground, or over loose stones, caused the evening to be far advanced before Torp, pointing downwards through a forest of trees, informed Nora that the lake was below them, and a little more than half an hour would take them to its shore. Invigorated by the intelligence, she hurried on through the darkening wood, on a path that in some places resembled a quagmire, in others was composed of flights of uneven stone steps, among which small rills meandered busily, or fell in tiny cascades. She no longer refused Torp's assistance when it was offered, and even during the last steep descent to the shore placed her hand in his, or on his shoulder— precisely as he desired her.

At length they reached the lake, out of which the surrounding mountains rose abruptly on all sides but the one opposite to them. The full moon struggling hard with the lingering clouds of the last thunder-storm, and at times forcing a way through them, cast furtive floods of light on the water and the fisherman's lonely dwelling, which had been built on the only patch of pasture land in the neighbourhood. It resembled an alpine hut in its isolation and surrounding meadows, while the deep dark lake, and background of lofty mountains, gave a grandeur to its simplicity that rendered it picturesque in the extreme.

From the lower windows of the house bright gleams of

red light were visible. Nora even thought she could distinguish the flickering flames on the kitchen hearth—but unfortunately the green fields, house, lights, and fires were on the opposite side of the lake, and Torp shouted long and loudly for a boat—in vain.

"They are at evening prayers, or at supper," suggested Nora.

"Very probably," he answered; "but if they are all praying aloud together, as the peasants generally do, I have little chance of being heard. The wind, too, is unfavourable—blows right into my mouth! I wish I could manage to alarm the dogs!" A succession of shrill whistles proving perfectly ineffectual, he added impatiently, "This will never do—we cannot stand shivering here in our wet clothes all night—"

"Can we not go round by the shore?" asked Nora.

"It is not possible," he replied. "At one side of us the mountains descend into the water like well-built walls, on the other there is a river, now of course flooded, and—no bridge. Just walk up and down these few yards of level ground here, to keep yourself warm, Miss Nixon, while I make another effort to procure one of those scooped-out trunks of trees that the people about here call boats."

Nora did as he requested, and unconsciously prepared her ears for a shout that would waken the echoes far and wide—instead of which she heard a plunge into the lake, the splashing of water, and, on turning round, could but just distinguish Torp's head, as he swam out towards the middle of the lake.

He had thrown his shooting jacket and boots on the bank, and placed his purse and watch on a stone, and Nora, careless of his well-meant exhortation to keep herself warm by exercise, sat—no—she actually laid herself down on the wet grass beside them. She had not allowed Torp to perceive, but she now confessed to herself, that she was fatigued beyond measure; wayworn, weatherbeaten, and exhausted, as she had never been before in her life.

The rain had ceased some time previously, and an occasional gleam of moonlight enabled her to follow the long furrow made in the water by the swimmer, so that she could judge pretty accurately of the time of his arrival at the boat-house. She once more heard him call the fisherman; but this time the response was quick and satisfactory, the door of the house opened, and men, women, children, and dogs rushed forth. A light glimmered in someone's hand, there was a confusion of voices, a barking of dogs, and not long after the steady sound of oars dipping regularly in the water.

An unshapely boat neared the shore, and on hearing Torp's voice, Nora instantly started to her feet. He was rowing vigorously, and when she entered the boat, and prepared to take a place in the stern, he observed, "If you know how to handle an oar, Miss Nixon, let me recommend you to take one now, and row across the lake, as the best preservative against cold."

Nora stepped across the bench, and took the oar out of the hand of the fisherman, notwithstanding the most earnest expostulations on his part, Torp, the while, neither interfering nor looking round.

Who can describe the surprise and curiosity of the assembled family standing at the boat-house to receive them, when they landed on the other side of the lake? Who can enumerate the questions?—the exclamations?

We decline the task, and leave all to the imagination of the reader.

CHAPTER XXIX

A Modern Idyl

IT is to be hoped that Nora, and even Torp, have excited sufficient interest to make the reader unwilling to leave them at the door of the fisherman's house in the state described by Job as "Wet with the showers of the mountains."* Nora's clothes were not only saturated with rain, but torn and soiled in a manner difficult to describe, and Torp had so recently emerged from the lake, that the water still trickled unceasingly from both his garments and hair.

The old fisherman, whose own curiosity had been in a great measure satisfied during his row across the lake, put an end to his wife's and daughter's questions and exclamations, by pushing them towards the staircase, and telling them to get dry clothes for the young lady—to give her the best they had, and the choice of their Sunday suits. He made the same offer an the part of his son to Torp, and the whole party began to mount the narrow steep stairs together.

While the fisherman's wife unlocked the door of her state-room, Nora turned to Torp, and, with unusual warmth of manner, thanked him for having saved her from

* *Job* xxiv. 8.

the calamity, if not peril, of passing the night without shelter on the mountains. "I am aware," she added, "that you put yourself into danger by coming to my rescue."

"Not so much as you suppose, Miss Nixon," said Torp, interrupting her; "my fishing and hunting expeditions have made me tolerably well acquainted with the country hereabouts. For you there was undoubtedly danger had you remained alone, but, being together, there was none, excepting, perhaps, that of your not having strength to reach this place for the night."

Charmed at his so magnanimously making light of his services, and relieving her mind of a weight of care and annoyance thereby, Nora extended her hand with a smile, and said, "I have incurred a debt of gratitude nevertheless, which—" here she paused a moment, for Torp, who had taken her proffered hand, let it fall with suddenness that surprised her, and he was already turning away, as she added, "which I can never in any way repay."

Though Torp's actions, and not his thoughts, have hitherto been chiefly deemed worthy of notice, the latter here deserve a place, to explain an ungraciousness so strongly in contrast to all he had said and done during the previous five or six hours. Alas for the vanity of human nature!—he had misunderstood the grateful glance of the dark eyes fixed on him so earnestly, and imagined nothing less than that he had found favour in them; and that, after the manner of sentimental young ladies, Nora might think it incumbent on her to bestow at least a portion of her heart on the man who had preserved her life! To put an end, therefore, to all such "stuff and nonsense," he scarcely looked at her while saying, "Really, Miss Nixon, you attach too much importance to this little adventure; the small service rendered you this day I should have considered it my duty, as a Christian and a man, to have offered to any one similarly situated."

"That ought not to lessen my sense of gratitude," rejoined Nora, in happy unconsciousness of the current of his thoughts; "and you must therefore allow me once more to thank you for having fulfilled the 'duties of a Christian and a man' in a way so essentially serviceable to me."

"Pray say no more about it," cried Torp, with an impatient gesture. "You seem to have forgotten that you released me from a very unpleasant imprisonment this morning. If I have saved you from spending the night on the mountains, it is but a return for a benefit received, and there is no occasion for gratitude or thanks on either side."

Struck even more by the incivility of his manner than his words, Nora turned abruptly to the attendant peasants, who, with wondering eyes and half-open mouths, had been bewildered listeners of this dialogue, in a, to them, unknown tongue, and saying she should be much obliged for any clothes they would lend her, entered the low wooden-walled room with the fisherman's two daughters, leaving Torp to make similar arrangements with their father.

Any one less acquainted with the Bavarian highlands than Nora would have had little hope of finding garments fit for her use in the humble abode of an evidently very poor fisherman. She had observed that the house—low, and chiefly built of wood—was very old, and the interior stained to the darkest brown by age and smoke; that though the fisherman and his wife wore stockings, the others had only shoes, and three or four little children had capered about in the wet grass before the house perfectly bare-footed. Yet not for one moment did she doubt that from the gaily-painted wardrobes in the best room all her wants could be supplied; and she smiled, and expressed the admiration expected, when the eldest girl, with innocent ostentation, opened wide the doors of the linen press so as to exhibit all its treasures, and then, by mistake as it were, pulled out drawers containing green felt hats with gold tassels, black bodices, and flaming coloured neckerchiefs! Nora's patience was, however, rewarded at last by a choice of coarse but white linen, blue and white stockings, and printed calico and bright-coloured stuff petticoats. From the elder girl she borrowed one of the latter, as it suited her in length; from the younger, a slim maiden of thirteen, a black bodice and a scarlet and green kerchief; a pair of well-knit stockings took the form of her feet, but no shoes could be found in which she could walk, until, after having dried and freshly plaited her hair, it occurred to the girls that "brother Hansel's new Sunday boots would not be a bit too small for the young lady;" and the Sunday boots of strong leather, double soled, well garnished with nails, and made to lace in front with thongs, were forthwith produced. Fortunately they proved neither too long, nor very much too wide; and Nora, perfectly convinced of the impossibility of ever again being able to make use of her own, was but too glad to avoid the contingency of being boot or shoeless the next day when the time came for her return to Almenau.

The passage outside the room was very dark, and as one of the girls remained behind to put everything in order again, and close the wardrobes, unceremoniously retaining the light for that purpose, Nora laid her hand on the arm of the other, and so groped her way to the staircase. At the foot of it, a red-flamed guttering candle in his hand, stood the fisherman's son, and near him Torp, completely equipped as a peasant, and looking remarkably well in a dress peculiarly calculated to show to advantage his well-proportioned muscular figure. With his arms folded, and head thrown back, he leaned against the open door of the kitchen, and Nora asked herself, was it possible that the calm, indolently-lounging personage before her could be the man whose unremitting energy and athletic strength she had during the day, so much against her inclination, been forced to admire? Greatly she rejoiced that he had spurned her thanks, and reminded her so opportunely that she had released him from imprisonment. And it was true, quite true, that she had been brought into an unpleasant predicament, and some danger, by her effort to relieve him from a situation just as unpleasant, and nearly as perilous, as her own had been subsequently. In short, as he had himself observed, she had been useful to him, and he to her, and now they were mutually free from all obligation.

"Anything you please," said Torp, at that moment, as if in answer to some question on the part of the fisherman's wife. "Give us anything you please, provided it be quickly. People who have not eaten for so many hours are not likely to be dainty, and a walk across the mountains from the Wild Alp in such weather would give any one an appetite."

The woman laughed, threw fresh wood on the hearth to hurry the process of cooking, and as the flickering flame lighted up Torp's features, he bore so strong a resemblance to his mother, especially as Nora remembered her sitting by the fireplace at The Willows on the memorable last evening there, that all her bitter feelings towards his family, and personal dislike to himself, returned with double force, and she passed on in silence to the dwelling-room, thinking how much she could have enjoyed so pleasant a termination to her mountain adventure had any one but Torp been her companion.

The sitting-room at the fisherman's was like all such apartments in peasants' cottages; but the ceiling, composed of beams of wood darkened by age, was lower, and the windows smaller than in any room Nora had yet seen; and through the latter the moonlight entered sparingly. As for convenience and warmth, the winter store of fuel-wood was piled against the walls of the house, merely leaving free the spaces occupied by the diminutive square window-frames. The fisherman and his younger children were seated on the wooden bench with which the sides of the great green tile stove were furnished. Above their heads, suspended on a rail, hung shirts, both large and small, worsted stockings and leggings, airing in preparation for the pilgrimage to the distant church the ensuing morning.

The children moved near to their father when Nora entered, and whispered eagerly, "She's got Ursi's best green gown and Lina's new black bodice; and oh, father! they've been and given her Hansl's spick and span new boots."

The last words attracted the attention of a bare-legged boy who, sitting astride on the bench at the table, was watching intently the flame of the candle, evidently prepared with a pair of old rusty iron snuffers to swoop down on the wick whenever it had attained a length that would enable him to do so without incurring a reprimand from his father. He turned round, slid nimbly from the bench, bent forward to ascertain the truth of what he had heard, and then, resting the forefinger of his left hand on his under teeth, sidled towards his father, all the while gazing at Nora from beneath his eyebrows with a mixture of curiosity and dismay.

As she took the place he had vacated, and drew him towards her by his shirt-sleeve, for jacket he had none, Torp entered the room.

"Hans," cried the fisherman, "take your finger out of your mouth, and tell the young lady she's welcome to the loan of your boots."

"It will not be for long," said Nora, smiling: "and when I send them back to you, Hans, you will find something that you like packed up in the same paper with them. Can you guess what it will be?"

Hans eyed her keenly, placed his thumbs beneath the

faded green braces of his tightly-fitting black leather shorts, yielded to the impulse given by her hand, and, on finding himself standing close beside her, asked shyly, "Is it a harmonica?"

"I think it is," she answered, "but I don't exactly know of what kind."

"You put it in your mouth and blow music," he rejoined, more confidently; "there were hundreds of them at the fair in Tyrol, but—they cost twelve kreutzers."

"Ah, exactly," said Nora; "and if there be anything else you would like, I can send it by the same opportunity."

"A great, great, big, long, smoked sausage," said the boy, to Nora's infinite amusement, and evidently gaining courage as she nodded her head and told him to go on.

"And a—bouquetel of real flowers" (he meant a bouquet of artificial ones, but Nora understood him)—"a bouquetel of real flowers for my holiday hat; and a—a fishing-line—and—and hooks," he continued, eagerly placing his hand on her arm to secure her attention; for just at that moment his mother entered the room, carrying in her hand a steaming iron pan, fresh from the kitchen fire, and containing a quantity of the chopped omelette called "schmarn". She deposited it on a tripod, placed on the table for the purpose, motioned to Torp to advance, gave him and Nora each a horn spoon and an enormous slice of very dark brown bread and then, placing her hands on her hips, uttered a sort of satisfied sigh, as she wished them a good appetite, and hoped they would not disdain what her poor house had to offer on so short a notice.

Nora not only reassured her, but flattered her vanity by immediately commencing to eat and praise with such thorough good will, that the whole family began to gather round her, while Torp, silently helping himself to his share from the other side of the pan, glanced towards her occasionally with a sort of amazement that, unknown to himself, began to verge on admiration.

When the remains of their repast had been removed, and Nora turned from him to talk to the fisherman and his wife about their cattle and crops, and then to the latter of her homespun linen and the children's school attendance; to the fisherman's son of the forest clearings in the neighbourhood, and the occupation that the sledging of the wood and charcoal gave the peasants in winter, Torp placed both his elbows on the table and leaned forward, surprised alike at her knowledge of such matters and the fluent highland *patois* in which she discussed them. He found himself wondering where she could have acquired both, when the fisherman drew him into the conversation by referring to his fishery, and describing his winter occupations. This subject interested Nora also, and she moved nearer to listen, taking up at the same time the ponderous half of a colossal blue stocking, and beginning to knit with a rapidity that only a German education could give.

For some reason which she would have found it difficult to explain, even to herself, Nora did not choose Torp to know how completely she was fatigued, so she forced herself to knit and listen until the effort became downrightly painful to her. The stocking seemed to widen immeasurably, and rise to her very eyes; the voices of the speakers sank into an indistinct murmur, like the hum of distant bees; one hand sought her forehead, to rub away the unwelcome drowsiness, but remained to support her drooping head; while the other, round which the blue thread was twisted in a manner incomprehensible to the uninitiated, at length fell powerless among the knitting-needles. A few faint struggles she made to raise her heavy eyelids, to look round her, to move—in vain; overcome by weariness, she first slumbered lightly, then slept profoundly.

The younger children had been taken off by their mother in succession; the elder girls had followed, and might be heard at work in the adjacent kitchen; the ticking of the clock in the wall became audible at intervals, for the fisherman alone continued to talk, Torp having ceased for some time to answer, even in monosyllables. He was, however, not sleeping, or even sleepy—on the contrary, very wide awake, though he no longer heard the voice of the speaker, or took cognizance of anything in the room, save the slumberer opposite him. Perhaps he had been attracted by the white hand and arm that appeared so strikingly inappropriate to the short, coarse linen sleeve; or the rounded figure that gave so much grace to a rustic costume of most ordinary materials; or the fair face in perfect repose; or the braids of shining black hair; or the long eyelashes, or—or— all together, perhaps. Certain it is that he might have seen Nora in London at fifty balls, and as many déjeuners, in the most splendid dresses that can be imagined; or spent a fortnight under the same roof, in the most distinguished and popular of country-houses, without her having had the power to interest and fascinate him as she had done that day, during the storm on the mountain, and in the dwelling-room of the fisherman's homely cottage.

And there was no mother or chaperon to put him on his guard, by looks of ill-concealed exaltation; no relations to point out personal and hint mental perfections—not even a friend to laugh at him! But, after all, what danger could there be for a fastidious man such as he, in the contemplation of a Miss Nora Nixon, especially when she happened to be asleep? So Torp gazed on, in a pleasant, dreamy sort of way, until the fisherman rose to wind up the clock.

Nora opened her eyes, smiled drowsily, "believed she was rather tired," and left the room in search of a candle. A minute afterwards he heard her speaking in the passage,

and, on looking out through the half-open door, soon discovered that she was making earnest inquiries respecting
the time that the cuirassier, Seppel, had been with the fisherman's family.

"Not here until six o'clock in the morning? Did he come
by the woodman's path, that was under water to-day, or—
or by the Wild Alp?"

"By the Alp. He told us he had slept in the loft of one of
the huts there for a couple of hours."

"But he may have left it very early," suggested Nora;
"before daylight most probably, or even during the night—
there was moonlight, you know."

"Oh, as to that, there's not a by-way on the mountains
unknown to him; but I suppose he wanted to find us all up
and together, to hear his good news, or else he would have
been sure to come on without stopping. Moonlight is his
delight, and," added the fisherman's wife, with a knowing
look, "Seppel has been often enough out in the mountains
about here at night to find his way in the dark, if necessary."

"Was he alone?" asked Nora, gravely.

"Alone! of course he was. He came here to invite us to
his betrothal."

"Are you quite sure," asked Nora, "that there were no
'boys' from Tyrol, or—other people with him?"

"Quite sure."

"And," continued Nora, hesitatingly, "he was not uneasy
in his manner, or in a hurry to leave you?"

"By no means. He was as merry as a grig, and took a
swim in the lake, and sang all the Almenau *Schnaderhüpfeln*,
and danced the *polky* as they do in Munich, and was as
fresh, and fresher than ever I saw him in my life, and that's
saying something!"

"Did he not say he had met people at the Alp?" asked

Nora, slowly, as if unwilling to disturb the pleasant impression made on her by the last speech; "some hunters, I mean, who were there last night?"

"No," answered the woman, thoughtfully, and looking round to her son and elder daughters, as if for confirmation. "I don't think he mentioned anything about them: but he said he had heard the report of a rifle when on his way here. Six years ago I should have had my suspicions, and asked him some questions; but now he has grown steady, and wouldn't, on any account, anger his father-in-law that is to be. If you think he was out with wild hunters, miss, you're mistaken. I can answer for him."

"I hope you may be right," said Nora, slowly mounting the staircase, at the top of which she turned round to say good night.

Torp, less fatigued, was soon after tempted to step out on the balcony, where he remained among the flower-pots and fishing-nets nearly two hours, in apparent admiration of the lake, mountains and moon. Why he afterwards went to his room, muttering the words, "stuff and nonsense," we have not time to take into consideration.

CHAPTER XXX

Post Horses Bring the Idyl to a Conclusion

WHEN Nora awoke the next morning, completely refreshed after a night of undisturbed rest, not a cloud was to be seen in the heavens. The mountains over which she had toiled the previous afternoon, together with those that inclosed so large a portion of the lake, were already glowing in the first rays of the rising sun, and standing out clear and distinct from a background of the deepest blue, while the fisherman's house still remained in complete shade. It was situated in the midst of green fields, at the entrance to a valley through which the overplus water of the lake found its way as a turbulent stream to the river Inn. There was pasturage in abundance for cattle, and a not inconsiderable herd were now in the neighbourhood of the house, collecting in groups round the hay-sheds on the meadows, before they commenced their daily wandering to the mountains. There clambering among the rocks or roaming in the woods, the sound of the deep-toned bells suspended round their necks gave constant indication of their whereabouts, and might be heard tinkling incessantly in the distance, until the loud, wild jodel of the fisherman's daughter assembled them, towards evening, at the skirts of the wood. During the summer months they generally remained out at night, not unfrequently, in unusually warm weather, returning home of their own accord during the daytime to the shelter of the long wooden cow-house attached to the dwelling. They liked standing in the lake, too, and regularly ate all the apples they could find under the trees in the orchards. In short, if Nora could have believed all that the fisherman's daughters told her, as she walked through the wet grass with them to look at their favourite cows, there never had been in this world such excellent, good-tempered, or intelligent animals.

"But here's the best fellow of all!" cried Ursi, stalking up to a great bull that stood ruminating at the cowhouse door, and throwing one arm over his neck, with the other she drew his great head towards her. "I brought him up myself and never let him be vexed, and now he follows me as steadily as the old bell-cow herself!"

Nora began to retire towards the house, not a little alarmed at the vicinity of the great animal, that even, while caressing and being caressed, could look so terrible.

The younger sister laughed. "Don't be fearful, miss," she said, encouragingly; "as long as Ursi has a bit of salt in her pocket he will not come near us!"

"You are afraid of him, too," said Nora.

"Oh no—he never minds me, and lets Hans beat him with a stick, when he is sent to drive him out of the potato-field or the oats."

Ursi, who was a stalwart young woman, with a waist and shoulders greatly resembling those of a man, seemed highly amused at Nora's avoidance of her favourite. In order to prove the truth of her last assertion concerning him, she moved on, and was, as she expected, followed by the bull, rubbing his head and shoulder against hers in a manner that would have thrown to the ground any less vigorous personage.

Nora retreated by stepping backwards, and stumbled against Torp, who had come to tell her that her guide, Michael, had arrived, and was waiting for orders.

"Oh, that's right," said Nora, "he can bring us some clothes—or at least take a message to Almenau. But how did he find out where we were?"

"He at first thought we had returned to the Alp," answered Torp, "and as he had the remnants of our provisions, thought it necessary to go there. On his return, the waterfall was dashing over the path, and then it occurred to him that—In short, he guessed what had happened, and was confirmed in the idea when he observed the removal of some large stones that I had displaced in springing on the sand; he followed us, arrived here late at night, made his way into the hay-loft, and is now at your service."

"I suppose we had better write," began Nora.

"Let us consider," he said, following her into the house, "let us first consider whether or not it be worth while. The pathway to the village is, you know, under water. If Michael have to go round through Tyrol, he cannot reach Almenau until late in the evening: it will not be early tomorrow when your clothes reach you, and you may find it necessary to remain here another day. Perhaps you have no objection to do so?"

"No objection?" cried Nora, interrupting him; "every possible objection! I cannot—will not—remain here if it can be avoided. It is of the greatest importance that I should see the forester and his son without delay—I must also endeavour to prevent the Crags peasant from taking any hasty step; you know he might refuse to resign—he might even disinherit—" She stopped suddenly, remembering that Torp could not understand her, and that he was the last person to whom she could explain her anxieties. "What do *you* mean to do?" she asked, abruptly.

"I shall return to Almenau to-day."

"In that dress?" she asked.

"I suppose so," he answered, looking down at his bare knees with a slight grimace.

"If it were not a holiday," said Nora, musingly, "and if we had not to pass through part of Tyrol—But after all there are only a couple of villages before we get into the Bavarian highlands again, and I *must* see the forester and Franz before I sleep this night."

Torp, who feared he had shown too much interest in her decision, now thought it necessary to appear supremely indifferent. "Had I my fishing-tackle," he said, walking to the door and looking out at the lake, "I could have spent a couple of days here pleasantly enough perhaps—without it, I should of course be bored to death."

Nora understood this speech in a way he had not intended. She supposed him unwilling to make arrangements for her return to Almenau, and when he looked round she was gone, and he had soon after the mortification to find that she had engaged the fisherman's son to take her and her guide Michael in a hay-cart to the nearest Tyrolean village, so that if he did not resolve to walk several miles unnecessarily he must request a place in her humble equipage, and receive as a favour what he might have offered to her.

To add to his annoyance, he soon perceived that she had resolved to give him no further opportunity of exhibiting either his indifference or unwillingness to a nearer acquaintance; for, while she remained at the fisherman's house, she effectually contrived to avoid him; not, however, in the downrightly rude manner to which he had recourse with her and her family, but by quietly withdrawing altogether from his presence. While he was left in solitary grandeur to breakfast on weak coffee and thick cream in the dwelling-room, Nora sat in the kitchen surrounded by the whole family; and when the fisherman's wife assembled her children to examine their dresses before they set out for church, she did the same by Nora, placing on her head the smartest little green hat in the house, and loudly declaring she was the prettiest girl she had seen for many a day.

What Nora afterwards said or did so completely to gain the hearts of the fisherman and his family is not recorded; certain it is that they gave her a large bouquet of *Alpenrosen*, too large for both her hands, that the children filled her pockets with apples, and that they were all, without exception, employed in arranging the hay-cart for her reception. The board which was to be her seat was covered with horse-cloths and jackets, over the straw beneath her feet the fisherman's son had spread his cloak, and soon after led from the stable a bay mare, whose foal of the preceding year showed a strong inclination to make the excursion with them. While he took his place in front as coachman, his legs dangling downwards in closest contact with the tail of his horse, Michael stretched himself on the straw in the back of the cart, beside a tolerably large butt containing fish to be sold to the village innkeeper, and during reiterated exclamations of "Adieu," and "May you reach home in safety," Nora was assisted, or rather lifted, into the vehicle by the fisherman himself.

Just as they were about to drive off, she looked up towards Torp, who was standing on the balcony, imagining himself forgotten, hesitated a moment, and then frankly proposed his going with them, as it would save him a very long walk.

"If you have a place for me," he answered, "I shall be much obliged, but you need not wait, for I can easily overtake you before you reach the end of the meadows."

The flush of annoyance was still on his cheek when he joined her at the entrance to the valley, and he long continued to walk beside her in a silent thoughtful sort of way, taking no sort of apparent interest in her conversation with the fisherman's son, and her guide of the previous day.

The road resembled the dry bed of a rivulet, being chiefly composed of the stones and sand left on it by the river after various inundations. On one side of them the swollen waters now rushed on, struggling with the impeding stones; on the other, the mountain rose abruptly, at times wooded, but not unfrequently exhibiting a succession of bare wild rocks, or a mixture of both, and seldom leaving more space than was absolutely necessary for the passage of the cart.

"If the road continue much longer like this," observed Nora, "I think we might just as well have walked."

"Oh, we shall get into the wood presently," said the fisherman's son, "and once on the road, there you shall see how Lizzie can step out."

And soon after they began gradually to ascend a long hill, or rather mountain, on a very rough narrow road. A steep descent followed, where Lizzie in fact stepped out in a manner that made it impossible for Nora to keep her seat without clinging to Torp's arm. She did so unconsciously at first, and he was more pleased than he chose to acknowledge to himself, or wished her to perceive; but he immediately laid aside his haughty manner as if it had been a garment, and when Lizzie became skittish, and made occasional clumsy attempts at a kick or shied at a felled tree, he laughed heartily, and held Nora's arm faster than ever. What perhaps most amused them both were the frequent expostulations of their driver with his bay mare; the idea of touching her with a whip never seemed to enter his mind, though he had one in his hand, which he continually cracked, and flourished in the air, in a remarkably carter-like manner, the surrounding mountains echoing quickly and distinctly the loud sharp sounds.

"Go on, Lizzie," he said, in a coaxing manner, as she

distrustfully eyed the upturned root of a prostrate beech tree, bearing a grotesque resemblance to a stooping human figure. "Go on, now, and don't be foolish before the strangers, after my praising you, and saying you could do everything but speak! It's a shame to see you cocking your ears after that fashion, for an old stump that you've passed by every week last winter, when we brought out the charcoal from the clearings to the iron-works. Oh, if you want to look at it, and sniff it, I'm sure I've no objection," he said, jumping down and leading her forward, while caressingly stroking her nose; "but," he added, "but instead of the lappet of red cloth for your collar that I promised you at the next fair, it's a pair of goggles, or a lorry to stick in your eye like the town folks, that you shall have, you shy old fool. She's as steady as an ox," he said, half apologetically, while resuming his seat, "as steady as an ox when we're sledging charcoal in winter!"

Notwithstanding various trifling delays of this kind, and longer ones where the road had been injured by the rain of the preceding day, Torp thought they reached the Tyrolean village in an astonishingly short time. As they drove up to the inn door, the landlady came bustling forward, and nodded a familiar greeting, but judging too hastily from appearances, showed infinitely more interest about the fish that she expected than the arrival of guests of so little apparent importance.

Torp and Nora were therefore for some time left to their own devices, and after having looked into the peasant room, which was crowded to excess, and where a civil but vain effort was made to find a place for them, they naturally went into the other reserved for persons of higher rank, and found in it a numerous assembly of well-dressed people and some travellers, who all turned round and seemed not a little surprised at their intention to join them.

"Perhaps there is a garden where we could dine alone," suggested Nora.

"There is," answered Torp. "I remember being here a couple of years ago with Waldemar."

"Then let us go to the kitchen and inquire about it and our dinner at the same time," said Nora.

And they moved away unconscious of the curiosity caused by the few words they had spoken in their native language.

It was long afterwards that Nora first became fully conscious of the comical position in which she was placed with Torp that day as they stood together by the hearth consulting with the cook about their dinner. Their similarity of taste and unanimity were remarkable, and a very simple repast had been ordered, when the landlady suddenly appeared, and proposed a few additions that convinced them both that she had had some conversation with Michael and the fisherman's son concerning them.

In the garden they were not so much alone as Nora had expected. The house was famous for its dinners, and a long wooden arcade and capacious summer-house were furnished with tables and guests. For Torp and Nora, however, a place was quickly arranged, and so complete was their peasant costume, that they might have escaped notice, had not the landlady chosen to serve them herself, and afterwards waited for an invitation from Nora to take a seat beside them.

"I think," she observed, turning to Torp, "I think you're the foreign gentleman who was here the year before last with the Count?"

"I was in this neighbourhood about two years ago," he answered, evasively.

"He was here last week," she continued, "and a large party of ladies and gentlemen from Herrenburg. There's to be a wedding in the family soon—perhaps two—if we may believe what the servants say."

Torp did not answer; but the landlady could not believe him as indifferent as he looked.

"They say," she continued, "the Count can have the lady from Vienna for the asking—that she's come on purpose—and the old Count is uncommon well satisfied with the match."

"Ah, indeed!" said Torp, carelessly, while Nora, strongly suspecting this lady from Vienna to be her friend Irene Schaumberg, would gladly have asked a question or two had he been absent.

"They have announced their intention of coming here to-day, and honouring our theatre with a visit," said the landlady.

"At what hour?" asked Torp, quickly.

"At two o'clock. And if you and the young lady would not disdain our village performance, you might as well remain for an hour or so to see it."

"I think," said Torp, turning to Nora, "I think the delay would scarcely be desirable for either of us."

"The play is much admired," interposed the landlady; "and the Count said he would go any distance to see our smith act the villain, and the workwoman do the duchess."

Nora smiled. She had no doubt that Waldemar had so spoken, but also no inclination to be seen by him and his friends, wandering about so adventurously in the guise of a peasant; so she became as anxious as Torp to avoid a meeting, and joined him in requesting the landlady to send an express to the nearest town for post horses.

When she had left them for this purpose, Torp informed Nora that the innkeeper and his wife had found it a good speculation to build a theatre; and he pointed, while speaking, towards a tolerably large wooden edifice at the end of a garden, adding, "Their house is crowded before and after the performances in a manner that amply indemnifies them for the outlay of capital."

"Under any other circumstances," observed Nora, "and in any other dress, I should have liked to remain here a few hours longer, in order to see this drama, or melodrama, in which the smith and workwoman have so distinguished themselves."

"I dare say we should have found it amusing enough," said Torp; "though why these peasants always choose dramas in which they have to represent princes and dukes and knights in armour, I have never been able to make out."

"Consider these dramas as a criterion of peasant civilisation," said Nora, "and you will no longer wonder at their taste."

"I do not understand you," said Torp.

"Do we not in infancy like tales of giants, and ogres, and fairies?" said Nora. "Learning to read and exercise our reason brings us farther on—to the Arabian Nights, or legends holy and profane. A smattering of knowledge, a very little history, takes us to the crusades, with all their array of kings, queens, princes, knights, and tournaments. This is the longest and brightest period, the manners, the dress, the glory of personal strength, courage, and honesty, the very superstition of that age."

"Ah, I see," cried Torp, interrupting her; "you consider the peasants in the mountains here to have attained somewhat about the degree of culture that we possess in our tenth or twelfth year."

"I cannot otherwise account for their theatrical taste," answered Nora. "At all events that they can enjoy such dramas is no small proof of peasant cultivation; that they are able to act them, and wonderfully well, too, is a still greater. Now I should like to know," she added, leaning her arms on the table and looking at him gravely, "I should like to know if our peasantry in England, Ireland, or Scotland could do as much?"

"I am decidedly inclined to doubt their histrionic talents," said Torp.

"Can you then tell me," she continued in the same tone, "what *are* the amusements or recreations of the lower orders in England, especially in the villages?"

"Really, Miss Nixon," said Torp, half laughing, "one might suppose you a foreigner making inquiries about the habits and customs of the inhabitants of the British Islands! It would be preposterous my offering to instruct a person of your intellect and information, and your question can only be put to extort the answer that our peasantry have no recreations of this description, and that I scarcely know whether or not they would be capable of enjoying them if they had."

"Excuse my ignorance," said Nora, quietly; "I have, in fact, had no opportunity of judging for myself, for London has been England to me."

"Ah, I had forgotten that," said Torp; "or rather I have latterly found it impossible to suppose an English and especially a London education, could have made you what you are."

He paused, perhaps expecting her to ask what he meant; but as she remained silent he added, of his own accord, "You give me the idea of a person who was in the habit of spending more than half the year abroad, and the rest of it in the wildest parts of the Highlands of Scotland."

Nora could not help smiling at a remark that proved she had been much more observed than she had supposed. "I have never been in Scotland, nor even in any of the country parts of England," she observed, after a moment's consideration. "The trees and grass of a dingy square have for many years represented woods and meadows to me, and solely through the medium of their sooty blighted vegetation have I been made aware of the gradual change of season going on beyond the houses of our overgrown metropolis."

"And yet," said Torp, "I am convinced you like these dingy squares, think London the most delightful place in the world, and make it a standard for all others."

"No, oh no!" said Nora, shaking her head.

"You surprise me," he rejoined, somewhat cavalierly, "for most London people consider their town *par excellence* a perfect paradise."

Not a little amused at finding herself civilly called a cockney, yet unwilling to enter into any explanation, Nora watched in silence and with some interest the effect which the supposition and recollections of her family would produce on her companion. He had been building a pyramid of small, bright, yellow-coloured apricots, and continued his occupation in an absent manner until a little boy placed a play-bill in Nora's hand, which she instantly began to study. Then Torp looked up, leaned slightly across the narrow table in order to read with her, and as she placed the paper between them, and they bent over it together, cockneys, Nixons, London, and England, seemed altogether to fade from his mind, and he became what she had learned to consider his better self again.

"I am much mistaken," he observed, with a laugh, "if that be not the very thing I saw in Brixley a couple of years ago."

"And what sort of a 'thing' is it?" asked Nora.

"Why, let me see—it was melodramatic—the duchess, I remember, sang very tolerably, and wore a red gown trimmed with a wonderful imitation of ermine—a yellowish cotton stuff with black spots."

"And the subject of the drama?" asked Nora.

"I am afraid I bestowed too much attention on the people with me, the audience in general, the theatre itself, and the persons of the peasant actors, to have any clear recollection of the drama. I remember there were a couple of large leather dolls, representing children, which were most inhumanly used, though whether they were to be killed outright or exposed in a wood to be found by a kind-hearted charcoal-burner, or brought up by a compassionate doe—"

"You are getting into the legend of Genoveva,"* said Nora, interrupting him.

"Ah, very true—there was a sort of resemblance I believe—at least, the duchess in the red gown was very unhappy about these children, or something else. I think, too, she was turned out of doors by her lord and master, a fellow with a long feather in his hat. The villain of the play was decidedly the best actor, with a few pieces of rather incongruous armour, a plumed helmet, and buskins. He 'strutted and fretted his hour upon the stage'† to every one's satisfaction; but whether in his character of robber-knight he only carried off the children, or actually attempted to murder them,—whether he merely provoked the jealousy of the marvellously dignified duke, or went the length of endeavouring to assassinate him in the lonely wood, I have not the slightest idea. That he had been foiled in all his atrocious attempts was made pleasantly evident by the ap-

---

* According to the legend, Count Siegfried of Andernach, returning from the Crusades, was persuaded to believe slanderous accusations against his wife Genoveva. He banished her from his castle after which she lived for some years in the forest, sustained by the animals and protected from danger by her virtue.

† "A poor player | That struts and frets his hour upon the stage, | And then is heard no more". *Macbeth*, Act V scene v lines 24-26.

pearance of the dolls, duchess, and duke in the last scene, while the villain himself, wounded and in a half-recumbent posture, confessed all his sins and misdemeanours in deep, broken, and sepulchral accents!"

"I think," said Nora, "that after so evident a proof of flagrant inattention to the drama itself, I may reasonably expect that your observations of other matters will prove unusually accurate."

"I grant, without hesitation," answered Torp, "that the fact of such theatres and performances being popular in the Bavarian Highlands and Tyrol interested me infinitely more than the actual representation going on in my presence, and that I made inquiries on the subject of every one likely to give me any information."

"And the result?" asked Nora.

"I found that, from time out of mind, these plays had been acted by the peasants about here. The original taste for them, and the habit of acting, seem to have been acquired from moralities and mysteries such as we saw at Ammergau; as in some plays a sort of explanatory *tableau vivant* still precedes each act, and a genius, holding a long-stalked lily, walks up and down before the foot-lights to expound its purport. There is a decided predilection for tragedy or serious drama, and all attempts have failed to procure popularity for modern plays or modern dresses; equally evident is the strong prejudice against prose compositions, and the more stilted the style and metre the more certain of applause."

"That I consider a matter of course," observed Nora, "when one takes into consideration that actors and audience are peasants with glowing fancies and partial educations."

"Yet the spirit of improvement or change is at work even here," said Torp, "and during the last few years some innovations have been attempted that are likely to cause an alteration in these performances calculated to make them, if not to the peasants, to us, at least, far less interesting. Formerly the actors were, as at Ammergau, altogether composed of the inhabitants of the village and the neighbouring peasants, who, not having much time at their disposal, only studied a couple of dramas each year, performing them with persevering regularity, on alternate holidays, at the end of the season, dividing as shareholders any profits that remained, and generally appropriating the amount to pay the expenses of a fête in which actors and audience mutually participated. Latterly there have been found enterprising men who have undertaken the management, supplied the dresses, paid the actors according to their capabilities, and not unfrequently tempted performers from the neighbouring towns to appear on their stages."

"I have not the slightest wish to see anything of *that* kind," said Nora, once more taking up the play-bill.

"They are, I believe, still quite primitive here," continued Torp; "and even at Brixley there were no actors or actresses from Innsbruck or the intervening towns. If, however, the stage is to be a sort of moral institution, a means of instructing the people, as has been so continually advocated in Germany, better actors and more variety in the choice of dramas might be perhaps desirable."

"I cannot think so," said Nora; "an amateur theatre interests more or less the whole parish, brings the people together for a common purpose, induces them to read and discuss what will suit them best, and is certainly a means of improving their manners. If, as you have given me to understand, you have carefully watched the conduct and appearance of a peasant audience in a peasant theatre, you must agree with me, and wish that our lower orders had similar tastes and similar amusements."

"It would never answer in England," said Torp. "Even supposing one half of our population found pleasure in theatres of this kind, the other would consider them a cause of umbrage, and regard them with indignation."

"What! even if they were moral or religious dramas?"

"About them there might be the greatest unanimity," replied Torp; "they would, most undoubtedly, be condemned at once as irreverent, if not impious."

"You are thinking of representations such as we saw at Ammergau," said Nora; "and I confess that, notwithstanding the intense interest and admiration I felt for *that* as an exceptional performance, had I the power I should forbid it and all others in which our Saviour's personal appearance might be supposed necessary."

"I am glad to hear you say so," observed Torp.

"But," continued Nora, "the drama at Ammergau has convinced me that religious subjects are eminently adapted for such theatres, such actors, and such audiences."

"Nothing of the kind would ever be tolerated in England," rejoined Torp.

"And why?"

"We are a religious people," he answered, "and consider the Bible so sacred that no person mentioned in it can with propriety be made to appear upon a stage."

"Is that your opinion also?" asked Nora.

"Not exactly," he replied; "but circumstances have obliged me to live almost constantly abroad, and chiefly in Germany, during the last ten years, so that many of my English prejudices have been modified or relinquished altogether, and I heartily wish that our lower orders had rational amusements of some kind or other to keep them out of the alehouses and gin-shops."

"I believe," said Nora, "Mr Hume* said something to that purport in the House of Commons once upon a time; but when one reads in statistical reports of hundreds of thousands who never enter a church in this religious country of ours, and more than as many who cannot read or write, one cannot help asking what amusements would be likely to suit such a people."

Torp shrugged his shoulders, drummed on the table, and then said, "I believe amusements could be found for them as well as for others, but not such as you, in your admiration of the peasantry here, would propose for them."

"You have guessed my thoughts," observed Nora, smiling. "I confess that I was planning gardens where they could hear good music, and drink beer and coffee with their wives. I should like to hear them sing merrily in chorus, and see them dance."

"We are not born singers and dancers, like the people here," said Torp. "You would have to teach us to be happy, Miss Nixon."

"I understand you," she replied. "You think it would be difficult to persuade English peasants that a waltz in the evening was a recreation after a hard day's work."

Torp nodded his head.

"And yet it is considered such here," she continued. "Those people who danced so gaily the other night at our inn had been up and at work before dawn, assembled in their church at six o'clock, and, with but a short rest about noon, had laboured incessantly the whole day. I was astonished to see them equal to such exertion after so much hard labour."

* Joseph Hume MP (1777-1855), radical politician and fighter for various social causes.

"So was I," said Torp. "They seem a robust race about Almenau, enjoy dancing to excess, and are as ready for a fight as if they had been born Irishmen."

"I cannot deny that," replied Nora. "Our landlady told me that some excesses which had taken place in the neighbourhood had caused the church festivals to be celebrated on the same day throughout Bavaria, in order to prevent a too great concourse of people in any one parish; and there is also some difficulty in obtaining permission from the land-judge to dance, excepting on occasions such as weddings, or shooting-matches, when the company are invited, and there is no likelihood of a brawl."

"These are the expedient restrictions of a patriarchal government," observed Torp; "but I need scarcely remind you, that our constitution allows no interference of this kind, even for a good purpose."

The landlady announced the arrival of the horses from the neighbouring town, and they both started up, equally anxious to accomplish their departure before the arrival of Waldemar and his friends. Neither made the slightest objection to the high old-fashioned yellow calash and long-legged half-harnessed horses that awaited them. Michael seated himself beside the grey and red liveried Tyrolean postilion, and they set off at a rate that promised a speedy return to Almenau.

At a short distance beyond the village they met a number of carriages containing ladies with gay bonnets and fluttering ribbons, and gentlemen in summer coats, and green or grey felt hats of fantastic forms. The carriages passed in quick succession, and evidently belonged to the same party; for, as the gentlemen in the first stood up to look after Torp and Nora, whom they supposed to be rich peasants taking their pleasure in a post-chaise, the others followed their example; and a gentleman in the last carriage, throw-

ing the reins to the servant beside him, sprang to the
ground and shouted "Halt!" to their postilion in a voice
that was not to be disobeyed.

Neither Torp nor Nora was surprised to see Waldemar,
though his amazement at the meeting was boundless. While
Nora explained, he murmured at intervals, "What an adventure! Why was I not with you? Oh that I had been in Torp's
place!—delightful—romantic"—and as she bent down towards him, and in a low voice mentioned her uneasiness
about long Seppel from the Crags—should the forester's
son prove implacable, and denounce him to the judge, he
instantly offered to return to Almenau for a couple of days
to defend him as far as lay in his power, and to use all his
influence to set matters to rights again.

"Thank you—oh, thank you!" cried Nora, extending her
hand to him with the warmth and unreserve that so surprise
and delight foreigners on the part of Englishwomen, especially when they happen to be young and handsome. "Be
sure you don't forget," she added, glancing at the carriage
that still waited for him in the distance; "for I am more interested in this affair than you can imagine, or I will venture
to tell you."

"If I am to act as counsel," said Waldemar, archly, "you
must give me your whole confidence."

"Is it not enough to say that this Seppel is, or rather was,
to be married to the forester's daughter?"

"Oh, it's the love affair that interests you," he rejoined,
laughing: "in that case you may venture to tell me all about
it, and be quite sure of my sympathy. But there seems to be
something else, too," he added, as the thought of how far
her cousin John was implicated made her colour deepen in
a very perceptible manner. His eyes sparkled, a sudden
flush passed across his features; but, without waiting for an
answer, he raised his hat, drew back, nodded laughingly to

Torp; and, while they drove off, stood looking after them as long as they remained in sight.

CHAPTER XXXI

The "Big Sausage"

A LL that Nora most feared had taken place. Rosel
had been unable to keep pace with her brother,
who, pressing forward, had reached home long before her, and required but a few words to inspire his father
with a fury equal to his own. Together they had gone to the
judge, Seppel had been summoned for examination, and
the presumptive evidence against him found so strong,
when corroborated by his own account of himself, that he
had been taken at once into custody.

The Crags peasant, affecting even more indignation than
he really felt, had openly condemned his son, declaring "he
had never expected anything else from so lawless a fellow,
who, he was convinced, had only been playing steady and
well-behaved in order to get possession of house and land;
but he might now go back to his regiment and the officers
who thought so much of him—it was the best thing he
could do, for not a rood of ground at the Crags should ever
belong to him!" To end all discussions and disputes with
his wife and neighbours on the subject, the old man had
carried his threat into immediate execution by taking the
steps necessary to put his younger son into immediate possession of the property.

Discord seemed to have changed the character of every
member of the forester's family. The cheerful Rosel hung

her head in deepest despondency, and, with eyes half closed by their swelled lids, listlessly and mechanically followed her mother's restless movements from place to place. The usual serenity of the latter had been completely disturbed by what she called the imprudent conduct of her "man" and "boy" in breaking off the marriage of Rosel, and giving up the thousand florins so generously offered by the young English lady! And for such a trifling offence too! for she could not be brought to consider imprisoning in an alpine hut in any other light, waxing in wrath as the others explained and expostulated, and ending by calling her son a blockhead, notwithstanding his forester learning, and her husband a fool, who would live to repent having destroyed the prospects of one child to humour the anger of another! Franz had snatched up his rifle and retreated to the wood, and the forester, after growling some unintelligible words intending to convey the idea that he was master of his house and children, and that no wildschuetz should ever darken his door, sneaked off to his workmen at the river, while his wife expended the remainder of her roused energy on her floors and furniture, scouring, rubbing, and dusting in a manner that had effectually prevented either of the offenders from again making his appearance during the day.

The work of cleanliness had been completed, but there were still damp boards and a strong smell of the fir-tree besoms and wisps so universally used in the Highlands for the purpose of sweeping and scouring, when Nora stopped at the forest-house to change her dress before she appeared at the inn or village. A sort of reserve had gradually crept over her and her companion as they had approached Almenau, and it was to Michael that she turned when alighting, with the request that he would tell Mr Nixon that she was quite safe, and would be with him in half an hour.

"The young English gentleman is gone to the Wild Alp

with some men from the village," said the forester's wife as Torp drove off; "they hoped to be able to cross the waterfall this afternoon, and never doubted your having remained in the Alp hut during the night."

While hastily relating her mountain adventure, Nora proceeded to her room, followed by Rosel and her mother. The latter immediately began a minute account of all that had occurred during the last two days, ending with bitter complaints of both husband and son, who had thought of nothing but satisfying their own revengeful feelings.

"Let us hope that Seppel's identity cannot be proved," observed Nora, consolingly. "They say his face was blackened with charcoal, and there was scarcely any light in the hut. Under such circumstances your son cannot venture to assert positively that his assailant was Seppel."

"But the foolish fellow has confessed—" began the forester's wife.

"Nothing—mother—nothing," cried Rosel; "he only said that he had slept for a few hours in one of the huts on the Alp, and heard the report of a gun or rifle somewhere on the mountain."

"I'm afraid that is enough, and more than enough, to confirm every one's suspicions," said her mother; "besides, Franz heard the others call him by his name."

"We have no less than nine Seppels in our village," rejoined Rosel, eagerly, "and the name is quite as common on the other side of the mountains. If they had said Kraft or Crags—"

"Kraft he may still be called," said her mother, interrupting her, "but Crags never. Before a week is over Anderl will be in possession of all that was to have been yours, and there is no use in talking more about the matter."

"If they cannot prove him guilty—" began Rosel.

"All the same," said her mother, despondingly. "You

know the old man only wants an excuse to do as he pleases."

"Count Waldemar is coming here to-morrow," observed Nora, "and has promised to do all he can for Seppel."

"The Count has ever been a friend to us, and may go bail for Seppel, and the judge may set him at liberty, but what's the use? Anderl will get the Crags, and Seppel, at the very most, five or six hundred florins from his father, and with that he cannot marry Rosel!"

"How much would be necessary to enable him to do so?" asked Nora.

"I don't know," answered the forester's wife, unconscious of the kind intention that prompted the question. "I don't know, and it is of little importance, for Rosel will never be allowed to marry a wildschuetz. I thought we were going to have two weddings in our family," she added, her voice trembling perceptibly; "but as misfortunes never come singly, I was hardly surprised when the miller's daughter told me to-day that all was at an end between her and Franz, as her father had promised her six years ago to black Seppel, who had it in writing, and signed by the miller himself; and that one might as well try to move a mountain as the Tyrolean, when he took anything into his head."

"I have heard something of this," said Nora; "but Madeleine has resolved not to marry this Seppel, and has told him so."

"It is hard to say what she may do," answered the forester's wife; "he's far richer than our Franz may ever be, and that may make her forget that he's a gloomy, churlish fellow, and has blood on his hands, as you may have heard from the people here."

"Michael mentioned his having shot his brother by accident," said Nora; "that for this reason he had left home, and made a vow never to touch a rifle again. I think a man in such a position more to be pitied than blamed."

"That's as may be," said the forester's wife, nodding her head sagaciously. "Now, if Crags Seppel were to shoot his brother Anderl by accident, what would you say?"

"That he was a most unfortunate man," answered Nora, perfectly understanding the drift of her question.

"Well, others would judge the deed less charitably, and it would be many a year before old Crags would forgive him."

"Oh, mother, mother! how can you talk in this way?" exclaimed Rosel, wringing her hands.

"I mean no disparagement to Seppel, child; he'll never do, or even think of, anything of the kind; but as to saying that he was not with the Tyroleans on the Wild Alp the day before yesterday, that is out of my power. You know he's a wildschuetz, Rosel, and nothing would ever restrain him, excepting, perhaps, a marriage with you, and the chance of an occasional hunt with your father or brother. You see even Miss Nora, who likes him for your sake, thinks—"

Nora, who was about to leave the room, stopped suddenly on hearing a violent burst of grief from Rosel. She turned back, put her hand on the arm of the weeping girl, and said, kindly, "If they cannot prove him guilty, Rosel, we are bound to believe what he himself says."

"I believe him now—on his word," cried Rosel.

"Of course you do," said Nora, smiling; "it would be very odd if you did not."

Nora, deprived of her round hat, was obliged to put on a gay little Paris bonnet to walk to the inn. Torp was looking out of his window as she entered, and seemed to have a peculiar pleasure in counting the voluminous flounces of her lilac muslin dress, and the various falls of lace and knots of fluttering ribbons that waved round her now well-gloved hands.

"I am glad she has doffed her mountain toggery before

Waldemar's arrival," thought the considerate friend; "it would have been all over with him had he seen her for any length of time in that peasant dress. What a precious fool *he* would have made of himself had he been in my place during the last two days!"

Nora found that neither her uncle nor Georgina required any explanation of her prolonged absence. They had heard from Adam that there were villages at the base, farmhouses on the sides of the mountains, a picturesque lake, and charming châlet on the Alp itself, where mademoiselle could perfectly well pass the night. Jack's uneasiness about her had been incomprehensible to them; and as he had entered into no explanation, and even confirmed Adam's account, they supposed he had only wanted an excuse to leave them and Almenau for a few days again. More at length, and with greater interest, they spoke of Captain Falkner, who had gone to his family to urge their return to St Benedict's.

"They may be expected about the end of next week," said Georgina; "and in the mean time every thing and person about the place is at our service. Papa was out fishing all day with the gardener, and I spent the afternoon in the drawing-room, where there is an excellent grand pianoforte of Mademoiselle de Falkner's. There are astonishingly few books in the house, and not one, as you know, in the beautiful library at the lake side,—but we shall change all that. Papa has planned a new approach, and thinks we shall have to build something, or make a plantation, to shut out that straggling hamlet that is so close to the monastery. There are some neighbouring farm-houses, too, which must be thrown down at once, as it would never do to have them visible from the drawing-room windows!"

"The houses of which you speak are not farms," said Nora; "they and the land about them are the property of the peasants living in them, and have been in their families for hundreds of years, perhaps. All the peasants about here are proprietors."

"I thought they belonged to the monastery, and that the people would be our tenants," said Georgina.

"They may have been something of the kind in former times," replied Nora; "but the forester, who seems to understand these things, tells me that they have been made free from feudal duties long ago, and from most others in the year 1848."

"Bless me!" cried Mr Nixon, "one might almost suppose the people here better off than in England! You don't mean to say, however, that if I chose to purchase and give a fair price, I could not have my choice of all the land about here?"

"The forests belong to the State," answered Nora; "and though the peasants can undoubtedly sell their ground if they please, they seldom do so if not overwhelmed by debts, and compelled by creditors."

"Oh," said Mr Nixon, "I really was preparing myself to hear that these peasant estates were entailed on the eldest heir male, and so forth."

"Not exactly," said Nora; "for, curiously enough, in some places and in some families it is the youngest son who inherits."

"That *is* curious," said Mr Nixon.

"Not more so than that many houses in the village have a right of trade," observed Nora.

"What does that mean?"

"That only a certain number of tradesmen are allowed to establish themselves in a town or village. For instance, one master-mason is considered sufficient for such a place as Almenau. The mason here died a few years ago, leaving a childless widow in possession of a red-balconied house with a mason's right of trade. The widow put an advertisement in the newspaper for a journeyman mason who could undertake the management of the business for her, with something more than a hint that if he gave satisfaction he might become master as well as manager. Several applied for the situation, producing certificates, and offering the most satisfactory recommendations. In the course of a few weeks the widow had made her choice, and given Almenau a mason."

"Do you know whether the certificates or her own inclinations were most taken into consideration?" asked Georgina, laughing.

"Probably the certificates," answered Nora; "the peasants are very calculating and prudent in their marriages; friends and relations are consulted. These often overlook strange disparity of age, and put personal inclination out of the question altogether. In this instance the choice seems to have been rational; the mason is a middle-aged industrious man, who, as the people here say, brought some money into the house, and now carries on the business to every one's satisfaction. I had some conversation with him concerning the expense of rebuilding the castle of Waltenburg, and found him very intelligent."

"Oh, ho!" cried Mr Nixon; "have you that crotchet in your head still?"

"Yes," said Nora: "the ruin I can easily obtain, but very little land in its immediate vicinity."

"You had better let Sam find out something at home for you, Nora. After all, there's no place like England."

"I leave Georgina to answer you," replied Nora, as they moved towards the dinner-table, where the trout and venison soon turned her uncle's thoughts into another channel.

While Torp the next morning loitered over his solitary breakfast under the lime trees in the garden of the inn, and

deliberated whether he should or should not take advantage
of the cloudy sky to fish in the stream between the forester's house and the road, he perceived Nora (the probability of whose appearance on the balcony overlooking the
said stream he had also unconsciously taken into consideration) walking quickly through the village. She had evidently
been making purchases in the little shop there, for not only
had she replaced the round flat hat lost in the storm on the
mountain by one equally huge and hideous, but she also
carried in her hand a parcel tied up peasant-like in a coloured cotton handkerchief, from one of the corners of
which there protruded a gay bunch of artificial flowers.

Torp began to pour out a fresh cup of the now cold coffee, and to heap an unnecessary number of lumps of sugar
into it, not overseeing, while doing so, a single movement
of the approaching figure; and he had no sooner convinced
himself that Nora was likely to pass without a glance towards him, or even a perception of his presence, than he
rose and advanced to the paling that separated the garden
from the road to wish her good morning.

"Good morning," she answered, depositing her parcel
on the top of the garden gate, and leaning her arms on it
while she added, "I have just heard of an opportunity of
sending back the clothes I borrowed to the fisherman's
family."

"And these bright-coloured things go with them, I suppose," replied Torp; "the 'real flowers' are, I know, for
Master Hanserl."

"Rightly guessed," said Nora; "I have got the harmonica,
too," she continued, diving into the parcel. "Madame
Cramer had the kindness to open a new packet fresh from
the manufactory for me, that I might have no objection to
trying them myself. It is wonderfully good for the price,"
she added, raising the little instrument to her mouth, and

breathing rather than blowing a succession of harmonious chords.

Torp smiled; and as he afterwards held it in his hand for a few seconds, he felt marvellously inclined to raise it to his own lips, and "blow music," as Hanserl had said; but he refrained.

"Everything I wanted," continued Nora, "was to be found at our wonderful little shop, excepting the 'great big sausage.' The half a yard of smoked pork that Hanserl so desired to have, can only be procured at the post town, and I find it impossible to get a messenger in the village, as the cloudy sky has made every man, women, and child turn out to bring in the corn already reaped, before the commencement of the expected rain. Had I known as much as I do now, between six and seven o'clock this morning, I could have found plenty of people to undertake my commission."

"Among the peasants coming out of church after matins?" said Torp.

"Yes," she answered, "for my frequent visits to the churchyard have made me familiar with the names and residences of most of the families about here. I have now a bowing acquaintance with all, and there are some with whom I am becoming almost intimate."

"I can guess who they are," said Torp: "first of all there is Florian, the painter and wood-carver; then the miller and his handsome daughter, and the old peasant called Crags, from the name of his property. By-the-by, that custom seems as common here as among the lairds of Scotland."

"Quite so," replied Nora; "the poorest peasant takes the name of his land, and it even devolves as a matter of course on any chance purchaser."

"Making altogether a confusion of names," observed Torp, "for most of the men have sobriquets also."

"*They* at least are easily learned and remembered," said Nora.

"I don't know that," he replied. "I have, for instance, had some trouble in getting acquainted with the different Seppels. There is black, or Tyrolee Sepp; red Sepp of the saw-mill; Sepp from the Rock-wall; and long Sepp, from the Crags; or target Sepp, or—wildschuetz Sepp, for by any of these names he is known."

"Poor fellow!" ejaculated Nora, "I hope you will not be obliged to give evidence against him."

"You need not be uneasy," he answered; "as I have only seen him occasionally in his cuirassier uniform coming out of church, I cannot be expected to know him in wildschuetz costume, and my suspicion that he was the leader of the poachers who found it necessary or convenient to imprison me will be no detriment to him. There was a small fellow," he continued after a pause, "who attacked me singly, and drew off when the others came on to give me fair play: he indeed made himself known to me in a manner not to be mistaken; but," he added, looking steadily at Nora's half-averted face, "but I have no intention of volunteering evidence of any kind, and the forester's son Franz seems not to have observed the individual of whom I speak."

Nora turned away in silence, and Torp no longer doubted her having gone to the Alp to release him.

"He seems to expect me to be grateful for his forbearance," thought Nora, "and is perfectly unconscious that his ill-natured refusal to let Jack have a day or two's sport has been the cause of all that has happened."

"Miss Nixon," said Torp, following her as she crossed the road, and was about to enter the inn, "if you will allow my servant to undertake your commission to the town, he will be most happy to be employed, and a walk will be good for his health."

So the man himself seemed to have thought, for on inquiry it was discovered he had gone out, and no one knew in what direction.

That Torp was an indulgent master had not escaped Nora's observation. His servant, who appeared to he a very exclusive personage, of rather studious habits, usually passed his time sauntering about in a contemplative manner with a small book in his hand, and a thicker and larger one in his pocket: this last Monsieur Adam the courier pronounced without hesitation to be a *dictionnaire de poche*, which, if true, may lead the reader to suppose he had on the present occasion sought some more quiet locality for the pursuit of his linguistic studies.

Torp seemed for a moment disconcerted, but only for a moment; the next he turned to Nora, proposed himself as substitute, and when she hesitated, said with a smile, "I require no orders, Miss Nixon; in a couple of hours you shall have the "biggest sausage" that can be found in the neighbouring town."

"After all," thought Nora, "there is—perhaps—some good in him."

CHAPTER XXXII

Alpenrosen

THE two hours had not elapsed, when Torp strode across the low bridge of planks conducting to the forest-house. Waldemar had arrived during his absence, and was now seated beside Nora on the long bench outside the door, where, with his elbow on his crossed knees, and his chin resting in the palm of his hand, he looked up into her face, so profoundly attentive to what she was saying, that he was unconscious of the approach of his friend until he actually stood before him.

Great was then his amusement when Torp drew the huge sausage from the pocket of his shooting jacket; still greater, when Nora thanked him gravely, and at some length, for having taken such a long warm walk to give pleasure to a poor little fisher-boy; Torp, the while, leaning calmly against the door-post, neither disclaiming nor explaining.

Nora afterwards turned to Waldemar, as it appeared, in continuation of their interrupted conversation. "If you could manage to see the judge, and procure Seppel's release to-day," she said, earnestly, "we might perhaps induce the Crags peasant to *defer*, at least, the resignation of his property. You perceive there is no positive evidence against Seppel, and a week or two may still set all to rights, as the forester and Franz seem both rather to repent their hasty denunciation."

"Your wishes are orders to me, Mees Nixone," replied
Waldemar, rising, "but let it be clearly understood," he
added, with a laughing glance towards Torp, "that I am
about to take this walk for *you*, and not for the cuirassier
and wildschuetz Seppel."

"Let us rather say for Rosel," suggested Nora; "for
Rosel, whom you have known so long!"

"No, Mees Nixone, I make no pretension to be a paragon man like Torp: I will not be good for nothing."

Nora laughed.

"I mean good—for goodness' sake."

Torp laughed.

"Hang your English!" cried Waldemar, bursting into
German; "we never thought of speaking it, Torp, until you
joined us. What I intended to say was, that I came here to-
day for your sake, Miss Nixon, and I am now going to the
judge also for your sake, and for yours alone."

"Well, well," cried Nora, impatiently, "for my sake and
for Rosel's sake, for everybody's sake; and, for goodness'
sake, do what you can in this unfortunate business."

The two men walked off together, Waldemar half expecting a renewal of Torp's former remonstrances, and
quite prepared to retaliate. Not a little was he therefore surprised when his companion, after a few minutes' silence,
asked him, with apparent interest, what he expected to be
able to do for the wildschuetz.

"The evidence against him seems merely presumptive,"
he answered, "and as he is the son of a respectable peasant,
and has a capital discharge from the colonel of his regiment, I shall go security for him. The forester and his son
will probably drop the prosecution, the old curmudgeon at
the Crags will perhaps relent, and we shall dance at Rosel's
wedding precisely in the manner projected by Mees Nora."

"Then, in fact, you think him innocent?" observed Torp.

Waldemar's glance was comical as he answered, "You know more about that matter than I do, Torp, but I am not disposed to ask you any questions. The fact is, I made up my mind beforehand to believe precisely what your fair countrywoman chose to tell me, and have avoided in any way urging her to be more explicit than she thought necessary. She pleaded for Seppel with consummate tact; dwelt on the attachment between him and Rosel from their childhood; the danger of his worldly prospects being ruined if his father were given so good an excuse for depriving him of the succession to the Crags; and mentioned her own wish to confide the grave of her cousin in the churchyard here to the care of this young man, could he be married to Rosel, and established on his father's property, before she and her family leave the village. Now, though I know he was—and think he may be still—a wildschuetz, the poor fellow wants to get married, and intends, as we all do, sooner or later, to reform and grow steady, and I am not the man to refuse to help him out of a scrape, when his cause is advocated in a manner that would move even a Stoic, such as you are!

"I thought," he added, perceiving that Torp stopped in a very determined manner when they reached the inn, "I thought you intended to accompany me into the town?"

"Once a day is enough for me," answered Torp; "and I must go there to-morrow, it seems, to give evidence against your protégé."

"Can you do so?" asked Waldemar. "Remember a man is not easily recognised when his face is blackened with charcoal."

"You have not much to fear from me," rejoined Torp, "for I am by no means sure that my antagonist was this long Seppel; there are enough tall peasants in the Highlands to make it difficult to identify him, though anywhere else in Bavaria he would be a marked man."

"Oh, ho!" cried Waldemar, laughing, "I perceive you have also been engaged as counsel for the defendant, as they say in England."

"No," answered Torp, "that philanthropical office has been confided to you alone; and I confess I should be rather puzzled, had I to undertake his defence, for although not *certain*, I have a strong *misgiving* that he was the fellow who joined the Tyroleans in flooring and handcuffing me, and I shall of course be obliged to say so if asked. Fortunately my suspicions will do him no harm."

"They will do him no good," said Waldemar, turning away; "but there is no use in our discussing this subject any longer. If you had consented to go into the town with me," he added, walking on, "I should have told you all about Falkner's love affair with your countrywoman, but I dare say you know all about it already."

"I know nothing more than we suspected before you left Almenau," said Torp, walking after him, apparently with some reluctance; "Falkner's sudden departure convinced me that some decisive step had been taken, and I concluded he was accepted, as the young lady still passed her days at St Benedict's, and whenever I chanced to meet her, was more carefully veiled than ever."

"Rightly guessed," said Waldemar; "and now tell me what the adorable Nora has been doing?"

"Wandering incessantly about the village and on the mountains," he answered; "and evidently entertaining a strong predilection for the society of the schoolmaster, shopkeeper, painter, priest, barefooted children, and peasants in general. It may interest you to know that her especial favourites are decidedly the wildschuetz and the young assistant forester."

"And," said Waldemar, thoughtfully, "it is very kind of her to interest herself so much for them. Few women in her place could or would enter into the joys and sorrows of people in a rank of life so inferior to their own, and her plans for assisting them are so rational, that I could have listened to her with pleasure for a couple of hours longer, had not you, as usual, interrupted us."

"I did so for the last time," answered Torp. "No *tête-à-tête* of yours with Miss Nixon shall ever again be disturbed by me."

"What does that mean?" asked Waldemar.

"Simply that I suppose you are free from the little entanglement of which you spoke some time ago, and that you intend to marry my unveiled countrywoman when Falkner takes the veiled one."

"The plan is more pleasant than feasible," said Waldemar. "Falkner has been uncommonly lucky on this occasion —he is really in love. The lady has fortune, and, to crown all, his father declares he took a fancy to her himself the very first and only time he ever saw her. I expected that at least his mother and sister would make objections; for you may remember the last evening they were at home, their annoyance at the general's bestowing a few civil words on the strangers when they came to see the monastery, and saying his old-fashioned politeness was perfectly intolerable."

Yes—Torp remembered the circumstance, and felt some qualms of conscience as the thought flashed across his mind, that his slighting manner towards the Nixons might have had undue weight with them.

"Well," continued Waldemar, "Falkner's sister Charlotte is now quite anxious to 'exercise her English' with her future sister-in-law. His mother is sure he has chosen judiciously; so the whole family and all my people will be here some time next week. The betrothal and marriage will considerably enliven the monastery; and who knows what may turn up for you or me during the festivities?"

"I have a great mind to decamp before they begin," said Torp. "Under such circumstances it will be impossible to avoid a nearer acquaintance with these Nixons."

"Spare yourself all uneasiness on that account, Torp," observed Waldemar, laughing; "for, without meaning to offend you, I must say the antipathy seems quite as great on their side as yours. Stay here, therefore, friend of my youth! and partake moderately, as beseems your wisdom, of such gaieties as St Benedict's may offer; and moreover bestow occasionally on me still some of the good and worldly admonitions with which I have ever found you so well provided,—for I fear—I greatly fear—I shall stand in need of such before long!"

They had reached the churchyard gate, and Torp ascended the few stone steps to it before he answered:

"My good and worldly admonitions shall be reserved for myself in future, Waldemar; if you can recall any of them when they are likely to be serviceable, so much the better for you—of a repetition there is not the slightest chance now or ever."

Waldemar laughed and walked on. Torp sauntered into the churchyard, and, before long, found himself standing before Arthur Nixon's grave. The alpine roses (*rhododendron*)* that Nora had received at the lake, and so carefully guarded during her drive to Almenau, had been formed into a wreath, and now hung bright and fresh on the black wooden cross. When Torp stooped to read the name and

---

* The German *Alpenrose* can mean either, as here, a flower of the genus *rhododendron* or the more celebrated *stella alpina*.

date that they encircled, he plucked a spray of the deep pink clustering blossoms, and examined it with an intenseness seldom bestowed on such objects excepting by botanists. Why, when he heard the sound of approaching footsteps, he stuffed it hastily into his waistcoat pocket, he perhaps asked himself, and found the answer unsatisfactory, for he again drew forth the little hardy branch, and with great waste of energy stripped it of all its brilliant array of flowers, flung the devastated stem on the ground, and left the churchyard with lips so closely pressed together, that the word "spooney" with difficulty forced a way between them.

He fished, as he had intended, in the stream close to the forester's house during the afternoon, not once bestowing even a cursory glance on the dwelling itself or its garden; so that when Waldemar, late in the afternoon, rushed up to him and asked where he could find Miss Nixon, Torp answered, with perfect veracity, that he did not know.

"She has not gone out, I hope?"

"I have not the least idea."

"Yet you must have seen her in the garden, or on the balcony, or at a window, had she remained at the forest-house."

"I am by no means sure of that," answered Torp, beginning to pack up his fishing-tackle with all the accuracy of an English angler; "for, without being furnished with eyes at the back of my head, I could not well throw my line at this side of the stream and know what was going on behind me."

Waldemar sprang up the rocks, vaulted over the garden-paling, and finding the arbour unoccupied, ran into the house. When he reappeared he seemed to have forgotten Torp; for, following the directions of the forester's wife, who accompanied him to the door, he turned into the path conducting to the mill, and was soon lost to sight.

Torp looked after him intently, musingly, then deliberately fastened a fresh fly on his line, and sauntered after his
impetuous friend, observing to the forester's wife, who
seemed to expect him to speak as he passed her, that "he
was going to try for a bite in some of the pools near the
mill."

CHAPTER XXXIII

The Old Char-à-Banc

ATYROLEAN fruit-seller, who had harnessed himself to a small cart filled with grapes and peaches, brought Nora a note from Jack, written with very pale ink, on remarkably coarse paper, and containing the following lines:—

DEAREST NORA,

When I left Almenau to go to your rescue at the Wild Alp, I made the necessary preparations for a pedestrian tour in Tyrol afterwards, but altogether forgot to mention my intention to our governor. I shall be absent about a week or ten days, according to circumstances; I intend, however, to return in time to give Georgy my blessing when the betrothal comes off. So make all straight like a brick, as you are and always have been. In case you should wish to communicate with me by letter or otherwise during the next week, I shall leave a few lines for you at the house of the sexton of St Hubert's, to let you know where I am to be found. A walk there will be little more than moderate exercise for one of your energetic habits. The man supplies pilgrims with coffee; and if you wish for a glass of Tyrolean wine, his grandson will take you across the frontiers in half-an-hour.

Ever your affectionate   —JACK

"Perhaps it is as well he is absent for a short time," thought Nora, as she walked towards the inn the next morning to make "all straight."

"An ill-timed tour," observed Mr Nixon, in a tone of vexation. "The Falkner family may return to the abbey to-morrow or the day after—they invite us to dinner as a matter of course—and where is my son John?"

"And, in fact, where is he?" asked Georgina, without turning from the window where she had been a careless listener of Nora's communication.

"Wandering about Tyrol," answered her father; "and not, as I supposed some time ago, with that young artist who has turned out to be a Count Somebody."

"Certainly not with him," observed Georgina, " for he is now in the garden with Mr Torp. And oh, Nora," she continued, "do look at the strange vehicle they have just drawn out of the wooden shed they call a coach-house!"

"In that same strange vehicle," said Nora, "I shall drive into the next town about an hour hence."

"You? for what purpose?"

"To be questioned by the judge of the district about a wildschuetz who happened to be on the Wild Alp a few hours before me, the day of the storm."

"A wildschuetz," observed Mr Nixon, "is aw—I suppose—aw——a sort of Freischuetz?"[*]

---

[*] Mr Nixon is clearly thinking of the opera *Der Freischütz* (1821) by Carl Maria von Weber (1786-1826) which had been given many times in London since its first performance there at the English Opera House in 1824. His musical knowledge did not apparently extend to Albert Lortzing's (1801-1851) opera *Der Wildschütz* which had been performed with great success in Leipzig in 1842—though he is hardly to be blamed for that as its first London performance, at Drury Lane, was not until 1895.

"No," answered Nora, "they would call him a poacher in England."

"And you are to be questioned about such a fellow—called up as witness before a judge—without my being made acquainted with a single circumstance of the case! This is, to say the least, a most extraordinary mode of proceeding. In what way was the requisition notified to you?"

"Count Waldemar told me yesterday."

"That is not a legal summons," observed Mr Nixon, with dignity, "and you have every right to dispute—"

"I believe," said Nora, interrupting him, "there *was* a man in a uniform with a printed paper at the forester's, and they sent a gend'arme into the wood to find him and his son. Rosel, who was with me on the Alp, has also been summoned, and Mr Torp too; so we are quite a company of witnesses, and Count Waldemar goes I believe as volunteer."

"I shall go as your uncle—my presence will protect you," said Mr Nixon.

Now, though Nora felt not a little nervous about the coming examination, and greatly feared that a good cross-examination might elicit more than she was disposed to confess, she did not expect that her uncle's presence would in any way lessen her embarrassment. Nevertheless she was glad that he proposed to accompany her, for she thought his appearance might prevent Waldemar from assuming the character of protector, and there had been something in the expression of Torp's face the day before, when he had discovered him sitting with her and Rosel at the mill, that had made an unpleasant impression on her.

The strange vehicle that had so surprised Georgina was one of those very antiquated char-à-bancs now only to be found in very out-of-the-way villages: their successors, the one-doored omnibus, is so little inviting, even for pic-nic parties or fishing excursions, that the most rattling market-cart of a peasant, affording an uninterrupted view of the wondrously romantic scenery, is preferable. Youthful recollections may perhaps cause some elderly people to over-value the advantages possessed by those old-fashioned carriages; it may be urged that the cushions were hard and the springs of primitive construction—we deny it not; but these disadvantages were more than neutralised by the rows of seats facing the horses, each apart and yet together; the open sides, with the long footboards that facilitated a change of place without interrupted movement, the lofty roof, the ease of ingress and egress in mountain districts, when either to spare the horses or relieve incipient impatience, steep hills are so often climbed on foot, the laughing pedestrians beguiling the ascent by plucking flowers, twisting wreaths round each other's hats, or with bright eyes and glowing cheeks looking back to recover breath and admire the scenery through which they have passed, and over which distance so soon begins to throw her veil of ultramarine blue.

The char-à-banc of Almenau was in a very neglected condition; no attempt had been made for many years to renew its pristine colours, so that the wheels and footboards had hardly a trace of paint left: the lithographs that, ingeniously transferred to the panels of the seats, had once glowed through the yellow varnish as highly-prized decorations, were now scratched and partially obliterated; yet the vehicle, strong in its clumsiness, seemed to defy time, and its air of rusticity accorded well with everything in and about the village.

Let us note and sketch this old carriage, and the still un-sophisticated manners of these Highland peasants. A few years hence an already projected railroad will pass within a couple of miles of the secluded hamlet, and instead of the solitary English fisherman or Munich artist, crowds of tourists may perhaps pour into the secluded valleys, and, attracted alike by the beauty and novelty of the scenes brought within their reach by the all-exploring locomotive, may turn these Bavarian Highlands and Tyrol into a second Switzerland;—hotels and boarding-houses may rise with the dimensions of barracks in all directions; every pebble on the path, and plant on the mountain side, may have its price;—and the stream that now, as if in recreation, dances lightly over the wheels of the isolated mill, may not long hence have to labour restlessly to turn those of a succession of factories.

"I should think," said Mr Nixon, looking at his watch, "that our letters and papers must be here by this time. Mr Torp has received his more than an hour ago."

"His letters do not come with ours," observed Georgina; "they are sent to him by an especial messenger in a sealed parcel from the post office, and his servant stands waiting for them at the inn door, as if they were political dispatches of the utmost importance."

"Ah! I was not aware of that," said Mr Nixon. "Now, if he were obliging, he would allow his messenger to take charge of our letters also."

"But he is not at all obliging," said Nora, following her uncle and Georgina to the garden.

Waldemar rose, and Torp bowed with unusual urbanity as they entered it, and soon after the latter even pushed the latest newspapers towards Mr Nixon, when he observed him eyeing them with a longing look. His spectacles were forthwith adjusted on the end of his nose, his head thrown back, and one of the newspapers held stiffly at that distance which so astonishes all near-sighted people, while he eagerly sought and then read attentively the "fashionable intelligence."

"It seems," he observed, after a pause, raising his eyebrows and looking over his spectacles towards Torp, whom he addressed as the possessor of the paper, "it seems that the Earl of Medway is in Tyrol, with some distinguished foreign friends, on a sporting excursion. I wonder is he likely to pass through this village before we leave it?"

Georgina turned to her father as if the intelligence were deeply interesting to her. Waldemar's eyes seemed to dance in his head as he asked if they were acquainted with the Medway family.

"Why, aw—we are—and we are not," answered Mr Nixon; "my daughter, Georgina, met them a good deal in society."

Waldemar turned to her inquiringly.

"I have been introduced to Lady Medway and her daughters," she said, "but they live too much abroad lately to admit of intimacy. The late Lord Medway I met frequently when he happened to be in England."

"And his brother?" asked Waldemar eagerly, "his brother?"

"Oh, you mean Charley Thorpe?"

"Yes, yes, I mean Charley; do you know anything of Charley?"

"From hearsay a good deal," replied Georgina, smiling. "He was generally considered the brains-carrier of the family—the Solomon and Solon."

"That is—clever?" said Waldemar, touching his forehead significantly.

"People supposed so, though they talked more of his eccentric exploits and herculean strength than of anything else."

"Ah! he was a boxer—an athlete," said Waldemar, amused.

"We have no objection to that sort of thing in England,"

rejoined Georgina; "and though ill-natured people said he used exercise and blankets like a jockey, and ate raw beef-steaks to keep himself in condition, he some way managed to make himself of immense importance and very fashionable, and was always an infinitely greater man than his brother, Lord Medway."

"What must he be now that he *is* Lord Madeaway!" suggested Waldemar.

"That is precisely what I should like to know," answered Georgina. "There is a sort of relationship between our family and his—"

Torp, who had been leaning on the table, gently rubbing his chin with an air of languid amusement, here interrupted her by calmly repeating the word "relationship?"

"I believe I ought rather to have said connection," continued Georgina, with slightly heightened colour; "but," she added, turning to Nora, "you at least can—"

"No," interposed Nora, quickly. "No, I wish for no acquaintance, and make no claim to any connection with the present Lord Medway."

"Perhaps you are right," said Georgina, with some pique; "for from all accounts he is a cold-hearted, calculating man, and it is certain was so resolutely bent on being himself Lord Medway, that he effectually prevented any of the many marriages projected by his brother from taking place."

Waldemar's countenance expressed surprise, but only for a moment; the next he shook his head so incredulously that Georgina thought it necessary to confirm her assertion.

"In this matter I have been too well informed to admit of a doubt," she said decidedly. "The stories of blankets and raw beef, the steeple-chases, shooting-matches, tree-felling, swimming for wagers, and all his other wild exploits may be at least half inventions; but that he considered himself his brother's keeper is certain; and that he made the poor invalid change his place of residence whenever there was a chance of his committing matrimony is a well-known fact."

To this speech Torp had listened apparently unmoved; but a perceptible paleness spread over his features when, after a moment's hesitation, he laid down the paper he had vainly been endeavouring to read, and fixing his eyes steadily on Georgina, said calmly, "Lord Medway is an acquaintance, a friend of mine, and I have reason to know that he never interfered in his brother's matrimonial plans but once, and on that occasion prevented him from—making an egregious fool of himself."

Georgina had not time to answer, for the innkeeper, leaning over the garden paling, informed them that a char-à-banc was ready for their reception,—that the forester and his family had arrived, and, if agreeable, the Crags peasant and his son Anderl would take the remaining places.

Mr Nixon rose with the others, and turned, as usual, to Nora for explanation.

"Oh!—ah! Are we to have more people with us than these two gentlemen? All right, is it? No other carriage in the village—oh, very well."

He assisted her to the seat immediately behind the coachman, who was no other than Boots equipped in his Sunday low-crowned beaver hat and his black velveteen jacket. Mr Nixon himself required some time to ensconce his bulky person in the remaining space beside her; but by allowing the tails of his coat to pend over the back of the seat, and a few other judicious arrangements, he was at last seated to his own satisfaction, though by no means to that of Waldemar, who, equally surprised and disconcerted at the unexpected additions to their party, took the vacant place beside Torp. The forester and his son, his wife and daughter, the Crags peasant and his son Anderl, occupied the remaining seats, and when the coachman, without a word of explanation, took up the old mountain miller as he trudged slowly along the road in the same direction, a more heterogeneous company could hardly be imagined, or a dozen of people easily found who, by an odd series of circumstances, had possessed and used the power of annoying each other in so determined a manner.

Nora, who had been apprehensive that her uncle might become loquacious and confidential, and in the course of conversation inform their English-speaking companions that she was his niece, which would at once betray her to Torp, was glad to perceive that the manner of the latter to Georgina had given umbrage, and that her uncle was as reserved as she could possibly have desired.

No one spoke, and all rejoiced as they rattled over the pavement of the town, and stopped at the entrance to the large building occupied by the judge.

In a long, vaulted, and paved hall, formed by a large portion of the ground floor, a couple of gens-d'armes were walking up and down, while some peasants, dispersed in groups, arranged their dress previous to making their appearance before the judge or one of his adjuncts. With persevering diligence they rubbed their right arm round the crowns of their hats, or dusted their shoes with pocket-handkerchiefs that rivalled the brightest Indian patterns in brilliancy of colours: their wives and daughters, whose presence had been required, were no less occupied in the setting to rights of their more elaborate toilets. The white kerchiefs were removed from the grenadier-like caps, the gilt helmets, the Munich cap, so strongly resembling a fish-tail both in form and composition, or the black silk kerchief that threatens to supersede all other head-dresses. These last were worn by some tied unbecomingly over the forehead as in Corsica: by others they were lightly wound round the back of the head in the manner of the Neapolitan peasants, or as they may be seen on the frescos at Pompeii; but all were now freshly tied, and the long ends made to float more wildly over the shoulders. The silver neck-chains, too, were drawn into view, and many a refractory stocking readjusted quite *sans-gêne* on legs of more than stout proportions.

Scarcely had the char-à-banc party had time to look round them before they were accosted by the fisherman from the Kerbstein lake and his wife: the latter rushed up to Rosel and her mother, and seizing their hands, began a long tearful condolence, breaking into occasional exclamations by no means calculated to promote the return of peace in the afflicted family. "To think that your own husband and son should bring such sorrow upon you! but the forester was always hot-tempered, and Franz is a chip of the old block it seems! A right reputable match it would have been for Rosel, and pleasant for all to have her at the Crags. Well, I suppose Franz himself having no luck at the mill, didn't choose his sister to have it all her own way. Hard enough—here we came, expecting a pleasure, and a feast, and a betrothal; and a gend'arme marches us up to the judge, and expects us to bear witness against the bridegroom that was to be,—the man who invited us, and is our godson into the bargain! We had our gifts prepared—small indeed, but such as beseems the occasion."

This was too much for Rosel and her mother—they burst into floods of tears. The forester turned to the fisherman, and began an eager explanation and justification of his son's conduct. Mr Nixon looked perfectly bewildered, Waldemar bored, for Nora appeared to have forgotten his presence, while Torp, standing a little apart, seemed not only suddenly to comprehend, but even in no small degree to sympathise in the feelings of the agitated speakers. His eyes were fixed intently on Nora, as she laid her hand on the old forester's arm, and in a few fervent words hoped that if Seppel should be acquitted by the land-judge, he would also be considered guiltless by him, and once more received into favour at the forest-house.

"I will do what I can, Miss Nora,—anything in reason, for your sake," he answered; and then perhaps willing to have so kind a mediatrix between him and his wife, he added, "If Seppel were not a wildschuetz, I don't know any one to whom I'd sooner have given my Rosel—but that's all over now, and no help for it. Old Crags has just gone up the stairs with his son Anderl, and before they come down again—"

"I know—I know," said Nora, interrupting him; "the mischief caused by your son's precipitancy in that quarter cannot be repaired, so we shall say no more about it; but promise me to bear no malice towards Seppel, to let Rosel speak to him again, and to give him work as wood-cleaver for a few weeks, in some place where he will not be exposed to temptation."

"I've no objection," said the forester. "Seppel is a good workman, and may go up next Monday to the clearance above the miller's alp—that is, if the accusation against him cannot be proved, or the Count goes security for him, as he has offered to do if it should be necessary."

Just then they all began to mount the stairs together, and were conducted into a large room where a number of young men were seated or standing at writing-tables provided with desks, ordinary writing materials, and quantities of sand, which they strewed about their tables and the floor in such profusion that the latter might be said to be sanded.

Many of these gentlemen (for such they all were by education if not by birth) had black linen covers drawn over the sleeves of their coats, and some had pens stuck behind their ears, and turned over the leaves of large books, or counted money in a manner that gave an official and business-like air to their proceedings, which did not fail to inspire Mr Nixon with respect. These were the practicants, who, having passed their theoretical law examination, had now to put their acquired knowledge into practice for a couple of years, and afterwards to submit to another examination before they could aspire to even the most insignificant situation under government. Among them there were some who received remuneration for their services from the judge, others were there as volunteers, and to a person aware of such arrangements the difference between them soon became perceptible; while the former bent over their desks scarcely conscious of, and perfectly indifferent to, the entrance of strangers, their pens continuing to move rapidly and uninterruptedly along the paper before them, the latter looked up, glanced meaningly at each other, ran their fingers through their hair, or twirled their moustaches. Nora's round hat and flounced dress seemed to produce a decided commotion; and when a servant opened the door of an adjoining chamber, and said the judge required the services of Baron Waltenburg as protocoller, a young man, the envied possessor of a blonde moustache rivalling in length that of the present king of Sardinia,[*] rose with undisguised alacrity to follow him out of the room, leaving on his table, for the amusement of his companions, the rough draft of a report in some criminal investigation, on the ample margins of which he had sketched with a pen a variety

[*] King Carlo Alberto of Piedmont-Sardinia. Though known as the Kings of Sardinia, the monarchy's main territory and power-base was Piedmont. Carlo Alberto's son Vittore Emanuele II in 1861 became the first King of united Italy.

of sylph-like female forms in round hats, with eyes of amazing dimensions not very artistically represented by elongated blots of ink.

The forester, his son, Torp, the fisherman and his wife, had been successively summoned, then Rosel with her mother, and at last Nora, who seemed to derive no sort of confidence from her uncle's presence, for she turned immediately to Waldemar with a look of alarm.

"I can introduce you to the judge," he said, in reply to her silent appeal, "but he will not give me permission to remain in the room."

Mr Nixon, who perceived that their turn was come, prepared himself for his appearance before the judge by twitching up his shirt collar, pulling down his waist-coat, and drawing Nora's arm within his in a dignified manner.

Waldemar accompanied them to the door, looked into the room for a moment, and nodding his head familiarly, said, "Fritz, allow me to introduce Mr and Mees Nixone."

Now Fritz was no other than the judge himself, who rose from his writing-table as they entered, and politely offered chairs. He was a middle-aged man, gentleman like and prepossessing in appearance, wearing a dark blue uniform with crimson facings, on which flashes of lightning were embroidered in gold; and this dress, added to a decided, authoritative manner, seemed so little to belong to a gentleman of the long-robe, according to Mr Nixon's English notions, that he immediately concluded another, and very unnecessary delay had occurred on his way into "court," and that the military-looking personage before him must be an officer, perhaps in command of the soldiers he had seen in the streets of the town. He therefore accepted the offered chair with a bow and a smile, spread out the tails of his coat, seated himself deliberately, and holding, or rather balancing his hat with both hands between his knees, looked calmly out of the nearest window, and civilly observed, "Long threatening comes at last; we are going to have rain now and no mistake!"

Young Baron Waltenburg, who was seated at an adjacent table arranging some sheets of foolscap, on which much close and even writing might be seen without any marginal sketches, found it necessary to bend his head and struggle with an untimely fit of laughter. The judge smiled, and murmured the word "English," while Nora hastily began an explanation to her uncle.

"Eh—what—no assizes—no jury!—This gentleman a judge, is he? ah—ah—very well. I suppose, though I know nothing of this affair, I had better tell him who I am and why I came here?" He rose, waved his hat, and began, "My name is Nixon—"

Nora felt greatly inclined to join in the only half-stifled laughter of the young practicant; but the dread of a cross-examination, such as the reports of the London papers had made familiar to her, overcame her disposition to mirth, and she interpreted gravely to her uncle the few words afterwards addressed to him in French by the judge.

"He regrets that he cannot speak English," she said, in a low voice; "but on the present occasion it is of the less importance, as he is aware that you cannot be required as a witness by either party."

Mr Nixon sat down.

When Nora then saw the judge refer to his notes, and the practicant lean forward, pen in hand, ready, as she supposed, to write down her words, she became so pale, and looked so frightened, that the former thought it incumbent on him to reassure her. He did so in German, which made her aware that Waldemar had spoken of her to him, and said he should only ask her a few questions likely to serve as corroboration to the depositions of her companion

Rosel, and their guide Michael.

Although he seemed perfectly aware that she had not personally assisted in the release of the Englishman, "Carl Torpe, Count of Medoei," and Franz Hartmann, assistant forester, in consequence of her having lingered behind the others on reaching the alp, yet he made her relate very circumstantially all she had seen after her arrival there. That she had sat for hours alone on the rocks afterwards he also appeared to know; but that, and her subsequent adventures in the storm, he passed over as irrelevant, though he was minute in his inquiries about what she had heard of Seppel at the fisherman's house, so much so, that she was heartily sorry she had asked any questions concerning him on that occasion.

At length there was a pause, and Nora hoped it was all over, when he added, "It was a singular piece of good fortune for the prisoners, your going to the Wild Alp just that day, mademoiselle: had Rosel Hartmann been the proposer of the excursion, I should have had reason to suspect that she had been sent there by—Seppel himself. She assures me, however, that the proposition came from you. Is this the case?"

"Yes," answered Nora, with an embarrassment that did not escape the questioner.

"It must have been rather a sudden resolution on your part," he continued, "for I understand another excursion had been projected for that day."

This appearing to Nora an observation, and not a question, she attempted no answer.

"I know you are interested for Seppel," he observed, not a little amused at her reserve, "and I perceive your reluctance to say anything to his disadvantage; nevertheless, I must ask you if, by chance or otherwise, you did not see him the evening before you went to the Wild Alp, and if he did not then request you to release *your* countryman, and *his* future brother-in-law from their unpleasant situation?"

"No," answered Nora, still so embarrassed at what she considered a prevarication on her part, that the judge thought it necessary to ask her when she had last seen Seppel. "I have not seen him," she replied, "since he left the village four days ago, to invite the fisherman at the Kerbstein lake to his betrothal."

"Did he send you any message by one of the peasants in the neighbourhood?"

"N–o."

"Or a hint through the medium of one of the Tyroleans who so frequently pass through the village?"

"No," again answered Nora, with an expression of relief, for she perceived the much-dreaded examination was at an end.

The judge rose, so did Mr Nixon, and Nora, feeling herself no longer in what her uncle called "court," immediately asked if there were any chance of Seppel's release.

"As you have not seen him, or received any message from him since this unpleasant occurrence took place," said the judge, smiling at her eagerness, "and as Count Waldemar offers to go security for him, I believe I can set him at liberty, provided he remains in the neighbourhood, ready to appear and answer any further charges that may be made against him in the course of time."

"Oh, none will be made I am sure," said Nora.

"Probably not," rejoined the judge; "I am even inclined to think that he has been unjustly accused on this occasion."

Nora looked down, pained with the consciousness of being better informed than he was.

"Almost all I have heard to-day," continued the judge, "is in his favour. Even the description given by the for-

ester's son of the brutal conduct of his antagonist, which he
repeated just now, when no longer under the influence of
angry excitement, seems so very unlike that of a man to his
future brother-in-law, and so completely in opposition to
Seppel's well-known character, that I am inclined to think
the whole gang were Tyroleans, and that one of them re-
venged himself for the unpleasant watchfulness of the forester, on the person of his son. Seppel himself assures me
he has not touched a fire-arm since he returned from Munich, and this morning I sent to the Crags for his rifle, and
examined it myself." He took it from his gun-rack while
speaking, and, forgetting that Mr Nixon could not understand him, turned politely towards him, and began to expatiate upon the proofs that it had not been loaded, or even
cleaned, for several months.

Mr Nixon, who had never loaded a gun in his life, and
was even more afraid of "dreadful accidents" than Nora of
cross-examinations, drew back, and edged so obviously towards the door, that the judge, concluding he was wearied,
merely added, as he turned to Nora, who seemed to wish to
hear more, "You alone could have convinced me of his
guilt, for had he, by word or message, tried to induce you to
go to the alp, it would have been impossible to have
doubted that, if not a principal actor, he had been at least a
party concerned in this disagreeable affair."

Nora had heard enough—she was glad to escape into
the adjoining room, though there she encountered the tranquil, scrutinising gaze of Torp, quite as disagreeable to her
now, as it had been some days previously to her cousin
Jack, and his wild companions on the alp.

The horses had been taken from the char-à-banc, and
while waiting for their re-appearance, Mr Nixon perceived
that the rain he had so facetiously predicted in the judge's
apartment was now falling in torrents, accompanied by cold

gusts of wind, that made him greatly rejoice in the warm paletot with which he had not forgotten to provide himself, and in which he now perambulated the hall, casting side-long, half-triumphant glances at the summer garments of his companions, and stopping occasionally to remind Nora of her folly in having refused to take a shawl with her. Perhaps it was the constant reiteration of these now useless remarks that made her so determinately avoid his vicinity on her way back to the village; certain it is that she took possession of the last seat but one, and beckoning to Rosel to take the vacant place beside her, was soon altogether engrossed by the occupation of consoling the despairing girl, whose worst fears had been confirmed by seeing the Crags peasant and his son Anderl walking off together to the Golden Lion, while long Seppel, once more at liberty, had been passed by both without the slightest notice, and now stood leaning against the gateway of the judge's house, his eyes fixed wistfully on the char-à-banc, and the people taking their places in it.

"Holloa, Sepp!" cried Waldemar, "there's room here beside our coachman for you, and don't look as if you had lost all hope of better days, because your father has cut you off with five hundred florins, instead of resigning his rocky acres to you, burdened with an alimentation for himself, that would have made your life a continual struggle with poverty. Cheer up, man,—the forester has promised to forget, and Franz to forgive, and something may turn up for you yet, of which there is at present little prospect."

He glanced back towards Nora while speaking, and received a smile and nod so animated and confidential that Torp felt provoked even to the length of accusing her of bestowing a too flattering degree of familiarity on his friend; yet he soon after forgot his disapprobation in honest appreciation of her forgetfulness of self and indifference to petty discomforts. The oil-cloth curtain, which she had supposed would defend her from wind and rain, happened, just beside the place where she was sitting, to be so completely torn, and in such a state of decay, that, after a few fruitless efforts to hold it together, she resigned herself quietly, and without a word of complaint, to the pelting of the pitiless storm, though her glance towards the clouds, and the dripping roof of the char-à-banc, showed plainly that she knew a very few minutes would complete the work of saturation. She moved nearer to Rosel, and began to speak in a low yet cheerful voice, and her words seemed to have a magical effect upon the latter, for her tears ceased to flow, she looked up eagerly, then smiled, seized Nora's hand, and, had not a struggle ensued, would certainly have raised it to her lips. Meanwhile, Torp had found it impossible to allow the muslin-clad shoulders and arms before him to remain unprotected: he leaned forward, with one hand held the tattered strips of oil-cloth partially together, with the other raised his broad-brimmed grey felt hat from his head, and so placed it and his own person that neither wind nor rain could reach Nora. Without touching, he was very close to her, and heard, or overheard—if we must use the word —what fully accounted for Rosel's ebullition of joy and gratitude, explained Waldemar's glance, and made the expression of Torp's own face soften in a very remarkable manner. No one, however, observed this, for he was sitting in the last seat alone, and Waldemar, the only person who thought of turning round occasionally, was just then giving Mr Nixon a history of the ruins of Waltenburg, which formed a prominent object in the landscape, and informing him that they belonged to the young practicant he had seen with the judge, and who, not having money to rebuild the castle, would gladly sell the remaining walls of the residence of his ancestors for almost anything he could get for them.

When they reached the village, and drew up before the door of the inn, Torp leaned back, clapped his supersaturated hat on his head, and resumed his usual air of serene impassibility. During the universal bustle attending the descent of the others from the open sides of the char-à-banc, Nora turned to him with a smile which he had no inclination to criticise, and said, significantly glancing towards his wet hat and shoulders, "I cannot let you suppose me unconscious of the manner in which you have shielded me from storm and rain during our drive, Mr Torp; and though I know you dislike being thanked, I must say I am very much obliged to you."

While half-a-dozen people assisted her to descend from the char-à-banc at the side next the inn, Torp sprang to the ground at the other, rushed into the house, up the stairs and into his room, flung his hat on the table, dragged off his clinging tweed jacket, and then strode up and down the room, gesticulating like a man in the most violent state of exasperation, and muttering words that, from the tone in which they were pronounced, might be supposed strong invectives mingled with threats of vengeance. "Infatuation —doltish infatuation! Absurd—inconsistent—preposterous! No escape in a small place of this kind, where people are literally shoved against each other! This village, this infernal little nest, will be my perdition! I shall leave it tomorrow with Waldemar, who, fortunately, *must* return to Herrenburg. Ah! there she is again."

He darted to the window, and perceived Nora looking up from beneath a red cotton umbrella, held over her by Waldemar. She was apparently answering some question addressed to her by Georgina from one of the windows of the inn.

"I must put on another dress," she said, gaily; "muslin is too cold for weather such as this."

And as she walked off with Waldemar at one side and long Seppel at the other a sudden change seemed to come over Torp; he looked after them, nodded his head two or three times in ironic approbation, and then soliloquised: "Why not? A man is a fool who avoids the society of an interesting and agreeable woman because he cannot or will not marry her. I did not understand what she was about until to-day; but it is now quite evident that, being employed by her father as deputy in the arrangements concerning his nephew's grave, she is bent on doing a benevolent action at the same time. Of course the old man has received *carte blanche* from Arthur Nixon's widow, or she could not have made the promise to the forester's daughter that I overheard to-day. Had I known all this sooner I might have spared myself some anxiety about Waldemar, and—made—myself—perhaps—a little less—disagreeable to her."

CHAPTER XXXIV

Pastime for a Rainy Day

"THE best friends must part, Torp," said Waldemar, the next morning, as he prepared to leave the village in a peasant's cabriolet, apparently but ill calculated to defend him from rain that poured down in a stream directed by the storm. "I hoped to have returned on foot," he added, "and expected to have had your company at least as far as St Hubert's. By-the-by, you can meet me there as soon as the weather clears up, as I intend to take a sketch of the curious old altars in the chapel. Oh, I was on the point of forgetting to mention that I told that adorable Mees Nora, to whom you have taken so unaccountable an aversion—"

"By no means," cried Torp, hastily. "My dislike is rather to the family, and especially to the one who caused dissension between my brother and me; but—a—I have no hesitation in saying that to this Miss Nixon I have no particular aversion."

"So much the better," said Waldemar, carelessly, "for I told her, in case she wanted advice or assistance during my absence, to apply to you."

"Advice and assistance?" repeated Torp, inquiringly.

"Why, yes—her own people cannot speak German, you know, and she intends to establish Rosel somewhere about here, and make her guardian of her cousin's grave. I enter warmly into her plan, but do not see any way of putting it into execution just now, for no peasant in the village or the neighbourhood is willing to sell his property. She spoke of Waltenburg—of giving the land to Rosel, and reserving the ruins for herself; and that might answer, but I have no time to ask Waltenburg what he considers the value of his roofless towers, strip of wood, and half-dozen fields. Now you might make yourself useful, and find out all about it. The price is not likely to cause much alarm; for Waltenburg does not expect much, and these Nixons are certainly enormously rich. Mees Nora can do what she pleases with 'papa,' that is evident."

"That was evident to me at Ammergau," said Torp, "when she went to the theatre there, though he and his other daughter remained at the inn in marked disapproval. And here, too, she seems on most occasions to do precisely what she pleases."

"I rejoice in her independence," cried Waldemar; "for, with every inclination to be civil, the old man puts my forbearance severely to the proof by his pomposity, the eldest daughter by her fastidiousness, and the student by his mercurial restlessness. I will have the Mees Nora alone."

"I suspect there are others who would take her on that condition as well as yourself," observed Torp, composedly.

"You do not mean that you would?" asked Waldemar.

"I was thinking just now of our friend Harry Darwin," replied Torp.

"Is not Darwin going to marry one of your sisters?"

"Yes; but he has confessed a six years' flirtation with one of these Miss Nixons (we can easily guess which) as an excuse for not having proposed sooner to my sister; and I now begin to fear that though Jane is a very good girl, and pretty withal, she will not make him quite forget this first long love of his."

"H–m! So you think Mees Nora has been six years in love with him?"

"Off and on—yes."

"Do you mean that she did not care much for him?"

"I mean there were some little heart episodes on her part during his frequent absences from England. He knew all about them, he says, but was enchained either by love or vanity until about two months ago, when, having proposed for my sister, he followed these people abroad to put an end to all their hopes and speculations."

"Mees Nora does not seem likely to die of a broken heart," observed Waldemar.

"On the contrary," said Torp, "she gives me the idea of a person in possession of a whole and even perfectly un-scathed one."

"Darwin is a coxcomb," continued Waldemar, "and fan-cies himself irresistible. The last time he was in Vienna he took it into his head that Irene Schaumberg was in love with him!"

"Did you undeceive him?"

"On the contrary, I rather encouraged him, got Irene to join me, and he afforded us incalculable amusement for some time."

"It is not improbable," said Torp, "that his imagination was at work in this affair with Miss Nixon too. At all events, I have a great mind to speak of him, and sound her on the subject when an opportunity offers."

"Do you care about the matter?" asked Waldemar, with some surprise.

"I ought to, when I consider that Harry will be my brother-in-law next Christmas," answered Torp, evasively. "I must say," he added, thoughtfully, "Jane's indifference on this subject appears to me now perfectly incomprehen-sible!"

"It is a lucky thing for us that women are so lenient on such occasions," rejoined Waldemar, lightly. "A man has but to offer his hand in an open business-like manner, and, if accepted, no questions are asked about his heart, which may have passed through a blast furnace, and be as riddled and worthless as the dross of metals, for all that mothers or daughters seem to care. *We* are not quite so unconcerned, Torp; and I confess I feel the greatest desire to know how much of her large warm heart and vivid imagination Mees Nora bestowed on your future brother-in-law. So commence your soundings at once, my good fellow, and let me know the result, without any of the reservations you may hereafter think it necessary to observe towards your sister."

He did not wait for an answer, but sprang into the little carriage, spoke a few parting words to the landlady, and drove off.

Torp lingered about the garden and door of the inn, and played with the hideous watch-dog, until chance procured him the information concerning Nora that for some undoubtedly good reason he had not chosen to demand. Madame Cramer sent "to let Miss Nora know that her son Florian had finished the renovation of the altar of St Hubert's chapel—perhaps she would step down and look at it before he began to pack it up."

"Miss Nora is not here," said the landlady, her hands resting, as usual, on her ample hips, "nor likely to be until the English dinner-hour. Who would go out in such weather as this, if they could avoid it? But you need not go on to the forest-house in the rain, Vevey," she added, benignantly, to the red-haired messenger, who seemed about to prolong her walk in that direction; "I can easily find some one going there who will do your errand."

"*I* shall be at the forester's in about a quarter of an hour," said Torp, "and can undertake to deliver your message."

"Florian told me to let the young lady know without de-lay," began Vevey, hesitatingly.

"And," observed the landlady severely, "and Florian never looked out of the window, or thought of you or the weather, when he did so, that's certain; while you, in your hurry to pleasure him, forgot to take an umbrella or cover your head with a kerchief!"

"It's but a stone's throw," said Vevey, turning away quickly.

"Stay," cried Torp, "there is nothing to prevent my go-ing at once. I was only waiting for letters." And he walked off at a pace that removed all Vevey's anxiety respecting unnecessary delay.

"Gone without an umbrella!" ejaculated the landlady. "That thin summer jacket of his will be well wet through before he reaches the forester's."

"Shall I run after him?" cried Vevey.

"No," said the landlady, "he might take it ill; for you see, Vevey, that Englishman is not like our count, who, out of pure gratitude for our care and attention, would offer to take two umbrellas instead of one. I know," she added with a laugh, "he'd leave them both at the forester's afterwards, if he did not lose them on the way; for in wraps and um-brellas the count's uncommon careless."

As Torp pushed open the door of the forest-house and unceremoniously proceeded to enter the dwelling-room, he was as thoroughly wet as the landlady had predicted, though apparently in no way incommoded by his plight, for it was with an air of more than usual serenity, almost suav-ity, that he entered the little apartment. The forester and his son were arranging a gun-rack at one end of the room, at the other sat Rosel, once more cheerful and blooming, sing-ing gaily, in a loud, clear voice, beside Nora, who, bending over a cithern placed on the table before her, was evidently endeavouring to play by ear the highland air that her companion warbled forth with its jodel and endless succession of verses. They were unconscious of Torp's entrance until the forester's fierce abuse of the weather attracted their attention, and his recommendation to Torp to get a woodman's mantle at Madame Cramer's induced them to look round.

Torp delivered his message to Nora.

Her fingers wandered over the strings of the cithern, while, between chords and snatches of the air she had been playing, she observed that the weather was almost inclement enough to deter her from a walk to the village, although a rummage in the shop, and a visit to Florian's atelier, were about as pleasant pastimes as could be found in Almenau on a rainy day.

"Do not let my wet coat discourage you, Miss Nixon," said Torp, seized with a sudden conviction that in her society the shop and atelier would afford him also just then some pleasant pastime; "with an umbrella, a warm shawl, and a pair of galoshes, you can brave the weather for so short a distance with perfect impunity."

"I must brave it, at all events, at six o'clock," she answered, musingly.

"Go to Florian's workshop to-morrow, Miss Nora," urged Rosel, coaxingly; "he'll not pack it to-day, for who'd begin anything of a Saturday?"

"And who," rejoined Nora, playfully, "who would go poking into ateliers and shops of a Sunday, Mademoiselle Rosel? Now I might wait until Monday morning perhaps—"

"No, Miss Nora," cried Rosel, hastily, "if the weather clear up at all we're going to St Hubert's on Monday, and you know—you know—"

"Yes, I know—I know," said Nora, smiling. "So lend me the great family umbrella, the yellow one that always puts me in mind of a fungus; and I think with a shawl, and a handkerchief tied over my head, I shall manage to get to Madame Cramer's."

She left the room with Rosel; and Torp, while awaiting her re-appearance, entered into conversation with the forester and his son. Five minutes, ten minutes, a quarter of an hour passed over, and Torp, unwilling to appear impatient, still talked on, waiting another full quarter of an hour before he opened the door of the room, and looked into the passage and up the staircase. Rosel was standing at the top of the latter, singing a popular verse of a very popular song, in which a too cautious and prudent lover is sarcastically advised to wrap up his heart in paper, bind it round with green ribbon, and put it carefully into some place where the dust cannot injure it.

Torp laughed, and asked if Miss Nixon were ready.

"Ready!" repeated Rosel, "she must be at Madame Cramer's by this time. I asked her," she continued, "I asked her if she would not take you or Franz to hold the umbrella, but she said she liked better being alone, as she could tuck up her gown pleasanter."

Torp left the forest-house with an air of perfect unconcern, but he remembered with some mortification that Nora had not thought about "tucking up her gown" the day before, when Waldemar had offered his services. The storm and rain, too, brought vividly to his recollection the day he had passed with her in precisely such weather among the mountains, and the evening afterwards at the fisherman's house; and he recalled, with feelings of regret, his ungracious, repulsive conduct at the latter place, and the fact that he had then and there been little less than gentlemanlike, in order to prove to her that a Miss Nixon had nothing to expect from him but Christian charity! He had forced her to retaliate: she had done so with ladylike indifference; and now what would he not give for another day's wandering under the same circumstances, or any opportunity to prove that he was not quite the churl she took him for! These thoughts strengthened his already formed resolution no longer so scrupulously to avoid her society during the short time they were still likely to be together in the village; and therefore, instead of reading his letters and looking over his newspapers, he hurried after her to Florian's atelier, and when there felt or feigned extraordinary interest in the renovated altar, and the legend of St Hubert related at some length by the highly flattered artist. When Nora regretted that the altar would not be in its place on Monday, and promised to make a pilgrimage to see it there before she left Almenau, Torp entered into a similar engagement, and said it was even very probable that he should accompany Florian to St Hubert's on Monday: "Where," he added, turning to Nora, "I believe you are also going about the same time?"

"If it be possible," she answered, not looking particularly delighted at the prospect of his society.

"I expect to find Waldemar in the chapel," he continued.

"Very likely," she replied; "he told me he intended to make coloured sketches of the altars there." While speaking it flashed across her mind that Torp might suppose a meeting with his friend was her inducement to go, "if it were possible," to St Hubert's; she therefore felt it necessary to explain, and added quietly, "I should have preferred waiting for finer weather than we are likely to have on Monday, but Seppel has received work as wood-cleaver from the forester, and must go on that day to the clearing in the neighbourhood of the miller's alp. St Hubert's is not much out of his way, and he and Rosel intend to pray in the chapel together, and make a vow."

"A sort of private betrothal," suggested Torp, "instead

of the public one that was to have taken place yesterday."

"Perhaps so," said Nora. "At all events the forester gave his consent at my request, and I have promised Seppel and Rosel to be present."

"And to pray with them?" asked Torp.

"Why not?" said Nora; "both with them and for them."

"Pray for me, too, Miss Nixon," said Torp.

"You are jesting and I am serious, Mr Torp," she answered, composedly; "but you cannot know, nor have I any inclination to explain to you, the strong personal interest I feel in the welfare of these people."

"Waldemar has informed me of your generous plans for them," said Torp, "and desired me to obtain the information you require about Waltenburg."

"I am much obliged to him and to you or your kind intentions," observed Nora, "but it is quite unnecessary that you should give yourself this trouble. The judge is expected here to-morrow, and from him I can hear not only all about Waltenburg, but of everything else that is to be had in the neighbourhood."

Torp felt half offended at not being employed, as he doubted not that Waldemar would have been had he remained in the village; but scarcely had Nora left the atelier, before he acknowledged to himself that she was quite right to refuse his services until he had removed the unpleasant impression made by his previous conduct on herself and her family. As to making advances of any kind to the latter, that was totally out of the question: he could merely learn to tolerate them for her sake, and with that effort on his part she must learn to be satisfied. Like his friend Waldemar, he "would have the Miss Nora alone," so he followed her to the shop, and found her standing behind the counter, an amused listener of the bargaining going on between Madame Cramer and an old peasant women about some printed calico, both appealing to her as umpire, and loudly deprecating, protesting, and expostulating, as they kreutzer-wise drew towards an agreement.

On the counter lay a green felt hat and a woodman's mantle. "The very thing I want!" cried Torp, taking up the latter and throwing it over his head, which after a struggle he succeeded in protruding through the slit made for that purpose: "long enough and a good fit too. Can I have it?" he asked, turning to Madame Cramer.

"No," said Nora, "that one belongs to me. I had it made for an acquaintance who wants it on Monday; but I can show you the material, and another can easily be ready before evening." She mounted the shop ladder, and took down a large pack of coarse, rough, dark green cloth, which she spread before him, feeling the texture and recommending it with all the earnestness of an experienced shopkeeper.

Torp was exceedingly amused, and not a little pleased, when she offered to give the necessary directions to have it made exactly like the one he had tried on, which was intended for long Seppel.

"I should like a hat such as you have chosen for him also," he said, beginning to try on the broad-brimmed, low-crowned, and narrow-rimmed, high-crowned hats that were piled over each other in heaps just behind him, turning continually to Nora, and apparently more inclined to consult her face than the slip of blue looking-glass placed near a window for the convenience of other customers.

"This will do," he said, at length; "and now, Miss Nixon, I should be infinitely obliged to you if you would remove this chamois beard from my English wide-awake, on which it is so exceedingly misplaced, and fasten it on this new and more picturesque hat, where, with a tuft of black-cock feathers, it will look equally spruce and appropriate!"

Nora felt that, having commenced playing at shopkeeping, she could not refuse to go on. "Have you feathers?" she asked.

"No, but I have shot such quantities of black-cock in Scotland, that I have no scruple in wearing bought ones."

Again Nora mounted the ladder, and, after a short search, found the box containing a few real, and a good many imitation chamois beards, some tufts of black-cock and other feathers, knots of green ribbon, with gold fringe, and a profusion of tinsel and spangles.

Torp seated himself on the counter, and looked on with an air of immense satisfaction. "Am I not to have a bunch of real flowers?" he asked.

"No, you are a sportsman, and not a peasant," she replied, without looking up.

"Is there nothing else you can give me?" he said, gazing round the shop, when he perceived her work nearly completed. "I am sure I want something else if I could only recollect what it is."

"Your bill, perhaps," suggested Nora, demurely.

"Exactly. You will write it for me—won't you?"

Nora drew some paper towards her, took up a pencil, wrote, counted, showed it to Madame Cramer, who nodded her head, and then handed it to Torp, who perceived, with astonishment, that it was faultlessly written in free *German* handwriting, which differs from the English as much as does the type of their books.

"Miss Nixon," he said eagerly, "you really must allow me to ask you how and where you have acquired this perfect knowledge of—"

But Nora did not choose to be questioned, and turned from him to sell a packet of snuff to the old schoolmaster, while Madame Cramer, taking her place, reiterated the promise that he should have his mantle that very evening. "There is not an hour's work upon it," she said, in explanation, "merely an opening for the head, a hook and eye to close it round the neck, and a seam on the shoulders! If the workwoman has not time, I'll stitch it up myself for you."

Torp lingered after the material for his mantle had been cut off, the counter cleared, and all the other customers had left the shop. He seemed to feel the most intense interest in the rows of penny trumpets, whistles, wooden cows, horses, sheep, and other rough toys that were ranged on a low shelf, in order to be within reach of children happy in the possession of a few kreutzers. Nora had seated herself on the ladder, and after vainly awaiting his departure for some time, said to Madame Cramer, in a low voice, "Have you spoken to the miller and his wife?"

"Yes."

"What did they say?"

"Just what I expected. They're more than willing to sell the mill, if they can get a good price for it. The miller, who is not good for much in the way of work, wishes to emigrate to Tyrol, and settle in the neighbourhood of Madeleine, now that she has consented to marry black Seppel—and, what is better than all, the Tyrolean himself approves of the plan, and has promised me fifty florins if I can manage to negotiate a fair price with you."

"And what does he consider a fair price?" asked Nora.

"The house, with the buildings belonging to the mill, he values at six thousand florins, the land round it, and the half of the Trift Alp, about as much more. He says the legal valuation is little less, and they can easily find a purchaser any day, if they advertise."

Torp turned round to see the impression that this communication made on Nora: the movement seemed to remind her of his presence, for she rose, took up long Seppel's mantle and hat from the counter, and paused before she said, "I am much obliged to you, Madame Cramer, for

the trouble you have taken in this matter, and now only request a short time to consider the proposal. On Tuesday,
however," she added, turning round at the door, "on Tuesday morning you shall have an answer, and in the afternoon
of the same day I shall go to the mill, and ask the people
there to show it to me."

Torp followed her out of the shop, and proposed carrying the mantle and hat with which she had, as he thought,
so unnecessarily burdened herself. She resigned them to his
care without demur or apology, graciously permitting him,
at the same time, to hold the wide-spreading yellow umbrella over her head while she walked to the inn in unusual
and profound silence; but when there she again took them
from him. Torp saw, or thought he saw, an expression of
more than amusement, a look of mirthful exultation, in her
dark eyes, that the demurely-smiling mouth vainly endeavoured to neutralise. Without listening to her thanks, he
passed on, mounted the stairs, and on entering his room
came to the hasty conclusion that she had mistaken his
waiting for her in the shop for vulgar curiosity, and his civility afterwards for—something more than civility—
women were so prone to fancy men in love with them!
"Now, though I do admire her," thought Torp, "I cannot
let her suppose that I have lost my heart, or mean to be
more than commonly polite, and it will be necessary for me
to convince her, without delay, that nothing but idleness
and bad weather made me follow her to Florian's atelier to-
day. Even if I go to St Hubert's on Monday I shall take care
to let her perceive that a meeting with Waldemar, and not
her society, is my inducement to make the excursion."

Among the letters that had arrived by that day's post
was one from his sister Jane: he took it up hastily, and read:
—"So glad you are enjoying yourself, and have such good
sport—remember Count Benndorff perfectly—dark eyes—

Roman nose—mazourka dancer. People said he was going to be married to a Countess Somebody, the widow of a friend or cousin of his. Harry Darwin is not yet with us. He *will* not write about his sister, so I suppose she has turned out a disagreeable person, and has been spoiled by her sudden accession to fortune. In his last letter he said he considered it scarcely generous my questioning him so often about the Gilbert Nixons—he did not know where they were now, but when he left them in Munich they intended to pass through Tyrol into Italy. Now, I do wish you could manage to meet them somewhere or other: they will of course be delighted to know you, and you can then write me a short description of the woman who has been my rival for six long years. I cannot remember ever having seen her in town, though Harry thinks I have: she has dark hair and eyes, and *he* says is ladylike and accomplished."

Torp put down the letter. "Actually requested to become acquainted with her!" he ejaculated. "Oh, Jane! for your sake I hope Harry may not often again see this rival of whom you write so flippantly."

In the mean time Nora had gone to her uncle Gilbert, and the look of exultation that had so alarmed Torp's pride was still on her countenance, as she explained her plans and expatiated on the pleasure she felt in being able to purchase the mountain mill, the place of all others that Rosel loved best in the neighbourhood. "Of course," she added, "a clause shall be inserted in the deed of gift, making it incumbent on every future possessor of the mill to take care of and decorate dear Arthur's grave. I believe I shall require something more than a thousand pounds for the purchase, and let you know in time, in case it should be necessary to write to England."

Mr Nixon opened his eyes very wide, made no attempt to conceal his astonishment, remonstrated at some length, and ended with the remark that he had never heard of anything so absurd as allowing the expense of keeping a grave in order so preposterously to exceed the price of the tombstone!

"Such was Arthur's desire," said Nora.

"My dear Nora, how *can* you know that?"

"He spoke to me several times on the subject."

"But he could not know that he would die here," expostulated Mr Nixon.

"He thought it was probable he might die abroad, and, when wishing for a simple tombstone, hoped that his grave might not be remarkable for its neglected state, as was the case with most English graves on the continent. To prevent this is *my* care, to insure the contrary *my* promise; and I think I have found the most effectual way of keeping it, if I do not resolve to rebuild the castle on the hill, and live here myself for the purpose."

Mr Nixon thought it better to attempt no further opposition.

CHAPTER XXXV

The Vow

IT was a rainy Sunday morning. Mr and Miss Nixon had not yet given any sign of wakefulness, though the neighbouring church bell had been for some time summoning the villagers to divine service, and noises of endless variety, and of a nature most likely to dispel sleep, had long succeeded each other without interruption. The Nixons had, however, become accustomed to the sound of rushing feet on uncarpeted stairs, and the tramping of nailed shoes on the floors of echoing corridors; and even the rough opening and shutting of the folding doors, or rather gates into the granary on the first floor of the house, and the frequent entrance and unloading of carts full of corn, had ceased materially to affect their slumbers; though it was perhaps a Sunday cessation of these last peculiarly disturbing sounds, with the accompanying stamping of horses' feet, and vociferous calls of the labourers, that enabled them to enjoy so long a sleep on the present occasion.

Torp was more wakeful. Stretched at full length on half a dozen chairs, he had so placed himself in the vicinity of an open window, that he could command an extensive view of the mountains that inclosed the village, and watch the different groups of peasants as they hurried over the fields and along the pathways, in all directions, towards the church. Most of them had to pass the inn, and had Torp been so disposed, he might have found subject for reflection in the gradual and not pleasing approaches towards Parisian fashions evident in the dress of many of them. It has been observed that these national costumes have at all times been modified by the changes in dress so frequent in the cities of Europe; but so slowly have the alterations been adopted, that an interval of thirty or forty years generally intervenes, and the large leg-of-mutton shaped sleeves and short petticoats worn by the women seem to confirm the supposition, though their bodices and head-dresses are of much more ancient date, and do not appear likely to be put aside for some years. The innovations attempted by the men are of a more serious and modern description, and peculiarly disadvantageous to both face and figure: a round black hat of any form that has been in fashion during the last ten years, a short-waisted coat with puckered sleeves, both manufactured by the privileged hatter and tailor of the village, and added to these, a pair of wide, ill-fitting trousers, that when but half worn out present an unpleasant picture of shabby gentility verging towards blackguardism.

Torp was too practical a man to waste either reflection or regret on the changes in the costume of peasants so little likely to be seen by him during the remainder of his life; he merely thought the old men looked withered and weather-beaten, the old women ugly and masculine. Waldemar was not at his side to point out the more picturesque figures; and before long he unconsciously began to mentally measure the colossal limbs and burly waists of all the passing women, overseeing many a young and handsome face while coming to the conclusion that the fair sex in and about Al-menau were of peculiarly clumsy proportions. As if to qualify in some degree this judgment, the slender figure of "the miller's Madeleine" became just then visible, as she tripped along the road accompanied by her parents and Tyrolean Seppel, attired in his brown national dress, broad belt, and high-crowned hat. They returned the salutations of their neighbours and friends cordially, but spoke not a word to each other as they hastened to pass the inn, followed at no great distance by the forester, his family, and Nora.

The latter party stopped beneath Torp's window for a few minutes, and seemed to discuss some subject with unusual earnestness. At length he heard Nora say, while she looked at her watch, "Plenty of time to reach the town before the church service there begins, and quite needless your subjecting yourself to so much unnecessary pain."

"I can bear it, Miss Nora," said Franz, in reply; "and that they shall see, especially the Tyrolean."

"He's right," said the forester; "they must see, or they won't believe that we can get over our disappointment."

The father and son walked on together, followed more slowly by Rosel and her mother. Nora looked after them thoughtfully until they were out of sight, waited until the last loiterers about the inn had gone to church, and then turned into a by-path that led directly to a small gate opening into the burial-ground. It was among the latest stragglers that she entered the crowded place of worship, and, concealed from the greater part of the congregation by one of the pillars supporting the organ-loft, heard the sermon that was preached quietly and impressively by the worthy priest, and in which peace and goodwill were strongly recommended, and earnest warnings offered against that "little member," the tongue. Nora was too well acquainted with the frame of mind then predominant in the village not to understand that much that was said was intended to counteract or suppress the loud animadversions in which most people indulged when speaking of the miller and his family, and every meaning glance exchanged among the peasants around, every moving arm that expressively nudged another, conveyed its meaning to her likewise.

Profound was the silence when soon after the banns of marriage were published between Joseph Mattner, possessor of the upper mill, near X——, in the Valley of the Inn, and Madeleine, daughter of Jacob Erdman, mountain miller, of the village of Almenau, &c, &c, and a sort of subdued commotion in the congregation, accompanied by an almost universal stretching of necks, became evident. A few stray glances sought the bent-down head of Madeleine, but most eyes were fixed on the forester and his family. The old man's furrowed features had assumed an air of defiance, his son's face and figure might have served for a model of stern and rigid self-control, yet Nora thought she detected a slight distension of the nostrils and a scarcely perceptible twitching of the moustache, which latter, according to Sir Charles Bell,[*] is capable of expression during passionate excitement, in consequence of the action of a muscle under the roots of the hair. There were probably not many such nice observers in the crowd, but Nora felt that her thoughts were being uttered, when a voice immediately behind her murmured in English, "Poor fellow! it is a hard trial; I am heartily sorry for him." These words were pronounced with so much warmth and feeling that she could not leave them unanswered.

"There was no help for it, if what the people here say be true," she whispered in reply, while leaving the church by the nearest door.

"What do they say?" asked Torp, following her.

[*] Sir Charles Bell (1774-1842), Scottish anatomist and author of *The Nervous System of the Human Body* (1830).

"That the miller is in the power of this Tyrolean, who is supposed to have had something to do with the burning of the old mill at a very critical juncture."

"Was there no investigation at the time?"

"Of course, but no proof could be obtained: the miller was from home, the Tyrolean actually lost all his clothes in the flames; and his efforts to save the few valuables belonging to the miller's wife and daughter told so much in his favour, that the suspicions would have died away, had not his imperious conduct at the mill kept them alive; and the breaking off of this marriage just now renewed them in every one's mind. I remember at Ammergau hearing some hints on the subject that excited my curiosity."

"Is it possible," cried Torp, "that even there you began to feel an interest in these people?"

"Why not?" she rejoined. "I heard they were inhabitants of the village to which we were going. Perhaps their ancestors had been, or they themselves might hereafter be laid in a grave next to the one confided to my charge;—that alone caused an indefinite feeling of interest, and my first visit to the churchyard made me feel as if I had had a presentiment —for you see the tombstone of the mountain miller family is the one next to that of my cousin Arthur; and I am not ashamed to confess that this circumstance has greatly increased my desire to see Rosel in possession of the mill."

"I should never have supposed you would attach importance to anything of this kind," said Torp; "it is, in fact, so very immaterial where one is buried, or who is one's neighbour when in the grave."

"That is an English idea; but in Germany people think differently," replied Nora.

"Most families in England have their tombs, or, at least, burying-places—" began Torp.

"You mean people of large fortune, and landed proprie-

tors," said Nora, "who have damp vaults under the
churches, which, only visited when the remains of a relation
are to be deposited in them, are regarded with horror by the
survivors. The greater number of people in England are,
however, buried in the churchyard nearest the place where
they die; and, even when monuments are erected by the
more wealthy, who ever thinks of visiting them, or caring
for them? Give me anything English but a grave!" She sat
down on the low wall while adding, "I hope I may yet find
a resting-place in the cheerful churchyard of some German
village—here, perhaps, beside my cousin Arthur."

"Well, I must say," rejoined Torp, seating himself beside
her, and stooping until he had obtained shelter under her
umbrella, "I must say the cheerfulness of this place is not
particularly remarkable to-day."

"It is quite as cheerful as elsewhere," persisted Nora.
"You will soon see it full of people, who, notwithstanding
the rain, will linger about the graves. In the afternoon many
of them will return: the church itself is seldom without
some pious visitor, for its doors are open at all hours during
the week; and, in fine weather, the sun shines here the live-
long day."

Torp looked at her intently, and smiled. "If," he said,
clasping his hands round his crossed knees, "if it were only
possible to imagine, I will not say believe, that the people
beneath these mounds could enjoy the—the sunshine and
—a—the company—"

"Not at all necessary," answered Nora, rising, as the
congregation began to issue in crowds from the church.
"Thoughts such as mine about churchyards are unconsciously cheering, consoling to the living; for few can ever
mentally so completely divest themselves of their bodies as
to be quite indifferent to what may become of them after
death. I have the weakness to wish that mine may rest in

sunshine; that, as I now stand by my cousin's grave, and think of him, relations and friends may stand by mine, and—" She stopped suddenly: the dreary thought that she had neither relations nor friends who would ever think of her grave, however they might perchance regret her death, came over her mind like a dark cloud; tears started to her eyes, and she turned hastily away to meet the forester and long Seppel, for whom she had been waiting.

"Downrightly and sincerely sentimental," thought Torp; "and some way, she has infected me too; for, after all, I rather like what she said about sunshine—and—aw—going to a fellow's grave and talking of him—"

Although Torp was quite resolved to convince Nora that his heart was still his own, and that she had no chance of obtaining from him more attention than civility required, he might have been seen by her, and her tolerably numerous escort, several times during the ascent to the chapel the next morning, had they been tempted to look around or beneath them. The fact was, Nora had observed his absence with great satisfaction when Florian had joined them, accompanied only by two men who were engaged to carry the renovated altar to St Hubert's, and she had hurried forward, hoping that Torp would be altogether deterred from making the excursion when he ascertained that he had been left to find his way alone to a place where there was but a slight chance of meeting his friend on such a gloomy day. She was mistaken. Torp was resolved to keep what he chose to consider an appointment with Waldemar, and we may suppose, as he did pertinaciously, that ignorance of the path was his sole inducement to follow so undeviatingly the well-known grey dress and wide-spreading hat.

Nora, as has been observed, did not look round her as

was her wont, for, although the weather had cleared during the night, dark wreaths of cloud still hung on the mountains, leaving only their bases and summits visible at intervals. The long-continued rain and storm had apparently completely weather-beaten the trees, the leaves clung to each other and drooped downwards, while on the branches of the less sensitive pines and firs large globules of water rolled backwards and forwards, ready to fall on the slightest provocation. Though the dripping trees in the wood and the marshy meadows beyond rather retarded and inconvenienced most members of the party, they braved the discomforts of the way exultingly, happy in the consciousness that they were taking what is called "advantage" of one of those "short cuts" in which most foresters delight, but which it would be better if women avoided, at least during or after rain. The guiding forester alone ventured to express the satisfaction he felt when they got upon the well-beaten path leading directly to the chapel and into Tyrol: he stamped his feet on the hard gravely ground, and began to point out a variety of objects to Nora that he had been judicious enough to avoid mentioning while she had been labouring after him, over the slippery roots of trees or through passages of coal-black mud.

A right pleasant and romantic path it was on which they now walked quickly forward, and when a new peak broke unexpectedly through the surrounding clouds they all hailed it as a harbinger of better weather. While they were still following the course of a small stream through a narrow gorge in the mountains, the sharp cry of a hawk attracted their attention. The forester stopped, unslung his rifle, and peered eagerly round: long Seppel sprang to his side, and pointed up the stream to where the bird, majestically soaring, seemed about to pass over their heads. "Try your hand, Sepp," cried the forester, magnanimously handing him the

rifle; and the young man, springing on a fragment of rock,
aimed and fired with a rapidity that delighted the old man,
who, as the bird fell at no great distance, splashed through
the water to pick it up; and, on seeing that it was quite dead,
and with scarcely a feather ruffled, he gave Seppel such a
slap on the shoulder and shove of approbation, that he sent
him reeling against Rosel, who stood the shock unshrink-
ingly, and, with sparkling eyes and smiling lips, called him
"a great awkward boy," and bade him "get out of her way."

Florian's two men, who had taken the opportunity of
resting, now raised their packs on their shoulders, and commenced the ascent to the chapel, the white spire of which
was visible far above them in the wood. Rosel and Nora
followed, leaving Seppel to assist the forester to bag the
bird and reload his rifle. These loiterers Torp joined, and,
after about three quarters of an hour's gradual but steep
ascent, they reached the isolated building. Rosel and Nora
had already entered; Seppel hurried after them; Torp followed slowly. The chapel was small, very massively built,
with long narrow windows at each side, and so surrounded
by trees that it was only on peculiarly bright days the sun's
rays could enter and light up its far-famed altars. Seppel and
Rosel knelt before the centre one, which was in a sort of
semi-circular protuberance in the building, and gorgeously
gilt and painted; the others, at each side, were more within
the church, one of them already renovated, the other about
to be restored to its place that day by Florian. Leaning with
her elbows on the railing that inclosed the vacant space
usually occupied by the latter, stood Nora, and Torp would
have given much to have obtained an undetected glance at
her face, as it rested on her clasped hands; but, true to his
resolution of taking no notice of her that could be avoided,
he waited patiently until Seppel and Rosel stood up, and
then advanced to the altar they had left, bowing very

slightly to Nora as he passed her. Quick as the salutation was on both sides, Torp perceived that hers was accompanied by a look of surprise totally unmixed with pleasure, in fact, rather the contrary; and while he stood, to all appearance, absorbed in the contemplation of the altar, he was considering, and deeply too, what he could have done or said to make his presence just then disagreeable.

Outside the chapel Rosel and Seppel were taking leave of each other. It was but for a week, yet they stood hand in hand, and seemed with difficulty to repress their tears.

"Come, Seppel, we must be moving," observed the forester, with an attempt at cheerfulness he was far from feeling, for every day and hour made him more regret having yielded to his choleric temper at a time when a little forbearance would have insured the happiness of his daughter. "It's only for a while, you know," he continued, "and to keep you out of temptation, as it were. Miss Nora has promised to set all to rights again, and she wouldn't have pledged herself if her papa had not allowed her."

Nora smiled at the doubt so shrewdly expressed, but gave no further affirmation than a slight nod of encouragement to Seppel, who, after vainly endeavouring to speak, held out his hand to her, and then slung his green linen pouch over his shoulder in a resolute manner. "God bless you, Rosel!" he said, with ill-concealed emotion; "on Saturday evening I shall be down in the village for a fresh supply of flour and butter, and to remain the Sunday. Take my greetings to my mother, and tell my father and brother I bear no malice."

"Where are you going, forester?" asked Torp, who was already at the door of the chapel.

"To the clearing above the miller's alp," he answered; "Seppel has offered to fell timber there, and must begin work with the other men about nine o'clock, so we have no time to lose."

"How far is the alp from here?"

"Two hours' smart walking," he replied. "The chapel was out of our way, but we can make up for lost time by cutting across the Rocky Horn."

"I have a great mind to go with you," said Torp, "if you can wait a few minutes until I have made some inquiries at the sexton's." Here he glanced towards Nora, and perceived an expression of such unmistakable satisfaction on her countenance, that he suddenly changed his mind, and, prompted alike by curiosity and mortification, resolved to remain and—watch her. He looked up towards the sky, however, before he added, "After all, perhaps I had better wait for finer weather; but don't forget to let me know the next time you go to the clearing above the miller's alp, as I want to see how you manage these things in Bavaria."

The forester and Seppel walked off at the steady quiet pace of highlanders when on their mountains; the latter looking back occasionally, as long as they were in sight, flourishing his hat in the air, and at length uttering the long loud popular jodel of his native village. Nora, who had been examining the altar as Florian unpacked it, now turned round, waved her handkerchief encouragingly above her head, looking so animated and hopeful, that Rosel, with tears still in her eyes, sprang forward, and gave the answering jodel; the altar-bearers shouted in the same strain; and even Torp found himself moved to raise his hat and utter a few of those long-drawn Ohs! and Ahs! which, from their frequent occurrence in the conversation of Englishmen, malicious Germans pretend to consider a part of our language.

"Meister Florian," said Nora, turning once more to the interrupted contemplation of the renovated altar-piece, "I wish you would carve me a copy of this alto-relievo, unpainted, and with any improvements you think necessary in the figures."

"If you can wait until next year," answered Florian, "and let me have the long winter evenings to work at it, I should have no objection to the undertaking, although I have never yet attempted anything on so large a scale."

"I should rather prefer your reducing the figures one half," said Nora, "as they are not to be viewed at a distance like these, but," she added, on perceiving Torp approaching, "we can talk the matter over at your house to-morrow —though, stay—not to-morrow, as I have promised to go to the mill on business—the day after—no—the day after, if things turn out, as I hope they will, I must go to the miller's alp,—but on Thursday I shall be quite at liberty. Let us say Thursday, Meister Florian, and now, if you will come with me to the sexton's house, you shall have a cup of his wife's best coffee."

Florian declined the invitation with evident regret. He could not leave the chapel until his work in it was completed.

"Can other people get coffee at the sexton's as well as you, Miss Nixon?" asked Torp.

"Anybody and everybody," she answered cheerfully, beginning the descent to the house, of which the chimney and roof were visible, at no great distance beneath them.

"Will you have the kindness, Miss Nixon," said Torp, making a last effort to convince her of his indifference to her society, "will you have the kindness to tell Waldemar that I shall be with him directly?"

"If I find him at the sexton's I shall give him your message," she answered, with such perfect unconcern, that Torp, unconsciously rejoicing in the perception of her indifference to his friend, stood looking after her even when the trees had hid her from his sight, and then, having

walked up and down the uneven plateau on which the
chapel was built, he sat down in the wooden porch of the
building, until he thought that he might descend to the sexton's without betraying too much *empressement* to join her.

Nora, seated before the house, at a small table that had
been brought out of one of the rooms, was, as he approached, just dismissing a boy, who had been standing
beside her, with the words, "Tell your grandfather I know
he must have a note or letter from the gentleman for me,
and then come back here directly, for I shall want you to
show me the way."

Whatever doubts Torp might have hitherto entertained
as to the nature of his feelings towards Nora, they were removed at that moment by a painful consciousness of sudden and intense jealousy. Not that he was so irrational as to
suppose that she had planned or even consented to a direct
rendezvous with Waldemar, though he had now no doubt
she had both hoped and expected to meet him. Her desire
to see him might be partly caused by a wish to consult him
about the purchase of Waltenburg or the mountain mill;
but that she had written to him was at least more than
probable, otherwise she could not be so certain that she
should find a letter from him at St Hubert's. And then—to
what place was the boy to show her the way?

Now Torp's presence was anything but agreeable to
Nora at that moment; so she left the table, and went to
meet the sexton, who was coming from the field, where he
had been digging potatoes, and contrived to join him while
still so distant from the house that their conversation could
not be overheard.

"I believe," she said, making a sign to him to keep on his
hat, "I believe you have got a note for me from the gentleman who is lodging at your son-in-law's house, on the
Tyrolean side of the frontiers?"

"Oh, you're the lady that's to call for the letter," he answered, deliberately taking a pinch of snuff; "and I was thinking of sending it to the village by Florian this very afternoon! Wastl," he added, turning to his grandson, who stood beside him, "tell your grandmother to give you the paper that's been lying so long on the dresser in the kitchen."

"The gentleman," he continued, accosting Nora, "the gentleman has had but little sport, and very rough weather, miss, and accordingly finds the time hang heavy; he came up here yesterday, and said he didn't know what to do with himself."

"I think he had better return to Almenau with me," said Nora.

"He's more likely to go further into Tyrol and take his pleasure, without having to consult forester or assistant forester," answered the sexton, taking another pinch of snuff.

Just then Wastl returned with a very slovenly soiled note. Nora opened it and read:—

Send the boy for me, and then come to a place called the Riven Rock. Should that tiresome fellow, Torp, be in the way, as usual, you must manage to get off without his observing you, as he is the last person I wish to meet just now.

"Have you time to go to this gentleman, who is lodging at your father's?" asked Nora, turning to Wastl.

"Oh, yes, plenty of time."

"And, when you have told him that I am here, will you return and show me the way to the Riven Rock?"

The boy nodded and ran off, and Nora, not choosing Torp to see her tear the note, and equally unwilling to put it, daubed with butter and smelling of cheese, into her

pocket, crumpled it in her hand into a pellet, which she
threw away, and then sat down and waited for her coffee,
with what Torp considered the perfection of self-
possession. He himself relapsed into the cold, imperturbable manner that had marked the commencement of their
acquaintance, but which was completely unobserved by
Nora, as she politely offered him coffee, and supplied him
with fresh rolls from Rosel's basket. While *they* talked of
shrines and chapels in the woods, and vows made and performed, *he* bent over and fed a hideous dog with cropped
ears and tail, and was so interested in this occupation that
he only looked up for a moment when Wastl unexpectedly
came back, and, running up to Nora, informed her, in a
panting and but too audible whisper, "that he had met the
gentleman from Tyrol coming up to St Hubert's, and that
he was now waiting for her at the Riven Rock."

Nora seemed annoyed, but not embarrassed, as she left
the table. Rosel entered the house, and Torp relaxing in his
attentions to the dog, the animal sniffed about under the
adjacent tree until he found the letter thrown there, in a
form that induced him first to snap it up, and, after a few
capers, to bound towards Torp, at whose feet he dropped
it.

Torp kicked it away with some violence.

The dog had evidently been taught to "seek;" he rushed
after and soon returned with the half-open letter, laid it on
the ground, and commenced barking and springing at a little distance, as if waiting for a continuation of the game.

Torp could now have read every word, but he did not
even glance at the handwriting, as he roughly crumpled it
up again, and, rising hastily, threw it as far away as possible.

"I won't believe this without stronger proof," he
thought. "Indiscreet she may be,—and romantic she is, in
her own peculiar way, but nothing worse. Yet I could al-

most wish that, after all, this rendezvous with Waldemar might prove a vulgar fact, and be ascertained with my own eyes in the course of the next half-hour—it would be the only certain means of preventing me from wasting a thought, still less a regret, on her for the rest of my life."

He descended the mountain in the direction that had been taken by her, and soon found himself among rocks of every description, excepting such as the one he sought, and had just resolved to go on into Tyrol, and make inquiries at the frontier inn, when he encountered Wastl walking slowly homewards, his head bent over one of his hands, in which he held a variety of small coins, that he counted over and over again with childish delight.

"Did the gentleman from Tyrol give you all that money?" asked Torp.

The boy looked up and nodded.

"Show me the way to the Riven Rock, and I will give you as much more."

Wastl turned round, walked about fifty yards, and then pointed downwards to a large grotesquely-shaped rock, that seemed to have burst asunder in some sudden manner, and so formed a narrow passage with accurately corresponding walls at each side.

Torp gave the promised kreutzers.

"If you go straight through the rock," said Wastl, "straight through to the end, and cry boo—oo—oo, they'll get a jolly fright!"

Torp half smiled, but did not profit by the advice; on the contrary, he made a considerable circuit, in order to approach them from the other side; and it was with a sort of grim satisfaction that he caught the first glimpses of the two figures seated beneath the overhanging rock, and speaking too eagerly to be aware of the approach of any one. The gentleman from Tyrol was playing rather cavalierly with the ribbons of Nora's hat; but though only seen in profile, there was no mistaking Waldemar's jaunty peasant dress, and Torp was just about to advance and accost him, when he remembered that he had promised his friend never again to interrupt a *tête-à-tête* with Nora. He therefore walked to some distance below them, and sauntered slowly past, as if unconscious of their presence, but firmly resolved to go on to the little inn on the frontiers, and there await Waldemar's return.

"Nora," cried Jack, "there he is, squinting up at us. I knew he would come after you to find out where I was hiding."

"He is not thinking of you," she answered quietly. "I am quite sure he is going to the inn, to make inquiries about that good-natured, gentlemanlike Count Waldemar, whom he expected to meet at St Hubert's to-day."

"Then I must return to the inn at once, to prevent his hearing more about me than is necessary."

"He knows all about you already, Jack, and was as silent as either of us could have desired."

"Suppose, however, Seppel should happen to come up and be seen by him—"

"Not the slightest danger. Seppel has just gone with the forester to the wood above the miller's alp."

Jack started to his feet with a look of uneasiness, and began to pace backwards and forwards impatiently.

"You fear, perhaps," said Nora, "that I am going to continue my jeremiade, as you call it, about Seppel, but you are mistaken. I was going to add that I have discovered a way of setting all to rights again."

"I always said you were a brick, Norry," cried Jack, "and, were you to talk for two hours, you could not make me more sorry than I am for this confounded occurrence—I mean misfortune. If I had not sworn to keep the secret I should now return with you, and acknowledge all to the judge."

"For what purpose?" asked Nora. "Seppel has been acquitted for want of evidence against him, and his brother is now in actual possession of the Crags."

"That's it," cried Jack, "that's what vexes me. I thought the worst that could come out of it would be a couple of days' arrest for the poor fellow, and never heard a word about the Crags until you explained the matter to me just now."

"Never—heard—a word about the Crags," repeated Nora; "that is strange, if, as you tell me, you saw him yesterday evening, for at that time the cession of the property was completed, and Seppel knew it. Could a feeling of generosity on his part—"

"No, no," cried Jack, interrupting her, "you don't understand me—he feared that I—that he—in short, I cannot, must not, dare not, explain. It has been a chapter of accidents from beginning to end, and there is no use in talking any more about it. I am sorry for what has happened, and the next time I have fifty pounds to spare, I shall give it to this poor fellow."

Nora smiled. She knew that Jack was never likely to have fifty pounds to spare.

"I will indeed, Nora. And now," he continued, seating himself again beside her, "tell me how you intend to make all straight."

She related her plan, and he warmly approved, calling her a dear, generous girl, and declaring, whatever other people might think, he considered it a fortunate circumstance that she had inherited their uncle's fortune instead of his brother Sam.

"But as to my going back with you to the village, Nora, you cannot expect me to think of such a thing, now that the weather is clearing up."

"Then promise me, at least, not to disgrace yourself by turning poacher again."

"I wish you would be civil, Nora, and remember that I prefer the word wildschuetz," he answered, laughing; "but, in point of fact, I am an innocent wildschuetz,—by accident, as one may say, and only occasionally, when not quite certain of the exact boundaries between Austria and Bavaria."

"What do you mean?"

"You see," he replied, gravely, "some peasants in Tyrol rent part of the chase about the frontiers here—perhaps they get it because it was suspected they would hunt at all events—perhaps not; that is no business of mine. For a trifling consideration, they have given me leave to shoot on their ground—and let me tell you, Nora, that I now infinitely prefer going out with a party of these daring fellows to any regular hunt with your friend Waldemar—that is, supposing him incumbered by such companions as the gruff old forester, and that cold-blooded curmudgeon Torp!"

"But," observed Nora, thoughtfully, "but if you were hunting in Tyrol, what brought you to the Wild Alp, which is completely on the Bavarian side of the mountains?"

"How sharp you are!" cried Jack, with a laugh; "you see, dear, the two countries are not separated by either paling or hedge, and there is a confusing similarity in their appearance hereabouts; so it happens occasionally, quite by accident of course, that one passes the frontiers, and all at once finds one's self turned into a wildschuetz, and, what is infinitely worse, into a target for the first Bavarian forester one chances to meet!"

"I am glad," observed Nora, "that you have become aware of the danger you incur on such occasions."

"All right," said Jack.

"All wrong," cried Nora, impatiently; "but fortunately Seppel is safe from further temptation."

Jack's eyes twinkled very knowingly.

"You mean that you can go or send to him," she said reproachfully.

"Well, it would not be a very difficult matter, I should think."

"Then let me tell you," she continued, gravely, "that by doing so you will frustrate all my plans for him—that the forester will never, after another offence of this kind, give his consent to his daughter's marriage with him—and that Rosel, for whom I feel personally interested, will be made more unhappy and hopeless than ever."

"I did not say I would do it," he observed deprecatingly.

"You have said enough to prevent my taking any further steps about the purchase of the mill until after your return to the village; I shall neither go to inspect it to-morrow, nor to visit the alp the day after, nor—"

"Come, come, Nora, I thought you would understand me without an hour's explanation. I could send or go to the alp easily enough, and I will even confess that I have a useful friend there; but surely you do not think me capable of trying to persuade your protégé to go out with us after all that has happened? I assure you he is safe as far as I am concerned, and if it be any relief to your mind, I can add that I neither want him nor wish for him. Let me, however, recommend you, in case there should be any talk of wild hunters in these parts again, to send some one up to the alp,—some one who, if it were necessary, could bear witness in his favour afterwards. I tell you what, Nora," he added, with a laugh, "persuade Rosel to go—and tell her to promise him, that at a certain hour of the night she will pop her head out of the window of the hut: they call that 'windowing,' here, and, if report may be trusted, your long Seppel has quite as decided a predilection for windowing as for hunting."

Nora could not help smiling at this suggestion, but she held her cousin's hand fast when he attempted to leave her, and said, entreatingly, "Return with me to Almenau, Jack, and give up these wild excursions; they are not reputable, however plausibly you may talk of them. Mr Torp is, I think, less repelling in his manner than at first, and I believe I might even venture to speak to him now about you, and request permission—"

"Request nothing for me," cried Jack, petulantly. "I detest that man, and would not accept a day's shooting if I had to thank him for it! You see, dear Nora, a woman cannot understand things like a man. I know perfectly well what I am about, and only regret not being able to assist you in the purchase of this mill, but my father will, I dare say, do all that is necessary; and aw—I say, Norry, just look here, will you?—don't you think I am getting a very respectable moustache? I wonder if I shall be obliged to shave it off when I go home?"

He stretched out his face towards her for inspection, in a rather provocative manner, received a light slap on his mouth from her glove, and then, fully persuaded that he had convinced her of the superiority of his sex to hers in general, and of his wisdom to hers in particular, he strode off towards Tyrol, while Nora slowly returned to the sexton's.

Need it be related how Torp with enduring patience waited the return of his friend to the inn? how he sprang up to meet him, and encountered Jack Nixon?

What he felt when he returned the scarcely perceptible salute of his sullen and purposely uncourteous countryman, may be imagined. Had any one been near him, he might have heard him murmur, as if in answer to some self-made reproach, "How the deuce could I think of him, when every one said he was in Innsbruck?"

CHAPTER XXXVI

Woodmen at Work

TORP was at the mill the next day before Nora: he was fishing in the stream below the house, and, as it appeared, with considerable success; but instead of turning away and pretending not to see her, as he would have done but a week previously, he looked up, accosted her cheerfully, packed up his fishing-rod while speaking, and accompanied her to the mill. Nora was neither pleased nor displeased at the meeting; the day before his presence had been a restraint and a bore, at the mill it was neither. He knew her motives for going there; and after having offered his services instead of Waldemar, she could only attribute his appearance to a wish to be useful, and felt in a manner constrained to receive what she considered an effort of civility on his part with a good grace.

Torp had seldom seen her to greater advantage than during this mill inspection, when, preceded by the miller and followed by Tyrolean Seppel, she visited every nook and corner of the building, listening with unwearied patience and evident intelligence to the long explanations of the machinery and latest improvements, given by the miller in a deep melancholy voice that well accorded with his sombre appearance. Torp was perfectly inattentive; he understood all at a glance, considered the works of rather primitive construction, the fall of water the most valuable part of the property, and by degrees completely concentrated his scrutiny and thoughts on Nora, whose long curved eyelashes, more than powdered with flour, seemed to possess a sort of fascination for him. When well covered both with flour and bran, they went to the saw-mill, and having there added a considerable quantity of dust to their garments, they entered the house, where Nora sat down with the miller, his wife, and black Seppel at the table in the dwelling-room, and deliberately looked over all the papers and documents offered her, taking notes in a business-like manner that equally amused and surprised Torp. He perceived she did not want him, yet he lingered and listened to the long discussion that followed about clear profits and probable losses, the number of cows kept, the alpine pasture, and the forest rights: his patience was not even exhausted by proposals on her part to buy most of the furniture of the house, as well as the farming utensils and part of the cattle; and though he did not accompany her through the rooms, he followed to the cow-house, and advised her to see the cattle on the alp, and to consult the forester before she decided on the purchase of live stock.

"You think me childishly impatient," she said, walking to the front of the house, "and you are right. I know that my evident desire to purchase will raise the price of everything I have been shown during the past hour; but I cannot conceal my wishes on this occasion, for it so happened that one of my first walks with Rosel in this neighbourhood was to the Crags, and on our way we stopped for half an hour here, and I remember then hearing her say that the mill was dearer to her than any place in the world, from its having been the play-ground of her infancy and early youth; that it was here the children from the Crags and the forest-house had met after school-hours; and that she could imagine nothing more delightful than sitting on the rocks below, or the timber ranged in heaps around the saw-mill, and listening to the rushing and splashing of the water. She appeared almost offended at my observing that the place was rather noisy!"

"It *is* noisy," said Torp; "but children like noise, and youthful reminiscences are a source of great enjoyment. Rosel has also, perhaps, some pleasant recollections of a later period, when a certain long-legged cuirassier may have taken post on the timber here?"

"Very likely," said Nora: "I believe she did say something to that purport; at all events, that she loves the place is certain, and I trust she may live long and happily in it, and heap up a fresh store of these pleasant recollections for her old age."

"She will have every reason to place your visit to Almenau among them," observed Torp, "and to be grateful in no common degree."

"I exact no gratitude," said Nora; "we have entered into an engagement, which, if kept by her and every future possessor of the mill, will make our obligations mutual."

"You must have been very much attached to Arthur Nixon," he said, as they afterwards walked towards the village together.

"He was one of my nearest relations," she answered, evasively.

"True," said Torp; "but as well as I can remember, he associated wonderfully little with his near relations."

"You knew him—well?" she said, half interrogatively.

"Oh, of course I knew him, for he latterly identified himself completely with his wife's family, and *they* are relations of mine, you know."

"I did *not* know it," said Nora, quietly.

"Ah, true—of course not—how could you? You do not even know my name yet, Miss Nixon."

Nora smiled, but without looking up, or appearing to consider the subject worth a question.

Piqued at such unexpected indifference, and perceiving, with infinite mortification, that his own person could not procure him the consideration he now began to desire from her, Torp thought it advisable to take advantage of the present occasion to at least partly make her acquainted with his position in the world, the advantages of which he had been too long a younger son not fully to appreciate. He began by repeating his last assertion, added in explanation that Waldemar had never been able to pronounce the English "th," and ended with the information that he was a Thorpe, and—very nearly related to the Medway family.

"In fact," said Nora, perfectly unmoved, "you now choose me to know that you *were* the Honourable Charles Thorpe, and are now Earl of Medway. I regret," she added, a little ironically, "I regret that I cannot pretend the astonishment you perhaps expected, but I am an indifferent actress, and have been too long aware of your real name to attach the importance to your communication that it perhaps deserves."

"So Waldemar betrayed me after all!" said Torp, biting his lip, and slightly frowning.

"No," she replied, "he understood too well your wish to remain unknown, in order to escape the probably expected obtrusiveness of our family. My informants were a Prussian lady and her daughter, to whom you were introduced on the Peissenberg."

"Ah! so long ago!" exclaimed Torp. "Then you knew who I was when those not very flattering remarks about a certain Charley Thorpe were made in the garden of the inn not long ago?"

"Undoubtedly."

"I have to thank you for your forbearance on that occasion," said Torp. "Your family took advantage of my incognito to say some very severe things of me, or rather to me."

"I must defend them from this accusation," said Nora, "by assuring you that they were, and are still, in utter ignorance of your true name."

"Do you mean that you never told them?" he asked, unable to conceal his astonishment.

"Never!" she replied, laughing lightly, but with a zest that annoyed him. "I thought if you chose to eclipse your glory, and play at mystery, it would be ungenerous of me to interfere with your plans, whatever they might be."

Torp felt completely put out of countenance; he thought the eyes of his companion began to sparkle mischievously, as if she rather enjoyed his discomfiture, and a long pause ensued.

"Perhaps," at length he observed, with some pique, "perhaps, Miss Nixon, I should have found more favour in your eyes, if, instead of having been Charles Thorpe, I had had the luck to be a Tom or Dick Torp?"

"Perhaps you might," said Nora; "but even as Mr *Torp* you have contrived to make yourself particularly disagreeable to me—to us all."

"In what way?" he asked, eagerly. "Surely the slight avoidance on my part, that may have been evident at the commencement of our acquaintance, cannot have made so unpleasant an impression on you?"

"It has made none at all," she answered, "for I did not wish it otherwise. But your determination not to allow Count Waldemar or the forester here to give our poor dear Jack a few days' sport has indeed made a more than unpleasant impression on me. It was scarcely to be expected that, at his age, he would remain a contented spectator of successes such as yours, and the consequences have been of a nature that, I confess, I am not likely to forget easily."

"I understand," said Torp, hastily; "I—I am very sorry —I shall speak to the forester about it directly, and—"

"Too late," said Nora, interrupting him; "I do not know where, in Tyrol, John may now be." She hesitated for a moment, and then added, "What is past can be remedied— what may yet occur—"

"Good heavens, Miss Nixon! surely you will not lay to my charge all that that wild boy may do? Perhaps he is still near St Hubert's; I will go there to-morrow—this evening, if you desire it—and entreat him to return here."

"He will not do for you what he refused me," said Nora; "but," she added, hastily, "do not misunderstand me, or suppose him in the company of wild hunters. He goes out with some Tyrolean peasants who rent the hunting-ground on the frontiers."

"And who pass them," observed Torp, "whenever they can do it with impunity."

"Jack may do so in ignorance," said Nora; "that is what I fear; and so much, that I shall write to him, and mention your proposal to speak to the forester. I can say you made the offer voluntarily; he forbade my speaking to you on the subject."

"Then you thought of asking me?"

"More than once; for, until yesterday, I feared he was with very reckless companions."

"I still suspect he is not with very steady ones," said Torp.

"At all events," rejoined Nora, "I shall write, and most probably the sexton at St Hubert's will know where to forward my letter; in the mean time, I must take care to have his companion, long Seppel, strictly watched."

They had reached the inn while speaking, and Nora, perceiving the judge in the garden, immediately joined him;

and, having renewed her acquaintance, drew her notes from her pocket, and began a conversation, which ended in her knowing what she might offer, and what ultimately give, for the mountain mill—and a resolution to go the next day to the alp belonging to it.

Great was her surprise when she mentioned her intention, in the course of the evening, to her uncle and Georgina, to find that they were willing to accompany her. They had heard that they could drive to the base of the mountain —that the path, chiefly through a forest, was less steep then usual to such places, and particularly carefully made—being used for the transport of wood in winter. No day could possibly suit them so well as the next; and, in short, they had made up their minds to see a real alp before they left the highlands.

"The Falkners are to return to St Benedict's to-morrow," said Georgina; "so we cannot well go to the lake —neither do we wish to be in the village when they pass through it."

"At what hour can you start?" asked Nora.

"After breakfast and post-time."

"That is ten o'clock," said Nora. "A drive of half an hour will take you to the mountain,—my uncle will require three hours to mount; so that I may suppose you will be on the alp between one and two o'clock: I shall be there long before noon, most probably."

"Why will you not go with us?"

"Because I am going first to St Hubert's chapel."

"What is to prevent us from visiting the chapel also?" asked Georgina. "I remember your telling me something about its antiquity and carved-wood altars, that rather excited my curiosity."

"Did I?" said Nora, musingly. "The way to the chapel is easy; but thence to the miller's alp would be too much for my uncle, or you either, Georgy. There is no path, and I shall require a guide who knows the country well, and can help me to scramble across the mountain called the 'Rocky Horn'."

"May I ask what induces you to go either to the chapel, where you were so lately, or over this Rocky Horn, if it be such a pathless wilderness?"

Nora did not choose to tell her that her brother Jack was roughing it in the mountains with Tyrolean peasants, instead of being, as she supposed, at Innsbruck; still less did she feel disposed to enter into an explanation of Torp's recent offer, and her fears that a letter from her would not be sufficient to induce her wilful cousin to return to the village, though she had some reasonable hopes of the result of another conference with him.

"I have long intended to make an excursion over the Rocky Horn," she replied, after a pause. "St Hubert's is the pleasantest, if not the nearest way to it. Then, as Rosel goes with me, I wish to pass the place where the woodmen are felling timber, that she may see a friend of hers who is at work there; and, all things considered, it will be much the same thing to you, I should suppose, if you find me at the alp when you arrive there."

During the evening Mr Nixon talked a good deal of his famous ascent of the "Peissenberg mountain," and seemed ready to undertake the Rocky Horn itself, had he received the slightest encouragement from Nora. The necessity of getting up at daybreak for the purpose alone deterred him from making at least the attempt; and he professed himself perfectly satisfied on hearing that the miller's alp was one of the highest in the neighbourhood, and peculiarly interesting, from its being half Tyrolean, near an extensive clearance in the forest, and surrounded by charcoal-burners.

Nora, Rosel, and their guide, left Almenau at a very early

hour the next morning, and reached St Hubert's in good time; but neither the sexton nor his grandson was at home, and the other members of the family could not tell her whether or not the "young gentleman" was still at the inn "on the other side." So Nora decided at once on taking her companions on, and breakfasting with them in Tyrol.

Her first question on reaching the inn was, "Is the foreign gentleman still here?"

"He is."

"Is he up?"

"Yes; he is drinking coffee and smoking a cigar in the little parlour."

"Bring us coffee there, too; and you, Rosel, go to the kitchen and see what they have got for Michael's breakfast."

Greatly pleased at finding her plans so successful, Nora moved lightly on to the little parlour, and, unceremoniously opening the door, exclaimed, "Here I am again, you tiresome, good-for-nothing thing!" Then she stopped, looked round the room, and stammered an excuse to Torp, who stood before her, apparently equally pleased and surprised, and colouring in a manner very unusual to him.

"You need not explain, Miss Nixon," he said, with his accustomed self-possession: "I am perfectly aware who it was you expected to meet. I hoped, by coming here yesterday evening, to have had a better chance; but, it seems, Mr John Nixon left this place the day after we were at St Hubert's, and the people here profess complete ignorance of his present place of abode, so that I have not been able to follow him."

"You have been very kind," said Nora; "and I am greatly obliged to you,—but what are we to do now?"

"Write to him," said Torp.

"Of what use, if they don't know where he is?"

"I believe, Miss Nixon, that letters often reach their destinations where there is no post, if a request to give the bearer a florin be distinctly written beside the address."

"But," said Nora, "to make it intelligible it must be written in German, and Jack cannot read German writing."

"Then let us put an English translation underneath," suggested Torp.

"Stupid—my not thinking of that," she rejoined, laughing, while she commenced a search for writing materials.

In an old portfolio some paper was found—then the dried-up ink hastily inundated with water, and, after some time, a pen procured, that enabled her to write a short and urgent note, to which Torp requested permission to add a couple of lines. Before signing his name, he looked up, and asked, "Am I Torp, or Medway, Miss Nixon?"

"Torp," she replied: "you can choose your own time to make yourself known to my family."

"The name is certainly not euphonious," he observed, when writing it as a signature.

"What's in a name?" she cried, gaily. "A rose by any other name—you know—"

"No, I do not know any such thing, Miss Nixon, for it seems to me that there is a good deal in a name."

"Especially in a titled one," she answered, rather sarcastically, while folding up their joint letter.

"I was not thinking of titles—I—I alluded to the melancholy fact of you and your family having taken a dislike to the *name* of Charles Thorpe; of himself you know too little to form an opinion." He paused, and then added, "You do not deny it?"

"I cannot," said Nora.

"You deliberately confess that you disliked without ever having seen me?"

"Yes," she replied, with a gravity that rather surprised

him.

"Is this right? is this just, Miss Nixon?"

"Perhaps not," she said, rising; "it is rather what you call 'a melancholy fact.' I wonder," she added, musingly, "to whom in this house I ought to confide our letter?"

"To the eldest son of our host," answered Torp; "I have very little doubt that he will deliver it both safely and quickly. One word more, Miss Nixon: may I ask if a personal acquaintance with Charles Thorpe has tended to remove this unreasonable antipathy to his name?"

"You seem to have forgotten my having mentioned yesterday that Mr Torp had contrived to make himself rather disagreeable on more occasions than one."

"Hang Torp," he cried, half laughing.

"I have no objection," said Nora.

"And Charles Thorpe?" he asked.

"Hang him, too, by all means," she answered, walking off with her letter, and leaving him in provoking uncertainty as to the progress he had made in her good opinion.

Perhaps it was a wish to obtain some information on this subject that induced Torp to leave the inn at the same time with Nora and her companions, and accompany them across the mountains. He did not, however, choose her to suppose so, and took the trouble to explain at some length that he had long intended to make this excursion, in order to see how the Bavarian foresters managed their fellings on the mountains. Why he was afterwards half offended with her for believing him implicitly, it would be hard to say, and he actually looked little less than angry when she turned from him to their guide, and requested the latter to give them all the information he had acquired concerning forest culture and the habits and employments of the woodmen. She knew that Michael had often been employed as feller and logman, and that he was still in the habit of sledging wood in winter, and found, as she had expected, but little solicitation necessary on her part to induce him to be loquacious on a subject so familiar and interesting to him.

Few people lead a more isolated, monotonous, obscure, and laborious life than these German woodmen, especially in the mountain districts, where their work is frequently performed with more danger than attends the enterprises of the most dauntless chamois-hunters; yet it is in such places that the employment is eagerly sought, and that during the winter months the young peasants leave their homes, when the fields lie buried in snow, and no longer require their care, to seek work for themselves, or their otherwise unemployed horses and oxen. The money so obtained is pure gain, which, with the possibility of returning occasionally to their families, makes them brave their hardships cheerfully. Many even find a sort of fascination in the wild scenery, the sociability of their comrades, and the pride of increased physical strength, so that they are induced ultimately, when they have no prospect of marriage, to become woodmen or charcoal-burners by profession. These men acquire, in the course of a few years, a peculiarly robust and powerful appearance; their shoulders are broad; strong muscles, like lines of whipcord, may be traced beneath the sunburnt skin of their arms; and no stretch of an English imagination can picture the dimensions of their short, thick, Saturday-clipped beards.

The way from St Hubert's to the miller's alp led Nora past all the various contrivances for expediting the mountain timber to the valleys; and, while her guide beguiled the way with explanations of the ice-channels, water-courses, sluices, weirs, and sledging-paths, she followed him, unconscious of fatigue, to the summit of the mountain where Seppel and his companions were at work. They arrived just in time to see the process of felling a pine of no common dimensions that had grown on a sort of promontory on the skirts of the wood, and, in consequence, found means to stretch its wide fat branches outwards, their weight giving the tree an inclination downwards that greatly added to its picturesque appearance. The woodmen scrambled up the crags; two of them laid the large sharp-toothed saw on the trunk, and the bark chipped off around the scarcely perceptible wound; more and more steadily it grated backwards and forwards, and small splinters darted, and yellow dust began to fall at each side; other woodmen advanced with poles, which they pressed against the trunk to direct the fall. The saw reached the middle of the tree, the pith is severed, and a shudder, as of agony, seemed to pass through the quivering branches as they rose and fell with every motion of the saw. More men pressed forward, and stemmed themselves resolutely against the now tottering trunk; a smashing and snapping of the branches among the trees behind, intermingled with the creaking of the trunk itself, warned the sawyers to take flight; the tree bent forward more and more; the branches waved frantically: for a moment it seemed to raise itself by a violent effort, the next fell prostrate, the shouts of human voices lost in the crash that for a few seconds effectually stunned the less-inured spectators.

The echoes were hardly silent when the woodmen sprang forward with saws and axes to commence the work of dismemberment. Seppel, who had been one of the sawyers, now approached Rosel, and, after some whispering, the latter asked Nora if she would not like to see the woodmen's shed, and proposed their resting there until the men came to cook their dinner.

Nora acquiesced willingly, but sent their guide to the miller's alp, with directions to return for her in case her relations should arrive sooner than she expected. It was not until Seppel and Rosel walked on to show the way, and Nora was in a manner left alone with Torp, that she became conscious of his more than usual thoughtfulness and taciturnity, and began to feel some qualms of conscience for having so completely forgotten his presence, and neglected him, after the effort he had made to relieve her anxiety respecting her cousin John. She therefore resolved to be polite and loquacious for the next hour at least, and made the most laudable efforts to appear so, but never had she during her life been less successful. It was in vain she racked her brain for questions or observations likely to interest him. He looked at her intently, but answered so absently, that she at length desisted, and left him to reflections of an apparently but little agreeable nature.

CHAPTER XXXVII

Quits

THE woodmen's summer hut was of very primitive construction. Altogether of wood, and very carelessly roofed, it contained but one large room, furnished with sleeping-places for about a dozen men,—a long stone hearth, that served alike for fireplace and table, being provided with rough hewn benches at each side,—and a rack against the wall of planks, on which hung the saucepan and iron cooking spoon of each workman, with the scrip that contained his week's provision.

Seppel's was immediately opened for Nora's inspection, and she found in it the remains of a loaf of brown bread, a small bag of white flour, and a round box made of maple wood, containing *schmalz*, that is, butter melted to oil, and then cooled, in which state it can be preserved for months without danger of its becoming rancid. This is, in fact, their substitute for meat; but only those who work hard, and in the open air, could venture to live so exclusively on food so butyraceous. The mode of preparing this woodman's fare is simple in the extreme. A portion of flour is mixed with fresh cold water and a little salt, the pan then placed on the fire, with a large slice of *schmalz*, which almost immediately assumes the appearance of oil, in which the dough or paste is turned until completely saturated with grease, and the morsels slightly browned and crusted.

When Seppel had explained all this, and began to replace his provisions in the bag, Nora turned to Torp, who was standing at the door watching a charcoal-burner, whose kiln was visible in the open space below the hut.

"These people," she said in a low voice, "lead a laborious life, and suffer all sorts of privations."

"Better than working in a coal-mine," he answered; "at least *I* should prefer it."

"Even in winter?" she asked.

"Yes. There is something inspiriting in warring against storm and snow, in places such as this—something pleasant in work so completely manly. The hardships and dangers are not greater than those of our sailors, and possess the advantage of personal freedom of action and motion. Had I been born here, and a peasant, I should undoubtedly have been either a forester or a woodman; and who knows," he added with a smile, glancing towards their companions, "who knows but I might have found a Rosel, to bestow her love and—a pocket full of cheese upon me?"

Nora looked round in time to catch a glimpse of the cheese, just as it was being transferred to the wallet. Some eggs followed, that must have been most troublesome to carry; and, when these had been satisfactorily arranged in the butter-box, Seppel took up a barrel, and said he must go to the spring for water, as his comrades would expect to find it, and a fire ready for them, when they left off work. Rosel followed him out of the hut, and Nora, not feeling disposed for a tête-à-tête with Torp, joined them, resolved to take the rest of which she began to feel so much in need at the spring. They stopped on their way for a moment to speak to the charcoal-burner; and as Nora then glanced upwards, she perceived Torp, with folded arms, and head bent down, striding backwards and forwards, in the small space before the woodmen's hut, in a manner that rather

excited her wonder, but made her suppose he had no intention of following them.

The spring was celebrated for its ice-cold, clear, and
sparkling water, and had therefore been covered with a
rough building resembling a grotto; some woodman, too, in
an idle hour, had formed a spout for the water, so that it
flowed fresh, and without exposure to the air, out of the
rock into the receptacle beneath, whence it trickled in various small channels down the side of the mountain. There
were rustic benches beneath the trees and moss-cushioned
rocks beside the fountain; and it was on one of these that
Nora seated herself, threw her hat on the ground, and drew
from her pocket a leather drinking-cup.

"No need of that, miss," said Seppel. "We have our
glass, and whoever breaks must replace it. As good luck
would have it, the last time Count Waldemar was out hunting in these parts with the English gentleman, they smashed
it some way or other between them, I suppose, for in the
evening we missed it, and the day after found two new
glasses here, thick and strong ones you see, and not likely to
fall to pieces for a chance knock against the rocks."

While Nora examined the glasses, and tried to guess
which had been chosen by Waldemar, Seppel filled his keg
with water, and Rosel amused herself gathering some beech
leaves, and fastening them ingeniously together with the
needle-like foliage of the nearest pine-tree, so as to form a
chaplet of such peculiarly classical appearance, that when
she encircled Nora's head with it, Torp, who was at the
moment approaching them, could hardly repress an exclamation of admiration. Perfectly unconscious of the light
decoration, Nora bent forward and filled a glass with water,
while Seppel shouldered his keg, and prepared to leave the
spring;—perhaps Rosel intended to accompany him, she
murmured something about helping to make a fire; but

Nora, who had already caught a glimpse of Torp, requested her to wait a few minutes longer, and pointed to a place on the rocks beside her.

"If Waldemar were here, Miss Nixon," observed Torp, as he drew near, "he would say that you looked like the nymph of the fountain."

"And you," answered Nora, "would think that I looked more like a wearied wayfarer resting at a shady spring."

"Be a nymph for the nonce," said Torp, smiling, "and give me a glass of this famous water."

Nora lazily stretched out her arm, let the water flow into and over the glass for a few seconds, and then held it towards him. He would have given much at that moment could he have detected the slightest shade of coquetry in her manner: but, with the most provoking unconsciousness of his glance of unconcealed admiration, she shook the water from her dripping hand, and then leaned back against the rocks, while deliberately drying her fingers in her handkerchief.

Perhaps Torp wished to rouse her, perhaps he thought of his sister Jane, perhaps he only thought of himself, when he observed with unusual significance of tone and manner, "I received a letter from Henry Darwin yesterday, Miss Nixon;—he is not yet aware of my having met you and your family here, and addressed his letter to Herrenburg in Tyrol, supposing me to be staying with the Benndorffs."

The colour that had overspread Nora's face at the commencement of this speech faded away, when she perceived that Torp was still ignorant of her being Harry's step-sister.

"I believe he is an old acquaintance—a friend of yours?" he continued.

"He scarcely deserves the name of friend," she answered, composedly.

"Yet you knew him long and intimately," persisted Torp.

"Long—but not intimately," she answered.

"You liked him—of course?" he said, half interrogatively.

"Not particularly."

"Yet you received his attentions."

"They were few enough," said Nora, with a look of
amusement, perfectly incomprehensible to Torp; "but,
however I might have valued them at one time of my life,
they became in later years perfectly worthless, and at last
equally disagreeable and troublesome."

"And,"—half soliloquised Torp, while he diligently drew
lines in the gravel with the iron point of his mountain
staff,—"and Harry fancied—supposed—no matter what!"

"No matter indeed," she rejoined; "he never did anything that could lead to a supposition that he really cared
for me, and scrupulously avoided all professions of a regard
which he would have been half ashamed to confess for any
one bearing the hated name of Nixon! His indifference
caused me, however, no unhappiness, for experience has
taught me not to waste a thought, still less a particle of affection, on any one, until he has said in the most unequivo-
cal manner, 'I like', or 'I love you'."

"Then pray waste, or rather bestow a thought on me
now, Miss Nixon," said Torp, "for, from my soul, I love
you!"

"You!" cried Nora, sitting upright, in unfeigned astonishment, and roused as much as he could possibly have expected. "You—surely you are jesting!"

"By no means. I wish to tell you, as unequivocally as you
can desire, that I love you."

Nora was silent: she shaded her eyes with one of her
hands, to hide the surprise that at first overpowered every
other feeling. Then came a confused recollection of her
long-cherished resentment towards the man who now

stood beside her, and of her ardent longing for an opportunity of making him suffer mortification such as he had
caused her ten years previously; but, instead of seizing the
offered opportunity of revenge with the eagerness that she
had expected, she perceived that a more Christian-like feeling had replaced her previous animosity, and before long
she found herself considering how she could best explain,
that though she no longer *dis*liked, she had not yet learned
to like him. She looked up at last, and perceived him leaning against the side of the grotto, awaiting her answer with
an air of such cool self-command, such calm confidence in
the result of her meditations, that her pride instantly took
alarm. He had so evidently misunderstood the cause of her
silence, that she was provoked with herself for having felt
anxious to spare his feelings, and consequently made no
effort to conceal her mirth when he observed, "You are
even more astonished than I expected, Miss Nixon; but I
hope for an answer nevertheless."

"An answer to what?" she asked, with admirable composure.

"I did not think you could be so malicious," said Torp,
good-humouredly. "What I have said can hardly be misunderstood, but if you require time to consider, or wish to
consult your family, say so: I can wait."

"I have no doubt of that," replied Nora, smiling archly.
"You are a perfect personification of patience at this moment."

Torp knew too much of women to augur well from such
complete self-possession on her part; he bit his lip and coloured, as the conviction flashed across his mind that if she
accepted him it would be for his coronet and fortune, and
not at all for himself.

"I require no time to consider," she continued, "nor is it
necessary for me to consult my family. Let me rather rec-

ommend you to forget what you have just said, while re-
minding you that, like your brother ten years ago, you are
proposing to 'make an egregious fool of yourself'."

"Perhaps so," answered Torp, "but—I love you!"

"Have you forgotten all your resolutions to avoid 'these
people,' as you called us?" continued Nora. "Have you considered the 'odious connection'?"

"Yes," he answered, without hesitation, "but—I love
you!"

"Has the possibility," said Nora, "just the mere possibility, never occurred to you, that your love might not be returned?"

"I have thought of that, too, Miss Nixon, and as Mr
Torp, or even Charles Thorpe, I should hardly have ventured to indulge a hope of a favourable hearing. When I
spoke, my reliance was placed quite as much, and now, I
regret to say, rests altogether, on what I have to offer with
myself, rather than on myself personally."

"I understand you, Lord Medway; but your rank will
have quite as little influence on me as my fortune on you."

"Had fortune been an object to me," said Torp, somewhat loftily, "I should have reserved, if not my heart, certainly the offer of my hand, for the sister of my friend and
relation, Harry Darwin."

"You have unconsciously done what you have just said,"
she rejoined, quietly, "for—I am Harry's sister Leonora."

Torp's start, and but half-suppressed exclamation of surprise, attracted the attention of Rosel, whose presence had
been less heeded than that of a child by either of them.
They knew that the girl, with all her intelligence, was to all
intents and purposes made deaf and dumb when listening
to a language unknown to her; and so low and calm had
been the voices of the speakers, so unruffled the manner of
both, that she had, until that moment, supposed them to be

discussing some topic devoid of all personal interest. She looked up just as Torp was saying, "So you are Leonora—half a Thorpe—and my cousin in spite of yourself? If I had not been impenetrably stupid, I might have guessed it the first day we met! And your dislike to me," he added, seating himself at the opposite side of the fountain—"your dislike to me originated in my interference with Medway's plans ten years ago—of course?"

"His plans were unknown to me," replied Nora; "but you may remember that at your instigation I was expelled your mother's house in a manner that was neither kind nor considerate. Without being consulted, or given the friendly advice to write to my nearer relations, I was forced upon them—sent to an uncle prejudiced against me, not only by my evident wish to ignore him, but still more by a letter from you, representing my at worst thoughtless conduct in a manner that threw upon me all the opprobrium of a detected intriguante."

"My mother—my sisters—" began Torp, and then stopped, evidently unwilling to excuse himself at their expense.

"I can now understand their anxiety and fears," she continued, "and forgive them and you for wishing to get rid of me. It is the recollection of the way in which I was dismissed, and the discovery of your traducing letter, which even after a lapse of ten years forced tears of indignation from my eyes, that still has power to mortify and pain me."

"You probably found this letter among your uncle's papers?" observed Torp, without looking up.

"Yes."

"And have preserved it as an antidote to any kind feelings you might ever be disposed to entertain for me?"

Nora did not answer; he had made a good guess.

"I had altogether forgotten having written a letter of

such offensive purport," he observed, after a pause. "My only consolation is, that by it, or through me, you have become one of the richest heiresses in England. I have, in fact, been the means of procuring you a brilliant lot in life, and greatly promoting your happiness."

"How can you tell?" said Nora, in a low, and rather melancholy voice; "wealth brings with it duties, unknown to, unthought of, by the poor. The responsibility is great, for to whom much is given, from them will much be required: a few thousand pounds would perhaps have made me happier."

"My thoughts were less Christian-like," said Torp, dryly; "I alluded to your almost unlimited choice in marriage."

"I do not intend to marry."

He looked up, and smiled incredulously.

"Do not misunderstand me," she continued, quietly; "I have made no rash vows; but I cannot forget that during the best years of my life, among those who loved, or fancied they loved me, not one had resolution or devotion enough to overcome the obstacles to a union with me—not one had the courage to pronounce the word marriage to a penniless orphan. That it is otherwise now, can be attributed to but one motive—and that is not flattering to my self-love."

"Far be it from me to undertake a defence of the motives of those who may hereafter aspire to the heart and hand you have just refused me," said Torp; "but if ever a man loved disinterestedly, and was made, by downright earnest devotion, to overlook all obstacles and conquer all his strongest prejudices, I am—I mean I *was*—that man, Leonora, when, believing you to be the daughter of Gilbert Nixon, I proposed to—" he paused, embarrassed by a deep blush that seemed to pass like a shadow over Nora's face.

"The effort was great, no doubt," she said, calmly; "and

it was unpardonable my not feeling as much flattered as surprised on this occasion."

"You are severe," said Torp; "but I have no hesitation in confessing that my struggles between passion and prudence have been great. Had I known who you really were sooner, I should have been spared, if not the pain, certainly the mortification, that I now feel, for nothing would ever have induced me to confess to Leonora, the heiress, that I loved her."

"Of that I am quite convinced," said Nora; "for my brother informed me before he left Munich, that you had already, in a gentlemanly manner, objected to my paternal connections, and declined my—fortune."

"So you have heard that too!" cried Torp; "then, indeed, I have nothing more to hope—the letter might have been forgiven—but this offence is, I know, unpardonable."

"You are mistaken," said Nora; "though I had the weakness to feel angry, for a few minutes, at having been so carelessly offered, and cavalierly rejected, I soon perceived that, under the circumstances, you could scarcely have spoken otherwise. I have also not the slightest doubt that had you known me to be Harry's sister, you would not only *not* have acknowledged liking me, but would even have *dis*liked me as cordially as—"

"As you do me," said Torp.

"No," she answered; "I believe I can now say that I have ceased to dislike you, and must confess that my ten years' resentment was wrong and unchristian-like. And now, Lord Medway—"

"Don't call me Lord Medway."

"Mr Torp."

"Nor Mr Torp: for you, I am henceforward neither."

"Do you not wish to preserve your incognito?"

"To others—yes—but when we are alone I expect you

to remember our relationship."

"I have had time to forget it," she rejoined, with some bitterness.

"You have had the same time to forget the offences of Charles Thorpe. Come, Leonora, be indeed a Christian, and tell me you forgive my having prevented you from taking the name of Medway ten years ago."

"That," said Nora, "I can easily forgive, for I never formed any plan of the kind."

"I believe you; but my mother," said Torp, musingly, and as if speaking his thoughts, "my mother said—and says still—that had you remained with her, Medway would have married you."

"It is not improbable," rejoined Nora; "for I will not attempt to deny that rank and fortune might, at that time, have tempted me in a manner they cannot do now. It was fortunate that she foresaw, and you prevented, so odious a connection—so terrible a *mésalliance!*"

"You do not understand me," explained Torp, with heightened colour; "no girl of sixteen could have been a proper match for Medway, who was so notoriously unsteady that our anxiety about him only ended with his life."

"Ah, you took that into consideration," said Nora, with pitiless irony; "perhaps also my foreign education, on which you enlarged so eloquently in your letter to my uncle? I now perceive plainly that all I heard of your intellect and discrimination during my short stay at The Willows was true, and—if then so profoundly calculating and discreet, what must you be now?"

"A patient target for the arrows of your sarcasm," answered Torp, hiding his intense mortification under an appearance of humility. "But I do not wish you to spare me, or be merciful; on the contrary, the best service you can now render me is to scoff and laugh at me to your heart's content. I will even give you fresh subject for mirth, by confessing that poor Medway himself could not have fallen more desperately and irretrievably in love, or become more extravagantly infatuated, than I have been ever since that unlucky evening at the fisherman's cottage! You see in me, Leonora, a contemptible spooney, whose chief employment of late has been to prowl about by day, in order to catch an occasional glimpse of your grey silk dress, and to wander before the forest-house by night, for the still rarer, and less satisfactory vision, of a shadow passing occasionally across the muslin curtain of a dimly-lighted window!"

What effect this speech produced on Nora, Torp had not time to ascertain, for at that moment he heard his name loudly called.

"Waldemar!" he exclaimed, rising from his lowly seat. "What has brought him here to-day?"

Waldemar, already close to them, was quite prepared to answer this question. He had been out hunting since day-break, had breakfasted at St Hubert's, heard there, by chance, of the party about to assemble at the miller's alp, and had crossed the Rocky Horn, in order to return to the village in the exhilarating society of his friend and Mees Nora, if she would permit it!

He sat down deliberately in the place previously occupied by Torp, and while filling a glass with water, and informing the latter that St Benedict's would soon be the scene of festivities, such as had never been dreamed of within its monastic precincts, his eyes were fixed on Nora with the thoughtful, studious, keen, yet by no means offensive, artistic stare, that had in a manner become habitual to him. She did not move until the well-known sketch-book was drawn from his pocket, and he entreated, "For the sake of all the nymphs that ever guarded fountains, rest on that rock ten minutes longer, Mees Nora; I would give anything for your head, with that green chaplet, and such wondrous light as we have at this moment!"

"I cannot sit for my picture just now," she replied, rising, "for by this time my guests are probably waiting for me at the hut." Then throwing the much-admired chaplet on the ground, and taking her hat from Rosel, she placed the latter carelessly on her head, and began a descent to the alp.

Waldemar sprang after her, and Torp was left alone beside the fountain. He looked after them as long as they were within sight, then resumed his seat, raising Nora's chaplet from the ground, and, while holding it in his hand, fell into a reverie of the most absorbing description. More than half an hour elapsed before he roused himself, as if from a deep sleep, and perceived that he had unconsciously encircled his wrists with the beech-leaf chain, as if he had intended to try its strength. He smiled somewhat grimly, as the fragile fetter yielded to the first slight movement of his hands; but the force he afterwards employed to fling it far away among the moss-covered rocks above the spring, must have received an impetus from some peculiarly irritating thought, for it was sufficient to have hurled to a much greater distance a stone of no common weight or dimensions.

CHAPTER XXXVIII

Pastoral Pleasures

MEANTIME Nora met Michael coming towards the spring, to inform her that "the old gentleman and the young lady were at the alp, and that the miller's daughter was with them, and was making coffee for them." She hurried forward, and found her uncle, a good deal overheated and tired, sitting on the bench outside the hut, while the flounces of Georgina's dress completely filled up the adjacent doorway, which formed a very rustic frame to so fashionable a figure.

"Nora," began Mr Nixon, "the gravel walk thus talked of was not what we expected. Georgy stuck in the mud, and stumbled on the rocks—"

"Oh, never mind Georgy," said Nora; "I was only afraid the excursion would be too much for you. Don't you think you had better sit inside the hut for a little while, that you may not catch cold?"

"The kitchen smokes," said Mr Nixon, "and the draught inside is more likely to give a cold than preserve one from it. This is no doubt a very picturesque and pleasant sort of place for people of a poetical turn of mind, Nora, but give me English gravel walks, and English shrubberies, and, above all, an English dairy! The girl there without stockings brought me a roll of butter weighing at least six pounds, and a loaf of bread as black as my boots, to stay my stomach until the coffee was made."

"I am glad you came here of your own accord," said Nora, as she began to unpack Michael's bag of provisions, and placed its contents on the bench beside him. "The enjoyment of excursions of this description is only to be acquired by degrees; and I am afraid you feel the discomforts, without having become conscious of the beauties of scenery that recompense most people for the toil of making their way to such a place as this."

"Well, as to the beauties you talk of," said Mr Nixon, testily, "I think the higher we got, the less we saw of them. At first we passed some whitewashed cottages, that looked astonishingly clean and comfortable, and with apple and damson trees in the orchards about them so overloaded with fruit that the branches were propped up in all directions—very creditable trees indeed—I was surprised to see them. Then we got upon a path covered with large stones —I tell you, Nora—each as big as a man's fist, and so round, that there was no such thing as walking on them without assistance. I took the arm of the fellow you engaged to guide us, and Georgy was right glad to cling to the miller's daughter—an uncommon handsome girl, that Madeleine Miller, or Miller Madeleine, as they call her, and full of fun, too—had her jokes all the way up the mountain with our man—I couldn't understand a word she said, nor Georgy either—stupid of Georgy, after all the lessons she has had from the captain."

"Very stupid," acquiesced Nora, not in the least knowing what he had said, and thinking only of the knives and forks, that she had just discovered had been forgotten. Waldemar instantly perceived her embarrassment, and suddenly appeared so interested in Mr Nixon's recital, that the latter turned completely to him, and continued:—

"Well, sir, this path brought us along one of your mountain streams—rocks, sir—nothing but rocks and pools of remarkably green water—they say that trout are to be found in them, to the weight of half a pound and more, but I hadn't my rod, that is, the captain's—so we only stopped occasionally to rest. It was an exceedingly wild, uncultivated place, altogether nothing but stone, and water, and woods without end; I could not help thinking it would be better if the land about here were more cultivated—but I don't venture to give an opinion, as I understand too little of such matters. We manage these things differently in England, however, and I only wish you could hear one of our agriculturists talk!"

"I am sure I should be very happy to do so," answered Waldemar.

"Everything seems to me on so small a scale here," continued Mr Nixon, waving his hand; "for instance, this dairy here—what are a couple of firkins of butter, and thirty or forty cheeses?"

"Very true," said Waldemar, "but it is enough for the miller's family and workmen, and I have even heard that they sell cheese and butter occasionally."

"Now, our farmers—" began Mr Nixon.

"Excuse me," said Waldemar; "the miller is not a farmer, he is a proprietor, and so are all the peasants about here. They have had the right of pasturage, and been in possession of their land, for upwards of three hundred years."

"Bless me!" cried Mr Nixon, suddenly struck with respect for the peasant proprietors, "quite what we call old families in England!"

"Quite *respectable*," said Waldemar, laughing; "that is the English word for it, I believe: but they are not what you call rich—quite the contrary; in fact, having only just enough to live upon, and supplying themselves with clothes and a few luxuries by the sale of overplus cattle, butter, or cheese, and in the mountain districts by charcoal-burning and forest work."

"But—aw," said Mr Nixon, "in England we should have roads through our forests, and here, what they call a wood-path is sometimes like a flight of steps in the rocks, or a mere clearance of trees, where one sinks ankle-deep in mud, or stumbles over projecting roots, or, worse than all, when a road is formed by the trunks of trees laid side by side."

"That is only when there are springs," observed Waldemar.

"That's the reason they were so slippery," cried Mr Nixon, "and either covered with green and brown slimy plants, or else the bark had peeled off, so that it was almost impossible to walk on them. I am convinced that no horse—"

"No horse ever trod them," said Waldemar; "they are only used for sledging in winter."

Nora left them just as he began an explanation which she foresaw would give him some trouble, as there were no English words for many of the commonest expressions of the foresters. His endeavours to make himself intelligible would have amused her at any other time, but she was not at all disposed to be amused just then,—she wished to be alone, and feared that hours might elapse before she could hope for undisturbed solitude. In the kitchen she found Madeleine jesting and laughing with the two guides, and, less charitably disposed than usual, she condemned her as a heartless coquette, not worthy the commiseration she had felt for her, or the regard of such a man as the forester's son.

Nora was unusually severe in her judgment on this occasion. She was not quite satisfied with herself, consequently more than usually disposed to find fault with others. The momentary triumph she had felt in showing Torp her indifference to himself, his rank, fortune, and family, had passed away, and given place to the conviction that she never had been, and never would be so devotedly and disinterestedly loved as by him, and that she had thrown away the only and very singular chance that was now ever likely to present itself of being chosen for herself alone. She had little doubt that she might have refused his proposal, and at the same time have secured him as a friend, and regretted the few bitter ironical words that had perhaps made him her enemy for life.

As soon as Georgina had perceived Waldemar advancing towards the hut with Nora, she had retreated to the sennerin's little sleeping-room, in order to arrange her hair and dress, for she was one of those women whose anxiety to please, and desire for the admiration of men, are insatiable. Never for one moment did she forget herself or her appearance, or cease to watch the impression she made on those around her, quite unconscious of the sacrifice of time, thought, and comfort she was making for most thankless observers, and the actual loss of pleasure, and perhaps profit, incurred by not bestowing her attention on others. She called Nora, and saw with wonder that her dress was looped up by an india-rubber girdle, so as to display, without reserve, a pair of thick-soled leather boots, made by the village shoemaker; while her straw hat, anything but improved in form by the various rents made in it, and the branches of trees with which it had lately come in contact, was pressed down on her forehead in a manner that proved how little her personal appearance occupied her mind.

"Well, Nora," she exclaimed, "I never saw such a figure as you have made yourself! I declare if you had not got such a lovely colour from your walk, you would not be fit to be looked at. For my part, I am so excessively tired and heated, and, as you see, so dreadfully flushed, that I cannot think of showing myself to Count Waldemar! It is incomprehensible to me what pleasure you can find in trudging through mud, and stumbling over stones to places such as this!"

"A few years hence you will think and speak differently," said Nora.

"Oh, never! I have no objection to these mountains—rather like them, in fact, for scenery—but they should be viewed from their basis or at a distance."

"Wait until you have resided some time at St Benedict's," said Nora, "and when I come to see you here you will be as proud of your alps and mountains as I could desire, and will force every one to visit them who visits you."

Georgina shook her head, and began to toss about the clothes of the sennerin, which were placed on a shelf behind the door.

"Why are you crumpling the poor girl's Sunday dress?" asked Nora.

"I am looking for a—a—oh, here it is!" and she pulled forth a few inches square of looking-glass, backed and framed with paper, that appeared to have already been in service on the walls of a room, and having placed it against the window, began to arrange her hair.

"You have completely spoiled the folds of the apron," said Nora, vainly endeavouring to set to rights the humble habiliments.

"No great matter," said Georgina, "if it belong to that creature who looks like a man in petticoats. The bodice lying there beneath the apron would fit a heavy dragoon. Such a waist as that girl's, and such feet, I never beheld: it is worth your while to go to the cow-house to look at her, as a matter of curiosity."

"I am going there at all events," said Nora, "as I intend to purchase some of the cows."

"I perceive," continued Georgina, "that Captain Falkner was jesting when he talked of the pleasures of an alpine party."

"Not at all," said Nora, "I am sure he was serious."

"He tried to look so, at all events," rejoined Georgina, "and made me suppose I should see a miniature Swiss châlet, where I have found a smoky cabin—and find a picturesque, ideal-looking girl in a smart costume, ready to offer glasses of thick cream and pats of fresh butter to everybody—instead of which a female grenadier came to welcome us, and afterwards stalked about with her bare legs, and but very slightly prolonged kilt, carrying a calf as if it were a baby, and slapping and fondling her cows and bulls as if they were children! and then, Nora, this *ranz des vaches* —this yoddal or yoodel, or whatever they call it—is—is something very trying to the nerves—something between a yell and a screech I think—and perfectly stunning."

"Captain Falkner will not like to hear you talk in this way," said Nora, smiling; "remember his father is a Bavarian highlander, and his mother a Tyrolean."

"I can't admire this yoodel," replied Georgina, "and must say the whooping and hallooing of our guide and the miller's daughter, as we came up the mountain, were perfectly deafening, though they thought they were making themselves particularly agreeable to us."

"I have no doubt of it," said Nora, " especially if there were an echo."

"They were frequently answered," said Georgina, "and quite distinctly, by people at a great distance, whom we could not see."

"And you found nothing pleasant—nothing exhilarating in that?"

"Not particularly—the distant shouts were less disagreeable, certainly, and to the echoes I should not have objected, if the piercing sounds that roused them had not had their origin so close to my ears."

Nora opened the door into the kitchen, and they saw the guides sitting on one side of the hearth, eating brown bread and milk from a yellow earthen pan, placed between them. As they looked up and exhibited their moustaches deeply fringed with cream, Nora gravely, in the German fashion, wished them "a good appetite," and was ceremoniously thanked by them in return, before she entered the cow-house, the door into which was open to admit of a conversation being carried on between the miller's daughter and the sennerin.

The cattle had returned to the hut for shade during the heat at noon, and were now lying on the ground ruminating, while a couple of goats trotted about restlessly, and, with the familiarity for which they are remarkable, immediately approached Nora, and commenced nibbling the flowers and grasses she had collected with some trouble during her passage over the Rocky Horn. She was unconscious of their depredations, unobservant of the occupation of the sennerin, unheedful of the loud dialogue carried on so close to her, although she stood between the speakers, for she was in thought once more at the spring, and Torp was again telling her how he had wandered about the inn and forest-house by day and night, and how, in spite of all she could say, he loved her. And she wished that Waldemar had not interrupted them, and that she had had time to remove the unpleasant impression which her last speech must have made on him.

The audacity of the goats at length attracted her attention, for one of them had mounted on some wood piled up near her, and was, with unparalleled impudence, tearing the floral decorations from her hat, so that, in order to put it and herself out of reach, she walked through the cow-house to the entrance used by the cattle, and having opened the door, began to meditate a visit to one of the other huts. That which belonged to a Tyrolean was separated from the miller's by a sort of gap or chasm in the mountain, apparently more wide than deep, for in it the roof of a third châlet was visible. The huts were, however, unusually far apart; and had not Nora had a remarkably good sight, she would not have been able to recognise Torp, as he stood at the door of the most distant one, with the sennerin, and moved his arms as if asking the names of the mountains around them, so, at least, she at first supposed; but she soon after came to the conclusion that he had been trying to find out a way to the village which would not oblige him to pass the hut then occupied by her and her relations, for he advanced a short way—stopped—seemed to speak to the woman, who, shading her eyes from the sun with one arm, pointed with the other to the ravine, and a moment after Nora saw him spring down the rocks and disappear.

"He is offended—deeply offended," she thought, "and not altogether without reason. Yet I do believe I should have had more forbearance, or, at least, been less vindictive, had he not provoked me beyond endurance by looking so proudly confident. After all, I was not so much to blame, and there is no use in thinking any more about the matter."

But she did think of it, and of him, so incessantly that her recollections of what afterwards occurred that day on the alp were never very clear. She remembered that Captain Falkner had joined them, that Georgina's discontent had vanished with marvellous celerity, so that she had laughed and enjoyed everything, especially her father's dismay when he had been obliged to drink his coffee out of something resembling a slop-basin. She also recollected that her uncle had monopolised Waldemar, and, with what he considered British frankness, had informed him that in England people considered most of the German nobility little better than tinkers and tailors, notwithstanding their stunning genealogies, and that, for his part, without boasting, he believed he could say there were few counts or barons that he could not buy "out-and-out."

"Provided they chose to sell," had been Waldemar's reply, and his forbearance had only increased Nora's annoyance.

In short, the events of the day had made an unpleasant impression on her, that remained even after she returned to the village, and induced her to refuse to take any part in the introductions and visitings which immediately commenced between the Falkner and Nixon families.

It was on this evening that the long-expected tombstone arrived from Munich, and was placed in the churchyard to be ready for erection the ensuing day. Mr Nixon and Georgina had neither time nor inclination to inspect it,—they were sure it was "all right,"—were very glad of its arrival, as they would now be at liberty to leave or stay at the village as they pleased,—they hoped Nora would accept the invitation to dine at St Benedict's the next day—she surely did not intend to spend the whole of it in the churchyard?

Yes; such was Nora's intention, and so absorbing the interest she felt on the occasion, that she did not even turn round, the ensuing day, when the carriage containing Waldemar's family passed, at no great distance, on the road to St Benedict's. There was also a second carriage, in which she might have seen the friend of her childhood, the Countess Schaumberg; but Nora had no thoughts just then beyond the marble monument, beside which she had taken her post. Even late in the afternoon, after the workmen had left the churchyard, she lingered at the gate, waiting for the wreath of dahlias and the festoons of ivy that Rosel was to bring her, and with which she intended to decorate the tombstone, for the first time, with her own hands.

And Rosel came, and the wreath was carefully deposited on some sculptured ornaments that seemed to have been made for the purpose, as Arthur had himself observed; the festoons were afterwards arranged, and then they withdrew to a little distance to judge of the effect.

"The tombstone is handsome, but very simple," said Nora, musingly. "Had he not chosen it himself I should hardly have been satisfied with it, although a more ornamented one would perhaps be misplaced in a village churchyard like this."

"That's true," said Rosel, eagerly; "it is the handsomest here, and with the fresh wreath that shall never fail, it will attract everybody's attention, and will show that *he* was honoured who lies beneath the sod, and that his grave is cared for, as the graves of those we have loved in life should be."

The workmen had trampled the grass away, and scattered stones and gravel round the tombstone.

"We must get fresh earth, Rosel," said Nora, "and some plants that will look well on All Saints' Day. I believe I should like a border of those dark-coloured pensées that you have in your garden, and some violets—I think—I am sure he must have liked violets."

CHAPTER XXXIX

Treats of Different Kinds of Love

NORA waited at the inn to see her uncle and Georgina, on their return from St Benedict's. "Well, Nora," exclaimed the latter, "who do you suppose Mr Torp turns out to be? No less a person than Lord Medway! What do you think of that?"

"Nothing," answered Nora: "he told me so himself the day before yesterday."

"And this tombstone, of course, made you forget all about it. Did he condescend to acknowledge your relationship?"

"After a manner—yes," replied Nora.

"To us he was grandly polite, but had evidently not forgotten our remarks in the garden. He made no inquiries about you, though people spoke both of you and your tombstone, at dinner, as the cause, they called it the fortunate cause, of our coming to, and remaining in the village."

"I suppose you were introduced to the Countess Schaumberg?" said Nora.

"Yes; she came just before dinner, but found time to make a most elaborate toilet. His lordship seemed rather on flirting terms with her; but Captain Falkner told me they are old Vienna acquaintances, and that she is, in fact, attached to Count Waldemar, to whom her husband was related, and who is guardian to her little daughter."

"Do you not think her very beautiful?" asked Nora.

"Not exactly; but she is handsome, and graceful, and dresses well, and is decidedly a very fashionable personage. Captain Falkner told me she is the best shot at a target, and the keenest sportswoman he ever saw; and I heard her myself talking of duck-shooting to Lord Medway and Count Waldemar."

"And her child?" asked Nora.

"A little fair-haired doll, that speaks better French than German, and shows her affection for Count Waldemar in the most open manner. But I thought, Nora, you would be more anxious to hear of my future relatives than these people."

"Of course I expect to hear all about them too," said Nora.

"The general you have seen," continued Georgina; "he is charming. I like him almost as well as Ernst—that is Captain Falkner, you know."

"No, I did not know it," said Nora, laughing, "but go on."

"Madame de Falkner is rather proud, I suspect; she is related to the Benndorffs, and through them to the Schaumbergs: they are all second or third cousins to each other."

"I consider that scarcely a relationship," observed Nora.

"They think otherwise," said Georgina; "and it was pleasant to see them so intimate and friendly with each other, though it made papa and me feel rather isolated."

"My uncle must have felt so, at all events," said Nora. "How did he contrive to make himself understood by people who probably only spoke French or German?"

"Some of them spoke a little English, and Ernst was very attentive, and acted as interpreter between him and the general for more than an hour. If Lord Medway had only been a little more civil, or rather a little less haughty, we should have got on famously."

"You surely did not want any notice from him at St Benedict's?" said Nora.

"Yes, dear, we should have liked it, and he knew it too, for papa spoke to him across the dinner-table, to show at least that he knew something of him and his connections, and even mentioned that Arthur, whose grave was in the village churchyard, had married into the Medway family. But what was the use of all that?—nobody understood what papa was saying, while they all saw the air of cold civility with which Lord Medway bowed his answers, for he seldom deigned to speak. You know what I mean, Nora?"

"Perfectly. It would have been better if my uncle had taken no notice of him whatever."

"Perhaps so," said Georgina; "but he is evidently a friend of the Benndorffs, and it seems the Falkners have taken an immense fancy to him. I heard Ernst's quiet little sister Charlotte calling him 'Ce charmant milord;' and, oh, Nora! if you had only seen him beside the Countess Schaumberg, looking so very *distingué* and handsome, and evidently liked by every one but ourselves, you would have regretted, as we did, having neglected the opportunity of making his acquaintance when he was supposed to be only a Mr Torp."

"I don't think I should," said Nora, "nor need you. He showed us too plainly that he did not want to know us; his manners remain the same, and the change is only in you and my uncle."

"Perhaps you are right," said Georgina, thoughtfully. "Count Waldemar was such a contrast!"

"He always has been," rejoined Nora.

"I wish he was not likely to be married to that Countess Schaumberg."

"Why so?"

"Because I think he has rather a fancy for you. The description he gave of your appearance, as you sat beside some spring near the miller's alp, was quite romantic, and attracted the attention of the countess, though Lord Medway was speaking to her, and looking at her in a way of which your acquaintance with him cannot enable you to form the slightest idea."

"And a—I dare say he was not particularly pleased at the interruption," observed Nora, wishing to hear more, but unwilling to ask in direct terms.

"I should have thought him downright angry, he grew so suddenly red, and afterwards so pale," she answered; "but I must have been mistaken, for when Count Waldemar appealed to him for corroboration of what he had said, he declared you were charming at all times, and in all places— at a spring or on an alp, in a wood or on a cart, but most of all when dressed as a peasant, after having been exposed for hours to any quantity of hail or rain that could be imagined! The countess understood him better than I did, and said she had heard of all that from Waldemar. I think some way she supposes you my sister, and Lord Medway did not take the trouble, or did not choose to explain—probably fearing the necessity of acknowledging a connection with our family. I wonder what he will do when you appear with us tomorrow at St Benedict's?"

"I don't mean to go."

"You must, for my betrothal is to take place, and we are to see Mademoiselle de Falkner's trousseau, and there is to be a ball in the evening, to which all the people in the neighbourhood have been invited a week ago."

"These gaieties," observed Nora, "will scarcely give you time to become acquainted with your future sister-in-law."

"Time and opportunity enough when we have joined our regiment," answered Georgina, laughing. "The most important thing to be considered now is our dress; she has asked me to be bridesmaid, and I intend to wear white with blue flowers and ribbons; white and blue are the Bavarian colours, you know—so I shall be quite national. But that is for the wedding, which is to take place the day after to-morrow; at the ball, I think, I shall appear in rose colour—it becomes me, and looks well at night. I hope you intend to lay aside your eternal half-mourning on this occasion."

"Ask Mrs Nesbitt what she has got for me," answered Nora. "When I call here on my way into the town to-morrow morning, you can let me know the result of your consultation."

"And what on earth takes you into the town to-morrow to tire and heat yourself, when you have a dinner and ball in prospect?"

"I wish to complete the purchase of the mill, and have a deed of gift drawn up, so that I can bestow it on Rosel whenever you and my uncle wish to leave the village. I have no excuse for detaining you here any longer."

"We shall now have to request you to remain here on our account," said Georgina; "but only until Captain Falkner's leave expires. He goes with us to Vienna, thence to his regiment, in order to give me time to collect one of these extensive German trousseaux, and then—"

"And then," said Nora, "you will ask *me* to be bridesmaid."

"I suppose so," answered Georgina, smiling; "and you will be the only one, if that tends to increase the honour and glory. Had Captain Falkner had time to come to England, we could have been married in good style, with bridesmaids and breakfast,—whereas now—"

"Now," said Nora, "you will be married in a quiet, unostentatious sort of way, that I should think infinitely preferable."

"There are some people at home I should have liked to have invited," said Georgina, pensively; "and a tour on the continent would have been pleasanter than joining a regiment in country quarters, where one's new dresses are superfluous."

"Ah! I had forgotten to take the dresses into consideration," said Nora.

"I have taken everything into consideration," continued Georgina; "and shall even avoid all unnecessary delay at Vienna for the purpose of—Can you guess?"

"No."

"For the purpose of being married before your brother."

"Georgina! Is it possible that anger or pique has in any way influenced—"

"Oh, not at all," said Georgina, interrupting her; "but I confess that I wish to be married before he is; and rejoice to think we shall not meet for years—if ever!"

"You must have had an odd kind of regard for him," observed Nora, musingly.

"Rather say a very common kind," rejoined Georgina. "It was made up of personal admiration, vanity, ambition, and interest; and would have borne test as well as that of Lady Jane's, which is probably of the same nature, with this difference—that I was more grateful for his notice, and more flattered by his preference, than she can possibly be."

"It seems to me," said Nora, "as if, even ten years ago, Lady Medway intended to make him her son-in-law in the course of time. He was evidently considered one of the family,—his picture hung up with those of her own children; and, even at The Willows, there was Harry's room, and Harry's cab, and Harry's wherry! They made me for some time suppose him a very important person."

"He has been so to me for many years," said Georgina; "but you need not tell him so, Nora,—there is no necessity for making him vainer than he is,—he would be capable of supposing I married Captain Falkner in a fit of despair; whereas I am merely glad that he will read of my marriage in the newspaper before his own takes place—he said Christmas to you, did he not?"

"I believe so," answered Nora, putting on her hat, as she perceived, from the window, that the forester and his son were standing at the garden-gate, waiting to accompany her to the forest-house. "I believe so; but I should think it matters little to you now who or when he marries."

As Nora stood with Rosel on the balcony of the forest-house that night, she was unusually silent, and looked so intently upwards towards the stars, that the latter, for some time, supposed her to be praying, and forbore to interrupt her. It was not until the glistening, dark eyes began to wander along the stream, and towards the road, that Rosel approached, and said, timidly, "Miss Nora, I have a request to make—a great favour to ask of you."

"What is it, Rosel? You are not likely to ask anything that I ought to refuse."

"It is hard, very hard, to explain. I am afraid you will think me presumptuous,—I—I cannot—dare not—say it."

"Then I have made you fear more than like me."

"No, no,—I do not fear you—I only fear you will think it unseemly in me, taking it quite for granted that you will put me in possession of the mountain-mill."

"By no means, Rosel. I am to see the judge, by appointment, to-morrow, and shall only, as you requested me, delay the gift until you have performed your vow in the chapel of St Hubert. If you wish to be in possession sooner, you have but to say so."

"On no account, dear Miss Nora—on no account," cried Rosel, eagerly; "nothing was further from my thoughts than that—I meant quite the contrary."

"You must speak more intelligibly, Rosel, if you expect me to understand you."

"I will—I will tell you everything, Miss Nora: my father said yesterday, that the—the wild hunters had been out again."

"When? where?" cried Nora, anxiously.

"On the frontiers—not far from the miller's alp."

"And your father?" said Nora.

"Was out last night, Miss Nora; but they had gone back into Tyrol. He came home by the alp to see if Seppel were there."

"And found him at work, I hope?"

"Yes,—but he said, if it had been a Saturday, and Seppel free, he would not easily have been persuaded that he had not been out for an hour or so. Now, Miss Nora, the wild hunters *may* cross the frontiers of a Saturday or Sunday night, and Seppel *may* be again suspected."

"That is," said Nora, "you cannot quite trust him, and think he may be led into temptation where he now is."

"Not so," cried Rosel; "he was not on the Wild Alp that unlucky morning."

Nora drummed a little on the balustrade of the balcony.

"He was *not*," persisted Rosel, "he swore he was not, and I believe him; neither will he join them now. But we have seen the consequences of his being suspected and not being able to clear himself, and that may happen again while he is going to or coming from the forest. I heard my father say, that if I were once in possession of the mill, and Seppel got into trouble again, he'd refuse his consent to our marriage; and he'd do it, Miss Nora, so great is his hatred of a wildschuetz—he'd do it, if he were on his deathbed, and refuse his blessing, too, if I did not promise to give up Seppel for ever—and what would the mill be to me without *him?* Oh, Miss Nora," she added, passionately, "give the mill to Seppel—put him in possession, and you will indeed secure our happiness."

"I understand you," said Nora; "you think your father less likely to entertain suspicions of Seppel the miller, than Seppel the wood-cleaver, and perhaps you are right—it is the way of the world; but it is not worldly-wise of you, Rosel, to resign everything to a man who is, as yet, nothing to you."

"Nothing to me!" exclaimed Rosel, "he is everything to me; and will not all that is his be mine?"

"It ought to be," said Nora, "especially every bit of his heart."

"Has been mine time out of mind," cried Rosel, confidently. "Dear Miss Nora, I see you understand me, and will grant my request."

"Of course," answered Nora, "I shall do what you tell me will best secure your happiness."

"And," continued Rosel, "all this may as well remain a secret between us, until we have been to the chapel at St Hubert's."

"As you please."

"My father might be angry with me, if he knew—" began Rosel.

"Very possibly," said Nora; "but he cannot dictate to me, and I shall do—what you wish."

"Thank you, oh, thank you!" cried Rosel. "Be assured that I shall never cease to pray for you, night and morning, as long as I live!"

"Do so," said Nora, extending her hand, "and begin at once. Good night!"

"How implicitly she trusts him—how thoroughly she identifies her welfare with his!" thought Nora. "This is love, genuine love, and not a compound of admiration, vanity, and interest, such as Georgina described. I wish I were quite convinced that this Seppel were worthy of her; but, after all, if she think him so, and continue as blind to his failings as hitherto, it is pretty much the same thing as far as she is concerned. I am not even quite sure that she does not like his very faults; she certainly does not love him less for having been a wild fellow and a wild hunter."

Nora entered her room, lit a candle, sat down beside the deal table on which she had placed it, and, drawing from her pocket the green leather note-book already mentioned, took from it Charles Thorpe's letter to her uncle, and was soon completely absorbed in its perusal, and the thoughts which it suggested.

And Torp—fortunately we are not obliged to follow the course of his thoughts after he left the spring. He loved like an Englishman, that is, earnestly and passionately; but being a strong-minded man, and proud withal, he had probably resolved to conquer an attachment so apparently hopeless. To judge by his actions, he considered stalking up and down his room the greater part of the night as the most efficacious mode of putting his intentions into practice. Waldemar had slept too soundly, after his long walk across the mountains, to observe his friend's intranquillity the first night of his return to the village, but on the second this was no longer the case; he had lounged about St Benedict's during the morning, had joined the family dinner-party, rowed the Countess Schaumberg on the lake afterwards, and smoked a cigar by moonlight with Torp. "All occupations," as he observed to his restless companion, when throwing open the door of communication between their rooms, "by no means calculated to make a man sleepy; therefore, if not disposed to rest, we may as well enjoy each other's society!" and then, with exaggerated politeness, he requested him to prolong his walk to the length of both rooms.

Torp complied, but his steady step shook the room, and

incommoded Waldemar, who, having turned over the leaves of his long-neglected portfolio, seemed now disposed, by the light of all the candles he could find, to add a new sketch to his collection. He looked up imploringly, then impatiently, and at last exclaimed, "I wish you'd be quiet, Torp, and sit down beside me as you used to do. Look here, I've been sketching something that, after what you said to-day at dinner, you will like to see, or I'm much mistaken."

He *was* mistaken. The sketch was Nora at the fountain, and Torp did not at all like to see it. "Now," he added, after a long pause, "when I have washed in a little colour to-morrow morning, I should like to know what you would give for this!"

"Nothing," said Torp; "I would not accept it if you offered it to me."

"You don't think it like!" cried Waldemar, throwing down his pencil, and holding the drawing at arm's length; "but wait until morning, and you will see it will be as good as any of the other sketches I have made of her, and they are not a few."

"It is already a good likeness," said Torp; " but I should prefer one of your landscapes, if you are disposed to be generous."

"No," replied Waldemar; "I still hope to be able to sell them to Mees Nora for a cup of coffee, though you must perceive I am rather avoiding her, according to your advice."

"I have not perceived any avoidance on your part," said Torp.

"What else do you call my leaving the village as I did, three weeks ago?"

"I call it going home when you were expected to do so, in order to meet a person to whom you have been all but engaged for nearly two years."

"Yes, but, my dear fellow, there is a great difference between all but, and actually engaged. I consider myself, to a certain extent, still free."

"I don't think you do, Waldemar."

"Quite as much as your cousin Darwin, who, at the end of six years, deserted this charming Mees Nora, in order to marry your no doubt equally charming sister, Lady Jane."

"Stay," cried Torp; "I must now inform you that my suppositions about *this* Miss Nixon were erroneous. It was the other one, Georgina I believe is her name, who was Harry's flame."

"I don't believe that," said Waldemar, laughing; "Darwin has better taste."

"You will believe it when I tell you that Nora, or, as we call her in our family, Leonora, is Harry's step-sister—you know his mother married again."

"Not I! I know nothing about these Nixons but what you have been pleased to tell me," said Waldemar, turning to Torp with a look of inquiry; and the latter then explained at some length, ending with the information that Nora had inherited an unusually large fortune from an uncle about a year previously.

"May I ask when and where you first discovered your relationship to this young lady?" asked Waldemar, fixing his keen eyes on the face of his companion.

"Then and there," answered Torp, placing his hand on the drawing that lay on the table between them.

"Upright as usual, Torp," said Waldemar, leaning back in his chair, and smiling. "I did you injustice for half a minute, and thought you had deceived me purposely on this occasion (all for my good, of course), but if you had I should never have forgiven you! Perhaps I ought also to confess that, when at home, it more than once flashed across my mind that you had wished to get rid of me, in order to have leisure to carry on a quiet flirtation with Mees Nora yourself. Now don't grow red, or be angry; the thought was natural enough, when I considered you were not the sort of man to pass nearly a month alone in a village of this kind, without some especial interest or occupation, and to my certain knowledge you had, during the whole time, only once been on the mountain with your rifle, and had had but little sport with your angle."

"Waldemar," said Torp, rising, "you wronged me by such a thought, for I advised you to avoid this temptation from pure friendship, and wish most sincerely I had gone with you, as you proposed, to Herrenburg. I remained here in the most perfect state of imaginary security, at first, then had to struggle hard with what I considered a mere passing fancy for this wayward girl, and finally yielded to a passion that more resembled infatuation than anything else. In short, I have been guilty of every imaginable absurdity."

"Am I to understand that, supposing her the daughter of this Gilbert, you—" Waldemar's open eyes and mouth finished the question.

"Understand that I have done everything that is rash and inconsistent."

"And is it possible that, knowing who you were, she actually—?"

"Actually refused and laughed at me," said Torp; "and I am glad she laughed, for otherwise I might have been tempted to try and make her like me; whereas now I shall just remain here long enough to convince her that I can live without her, and then she may bestow herself and her fortune on whomsoever she pleases."

"Oh, that's the way of it—is it?" said Waldemar, first glancing at the flushed countenance of his friend, and then bending over his drawing.

Torp strode up and down the room with folded arms, until a succession of odd sounds made him suddenly stop before his companion. Waldemar was convulsed with suppressed laughter.

"It's a capital joke, isn't it?" said Torp, grimly.

"My dear fellow," cried Waldemar, vainly endeavouring to regain his composure, "I beg your pardon a thousand times, but really the idea of *your* falling into love in this way is so irresistibly comical, that I cannot behave as I ought on the occasion. You have so long been an oracle to me—to all of us poor soft-hearted mortals—that I could as easily have imagined a priestess of Apollo, fresh from her tripod, dancing a polka or mazourka, as you—"

"Pshaw!" cried Torp, striding indignantly to the door of his room.

"I say, Torp—don't be angry—upon my life I'm sorry you've come to grief in this way."

"*I* am sorry I told you anything about it," said Torp. "It was an unnecessary anxiety to convince you of my probity, and a wish to show you the danger you had escaped, that induced me to make so humiliating a confession."

"I see," replied Waldemar. "I ought to have thanked you for the good advice you gave me, and wisely drawn the conclusion, that where you had become a fool, I should have proved a madman; where you were laughed at, I should have been—whatever is worse on an occasion of this kind."

"There is nothing worse," muttered Torp.

"Then let me tell you, Torp, that I should *not* be laughed at by Mees Nora. She knows perfectly well how much I like and admire her, for I never attempted any concealment, and she would believe me serious, and answer me seriously, if I told her so to-morrow. Now, you commenced by treating her and her relations with hauteur—then I can imagine you absolutely odious during what you call your state of perfect security—how you got on when struggling you know best; you are a strong man, Torp, and I should think your kicks and cuffs may have hurt more than you suppose; finally, by your own account, you became infatuated, and I am sure you must have been, when, under such circumstances, you expected your fair countrywoman to be anything but astonished or amused at hearing you talk of love."

"I was aware of all this," said Torp; "and therefore told her that I relied more on what I had to offer with myself than—"

"Soh!" cried Waldemar, interrupting him, "you were explicit and rational too! She must be very good-tempered to have laughed instead of being angry. I think I see you, Torp, grandly informing her, that notwithstanding her connections and so forth, you condescend to like her—and would marry her; that though you had not taken any trouble to gain her affections, you had no doubt she would accept you, because you were 'a *lord*,' and so forth. Now these things may be understood, but ought never to be expressed, or even hinted—and I am sure, quite sure, your looks were still more arrogant than your words. Oh, Charley, Charley, if you cannot learn to be humble for a while, at least, you must give up all thoughts of the adorable Nora!"

"I have already done so," said Torp; "neither she nor you shall ever have cause to laugh at me again—and now good night."

CHAPTER XL

A Huntress with Two Strings to her Bow

I NTIMATE as Nora had been with Irene Schaumberg ten years previously, she was too well aware of the changes which a separation of such length, at their ages, was likely to produce in the feelings—and the alterations which time must naturally have made in her own person—to expect either a joyful or instantaneous recognition on the part of her friend. To claim acquaintance, and afterwards have to enter into explanations in the presence of Torp and Waldemar, would not be agreeable; therefore she had deemed it expedient to write, and prepare the companion of her childhood for the meeting which was to take place that day, before dinner, at St Benedict's.

Georgina was particularly anxious to see what effect Nora's appearance would have on Torp. She supposed he would feel himself compelled, at least in *her* favour, to relax somewhat in his dignity. Great was, therefore, her indignation when she perceived, that after a cold formal bow, he seemed to lose all consciousness of their presence, apparently as determined to decline relationship as acquaintance with any of them.

The presentations to the Falkners and Benndorffs had scarcely been gone through by Nora, when the sound of rustling silk became audible, and through the open door of an adjoining room a fair-haired, graceful woman, magnifi-

cently dressed, came forward, and advancing directly towards her, encircled her with the whitest and most pro-
fusely braceleted arms imaginable, while, lightly kissing her
on each cheek, she murmured, "*Chère* Nora—*quel plaisir!*"

"Nora!" cried a young officer who was present; "our
Nora?"

Nora extended her hand to him with a smile, as she said,
"I am very glad to see you, though I have not the least idea
whether you are Otto, who used to torment me, or Adolph
who quarrelled, or Ferdinand who learned to dance with
me."

"I am happy to say that I am the last named, and hope
this evening to prove that I have not forgotten the instruction we received together so many years ago."

"I have almost forgotten how to dance," said Nora, "for
I have not been at a ball these ten years."

"Ah," said Irene, "that is the reason you look so well
and so young, Nora. Nothing is so injurious to the appearance as heated ball-rooms and late hours."

This little scene, and the explanations which it caused,
gave animation to the conversation until they went to dinner. Waldemar had not yet made his appearance, but some
manoeuvring on the part of the elders of the family kept a
place beside Irene vacant for him, and Nora thought she
perceived a slight degree of annoyance, or unwillingness on
his part, as he some time afterwards took possession of it.

"You see, Waldemar," said Irene, with a gay smile, "you
see the consequences of want of punctuality. Your father
has condemned you to sit beside me for the next hour as a
punishment; but after all," she added, as he drew his chair
to the table, "it is better than being put in the corner, you
know."

Waldemar murmured something about its being a vast
deal better, hoped all his misdemeanours might be pun-

ished in the same way, and then leaned back to give directions to a servant about some soup.

"Waldemar, you shall have some venison presently," cried his father, eagerly; "a fair hand killed it for you."

"If you mean my hand," said Irene, "I am afraid I must confess I never thought less of your son than on the day of our last hunt at Herrenburg. By-the-by, I forget why you were not with us," she added, turning to Waldemar; "something about a wildschuetz, was it not?"

"No," he replied; "the wildschuetz affair was ages ago. I went to St Hubert's that day, hoping to meet Torp, and followed him to the miller's alp."

"Miller's alp? Is not that the place where General Falkner promised me a hunt?"

"More likely in the neighbourhood of the Wild Alp," answered Waldemar. "I dare say our good old forester, or his son, has something in store for us, if that long-legged fellow who took Torp prisoner does not get the start of us."

"You mean the famous wildschuetz?"

"Yes."

"I hear he has been out again," observed General Falkner.

Nora's conversation with Count Ferdinand suddenly ceased, and she looked up eagerly.

"He was out on the frontiers," continued the general, "and the forester went to look after him, not in the best temper imaginable, as you may suppose. He could not, however, find a trace either of him or his companions, though he visited all his charcoal-burners and woodmen, suspecting one of them of conniving, if not of being a party concerned."

"But he found nothing to confirm his suspicions?" interposed Nora.

"Nothing; nor in the alp huts either, though that is

scarcely to be wondered at, as the sennerins seldom betray a wildschuetz. As soon as our festivities are over," he added, turning to the countess, "you shall have the promised hunt; in the mean time, I can offer you some duck-shooting at the marsh beyond the lake. A couple of men were sent up there to-day, and they have erected a fir-tree shed for you."

"And Waldemar," said old Count Benndorff, "I have promised the general that you will take the place of his son while we remain here. Ernst cannot leave his fair fiancée, so the duty and pleasure of accompanying Irene falls to your lot, and very much flattered you ought to be, if she accept you for her companion."

"Of course I feel immensely flattered," said Waldemar, bending over his plate.

"You look more bored than flattered," said Irene, laughing; "but the fact is, if the general has taken the trouble to make arrangements for me, I feel bound to go out duck-shooting, and this very evening too. It is, however, the last time I shall put your patience to the proof, so you need not look so disconsolate."

Waldemar had just begun to protest and explain, when a remarkably pretty girl of about seven years old, came bounding into the room; she seemed alarmed at seeing so many strangers, and pushed herself shyly between him and Irene, placing her hand on the arm of the latter.

"What does this mean?" asked her mother, pushing back the profusion of blonde ringlets that concealed the face of the child; "have you nothing to say to Waldemar, now that he is beside you, though you never cease talking of him when he is absent?"

The little girl held out her hand to Waldemar, but did not speak.

"We are only modest before company," he said, drawing her towards him; "no one knows that we have been playing at hide-and-seek in the cloisters instead of dressing for dinner."

"Ah, soh!" ejaculated the old count, with evident satisfaction.

"And pray, mademoiselle, who gave you leave to make your appearance so early?" asked her mother.

"Waldemar told me I might come whenever I liked," she replied, in French, which, like all children in her rank of life in Germany, she spoke infinitely better than German.

And immediately every one present began to speak in the same language, excepting Mr Nixon and Madame de Falkner, the latter having undertaken to speak English with him. It was a curious conversation that they carried on together; both spoke, but without being able to make themselves intelligible to each other; however, they laughed a good deal, and Mr Nixon evidently thought that anything was better than nothing, for, even after they had entered the adjoining room to drink coffee, he followed her, and Nora heard him vainly endeavouring to explain how odd it appeared to him dining so early, seven or eight o'clock in the evening being the usual hour in England.

"Yees," replied Madame de Falkner, "we shall dance on zee ball at that time."

Irene tapped Nora on the shoulder. "You must come to my room for a couple of hours," she said, caressingly; "I want to have a talk of old times with you."

Nora followed her through a long suite of large and lofty rooms to the one she had so much admired on her first visit to the monastery. Several persons, in felt shoes, were polishing the floor, already so slippery that it was more adapted for dancing than walking. The gardener was decorating the marble fountain at the end with all the treasures of his not very extensive greenhouse, but they were tastefully arranged, and already spread a delicious perfume around.

"Perhaps you would like to look at Charlotte's trousseau," said Irene, opening the door of an adjoining apartment, where they were soon joined by almost the whole dinner-party, and where Mr Nixon, at first innocently supposing himself at a sort of fancy fair, got up for some charitable purpose, looked round him in dismay at the heaps of linen and dozens of articles of dress which were arranged with taste on tables placed against the wall, seeking in vain those useless little nothings for which elderly gentlemen are expected to give their sovereigns.

Georgina relieved his mind by an explanation, but alarmed him again by the information that she must have a trousseau of precisely the same description.

"Bless my soul, Georgy," he exclaimed, "you don't expect me to give you table-cloths, and pillow-cases, when you are marrying into such a family as this, and Captain Falkner the eldest son, too!"

Georgina said she believed it was expected that she should provide house-linen for the rest of her life. Some one had told her that quite old people went on using the things they had received for their trousseau, and surely if Madame de Falkner thought it necessary to give all these things to her daughter, who was going to marry a Count Benndorff, he could not do less for her, and she had already asked for a list of everything in the room.

"I tell you what, Georgy," cried Mr Nixon, "I don't understand these things, so I'll give you a silver tea-service and a reasonable sum of money, and if you choose to buy linen instead of lace, that's your affair, not mine."

"Oh, Nora, did you ever hear anything so shabby?" said Georgina.

"Never mind," answered Nora, "we shall have a German trousseau all the same,—it is a very good rational old custom well worthy of imitation, even to the tying up of the parcels with coloured ribbon, and the putting labels on them to prevent confusion. Look here, 'Table-cloth for twelve—napkins to match—Turtle-dove pattern'!"

"Come, Nora," said Irene, "examine these handkerchiefs, and then let us go. Do you remember assisting me to hem some of mine, ten years ago, when I was a fiancée, and my solemnly promising to do the same for you when you should be in the same—predicament?"

They had reached the door, beside which Torp was standing, an amused spectator of the scene before him, and especially enjoying the pranks of Waldemar, who had paraded the room with two or three parasols, tried on the shawls, caps, and bonnets, and was now standing as if transfixed in admiration of the bridal wreath, which he held daintily on the outspread fingers of both hands.

"By-the-by, Nora," continued Irene, "for all I know, you may be a fiancée now—in fact, I am sure you must be, for how else could Ernst Falkner have chosen your cousin instead of you! There is some mystery here, don't you think so, Monsieur Torp,—je veux dire Milor Medvie?"

"The mystery is easily explained," he answered; "Falkner had daily opportunities of seeing one Miss Nixon, while the other found occupation elsewhere."

"Ah, true, Nora made excursions on the mountains, and into Tyrol,—I remember seeing you together in very becoming masquerade dresses."

"Count Waldemar can tell you," said Nora, quickly, "that mere accident brought us together on that occasion, and it was a matter of necessity our wearing the dresses of which you speak."

"Oh, Waldemar!" cried Irene, looking up and laughing, and as Nora followed the direction of her eyes, she perceived that he had raised his little ward sufficiently high to admit of her dropping the wreath of orange flowers and myrtle upon Torp's broad forehead, where it lay without a movement on his part to remove it.

Nora walked on—Irene soon followed, observing, as they mounted the stair together, "If the characters of those two men were mixed, we should have something very near perfection. There are times when I scarcely know which I like best."

Pleasant were the reminiscences of their youth—endless Nora's inquiries about their mutual acquaintances. It was when speaking of them that she slowly and unwillingly began to discover the changes which time, prosperity, and constant intercourse with the world of fashion had made in the mind and manners of her friend. The innocent, warm-hearted, unaffected girl, had become what she herself called a "*grande dame*." She spoke without the slightest reserve, and with hardly concealed exultation, of her brilliant position in the world; and so great was her egotism, so desirous was she to expatiate on the delights of Vienna and its society, that she scarcely listened to the short account which Nora gave of her quiet life in London. That she considered herself a person of immense importance was evident; and Nora doubted not that this was the case in the circle in which she moved, for she possessed in no common degree all the advantages there most highly valued—rank, riches, and personal beauty.

Yet, charmed by her graceful manners and fluent conversation, it was long before Nora admitted the perfect worldliness and selfishness of her companion, and, flattered by her unreserved confidence, still longer before she obtained a complete consciousness of her overweening self-esteem and vanity. The whole afternoon passed away in gay descriptions of her success in society during her husband's lifetime—of the manner in which she had punished people who had dared to brave her despotism—and of the heartaches she had caused! Evening was drawing near when she began to speak of the more interesting period of her widowhood, and it was then that her communications first inspired Nora with profound interest, for Torp and Waldemar assumed prominent places in the narrative. She had known and liked them for many years. Old Count Benndorff had been her husband's uncle and guardian—Waldemar, his cousin, had frequently spent the winter with them in Vienna. "In fact, so intimate were we," she said, with a light laugh, "that I really could not at first quite comprehend why he might not continue to come to my house and stay there as he had previously done, and was very angry at the reports which were so soon circulated of our mutual attachment and probable engagement. In the course of time, however, they were not altogether without foundation. Waldemar, you must know, is an unexceptionable *parti*, and, had I wished it, there is no doubt that we should soon have been affianced, for his heart is always on his lips and in his eyes, but—but—Nora, if I go on you must promise never to betray me."

"I don't suppose I shall ever have an opportunity," said Nora.

"Probably not—still you must promise!"

"I think you had better not tell me—I believe I should rather not hear—" began Nora.

"It would be a great relief to speak to some one," rejoined Irene, "and you could give me information which I much want."

"Go on, then," said Nora; "I promise to keep your secret."

"Fancy, my dear girl, my discovering that I loved some one else in the most absurd and unaccountable manner, and who do you think was this person?"

Nora paused for a moment before she answered, "From

all you have said just now, I must suppose you refer to Lord Medway."

"Exactly!—but, my dear creature, he was not Lord Medvie then—he was Monsieur Torp—what you call younger son—*cadet de famille*—poor, everything that was exceptionable, and the contrary to Waldemar—so I—I resolved to overcome the foolish fancy."

"And he?" asked Nora.

"He knew nothing about the matter. I was aware that he admired and liked me, for he said so unreservedly, and often enough. We have always been the best friends imaginable, but nothing more—as yet."

"So—" said Nora, with some surprise, "he—he did not—"

"No, perhaps never thought of me, yet, strange to say, I liked him all the better for his stoicism. It would have been a glorious conquest, and I longed to put his cool head and imperturbable serenity to the test—but I refrained."

"You were right," said Nora; "I suppose you declined his visits and avoided him as much as possible?"

"Not exactly. I mentioned to him and Waldemar, in the course of conversation, that no widow ought to think of marriage for at least two years after her husband's death, and then we got on quite pleasantly together until he was removed to Italy, and Waldemar went with him there, and afterwards to England. More than two years have elapsed since that time," continued Irene; "the marriage of Waldemar's brother to Charlotte Falkner afforded me a good excuse for going to the Benndorffs. Monsieur Torp has become *milord* Medvie, and my prudent scruples are at an end. I expected to meet him at Herrenburg, and had resolved, for his sake, to give up hunting, or even shooting at a target, having by chance heard that he has a horror of what he calls masculine women."

"And Count Waldemar?" asked Nora.

"Oh! he does not mind—rather likes that sort of thing, I believe. His intercourse with Lord Medvie, or his visit to England, has greatly improved him; he has grown much more steady and quiet, and seems as little in a hurry as myself to come to an explanation: nevertheless, I don't intend to give him an opportunity if I can help it; so I have requested my brother Ferdinand to go with me this evening to the marsh; as with a Hungarian chasseur, who can speak but little German and no French, our *tête-à-tête* would be as complete as if we were alone."

"You naturally wish to avoid paining him by a refusal," observed Nora, gravely.

"I want to gain time," replied Irene, laughing, "because I —don't feel quite so sure of *ce grand Charles* as I could wish; but I suppose he can be cajoled like other men. They are all vain, more or less, Nora—very nearly as vain as we are, and only a *little* wiser."

"I suppose," said Nora, with some hesitation, "you have considered the—a—possibility of Lord Medway's having already—disposed of his heart—or at least not being sufficiently fancy free to—"

"To be sure—of course I have thought of all that," interposed Irene, "and questioned Waldemar directly after he came to Herrenburg. He assured me that milord is not engaged, nor likely to be, as he has become more fastidious than ever, and so full of fancies about what the future *milady* is to be, that Waldemar is prepared to fall down in adoration of her perfections whenever she is made known to the world!"

"And this fastidiousness has not alarmed you?" asked Nora.

"Not at all; love is blind, or rather blinded by a bandage, which is sometimes drawn over his ears, so that he is made deaf too. Now, without being either blind or deaf, a man might take a fancy to me, Nora; and I am greatly mistaken if milord has not lived long enough abroad to have got over all absurd prejudices in favour of his stiff, cold country-women!"

She bent over the table to look at her watch, and then rang the bell. "I believe it is time to change my dress," she added; "but you must not leave me. I want to ask you a hundred questions about England,—the carnival is very gay there, is it not?"

"There is no carnival."

"Well, the season—or whatever you call it?"

"It may be gay," said Nora, "but I know nothing about it."

"Ah, true—you were living with an old uncle whose wife was dead, and you had no one to go out with; but the country houses, full of guests, must be delightful."

"I don't know."

"I suppose, at least, I shall be in the best society?"

The entrance of her maid prevented her from observing Nora's silence, or look of astonishment; and she was, for some time afterwards, completely occupied in disembarrassing herself of the thousand details of her elaborate demi-toilette.

Nora went to a window and made some observation about the beauty of the sunset, the lake, and wooded mountains.

"I perceive your taste in scenery has not changed," replied Irene; "indeed you are quite what you used to be, if it were not for the English reserve—not to say coldness of manner—that you have acquired."

"Reserve!" repeated Nora. "I never heard that I was reserved!"

"You were not, but you are now. Here have I forgotten

our ten years' separation, and talked to you as if we had never been apart; while you have listened and looked at me as if I were some strange being, whose character you were trying to understand."

Nora made no attempt to deprecate. She *had* been studying her friend; and now, while standing at the window, modified her previous rigorous judgment of her by the recollection that, ten years previously, they had greatly resembled each other in disposition; and that, perhaps, or rather, most probably, had she been subjected to the allurements and temptations of the world like Irene, her thoughts and actions would have become similar. She no longer regretted the years spent in tranquil retirement with her uncle in Russell-square—and believed the old house there had been to her a sanctuary.

When she looked round, Irene was already dressed in a pair of loose trousers, and what appeared a very short green riding-habit; on her head she placed a remarkably pretty and picturesque hat, also green, with black cocks' feathers, and chamois beard; and, if Nora thought this hunting-attire somewhat fantastical, she felt obliged to acknowledge that it was very becoming to a figure so symmetrical as that of Irene.

"I like the dress, too," said the latter; "and Waldemar says I only want a falcon on my wrist to make it perfect,— but the—the other does *not* like it, I suspect; so, if you have no objection, we will go down the back staircase, and take refuge in the boat-house."

To the boat-house they went, and there found the chasseur, with fowling-piece and dogs. Irene sent him to summons her brother and Count Waldemar; but scarcely had he left them, when Torp approached, and announced himself as substitute for the latter, who had been detained by business.

"Where?" she asked, abruptly.

"In the town, or the village. He went to speak to Baron Waltenburg about the sale of the ruins of the castle."

"Could he not have spoken to him at the ball to-night? I am sure he is invited."

"Most probably—but they are going to examine the ruins with an architect; and Waldemar thought, for once in a way, you would be satisfied with me as substitute. I fear he was mistaken."

"Not at all," cried Irene, hastily—and she blushed beautifully, while she added, "I am only sorry you have seen me in this dress, or, rather, going out in this way; for I know you dislike and disapprove of everything unfeminine. I am beginning, myself, to think these amusements very unladylike, and seriously meditate giving them up altogether."

"Your dress," said Torp, stooping to caress one of the dogs, "is exceedingly becoming; and I am well acquainted with it from Waldemar's sketch-book. As to what is ladylike or not, my ideas have greatly changed of late,—so much depends on the way in which things are done, and the person who—"

Nora heard no more; unobserved, as she thought, by either of the speakers, she had turned to the monastery, and was, soon after, on her way to the village.

The neighbouring town furnished musicians and guests for the ball; the latter were numerous—and among them so many good dancers, that Nora scarcely had time to rest during the evening. As this constitutes happiness to women of German education, she might have been supposed to have enjoyed herself in an unusual degree,—that she appeared to do so—perhaps, even wished to make others think so—is certain; but the reader must be informed that a foolish desire, on her part, to watch the progress of her friend's designs on Torp completely destroyed her pleasure.

The interest that she began to feel about him was singular enough—still more so, that she was perfectly conscious of it; she even saw through his design of convincing her that his disappointment could be easily borne, and would be soon forgotten; and she was quite aware that, circumstanced as he was just then, the evident predilection of such a woman as Irene Schaumberg must be very flattering, and particularly agreeable, when shown in *her* presence. They were seated together at a window,—neither danced nor looked at the dancers,—and hour after hour passed over in conversation that never seemed to flag.

Waldemar, at first, appeared exceedingly amused at this flirtation, and devoted himself to Nora; but, later in the evening, she heard his brother remonstrating with him, and pointing out the absurdity of his position.

"It may be absurd," said Waldemar; "but I see no remedy—for I have no right to interfere. You can signify your displeasure to Charlotte Falkner, to whom you are going to be married to-morrow; or, seeing that Ernst placed a ring of betrothal on Miss Nixon's finger after dinner to-day, he may show anger or jealousy, should she dance again with Waltenburg; but what would Irene say were I to order her not to talk any more to Torp, whom she has known as long, and almost as intimately, as she knows me?"

"You have neglected her of late, Waldemar," said his brother; "shirked the duck-shooting this evening on some frivolous pretence, and have not asked her to dance—though you know there is nothing she resents so much."

At this moment Waldemar's mother came towards him, and, perhaps, said something to the same purport, for he shrugged his shoulders and walked off in the direction of the window.

Nora watched the scene that followed with intense interest. Waldemar spoke, but seemed scarcely to be heard by

Irene; he persisted, and she shook her head and raised her hand, as if to wave him off; he seated himself on a chair near hers, and she turned from him with a very significant gesture of annoyance; then his eyes flashed, and he said something that seemed to provoke an angry reply. Torp rose, laughed, and left them. A few more words were spoken, and then Irene stood up haughtily, and walked across the room towards Nora, whispering, as she passed her, "the die is cast; I have quarrelled with Waldemar for presuming to suppose he had a right to be jealous, and can now only hope that all may go on sweetly with the other. I trust these men will not have any disagreement on my account."

They had none; but both perambulated their respective rooms for more than an hour after their return to the inn; the door between them, however, remained closed.

CHAPTER XLI

On Guard

ABOUT noon the next day a well-arranged procession moved from one of the reception-rooms at St Benedict's down the tastefully decorated stone staircase that led to the church of the monastery. The programme had deprived General Falkner of at least an hour's sleep during the night; but he was more than indemnified when he perceived the accuracy with which it was followed, and glanced at the brilliant appearance of his guests, who, to gratify him, and do honour to the family, were all magnificently dressed; most of the gentlemen in glittering uniforms, and the ladies no less splendid in brocaded silk and *moire antique*.

There was no weeping. The fair bride seemed to have exhausted her store of tears during the morning, if one might judge by her still red eyelids and very crimson lips, and now appeared becomingly serene. Her father carefully concealed any regret he felt at parting with his only daughter; and though her mother occasionally raised her transparent handkerchief to her eyes, it was difficult to discover any cause for the movement, excepting, perhaps, that the sunbeams were not sufficiently moderated by the coloured glass through which they shone. Georgina was exceedingly attentive to the ceremony. Mr Nixon gazed round him, and made reflections on the difference between the vast place of worship in which he stood, with its statues, pictures, and numerous altars, and the chapel that he was in the habit of frequenting in London, and came to the conclusion that the latter was infinitely—more comfortable!

The marriage ceremony was succeeded by a dinner, which Nora thought as tedious as it was sumptuous; for when she was following the bridal party out of the church, Rosel had left the crowd of spectators to whisper that her father had again heard of the wildschuetz, and had suddenly left home with her brother. Instantly, and greatly alarmed on John's account, Nora had yielded without hesitation to Rosel's urgent entreaties to spend the night on the miller's alp, in order, if necessary to be able to bear witness in favour of Seppel, and had only stipulated that they were to be accompanied by her mother. In consequence of this arrangement every moment became of importance to Nora, as tending to increase her chance of having to wander in the woods after sunset; therefore, the moment she found herself at liberty, after attempting a hurried sort of explanation to her uncle and cousin, not one word of which they understood, she set off on foot to the forest-house, changed her dress with the rapidity of a Cinderella, and might soon after have been seen with her iron-shod staff, climbing the mountain behind the mill; not stopping to look around her, or talking to her companions, as was her custom, but hastening onward, silent and abstracted.

When recollections of all she had heard and seen during the last two days took possession of her thoughts for a few minutes, they were chased by anxiety about her cousin John. She feared, and not without reason, a rencounter between him and his companions on the one side, and the forester and Franz on the other; and at one time her fears so far got the better of her prudence that, had Rosel been able to tell her in what direction her father had gone, she would have followed, and confessed all to him.

The sun was already below the horizon as they left the steep path in the forest, and began the ascent of the more gentle slope on which the huts were situated. The summit of the mountains beyond were still glowing in purple light, but all beneath had fallen into shade, and the cool evening breeze swept lightly over the already damp grass. The tinkling of bells became audible in all directions, showing the course taken by each herd, as it wandered forth for the night, so that the rocks, the skirts of the wood, and even far up on the sides of the mountains seemed suddenly full of life and animation. The sennerins stood at the doors of their huts and jodeled loudly and cheerfully, occasionally pausing to hear the echo or the answering jodel from the woodmen, as they left off work; but there was one who stood there mute and melancholy, listening to the familiar sounds, and gazing, perhaps for the last time, on the well-known landscape. It was Madeleine, the miller's daughter, who, however, no sooner perceived Nora than she hastened down the hill, seeming to think it necessary to apologise for her presence. "I know," she added, "that my father sold the alp with the hill yesterday, and that you have taken the cattle at a valuation; but I felt a longing to see the old place once more, and my mother said I ought to look after our cheese and butter, that we might know what we had to take with us into Tyrol. The sennerin has heard that I was only a guest, as it were, now—and—"

"Not so," said Nora; "the alp is yours as long as you remain at the mill."

"That will only be until next week," observed Madeleine, with a sigh.

"And by that time," continued Nora, "the cattle will at all events be driven down for the winter, so you see we expect you to supply us with milk and butter both now and to-morrow morning."

"Everything but a bed," said Madeleine. "I am afraid you will hardly be able to sleep on the straw mattress of the sennerin."

"We don't want beds," said Nora; "we have no intention of sleeping to night—have we, Rosel?"

"No," she answered, smiling, "and there's another who mus'nt sleep either, and we are going for him as soon as the moon gets over the Rocky Horn."

"Long Seppel?" suggested Madeleine, with a faint smile.

"You've guessed it," said Rosel's mother. "The wild hunters are on this side of the frontiers they say, and Miss Nora thinks if so be suspicion should again fall on Seppel, we can stand up for him, and say he was with us the live-long night!"

"Has the forester gone in search of the wildschuetz?" asked Madeleine.

"Yes, and Franz too; he would not let his father go alone, because this wildschuetz is seldom without companions."

"Good heavens!" exclaimed Madeleine, "if they should happen to meet at the votive tablet where your eldest brother was shot—there may be bloodshed."

"Are they on the Wild Alp?" asked Rosel, with a look of alarm. "My father seemed very fierce, but would not say where he was going. There is little chance of escape for any wildschuetz he may meet on that mountain."

"But," said Nora, looking up suddenly, "who told Madeleine that the wild hunters were there?"

Madeleine blushed deeply, and answered that a Tyrolean, who had been at the mill that morning, had seen them, and said they were a large party, and had dogs with them to drive the deer across the frontiers.

"And Franz and his father have not taken any one with

them," exclaimed Rosel's mother, uneasily.

"Oh, I hope—I trust—they may not meet," cried Madeleine, evidently sharing her anxiety. "The forester will perhaps go on to the huts, and then the others intend to keep along the frontier line, and may not be very far from this about daybreak."

"Your informant was so accurate," observed Nora, "that I suspect be must be one of the party."

"Perhaps so," she answered, with a look of intelligence; "but," she added in a whisper, "I don't mind telling you all I know, as you are not likely to have me questioned by the judge, seeing that I might be made to say more than would be agreeable to you and yours."

Nora looked at her inquiringly.

"Some people," she continued, in the same significant manner, "some people talk of a tall wildschuetz, and others of a small one, and lately they've been mostly seen together."

"Are they to be together in this neighbourhood to-night?" asked Nora, quickly.

"Somewhere between this and the Wild Alp," she answered.

"We must secure Seppel at once, and if possible bring him here," cried Nora, turning to Rosel and her mother.

To this arrangement neither objected, though the latter was evidently both heated and tired, and they were soon on their way to the woodmen's shed.

On arriving there, they found that most of the workmen had retired for the night, the others were smoking, but Seppel was neither among the sleepers nor smokers—he had gone down to the charcoal-burners, they said, to take charge of the kiln for the night, as the man was ill, and had been obliged to go home. To the charcoal kiln Nora and her companions immediately went, and as the moon rose bright and clear above the jagged summit of the Rocky Horn, the black pile, and waving smoke above it, the wooden shed and surrounding trees were covered with a flood of light; but no human being was to be seen. It was in vain that Nora walked round the kiln, and the others examined the shed, which was almost completely filled with charcoal, no Seppel could be found; and after a close inspection of every rock and heap of wood around them, Nora put her hand on Rosel's arm, and asked gravely, "What do you expect me to think now?"

"Think!" she repeated, "think, that he has gone to the fountain; he is not likely to drink the water here, when there is fresher and better to be had within a stone's throw."

Nora and the forester's wife seated themselves on the rough bench beneath the overhanging gable roof of the shed. "I fear," she said, dejectedly, "I fear he is not so near as you imagine, but I am quite willing to wait here until you have convinced yourself that he is not at the fountain."

"Surely, Miss Nora, you cannot suppose that he would undertake the charge of a charcoal kiln on the borders of the forest, and leave it for any length of time by night or by day?"

"Perhaps he ought not," said Nora, "and you can scarcely be more unwilling than I am to believe that Seppel is still a wildschuetz; but from first to last appearances and circumstances have been strongly against him—more so, Rosel, than you suppose, or than I am at liberty to tell you."

"That may be," she answered; "but I cannot and will not believe that he has deceived me. Let me only step down to the spring and convince you that he is within call."

"Do so," said Nora; "I am more than willing to be convinced, and hope with all my heart that he may answer you."

Five minutes, ten minutes, passed over before Nora's

not particularly pleasant reflections were interrupted by the sound of Rosel's loud clear call, the same peculiar successions of tones she had used when on her way to the Crags for the first time with Nora, soon after the arrival of the latter at the village. A faint echo repeated the notes in a confused uncertain manner, and as it died away, Nora thought she heard the sound of something near her moving. She stood up and looked round—again Rosel's voice, more loud than ever, was heard beneath; but scarcely had the last note been uttered before the wooden walls of the shed were shaken in a remarkable manner, and Nora and the forester's wife, fearing that the roof was about to fall on their heads, sprang from beneath it, and gazed upwards in some alarm. Then it was that they perceived for the first time, just beneath the gable, a sort of framework of boards, that by a great stretch of imagination might have been called a balcony, and in this narrow place Seppel seemed to have made his bed, for he was raising himself from a recumbent posture, and staring round him like a man wakened from heavy slumber. A moment afterwards his long legs were dangling over the side, until they reached a ladder at some distance beneath, whence, flourishing his arms in the air, he shouted vociferously; afterwards, to Nora's infinite amusement, he sprang to the ground, and approaching her deferentially, he raised his hand to his temple, in military salute.

"I am very glad to see you, Seppel," she said, smiling, "for I was afraid that the bright moonlight might have tempted you once more to go out with that reckless—"

"Miss Nora," he said, interrupting her eagerly, "I was not out last month, nor can any weather induce me to break the vow I made at St Hubert's. Rosel," he added reproachfully, as he turned to the panting girl who then joined them, "did you too mistrust me?"

"No, no—not for a moment—I thought to find you at the spring."

"Can you tell me where my cousin is just now?" asked Nora, a little impatiently.

"You mean the young gentleman?" said Seppel with a perplexed air.

"Yes. I want to see him, or send him a letter without delay."

"Give it to the Tyrolean sennerin, Miss Nora. She saw him last Sunday, when she went down to the valley. She'll deliver it safely, and bring you an answer, too, if you require one."

Nora perceived he was determined not to commit himself in any way, and that she must apply to the sennerin in the morning for information. "What are we to do now?" she said, turning to Rosel. "If Seppel cannot leave his charcoal, who is to watch him?"

Rosel, of course, did not know.

"Could not one of the other woodmen take his place for to-night," suggested Rosel's mother, "and then he would be at liberty to return with us to the alp."

"There's not a charcoal-burner among them," said Seppel; "but if you cannot make up your mind to trust me, maybe it would be as well to leave Rosel here on guard as it were, at least until after nightfall, and again about daybreak she might go the rounds—these are the hours of strong temptation for a wildschuetz, which, however, with your leave, I beg to say I am not—and havn't been for many a year."

"What is to be done now?" asked Nora, turning to the forester's wife, who had again seated herself on the bench, and was yawning unrestrainedly.

At that moment they were startled by the report of distant firearms.

"Where's that?" cried Rosel.

"Between this and St Hubert's I should think," answered Seppel: "perhaps the forester has brought down a buck."

"Not likely," said Rosel, "for he has lately been watching one in that direction for the lady from Vienna, who is going out next week with Count Waldemar. I'm afraid it must be the wild hunters."

"Well, I shouldn't wonder if it were," said Seppel; "and precious bunglers they must be to require so much lead for a single buck, on such a night as this, when one can aim as at a target."

"Anything," rejoined Rosel, "is better than a meeting with my father and Franz. I hope they have shot the buck, and made good their escape into Tyrol, though my father will be as mad as a March hare for a week to come."

"I think, Miss Nora," said the forester's wife, "we may now leave Seppel to attend to his charcoal. If he should be asleep when we return here, instead of alarming him, Rosel must mount the ladder, and make his face as black as a chimney-sweeper's."

They returned to the alp, and, after a frugal supper, Nora crossed the ravine with Madeleine, and questioned the Tyrolean sennerin about her cousin John. The girl, however, could give no information concerning him, excepting that he was well, and not likely to return to Almenau for some time. She accompanied Nora back to the miller's hut, and remained there until Rosel and her mother retired to the sleeping-room, where they shared a palliasse on the floor with Madeleine. Nora, who professed to be neither tired nor drowsy, then seated herself outside the open door of the hut, and looked at the moon and stars, the trees and distant mountains, listening to the sound of the cattle-bells, while thinking of Seppel and Rosel, Jack and the wildschuetz, the forester and his son, Torp and

Irene, Waldemar, St Benedict's, and the ball there. It was
strange, she thought, to feel so little fatigued, after having
danced so much and slept but a few hours the previous
night—she supposed her anxiety about Jack kept her
awake—she would go to the Tyrolean sennerin at the other
side of the ravine in—the—morning. Very odd that the
moon seemed to dance up and down—no, it was only the
reflection in the water of the spring, retained in the hol-
lowed trunk of a tree, for the use of the cattle—and now
the wood seemed to slide backwards and forwards—
Macbeth—Wood of Dunsinane—Austrian troops on the
march with green branches in their helmets—national customs—singular—effects—of—moon—light—

    Nora slept.

CHAPTER XLII

Jack's Last Exploit

NORA slept, and so soundly, that hours passed over as if they had been so many minutes. She was awakened by the murmuring of voices not far distant from her, and, on opening her eyes, she perceived two men at the fountain below the hut. One sat at the end of the water-trough, in a desponding attitude, the other stood leaning lightly against the upright stem that served as conductor to the water, which flowed incessantly, and in a profusion only common in wooded mountainous districts. As soon as Nora discovered them to be the forester and his son, she rose and approached them; the former raised his hat for a moment, and then, replacing it on his head, drew it over his eyebrows with a vehement jerk; the latter held his in his hand, while expressing some surprise at finding her at the alp.

"I heard of your having gone out, and became so uneasy about Seppel, and a—in short, I made Rosel and her mother come up here with me, and we went directly to see Seppel, who has taken charge of the charcoal kiln for the night."

"It was there he blackened his face," muttered the forester, with closed teeth.

"We found him sleeping as quietly as we could have desired," continued Nora, "and intend to go again to the kiln before midnight."

"Then you must wait four-and-twenty hours, Miss Nora, for midnight is long past."

Nora looked at her watch, and found he was right. "I am afraid," she began, hesitatingly, "they have shot the roebuck you were keeping for the general."

"The buck's safe," replied the forester, grimly, "and so is Franz, though they aimed well, considering the distance;" while speaking, he snatched the hat from his son's hand, and put his fingers through two holes in it, as if to show the direction taken by the bullet.

"Good heavens! you have had a conflict with the wild-schuetz after all!"

"Yes," said the forester, sternly; "the long schuetz fired at Franz, and—and then—I shot him—dead, I believe, or wounded him mortally. They were six to two, and he need not have fired; 'tis true, I shot their dog—but it was not his dog—Seppel has no dog—"

"It was not Seppel—it was certainly not Seppel," cried Nora, eagerly; "we were with him when the shots were fired, and heard them distinctly, notwithstanding the distance."

"Not Seppel," cried the forester, springing up; "I'd give all I'm worth to be sure of that! If I had not been made frantic by seeing him aim deliberately at Franz, while the others were shouting to me, and if the bullet had not so nearly done its work, I'd not have fired. Six to two was fearful odds, and we had to fly for our lives afterwards."

"Come at once to the charcoal kiln," said Nora, "and convince yourself that Seppel is alive and well."

In expectation, perhaps, of another visit from Rosel and Nora, Seppel had not returned to his balcony, but lay stretched at full length on the bench beneath, his hands clasped under his head by way of pillow, and sleeping as soundly as hard work and exposure to the air could make him. The forester signed that he should not be wakened, and then leaned on his staff and contemplated the man, whose supposed death had caused him such deep regret during the last few hours, notwithstanding all his efforts to convince himself that a wildschuetz was no loss, and that his daughter could never have married him.

Meanwhile Nora had drawn Franz aside, and asked for some clear account of what had happened.

"It is easily given," he said, gravely; "we heard that the long wildschuetz had been seen again in the neighbourhood of the Wild Alp, but my father rightly judged that it was probable he was hunting the buck we have been preserving for the general and his guests, at St Benedict's, so we went at once to a well-known grazing-place among the rocks, between this and St Hubert's, and, sure enough, hardly had we got within rifle shot of the frontier, before we saw one of the dogs of these fellows hunting our game across the boundary for them. My father shot the dog, and had but just time to load again, before the Tyroleans, who must have heard the report of the rifle, came in sight. I think they supposed us stronger than we were, for there were rocks enough to have concealed a dozen men behind us, and that made them keep at a distance, and commence a dispute; they said they were on Tyrolean ground, we *knew* we were on Bavarian; in the heat of argument the rifles were raised —my father says the long schuetz aimed at me, at all events he fired the first shot, and his bullet went through my hat. You know what followed."

"Do you think they were all Tyroleans?" asked Nora, anxiously.

"No; the man that we took for Seppel and another fellow, had grey Bavarian jackets, and wore hats like mine."

"I suppose," said Nora, "that no one else was wounded,

as you did not fire."

"Yes, I did, but without aiming, and suspect I must have
hit one of them, for they fired a few random shots after us
during our retreat. As they were all more or less disguised
with false beards, kerchiefs, charcoal, or brick-dust, I think
they would even have pursued us, had their leader been less
dangerously wounded. If he had any life in him they most
probably carried him across the frontiers to the nearest surgeon."

"A horrible business altogether," said Nora. "Your father seems to feel it greatly."

"As long as he thought it was Seppel, whom he has
known from a child, who was my murdered brother's
playmate, and my sister's future husband, he took it to heart
greatly, and was several times so overcome, that we were
twice as long as need be on our way here; but I am much
mistaken, if he will not now go home and inform the
forstmeister and judge, without any feeling of compunction, that he has shot a notorious wildschuetz, and is ready
to stand his trial."

"And what will happen then?" asked Nora.

"He will plead self-defence and my defence; I can swear
that the wildschuetz fired the first shot, and then he will be
acquitted."

"Come, Franz," said the forester, in a low voice as he
joined them, "our way now is down hill and without delay."

"Father," observed Franz, glancing towards the sleeper,
"I now see that I accused Seppel unjustly, and that the
judge was right when he said there was no convincing evidence against him. It was the wildschuetz we saw tonight,
who was on the Wild Alp; he would have murdered me
there, had he dared, and only failed in this last attempt, I do
believe, by a special interposition of Providence. I wonder
how I have made myself such a bitter enemy, for I have not

been long enough assistant forester to become implacably hated by these men as yet!"

"It was odd enough," said the forester, musingly, "odd enough that you were aimed at, when I was standing by; but there was no mistake, Franz—that fellow wanted your life-blood."

Day was beginning to dawn as they approached the alp again. The forester carried his hat in his hand, to let the cold morning air blow on his flushed and haggard face; his son had been long silent, and Nora wished they would both leave her, as she wanted to question the Tyrolean sennerin about Jack, and the woman was now walking round her hut, and shouting her *ranz des vaches* in all directions. The cattle began to assemble; they issued from the wood, wound round the rocks, or ascended from the depths of the valley below.

"Franz," said the forester, hurrying forward, "I shall return to the village by the shortest way;" and he turned to the path that Nora had once seen Torp take with equal impetuosity.

"I shall accompany Miss Nora to the miller's hut, father, and then follow you," he answered, walking on gravely before. Nora, and stopping to assist her more frequently than was necessary.

They passed the Tyrolean sennerin, who nodded her morning greeting, and continued to shout her *ranz des vaches*, even while she turned after Nora, and mysteriously drawing a piece of folded paper from beneath the folds of her neck-kerchief, made signs to her to ask no questions in the presence of her companion.

Nora glanced at the address, which was written with a pencil. It was Jack's handwriting; and, relieved of much of her anxiety, she dropped the paper into her pocket, and then followed Franz, who was waiting to assist her down the side of the ravine that separated them from the miller's hut. Her entreaties that he would not give himself so much trouble, were vain; he mounted the other side and accompanied her to the hut. As they approached it, Nora saw him start and hesitate, and on looking up perceived a man seated on the bench outside; he was leaning against the wood piled there, and seemed to have considered it too early to expect admittance, for the door was still closed, and while waiting for daylight he had apparently fallen asleep.

"Who is it?" asked Nora.

"Black Seppel, from the mill," he answered, gloomily; "he has come to visit Madeleine."

"Who, it seems, is not yet up," said Nora.

"She is; I saw her at the other side of the house as we came up the rocks."

Nora now understood why he had persisted in his attentions to her, and was not a little surprised when Madeleine came to meet them, and invited Franz to enter the hut through the cow-house. He stopped at the door, however, and observed abruptly, "Black Seppel is waiting for admittance at the hut door."

"I know it,—he has been there this long time. He told me he would come here about day-break."

"And, knowing this," said Franz, sternly, "you sent me word I should find you on the alp, and that you hoped I would not pass your hut without speaking to you? Oh Madeleine, Madeleine, have you not caused calamities enough without adding a meeting just now between Seppel and me, when you know how full of jealousy and anger we are, and how mortally we hate each other?"

"Don't speak so harshly, Franz; I did not know he was coming here when I sent the sennerin to you. My mother never leaves me for a moment, and he and my father are always watching me, so that I have never been able to see you since the day I was obliged to say that I must give you up for ever."

"And what else have you to say now?" asked Franz, coldly.

"That I *have* loved you, and will ever love you better than any one in the world," she replied, bursting into tears.

"Yet people in the village, those who know you better than I do, Madeleine, assert that this is not the case, and say there is scarcely a young man in the parish, who has not had hopes of being chosen by you, at one time or other."

"I never—loved—any one—but you," sobbed Madeleine.

"There was Anderl of the Crags," said Franz.

"The churl! I never thought of him."

"And Florian?"

"I laughed at him—and you laughed with me, Franz."

"But I did not laugh at Black Seppel, the Tyrolean," said Franz; "and people tell me now you said often and publicly, that he was a man of the right sort, of whom every one was afraid but yourself; but that you could lead him as if he were a child, and you even exhibited your power over him on several occasions in a very remarkable manner. I hope it may last, Madeleine—I wish you every happiness, and now, farewell."

"Stay, oh stay!" she cried, beseechingly. "What you have said is true, quite true, but I was forced to act as I did; he'd have worried my father's life out, if I had not kept fair with him. You know he stood by us in our poverty, and we could not compel him to leave us afterwards."

"This may be the case," said Franz, evidently moved at her distress, and flattered by her professions of affection. "Still—still you might have broken off with me to satisfy your father, without having yourself betrothed to the Tyrolean the very next day! That was what showed me what you

were, Madeleine;" he continued, working himself into anger
at the recollection, "and the people are right after all, who
say you never cared for me, and only sought a plausible pretext to give me up for the now rich Seppel—the miller
from the valley of the Inn!"

"Franz, Franz!" she cried, passionately, "if ever I acted
well in my life, it was on that occasion, and if I have been
foolish and vain, my punishment will be hard and long.
Only say that you forgive me, and that you believe I love
you, and I will bear without murmuring all the trials that I
know are before me."

Meantime Nora had entered the hut, and by the grey
light that found its way as yet but sparingly through
the small windows, with difficulty deciphered her cousin
John's note.

Dearest Norry,
Tell the governor anything you can invent for me in a
hurry, for I cannot return to the village for some days. We
have had hot work with those blackguards, the foresters,
and of the poor fellow who was killed, you will hear soon
enough. I represent the wounded—but don't be alarmed, it
is of no consequence, only a small slice of flesh out of my
left arm, and as the landlord's son at the inn beyond St
Benedict's is a famous fellow for binding up scratches of
this kind, and won't peach for many reasons, I am on my
way there now, and shall write to you again in a day or two.
Don't on any account come to me, as it might create suspicion, and this time I am in a fix and no mistake.

"What can I do?" thought Nora, "this innkeeper's son is
probably an ignorant peasant, and, if Jack's wound should
be illtreated, all the responsibility of the neglect will fall on

me. My going to him might, as he says, create suspicion, and would be useless, as he ought to be taken to some town —to Innsbruck, perhaps—for advice. There is but one person to whom I can apply—and that is—Charles Thorpe. Oh, how unwillingly I do it—but there is no alternative, and—if I make haste, Franz can take a few lines from me to him—in time to prevent his making any excursion, or going out to shoot with Irene, before I have seen him."

She tore a leaf out of her pocket-book, and wrote with a pencil:—

Something very unpleasant has occurred, and I should be much obliged by your meeting me at the forest-house any time after nine o'clock this morning.   —LEONORA
Frontier Alp—Miller Hut—4 o'clock AM

When Nora ran out with her note, Franz was holding Madeleine's hands, and looking at her earnestly. "I believe —and I—forgive you," he said slowly. "I pity you, and oh, Madeleine!" he added, vehemently, "I love you still—far, far more than I dare to tell you!" He drew her towards him for a moment, then freeing himself with a sort of desperate effort from her detaining hand, rushed from the hut, leaving her so overwhelmed with grief, that she was perfectly unconscious of Nora's presence, as she passed her in pursuit of Franz.

Nora did not expect—did not, perhaps, wish—to overtake him immediately; but as he swung himself recklessly down the rocks of the ravine, she called his name loudly, threw her note as far as she could after him, saw that he returned to pick it up, and then slowly retraced her steps to the hut.

Madeleine had not time for the indulgence of her grief; Nora found her, on her return, among the assembled cattle, talking, with perhaps forced composure, to the sennerin, who was milking the cows: she averted her face, as if she feared that the very evident traces of tears on it might be observed, and taking up some sticks that lay on the ground, said she would light a fire and make coffee.

Nora followed her to the hearth, and saw, through the open door of the sleeping-room, that Rosel and her mother still rested undisturbed on their straw mattress, looking warm and placid, while *she*, though infinitely less personally interested in all that had just occurred, felt feverish, anxious, and restless. Having observed that the front door, when opened to admit the morning air, made the chimney smoke, she left the hut altogether, and drew the door to as she went out. For a moment she could have supposed it evening again; once more the moon was pale and cloud-like, the woods beneath looked dark and indistinct, the ground about her, still in shade, was damp with dew, and the rocks that formed the summit of the mountains were glowing afresh in violet blue, but instead of darkening coldly into night, the colour lightened and brightened, until they shone resplendent in golden yellow. Rapidly the day-light now spread around, long shadows seemed to start from the trees and rocks, and while Nora slowly walked to the spring, and dipped her hands into the ice-cold water, with which the capacious wooden trough was filled, a flood of light swept over the hut and all in its vicinity, red sun-beams sparkled on the little windows, and Madeleine, as if tempted by the cheerful gleam that had so suddenly penetrated into the interior, appeared for a moment at the door, glanced towards the Tyrolean as he leaned against the pile of wood which still kept him half in the shade, but perhaps perceiving, as Nora had done, that his hat was drawn over his eyebrows, and his head bent on his breast, so that nothing but a bearded chin was visible, she made no attempt to rouse him from slumbers so profound, and entering the hut again, closed the door as before.

Meanwhile, Nora continued her ablutions, and felt greatly refreshed; she sat down afterwards on a protruding rock below the fountain, to arrange her hair, and, after having completed her rustic toilet, weariness induced her to stretch out her feet, and lay herself at full length on the hard resting-place. It was, probably, this circumstance, added to her grey dress, the absence of all coloured ribbons, and the intervening fountain, that made her unperceived by the old miller, as he hurried with evident effort up the slope to the hut. His manner, however, instantly attracted her attention; for, after glancing furtively round him, he advanced towards the sleeper—slowly, warily, reluctantly—then sat down on the bench beside him, and moved stealthily and irresolutely backwards and forwards—at one time sitting bolt upright, as if listening to some noise within the hut, then sidling-up to the Tyrolean, bending down and peering into his face; at length, he raised his hand, thrust it cautiously into the bosom of the unconscious man, and, after a search of a few seconds, drew forth a small paper packet, which, probably from agitation, he let fall to the ground. Snatching it up he retreated by the way he had come; and, before Nora had recovered from her astonishment at what she had witnessed, he was again approaching the alp, tremulously calling his daughter's name, and hastening towards the weather-beaten clump of fir-trees behind the hut, which he entered through the cowhouse.

It required but little reflection to enable Nora to understand the motives of the theft she had seen committed. The miller had put himself in possession of the papers that would convict him of having consented to, if not instigated, the burning of his mill; and the poor old man had been so tyrannically treated by the Tyrolean, that she could not help rejoicing in his regained freedom, and the chance given him of restoring the money he had dishonestly acquired. She moved a little further down the hill, that she might not be supposed to have seen what had passed, and was so completely out of sight, that Madeleine sent Rosel to look for her. As the latter ran towards her, gaily singing, Nora felt it impossible just then to damp her mirth, by telling her all she knew about her father; so she only mentioned having visited Seppel again towards daybreak, and having found him sleeping beside his kiln.

And Rosel laughed, and talked, and sang; and the cattle dispersed over the alp, lowing loudly, and a couple of cows, with large copper bells, trotted past towards the spring, the goats springing after them, bleating, and, in the midst of all, the Tyrolean lounged lazily on the bench, as if unwilling to rouse himself.

"He sleeps as soundly as Seppel at the charcoal kiln last night," said Rosel, in reply to Nora's expressions of surprise, as they approached the hut. "He told Madeleine he would come here this morning; but, though she professes to prefer his absence to his company, I don't think she is quite pleased to see him sleeping, as she says he has done for the last two hours, under her window, without a word of greeting, as if he did not care to notice now that he is sure of her. I am no friend of his, as you may well suppose; but I told her when a man is downright tired, it is better to leave him in peace."

"That man," said Nora, slowly, "is not tired—is not sleeping—he is—dead!"

She had observed that not the slightest change of position had taken place from the time she had first seen him, and now perceived that, when the old man had abstracted the letters, he had laid bare part of a shirt saturated with blood. Even while she spoke, a light seemed to break upon her, and the conviction flashed across her mind, that the man before her was the wildschuetz Seppel!

Rosel raised the hat from his brows, and exposed the features of a corpse. The colour forsook her face as she turned to Nora, and asked, in a scarcely audible voice, "Who has done this? Not Franz—not my brother—"

"No," answered Nora; "but," she added, reluctantly, "I saw your father this morning, and he told me he had, in self-defence, shot the wildschuetz, about whom we have talked so much lately. I think it more than probable that this is the man."

"This man was no wildschuetz," said Rosel; "he made a vow, the day he shot his brother by accident, never to touch gun, rifle, or fowling-piece again as long as he lived. A Tyrolean has courage to do anything but break a vow, Miss Nora. My father is in trouble, at all events; I fear that my brother may know something of this man's death; so, if you will not take it amiss, I should like to return home without delay."

"Go," said Nora. "After I have spoken a few words to the miller, I shall follow, and, I hope, overtake you before you reach the cascades."

Rosel sprang down the hill, and was soon out of sight. Nora looked into the hut and made a sign to the miller to join her, which he obeyed, with evident reluctance.

"You know what has happened," said Nora, pointing to the Tyrolean.

"Yes—one of them called at the mill, soon after midnight, and told me."

"So, this Seppel was the wildschuetz after all," said Nora; "yet Rosel could not believe it possible, because he had made a vow never to touch a gun or rifle as long as he lived."

"No more he did," answered the miller; "he always carried a long pistol, with the butt-end of a gun screwed on it!"

"And you knew this," said Nora, reproachfully, "and allowed Seppel from the Crags to suffer for his fault!"

"I could not help myself," said the old man, querulously; "I was under obligations, and could not betray him; so, on pretence of visiting his father, he has lately had his sport regular, like the forester, or forstmeister himself! *I* never touched the venison he brought home to us on occasions; but I cannot answer for my wife and daughter—it's the nature of women to like game from a wildschuetz, and silk kerchiefs from a smuggler."

"So he was a smuggler, too?"

"In a small way—with tobacco and silk; but I hope you won't mention this, or say anything about me or my family to the judge, Miss Nora—for he'd make me confess everything in no time. I'd be sorry, indeed, to bring the young Englishman into trouble, and he's a marked man now that he has fired at the forester, and got a wound in his arm. It's better to keep quiet, and say nothing about the matter to friend or foe, and in a few days we shall have left the village altogether, either for Tyrol or Munich."

"Munich!" repeated Nora, "what induces you to think of Munich?"

"I don't know why we should go to Tyrol now," he said, pointing to the Tyrolean; "in Munich, we shall be *preevateers* (*privatiers*), and something may turn up for Madeleine. If my wife and daughter, and the man that's now sitting dead on this bench, had not been against me, I'd have gone to America six years ago. I think I'd have felt more peaceful and happy there. It's a fine land they say, and people don't concern themselves so much about their neighbours' affairs as they do here. I've had an unquiet life of late, Miss Nora —what with my daughter, and that man there, and the evil speaking, and the 'nonmous letters, I've been harassed a'most to death."

Nora knew that a consciousness of crime had caused the old man's misery, and felt glad when he added that he and his wife intended to speak to "his reverence" the next day, and follow his advice whatever it might cost them.

She understood this to refer to the restitution of the money paid by the insurance office, but no look of consciousness betrayed her knowledge of his affairs.

At this moment Madeleine called out, "Father, you are keeping Miss Nora from her coffee all this time, and it is getting cold. Seppel, I suppose, is awake at last, and expecting his breakfast—tell him he may come for it when he chooses."

The miller and Nora looked at each other, and the latter, unwilling to witness the effect which the communication, that was now unavoidable, would have on Madeleine, took up her staff, and requesting him to tell the forester's wife to follow her as quickly as possible, she turned abruptly from the hut, and commenced a rapid descent of the mountain.

It was still early when Nora and her companion approached the forest-house, yet Torp was already there, apparently waiting for her as he leaned against the garden-paling, and looked towards the wood, through which her path lay;—he advanced to meet her, too, but stopped suddenly as she pronounced the name he had requested her *not* to call him. Unconscious of the cause of his frigid bow, Nora commenced an embarrassed apology for the liberty she had taken in requesting him to meet her, ending with the assurance that nothing but dire necessity would have induced her to apply to him on the present occasion.

No statue could have been more immovable than Torp at that moment.

"I want your assistance," she continued, with evident effort, "but I begin to fear that I have not courage to ask it."

Torp's features relaxed a little: "Let me assure you," he answered, with calm politeness, "that I am quite ready to be made use of in any way you may require."

"Unfortunately," said Nora, with ill-concealed annoyance—"unfortunately you are the only person to whom I can confide all my difficulties and fears, without reserve— you alone can understand the whole state of the case, without explanations, and assist me without exciting unpleasant suspicions."

"Reasons enough for employing me," said Torp; "and now let me know in what way I can make myself useful."

"You have heard of the wildschuetz, who was shot last night!"

"Yes; and I was glad to hear it was not the young cuirassier, about whom you have felt so much interest lately."

"Thank you," said Nora. "The wildschuetz proves to have been black Seppel, the miller's man; but unhappily my cousin John was with him, and has let me know that he has been wounded in this unlucky affair—he says slightly, though as he cannot return here, and is under the care of an ignorant peasant—"

"Where?" cried Torp, interrupting her with every appearance of the greatest sympathy.

"At the little inn on the frontiers. You see I cannot help myself—that I am compelled to request you to go to him, and—and—if necessary to take him to Innsbruck for advice."

"Of course. I shall not lose a moment; and you shall hear from me this evening: the sexton's son can be my messenger, and I hope the bearer of good tidings. Console yourself at present with the thought that if he had been severely wounded, he could hardly have made his way across the mountains to Saint Hubert's."

"True," said Nora; "but if the wound be indeed so slight

as he represents it, why does he not return here?"

"For many reasons," said Torp, "which he did not think it prudent to write, nor have I time now to explain to you, as I must be off without delay."

He raised his hat, slightly, in the reluctant way peculiar to Englishmen, and turned from her even more quickly than he had approached.

"Proud man!" thought Nora, "I see you will never forgive me; but you have no objection to place me under an obligation that I cannot repay, and for which you will receive my thanks with haughty composure. Oh, Jack, Jack! you have put my regard for you to a severe test! No one will ever know what I have suffered during the last quarter of an hour!"

CHAPTER XLIII

The Break-Up

THE promised letter arrived in the course of the evening; it was without formal commencement, and without signature; gave a perfectly satisfactory account of Jack and his wounded arm, but said that, after mature consideration, they had resolved to go on to Innsbruck to consult a surgeon, and also to be out of the way, in case a strict investigation of the wildschuetz affair should be undertaken by the judge.

The forester related circumstantially all that had occurred, and what he said was corroborated by his son in a manner to force conviction of the truth of their statements. Not one of the Tyroleans concerned in the transaction could be discovered; even the dog that might have led to their detection had been removed, and nothing was found where the conflict had taken place but the long pistol already mentioned. The miller was, of course, questioned; but, relying on Nora's silence, his evidence was not calculated to throw much light on the subject. "Seppel had been chief workman at the mill for six years, as every one in the village knew; was a clever, industrious man, went often to see his family in Tyrol, especially lately, since his father had resigned his mill to him; might have been a wildschuetz for all he knew: supposed he was, as he had been found in such company." The judge smiled significantly, said the miller could tell more if he chose, but that it was not necessary; there was evidence enough to prove that the man had been a notorious wildschuetz for nearly as many years as he had been in the village; that his figure, his name, and especially his conduct to the assistant-forester on the Wild Alp left no doubt of his having been the leader of the gang who had there behaved in such an unwarrantable manner; his having aimed at Franz instead of his father on the last occasion made it equally evident that motives of personal hatred and jealousy would have tempted him to commit murder, had an occasion presented itself. The forester and his son had unquestionably fired in self-defence, and, if no one from Tyrol appeared to witness against them, they were to be acquitted.

No one appeared—not even at the funeral. The wild-schuetz' friends feared they might be suspected of having been his companions in his mountain wanderings, and wisely remained at home. His father was bedridden—his mother unable to leave him; so the miller appeared as chief mourner on the occasion, and it was generally understood that he mourned not at all.

The departure of the miller and his family a few days afterwards for Munich created more sensation. There was much leave-taking, some weeping, and innumerable invitations given to the October fête, and the lodging which their cousin in Munich had taken for them. Franz disappeared for some days, and it was more than hinted that he too had gone to Munich. Good-natured people said it was to make himself useful to the miller, who was a child in business, and did not know what to do with the heaps of money he had got from the English lady for the mill; others, disposed to judge less kindly, were heard to surmise that he had gone to procure a fresh promise of marriage from Madeleine, before she had had time to attract the attention of the young burghers of Munich. It concerns us not. He returned home within the week, looking as quiet, cheerful, and self-possessed as he had been at Ammergau, and apparently exclusively interested in the affair of his sister, whose approaching marriage now formed the principal topic of conversation in the village.

After the events related having completely cleared Seppel from all suspicion of being a wildschuetz, Nora conferred the mill, and all belonging to it, on him, in the least ostentatious manner possible, the first time he returned from his work in the forest; so that, as he said himself at the forest-house in the evening, "He had come down the mountain a homeless labourer, and should go to bed a rich miller!"

"A miller who has to learn his trade," observed the forester, laughing. "Now, I could have given you a certificate, Seppel, that, had Miss Nora made you assistant forester instead of miller, you'd have taken to the work as naturally as a chamois to the rocks."

"It won't require a conjuror to make a miller of me," rejoined Seppel; "and as all the people at the mill remain there, and the water and the wheels work on as heretofore, I suppose the business will go on much as usual. If Rosel were with me, of course things would get on still better; for without her the house will soon be in disorder; and what I'm to do when the cows come from the alp, I'm sure I don't know!"

"Listen to the rich peasant talking of his people and his cows!" cried the forester, laughing, and they all laughed, and were very happy, and Rosel repeated every word they said to Nora, and made her promise to spend the afternoon of the ensuing day at the mill.

Seppel seemed to think a white cap and a certain quantity of flour on his garments and face necessary for the representation of a miller. His moustaches, too, were amply powdered, and he appeared to have an immense quantity of work to do when Nora and Rosel came to visit him; the latter laughed with childish delight as she saw him rush up and down the ladders, carry sacks from one place to another, and make believe to have scarcely time to speak to her! Nora, too, was amused, but enjoyed much more Rosel's quieter satisfaction, as she explained the little alterations she intended to make in the house arrangements, and milked the cows, and prepared the supper for the miller and his men. Leaving her so employed, Nora seated herself on the planks near the saw-mill, and had not been long there when a carriage stopped on the road (that, as the reader may remember, formed a sort of shelf upon the opposite mountain), and, a man springing from it, ran down the green slope to the mill; and, bounding over the bridge and across the stream, boisterously embraced her, with the assurance that he would never play at wildschuetz again as long as he lived.

"And your arm, Jack?"

"Almost quite well. Medway's a famous fellow, Norry, and you must like him now, if only for my sake,—he has no sort of dislike to you, that's clear! And didn't I tell him what a darling you were, and how uncle Stephen did not want to have you at first, and couldn't live without you afterwards, and how you kept his house, and took care of him when he was ill, and managed his affairs for him latterly! I told him your coming into such a fortune hadn't changed you a bit, and that you were always ready to help a fellow out of a scrape." Here he looked up, and made a sign that the carriage should drive on.

"We're the best friends possible," he continued, sitting himself astride on the planks; "quite intimate, latterly, and you can't imagine how jolly he can be when he chooses. I now believe all the stories they tell of him, for I am sure he is up to anything, for all his quiet looks. He gave me a capital account of the ball at St Benedict's, and said you looked lovely in an evening dress, which he had not expected."

"Why should I not look well in an evening dress?" asked Nora.

"Oh! I'm sure I don't know; perhaps he thought it unlikely, because he had only seen you tramping about in hob-nailed boots, and that odious straw hat! He knew more about us than I supposed; and, when I spoke of Sam, asked me if he was the man that people said you intended to marry."

"People never said any such thing!" cried Nora.

"Well, I told him I was surprised he knew anything about that matter, for Sam could keep a secret as well as most people, especially if it concerned himself."

"And you allowed him to suppose—" began Nora, indignantly.

"Not at all!" cried Jack, interrupting her. "I told him you put an extinguisher on Sam at once; but that you were uncommonly fond of me, and that if I were ten years older you'd marry me to-morrow!"

"It seems you were very communicative," said Nora, laughing.

"We were more than a week together, and must talk of something or other, you know."

"And what did he tell you in return?"

"Why, nothing particular, excepting that he regretted not having become better acquainted with us all, and was particularly sorry that *you* had taken such a dislike to him, so I have promised to make you friends the first time you meet, and told him you often said there were few things you would not do for me, because I was the first person who loved you after you came among us."

"I am glad you said that, Jack, and it is quite true. I do like you, though you are as wild, idle, and troublesome an animal as it is possible to imagine. And now let us return to the village. You will probably have to go this evening to Saint Benedict's, to make the acquaintance of your future relations."

"And you will be civil to Torp—I mean Medway, for my sake, Nora, and not let him suppose that I boasted of influence that I do not possess. He is really anxious to make up to us now, and has promised that I shall have a hunt with Waldemar and a countess somebody to-morrow. But the queerest thing of all, Nora, is—that he told me we should in all probability hunt the very roebuck below the Wild Alp that cost the wildschuetz his life, and has given me a mark on my arm that I shall carry to my grave."

As they drew near the inn, John looked round for his new friend, and soon discovered him sitting in the garden at a table covered with letters, that had accumulated during his absence. "Lord Medway," he cried, eagerly, "here's Nora been telling me not to make foolish speeches about friendship, for that she has no sort of dislike to you—it's all a mistake, she says."

"I am very glad to hear it," said Torp, advancing towards them.

"John—John," cried Mr Nixon and Georgina, from one of the windows of the inn.

"At all events," said John, "as you see I cannot wait for explanations, just shake hands and show that you are friends; you may fight it out—I mean talk the matter over as long as you like afterwards."

Torp and Nora extended their hands at the same moment. Jack laughed and ran into the house.

"Let us be friends, Leonora," said Torp, cordially; "it will be a more natural state of things, and pleasanter for us both. Destroy the letter I wrote ten years ago to your uncle —I can assure you that any annoyance or mortification it may have caused you was repaid with interest at the wood-man's fountain, and we may now begin our acquaintance again, as cousins or friends—or anything you please."

Nora drew her note-book from her pocket, and silently took from it the letter of which he had spoken, and on which the marks of age, perhaps also of frequent perusal, were evident.

"Thank you," said Torp. "I perceive I might have stolen the odious scrawl six weeks ago, when I found your note-book in the forester's parlour. I had very little idea then of the importance of the contents to me."

Just then, a servant came to tell her that her uncle was waiting dinner.

"Before I go," she said, turning to Torp, "let me thank you for the care you have taken of this wild cousin of mine."

"Quite unnecessary," he answered. "I felt myself partly to blame, for what had happened, and was glad of an opportunity to repair the mischief I had caused."

In the evening they met again at Saint Benedict's, where plans and arrangements were made for the breaking up of the whole party. Captain Falkner had but one day more to spend at home, and wished Mr Nixon and his family to travel to Vienna, at the same time with him, and to this no objection could be made, as Nora had now concluded, in a satisfactory manner, the business that had brought them to Almenau.

"Give me but to-morrow to go once more to St Hubert's," she said to her uncle, with a smile, "and I am ready to start for Vienna at any hour the ensuing day."

"And give me," cried John, "give me also to-morrow for the hunt Lord Medway has got the general to offer me."

"Who hunts to-morrow?" asked Irene.

"Mr John Nixon will join us, if you have no objection," answered Torp.

"Oh none whatever," she said. "I shall not be of the party, as I intend to confine myself to target-shooting in future."

Torp expressed some surprise, but none of the approbation she had perhaps expected.

"And you?" she said,—"are you too going to Vienna with the others?"

"No. As nobody is going to marry me, I don't know what I should do there at this time of year."

"You had better pay your promised visit to the Benndorffs," she observed, lightly: "and don't be too much flattered if I say I hope you will, as I have promised to return with them to Herrenburg."

"That I expected," said Torp, laughing. "Waldemar will be pardoned, and the last act of the comedy played on the terrace overlooking the river Inn."

"You are mistaken," she said, seriously. "During the ten days you have been absent, he has been trying his utmost to make me jealous, by paying attention to Nora Nixon, and instead of piquing me, as he expected, he has convinced me that I never really cared for him at all."

"*Indeed!*" said Torp, so earnestly, and with such evident interest, that she was induced to be more explicit, and added—

"There never was any actual engagement between us, you know. He is free, and I am free, without any further explanation being necessary."

"And—and Leonora?" asked Torp.

"Leonora!" she repeated. "Are you so intimate that you can call her Leonora?"

"Oh, not at all intimate, but we are second cousins, and

that gives a right, if one choose to use it."

"She never mentioned this relationship," observed Irene, musingly.

"Perhaps you did not chance to speak of me," suggested Torp.

"On the contrary, you were frequently the subject of conversation."

Torp coloured violently,—he feared that Nora might have been as little reserved with *her* friend as he had been with his. "Then she told you of her dislike to me—" he began, after a pause.

"She told me nothing—absolutely nothing," said Irene. "I could not even find out whether or not she liked Waldemar."

Torp regained his composure, but his inattention to what she afterwards said was so remarkable, that he was obliged to apologise repeatedly, and in the end, supposing him interested in the routes to Vienna, which were being discussed at the tea-table, she proposed his giving an opinion on a subject with which he was so perfectly well acquainted.

He left her, but it was to watch Nora and Waldemar, as they studied a map of Tyrol together, evidently intent on cheating Mr Nixon into a tour through the Valley of the Inn, before they allowed him to find the road that would bring their journey to a speedy conclusion.

CHAPTER XLIV

Who Wins the Wager?

IT was on a bright mild morning in autumn that Nora commenced her last walk through scenes that had become alike familiar and interesting to her. The change of season had as yet made so little alteration in the aspect of the country, that it had been almost unthought of, and quite unperceived. There were no long tracts of stubble to remind them of the approach of winter; for in these highlands but a few days after the reapers have left the cornfields, fresh grass springs up luxuriantly, to give the ground once more its rich green covering, and not unfrequently a second harvest of the beautiful and delicate plants that belong to alpine regions. The few white clouds that variegated the deep blue sky served but to cast light and fleeting shadows on the mountains, meadows, and woods, making the succeeding sunbeams appear still brighter by contrast, and a light breeze gently waved the shining gossamer thread that hung on weed, bush, and bramble, or bore it aloft, to float in wavy endless lengths in the air. The red, yellow, and purple tinted leaves of the maple and beech contrasted well with the fresh green of the pine and fir; and among the branches of the scarlet-berried mountain ash, or the clustering fruit of the berberis, the cheerful chirp of a bird might be heard, as if in exultation at the continuance of warmth and sunshine.

They reached St Hubert's at a later hour than on a former occasion; this time, however, Seppel had no prolongation of his walk, no separation from Rosel in prospect. His happiness had been made evident on the way by a succession of whoops and shouts, and long-prolonged jodels; but, as he approached the chapel, he became tranquil and thoughtful; and, on entering the little building, he knelt as reverently, and seemed quite as fervid in prayer and thanksgiving as Rosel herself.

Nora turned towards the side-altar that had been renovated by Florian, and had scarcely had time to examine the repairs of St Hubert's plumed hat, and the stag with the golden cross between his antlers, when she heard some one enter the chapel, and then, as if fearing to disturb its occupants, quickly retire again. On looking round, she perceived Torp standing at the door, and instantly the idea took possession of her mind, that some accident had occurred, and that he was come to break it to her.

"What has happened?" she asked, anxiously, when scarcely outside the chapel.

"Nothing—nothing, I assure you," answered Torp, following her to the low wall that inclosed one side of the ground round the building.

"Then why are you here?" she asked, her face still pale with alarm.

"For the purpose of seeing and speaking to you, if you have no objection."

"Oh!" said Nora, recovering her colour immediately. "I thought of nothing but that tiresome Jack when I saw you. Knowing he had gone out at daybreak this morning with you and the others, and seeing you here now alone, led to the hasty conclusion that something unpleasant had occurred."

"I am not alone," said Torp. "Waldemar is with me—

that is, he is now at the sexton's. We agreed to leave your cousin and Count Ferdinand the honour and glory of bringing down this much-talked-of roebuck; so they have gone off with the forester and his son beyond the Wild Alp,— and here we are, with every intention of accompanying you home whenever it is your pleasure to leave St Hubert's."

"I have only just arrived," said Nora; "but there is nothing to prevent our going to the sexton's if you prefer it to remaining here. Rosel will be at no loss to know where to find me."

"Let us remain here," said Torp, seating himself beside her on the wall, stretching out his feet, and folding his arms in a very resolute manner. "Will you," he added, after a pause, "will you consider that I presume too much on our relationship, or friendship, if I ask what are your plans for the winter?"

"By no means," answered Nora; "but I scarcely know them myself yet. I believe I should like to travel if I could find an eligible companion; for I have no ties, no one thing or person, to make one place more desirable to me than another. You return to England, of course?"

"I don't know," he replied, musingly; "my movements depend on yours, for some time at least."

Nora felt rather curious to know in what way, but did not deem it advisable to ask.

"If you remain abroad," he continued, "I shall return home,—if you go to England I shall remain in Germany, or spend the winter in Italy."

"An odd way of commencing our projected friendship," observed Nora, without looking up.

"My feelings towards you," said Torp, earnestly, "have not yet subsided into friendship, and until they have, we are better apart." He paused, and then added, "You will probably be induced to reside with Jane and Harry Darwin after their marriage?"

"Certainly not," replied Nora. "I do not choose to spend the rest of my life in London and Paris, with summer excursions in a yacht, as I know they intend to do. The world of fashion has ever been a source of danger and temptation to the Nixon family, and I have resolved to avoid it altogether."

"There is," said Torp, after a long pause, "there is one thing more which circumstances oblige me to say,—something that I ought to recommend, and know not how."

"It is difficult to imagine what it can be," said Nora, "excepting, perhaps, that you know of some house to be let, or sold, or of some respectable widow willing to be the companion of a wayward heiress."

"I was about to speak of a respectable *man* who wishes for the situation you have mentioned," replied Torp.

Nora felt her heart beat violently, but her agitation subsided as he continued:

"I need scarcely say that I allude to Waldemar. He has only been a week or ten days free from a sort of tacit engagement that has existed for a long time between him and the Countess Schaumberg, and now fears that the reserve which he was obliged to observe at the commencement of his acquaintance with you, may have prejudiced you against him. In short, to speak plainly, he thinks that appearances may lead you to suppose that he avoided a declaration of his regard, until he had ascertained the amount of your fortune."

"Are you making a proposal of marriage for your friend?" asked Nora, with forced composure.

"No," answered Torp, "he is ignorant of my intentions to speak to you about him, but I think it necessary to do so as a sort of expiation for the injudicious advice that I gave him some time ago. Supposing you the daughter of Gilbert

Nixon, I not only told him that your fortune would not be sufficient to make his father overlook your want of rank, but tried to prejudice him against your relations, and even yourself, completing my absurd interference by using all my influence to induce him to return to his family, with whom I knew the Countess Schaumberg was then staying. I hope," he added, with heightened colour, "I hope you understand the motives that have induced me to enter into this explanation, and make a confession which, I am quite aware, will not increase your regard for me."

"It will not lessen it," replied Nora, "for chance has already made me aware of almost all you have told me."

"Then you were not prejudiced against him?"

"Not in the least."

"Yet he complains of increasing reserve on your part during the last ten days—that is, precisely since he has been at liberty to let you perceive his intentions: your preference for him has, however, on all occasions, been so evident, that I think he must be mistaken."

"He was not mistaken," said Nora.

Torp looked at her eagerly, inquiringly, but to his infinite chagrin, perceived her eyes fixed on Seppel and Rosel, as they just then descended from the chapel.

"Have you prayed for me as you promised, Rosel?" she asked, advancing to meet her.

"That I have!" answered Rosel. "I prayed that you might be as happy as you deserved to be."

"Choose another form of prayer next time, dear girl," rejoined Nora, "for I have been happy beyond my deserts all my life."

"Miss Nora," interposed Seppel, a little shyly, but with a beaming countenance, "I prayed for you too, and with all my heart, that you might be as happy—as you have made us."

"Thank you," said Nora, with a cordial smile; "to judge by your face at this moment, my portion of happiness would in that case be no common one."

"Are you going, Leonora?" asked Torp, perceiving her begin to walk away with them.

"Are you coming?" she asked in return, waiting until he had joined her at the gate of the inclosure.

Torp stopped there, and said resolutely, "We were speaking of Waldemar, Leonora, and I feel bound to tell you what a good-hearted, excellent sort of fellow he is."

Nora would have been annoyed, perhaps even irritated, at his cool, business-like manner, had she not felt convinced that he considered himself to be fulfilling a solemn act of expiation. The absurdity of their mutual position struck her, however, so forcibly, that she had some difficulty in keeping her countenance as she replied, that she had never doubted Count Waldemar's excellent qualities.

"You are also aware of his present position and splendid prospects?"

"Perfectly."

"Then may I ask the cause of the reserve of which he speaks so despondingly?"

"You may not," she answered, abruptly.

Torp opened the gate—he looked very grave, almost offended; and unwilling that they should part in anger, she observed, as they walked towards the sexton's, "that having heard from the forester of Count Waldemar's engagement to Irene Schaumberg, she had never thought of him otherwise than as the future husband of her former friend."

"Ah!" said Torp, "I understand—it was the constraint of a new position."

"There was no constraint," said Nora, and then they walked on in silence to the house, where they found Wal-

demar established, with his drawing materials before him, at
the rough planks that formed a table.

Perhaps it was the desire to prove the absence of the
supposed restraint, that induced her to sit down near Waldemar, and examine a drawing that he had just made of the
Riven Rock. He took from his pouch the portfolio she had
examined at the forest-house and so much wished to possess, and with playful ostentation began to place the various
sketches and drawings before her.

"Will you buy them?" he asked, gaily.

"Most willingly. Name your price."

"Answered like a rich Englishwoman," said Waldemar;
"but they are not to be had for gold. I believe," he added,
while he leaned his chin on the tip of his pencil, "I believe I
once before mentioned that they were to be had for a cup
of coffee."

"Seriously spoken?" asked Nora.

"Most seriously,—but this coffee must be made by your
fair hands, and brought to me by yourself; nay, to make the
enjoyment complete, I must also request you to sit by me
while I drink it!"

"What an odd idea!" exclaimed Nora. "You had better
take into consideration, that coffee made by me will
scarcely be particularly good."

"That is of no consequence whatever," said Waldemar,
quickly. "*You* have taken a fancy to my sketches, and I have
taken a fancy to drink coffee made by an Englishwoman."

"If you had said tea—" began Nora.

"Perhaps I should if I had been an Englishman, and my
drawings of people and places in England; but, for a German, and for alpine sketches, you must, yourself, allow that
coffee is more appropriate."

"A cup of coffee seems to me so altogether *in*appropriate," said Nora, "that I cannot help thinking that more is

meant than meets the ear."

"You cannot imagine the supreme pleasure which a cup of coffee, made by you, would give me!"

"Not in the least. You must have some hidden motive, or—" At this moment she turned towards Torp. He was endeavouring to look indifferent with all his might; but his face was unusually flushed as he bent over the sketches in question. Nora hesitated for a moment, looked from one to the other, and then added, slowly, "There is something here that I do not understand,—under such circumstances I— decline making the coffee."

"Torp," cried Waldemar, half laughing, "your jealous face has spoiled all!"

"Jealous!" repeated Torp; "not at all. Time enough for that when you have got the coffee."

"Just take yourself off, will you, and let me try my powers of persuasion alone."

Torp made a lazy movement, as if about to obey this command.

"Stay," cried Nora. "I now insist on knowing what you both mean."

Torp stayed, but remained silent. Waldemar closed his drawing-book. "My sketches, it seems, are not considered worth even a cup of bad coffee," he said, beginning to replace them in the portfolio; "however, I can patiently bear the mortification—for the contemplation of them will, I hope, often afford me pleasure when drinking a cup of good!"

"Then," said Nora, frankly, "then you have not, as I began to suppose, made me the subject of a wager."

It was now Waldemar's turn to blush. Nora looked in vain to Torp for explanation,—he was apparently absorbed in the contents of the portfolio. The silence of both naturally confirmed her suspicions—and she turned, with an air of displeasure, to Waldemar, while she said, "Most willingly would I have tried to make coffee for you, had it been merely to gratify an eccentric wish, but to find myself the subject of a wager, is so far from agreeable, that I shall certainly not assist you to win it. You have lost—whatever it may be."

"I have lost more than my wager, if I cannot persuade you to gratify this wish of mine," said Waldemar, gravely. "When I now repeat my request, it is not to gain a wager, which I cannot deny having made with Torp the day after I first saw you. I desire your compliance now as a special mark of your favour, or rather as a sign that you like me better than your cousin and countryman here! The drawings are yours, at all events; for if you refuse my request, after what I have just said, they will hereafter be a source of more pain than pleasure to me."

"This is absurd," cried Nora, rising, and greatly annoyed at the increasing seriousness of both her companions. "Surely," she added, appealing to Torp, "surely you do not mean to embarrass me, by attaching importance to what I may do on this occasion?"

Now Torp was, at the moment, looking at Waldemar's sketch of Nora, as she sat at the woodman's fountain; he moved it, so that she could recognize her portrait; and he was convinced she did so instantly—for she grew very pale; and, as if to change the current of his thoughts, covered it hastily with the beautifully-finished drawing of the Kerbstein lake and fisherhouse, that she happened at the moment, to have in her hand. Her confusion was, however, boundless, when she perceived that Torp understood her as if she had spoken, and said more—much more than she had ventured to think at the moment; for he leaned forward, and, looking up, said with a significance that was not to be mistaken, "Make the coffee for him, Nora, and you will confer a favour on me, too!"

"Confound you," cried Waldemar, springing up with undisguised annoyance; "this is what may be called turning the tables with a vengeance. Coffee made at his command, Mees Nixone, would be so little what I hoped to receive from you, that I prefer, this time, some of that which the sexton's wife has probably made for us all."

He walked towards the house as he spoke, but stopped, when sufficiently within it to enable him to look back unperceived. He saw Torp stretch his hand across the table to Nora—saw hers extended in return; there was no perceptible movement of Torp's lips; his face, however, was eloquent enough, though seen but for a moment before he bent his head over the hand he held fast in both of his. Not one word had been spoken.

> For, it is with feelings as with waters—
> The shallow murmur, but the deep are dumb.[*]

"So," muttered Waldemar, to whom this pantomime had been painfully intelligible, "so I have lost her as well as my wager. She does not know how much I love her—nor Torp either—and they never shall know. It will be very odd if I cannot dissemble for the four-and-twenty hours we shall still be together." And he returned to them, soon afterwards, apparently as gay as ever; and, during their return to the village, might have been supposed the happiest of the party!

---

[*] The second line is from "The Silent Lover" by Sir Walter Ralegh (c1552-1618): "Passions are liken'd best to floods and streams | The shallow murmur, but the deep are dumb."